Peggy Duthie.

THE COMPLETE SHORT STORIES OF
W. SOMERSET MAUGHAM

VOL. II

By W. SOMERSET MAUGHAM

The Collected Plays

THE COMPLETE
SHORT STORIES

of

W. SOMERSET
MAUGHAM

❖

VOL. II

WILLIAM HEINEMANN LTD
MELBOURNE :: LONDON :: TORONTO

FIRST PUBLISHED 1951

PRINTED IN GREAT BRITAIN
AT THE WINDMILL PRESS
KINGSWOOD, SURREY

Contents

VOL. II

———————————————— ❖ ————————————————

Preface

IN this, the second volume of my collected stories, I have made a
somewhat different arrangement from that which I have made in
the other two. In those I put the stories I wrote in which the scene
was laid in Malaya. These are so long that I thought it would give
the reader a rest if I interspersed them with short ones set in other
parts of the world, so I divided them in each volume into four groups.
But I wrote a batch of stories dealing with the adventures of an
agent in the Intelligence Department during the First World War.
I gave him the name of Ashenden. Since they are connected by this
character of my invention I have thought it well, notwithstanding
their great length, to put them all together. They are founded on
experiences of my own during that war, but I should like to
impress upon the reader that they are not what the French call
reportage, but works of fiction. Fact, as I said in the preface to the
volume in which these stories appeared, is a poor story-teller. It
starts a story at haphazard, generally long before the beginning,
rambles on inconsequently and tails off, leaving loose ends hanging
about, without a conclusion. The work of an agent in the
Intelligence Department is on the whole monotonous. A lot of
it is uncommonly useless. The material it offers for stories is
scrappy and pointless; the author has himself to make it coherent,
dramatic and probable. That is what I have tried to do in this
particular series.

There is one more point I want to make. The reader will notice
that many of my stories are written in the first person singular.
That is a literary convention which is as old as the hills. It was used
by Petronius Arbiter in the *Satyricon* and by many of the story-
tellers in *The Thousand and One Nights*. Its object is of course to
achieve credibility, for when someone tells you what he states
happened to himself you are more likely to believe that he is telling
the truth than when he tells you what happened to somebody
else. It has besides the merit from the story-teller's point of view
that he need only tell you what he knows for a fact and can leave
to your imagination what he doesn't or couldn't know. Some of

the older novelists who wrote in the first person were in this respect very careless. They would narrate long conversations that they couldn't possibly have heard and incidents which in the nature of things they couldn't possibly have witnessed. Thus they lost the great advantage of verisimilitude which writing in the first person singular offers. But the *I* who writes is just as much a character in the story as the other persons with whom it is concerned. He may be the hero or he may be an onlooker or a confidant. But he is a character. The writer who uses this device is writing fiction and if he makes the *I* of his story a little quicker on the uptake, a little more level-headed, a little shrewder, a little braver, a little more ingenious, a little wittier, a little wiser than he, the writer, really is, the reader must show indulgence. He must remember that the author is not drawing a faithful portrait of himself, but creating a character for the particular purposes of his story.

❖

The Alien Corn

I HAD known the Blands a long time before I discovered that they had any connection with Ferdy Rabenstein. Ferdy must have been nearly fifty when I first knew him and at the time of which I write he was well over seventy. He had altered little. His hair, coarse but abundant and curly, was white, but he had kept his figure and held himself as gallantly as ever. It was not hard to believe that in youth he had been as beautiful as people said. He had still his fine Semitic profile and the lustrous black eyes that had caused havoc in so many a Gentile breast. He was very tall, lean, with an oval face and a clear skin. He wore his clothes very well and in evening dress, even now, he was one of the handsomest men I had ever seen. He wore then large black pearls in his shirt-front and platinum and sapphire rings on his fingers. Perhaps he was rather flashy, but you felt it was so much in character that it would have ill become him to be anything else.

"After all, I am an Oriental," he said. "I can carry a certain barbaric magnificence."

I have often thought that Ferdy Rabenstein would make an admirable subject for a biography. He was not a great man, but within the limits he set himself he made of his life a work of art. It was a masterpiece in little, like a Persian miniature, and derived its interest from its perfection. Unfortunately the materials are scanty. They would consist of letters that may very well have been destroyed and the recollections of people who are old now and will soon be dead. His memory is extraordinary, but he would never write his memoirs, for he looks upon his past as a source of purely private entertainment; and he is a man of the most perfect discretion. Nor do I know anyone who could do justice to the subject but Max Beerbohm. There is no one else in this hard world of to-day who can look upon the trivial with such tender sympathy and wring such a delicate pathos from futility. I wonder that Max, who must have known Ferdy much better than I, and long before, was never tempted to exercise his exquisite fancy on such a theme. He was born for Max to write about.

A*

And who should have illustrated the elegant book that I see in my mind's eye but Aubrey Beardsley? Thus would have been erected a monument of triple brass and the ephemera imprisoned to succeeding ages in the amber's translucency.

Ferdy's conquests were social and his venue was the great world. He was born in South Africa and did not come to England till he was twenty. For some time he was on the Stock Exchange, but on the death of his father he inherited a considerable fortune, and retiring from business devoted himself to the life of a man about town. At that period English society was still a closed body and it was not easy for a Jew to force its barriers, but to Ferdy they fell like the walls of Jericho. He was handsome, he was rich, he was a sportsman and he was good company. He had a house in Curzon Street, furnished with the most beautiful French furniture, and a French chef, and a brougham. It would be interesting to know the first steps in his wonderful career: they are lost in the dark abysm of time. When I first met him he had been long established as one of the smartest men in London: this was at a very grand house in Norfolk to which I had been asked as a promising young novelist by the hostess who took an interest in letters, but the company was very distinguished and I was over-awed. We were sixteen, and I felt shy and alone among these Cabinet Ministers, great ladies and peers of the realm who talked of people and things of which I knew nothing. They were civil to me, but indifferent, and I was conscious that I was somewhat of a burden to my hostess. Ferdy saved me. He sat with me, walked with me and talked with me. He discovered that I was a writer and we discussed the drama and the novel; he learnt that I had lived much on the Continent and he talked to me pleasantly of France, Germany and Spain. He seemed really to seek my society. He gave me the flattering impression that he and I stood apart from the other members of the company and by our conversation upon affairs of the spirit made that of the rest of them, the political situation, the scandal of somebody's divorce and the growing disinclination of pheasants to be killed, seem a little ridiculous. But if Ferdy had at the bottom of his heart a feeling of ever so faint a contempt for the hearty British gentry that surrounded us I am sure that it was only to me that he allowed an inkling of it to appear, and looking back I cannot but wonder whether it was not after all a suave and very delicate compliment that he paid me. I think of course that he liked to exercise his charm and I dare say the obvious pleasure his conversation gave me gratified him, but he could have had no motive for taking so much trouble over an obscure novelist other than his real interest in art and letters. I felt that he and I at bottom were equally alien in that company, I because I was a writer and he because he was a Jew, but I envied the ease with which he bore himself. He was completely at home. Everyone called him Ferdy. He seemed to be always in good spirits. He was never at a loss for a quip, a jest or a repartee. They liked him in that house because he made them laugh, but never made them uncomfortable by talking over their heads. He brought a faint savour of Oriental romance into their lives, but so cleverly that they only felt more English. You could never be dull when he was by and with him present you were safe from the fear of the devastating silences that sometimes overwhelm a British company. A pause looked inevitable and Ferdy Rabenstein had broken into a topic that interested everyone. An invaluable asset to any party. He had an inexhaustible fund of Jewish stories. He was a very good mimic and he assumed the Yiddish accent and reproduced the Jewish gestures to perfection; his head sank into his body, his face grew cunning, his voice oily, and he was a rabbi or an old clothes merchant or a smart commercial traveller or a fat procuress in Frankfort. It was as good as a play. Because he was himself a Jew and insisted on it you laughed without reserve, but for my own part not without an under-current of discomfort. I was not quite sure of a sense of humour that made such cruel fun of his own race. I discovered afterwards that Jewish stories were his speciality and I seldom met him anywhere without hearing him tell sooner or later the last he had heard.

But the best story he told me on this occasion was not a Jewish one. It struck me so that I have never forgotten it, but for one reason or another I have never had occasion to tell it again. I give it here because it is a curious little incident concerning persons whose names at least will live in the social history of the Victorian Era and I think it would be a pity if it were lost. He told me then that once when quite a young man he was staying in the country. in a house where Mrs. Langtry, at that time at the height of her beauty and astounding reputation, was also a guest. It happened to be within driving distance of that in which lived the Duchess of Somerset, who had been Queen of Beauty at the Eglinton Tournament, and knowing her slightly, it occurred to him that

it would be interesting to bring the two women together. He
suggested it to Mrs. Langtry, who was willing, and forthwith
wrote to the Duchess asking if he might bring the celebrated
beauty to call on her. It was fitting, he said, that the loveliest
woman of this generation (this was in the 'eighties) should pay
her respects to the loveliest woman of the last. "Bring her by all
means," answered the Duchess, "but I warn you that it will be a
shock to her." They drove over in a carriage and pair, Mrs.
Langtry in a close-fitting blue bonnet with long satin strings,
which showed the fine shape of her head and made her blue
eyes even bluer, and were received by a little ugly old hag who
looked with irony out of her beady eyes at the radiant beauty who
had come to see her. They had tea, they talked and they drove
home again. Mrs. Langtry was very silent and when Ferdy looked
at her he saw that she was quietly weeping. When they got back
to the house she went to her room and would not come down to
dinner that night. For the first time she had realised that beauty
dies.

Ferdy asked me for my address and a few days after I got back
to London invited me to dinner. There were only six of us, an
American woman married to an English peer, a Swedish painter,
an actress and a well-known critic. We ate very good food and
drank excellent wine. The conversation was easy and intelligent.
After dinner Ferdy was persuaded to play the piano. He only
played Viennese waltzes, I discovered later that they were his
speciality, and the light, tuneful and sensual music seemed to
accord well with his discreet flamboyance. He played without
affectation, with a lilt, and he had a graceful touch. This was the
first of a good many dinners I had with him, he would ask me two
or three times a year, and as time passed I met him more and more
frequently at other people's houses. I rose in the world and
perhaps he came down a little. Of late years I had sometimes found
him at parties where other Jews were and I fancied that I read in his
shining liquid eyes, resting for a moment on these members of
his race, a certain good-natured amusement at the thought of what
the world was coming to. There were people who said he was a
snob, but I do not think he was; it just happened that in his early
days he had never met any but the great. He had a real passion
for art and in his commerce with those that produced it was at his
best. With them he had never that faint air of persiflage which

when he was with very grand persons made you suspect that he was never quite the dupe of their grandeur. His taste was perfect and many of his friends were glad to avail themselves of his knowledge. He was one of the first to value old furniture and he rescued many a priceless piece from the attics of ancestral mansions and gave it an honourable place in the drawing-room. It amused him to saunter round the auction rooms and he was always willing to give his advice to great ladies who desired at once to acquire a beautiful thing and make a profitable investment. He was rich and good-natured. He liked to patronise the arts and would take a great deal of trouble to get commissions for some young painter whose talent he admired or an engagement to play at a rich man's house for a violinist who could in no other way get a hearing. But he never let his rich man down. His taste was too good to deceive and civil though he might be to the mediocre he would not lift a finger to help them. His own musical parties, very small and carefully chosen, were a treat.

He never married.

"I am a man of the world," he said, "and I flatter myself that I have no prejudices, *tous les goûts sont dans la nature*, but I do not think I could bring myself to marry a Gentile. There's no harm in going to the opera in a dinner jacket, but it just would never occur to me to do so."

"Then why didn't you marry a Jewess?"

(I did not hear this conversation, but the lively and audacious creature who thus tackled him told me of it.)

"Oh, my dear, our women are so prolific. I could not bear the thought of peopling the world with a little Ikey and a little Jacob and a little Rebecca and a little Leah and a little Rachel."

But he had had affairs of note and the glamour of past romance still clung to him. He was in his youth of an amorous complexion. I have met old ladies who told me that he was irresistible, and when in reminiscent mood they talked to me of this woman and that who had completely lost her head over him, I divined that, such was his beauty, they could not find it in their hearts to blame them. It was interesting to hear of great ladies that I had read of in the memoirs of the day or had met as respectable dowagers garrulous over their grandsons at Eton or making a mess of a hand at bridge and bethink myself that they had been consumed with sinful passion for the handsome Jew. Ferdy's most notorious amour was with the Duchess of Hereford, the loveliest, the most gallant and dashing of the beauties of the end of Queen Victoria's reign. It lasted for twenty years. He had doubtless flirtations meanwhile, but their relations were stable and recognised. It was proof of his marvellous tact that when at last they ended he exchanged an ageing mistress for a loyal friend. I remember meeting the pair not so very long ago at luncheon. She was an old woman, tall and of a commanding presence, but with a mask of paint on a ravaged face. We were lunching at the Carlton and Ferdy, our host, came a few minutes late. He offered us a cocktail and the Duchess told him we had already had one.

"Ah, I wondered why your eyes were so doubly bright," he said.

The old raddled woman flushed with pleasure.

My youth passed, I grew middle-aged, I wondered how soon I must begin to describe myself as elderly; I wrote books and plays, I travelled, I underwent experiences, I fell in love and out of it; and still I kept meeting Ferdy at parties. War broke out and was waged, millions of men were killed and the face of the world was changed. Ferdy did not like the war. He was too old to take part in it, and his German name was awkward, but he was discreet and took care not to expose himself to humiliation. His old friends were faithful to him and he lived in a dignified but not too strict seclusion. But then peace came and with courage he set himself to making the best of changed conditions. Society was mixed now, parties were rowdy, but Ferdy fitted himself to the new life. He still told his funny Jewish stories, he still played charmingly the waltzes of Strauss, he still went round auction rooms and told the new rich what they ought to buy. I went to live abroad, but whenever I was in London I saw Ferdy and now there was something a little uncanny in him. He did not give in. He had never known a day's illness. He seemed never to grow tired. He still dressed beautifully. He was interested in everybody. His mind was alert and people asked him to dinner, not for old times' sake, but because he was worth his salt. He still gave charming little concerts at his house in Curzon Street.

It was when he invited me to one of these that I made the discovery that started the recollections of him I have here set down. We were dining at a house in Hill Street, a large party, and the women having gone upstairs Ferdy and I found ourselves side by side. He told me that Lea Makart was coming to play for him on the following Friday evening and he would be glad if I would come.

"I'm awfully sorry," I said, "but I'm going down to the Blands."

"What Blands?"

"They live in Sussex at a place called Tilby."

"I didn't know you knew them."

He looked at me rather strangely. He smiled. I didn't know what amused him.

"Oh, yes, I've known them for years. It's a very nice house to stay at."

"Adolph is my nephew."

"Sir Adolphus?"

"It suggests one of the bucks of the Regency, doesn't it? But I will not conceal from you that he was named Adolf."

"Everyone I know calls him Freddy."

"I know, and I understand that Miriam, his wife, only answers to the name of Muriel."

"How does he happen to be your nephew?"

"Because Hannah Rabenstein, my sister, married Alfons Bleikogel, who ended life as Sir Alfred Bland, first Baronet, and Adolf, their only son, in due course became Sir Adolphus Bland, second Baronet."

"Then Freddy Bland's mother, the Lady Bland who lives in Portland Place, is your sister?"

"Yes, my sister Hannah. She was the eldest of the family. She's eighty, but in full possession of her faculties and a remarkable woman."

"I've never met her."

"I think your friends the Blands would just as soon you didn't. She has never lost her German accent."

"Do you never see them?" I asked.

"I haven't spoken to them for twenty years. I am such a Jew and they are so English." He smiled. "I could never remember that their names were Freddy and Muriel. I used to come out with an Adolf or a Miriam at awkward moments. And they didn't like my stories. It was better that we should not meet. When the war broke out and I would not change my name it was the last straw. It was too late, I could never have accustomed my friends to think of me as anything but Ferdy Rabenstein; I was quite content. I was not ambitious to be a Smith, a Brown or a Robinson."

Though he spoke facetiously, there was in his tone the faintest possible derision and I felt, hardly felt even, the sensation was so shadowy, that, as it had often vaguely seemed to me before, there was in the depth of his impenetrable heart a cynical contempt for the Gentiles he had conquered.

"Then you don't know the two boys?" I said.

"No."

"The eldest is called George, you know. I don't think he's so clever as Harry, the other one, but he's an engaging youth. I think you'd like him."

"Where is he now?"

"Well, he's just been sent down from Oxford. I suppose he's at home. Harry's still at Eton."

"Why don't you bring George to lunch with me?"

"I'll ask him. I should think he'd love to come."

"It has reached my ears that he's been a little troublesome."

"Oh, I don't know. He wouldn't go into the army, which is what they wanted. They rather fancied the Guards. And so he went to Oxford instead. He didn't work and he spent a great deal of money and he painted the town red. It was all quite normal."

"What was he sent down for?"

"I don't know. Nothing of any consequence."

At that moment our host rose and we went upstairs. When Ferdy bade me good-night he asked me not to forget about his great-nephew.

"Ring me up," he said. "Wednesday would suit me. Or Friday."

Next day I went down to Tilby. It was an Elizabethan mansion standing in a spacious park, in which roamed fallow deer, and from its windows you had wide views of rolling downs. It seemed to me that as far as the eye could reach the land belonged to the Blands. His tenants must have found Sir Adolphus a wonderful landlord, for I never saw farms kept in such order, the barns and cow-sheds were spick and span and the pigsties were a picture; the public-houses looked like old English water-colours and the cottages he had built on the estate combined admirably picturesqueness and convenience. It must have cost him a pot of money to run the place on these lines. Fortunately he had it. The park with its grand old trees (and its nine-hole golf course) was tended like a garden, and the wide-stretching gardens were the pride of the neighbourhood. The magnificent house, with its steep roofs and mullioned windows, had been restored by the most celebrated architect in England and furnished by Lady Bland, with taste and knowledge, in a style that perfectly fitted it.

"Of course it's very simple," she said. "Just an English house in the country."

The dining-room was adorned with old English sporting pictures and the Chippendale chairs were of incredible value. In the drawing-room were portraits by Reynolds and Gainsborough and landscapes by Old Crome and Richard Wilson. Even in my bedroom with its four-post bed were water-colours by Birket Foster. It was very beautiful and a treat to stay there, but though it would have distressed Muriel Bland beyond anything to know it, it entirely missed oddly enough the effect she had sought. It did not give you for a moment the impression of an English house. You had the feeling that every object had been bought with a careful eye to the general scheme. You missed the dull Academy portraits that hung in the dining-room beside a Carlo Dolci that an ancestor had brought back from the grand tour, and the water-colours painted by a great aunt that cluttered up the drawing-room so engagingly. There was no ugly Victorian sofa that had always been there and that it never occurred to anybody to take away and no needlework chairs that an unmarried daughter had so painstakingly worked at about the time of the Great Exhibition. There was beauty but no sentiment.

And yet how comfortable it was and how well looked after you were! And what a cordial greeting the Blands gave you! They seemed really to like people. They were generous and kindly. They were never happier than when they were entertaining the county, and though they had not owned the property for more than twenty years they had established themselves firmly in the favour of their neighbours. Except perhaps in their splendour and the competent way in which the estate was run there was nothing to suggest that they had not been settled there for centuries.

Freddy had been at Eton and Oxford. He was now in the early fifties. He was quiet in manner, courtly, very clever, I imagine, but a trifle reserved. He had great elegance, but it was not an English elegance; he had grey hair and a short pointed grey beard, fine dark eyes and an aquiline nose. He was just above middle height; I don't think you would have taken him for a Jew, but rather for a foreign diplomat of some distinction. He was a man of character, but gave you, strangely enough, notwithstanding the success he had had in life, an impression of faint melancholy. His successes had been financial and political; in the world of sport, for all his perseverance, he had never shone. For many years he had followed hounds, but he was a bad rider and I think it must have been a relief to him when he could persuade himself that middle age and pressure of business forced him to give up hunting. He had excellent shooting and gave grand parties for it, but he was a poor shot; and despite the course in his park he never succeeded in being more than an indifferent golfer. He knew only too well how much these things meant in England and his incapacity was a bitter disappointment to him. However George would make up for it.

George was scratch at golf, and though tennis was not his game he played much better than the average; the Blands had had him taught to shoot as soon as he was old enough to hold a gun and he was a fine shot; they had put him on a pony when he was two and Freddy, watching him mount his horse, knew that out hunting when the boy came to a fence he felt exhilaration and not that sickening feeling in the pit of his stomach which, though he had chased the fox with such grim determination, had always made the sport a torture to him. George was so tall and slim, his curly hair, of a palish brown, was so fine, his eyes were so blue, he was the perfect type of the young Englishman. He had the engaging candour of the breed. His nose was straight, though perhaps a trifle fleshy, and his lips were perhaps a little full and sensual, but he had beautiful teeth, and his smooth skin was like ivory. George was the apple of his father's eye. He did not like Harry, his second son, so well. He was rather stocky, broad-shouldered and strong for his age, but his black eyes, shining with cleverness, his coarse dark hair and his big nose revealed his race. Freddy was severe with him, and often impatient, but with George he was all indulgence. Harry would go into the business, he had brains and push, but George was the heir. George would be an English gentleman.

George had offered to motor me down in the roadster his father had given him as a birthday present. He drove very fast and we arrived before the rest of the guests. The Blands were sitting on the lawn and tea was laid out under a magnificent cedar.

"By the way," I said presently, "I saw Ferdy Rabenstein the other day and he wants me to bring George to lunch with him."

I had not mentioned the invitation to George on the way because

I thought that if there had been a family coldness I had better address his parents as well.

"Who in God's name is Ferdy Rabenstein?" said George.

How brief is human glory! A generation back such a question would have seemed grotesque.

"He's by way of being your great-uncle," I replied.

A glance had passed from father to mother when I first spoke.

"He's a horrid old man," said Muriel.

"I don't think it's in the least necessary for George to resume relationships that were definitely severed before he was born," said Freddy with decision.

"Anyhow I've delivered the message," said I, feeling somewhat snubbed.

"I don't want to see the old blighter," said George.

The conversation was broken off by the arrival of other guests and in a little while George went off to play golf with one of his Oxford friends.

It was not till next day that the matter was referred to again. I had played an unsatisfactory round with Freddy Bland in the morning and several sets of what is known as country-house tennis in the afternoon and was sitting alone with Muriel on the terrace. In England we have so much bad weather that it is only fair that a beautiful day should be more beautiful than anywhere in the world and this June evening was perfect. The blue sky was cloudless and the air was balmy; before us stretched green rolling downs, and woods, and in the distance you saw the red roofs of a little village church. It was a day when to be alive was sufficient happiness. Detached lines of poetry hovered vaguely in my memory. Muriel and I had been chatting desultorily.

"I hope you didn't think it rather horrid of us to refuse to let George lunch with Ferdy," she said suddenly. "He's such a fearful snob, isn't he?"

"D'you think so? He's always been very nice to me."

"We haven't been on speaking terms for twenty years. Freddy never forgave him for his behaviour during the war. So unpatriotic, I thought, and one really must draw the line somewhere. You know, he absolutely refused to drop his horrible German name. With Freddy in Parliament and running munitions and all that sort of thing it was quite impossible. I don't know why he should want to see George. He can't mean anything to him."

"He's an old man. George and Harry are his great-nephews. He must leave his money to someone."

"We'd rather not have his money," said Muriel coldly.

Of course I didn't care a row of pins whether George went to lunch with Ferdy Rabenstein, and I was quite willing to let the matter drop, but evidently the Blands had talked it over and Muriel felt that some explanation was due to me.

"Of course you know that Freddy has Jewish blood in him," she said.

She looked at me sharply. Muriel was rather a big blonde woman and she spent a great deal of time trying to keep down the corpulence to which she was predisposed. She had been very pretty when young and even now was a comely person; but her round blue eyes, slightly prominent, her fleshy nose, the shape of her face and the back of her neck, her exuberant manner, betrayed her race. No Englishwoman, however fair-haired, ever looked like that. And yet her observation was designed to make me take it for granted that she was a Gentile. I answered discreetly:

"So many people have nowadays."

"I know. But there's no reason to dwell on it, is there? After all, we're absolutely English; no one could be more English than George, in appearance and manner and everything; I mean, he's such a fine sportsman and all that sort of thing, I can't see any object in his knowing Jews just because they happen to be distant connections of his."

"It's very difficult in England now not to know Jews, isn't it?"

"Oh, I know, in London one does meet a good many, and I think some of them are very nice. They're so artistic. I don't go so far as to say that Freddy and I deliberately avoid them, of course I wouldn't do that, but it just happens that we don't really know any of them very well. And down here, there simply aren't any to know."

I could not but admire the convincing manner in which she spoke. It would not have surprised me to be told that she really believed every word she said.

"You say that Ferdy might leave George his money. Well, I don't believe it's so very much anyway; it was quite a comfortable fortune before the war, but that's nothing nowadays. Besides we're hoping that George will go in for politics when he's a little older, and I don't think it would do him any good in the constituency to inherit money from a Mr. Rabenstein."

"Is George interested in politics?" I asked, to change the conversation.

"Oh, I do hope so. After all, there's the family constituency waiting for him. It's a safe Conservative seat and one can't expect Freddy to go on with the grind of the House of Commons indefinitely."

Muriel was grand. She talked already of the constituency as though twenty generations of Blands had sat for it. Her remark, however, was my first intimation that Freddy's ambition was not satisfied.

"I suppose Freddy would go to the House of Lords when George was old enough to stand."

"We've done a good deal for the party," said Muriel.

Muriel was a Catholic and she often told you that she had been educated in a convent—"Such sweet women, those nuns, I always said that if I had a daughter I should have sent her to a convent too"—but she liked her servants to be Church of England, and on Sunday evenings we had what was called supper because the fish was cold and there was ice-cream, so that they could go to church, and we were waited on by two footmen instead of four. It was still light when we finished and Freddy and I, smoking our cigars, walked up and down the terrace in the gloaming. I suppose Muriel had told him of her conversation with me, and it may be that his refusal to let George see his great-uncle still troubled him, but being subtler than she he attacked the question more indirectly. He told me that he had been very much worried about George. It had been a great disappointment that he had refused to go into the army.

"I should have thought he'd have loved the life," he said.

"And he would certainly have looked marvellous in his Guards uniform."

"He would, wouldn't he?" returned Freddy, ingenuously. "I wonder he could resist that."

He had been completely idle at Oxford; although his father had given him a very large allowance, he had got monstrously into debt; and now he had been sent down. But though he spoke so tartly I could see that he was not a little proud of his scapegrace son, he loved him with oh, such an unEnglish love, and in his heart it flattered him that George had cut such a dash.

"Why should you worry?" I said. "You don't really care if George has a degree or not."

Freddy chuckled.

"No, I don't suppose I do really. I always think the only important thing about Oxford is that people know you were there, and I dare say that George isn't any wilder than the other young men in his set. It's the future I'm thinking of. He's so damned idle. He doesn't seem to want to do anything but have a good time."

"He's young, you know."

"He's not interested in politics, and though he's so good at games he's not even very keen on sport. He seems to spend most of his time strumming the piano."

"That's a harmless amusement."

"Oh, yes, I don't mind that, but he can't go on loafing indefinitely. You see, all this will be his one day." Freddy gave a sweeping gesture that seemed to embrace the whole county, but I knew that he did not own it all yet. "I'm very anxious that he should be fit to assume his responsibilities. His mother is very ambitious for him, but I only want him to be an English gentleman."

Freddy gave me a sidelong glance as though he wanted to say something but hesitated in case I thought it ridiculous; but there is one advantage in being a writer that, since people look upon you as of no account, they will often say things to you that they would not to their equals. He thought he would risk it.

"You know, I've got an idea that nowhere in the world now is the Greek ideal of life so perfectly cultivated as by the English country gentleman living on his estates. I think his life has the beauty of a work of art."

I could not but smile when I reflected that it was impossible for the English country gentleman in these days to do anything of the sort without a packet of money safely invested in American Bonds, but I smiled with sympathy. I thought it rather touching that this Jewish financier should cherish so romantic a dream.

"I want him to be a good landlord. I want him to take his part in the affairs of the country. I want him to be a thorough sportsman."

"Poor mutt," I thought, but said: "Well, what are your plans for George now?"

"I think he has a fancy for the diplomatic service. He's suggested going to Germany to learn the language."

"A very good idea, I should have thought."

"For some reason he's got it into his head that he wants to go to Munich."

"A nice place."

Next day I went back to London and shortly after my arrival rang up Ferdy.

"I'm sorry, but George isn't able to come to lunch on Wednesday."

"What about Friday?"

"Friday's no good either." I thought it useless to beat about the bush. "The fact is, his people aren't keen on his lunching with you."

There was a moment's silence. Then:

"I see. Well, will you come on Wednesday anyway?"

"Yes, I'd like to," I answered.

So on Wednesday at half-past one I strolled round to Curzon Street. Ferdy received me with the somewhat elaborate graciousness that he cultivated. He made no reference to the Blands. We sat in the drawing-room and I could not help reflecting what an eye for beautiful objects that family had. The room was more crowded than the fashion of to-day approves and the gold snuff-boxes in vitrines, the French china, appealed to a taste that was not mine; but they were no doubt choice pieces; and the Louis XV suite, with its beautiful *petit point*, must have been worth an enormous lot of money. The pictures on the walls by Lancret, Pater and Watteau did not greatly interest me, but I recognised their intrinsic excellence. It was a proper setting for this aged man of the world. It fitted his period. Suddenly the door opened and George was announced. Ferdy saw my surprise and gave me a little smile of triumph.

"I'm very glad you were able to come after all," he said as he shook George's hand.

I saw him in a glance take in his great-nephew whom he saw to-day for the first time. George was very well dressed. He wore a short black coat, striped trousers and the grey double-breasted waistcoat which at that time was the mode. You could only wear it with elegance if you were tall and thin and your belly was slightly concave. I felt sure that Ferdy knew exactly who George's tailor was and what haberdasher he went to and approved of them. George, so smart and trim, wearing his clothes so beautifully, certainly looked very handsome. We went down to luncheon. Ferdy had the social graces at his fingers' ends and he put the boy at his ease, but I saw that he was carefully appraising him; then, I do not know why, he began to tell some of his Jewish stories. He told them with gusto and with his wonderful mimicry. I saw George flush, and though he laughed at them, I could see that it was with embarrassment. I wondered what on earth had induced Ferdy to be so tactless. But he was watching George and he told story after story. It looked as though he would never stop. I wondered if for some reason I could not grasp he was taking a malicious pleasure in the boy's obvious discomfiture. At last we went upstairs and to make things easier I asked Ferdy to play the piano. He played us three or four little waltzes. He had lost none of his exquisite lightness nor his sense of their lilting rhythm. Then he turned to George.

"Do you play?" he asked him.

"A little."

"Won't you play something?"

"I'm afraid I only play classical music. I don't think it would interest you."

Ferdy smiled slightly, but did not insist. I said it was time for me to go and George accompanied me.

"What a filthy old Jew," he said as soon as we were in the street. "I hated those stories of his."

"They're his great stunt. He always tells them."

"Would you if you were a Jew?"

I shrugged my shoulders.

"How is it you came to lunch after all?" I asked George.

He chuckled. He was a light-hearted creature, with a sense of humour, and he shook off the slight irritation his great-uncle had caused him.

"He went to see Granny. You don't know Granny, do you?"

"No."

"She treats daddy like a kid in Etons. Granny said I was to go to lunch with great-uncle Ferdy and what Granny says goes."

"I see."

A week or two later George went to Munich to learn German. I happened then to go on a journey and it was not till the following spring that I was again in London. Soon after my arrival I found myself sitting next to Muriel Bland at dinner. I asked after George.

"He's still in Germany," she said.

"I see in the papers that you're going to have a great beano at Tilby for his coming of age."

"We're going to entertain the tenants and they're making George a presentation."

She was less exuberant than usual, but I did not pay much attention to the fact. She led a strenuous life and it might be that she was tired. I knew she liked to talk of her son, so I continued.

"I suppose George has been having a grand time in Germany," I said.

She did not answer for a moment and I gave her a glance. I was surprised to see that her eyes were filled with tears.

"I'm afraid George has gone mad," she said.

"What *do* you mean?"

"We've been so frightfully worried. Freddy's so angry, he won't even discuss it. I don't know what we're going to do."

Of course it immediately occurred to me that George, who, I supposed, like most young Englishmen sent to learn the language, had been put with a German family, had fallen in love with the daughter of the house and wanted to marry her. I had a pretty strong suspicion that the Blands were intent on his making a very grand marriage.

"Why, what's happened?" I asked.

"He wants to become a pianist."

"A what?"

"A professional pianist."

"What on earth put that idea in his head?"

"Heaven knows. We didn't know anything about it. We thought he was working for his exam. I went out to see him. I thought I'd like to know that he was getting on all right. Oh, my dear. He looks like nothing on earth. And he used to be so smart; I could have cried. He told me he wasn't going in for the exam. and had never had any intention of doing so; he'd only suggested the diplomatic service so that we'd let him go to Germany and he'd be able to study music."

"But has he any talent?"

"Oh, that's neither here nor there. Even if he had the genius of Paderewski we couldn't have George traipsing around the country playing at concerts. No one can deny that I'm very artistic, and so is Freddy, we love music and we've always known a lot of artists, but George will have a very great position, it's out of the question. We've set our hearts on his going into

Parliament. He'll be very rich one day. There's nothing he can't aspire to."

"Did you point all that out to him?"

"Of course I did. He laughed at me. I told him he'd break his father's heart. He said his father could always fall back on Harry. Of course I'm devoted to Harry, and he's as clever as a monkey, but it was always understood that he was to go into the business; even though I am his mother I can see that he hasn't got the advantages that George has. Do you know what he said to me? He said that if his father would settle five pounds a week on him he would resign everything in Harry's favour and Harry could be his father's heir and succeed to the baronetcy and everything. It's too ridiculous. He said that if the Crown Prince of Roumania could abdicate a throne he didn't see why he couldn't abdicate a baronetcy. But you can't do that. Nothing can prevent him from being third baronet and if Freddy should be granted a peerage from succeeding to it at Freddy's death. Do you know, he even wants to drop the name of Bland and take some horrible German name."

I could not help asking what.

"Bleikogel or something like that," she answered.

That was a name I recognised. I remembered Ferdy telling me that Hannah Rabenstein had married Alfons Bleikogel who became eventually Sir Alfred Bland, first Baronet. It was all very strange. I wondered what had happened to the charming and so typically English boy whom I had seen only a few months before.

"Of course when I came home and told Freddy he was furious. I've never seen him so angry. He foamed at the mouth. He wired to George to come back immediately and George wired back to say he couldn't on account of his work."

"Is he working?"

"From morning till night. That's the maddening part of it. He never did a stroke of work in his life. Freddy used to say he was born idle."

"H'm."

"Then Freddy wired to say that if he didn't come he'd stop his allowance and George wired back: 'Stop it.' That put the lid on. You don't know what Freddy can be when his back is up."

I knew that Freddy had inherited a large fortune, but I knew also that he had immensely increased it, and I could well imagine that behind the courteous and amiable Squire of Tilby there was a ruthless man of affairs. He had been used to having his own way and I could believe that when crossed he would be hard and cruel.

"We'd been making George a very handsome allowance, but you know how frightfully extravagant he was. We didn't think he'd be able to hold out long and in point of fact within a month he wrote to Ferdy and asked him to lend him a hundred pounds. Ferdy went to my mother-in-law, she's his sister, you know, and asked her what it meant. Though they hadn't spoken for twenty years Freddy went to see him and begged him not to send George a penny, and he promised he wouldn't. I don't know how George has been making both ends meet. I'm sure Freddy's right, but I can't help being rather worried. If I hadn't given Freddy my word of honour that I wouldn't send him anything I think I'd have slipped a few notes in a letter in case of accident. I mean, it's awful to think that perhaps he hasn't got enough to eat."

"It'll do him no harm to go short for a bit."

"We were in an awful hole, you know. We'd made all sorts of preparations for his coming of age, and I'd issued hundreds of invitations. Suddenly George said he wouldn't come. I was simply frantic. I wrote and wired. I would have gone over to Germany only Freddy wouldn't let me. I practically went down on my bended knees to George. I begged him not to put us in such a humiliating position. I mean, it's the sort of thing it's so difficult to explain. Then my mother-in-law stepped in. You don't know her, do you? She's an extraordinary old woman. You'd never think she was Freddy's mother. She was German originally, but of very good family."

"Oh?"

"To tell you the truth I'm rather frightened of her. She tackled Freddy and then she wrote to George herself. She said that if he'd come home for his twenty-first birthday she'd pay any debts he had in Munich and we'd all give a patient hearing to anything he had to say. He agreed to that and we're expecting him one day next week. But I'm not looking forward to it, I can tell you."

She gave a deep sigh. When we were walking upstairs after dinner Freddy addressed me.

"I see Muriel has been telling you about George. The damned fool! I have no patience with him. Fancy wanting to be a pianist. It's so ungentlemanly."

"He's very young, you know," I said soothingly.

"He's had things too easy for him. I've been much too

indulgent. There's never been a thing he wanted that I haven't given him. I'll learn him."

The Blands had a discreet apprehension of the uses of advertisement and I gathered from the papers that the celebrations at Tilby of George's twenty-first birthday were conducted in accordance with the usage of English county families. There was a dinner-party and a ball for the gentry and a collation and a dance in marquees on the lawn for the tenants. Expensive bands were brought down from London. In the illustrated papers were pictures of George surrounded by his family being presented with a solid silver tea-set by the tenantry. They had subscribed to have his portrait painted, but since his absence from the country had made it impossible for him to sit, the tea-service had been substituted. I read in the columns of the gossip writers that his father had given him a hunter, his mother a gramophone that changed its own records, his grandmother the dowager Lady Bland an *Encyclopædia Britannica* and his great-uncle Ferdinand Rabenstein a *Virgin and Child* by Pellegrino da Modena. I could not help observing that these gifts were bulky and not readily convertible into cash. From Ferdy's presence at the festivities I concluded that George's unaccountable vagary had effected a reconciliation between uncle and nephew. I was right. Ferdy did not at all like the notion of his great-nephew becoming a professional pianist. At the first hint of danger to its prestige the family drew together and a united front was presented to oppose George's designs. Since I was not there I only know from hearsay what happened when the birthday celebrations were over. Ferdy told me something and so did Muriel, and later George gave me his version. The Blands had very much the impression that when George came home and found himself occupying the centre of the stage, when, surrounded by splendour, he saw for himself once more how much it meant to be the heir of a great estate, he would weaken. They surrounded him with love. They flattered him. They hung on his words. They counted on the goodness of his heart and thought that if they were very kind to him he would not have the courage to cause them pain. They seemed to take it for granted that he had no intention of going back to Germany and in conversation included him in all their plans. George did not say very much. He seemed to be enjoying himself. He did not open a piano. Things looked as though they were going very well. Peace descended on the troubled house. Then one day at luncheon when they were discussing a garden-party to which they had all been asked for one day of the following week, George said pleasantly:

"Don't count on me. I shan't be here."

"Oh, George, why not?" asked his mother.

"I must get back to my work. I'm leaving for Munich on Monday."

There was an awful pause. Everyone looked for something to say, but was afraid of saying the wrong thing, and at last it seemed impossible to break it. Luncheon was finished in silence. Then George went into the garden and the others, old Lady Bland and Ferdy, Muriel and Sir Adolphus, into the morning-room. There was a family council. Muriel wept. Freddy flew into a temper. Presently from the drawing-room they heard the sound of someone playing a nocturne of Chopin. It was George. It was as though now he had announced his decision he had gone for comfort, rest and strength to the instrument he loved. Freddy sprang to his feet.

"Stop that noise," he cried. "I won't have him play the piano in my house."

Muriel rang for a servant and gave him a message.

"Will you tell Mr. Bland that her ladyship has a bad headache and would he mind not playing the piano."

Ferdy, the man of the world, was deputed to have a talk with George. He was authorised to make him certain promises if he would give up the idea of becoming a pianist. If he did not wish to go into the diplomatic service his father would not insist, but if he would stand for Parliament he was prepared to pay his election expenses, give him a flat in London and make him an allowance of five thousand a year. I must say it was a handsome offer. I do not know what Ferdy said to the boy. I suppose he painted to him the life that a young man could lead in London on such an income. I am sure he made it very alluring. It availed nothing. All George asked was five pounds a week to be able to continue his studies and to be left alone. He was indifferent to the position that he might some day enjoy. He didn't want to hunt. He didn't want to shoot. He didn't want to be a Member of Parliament. He didn't want to be a millionaire. He didn't want to be a baronet. He didn't want to be a peer. Ferdy left him defeated and in a state of considerable exasperation.

After dinner that evening there was a battle royal. Freddy was a quick-tempered man, unused to opposition, and he gave George the rough side of his tongue. I gather that it was very rough indeed. The women who sought to restrain his violence were sternly silenced. Perhaps for the first time in his life Freddy would not listen to his mother. George was obstinate and sullen. He had made up his mind and if his father didn't like it he could lump it. Freddy was peremptory. He forbade George to go back to Germany. George answered that he was twenty-one and his own master. He would go where he chose. Freddy swore he would not give him a penny.

"All right, I'll earn money."

"You! You've never done a stroke of work in your life. What do you expect to do to earn money?"

"Sell old clothes," grinned George.

There was a gasp from all of them. Muriel was so taken aback that she said a stupid thing.

"Like a Jew?"

"Well, aren't I a Jew? And aren't you a Jewess and isn't daddy a Jew? We're all Jews, the whole gang of us, and everyone knows it and what the hell's the good of pretending we're not?"

Then a very dreadful thing happened. Freddy burst suddenly into tears. I'm afraid he didn't behave very much like Sir Adolphus Bland, Bart., M.P., and the good old English gentleman he so much wanted to be, but like an emotional Adolf Bleikogel who loved his son and wept with mortification because the great hopes he had set on him were brought to nothing and the ambition of his life was frustrated. He cried noisily with great loud sobs and pulled his beard and beat his breast and rocked to and fro. Then they all began to cry, old Lady Bland and Muriel, and Ferdy, who sniffed and blew his nose and wiped the tears streaming down his face, and even George cried. Of course it was very painful, but to our rough Anglo-Saxon temperament I am afraid it must seem also a trifle ridiculous. No one tried to console anybody else. They just sobbed and sobbed. It broke up the party.

But it had no result on the situation. George remained obdurate. His father would not speak to him. There were more scenes. Muriel sought to excite his pity; he was deaf to her piteous entreaties, he did not seem to mind if he broke her heart, he did not care two hoots if he killed his father. Ferdy appealed to him as a sportsman and a man of the world. George was flippant and indeed personally offensive. Old Lady Bland with her guttural German accent and strong common-sense argued with him, but he would not listen to reason. It was she, however, who at last found a way out. She made George acknowledge that it was no use to throw away all the beautiful things the world laid at his feet unless he had talent. Of course he thought he had, but he might be mistaken. It was not worth while to be a second-rate pianist. His only excuse, his only justification, was genius. If he had genius his family had no right to stand in his way.

"You can't expect me to show genius already," said George. "I shall have to work for years."

"Are you sure you are prepared for that?"

"It's my only wish in the world. I'll work like a dog. I only want to be given my chance."

This was the proposition she made. His father was determined to give him nothing and obviously they could not let the boy starve. He had mentioned five pounds a week. Well, she was willing to give him that herself. He could go back to Germany and study for two years. At the end of that time he must come back and they would get some competent and disinterested person to hear him play, and if then that person said he showed promise of becoming a first-rate pianist no further obstacles would be placed in his way. He would be given every advantage, help and encouragement. If on the other hand that person decided that his natural gifts were not such as to ensure ultimate success he must promise faithfully to give up all thoughts of making music his profession and in every way accede to his father's wishes. George could hardly believe his ears.

"Do you mean that, Granny?"

"I do."

"But will daddy agree?"

"I vill see dat he does," she answered.

George seized her in his arms and impetuously kissed her on both cheeks.

"Darling," he cried.

"Ah, but de promise?"

He gave her his solemn word of honour that he would faithfully abide by the terms of the arrangement. Two days later he went back to Germany. Though his father consented unwillingly to his going, and indeed could not help doing so, he would not be reconciled to him and when he left refused to say good-bye to him.

I imagine that in no manner could he have caused himself such pain. I permit myself a trite remark. It is strange that men, inhabitants for so short a while of an alien and inhuman world should go out of their way to cause themselves so much unhappiness.

George had stipulated that during his two years of study his family should not visit him, so that when Muriel heard some months before he was due to come home that I was passing through Munich on my way to Vienna, whither business called me, it was not unnatural that she should ask me to look him up. She was anxious to have first-hand information about him. She gave me George's address and I wrote ahead, telling him I was spending a day in Munich, and asked him to lunch with me. His answer awaited me at the hotel. He said he worked all day and could not spare the time to lunch with me, but if I would come to his studio about six he would like so show me that and if I had nothing better to do would love to spend the evening with me. So soon after six I went to the address he gave me. He lived on the second floor of a large block of flats and when I came to his door I heard the sound of piano-playing. It stopped when I rang and George opened the door for me. I hardly recognised him. He had grown very fat. His hair was extremely long, it curled all over his head in picturesque confusion; and he had certainly not shaved for three days. He wore a grimy pair of Oxford bags, a tennis shirt and slippers. He was not very clean and his finger-nails were rimmed with black. It was a startling change from the spruce, slim youth so elegantly dressed in such beautiful clothes that I had last seen. I could not but think it would be a shock to Ferdy to see him now. The studio was large and bare; on the walls were three or four unframed canvases of a highly cubist nature, there were several arm-chairs much the worse for wear, and a grand piano. Books were littered about and old newspapers and art magazines. It was dirty and untidy and there was a frowzy smell of stale beer and stale smoke.

"Do you live here alone?" I asked.

"Yes, I have a woman who comes in twice a week and cleans up. But I make my own breakfast and lunch."

"Can you cook?"

"Oh, I only have bread and cheese and a bottle of beer for lunch. I dine at a *Bierstube*."

It was pleasant to discover that he was very glad to see me. He seemed in great spirits and extremely happy. He asked after his relations and we talked of one thing and another. He had a lesson twice a week and for the rest of the time practised. He told me that he worked ten hours a day.

"That's a change," I said.

He laughed.

"Daddy said I was born tired. I wasn't really lazy. I didn't see the use of working at things that bored me."

I asked him how he was getting on with the piano. He seemed to be satisfied with his progress and I begged him to play to me.

"Oh, not now, I'm all in, I've been at it all day. Let's go out and dine and come back here later and then I'll play. I generally go to the same place, there are several students I know there, and it's rather fun."

Presently we set out. He put on socks and shoes and a very old golf coat, and we walked together through the wide quiet streets. It was a brisk cold day. His step was buoyant. He looked round him with a sigh of delight.

"I love Munich," he said. "It's the only city in the world where there's art in the very air you breathe. After all, art is the only thing that matters, isn't it? I loathe the idea of going home."

"All the same I'm afraid you'll have to."

"I know. I'll go all right, but I'm not going to think about it till the time comes."

"When you do, you might do worse than get a haircut. If you don't mind my saying so you look almost too artistic to be convincing."

"You English, you're such Philistines," he said.

He took me to a rather large restaurant in a side street, crowded even at that early hour with people dining and furnished heavily in the German medieval style. A table covered with a red cloth, well away from the air, was reserved for George and his friends and when we went to it four or five youths were at it. There was a Pole studying Oriental languages, a student of philosophy, a painter (I suppose the author of George's cubist pictures), a Swede, and a young man who introduced himself to me, clicking his heels, as Hans Reiting, *Dichter*, namely Hans Reiting, poet. Not one of them was more than twenty-two and I felt a trifle out of it. They all addressed George as *du* and I noticed that his German was extremely fluent. I had not spoken it for some time and mine was rusty, so that I could not take much part in the lively conversation. But nevertheless I thoroughly enjoyed myself. They ate sparingly, but drank a good deal of beer. They talked of art and women. They were very revolutionary and though gay very much in earnest. They were contemptuous of everyone you had ever heard of, and the only point on which they all agreed was that in this topsy-turvy world only the vulgar could hope for success. They argued points of technique with animation, and contradicted one another, and shouted and were obscene. They had a grand time.

At about eleven George and I walked back to his studio. Munich is a city that frolics demurely and except about the Marienplatz the streets were still and empty. When we got in he took off his coat and said:

"Now I'll play to you."

I sat in one of the dilapidated arm-chairs and a broken spring stuck into my behind, but I made myself as comfortable as I could. George played Chopin. I know very little of music and that is one of the reasons for which I have found this story difficult to write. When I go to a concert at the Queen's Hall and in the intervals read the programme it is all Greek to me. I know nothing of harmony and counterpoint. I shall never forget how humiliated I felt once when, having come to Munich for a Wagner Festival, I went to a wonderful performance of *Tristan und Isolde* and never heard a note of it. The first few bars sent me off and I began to think of what I was writing, my characters leapt into life and I heard their long conversations, I suffered their pains and was a party to their joy; the years swept by and all sorts of things happened to me, the spring brought me its rapture and in the winter I was cold and hungry; and I loved and I hated and I died. I suppose there were intervals in which I walked round and round the garden and probably ate *Schinken-Brödchen* and drank beer, but I have no recollection of them. The only thing I know is that when the curtain for the last time fell I woke with a start. I had had a wonderful time, but I could not help thinking it was very stupid of me to come such a long way and spend so much money if I couldn't pay attention to what I heard and saw.

I knew most of the things George played. They were the familiar pieces of concert programmes. He played with a great deal

of dash. Then he played Beethoven's *Appassionata*. I used to
play it myself when I played the piano (very badly) in my far
distant youth and I still knew every note of it. Of course it is a
classic and a great work, it would be foolish to deny it, but I
confess that at this time of day it leaves me cold. It is like *Paradise
Lost*, splendid, but a trifle stolid. This too George played with
vigour. He sweated profusely. At first I could not make out what
was the matter with his playing, something did not seem to me
quite right, and then it struck me that the two hands did not
exactly synchronise, so that there was ever so slight an interval
between the bass and the treble; but I repeat, I am ignorant of these
things; what disconcerted me might have been merely the effect
of his having drunk a good deal of beer that evening or indeed
only my fancy. I said all I could think of to praise him.

"Of course I know I need a lot more work. I'm only a beginner,
but I know I can do it. I feel it in my bones. It'll take me ten
years, but then I shall be a pianist."

He was tired and came away from the piano. It was after midnight
and I suggested going, but he would not hear of it. He opened a
couple of bottles of beer and lit his pipe. He wanted to talk.

"Are you happy here?" I asked him.

"Very," he answered gravely. "I'd like to stay for ever. I've
never had such fun in my life. This evening, for instance. Wasn't
it grand?"

"It was very jolly. But one can't go on leading the student's
life. Your friends here will grow older and go away."

"Others'll come. There are always students here and people like
that."

"Yes, but you'll grow older too. Is there anything more lamentable than the middle-aged man who tries to go on living the under-
graduate's life? The old fellow who wants to be a boy among
boys, and tries to persuade himself that they'll accept him as one
of themselves—how ridiculous he is. It can't be done."

"I feel so at home here. My poor father wants me to be an
English gentleman. It gives me gooseflesh. I'm not a sportsman.
I don't care a damn for hunting and shooting and playing cricket.
I was only acting."

"You gave a very natural performance."

"It wasn't till I came here that I knew it wasn't real. I loved
Eton, and Oxford was a riot, but all the same I knew I didn't
belong. I played the part all right, because acting's in my blood,

but there was always something in me that wasn't satisfied. The house in Grosvenor Square is a freehold and daddy paid a hundred and eighty thousand pounds for Tilby; I don't know if you understand what I mean, I felt they were just furnished houses we'd taken for the season and one of these days we'd pack up and the real owners would come back."

I listened to him attentively, but I wondered how much he was describing what he had obscurely felt and how much he imagined now in his changed circumstances that he had felt.

"I used to hate hearing great-uncle Ferdy tell his Jewish stories. I thought it so damned mean. I understand now; it was a safety valve. My God, the strain of being a man about town. It's easier for daddy, he can play the old English squire at Tilby, but in the City he can be himself. He's all right. I've taken the make-up off and my stage clothes and at last I can be my real self too. What a relief! You know, I don't like English people. I never really know where I am with you. You're so dull and conventional. You never let yourselves go. There's no freedom in you, freedom of the soul, and you're such funks. There's nothing in the world you're so frightened of as doing the wrong thing."

"Don't forget that you're English yourself, George," I murmured. He laughed.

"I? I'm not English. I haven't got a drop of English blood in me. I'm a Jew and you know it, and a German Jew into the bargain. I don't want to be English. I want to be a Jew. My friends are Jews. You don't know how much more easy I feel with them. I can be myself. We did everything we could to avoid Jews at home; Mummy, because she was blonde, thought she could get away with it and pretended she was a Gentile. What rot! D'you know, I have a lot of fun wandering about the Jewish parts of Munich and looking at the people. I went to Frankfort once, there are a lot of them there, and I walked about and looked at the frowzy old men with their hooked noses and the fat women with their false hair. I felt such a sympathy for them, I felt I belonged to them, I could have kissed them. When they looked at me I wondered if they knew that I was one of them. I wish to God I knew Yiddish. I'd like to become friends with them, and go into their houses and eat Kosher food and all that sort of thing. I wanted to go to a synagogue, but I was afraid I'd do the wrong thing and be kicked out. I like the smell of the Ghetto and the sense of life, and the mystery and the dust and the squalor and the romance. I shall never get the longing for it out of my head now. That's the real thing. All the rest is only pretence."

"You'll break your father's heart," I said.

"It's his or mine. Why can't he let me go? There's Harry. Harry would love to be squire of Tilby. He'd be an English gentleman all right. You know, mummy's set her heart on my marrying a Christian. Harry would love to. He'll found the good old English family all right. After all, I ask so little. I only want five pounds a week, and they can keep the title and the park and the Gainsboroughs and the whole bag of tricks."

"Well, the fact remains that you gave your solemn word of honour to go back after two years."

"I'll go back all right," he said sullenly. "Lea Makart has promised to come and hear me play."

"What'll you do if she says you're no good?"

"Shoot myself," he said gaily.

"What nonsense," I answered in the same tone.

"Do *you* feel at home in England?"

"No," I said, "but then I don't feel at home anywhere else."

But he was quite naturally not interested in me.

"I loathe the idea of going back. Now that I know what life has to offer I wouldn't be an English country gentleman for anything in the world. My God, the boredom of it!"

"Money's a very nice thing and I've always understood it's very pleasant to be an English peer."

"Money means nothing to me. I want none of the things it can buy, and I don't happen to be a snob."

It was growing very late and I had to get up early next day. It seemed unnecessary for me to pay too much attention to what George said. It was the sort of nonsense a young man might very well indulge in when thrown suddenly among painters and poets. Art is strong wine and needs a strong head to carry it. The divine fire burns most efficiently in those who temper its fury with horse sense. After all, George was not twenty-three yet. Time teaches. And when all was said and done his future was no concern of mine. I bade him good-night and walked back to my hotel. The stars were shining in the indifferent sky. I left Munich in the morning.

I did not tell Muriel on my return to London what George had said to me, or what he looked like, but contented myself with assuring her that he was well and happy, working very hard, and seemed to be leading a virtuous and sober life. Six months later he came home. Muriel asked me to go down to Tilby for the week-end: Ferdy was bringing Lea Makart to hear George play and he particularly wished me to be there. I accepted. Muriel met me at the station.

"How did you find George?" I asked.

"He's very fat, but he seems in great spirits. I think he's pleased to be back again. He's been very sweet to his father."

"I'm glad of that."

"Oh, my dear, I do hope Lea Makart will say he's no good. It'll be such a relief to all of us."

"I'm afraid it'll be a terrible disappointment to him."

"Life is full of disappointments," said Muriel crisply. "But one learns to put up with them."

I gave her a smile of amusement. We were sitting in a Rolls, and there was a footman as well as a chauffeur on the box. She wore a string of pearls that had probably cost forty thousand pounds. I recollected that in the birthday honours Sir Adolphus Bland had not been one of the three gentlemen on whom the King had been pleased to confer a peerage.

Lea Makart was able to make only a flying visit. She was playing that evening at Brighton and would motor over to Tilby on the Sunday morning for luncheon. She was returning to London the same day because she had a concert in Manchester on the Monday. George was to play in the course of the afternoon.

"He's practising very hard," his mother told me. "That's why he didn't come with me to meet you."

We turned in at the park gates and drove up the imposing avenue of elms that led to the house. I found that there was no party.

I met the dowager Lady Bland for the first time. I had always been curious to see her. I had had in my mind's eye a somewhat sensational picture of an old, old Jewish woman who lived alone in her grand house in Portland Place and, with a finger in every pie, ruled her family with a despotic hand. She did not disappoint me. She was of a commanding presence, rather tall, and stout without being corpulent. Her countenance was markedly Hebraic. She wore a rather heavy moustache and a wig of a peculiarly metallic brown. Her dress was very grand, of black brocade, and she had a row of large diamond stars on her breast and round her neck a chain of diamonds. Diamond rings gleamed on her wrinkled hands. She spoke in a rather loud harsh voice and with a strong German accent. When I was introduced to her she fixed me with shining eyes. She summed me up with despatch and to my fancy at all events made no attempt to conceal from me that the judgment she formed was unfavourable.

"You have known my brother Ferdinand for many years, is it not so?" she said, rolling a guttural R. "My brother Ferdinand has always moved in very good society. Where is Sir Adolphus, Muriel? Does he know your guest is arrived? And will you not send for George? If he does not know his pieces by now he will not know them by to-morrow."

Muriel explained that Freddy was finishing a round of golf with his secretary and that she had had George told I was there. Lady Bland looked as though she thought Muriel's replies highly unsatisfactory and turned again to me.

"My daughter-in-law tells me you have been in Italy?"

"Yes, I've only just come back."

"It is a beautiful country. How is the King?"

I said I did not know.

"I used to know him when he was a little boy. He was not very strong then. His mother, Queen Margherita, was a great friend of mine. They thought he would never marry. The Duchess of Aosta was very angry when he fell in love with that Princess of Montenegro."

She seemed to belong to some long-past period of history, but she was very alert and I imagine that little escaped her beady eyes. Freddy, very spruce in plus-fours, presently came in. It was amusing and yet a little touching to see this grey-bearded man, as a rule somewhat domineering, so obviously on his best behaviour with the old lady. He called her Mamma. Then George came in. He was as fat as ever, but he had taken my advice and had his hair cut; he was losing his boyish looks, but he was a powerful and well set-up young man. It was good to see the pleasure he took in his tea. He ate quantities of sandwiches and great hunks of cake. He had still a boy's appetite. His father watched him with a tender smile and as I looked at him I could not be surprised at the attachment which they all so obviously felt for him. He had an ingenuousness, a charm and an enthusiasm which were certainly very pleasant. There was about him a generosity of demeanour, a frankness and a natural cordiality which could not but make people take to him. I do not know whether it was owing to a hint from his grandmother or merely of his own good nature, but it was plain that he was going out of his way to be nice to his father; and in his father's soft eyes, in the way he hung upon the boy's words, in his pleased, proud and happy look, you felt how bitterly the estrangement of the last two years had weighed on him. He adored George.

We played golf in the morning, a three-ball match, since Muriel, having to go to Mass, could not join us, and at one Ferdy arrived in Lea Makart's car. We sat down to luncheon. Of course Lea Makart's reputation was well known to me. She was acknowledged to be the greatest woman pianist in Europe. She was a very old friend of Ferdy's, who with his interest and patronage had greatly helped her at the beginning of her career, and it was he who had arranged for her to come and give her opinion of George's chances. At one time I went as often as I could to hear her play. She had no affectations; she played as a bird sings, without any appearance of effort, very naturally, and the silvery notes dripped from her light fingers in a curiously spontaneous manner, so that it gave you the impression that she was improvising those complicated rhythms. They used to tell me that her technique was wonderful. I could never make up my mind how much the delight her playing gave me was due to her person. In those days she was the most ethereal thing you could imagine, and it was surprising that a creature so sylphlike should be capable of so much power. She was very slight, pale, with enormous eyes and magnificent black hair, and at the piano she had a child-like wistfulness that was most appealing. She was very beautiful in a hardly human way and when she played, a little smile on her closed lips, she seemed to be remembering things she had heard in another world. Now, however, a woman in the early forties, she was sylphlike no more; she was stout and her face had broadened; she had no longer that lovely remoteness, but the authority of her long succession of triumphs. She was brisk, business-like and somewhat over-whelming. Her vitality lit her with a natural spotlight as his sanctity surrounds the saint with a halo. She was not interested in anything very much but her own affairs, but since she had humour and knew the world she was able to invest them with gaiety. She held the conversation, but did not absorb it. George talked little. Every now and then she gave him a glance, but did not try to draw him in. I was the only Gentile at the table. All but old Lady Bland spoke perfect English, yet I could not help feeling that they did not speak like English people; I think they rounded their vowels more than we do, they certainly spoke louder, and the words seemed not to fall, but to gush from their lips. I think if I had been in another room where I could hear the tone but not the words of their speech I should have thought it was in a foreign language that they were conversing. The effect was slightly disconcerting.

Lea Makart wished to set out for London at about six, so it was arranged that George should play at four. Whatever the result of the audition, I felt that I, a stranger in the circle which her departure must render exclusively domestic, would be in the way and so, pretending an early engagement in town next morning, I asked her if she would take me with her in her car.

At a little before four we all wandered into the drawing-room. Old Lady Bland sat on a sofa with Ferdy; Freddy, Muriel and I made ourselves comfortable in arm-chairs; and Lea Makart sat by herself. She chose instinctively a high-backed Jacobean chair that had somewhat the air of a throne, and in a yellow dress, with her olive skin, she looked very handsome. She had magnificent eyes. She was very much made up and her mouth was scarlet.

George gave no sign of nervousness. He was already seated at the piano when I went in with his father and mother, and he watched us quietly settling ourselves down. He gave me the shadow of a smile. When he saw that we were all at our ease he began to play. He played Chopin. He played two waltzes that were familiar to me, a polonaise and an *étude*. He played with a great deal of brio. I wish I knew music well enough to give an exact description of his playing. It had strength, and a youthful exuberance, but I felt that he missed what to me is the peculiar charm of Chopin, the tenderness, the nervous melancholy, the wistful gaiety and the slightly faded romance that reminds me always of an Early Victorian keepsake. And again I had the vague sensation, so slight that it almost escaped me, that the two hands did not quite synchronise. I looked at Ferdy and saw him give his sister a look of faint surprise, Muriel's eyes were fixed on the pianist, but presently she dropped them and for the rest of the time stared at the floor. His father looked at him too, and his eyes were steadfast, but unless I was much mistaken he went pale and his face betrayed something like dismay. Music was in the blood of all of them, all their lives they had heard the greatest pianists in the world, and they judged with instinctive precision.

B*

The only person whose face betrayed no emotion was Lea Makart. She listened very attentively. She was as still as an image in a niche.

At last he stopped and turning round on his seat faced her. He did not speak.

"What is it you want me to tell you?" she asked.

They looked into one another's eyes.

"I want you to tell me whether I have any chance of becoming in time a pianist in the first rank."

"Not in a thousand years."

For a moment there was dead silence. Freddy's head sank and he looked down at the carpet at his feet. His wife put out her hand and took his. But George continued to look steadily at Lea Makart.

"Ferdy has told me the circumstances," she said at last. "Don't think I'm influenced by them. Nothing of this is very important." She made a great sweeping gesture that took in the magnificent room with the beautiful things it contained and all of us. "If I thought you had in you the makings of an artist I shouldn't hesitate to beseech you to give up everything for art's sake. Art is the only thing that matters. In comparison with art, wealth and rank and power are not worth a straw." She gave us a look so sincere that it was void of insolence. "We are the only people who count. We give the world significance. You are only our raw material."

I was not too pleased to be included with the rest under that heading, but that is neither here nor there.

"Of course I can see that you've worked very hard. Don't think it's been wasted. It will always be a pleasure to you to be able to play the piano and it will enable you to appreciate great playing as no ordinary person can hope to do. Look at your hands. They're not a pianist's hands."

Involuntarily I glanced at George's hands. I had never noticed them before. I was astounded to see how podgy they were and how short and stumpy the fingers.

"Your ear is not quite perfect. I don't think you can ever hope to be more than a very competent amateur. In art the difference between the amateur and the professional is immeasurable."

George did not reply. Except for his pallor no one would have known that he was listening to the blasting of all his hopes. The silence that fell was quite awful. Lea Makart's eyes suddenly filled with tears.

"But don't take my opinion alone," she said. "After all, I'm not infallible. Ask somebody else. You know how good and generous Paderewski is. I'll write to him about you and you can go down and play to him. I'm sure he'll hear you."

George now gave a little smile. He had very good manners and whatever he was feeling did not want to make the situation too difficult for others.

"I don't think that's necessary, I am content to accept your verdict. To tell you the truth it's not so very different from my master's in Munich."

He got up from the piano and lit a cigarette. It eased the strain. The others moved a little in their chairs. Lea Makart smiled at George.

"Shall I play to you?" she said.

"Yes, do."

She got up and went to the piano. She took off the rings with which her fingers were laden. She played Bach. I do not know the names of the pieces, but I recognised the stiff ceremonial of the frenchified little German courts and the sober, thrifty comfort of the burghers, and the dancing on the village green, the green trees that looked like Christmas trees, and the sunlight on the wide German country, and a tender cosiness; and in my nostrils there was a warm scent of the soil and I was conscious of a sturdy strength that seemed to have its roots deep in mother earth, and of an elemental power that was timeless and had no home in space. She played beautifully, with a soft brilliance that made you think of the full moon shining at dusk in the summer sky. With another part of me I watched the others and I saw how intensely they were conscious of the experience. They were rapt. I wished with all my heart that I could get from music the wonderful exaltation that possessed them. She stopped, a smile hovered on her lips, and she put on her rings. George gave a little chuckle.

"That clinches it, I fancy," he said.

The servants brought in tea and after tea Lea Makart and I bade the company farewell and got into the car. We drove up to London. She talked all the way, if not brilliantly at all events with immense gusto; she told me of her early years in Manchester and of the struggle of her beginnings. She was very interesting. She never even mentioned George; the episode was of no consequence, it was finished and she thought of it no more.

We little knew what was happening at Tilby. When we left

George went out on the terrace and presently his father joined him. Freddy had won the day, but he was not happy. With his more than feminine sensitiveness he felt all that George was feeling, and George's anguish simply broke his heart. He had never loved his son more than then. When he appeared George greeted him with a little smile. Freddy's voice broke. In a sudden and over-whelming emotion he found it in him to surrender the fruits of his victory.

"Look here, old boy," he said, "I can't bear to think that you've had such a disappointment. Would you like to go back to Munich for another year and then see?"

George shook his head.

"No, it wouldn't be any good. I've had my chance. Let's call it a day."

"Try not to take it too hard."

"You see, the only thing in the world I want is to be a pianist. And there's nothing doing. It's a bit thick if you come to think of it."

George, trying so hard to be brave, smiled wanly.

"Would you like to go round the world? You can get one of your Oxford pals to go with you and I'll pay all the expenses. You've been working very hard for a long time."

"Thanks awfully, daddy, we'll talk about it. I'm just going for a stroll now."

"Shall I come with you?"

"I'd rather go alone."

Then George did a strange thing. He put his arm round his father's neck, and kissed him on the lips. He gave a funny little moved laugh and walked away. Freddy went back to the drawing-room. His mother, Ferdy and Muriel were sitting there.

"Freddy, why don't you marry the boy?" said the old lady. "He is twenty-three. It would take his mind off his troubles and when he is married and has a baby he will soon settle down like every-body else."

"Whom is he to marry, mamma?" asked Sir Adolphus, smiling.

"That's not so difficult. Lady Frielinghausen came to see me the other day with her daughter Violet. She is a very nice maiden and she will have money of her own. Lady Frielinghausen gave me to understand that her Sir Jacob would come down very hand-some if Violet made a good match."

Muriel flushed.

"I hate Lady Frielinghausen. George is much too young to marry. He can afford to marry anyone he likes."

Old Lady Bland gave her daughter a strange look.

"You are a very foolish girl, Miriam," she said, using the name Muriel had long discarded. "As long as I am here I shall not allow you to commit a foolishness."

She knew as well as if Muriel had said it in so many words that she wanted George to marry a Gentile, but she knew also that so long as she was alive neither Freddy nor his wife would dare to suggest it.

But George did not go for a walk. Perhaps because the shooting season was about to open he took it into his head to go into the gun-room. He began to clean the gun that his mother had given him on his twentieth birthday. No one had used it since he went to Germany. Suddenly the servants were startled by a report. When they went into the gun-room they found George lying on the floor shot through the heart. Apparently the gun had been loaded and George while playing about with it had accidentally shot himself. One reads of such accidents in the paper often.

❖

The Creative Impulse

I SUPPOSE that very few people know how Mrs. Albert Forrester came to write *The Achilles Statue*; and since it has been acclaimed as one of the great novels of our time I cannot but think that a brief account of the circumstances that gave it birth must be of interest to all serious students of literature; and indeed, if, as the critics say, this is a book that will live, the following narrative, serving a better purpose than to divert an idle hour, may be regarded by the historian of the future as a curious footnote to the literary annals of our day.

Everyone of course remembers the success that attended the publication of *The Achilles Statue*. Month after month printers were kept busy printing, binders were kept busy binding, edition after edition; and the publishers, both in England and America, were hard put to it to fulfil the pressing orders of the booksellers. It was promptly translated into every European tongue and it has been recently announced that it will soon be possible to read it in Japanese and in Urdu. But it had previously appeared serially in magazines on both sides of the Atlantic and from the editors of these Mrs. Albert Forrester's agent had wrung a sum that can only be described as thumping. A dramatisation of the work was made, which ran for a season in New York, and there is little doubt that when the play is produced in London it will have an equal success. The film rights have been sold at a great price. Though the amount that Mrs. Albert Forrester is reputed (in literary circles) to have made is probably exaggerated, there can be no doubt that she will have earned enough money from this one book to save her for the rest of her life from any financial anxiety.

It is not often that a book meets with equal favour from the public and the critics, and that she, of all persons, had (if I may so put it) squared the circle must have proved the more gratifying to Mrs. Albert Forrester, since, though she had received the commendation of the critics in no grudging terms (and indeed had come to look upon it as her due) the public had always remained strangely insensibile to her merit. Each work she published, a slender volume beautifully printed and bound in white buckram, was hailed as a masterpiece, always to the length of a column, and in the weekly reviews which you see only in the dusty library of a very long-established club even to the extent of a page; and all well-read persons read and praised it. But well-read persons apparently do not buy books, and she did not sell. It was indeed a scandal that so distinguished an author, with an imagination so delicate and a style so exquisite, should remain neglected of the vulgar. In America she was almost completely unknown; and though Mr. Carl van Vechten had written an article berating the public for its obtuseness, the public remained callous. Her agent, a warm admirer of her genius, had blackmailed an American publisher into taking two of her books by refusing, unless he did so, to let him have others (trashy novels doubtless) that he badly wanted, and they had been duly published. The reception they received from the press was flattering and showed that in America the best minds were sensitive to her talent; but when it came to the third book the American publisher (in the coarse way publishers have) told the agent that any money he had to spare he preferred to spend on synthetic gin.

Since *The Achilles Statue* Mrs. Albert Forrester's previous books have been republished (and Mr. Carl van Vechten has written another article pointing out sadly, but firmly, that he had drawn the attention of the reading world to the merits of this exceptional writer fully fifteen years ago), and they have been so widely advertised that they can scarcely have escaped the cultured reader's attention. It is unnecessary, therefore, for me to give an account of them; and it would certainly be no more than cold potatoes after those two subtle articles by Mr. Carl van Vechten. Mrs. Albert Forrester began to write early. Her first work (a volume of elegies) appeared when she was a maiden of eighteen; and from then on she published, every two or three years, for she had too exalted a conception of her art to hurry her production, a volume either of verse or prose. When *The Achilles Statue* was written she had reached the respectable age of fifty-seven, so that it will be readily surmised that the number of her works was considerable. She had given the world half a dozen volumes of verse, published under Latin titles, such as *Felicitas*, *Pax Maris* and *Aes Triplex*, all of the graver kind, for her muse, disinclined to skip on a light, fantastic toe, trod a somewhat solemn measure. She remained faithful to the Elegy, and the Sonnet claimed much of her attention; but her chief distinction was to revive the Ode, a form of poetry that the poets of the present day somewhat neglect; and it may be asserted with confidence that her *Ode to President Fallières* will find a place in every anthology of English verse. It is admirable not only for the noble sonority of its rhythms, but also for its felicitous description of the pleasant land of France. Mrs. Albert Forrester wrote of the valley of the Loire with its memories of du Bellay, of Chartres and the jewelled windows of its cathedral, of the sun-swept cities of Provence, with a sympathy all the more remarkable since she had never penetrated further into France than Boulogne, which she visited shortly after her marriage on an excursion steamer from Margate. But the physical mortification of being extremely seasick and the intellectual humiliation of discovering that the inhabitants of that popular seaside resort could not understand her fluent and idiomatic French made her determine not to expose herself a second time to experiences that were at once undignified and unpleasant; and she never again embarked on the treacherous element which she, however, sang (*Pax Maris*) in numbers both grave and sweet.

There are some fine passages too in the *Ode to Woodrow Wilson*, and I regret that, owing to a change in her sentiments towards that no doubt excellent man, the author decided not to reprint it. But I think it must be admitted that Mrs. Albert Forrester's most distinguished work was in prose. She wrote several volumes of brief, but perfectly constructed, essays on such subjects as Autumn in Sussex, Queen Victoria, Death, Spring in Norfolk, Georgian Architecture, Monsieur de Diaghileff and Dante; she also wrote works, both erudite and whimsical, on the Jesuit Architecture of the XVIIth Century and on the Literary Aspect of the Hundred Years' War. It was her prose that gained her that body of devoted admirers, fit though few, as with her rare gift of phrase she herself put it, that proclaimed her the greatest master of the English language that this century has seen. She admitted herself that it was her style, sonorous yet racy, polished yet eloquent, that was her strong point; and it was only in her prose that she had occasion to exhibit the delicious, but restrained, humour that her readers found so irresistible. It was not a humour of ideas, nor even a humour of words; it was much more subtle than that, it was a humour of punctuation: in a flash of inspiration she had discovered the comic possibilities of the semi-colon, and of this she had made abundant and exquisite use. She was able to place it in such a way that if you were a person of culture with a keen sense of humour, you did not exactly laugh through a horse-collar, but you giggled delightedly, and the greater your culture the more delightedly you giggled. Her friends said that it made every other form of humour coarse and exaggerated. Several writers had tried to imitate her; but in vain: whatever else you might say about Mrs. Albert Forrester you were bound to admit that she was able to get every ounce of humour out of the semi-colon and no one else could get within a mile of her.

Mrs. Albert Forrester lived in a flat not far from the Marble Arch, which combined the advantage of a good address and a moderate rent. It had a handsome drawing-room on the street and a large bedroom for Mrs. Albert Forrester, a darkish dining-room at the back and a small poky bedroom, next door to the kitchen, for Mr. Albert Forrester, who paid the rent. It was in the handsome drawing-room that Mrs. Albert Forrester every Tuesday afternoon received her friends. It was a severe and chaste apartment. On the walls was a paper designed by William Morris himself and on this, in plain black frames, mezzotints collected before mezzotints grew expensive; the furniture was of the Chippendale period, but for the roll-top desk, vaguely Louis XVI in character, at which Mrs. Albert Forrester wrote her works. This was pointed out to visitors the first time they came to see her, and there were few who looked at it without emotion. The carpet was thick and the lights discreet. Mrs. Albert Forrester sat in a straight-backed grandfather's chair covered with red damask. There was nothing ostentatious about it, but since it was the only comfortable chair in the room it set her apart as it were and above her guests. Tea was dispensed by a female of uncertain age, silent and colourless, who was never introduced to anyone but who was known to look upon it as a privilege to be allowed to save Mrs. Albert Forrester from the irksome duty of pouring out tea. She was thus able to devote herself entirely to conversation, and it must be admitted that her conversation was excellent. It was not sprightly; and since it is difficult to indicate punctuation in speech it may have seemed to some slightly lacking in humour, but it was of wide range, solid, instructive and interesting. Mrs. Albert Forrester was well acquainted with social science, jurisprudence and theology. She had read much and her memory was retentive. She had a pretty gift for quotation, which is a serviceable substitute for wit, and having for thirty years known more or less intimately a great many distinguished people, she had a great many interesting anecdotes to tell, which she placed with tact and which she did not repeat more than was pardonable. Mrs. Albert Forrester had the gift of attracting the most varied persons and you were liable at one and the same time to meet in her drawing-room an ex-Prime Minister, a newspaper proprietor and the ambassador of a First Class Power. I always imagined that these great people came because they thought that here they rubbed shoulders with Bohemia, but with a Bohemia sufficiently neat and clean for them to be in no danger that the dirt would come off on them. Mrs. Albert Forrester was deeply interested in politics and I myself heard a Cabinet Minister tell her frankly that she had a masculine intelligence. She had been opposed to Female Suffrage, but when it was at last granted to women she began to dally with the idea of going into Parliament. Her difficulty was that she did not know which party to choose.

"After all," she said, with a playful shrug of her somewhat massive shoulders, "I cannot form a party of one."

Like many serious patriots, in her inability to know for certain which way the cat would jump she held her political opinions in suspense; but of late she had been definitely turning towards Labour as the best hope of the country, and if a safe seat were offered her it was felt fairly certain that she would not hesitate to come out into the open as a champion of the oppressed proletariat.

Her drawing-room was always open to foreigners, to Czecho-Slovaks, Italians and Frenchmen if they were distinguished and to Americans even if they were obscure. But she was not a snob and you seldom met there a duke unless he was of a peculiarly serious turn and a peeress only if in addition to her rank she had the passport of some small social solecism such as having been divorced, written a novel or forged a cheque, which might give her claim on Mrs. Albert Forrester's catholic sympathies. She did not much care for painters, who were shy and silent; and musicians did not interest her: even if they consented to play, and if they were celebrated they were too often reluctant, their music was a hindrance to conversation: if people wanted music they could go to a concert; for her part she preferred the more subtle music of the soul. But her hospitality to writers, especially if they were promising and little known, was warm and constant. She had an eye for budding talent and there were few of the famous writers who from time to time drank a dish of tea with her whose first efforts she had not encouraged and whose early steps she had not guided. Her own position was too well assured for her to be capable of envy, and she had heard the word genius attached to her name too often to feel a trace of jealousy because the talents of others brought them a material success that was denied to her.

Mrs. Albert Forrester, confident in the judgment of posterity, could afford to be disinterested. With these elements then it is no wonder that she had succeeded in creating something as near the French Salon of the Eighteenth Century as our barbarous nation has ever reached. To be invited to "eat a bun and drink a cup of tea on Tuesday" was a privilege that few failed to recognise; and when you sat on your Chippendale chair in the discreetly lit but austere room, you could not but feel that you were living literary history. The American Ambassador once said to Mrs. Albert Forrester:

"A cup of tea with you, Mrs. Forrester, is one of the richest intellectual treats which it has ever been my lot to enjoy."

It was indeed on occasion a trifle overwhelming. Mrs. Albert Forrester's taste was so perfect, she so inevitably admired the right thing and made the just observation about it, that sometimes you almost gasped for air. For my part I found it prudent to fortify myself with a cocktail or two before I exposed myself to the rarefied atmosphere of her society. Indeed, I very nearly found myself for ever excluded from it, for one afternoon, presenting myself at the door, instead of asking the maid who opened it: "Is Mrs. Forrester at home?" I asked: "Is there Divine Service to-day?"

Of course it was said in pure inadvertence, but it was unfortunate that the maid sniggered and one of Mrs. Albert Forrester's most devoted admirers, Ellen Hannaway, happened to be at the moment in the hall taking off her goloshes. She told my hostess what I had said before I got into the drawing-room, and as I entered Mrs. Albert Forrester fixed me with an eagle eye.

"Why did you ask if there was Divine Service to-day?" she inquired.

I explained that I was absent-minded, but Mrs. Albert Forrester held me with a gaze that I can only describe as compelling.

"Do you mean to suggest that my parties are . . ." she searched for a word. "Sacramental?"

I did not know what she meant, but did not like to show my ignorance before so many clever people, and I decided that the only thing was to seize my trowel and the butter.

"Your parties are like you, dear lady, perfectly beautiful and perfectly divine."

A little tremor passed through Mrs. Albert Forrester's substantial frame. She was like a man who enters suddenly a room filled with hyacinths; the perfume is so intoxicating that he almost staggers. But she relented.

"If you were trying to be facetious," she said, "I should prefer you to exercise your facetiousness on my guests rather than on my maids. . . . Miss Warren will give you some tea."

Mrs. Albert Forrester dismissed me with a wave of the hand, but she did not dismiss the subject, since for the next two or three years whenever she introduced me to someone she never failed to add:

"You must make the most of him, he only comes here as a penance. When he comes to the door he always asks: Is there Divine Service to-day? So amusing, isn't he?"

But Mrs. Albert Forrester did not confine herself to weekly tea-parties: every Saturday she gave a luncheon of eight persons; this according to her opinion being the perfect number for general conversation and her dining-room conveniently holding no more. If Mrs. Albert Forrester flattered herself upon anything it was not that her knowledge of English prosody was unique, but that her luncheons were celebrated. She chose her guests with care and an invitation to one of them was more than a compliment, it was a consecration. Over the luncheon-table it was possible to keep the conversation on a higher level than in the mixed company of a tea-party and few can have left her dining-room without taking away with them an enhanced belief in Mrs. Albert Forrester's ability and a brighter faith in human nature. She only asked men, since, stout enthusiast for her sex as she was and glad to see women on other occasions, she could not but realise that they were inclined at table to talk exclusively to their next-door neighbours and thus hinder the general exchange of ideas that made her own parties an entertainment not only of the body but of the soul. For it must be said that Mrs. Albert Forrester gave you uncommonly good food, excellent wine and a first-rate cigar. Now to anyone who has partaken of literary hospitality this must appear very remarkable, since literary persons for the most part think highly and live plainly; their minds are occupied with the things of the spirit and they do not notice that the roast mutton is underdone and the potatoes cold: the beer is all right, but the wine has a sobering effect, and it is unwise to touch the coffee. Mrs. Albert Forrester was pleased enough to receive compliments on the fare she provided.

"If people do me the honour to break bread with me," she said, "it is only fair that I should give them as good food as they can get at home."

But if the flattery was excessive she deprecated it.

"You really embarrass me when you give me a meed of praise which is not my due. You must praise Mrs. Bulfinch."

"Who is Mrs. Bulfinch?"

"My cook."

"She's a treasure then, but you're not going to ask me to believe that she's responsible for the wine."

"Is it good? I'm terribly ignorant of such things; I put myself entirely in the hands of my wine merchant."

But if mention was made of the cigars Mrs. Albert Forrester beamed.

"Ah, for them you must compliment Albert. It is Albert who chooses the cigars and I am given to understand that no one knows more about a cigar than Albert."

She looked at her husband, who sat at the end of the table, with the proud bright eyes of a pedigree hen (a Buff Orpington for choice) looking at her only chick. Then there was a quick flutter of conversation as the guests, anxious to be civil to their host and relieved at length to find an occasion, expressed their appreciation of his peculiar merit.

"You're very kind," he said. "I'm glad you like them."

Then he would give a little discourse on cigars, explaining the excellencies he sought and regretting the deterioration in quality which had followed on the commercialisation of the industry. Mrs. Albert Forrester listened to him with a complacent smile, and it was plain that she enjoyed this little triumph of his. Of course you cannot go on talking of cigars indefinitely and as soon as she perceived that her guests were growing restive she broached a topic of more general, and it may be of more significant, interest. Albert subsided into silence. But he had had his moment.

It was Albert who made Mrs. Forrester's luncheons to some less attractive than her tea-parties, for Albert was a bore; but though without doubt perfectly conscious of the fact, she made a point that he should come to them and in fact had fixed upon Saturdays (for the rest of the week he was busy) in order that he should be able to. Mrs. Albert Forrester felt that her husband's presence on these festive occasions was an unavoidable debt that she paid to her own self-respect. She would never by a negligence admit to the world that she had married a man who was not spiritually her equal, and it may be that in the silent watches of the nights she asked herself where indeed such could have been found. Mrs. Albert Forrester's friends were troubled by no such reticence and they said it was dreadful that such a woman should be burdened with such a man. They asked each other how she had ever come to marry him and (being mostly celibate) answered despairingly that no one ever knew why anybody married anybody else.

It was not that Albert was a verbose and aggressive bore; he did not buttonhole you with interminable stories or pester you with pointless jokes; he did not crucify you on a platitude or hamstring you with a commonplace; he was just dull. A cipher. Clifford Boyleston, for whom the French Romantics had no secrets and who was himself a writer of merit, had said that when you looked into a room into which Albert had just gone there was nobody there. This was thought very clever by Mrs. Albert Forrester's friends and Rose Waterford, the well-known novelist and the most fearless of women, had ventured to repeat it to Mrs. Albert Forrester. Though she pretended to be annoyed, she had not been able to prevent the smile that rose to her lips. Her behaviour towards Albert could not but increase the respect in which her friends held her. She insisted that whatever in their secret hearts they thought of him, they should treat him with the decorum that was due to her husband. Her own demeanour was admirable. If he chanced to make an observation she listened to him with a pleasant expression and when he fetched her a book that she wanted or gave her his pencil to make a note of an idea that had occurred to her, she always thanked him. Nor would she allow her friends pointedly to neglect him, and though, being a woman of tact, she saw that it would be asking too much of the world if she took him about with her always, and she went out much alone, yet her friends knew that she expected them to ask him to dinner at least once a year. He always accompanied her to public banquets when she was going to make a speech, and if she delivered a lecture she took care that he should have a seat on the platform.

Albert was, I believe, of average height, but perhaps because you never thought of him except in connection with his wife (of imposing dimensions) you only thought of him as a little man. He

was spare and frail and looked older than his age. This was the
same as his wife's. His hair, which he kept very short, was white
and meagre, and he wore a stubby white moustache; his was a
face, thin and lined, without a noticeable feature; and his blue
eyes, which once might have been attractive, were now pale and
tired. He was always very neatly dressed in pepper-and-salt
trousers, which he chose always of the same pattern, a black coat
and a grey tie with a small pearl pin in it. He was perfectly
unobtrusive, and when he stood in Mrs. Albert Forrester's
drawing-room to receive the guests whom she had asked to
luncheon you noticed him as little as you noticed the quiet and
gentlemanly furniture. He was well-mannered and it was with a
pleasant, courteous smile that he shook hands with them.

"How do you do? I'm very glad to see you," he said if they were
friends of some standing. "Keeping well, I hope?"

But if they were strangers of distinction coming for the first
time to the house, he went to the door as they entered the drawing-
room, and said:

"I am Mrs. Albert Forrester's husband. I will introduce you to
my wife."

Then he led the visitor to where Mrs. Albert Forrester stood,
with her back to the light, and she with a glad and eager gesture
advanced to make the stranger welcome.

It was agreeable to see the demure pride he took in his wife's
literary reputation and the self-effacement with which he furthered
her interests. He was always there when he was wanted and never
when he wasn't. His tact, if not deliberate, was instinctive. Mrs.
Albert Forrester was the first to acknowledge his merits.

"I really don't know what I should do without him," she said.
"He's invaluable to me. I read him everything I write and his
criticisms are often very useful."

"Molière and his cook," said Miss Waterford.

"Is that funny, dear Rose?" asked Mrs. Forrester, somewhat
acidly.

When Mrs. Albert Forrester did not approve of a remark, she
had a way that put many persons to confusion of asking you
whether it was a joke which she was too dense to see. But it was
impossible to embarrass Miss Waterford. She was a lady who in
the course of a long life had had many affairs, but only one passion,
and this was for printer's ink. Mrs. Albert Forrester tolerated
rather than approved her.

"Come, come, my dear," she replied, "you know very well that he wouldn't exist without you. He wouldn't know us. It must be wonderful to him to come in contact with all the best brains and the most distinguished people of our day."

"It may be that the bee would perish without the hive which shelters it, but the bee nevertheless has a significance of its own."

And since Mrs. Albert Forrester's friends, though they knew all about art and literature, knew little about natural history, they had no reply to this observation. She went on.

"He doesn't interfere with me. He knows subconsciously when I don't want to be disturbed and, indeed, when I am following out a train of thought I find his presence in the room a comfort rather than a hindrance to me."

"Like a Persian cat," said Miss Waterford.

"But like a very well-trained, well-bred, and well-mannered Persian cat," answered Mrs. Forrester severely, thus putting Miss Waterford in her place.

But Mrs. Albert Forrester had not finished with her husband.

"We who belong to the intelligentsia," she said, "are apt to live in a world too exclusively our own. We are interested in the abstract rather than in the concrete, and sometimes I think that we survey the bustling world of human affairs in too detached a manner and from too serene a height. Do you not think that we stand in danger of becoming a little inhuman? I shall always be grateful to Albert because he keeps me in contact with the man in the street."

It was on account of this remark, to which none of her friends could deny the rare insight and subtlety that characterised so many of her utterances, that for some time Albert was known in her immediate circle as The Man in the Street. But this was only for a while, and it was forgotten. He then became known as The Philatelist. It was Clifford Boyleston, with his wicked wit, who invented the name. One day, his poor brain exhausted by the effort to sustain a conversation with Albert, he had asked in desperation:

"Do you collect stamps?"

"No," answered Albert mildly. "I'm afraid I don't."

But Clifford Boyleston had no sooner asked the question than he saw its possibilities. He had written a book on Baudelaire's aunt by marriage, which had attracted the attention of all who were interested in French literature, and was well known in his exhaustive studies of the French spirit to have absorbed a goodly share of the Gallic quickness and the Gallic brilliancy. He paid no attention to Albert's disclaimer, but at the first opportunity informed Mrs. Albert Forrester's friends that he had at last discovered Albert's secret. He collected stamps. He never met him afterwards without asking him:

"Well, Mr. Forrester, how is the stamp collection?" Or: "Have you been buying any stamps since I saw you last?"

It mattered little that Albert continued to deny that he collected stamps, the invention was too apt not to be made the most of; Mrs. Albert Forrester's friends insisted that he did, and they seldom spoke to him without asking him how he was getting on. Even Mrs. Albert Forrester, when she was in a specially gay humour, would sometimes speak of her husband as The Philatelist. The name really did seem to fit Albert like a glove. Sometimes they spoke of him thus to his face and they could not but appreciate the good nature with which he took it; he smiled unresentfully and presently did not even protest that they were mistaken.

Of course Mrs. Albert Forrester had too keen a social sense to jeopardise the success of her luncheons by allowing her more distinguished guests to sit on either side of Albert. She took care that only her older and more intimate friends should do this, and when the appointed victims came in she would say to them:

"I know you won't mind sitting by Albert, will you?"

They could only say that they would be delighted, but if their faces too plainly expressed their dismay she would pat their hands playfully and add:

"Next time you shall sit by me. Albert is so shy with strangers and you know so well how to deal with him."

They did: they simply ignored him. So far as they were concerned the chair in which he sat might as well have been empty. There was so sign that it annoyed him to be taken no notice of by persons who after all were eating food he paid for, since the earnings of Mrs. Forrester could certainly not have provided her guests with spring salmon and forced asparagus. He sat quiet and silent, and if he opened his mouth it was only to give a direction to one of the maids. If a guest were new to him he would let his eyes rest on him in a stare that would have been embarrassing if it had not been so childlike. He seemed to be asking himself what this strange creature was; but what answer his mild scrutiny gave him he never revealed. When the conversation grew animated he would look from one speaker to the other, but again you could not tell from his thin, lined face what he thought of the fantastic notions that were bandied across the table.

Clifford Boyleston said that all the wit and wisdom he heard passed over his head like water over a duck's back. He had given up trying to understand and now only made a semblance of listening. But Harry Oakland, the versatile critic, said that Albert was taking it all in; he found it all too, too marvellous, and with his poor, muddled brain he was trying desperately to make head or tail of the wonderful things he heard. Of course in the City he must boast of the distinguished persons he knew, perhaps there he was a light of learning and letters, an authority on the ideal; it would be perfectly divine to hear what he made of it all. Harry Oakland was one of Mrs. Albert Forrester's staunchest admirers, and had written a brilliant and subtle essay on her style. With his refined and even beautiful features he looked like a San Sebastian who had had an accident with a hair-restorer; for he was uncommonly hirsute. He was a very young man, not thirty, but he had been in turn a dramatic critic, and a critic of fiction, a musical critic and a critic of painting. But he was getting a little tired of art and threatened to devote his talents in future to the criticism of sport.

Albert, I should explain, was in the City and it was a misfortune that Mrs. Forrester's friends thought she bore with meritorious fortitude that he was not even rich. There would have been something romantic in it if he had been a merchant prince who held the fate of nations in his hand or sent argosies, laden with rare spices, to those ports of the Levant the names of which have provided many a poet with so rich and rare a rhyme. But Albert was only a currant merchant and was supposed to make no more than just enabled Mrs. Albert Forrester to conduct her life with distinction and even with liberality. Since his occupation kept him in his office till six o'clock he never managed to get to Mrs. Albert Forrester's Tuesdays till the most important visitors were gone. By the time he arrived, there were seldom more than three or four of her more intimate friends in the drawing-room, discussing with freedom and humour the guests who had departed, and when they heard Albert's key in the front door they realised with one accord that it was late. In a moment he opened the door in his hesitating way and looked mildly in. Mrs. Albert Forrester greeted him with a bright smile.

"Come in, Albert, come in. I think you know everybody here."

Albert entered and shook hands with his wife's friends.

"Have you just come from the City?" she asked eagerly, though she knew there was nowhere else he could have come from. "Would you like a cup of tea?"

"No, thank you, my dear. I had tea in my office."

Mrs. Albert Forrester smiled still more brightly and the rest of the company thought she was perfectly wonderful with him.

"Ah, but I know you like a second cup. I will pour it out for you myself."

She went to the tea-table and, forgetting that the tea had been stewing for an hour and a half and was stone cold, poured him out a cup and added milk and sugar. Albert took it with a word of thanks, and meekly stirred it, but when Mrs. Forrester resumed the conversation which his appearance had interrupted, without tasting it put it quietly down. His arrival was the signal for the party finally to break up and one by one the remaining guests took their departure. On one occasion, however, the conversation was so absorbing and the point at issue so important that Mrs. Albert Forrester would not hear of their going.

"It must be settled once for all. And after all," she remarked in a manner that for her was almost arch, "this is a matter on which Albert may have something to say. Let us have the benefit of his opinion."

It was when women were beginning to cut their hair and the subject of discussion was whether Mrs. Albert Forrester should or should not shingle. Mrs. Albert Forrester was a woman of authoritative presence. She was large-boned and her bones were well covered; had she not been so tall and strong it might have suggested itself to you that she was corpulent. But she carried her weight gallantly. Her features were a little larger than life-size and it was this that gave her face doubtless the look of virile intellectuality that it certainly possessed. Her skin was dark and you might have thought that she had in her veins some trace of Levantine blood: she admitted that she could not but think there was in her a gypsy strain and that would account, she felt, for the wild and lawless passion that sometimes characterised her poetry. Her eyes were large and black and bright, her nose like the great Duke of Wellington's, but more fleshy, and her chin square and determined. She had a big mouth, with full red lips, which owed nothing to cosmetics, for of these Mrs. Albert Forrester had never deigned to make use; and her hair, thick, solid and grey, was piled on the top of her head in such a manner as to increase her already commanding height. She was in appearance an imposing, not to say an alarming, female.

She was always very suitably dressed in rich materials of sombre hue and she looked every inch a woman of letters; but in her discreet way (being after all human and susceptible to vanity) she followed the fashions and the cut of her gowns was modish. I think for some time she had hankered to shingle her hair, but she thought it more becoming to do it at the solicitation of her friends than on her own initiative.

"Oh, you must, you must," said Harry Oakland, in his eager, boyish way. "You'd look too, too wonderful."

Clifford Boyleston, who was now writing a book on Madame de Maintenon, was doubtful. He thought it a dangerous experiment.

"I think," he said, wiping his eye-glasses with a cambric handkerchief, "I think when one has made a type one should stick to it. What would Louis XIV have been without his wig?"

"I'm hesitating," said Mrs. Forrester. "After all, we must move with the times. I am of my day and I do not wish to lag behind. America, as Wilhelm Meister said, is here and now." She turned brightly to Albert. "What does my lord and master say about it? What is your opinion, Albert? To shingle or not to shingle, that is the question."

"I'm afraid my opinion is not of great importance, my dear," he answered mildly.

"To me it is of the greatest importance," answered Mrs. Albert Forrester, flatteringly.

She could not but see how beautifully her friends thought she treated The Philatelist.

"I insist," she proceeded, "I insist. No one knows me as you do, Albert. Will it suit me?"

"It might," he answered. "My only fear is that with your—statuesque appearance short hair would perhaps suggest,—well, shall we say, the Isle of Greece where burning Sappho loved and sung."

There was a moment's embarrassed pause. Rose Waterford smothered a giggle, but the others preserved a stony silence. Mrs. Forrester's smile froze on her lips. Albert had dropped a brick.

"I always thought Byron a very mediocre poet," said Mrs. Albert Forrester at last.

The company broke up. Mrs. Albert Forrester did not shingle, nor indeed was the matter ever again referred to.

It was towards the end of another of Mrs. Albert Forrester's Tuesdays that the event occurred that had so great an influence on her literary career.

It had been one of her most successful parties. The leader of the Labour Party had been there and Mrs. Albert Forrester had gone as far as she could without definitely committing herself to intimate to him that she was prepared to throw in her lot with Labour. The time was ripe and if she was ever to adopt a political career she must come to a decision. A member of the French Academy had been brought by Clifford Boyleston and, though she knew he was wholly unacquainted with English, it had gratified her to receive his affable compliment on her ornate and yet pellucid style. The American Ambassador had been there and a young Russian prince whose authentic Romanoff blood alone prevented him from looking a gigolo. A duchess who had recently divorced her duke and married a jockey had been very gracious; and her strawberry leaves, albeit sere and yellow, undoubtedly added tone to the assembly. There had been quite a galaxy of literary lights. But now all, all were gone but Clifford Boyleston, Harry Oakland, Rose Waterford, Oscar Charles and Simmons. Oscar Charles was a little, gnome-like creature, young but with the wizened face of a cunning monkey, with gold spectacles, who earned his living in a government office but spent his leisure in the pursuit of literature. He wrote little articles for the sixpenny weeklies and had a spirited contempt for the world in general. Mrs. Albert Forrester liked him, thinking he had talent, but though he always expressed the keenest admiration for her style (it was indeed he who had named her the mistress of the semi-colon), his acerbity was so general that she also somewhat feared him. Simmons was her agent; a round-faced man who wore glasses so strong that his eyes behind them looked strange and misshapen. They reminded you of the eyes of some uncouth crustacean that you had seen in an aquarium. He came regularly to Mrs. Albert Forrester's parties, partly because he had the greatest admiration for her genius and partly because it was convenient for him to meet prospective clients in her drawing-room.

Mrs. Albert Forrester, for whom he had long laboured with but a trifling recompense, was not sorry to put him in the way of earning an honest penny, and she took care to introduce him, with warm expressions of gratitude, to anyone who might be supposed to have literary wares to sell. It was not without pride that she remembered that the notorious and vastly lucrative memoirs of Lady St. Swithin had been first mooted in her drawing-room.

They sat in a circle of which Mrs. Albert Forrester was the centre and discussed brightly and, it must be confessed, somewhat maliciously the various persons who had been that day present. Miss Warren, the pallid female who had stood for two hours at the tea-table, was walking silently round the room collecting cups that had been left here and there. She had some vague employment, but was always able to get off in order to pour out tea for Mrs. Albert Forrester, and in the evening she typed Mrs. Albert Forrester's manuscripts. Mrs. Albert Forrester did not pay her for this, thinking quite rightly that as it was she did a great deal for the poor thing; but she gave her the seats for the cinema that were sent her for nothing and often presented her with articles of clothing for which she had no further use.

Mrs. Albert Forrester in her rather deep, full voice was talking in a steady flow and the rest were listening to her with attention. She was in good form and the words that poured from her lips could have gone straight down on paper without alteration. Suddenly there was a noise in the passage as though something heavy had fallen and then the sound of an altercation.

Mrs. Albert Forrester stopped and a slight frown darkened her really noble brow.

"I should have thought they knew by now that I will not have this devastating racket in the flat. Would you mind ringing the bell, Miss Warren, and asking what is the reason of this tumult?"

Miss Warren rang the bell and in a moment the maid appeared. Miss Warren at the door, in order not to interrupt Mrs. Albert Forrester, spoke to her in undertones. But Mrs. Albert Forrester somewhat irritably interrupted herself.

"Well, Carter, what is it? Is the house falling down or has the Red Revolution at last broken out?"

"If you please, ma'am, it's the new cook's box," answered the maid. "The porter dropped it as he was bringing it in and the cook got all upset about it."

"What do you mean by 'the new cook'?"

"Mrs. Bulfinch went away this afternoon, ma'am," said the maid.

Mrs. Albert Forrester stared at her.

"This is the first I've heard of it. Had Mrs. Bulfinch given notice? The moment Mr. Forrester comes in tell him that I wish to speak to him."

"Very good, ma'am."

The maid went out and Miss Warren slowly returned to the tea-table. Mechanically, though nobody wanted them, she poured out several cups of tea.

"What a catastrophe!" cried Miss Waterford.

"You must get her back," said Clifford Boyleston. "She's a treasure, that woman, a remarkable cook, and she gets better and better every day."

But at that moment the maid came in again with a letter on a small plated salver and handed it to her mistress.

"What is this?" said Mrs. Albert Forrester.

"Mr. Forrester said I was to give you this letter when you asked for him, ma'am," said the maid.

"Where is Mr. Forrester then?"

"Mr. Forrester's gone, ma'am," answered the maid as though the question surprised her.

"Gone? That'll do. You can go."

The maid left the room and Mrs. Albert Forrester, with a look of perplexity on her large face, opened the letter. Rose Waterford has told me that her first thought was that Albert, fearful of his wife's displeasure at the departure of Mrs. Bulfinch, had thrown himself in the Thames. Mrs. Albert Forrester read the letter and a look of consternation crossed her face.

"Oh, monstrous," she cried. "Monstrous! Monstrous!"

"What is it, Mrs. Forrester?"

Mrs. Albert Forrester pawed the carpet with her foot like a restive, high-spirited horse pawing the ground, and crossing her arms with a gesture that is indescribable (but that you sometimes see in a fishwife who is going to make the very devil of a scene) bent her looks upon her curious and excessively startled friends.

"Albert has eloped with the cook."

There was a gasp of dismay. Then something terrible happened. Miss Warren, who was standing behind the tea-table, suddenly choked. Miss Warren, who never opened her mouth and whom no one ever spoke to, Miss Warren, whom not one of them, though he had seen her every week for three years, would have recognised in the street, Miss Warren suddenly burst into uncontrollable laughter. With one accord, aghast, they turned and stared at her. They felt as Balaam must have felt when his ass broke into speech. She positively shrieked with laughter. There was a nameless horror about the sight, as though something had on a sudden gone wrong with a natural phenomenon, and you were just as startled as though the chairs and tables without warning began to skip about the floor in an antic dance. Miss Warren tried to contain herself, but the more she tried the more pitilessly the laughter shook her, and seizing a handkerchief she stuffed it in her mouth and hurried from the room. The door slammed behind her.

"Hysteria," said Clifford Boyleston.

"Pure hysteria, of course," said Harry Oakland.

But Mrs. Albert Forrester said nothing.

The letter had dropped at her feet and Simmons, the agent, picked it up and handed it to her. She would not take it.

"Read it," she said. "Read it aloud."

Mr. Simmons pushed his spectacles up on his forehead and holding the letter very close to his eyes read as follows:

My Dear,

Mrs. Bulfinch is in need of a change and has decided to leave, and as I do not feel inclined to stay on here without her I am going too. I have had all the literature I can stand and I am fed up with art.

Mrs. Bulfinch does not care about marriage, but if you care to divorce me she is willing to marry me. I hope you will find the new cook satisfactory. She has excellent references. It may save you trouble if I inform you that Mrs. Bulfinch and I are living at 411, Kennington Road, S.E.

Albert.

No one spoke. Mr. Simmons slipped his spectacles back on to the bridge of his nose. The fact was that none of them, brilliant as they were and accustomed to find topics of conversation to suit every occasion, could think of an appropriate remark. Mrs. Albert Forrester was not the kind of woman to whom you could offer condolences and each was too much afraid of the other's ridicule to venture upon the obvious. At last Clifford Boyleston came bravely to the rescue.

"One doesn't know what to say," he observed.

There was another silence and then Rose Waterford spoke.

"What does Mrs. Bulfinch look like?" she asked.

"How should I know?" answered Mrs. Albert Forrester, somewhat peevishly. "I have never looked at her. Albert always engaged the servants, she just came in for a moment so that I could see if her aura was satisfactory."

"But you must have seen her every morning when you did the housekeeping."

"Albert did the housekeeping. It was his own wish, so that I might be free to devote myself to my work. In this life one has to limit oneself."

"Did Albert order your luncheons?" asked Clifford Boyleston.

"Naturally. It was his province."

Clifford Boyleston slightly raised his eyebrows. What a fool he had been never to guess that it was Albert who was responsible for Mrs. Forrester's beautiful food! And of course it was owing to him that the excellent Chablis was always just sufficiently chilled to run coolly over the tongue, but never so cold as to lose its bouquet and its savour.

"He certainly knew good food and good wine."

"I always told you he had his points," answered Mrs. Albert Forrester, as though he were reproaching her. "You all laughed at him. You would not believe me when I told you that I owed a great deal to him."

There was no answer to this and once more silence, heavy and ominous, fell on the party. Suddenly Mr. Simmons flung a bombshell.

"You must get him back."

So great was her surprise that if Mrs. Albert Forrester had not been standing against the chimney-piece she would undoubtedly have staggered two paces to the rear.

"What on earth do you mean?" she cried. "I will never see him again as long as I live. Take him back? Never. Not even if he came and begged me on his bended knees."

"I didn't say take him back; I said, get him back."

But Mrs. Albert Forrester paid no attention to the misplaced interruption.

"I have done everything for him. What would he be without me? I ask you. I have given him a position which never in his remotest dreams could he have aspired to."

None could deny that there was something magnificent in the indignation of Mrs. Albert Forrester, but it appeared to have little effect on Mr. Simmons.

"What are you going to live on?"

Mrs. Albert Forrester flung him a glance totally devoid of amiability.

"God will provide," she answered in freezing tones.

"I think it very unlikely," he returned.

Mrs. Albert Forrester shrugged her shoulders. She wore an outraged expression. But Mr. Simmons made himself as comfortable as he could on his chair and lit a cigarette.

"You know you have no warmer admirer of your art than me," he said.

"Than I," corrected Clifford Boyleston.

"Or than you," went on Mr. Simmons blandly. "We all agree that there is no one writing now whom you need fear comparison with. Both in prose and verse you are absolutely first class. And your style—well, everyone knows your style."

"The opulence of Sir Thomas Browne with the limpidity of Cardinal Newman," said Clifford Boyleston. "The raciness of John Dryden with the precision of Jonathan Swift."

The only sign that Mrs. Albert Forrester heard was the smile that hesitated for a brief moment at the corners of her tragic mouth.

"And you have humour."

"Is there anyone in the world," cried Miss Waterford, "who can put such a wealth of wit and satire and comic observation into a semi-colon?"

"But the fact remains that you don't sell," pursued Mr. Simmons imperturbably. "I've handled your work for twenty years and I tell you frankly that I shouldn't have grown fat on my commission, but I've handled it because now and again I like to do what I can for good work. I've always believed in you and I've hoped that sooner or later we might get the public to swallow you. But if you think you can make your living by writing the sort of stuff you do I'm bound to tell you that you haven't a chance."

"I have come into the world too late," said Mrs. Albert Forrester. "I should have lived in the eighteenth century when the wealthy patron rewarded a dedication with a hundred guineas."

"What do you suppose the currant business brings in?"

Mrs. Albert Forrester gave a little sigh.

"A pittance. Albert always told me he made about twelve hundred a year."

"He must be a very good manager. But you couldn't expect

him on that income to allow you very much. Take my word for it, there's only one thing for you to do and that's to get him back."

"I would rather live in a garret. Do you think I'm going to submit to the affront he has put upon me? Would you have have me battle for his affections with my cook? Do not forget that there is one thing which is more valuable to a woman like me than her ease and that is her dignity."

"I was just coming to that," said Mr. Simmons coldly.

He glanced at the others and those strange, lopsided eyes of his looked more than ever monstrous and fish-like.

"There is no doubt in my mind," he went on, "that you have a very distinguished and almost unique position in the world of letters. You stand for something quite apart. You never prostituted your genius for filthy lucre and you have held high the banner of pure art. You're thinking of going into Parliament. I don't think much of politics myself, but there's no denying that it would be a good advertisement and if you get in I daresay we could get you a lecture tour in America on the strength of it. You have ideals and this I can say, that even the people who've never read a word you've written respect you. But in your position there's one thing you can't afford to be and that's a joke."

Mrs. Albert Forrester gave a distinct start.

"What on earth do you mean by that?"

"I know nothing about Mrs. Bulfinch and for all I know she's a very respectable woman, but the fact remains that a man doesn't run away with his cook without making his wife ridiculous. If it had been a dancer or a lady of title I daresay it wouldn't have done you any harm, but a cook would finish you. In a week you'd have all London laughing at you, and if there's one thing that kills an author or a politician it is ridicule. You must get your husband back and you must get him back pretty damned quick."

A dark flush settled on Mrs. Albert Forrester's face, but she did not immediately reply. In her ears there rang on a sudden the outrageous and unaccountable laughter that had sent Miss Warren flying from the room.

"We're all friends here and you can count on our discretion."

Mrs. Forrester looked at her friends and she thought that in Rose Waterford's eyes there was already a malicious gleam. On the wizened face of Oscar Charles was a whimsical look. She wished that in a moment of abandon she had not betrayed her secret.

Mr. Simmons, however, knew the literary world and allowed his eyes to rest on the company.

"After all you are the centre and head of their set. Your husband has not only run away from you but also from them. It's not too good for them either. The fact is that Albert Forrester has made you all look a lot of damned fools."

"All," said Clifford Boyleston. "We're all in the same boat. He's quite right, Mrs. Forrester, The Philatelist must come back."

"*Et tu, Brute.*"

Mr. Simmons did not understand Latin and if he had would probably not have been moved by Mrs. Albert Forrester's exclamation. He cleared his throat.

"My suggestion is that Mrs. Albert Forrester should go and see him to-morrow, fortunately we have his address, and beg him to reconsider his decision. I don't know what sort of things a woman says on these occasions, but Mrs. Forrester has tact and imagination and she must say them. If Mr. Forrester makes any conditions she must accept them. She must leave no stone unturned."

"If you play your cards well there is no reason why you shouldn't bring him back here with you to-morrow evening," said Rose Waterford lightly.

"Will you do it, Mrs. Forrester?"

For two minutes, at least, turned away from them, she stared at the empty fireplace; then, drawing herself to her full height, she faced them.

"For my art's sake, not for mine. I will not allow the ribald laughter of the Philistine to besmirch all that I hold good and true and beautiful."

"Capital," said Mr. Simmons, rising to his feet, "I'll look in on my way home to-morrow and I hope to find you and Mr. Forrester billing and cooing side by side like a pair of turtledoves."

He took his leave, and the others, anxious not to be left alone with Mrs. Albert Forrester and her agitation, in a body followed his example.

It was latish in the afternoon next day when Mrs. Albert Forrester, imposing in black silk and a velvet toque, set out from her flat in order to get a bus from the Marble Arch that would take her to Victoria Station. Mr. Simmons had explained to her by telephone how to reach the Kennington Road with expedition and economy.

She neither felt nor looked like Delilah. At Victoria she took the tram that runs down the Vauxhall Bridge Road. When she crossed the river she found herself in a part of London more noisy, sordid and bustling than that to which she was accustomed, but she was too much occupied with her thoughts to notice the varied scene. She was relieved to find that the tram went along the Kennington Road and asked the conductor to put her down a few doors from the house she sought. When it did and rumbled on leaving her alone in the busy street, she felt strangely lost, like a traveller in an eastern tale set down by a djinn in an unknown city. She walked slowly, looking to right and left, and notwithstanding the emotions of indignation and embarrassment that fought for the possession of her somewhat opulent bosom, she could not but reflect that here was the material for a very pretty piece of prose. The little houses held about them the feeling of a bygone age when here it was still almost country, and Mrs. Albert Forrester registered in her retentive memory a note that she must look into the literary associations of the Kennington Road. Number four hundred and eleven was one of a row of shabby houses that stood some way back from the street; in front of it was a narrow strip of shabby grass, and a paved way led up to a latticed wooden porch that badly needed a coat of paint. This and the straggling, stunted creeper that grew over the front of the house gave it a falsely rural air which was strange and even sinister in that road down which thundered a tumultuous traffic. There was something equivocal about the house that suggested that here lived women to whom a life of pleasure had brought an inadequate reward.

The door was opened by a scraggy girl of fifteen with long legs and a tousled head.

"Does Mrs. Bulfinch live here, do you know?"

"You've rung the wrong bell. Second floor." The girl pointed to the stairs and at the same time screamed shrilly: "Mrs. Bulfinch, a party to see you. Mrs. Bulfinch."

Mrs. Albert Forrester walked up the dingy stairs. They were covered with torn carpet. She walked slowly, for she did not wish to get out of breath. A door opened as she reached the second floor and she recognised her cook.

"Good-afternoon, Bulfinch," said Mrs. Albert Forrester, with dignity. "I wish to see your master."

Mrs. Bulfinch hesitated for the shadow of a second, then held the door wide open.

"Come in, ma'am." She turned her head. "Albert, here's Mrs. Forrester to see you."

Mrs. Forrester stepped by quickly and there was Albert sitting by the fire in a leather-covered, but rather shabby, arm-chair, with his feet in slippers, and in shirt-sleeves. He was reading the evening paper and smoking a cigar. He rose to his feet as Mrs. Albert Forrester came in. Mrs. Bulfinch followed her visitor into the room and closed the door.

"How are you, my dear?" said Albert cheerfully. "Keeping well, I hope."

"You'd better put on your coat, Albert," said Mrs. Bulfinch. "What will Mrs. Forrester think of you, finding you like that? I never."

She took the coat, which was hanging on a peg, and helped him into it; and like a woman familiar with the peculiarities of masculine dress pulled down his waistcoat so that it should not ride over his collar.

"I received your letter, Albert," said Mrs. Forrester.

"I supposed you had, or you wouldn't have known my address, would you?"

"Won't you sit down, ma'am?" said Mrs. Bulfinch, deftly dusting a chair, part of a suite covered in plum-coloured velvet, and pushing it forwards.

Mrs. Albert Forrester with a slight bow seated herself.

"I should have preferred to see you alone, Albert," she said.

His eyes twinkled.

"Since anything you have to say concerns Mrs. Bulfinch as much as it concerns me I think it much better that she should be present."

"As you wish."

Mrs. Bulfinch drew up a chair and sat down. Mrs. Albert Forrester had never seen her before but with a large apron over a print dress. She was wearing now an open-work blouse of white silk, a black skirt, and high-heeled, patent-leather shoes with silver buckles. She was a woman of about five-and-forty, with reddish hair and a reddish face, not pretty, but with a good-natured look, and buxom. She reminded Mrs. Albert Forrester of a serving-wench, somewhat overblown, in a jolly picture by an old Dutch master.

"Well, my dear, what have you to say to me?" asked Albert.

Mrs. Albert Forrester gave him her brightest and most

affable smile. Her great black eyes shone with tolerant good-humour.

"Of course you know that this is perfectly absurd, Albert. I think you must be out of your mind."

"Do you, my dear? Fancy that."

"I'm not angry with you, I'm only amused, but a joke's a joke and should not be carried too far. I've come to take you home."

"Was my letter not quite clear?"

"Perfectly. I ask no questions and I will make no reproaches. We will look upon this as a momentary aberration and say no more about it."

"Nothing will induce me ever to live with you again, my dear." said Albert in, however, a perfectly friendly fashion.

"You're not serious?"

"Quite."

"Do you love this woman?"

Mrs. Albert Forrester still smiled with an eager and somewhat metallic brightness. She was determined to take the matter lightly. With her intimate sense of values she realised that the scene was comic. Albert looked at Mrs. Bulfinch and a smile broke out on his withered face.

"We get on very well together, don't we, old girl?"

"Not so bad," said Mrs. Bulfinch.

Mrs. Albert Forrester raised her eyebrows; her husband had never in all their married life called *her* "old girl": nor indeed would she have wished it.

"If Bulfinch has any regard or respect for you she must know that the thing is impossible. After the life you've led and the society you've moved in she can hardly expect to make you permanently happy in miserable furnished lodgings."

"They're not furnished lodgings, ma'am," said Mrs. Bulfinch. "It's all me own furniture. You see, I'm very independent-like and I've always liked to have a home of me own. So I keep these rooms on whether I'm in a situation or whether I'm not, and so I always have some place to go back to.'

"And a very nice cosy little place it is," said Albert.

Mrs. Albert Forrester looked about her. There was a kitchen range in the fireplace on which a kettle was simmering and on the mantelshelf was a black marble clock flanked by black marble candelabra. There was a large table covered with a red cloth, a dresser, and a sewing-machine. On the walls were photographs and framed pictures from Christmas supplements. A door at the back, covered with a red plush portière, led into what, considering the size of the house, Mrs. Albert Forrester (who in her leisure moments had made a somewhat extensive study of architecture) could not but conclude was the only bedroom. Mrs. Bulfinch and Albert lived in a contiguity that allowed no doubt about their relations

"Have you not been happy with me, Albert?" asked Mrs. Forrester in a deeper tone.

"We've been married for thirty-five years, my dear. It's too long. It's a great deal too long. You're a good woman in your way, but you don't suit me. You're literary and I'm not. You're artistic and I'm not.'

"I've always taken care to make you share in all my interests. I've taken great pains that you shouldn't be overshadowed by my success. You can't say that I've ever left you out of things."

"You're a wonderful writer, I don't deny it for a moment, but the truth is I don't like the books you write."

"That, if I may be permitted to say so, merely shows that you have very bad taste. All the best critics admit their power and their charm."

"And I don't like your friends. Let me tell you a secret, my dear. Often at your parties I've had an almost irresistible impulse to take off all my clothes just to see what would happen."

"Nothing would have happened," said Mrs. Albert Forrester with a slight frown. "I should merely have sent for the doctor."

"Besides you haven't the figure for that, Albert," said Mrs. Bulfinch.

Mr. Simmons had hinted to Mrs. Albert Forrester that if the need arose she must not hesitate to use the allurements of her sex in order to bring back her erring husband to the conjugal roof, but she did not in the least know how to do this. It would have been easier, she could not but reflect, had she been in evening dress.

"Does the fidelity of five-and-thirty years count for nothing? I have never looked at another man, Albert. I'm used to you. I shall be lost without you."

"I've left all my menus with the new cook, ma'am. You've only got to tell her how many to luncheon and she'll manage," said Mrs. Bulfinch. "She's very reliable and she has as light a hand with pastry as anyone I ever knew."

Mrs. Albert Forrester began to be discouraged. Mrs. Bulfinch's remark, well-meant no doubt, made it difficult to bring the conversation on to the plane on which emotion could be natural.

"I'm afraid you're only wasting your time, my dear," said Albert. "My decision is irrevocable. I'm not very young any more and I want someone to take care of me. I shall of course make you as good an allowance as I can. Corinne wants me to retire."

"Who is Corinne?" asked Mrs. Forrester with the utmost surprise.

"It's my name," said Mrs. Bulfinch. "My mother was half French."

"That explains a great deal," replied Mrs. Forrester, pursing her lips, for though she admired the literature of our neighbours she knew that their morals left much to be desired.

"What I say is, Albert's worked long enough, and it's about time he started enjoying himself. I've got a little bit of property at Clacton-on-Sea. It's a very healthy neighbourhood and the air is wonderful. We could live there very comfortable. And what with the beach and the pier there's always something to do. They're a very nice lot of people down there. If you don't interfere with nobody, nobody'll interfere with you."

"I discussed the matter with my partners to-day and they're willing to buy me out. It means a certain sacrifice. When everything is settled I shall have an income of nine hundred pounds a year. There are three of us, so it gives us just three hundred a year apiece."

"How am I to live on that?" cried Mrs. Albert Forrester. "I have my position to keep up."

"You have a fluent, a fertile and a distinguished pen, my dear."

Mrs. Albert Forrester impatiently shrugged her shoulders.

"You know very well that my books don't bring me in anything but reputation. The publishers always say that they lose by them and in fact they only publish them because it gives them prestige."

It was then that Mrs. Bulfinch had the idea that was to have consequences of such magnitude.

"Why don't you write a good thrilling detective story?" she asked.

"Me?" exclaimed Mrs. Albert Forrester, for the first time in her life regardless of grammar.

"It's not a bad idea," said Albert. "It's not a bad idea at all."

c*

"I should have the critics down on me like a thousand of bricks."

"I'm not so sure of that. Give the highbrow the chance of being lowbrow without demeaning himself and he'll be so grateful to you, he won't know what to do."

"For this relief much thanks," murmured Mrs. Albert Forrester reflectively.

"My dear, the critics'll eat it. And written in your beautiful English they won't be afraid to call it a masterpiece."

"The idea is preposterous. It's absolutely foreign to my genius. I could never hope to please the masses."

"Why not? The masses want to read good stuff, but they dislike being bored. They all know your name, but they don't read you because you bore them. The fact is, my dear, you're dull."

"I don't know how you can say that, Albert," replied Mrs. Albert Forrester, with as little resentment as the equator might feel if someone called it chilly. "Everyone knows and acknowledges that I have an exquisite sense of humour and there is nobody who can extract so much good wholesome fun from a semi-colon as I can."

"If you can give the masses a good thrilling story and let them think at the same time that they are improving their minds you'll make a fortune."

"I've never read a detective story in my life," said Mrs. Albert Forrester. "I once heard of a Mr. Barnes of New York and I was told that he had written a book called *The Mystery of a Hansom Cab.* But I never read it."

"Of course you have to have the knack," said Mrs. Bulfinch. "The first thing to remember is that you don't want any love-making, it's out of place in a detective story, what you want is murder, and sleuth-hounds, and you don't want to be able to guess who done it till the last page.'

"But you must play fair with your reader, my dear," said Albert. "It always annoys me when suspicion has been thrown on the secretary or the lady of title and it turns out to be the second footman who's never done more than say, 'The carriage is at the door.' Puzzle your reader as much as you can, but don't make a fool of him."

"I love a good detective story," said Mrs. Bulfinch. "Give me a lady in evening dress, just streaming with diamonds, lying on the library floor with a dagger in her heart, and I know I'm going to have a treat."

"There's no accounting for tastes," said Albert. "Personally, I prefer a respectable family solicitor, with side-whiskers, gold watch-chain, and a benign appearance, lying dead in Hyde Park."

"With his throat cut?" asked Mrs. Bulfinch eagerly.

"No, stabbed in the back. There's something peculiarly attractive to the reader in the murder of a middle-aged gentleman of spotless reputation. It is pleasant to think that the most apparently blameless of us have a mystery in our lives."

"I see what you mean, Albert," said Mrs. Bulfinch. "He was the repository of a fatal secret."

"We can give you all the tips, my dear," said Albert, smiling mildly at Mrs. Albert Forrester. "I've read hundreds of detective stories."

"You!"

"That's what first brought Corinne and me together. I used to pass them on to her when I'd finished them."

"Many's the time I've heard him switch off the electric light as the dawn was creeping through the window and I couldn't help smiling to myself as I said: 'There, he's finished it at last, now he can have a good sleep."

Mrs. Albert Forrester rose to her feet. She drew herself up.

"Now I see what a gulf separates us," she said, and her fine contralto shook a little. "You have been surrounded for thirty years with all that was best in English literature and you read hundreds of detective novels."

"Hundreds and hundreds," interrupted Albert with a smile of satisfaction.

"I came here willing to make any reasonable concession so that you should come back to your home, but now I wish it no longer. You have shown me that we have nothing in common and never had. There is an abyss between us."

"Very well, my dear," said Albert gently, "I will submit to your decision. But you think over the detective story."

"I will arise and go now," she murmured, "and go to Innisfree."

"I'll just show you downstairs," said Mrs. Bulfinch. "One has to be careful of the carpet if one doesn't exactly know where the holes are."

With dignity, but not without circumspection, Mrs. Albert Forrester walked downstairs and when Mrs. Bulfinch opened the door and asked her if she would like a taxi she shook her head.

"I shall take the tram."

"You need not be afraid that I won't take good care of Mr. Forrester, ma'am," said Mrs. Bulfinch pleasantly. "He shall have every comfort. I nursed Mr. Bulfinch for three years during his last illness and there's very little I don't know about invalids. Not that Mr. Forrester isn't very strong and active for his years. And of course he'll have a hobby. I always think a man should have a hobby. He's going to collect postage-stamps."

Mrs. Albert Forrester gave a little start of surprise. But just then a tram came in sight and, as a woman (even the greatest of them) will, she hurried at the risk of her life into the middle of the road and waved frantically. It stopped and she climbed in. She did not know how she was going to face Mr. Simmons. He would be waiting for her when she got home. Clifford Boyleston would probably be there too. They would all be there and she would have to tell them that she had miserably failed. At that moment she had no warm feeling of friendship for her little group of devoted admirers. Wondering what the time was, she looked up at the man sitting opposite her to see whether he was the kind of person she could modestly ask, and suddenly started; for sitting there was a middle-aged gentleman of the most respectable appearance, with side-whiskers, a benign expression and a gold watch-chain. It was the very man whom Albert had described lying dead in Hyde Park and she could not but jump to the conclusion that he was a family solicitor. The coincidence was extraordinary and really it looked as though the hand of fate were beckoning to her. He wore a silk hat, a black coat and pepper-and-salt trousers, he was somewhat corpulent, of a powerful build, and by his side was a despatch-case. When the tram was half-way down the Vauxhall Bridge Road he asked the conductor to stop and she saw him go down a small, mean street. Why? Ah, why? When it reached Victoria, so deeply immersed in thought was she, until the conductor somewhat roughly told her where she was, she did not move. Edgar Allan Poe had written detective stories. She took a bus. She sat inside, buried in reflection, but when it arrived at Hyde Park Corner she suddenly made up her mind to get out. She couldn't sit still any longer. She felt she must walk. She entered the gates, walking slowly, and looked about her with an air that was at once intent and abstracted. Yes, there was Edgar Allan Poe; no one could deny that. After all he had invented the genre, and everyone knew how great his influence had been on the Parnassians. Or was it the Symbolists? Never mind. Baudelaire and all that. As she passed the Achilles Statue she stopped for a minute and looked at it with raised eyebrows.

At length she reached her flat and opening the door saw several hats in the hall. They were all there. She went into the drawing-room

"Here she is at last," cried Miss Waterford.

Mrs. Albert Forrester advanced, smiling with animation, and shook the proffered hands. Mr. Simmons and Clifford Boyleston were there, Harry Oakland and Oscar Charles.

"Oh, you poor things, have you had no tea?" she cried brightly. "I haven't an idea what the time is, but I know I'm fearfully late."

"Well?" they said. "Well?"

"My dears, I've got something quite wonderful to tell you. I've had an inspiration. Why should the devil have all the best tunes?"

"What *do* you mean?"

She paused in order to give full effect to the surprise she was going to spring upon them. Then she flung it at them without preamble.

"I'M GOING TO WRITE A DETECTIVE STORY."

They stared at her with open mouths. She held up her hand to prevent them from interrupting her, but indeed no one had the smallest intention of doing so.

"I am going to raise the detective story to the dignity of Art. It came to me suddenly in Hyde Park. It's a murder story and I shall give the solution on the very last page. I shall write it in an impeccable English, and since it's occurred to me lately that perhaps I've exhausted the possibilities of the semi-colon, I am going to take up the colon. No one yet has explored its potentialities. Humour and mystery are what I aim at. I shall call it *The Achilles Statue*."

"What a title!" cried Mr. Simmons, recovering himself before any of the others. "I can sell the serial rights on the title and your name alone."

"But what about Albert?" asked Clifford Boyleston.

"Albert?" echoed Mrs. Forrester. "Albert?"

She looked at him as though for the life of her she could not think what he was talking about. Then she gave a little cry as if she had suddenly remembered.

"Albert! I knew I'd gone out on some errand and it absolutely slipped my memory. I was walking through Hyde Park and I had this inspiration. What a fool you'll all think me!"

"Then you haven't seen Albert?"

"My dear, I forgot all about him." She gave an amused laugh. "Let Albert keep his cook. I can't bother about Albert now. Albert belongs to the semi-colon period. I am going to write a detective story.'

"My dear, you're too, too wonderful," said Harry Oakland.

Virtue

THERE are few things better than a good Havana. When I was young and very poor and smoked a cigar only when somebody gave me one, I determined that if ever I had money I would smoke a cigar every day after luncheon and after dinner. This is the only resolution of my youth that I have kept. It is the only ambition I have achieved that has never been embittered by disillusion. I like a cigar that is mild, but full-flavoured, neither so small that it is finished before you have become aware of it nor so large as to be irksome, rolled so that it draws without consciousness of effort on your part, with a leaf so firm that it doesn't become messy on your lips and in such condition that it keeps its savour to the very end. But when you have taken the last pull and put down the shapeless stump and watched the final cloud of smoke dwindle blue in the surrounding air it is impossible, if you have a sensitive nature, not to feel a certain melancholy at the thought of all the labour, the care and pains that have gone, the thought, the trouble, the complicated organisation that have been required to provide you with half an hour's delight. For this men have sweltered long years under tropical suns and ships have scoured the seven seas. These reflections become more poignant still when you are eating a dozen oysters (with half a bottle of dry white wine) and they become almost unbearable when it comes to a lamb cutlet. For these are animals and there is something that inspires awe in the thought that since the surface of the earth became capable of supporting life from generation to generation for millions upon millions of years creatures have come into existence to end at last upon a plate of crushed ice or on a silver grill. It may be that a sluggish fancy cannot grasp the dreadful solemnity of eating an oyster and evolution has taught us that the bivalve has through the ages kept itself to itself in a manner that inevitably alienates sympathy. There is an aloofness in it that is offensive to the aspiring spirit of man and a self-complacency that is obnoxious to his vanity. But I do not know how anyone can look upon a lamb cutlet without thoughts too deep for tears: here man himself has taken a hand and the history of the race is bound up with the tender morsel on your plate.

And sometimes even the fate of human beings is curious to consider. It is strange to look upon this man or that, the quiet ordinary persons of every day, the bank clerk, the dustman, the middle-aged girl in the second row of the chorus, and think of the interminable history behind them and of the long, long series of hazards by which from the primeval slime the course of events has brought them at this moment to such and such a place. When such tremendous vicissitudes have been needed to get them here at all one would have thought some huge significance must be attached to them; one would have thought that what befell them must matter a little to the Life Spirit or whatever else it is that has produced them. An accident befalls them. The thread is broken. The story that began with the world is finished abruptly and it looks as though it meant nothing at all. A tale told by an idiot. And is it not odd that this event, of an importance so dramatic, may be brought about by a cause so trivial?

An incident of no moment, that might easily not have happened, has consequences that are incalculable. It looks as though blind chance ruled all things. Our smallest actions may affect profoundly the whole lives of people who have nothing to do with us. The story I have to tell would never have happened if one day I had not walked across the street. Life is really very fantastic and one has to have a peculiar sense of humour to see the fun of it.

I was strolling down Bond Street one spring morning and having nothing much to do till lunch-time thought I would look in at Sotheby's, the auction rooms, to see whether there was anything on show that interested me. There was a block in the traffic and I threaded my way through the cars. When I reached the other side I ran into a man I had known in Borneo coming out of a hatter's.

"Hullo, Morton," I said. "When did you come home?"

"I've been back about a week."

He was a District Officer. The Governor had given me a letter of introduction to him and I wrote and told him I meant to spend a week at the place he lived at and should like to put up at the government rest-house. He met me on the ship when I arrived and asked me to stay with him. I demurred. I did not see how I could spend a week with a total stranger, I did not want to put him to the expense of my board, and besides I thought I should have more freedom if I were on my own. He would not listen to me.

"I've got plenty of room," he said, "and the rest-house is beastly. I haven't spoken to a white man for six months and I'm fed to the teeth with my own company."

But when Morton had got me and his launch had landed us at the bungalow and he had offered me a drink he did not in the least know what to do with me. He was seized on a sudden with shyness and his conversation, which had been fluent and ready, ran dry. I did my best to make him feel at home (it was the least I could do, considering that it was his own house) and asked him if he had any new records. He turned on the gramophone and the sound of rag-time gave him confidence.

His bungalow overlooked the river and his living-room was a large verandah. It was furnished in the impersonal fashion that characterised the dwellings of government officials who were moved here and there at little notice according to the exigencies of the service. There were native hats as ornaments on the walls and the horns of animals, blow-pipes and spears. In the book-shelf were detective novels and old magazines. There was a cottage piano with yellow keys. It was very untidy, but not uncomfortable.

Unfortunately I cannot very well remember what he looked like. He was young, twenty-eight, I learnt later, and he had a boyish and attractive smile. I spent an agreeable week with him. We went up and down the river and we climbed a mountain. We had tiffin one day with some planters who lived twenty miles away and every evening we went to the club. The only members were the managers of a kutch factory and his assistants, but they were not on speaking terms with one another and it was only on Morton's representations that they must not let him down when he had a visitor that we could get up a rubber of bridge. The atmosphere was strained. We came back to dinner, listened to the gramophone and went to bed. Morton had little office work and one would have thought the time hung heavy on his hands, but he had energy and high spirits; it was his first post of the sort and he was happy to be independent. His only anxiety was lest he should be transferred before he had finished a road he was building. This was the joy of his heart. It was his own idea and he had wheedled the government into giving him the money to make it; he had surveyed the country himself and traced the path. He had solved unaided the technical problems that presented themselves. Every morning, before he went to his office, he drove out in a rickety old Ford to where the coolies were working and watched the progress that had been made since the day before. He thought of nothing else. He dreamt of it at night. He reckoned that it would be finished in a year and he did not want to take his leave till then. He could not have worked with more zest if he had been a painter or a sculptor creating a work of art. I think it was this eagerness that made me take a fancy to him. I liked his zeal. I liked his ingenuousness. And I was impressed by the passion for achievement that made him indifferent to the solitariness of his life, to promotion and even to the thought of going home. I forget how long the road was, fifteen or twenty miles, I think, and I forget what purpose it was to serve. I don't believe Morton cared very much. His passion was the artist's and his triumph was the triumph of man over nature. He learnt as he went along. He had the jungle to contend against, torrential rains that destroyed the labour of weeks, accidents of topography; he had to collect his labour and hold it together; he had inadequate funds. His imagination sustained him. His labours gained a sort of epic quality and the vicissitudes of the work were a great saga that unrolled itself with an infinity of episodes.

His only complaint was that the day was too short. He had office duties, he was judge and tax collector, father and mother (at twenty-eight) of the people in his district; he had now and then to make tours that took him away from home. Unless he was on the spot nothing was done. He would have liked to be there twenty-four hours a day driving the reluctant coolies to further effort. It so happened that shortly before I arrived an incident had occurred that filled him with jubilation. He had offered a contract to a Chinese to make a certain section of the road and the Chinese had asked more than Morton could afford to pay. Notwithstanding interminable discussions they had been unable to arrive at an agreement and Morton with rage in his heart saw his work held up. He was at his wits' end. Then going down to his office one morning, he heard that there had been a row in one of the Chinese gambling houses the night before. A coolie had been badly wounded and his assailant was under arrest. This assailant was the contractor. He was brought into court, the evidence was clear and Morton sentenced him to eighteen months' hard labour.

"Now he'll have to build the blasted road for nothing," said Morton, his eyes glistening when he told me the story.

We saw the fellow at work one morning, in the prison sarong, unconcerned. He was taking his misfortunes in good part.

"I've told him I'll remit the rest of his sentence when the road's finished," said Morton, "and he's as pleased as Punch. Bit of a snip for me, eh, what?"

When I left Morton I asked him to let me know when he came to England and he promised to write to me as soon as he landed. On the spur of the moment one gives these invitations and one is perfectly sincere about them. But when one is taken at one's word a slight dismay seizes one. People are so different at home from what they are abroad. There they are easy, cordial and natural. They have interesting things to tell you. They are immensely kind. You are anxious when your turn comes to do something in return for the hospitality you have received. But it is not easy. The persons who were so entertaining in their own surroundings are very dull in yours. They are constrained and shy. You introduce them to your friends and your friends find them a crashing bore. They do their best to be civil, but sigh with relief when the strangers go and the conversation can once more run easily in its accustomed channels. I think the residents in far places early in their careers understand the situation pretty well, as the result maybe of bitter and humiliating experiences, for I have found that they seldom take advantage of the invitation which on some outstation on the edge of the jungle has been so cordially extended to them and by them as cordially accepted. But Morton was different. He was a young man and single. It is generally the wives that are the difficulty; other women look at their drab clothes, in a glance take in their provincial air, and freeze them with their indifference. But a man can play bridge and tennis, and dance. Morton had charm. I had had no doubt that in a day or two he would find his feet.

"Why didn't you let me know you were back?" I asked him.

"I thought you wouldn't want to be bothered with me," he smiled.

"What nonsense!"

Of course now as we stood in Bond Street on the kerb and chatted for a minute he looked strange to me. I had never seen him in anything but khaki shorts and a tennis shirt, except when we got back from the club at night and he put on a pyjama jacket and a sarong for dinner. It is as comfortable a form of evening dress as has ever been devised. He looked a bit awkward in his blue serge suit. His face against a white collar was very brown.

"How about the road?" I asked him.

"Finished. I was afraid I'd have to postpone my leave, we struck one or two snags towards the end, but I made 'em hustle and the day before I left I drove the Ford to the end and back without stopping."

I laughed. His pleasure was charming.

"What have you been doing with yourself in London?"

"Buying clothes."

"Been having a good time?"

"Marvellous. A bit lonely, you know, but I don't mind that. I've been to a show every night. The Palmers, you know, I think you met them in Sarawak, were going to be in town and we were going to do the play together, but they had to go to Scotland because her mother's ill."

His words, said so breezily, cut me to the quick. His was the common experience. It was heartbreaking. For months, for long months before it was due, these people planned their leave and when they got off the ship they were in such spirits they could hardly contain themselves. London. Shops and clubs and theatres and restaurants. London. They were going to have the time of their lives. London. It swallowed them. A strange turbulent city, not hostile but indifferent, and they were lost in it. They had no friends. They had nothing in common with the acquaintances they made. They were more lonely than in the jungle. It was a relief when at a theatre they ran across someone they had known in the East (and perhaps been bored stiff by or disliked) and they could fix up an evening together and have a good laugh and tell one another what a grand time they were having and talk of common friends and at last confide to one another a little shyly that they would not be sorry when their leave was up and they were once again in harness. They went to see their families and of course they were glad to see them, but it wasn't the same as it had been, they did feel a bit out of it, and when you came down to brass tacks the life people led in England was deadly. It was grand fun to come home, but you couldn't live there any more, and sometimes you thought of your bungalow overlooking the river and your tours of the district and what a lark it was to run over once in a blue moon to Sandakan or Kuching or Singapore.

And because I remembered what Morton had looked forward to when, the road finished and off his chest, he went on leave I could not but feel a pang when I thought of him dining by himself in a dismal club where he knew nobody or alone in a restaurant in Soho and then going off to see a play with no one by his side with whom he could enjoy it and no one to have a drink with during the interval. And at the same time I reflected that even if I had known he was in London I could have done nothing much for him, for during the last week I had not had a moment free. That very evening I was dining with friends and going to a play, and the next day I was going abroad.

"What are you doing to-night?" I asked him.

"I'm going to the Pavilion. It's packed jammed full, but there's a fellow over the road who's wonderful and he's got me a ticket that had been returned. You can often get one seat, you know, when you can't get two."

"Why don't you come and have supper with me? I'm taking some people to the Haymarket and we're going on to Ciro's afterwards."

"I'd love to."

We arranged to meet at eleven and I left him to keep an engagement.

I was afraid the friends I had asked him to meet would not amuse Morton very much, for they were distinctly middle-aged, but I could not think of anyone young that at this season of the year I should be likely to get hold of at the last moment. None of the girls I knew would thank me for asking her to supper to dance with a shy young man from Malaya. I could trust the Bishops to do their best for him, and after all it must be jollier for him to have supper in a club with a good band where he could see pretty women dancing than to go home to bed at eleven because he had nowhere else in the world to go. I had known Charlie Bishop first when I was a medical student. He was then a thin little fellow with sandy hair and blunt features; he had fine eyes, dark and gleaming, but he wore spectacles. He had a round, merry, red face. He was very fond of the girls. I suppose he had a way with him, for with no money and no looks, he managed to pick up a succession of young persons who gratified his roving desires. He was clever and bumptious, argumentative and quick-tempered. He had a caustic tongue. Looking back, I should say he was a rather disagreeable young man, but I do not think he was a bore. Now, half-way through the fifties, he was inclined to be stout and he was very bald, but his eyes behind the gold-rimmed spectacles were still bright and alert. He was dogmatic and somewhat conceited, argumentative still and caustic, but he was good-natured and amusing. After you have known a person so long his idiosyncrasies cease to trouble you. You accept them as you accept your own physical defects. He was by profession a pathologist and now and then he sent me a slim book he had just published. It was severe and extremely technical and grimly illustrated with photographs of bacteria. I did not read it. I gathered from what I sometimes heard that Charlie's views on the subjects with which he dealt were unsound. I do not believe that he was very popular with the other members of his profession, he made no secret of the fact that he looked upon them as a set of incompetent idiots; but he had his job, it brought him in six or eight hundred a year, I think, and he was completely indifferent to other people's opinion of him.

I liked Charlie Bishop because I had known him for thirty years, but I liked Margery, his wife, because she was very nice. I was extremely surprised when he told me he was going to be married. He was hard on forty at the time and so fickle in his affections that I had made up my mind he would remain single. He was very fond of women, but he was not in the least sentimental, and his aims were loose. His views on the female sex would in these idealistic days be thought crude. He knew what he wanted and he asked for it, and if he couldn't get it for love or money he shrugged his shoulders and went his way. To be brief, he did not look to women to gratify his ideal but to provide him with fornication. It was odd that though small and plain he found so many who were prepared to grant his wishes. For his spiritual needs he found satisfaction in unicellular organisms. He had always been a man who spoke to the point, and when he told me he was going to marry a young woman called Margery Hobson I did not hesitate to ask him why. He grinned.

"Three reasons. First, she won't let me go to bed with her without. Second, she makes me laugh like a hyena. And third, she's alone in the world, without a single relation, and she must have someone to take care of her."

"The first reason is just swank and the second is eyewash. The third is the real one and it means that she's got you by the short hairs."

His eyes gleamed softly behind his large spectacles.

"I shouldn't be surprised if you weren't dead right."

"She's not only got you by the short hairs but you're as pleased as Punch that she has."

"Come and lunch to-morrow and have a look at her. She's easy on the eye."

Charlie was a member of a cock-and-hen club which at that time I used a good deal and we arranged to lunch there. I found Margery a very attractive young woman. She was then just under thirty. She was a lady. I noticed the fact with satisfaction, but with a certain astonishment, for it had not escaped my notice that Charlie was attracted as a rule by women whose breeding left something to be desired. She was not beautiful, but comely, with fine dark hair and fine eyes, a good colour and a look of health. She had a pleasant frankness and an air of candour that were very taking. She looked honest, simple and dependable. I took an immediate liking to her. She was easy to talk to and though she did not say anything very brilliant she understood what other people were talking about; she was quick to see a joke and she was not shy. She gave you the impression of being competent and business-like. She had a happy placidity that suggested a good temper and an excellent digestion.

They seemed extremely pleased with one another. I had asked myself when I first saw her why Margery was marrying this irritable little man, baldish already and by no means young, but I discovered very soon that it was because she was in love with him. They chaffed one another a good deal and laughed a lot and every now and then their eyes met more significantly and they seemed to exchange a little private message. It was really rather touching.

A week later they were married at a registrar's office. It was a very successful marriage. Looking back now after sixteen years I could not but chuckle sympathetically at the thought of the lark they had made of their life together. I had never known a more devoted couple. They had never had very much money. They never seemed to want any. They had no ambitions. Their life was a picnic that never came to an end. They lived in the smallest flat I ever saw, in Panton Street, a small bedroom, a small sitting-room and a bathroom that served also as a kitchen. But they had no sense of home, they ate their meals in restaurants, and only had breakfast in the flat. It was merely a place to sleep in. It was comfortable, though a third person coming in for a whisky and soda crowded it, and Margery with the help of a charwoman kept it as neat as Charlie's untidiness permitted, but there was not a single thing in it that had a personal note. They had a tiny car and whenever Charlie had a holiday they took it across the Channel and started off, with a bag each for all their luggage, to drive wherever the fancy took them. Breakdowns never disturbed them, bad weather was part of the fun, a puncture was no end of a joke and if they lost their way and had to sleep out in the open they thought they were having the time of their lives.

Charlie continued to be irascible and contentious, but nothing he did ever disturbed Margery's lovely placidity. She could calm him with a word. She still made him laugh. She typed his monographs on obscure bacteria and corrected the proofs of his articles in the scientific magazines. Once I asked them if they ever quarrelled.

"No," she said, "we never seem to have anything to quarrel about. Charlie has the temper of an angel."

"Nonsense," I said, "he's an overbearing, aggressive and cantankerous fellow. He always has been."

She looked at him and giggled and I saw that she thought I was being funny.

"Let him rave," said Charlie. "He's an ignorant fool and he uses words of whose meaning he hasn't the smallest idea."

They were sweet together. They were very happy in one another's company and were never apart if they could help it. Even after the long time they had been married Charlie used to get into the car every day at luncheon-time to come west and meet Margery at a restaurant. People used to laugh at them, not unkindly, but perhaps with a little catch in the throat, because when they were asked to go and spend a week-end in the country Margery would write to the hostess and say they would like to come if they could be given a double bed. They had slept together for so many years that neither of them could sleep alone. It was often a trifle awkward. Husbands and wives as a rule not only demanded separate rooms, but were inclined to be peevish if asked to share the same bathroom. Modern houses were not arranged for domestic couples, but among their friends it became an understood thing that if you wanted the Bishops you must give them a room with a double bed. Some people of course thought it a little indecent, and it was never convenient, but they were a pleasant pair to have to stay and it was worth while to put up with their crankiness. Charlie was always full of spirits and in his caustic way extremely amusing and Margery was peaceful and easy. They were no trouble to entertain.

Nothing pleased them more than to be left to go out together for a long ramble in the country.

When a man marries, his wife sooner or later estranges him from his old friends, but Margery on the contrary increased Charlie's intimacy with them. By making him more tolerant she made him a more agreeable companion. They gave you the impression not of a married couple, but, rather amusingly, of two middle-aged bachelors living together; and when Margery, as was the rule, found herself the only woman among half a dozen men, ribald, argumentative and gay, she was not a bar to good-fellowship but an asset. Whenever I was in England I saw them. They generally dined at the club of which I have spoken and if I happened to be alone I joined them.

When we met that evening for a snack before going to the play I told them I had asked Morton to come to supper.

"I'm afraid you'll find him rather dull," I said. "But he's a very decent sort of boy and he was awfully kind to me when I was in Borneo."

"Why didn't you let me know sooner?" cried Margery. "I'd have brought a girl along."

"What do you want a girl for?" said Charlie. "There'll be you."

"I don't think it can be much fun for a young man to dance with a woman of my advanced years," said Margery.

"Rot. What's your age got to do with it?" He turned to me. "Have you ever danced with anyone who danced better?"

I had, but she certainly danced very well. She was light on her feet and she had a good sense of rhythm.

"Never," I said heartily.

Morton was waiting for us when we reached Ciro's. He looked very sunburned in his evening clothes. Perhaps it was because I knew that they had been wrapped away in a tin box with moth balls for four years that I felt he did not look quite at home in them. He was certainly more at ease in khaki shorts. Charlie Bishop was a good talker and liked to hear himself speak. Morton was shy. I gave him a cocktail and ordered some champagne. I had a feeling that he would be glad to dance, but was not quite sure whether it would occur to him to ask Margery. I was acutely conscious that we all belonged to another generation.

"I think I should tell you that Mrs. Bishop is a beautiful dancer," I said.

"Is she?" He flushed a little. "Will you dance with me?"

She got up and they took the floor. She was looking peculiarly nice that evening, not at all smart, and I do not think her plain black dress had cost more than six guineas, but she looked a lady. She had the advantage of having extremely good legs and at that time skirts were still being worn very short. I suppose she had a little make-up on, but in contrast with the other women there she looked very natural. Shingled hair suited her; it was not even touched with white and it had an attractive sheen. She was not a pretty woman, but her kindliness, her wholesome air, her good health gave you, if not the illusion that she was, at least the feeling that it didn't at all matter. When she came back to the table her eyes were bright and she had a heightened colour.

"How does he dance?" asked her husband.

"Divinely."

"You're very easy to dance with," said Morton.

Charlie went on with his discourse. He had a sardonic humour and he was interesting because he was himself so interested in what he said. But he spoke of things that Morton knew nothing about and though he listened with a civil show of interest I could see that he was too much excited by the gaiety of the scene, the music and the champagne to give his attention to conversation. When the music struck up again his eyes immediately sought Margery's. Charles caught the look and smiled.

"Dance with him, Margery. Good for my figure to see you take exercise."

They set off again and for a moment Charlie watched her with fond eyes.

"Margery's having the time of her life. She loves dancing and it makes me puff and blow. Not a bad youth."

My little party was quite a success and when Morton and I, having taken leave of the Bishops, walked together towards Piccadilly Circus he thanked me warmly. He had really enjoyed himself. I said good-bye to him. Next morning I went abroad.

I was sorry not to have been able to do more for Morton and I knew that when I returned he would be on his way back to Borneo. I gave him a passing thought now and then, but by the autumn when I got home he had slipped my memory. After I had been in London a week or so I happened to drop in one night at the club to which Charlie Bishop also belonged. He was sitting with three or four men I knew and I went up. I had not seen any of them since my return. One of them, a man called Bill Marsh, whose wife, Janet, was a great friend of mine, asked me to have a drink.

"Where have you sprung from?" asked Charlie. "Haven't seen you about lately."

I noticed at once that he was drunk. I was astonished. Charlie had always liked his liquor, but he carried it well and never exceeded. In years gone by, when we were very young, he got tight occasionally, but probably more than anything to show what a great fellow he was, and it is unfair to bring up against a man the excesses of his youth. But I remembered that Charlie had never been very nice when he was drunk: his natural aggressiveness was exaggerated then and he talked too much and too loud; he was very apt to be quarrelsome. He was very dogmatic now, laying down the law and refusing to listen to any of the objections his rash statements called forth. The others knew he was drunk and were struggling between the irritation his cantankerousness aroused in them and the good-natured tolerance which they felt his condition demanded. He was not an agreeable object. A man of that age, bald and fattish, with spectacles, is disgusting drunk. He was generally rather dapper, but he was untidy now and there was tobacco ash all over him. Charlie called the waiter and ordered another whisky. The waiter had been at the club for thirty years.

"You've got one in front of you, sir."

"Mind your own damned business," said Charlie Bishop. "Bring me a double whisky right away or I'll report you to the secretary for insolence."

"Very good, sir," said the waiter.

Charlie emptied his glass at a gulp, but his hand was unsteady and he spilled some of the whisky over himself.

"Well, Charlie, old boy, we'd better be toddling along," said Bill Marsh. He turned to me. "Charlie's staying with us for a bit."

I was more surprised still. But I felt that something was wrong and thought it safer not to say anything.

"I'm ready," said Charlie. "I'll just have another drink before I go. I shall have a better night if I do."

It did not look to me as though the party would break up for some time, so I got up and announced that I meant to stroll home.

"I say," said Bill, as I was about to go, "you wouldn't come and dine with us to-morrow night, would you, just me and Janet and Charlie?"

"Yes, I'll come with pleasure," I said.

It was evident that something was up.

The Marshes lived in a terrace on the East side of Regent's Park. The maid who opened the door for me asked me to go in to Mr. Marsh's study. He was waiting for me there.

"I thought I'd better have a word with you before you went upstairs," he said as he shook hands with me. "You know Margery's left Charlie?"

"No!"

"He's taken it very hard. Janet thought it was so awful for him alone in that beastly little flat that we asked him to stay here for a bit. We've done everything we could for him. He's been drinking like a fish. He hasn't slept a wink for a fortnight."

"But she hasn't left him for good?"

I was astounded.

"Yes. She's crazy about a fellow called Morton."

"Morton. Who's he?"

It never struck me it was my friend from Borneo.

"Damn it all, you introduced him and a pretty piece of work you did. Let's go upstairs. I thought I'd better put you wise."

He opened the door and we went out. I was thoroughly confused.

"But look here," I said.

"Ask Janet. She knows the whole thing. It beats me. I've got no patience with Margery, and he must be a mess."

He preceded me into the drawing-room. Janet Marsh rose as I entered and came forward to greet me. Charlie was sitting at the window, reading the evening paper; he put it aside as I went up to him and shook his hand. He was quite sober and he spoke in his usual rather perky manner, but I noticed that he looked very ill. We had a glass of sherry and went down to dinner. Janet was a woman of spirit. She was tall and fair and good to look at. She kept the conversation going with alertness. When she left us to drink a glass of port it was with instructions not to stay more than ten minutes. Bill, as a rule somewhat taciturn, exerted himself now to talk. I tumbled to the game. I was hampered by my ignorance of what exactly had happened, but it was plain that the Marshes wanted to prevent Charlie from brooding, and I did my best to interest him. He seemed willing to play his part, he was always fond of holding forth, and he discussed, from the pathologist's standpoint, a murder that was just then absorbing the public. But he spoke without life. He was an empty shell, and one had the feeling that though for the sake of his host he forced himself to speak, his thoughts were elsewhere. It was a relief when a knocking on the floor above indicated to us that Janet was getting impatient. This was an occasion when a woman's presence eased the situation. We went upstairs and played family bridge. When it was time for me to go Charlie said he would walk with me as far as the Marylebone Road.

"Oh, Charlie, it's so late, you'd much better go to bed," said Janet.

"I shall sleep better if I have a stroll before turning in," he replied.

She gave him a worried look. You cannot forbid a middle-aged professor of pathology from going for a little walk if he wants to. She glanced brightly at her husband.

"I daresay it'll do Bill no harm."

I think the remark was tactless. Women are often a little too managing. Charlie gave her a sullen look.

"There's absolutely no need to drag Bill out," he said with some firmness.

"I haven't the smallest intention of coming," said Bill, smiling. "I'm tired out and I'm going to hit the hay."

I fancy we left Bill Marsh and his wife to a little argument.

"They've been frightfully kind to me," said Charlie, as we walked along by the railings. "I don't know what I should have done without them. I haven't slept for a fortnight."

I expressed regret but did not ask the reason, and we walked for a little in silence. I presumed that he had come with me in order to talk to me of what had happened, but I felt that he must take his own time. I was anxious to show my sympathy, but afraid of saying the wrong thing; I did not want to seem eager to extract confidences from him. I did not know how to give him a lead. I was sure he did not want one. He was not a man given to beating about the bush. I imagined that he was choosing his words. We reached the corner.

"You'll be able to get a taxi at the church," he said. "I'll walk on a bit further. Good-night."

He nodded and slouched off. I was taken aback. There was nothing for me to do but to stroll on till I found a cab. I was having my bath next morning when a telephone call dragged me out of it, and with a towel round my wet body I took up the receiver. It was Janet.

"Well, what do you think of it all?" she said. "You seem to have kept Charlie up pretty late last night. I heard him come home at three."

"He left me at the Marylebone Road," I answered. "He said nothing to me at all."

"Didn't he?"

There was something in Janet's voice that suggested that she was prepared to have a long talk with me. I suspected she had a telephone by the side of her bed.

"Look here," I said quickly. "I'm having my bath."

"Oh, have you got a telephone in your bathroom?" she answered eagerly, and I think with envy.

"No, I haven't." I was abrupt and firm. "And I'm dripping all over the carpet."

"Oh!" I felt disappointment in her tone and a trace of irritation. "Well, when can I see you? Can you come here at twelve?"

It was inconvenient, but I was not prepared to start an argument. "Yes, good-bye."

I rang off before she could say anything more. In heaven when the blessed use the telephone they will say what they have to say and not a word beside.

I was devoted to Janet, but I knew that there was nothing that thrilled her more than the misfortunes of her friends. She was only too anxious to help them, but she wanted to be in the thick of their difficulties. She was the friend in adversity. Other people's business was meat and drink to her. You could not enter upon a love affair without finding her somehow your confidante nor be mixed up in a divorce case without discovering that she too had a finger in the pie. Withal she was a very nice woman. I could not help then chuckling in my heart when at noon I was shown in to Janet's drawing-room and observed the subdued eagerness with which she received me. She was very much upset by the catastrophe that had befallen the Bishops, but it was exciting, and she was tickled to death to have someone fresh to whom she could tell all about it. Janet had just that business-like expectancy that a mother has when she is discussing with the family doctor her married daughter's first confinement. Janet was conscious that the matter was very serious, and she would not for a moment have been thought to regard it flippantly, but she was determined to get every ounce of value out of it.

"I mean, no one could have been more horrified than I was when Margery told me she'd finally made up her mind to leave Charlie," she said, speaking with the fluency of a person who has said the same thing in the same words a dozen times at least. "They were the most devoted couple I'd ever known. It was a perfect marriage. They got on like a house on fire. Of course Bill and I are devoted to one another, but we have awful rows now and then. I mean, I could kill him sometimes."

"I don't care a hang about your relations with Bill," I said. "Tell me about the Bishops. That's what I've come here for."

"I simply felt I must see you. After all you're the only person who can explain it."

"Oh, God, don't go on like that. Until Bill told me last night I didn't know a thing about it."

"That was my idea. It suddenly dawned on me that perhaps you didn't know and I thought you might put your foot in it too awfully."

"Supposing you began at the beginning," I said.

"Well, you're the beginning. After all you started the trouble. You introduced the young man. That's why I was so crazy to see you. You know all about him. I never saw him. All I know is what Margery has told me about him."

"At what time are you lunching?" I asked.

"Half-past one."

"So am I. Get on with the story."

But my remark had given Janet an idea.

"Look here, will you get out of your luncheon if I get out of mine. We could have a snack here. I'm sure there's some cold meat in the house, and then we needn't hurry. I don't have to be at the hairdresser's till three."

"No, no, no," I said. "I hate the notion of that. I shall leave here at twenty minutes past one at the latest."

"Then I shall just have to race through it. What do *you* think of Gerry?"

"Who's Gerry?"

"Gerry Morton. His name's Gerald."

"How should I know that?"

"You stayed with him. Weren't there any letters lying about?"

"I daresay, but I didn't happen to read them," I answered somewhat tartly.

"Oh, don't be so stupid. I meant the envelopes. What's he like?"

"All right. Rather the Kipling type, you know. Very keen on his work. Hearty. Empire-builder and all that sort of thing."

"I don't mean that," cried Janet, not without impatience. "I mean, what does he look like?"

"More or less like everybody else, I think. Of course I should recognise him if I saw him again, but I can't picture him to myself very distinctly. He looks clean."

"Oh, my God," said Janet. "Are you a novelist or are you not? What's the colour of his eyes?"

"I don't know."

"You must know. You can't spend a week with anyone without knowing if their eyes are blue or brown. Is he fair or dark?"

"Neither."

"Is he tall or short?"

"Average, I should say."

"Are you trying to irritate me?"

"No. He's just ordinary. There's nothing in him to attract your attention. He's neither plain nor good-looking. He looks quite decent. He looks a gentleman."

"Margery says he has a charming smile and a lovely figure."

"I dare say."

"He's absolutely crazy about her."

"What makes you think that?" I asked dryly.

"I've seen his letters."

"Do you mean to say she's shown them to you?"

"Why, of course."

It is always difficult for a man to stomach the want of reticence that women betray in their private affairs. They have no shame. They will talk to one another without embarrassment of the most intimate matters. Modesty is a masculine virtue. But though a man may know this theoretically, each time he is confronted with women's lack of reserve he suffers a new shock. I wondered what Morton would think if he knew that not only were his letters read by Janet Marsh as well as by Margery, but that she had been kept posted from day to day with the progress of his infatuation. According to Janet he had fallen in love with Margery at first sight. The morning after they had met at my little supper party at Ciro's he had rung up and asked her to come and have tea with him at some place where they could dance. While I listened to Janet's story I was conscious of course that she was giving me Margery's view of the circumstances and I kept an open mind. I was interested to observe that Janet's sympathies were with Margery. It was true that when Margery left her husband it was her idea that Charlie should come to them for two or three weeks rather than stay on in miserable loneliness in the deserted flat and she had been extraordinarily kind to him. She lunched with him almost every day, because he had been accustomed to lunch every day with Margery; she took him for walks in Regent's Park and made Bill play golf with him on Sundays. She listened with wonderful patience to the story of his unhappiness and did what she could to console him. She was terribly sorry for him. But all the same she was definitely on Margery's side and when I expressed my disapproval of her she came down on me like a thousand of bricks. The affair thrilled her. She had been in it from the beginning when Margery, smiling, flattered and a little doubtful, came and told her that she had a young man to the final scene when Margery, exasperated and distraught, announced that she could not stand the strain any more and had packed her things and moved out of the flat.

"Of course, at first I couldn't believe my ears," she said. "You know how Charlie and Margery were. They simply lived in one another's pockets. One couldn't help laughing at them, they were so devoted to one another. I never thought him a very nice little man and heaven knows he wasn't very attractive physically, but one couldn't help liking him because he was so awfully nice to Margery. I rather envied her sometimes. They had no money and they lived in a hugger-mugger sort of way, but they were frightfully happy. Of course I never thought anything would come of it. Margery was rather amused. 'Naturally I don't take it very seriously,' she told me, 'but it is rather fun to have a young man at my time of life. I haven't had any flowers sent me for years. I had to tell him not to send any more because Charlie would think it so silly. He doesn't know a soul in London and he loves dancing and he says I dance like a dream. It's miserable for him going to the theatre by himself all the time and we've done two or three matinées together. It's pathetic to see how grateful he is when I say I'll go out with him.' 'I must say,' I said, 'he sounds rather a lamb.' 'He is,' she said. 'I knew you'd understand. You don't blame me, do you?' 'Of course not, darling,' I said, 'surely you know me better than that. I'd do just the same in your place.' "

Margery made no secret of her outings with Morton and her husband chaffed her good-naturedly about her beau. But he thought him a very civil, pleasant-spoken young man and was glad that Margery had someone to play with while he was busy. It never occurred to him to be jealous. The three of them dined together several times and went to a show. But presently Gerry Morton begged Margery to spend an evening with him alone; she said it was impossible, but he was persuasive, he gave her no peace; and at last she went to Janet and asked her to ring up Charlie one day and ask him to come to dinner and make a fourth at bridge. Charlie would never go anywhere without his wife, but the Marshes were old friends, and Janet made a point of it. She invented some cock-and-bull story that made it seem important that he should consent. Next day Margery and she met. The evening had been wonderful. They had dined at Maidenhead and danced there and then had driven home through the summer night.

"He says he's crazy about me," Margery told her.

"Did he kiss you?" asked Janet.

"Of course," Margery chuckled. "Don't be silly, Janet. He is awfully sweet and, you know, he has such a nice nature. Of course I don't believe half the things he says to me."

"My dear, you're not going to fall in love with him."

"I have," said Margery.

"Darling, isn't it going to be rather awkward?"

"Oh, it won't last. After all he's going back to Borneo in the autumn."

"Well, one can't deny that it's made you look years younger."

"I know, and I feel years younger."

Soon they were meeting every day. They met in the morning and walked in the Park together or went to a picture gallery. They separated for Margery to lunch with her husband and after lunch met again and motored into the country or to some place on the river. Margery did not tell her husband. She very naturally thought he would not understand.

"How was it you never met Morton?" I asked Janet.

"Oh, she didn't want me to. You see, we belong to the same generation, Margery and I. I quite understand that."

"I see."

"Of course I did everything I could. When she went out with Gerry she was always supposed to be with me."

I am a person who likes to cross a "t" and dot an "i".

"Were they having an affair?" I asked.

"Oh, no. Margery isn't that sort of woman at all."

"How do you know?"

"She would have told me."

"I suppose she would."

"Of course I asked her. But she denied it point-blank and I'm sure she was telling me the truth. There's never been anything of that sort between them at all."

"It seems rather odd to me."

"Well, you see, Margery is a very good woman."

I shrugged my shoulders.

"She was absolutely loyal to Charlie. She wouldn't have deceived him for anything in the world. She couldn't bear the thought of having any secret from him. As soon as she knew she was in love with Gerry she wanted to tell Charlie. Of course I begged her not to. I told her it wouldn't do any good and it would only make Charlie miserable. And after all, the boy was going away in a couple of months, it didn't seem much good to make a lot of fuss about a thing that couldn't possibly last."

But Gerry's imminent departure was the cause of the crash. The Bishops had arranged to go abroad as usual and proposed to motor through Belgium, Holland and the North of Germany. Charlie was busy with maps and guides. He collected information from friends about hotels and roads. He looked forward to his holiday with the bubbling excitement of a schoolboy. Margery listened to him discussing it with a sinking heart. They were to be away four weeks and in September Gerry was sailing. She could not bear to lose so much of the short time that remained to them and the thought of the motor tour filled her with exasperation. As the interval grew shorter and shorter she grew more and more nervous. At last she decided that there was only one thing to do.

"Charlie, I don't want to come on this trip," she interrupted him suddenly, one day when he was talking to her of some restaurant he had just heard of. "I wish you'd get someone else to go with you."

He looked at her blankly. She was startled at what she had said and her lips trembled a little.

"Why, what's the matter?"

"Nothing's the matter. I don't feel like it. I want to be by myself for a bit."

"Are you ill?"

She saw the sudden fear in his eyes. His concern drove her beyond her endurance."

"No. I've never been better in my life. I'm in love."

"You? Whom with?"

"Gerry."

He looked at her in amazement. He could not believe his ears. She mistook his expression.

"It's no good blaming me. I can't help it. He's going away in a few weeks. I'm not going to waste the little time he has left."

He burst out laughing.

"Margery, how can you make such a damned fool of yourself? You're old enough to be his mother."

She flushed.

"He's just as much in love with me as I am with him."

"Has he told you so?"

"A thousand times."

"He's a bloody liar, that's all."

He chuckled. His fat stomach rippled with mirth. He thought it a huge joke. I daresay Charlie did not treat his wife in the proper way. Janet seemed to think he should have been tender and compassionate. *He should have understood.* I saw the scene that was in her mind's eye, the stiff upper lip, the silent sorrow, and the final renunciation. Women are always sensitive to the beauty of the self-sacrifice of others. Janet would have sympathised also if he had flown into a violent passion, broken one or two pieces of furniture (which he would have had to replace), or given Margery a sock in the jaw. But to laugh at her was unpardonable. I did not point out that it is very difficult for a rather stout and not very tall professor of pathology, aged fifty-five, to act all of a sudden like a cave-man. Anyhow, the excursion to Holland was given up and the Bishops stayed in London through August. They were not very happy. They lunched and dined together every day because they had been in the habit of doing so for so many years and the rest of the time Margery spent with Gerry. The hours she passed with him made up for all she had to put up with and she had to put up with a good deal. Charlie had a ribald and sarcastic humour and he made himself very funny at her expense and at Gerry's. He persisted in refusing to take the matter seriously. He was vexed with Margery for being so silly, but apparently it never occurred to him that she might have been unfaithful to him. I commented upon this to Janet.

"He never suspected it even," she said. "He knew Margery much too well."

The weeks passed and at last Gerry sailed. He went from Tilbury and Margery saw him off. When she came back she cried for forty-eight hours. Charlie watched her with increasing exasperation. His nerves were much frayed.

"Look here, Margery," he said at last, "I've been very patient with you, but now you must pull yourself together. This is getting past a joke."

"Why can't you leave me alone?" she cried. "I've lost everything that made life lovely to me."

"Don't be such a fool," he said.

I do not know what else he said. But he was unwise enough to tell her what he thought of Gerry and I gather that the picture he drew was virulent. It started the first violent scene they had ever had. She had borne Charlie's jibes when she knew that she would see Gerry in an hour or next day, but now that she had lost him for ever she could bear them no longer. She had held herself in for weeks: now she flung her self-control to the winds. Perhaps she never knew exactly what she said to Charlie. He had always been irascible and at last he hit her. They were both frightened when he had. He seized a hat and flung out of the flat. During all that miserable time they had shared the same bed, but when he came back, in the middle of the night, he found that she had made herself up a shake-down on the sofa in the sitting-room.

"You can't sleep there," he said. "Don't be so silly. Come to bed."

"No, I won't, let me alone."

For the rest of the night they wrangled, but she had her way and now made up her bed every night on the sofa. But in that tiny flat they could not get away from one another; they could not even get out of sight or out of hearing of one another. They had lived in such intimacy for so many years that it was an instinct for them to be together. He tried to reason with her. He thought her incredibly stupid and argued with her interminably in the effort to show her how wrong-headed she was. He could not leave her alone. He would not let her sleep, and he talked half through the night till they were both exhausted. He thought he could talk her out of love. For two or three days at a time they would not speak to one another. Then one day, coming home, he found her crying bitterly; the sight of her tears distracted him; he told her how much he loved her and sought to move her by the recollection of all the happy years they had spent together. He wanted to let bygones be bygones. He promised never to refer to Gerry again. Could they not forget the nightmare they had been through? But the thought of all that a reconciliation implied revolted her. She told him she had a racking headache and asked him to give her a sleeping draught. She pretended to be still asleep when he went out next morning, but the moment he was gone she packed up her things and left. She had a few trinkets that she had inherited and by selling them she got a little money. She took a room at a cheap boarding-house and kept her address a secret from Charlie.

It was when he found she had left him that he went all to pieces. The shock of her flight broke him. He told Janet that his loneliness was intolerable. He wrote to Margery imploring her to come back, and asked Janet to intercede for him; he was willing to promise anything; he abased himself. Margery was obdurate.

"Do you think she'll ever go back?" I asked Janet.

"She says not."

I had to leave then, for it was nearly half-past one and I was bound for the other end of London.

Two or three days later I got a telephone message from Margery asking if I could see her. She suggested coming to my rooms. I asked her to tea. I tried to be nice to her; her affairs were no business of mine, but in my heart I thought her a very silly woman and I dare say my manner was cold. She had never been handsome and the passing years had changed her little. She had still those fine dark eyes and her face was astonishingly unlined. She was very simply dressed and if she wore make-up it was so cunningly put on that I did not perceive it. She had still the charm she had always had of perfect naturalness and of a kindly humour.

"I want you to do something for me if you will," she began without beating about the bush.

"What is it?"

"Charlie is leaving the Marshes to-day and going back to the flat. I'm afraid his first few days there will be rather difficult; it would be awfully nice of you if you'd ask him to dinner or something."

"I'll have a look at my book."

"I'm told he's been drinking heavily. It's such a pity. I wish you could give him a hint."

"I understand he's had some domestic worries of late," I said, perhaps acidly.

Margery flushed. She gave me a pained look. She winced as though I had struck her.

"Of course you've known him ever so much longer than you've known me. It's natural that you should take his part."

"My dear, to tell you the truth I've known him all these years chiefly on your account. I have never very much liked him, but I thought you were awfully nice."

She smiled at me and her smile was very sweet. She knew that I meant what I said.

"Do you think I was a good wife to him?"

"Perfect."

"He used to put people's backs up. A lot of people didn't like him, but I never found him difficult."

"He was awfully fond of you."

"I know. We had a wonderful time together. For sixteen years we were perfectly happy." She paused and looked down. "I had to leave him. It became quite impossible. That cat-and-dog life we were leading was too awful."

"I never see why two persons should go on living together if they don't want to."

"You see, it was awful for us. We'd always lived in such close intimacy. We could never get away from one another. At the end I hated the sight of him."

"I don't suppose the situation was easy for either of you."

"It wasn't my fault that I fell in love. You see, it was quite a different love from the one I'd felt for Charlie. There was always something maternal in that and protective. I was so much more reasonable than he was. He was unmanageable, but I could always manage him. Gerry was different." Her voice grew soft and her face was transfigured with glory. "He gave me back my youth. I was a girl to him and I could depend on his strength and be safe in his care."

"He seemed to me a very nice lad," I said slowly. "I imagine he'll do well. He was very young for the job he had when I ran across him. He's only twenty-nine now, isn't he?"

She smiled softly. She knew quite well what I meant.

"I never made any secret of my age to him. He says it doesn't matter."

I knew this was true. She was not the woman to have lied about her age. She had found a sort of fierce delight in telling him the truth about herself.

"How old are you?"

"Forty-four."

"What are you going to do now?"

"I've written to Gerry and told him I've left Charlie. As soon as I hear from him I'm going out to join him."

I was staggered.

"You know, it's a very primitive little colony he's living in. I'm afraid you'll find your position rather awkward."

"He made me promise that if I found my life impossible after he left I'd go to him."

"Are you sure you're wise to attach so much importance to the things a young man says when he's in love?"

Again that really beautiful look of exaltation came into her face.

"Yes, when the young man happens to be Gerry."

My heart sank. I was silent for a moment. Then I told her the story of the road Gerry Morton had built. I dramatised it, and I think I made it rather effective.

"What did you tell me that for?" she asked when I finished.

"I thought it rather a good story."

She shook her head and smiled.

"No, you wanted to show me that he was very young and enthusiastic, and so keen on his work that he hadn't much time to waste on other interests. I wouldn't interfere with his work. You don't know him as I do. He's incredibly romantic. He looks upon himself as a pioneer. I've caught from him something of his excitement at the idea of taking part in the opening up of a new country. It *is* rather splendid, isn't it? It makes life here seem very humdrum and commonplace. But of course it's very lonely there. Even the companionship of a middle-aged woman may be worth having."

"Are you proposing to marry him?" I asked.

"I leave myself in his hands. I want to do nothing that he does not wish."

She spoke with so much simplicity, there was something so touching in her self-surrender, that when she left me I no longer felt angry with her. Of course I thought her very foolish, but if the folly of men made one angry one would pass one's life in a state of chronic ire. I thought all would come right. She said

Gerry was romantic. He was, but the romantics in this workaday world only get away with their nonsense because they have at bottom a shrewd sense of reality: the mugs are the people who take their vapourings at their face value. The English are romantic; that is why other nations think them hypocritical; they are not: they set out in all sincerity for the Kingdom of God, but the journey is arduous and they have reason to pick up any gilt-edged investment that offers itself by the way. The British soul, like Wellington's armies, marches on its belly. I supposed that Gerry would go through a bad quarter of an hour when he received Margery's letter. My sympathies were not deeply engaged in the matter and I was only curious to see how he would extricate himself from the pass he was in. I thought Margery would suffer a bitter disappointment; well, that would do her no great harm, and then she would go back to her husband and I had no doubt the pair of them, chastened, would live in peace, quiet and happiness for the rest of their lives.

The event was different. It happened that it was quite impossible for me to make any sort of engagement with Charlie Bishop for some days, but I wrote to him and asked him to dine with me one evening in the following week. I proposed, though with misgiving, that we should go to a play; I knew he was drinking like a fish, and when tight he was noisy. I hoped he would not make a nuisance of himself in the theatre. We arranged to meet at our club and dine at seven because the piece we were going to began at a quarter past eight. I arrived. I waited. He did not come. I rang up his flat, but could get no reply, so concluded that he was on his way. I hate missing the beginning of a play and I waited impatiently in the hall so that when he came we could go straight upstairs. To save time I had ordered dinner. The clock pointed to half-past seven, then a quarter to eight; I did not see why I should wait for him any longer, so walked up to the dining-room and ate my dinner alone. He did not appear. I put a call through from the dining-room to the Marshes and presently was told by a waiter that Bill Marsh was at the end of the wire.

"I say, do you know anything about Charlie Bishop?" I said. "We were dining together and going to a play and he hasn't turned up."

"He died this afternoon?"

"What?"

My exclamation was so startled that two or three people within earshot looked up. The dining-room was full and the waiters were hurrying to and fro. The telephone was on the cashier's desk and a wine waiter came up with a bottle of hock and two long-stemmed glasses on a tray and gave the cashier a chit. The portly steward showing two men to a table jostled me.

"Where are you speaking from?" asked Bill.

I suppose he heard the clatter that surrounded me. When I told him he asked me if I could come round as soon as I had finished my dinner. Janet wanted to speak to me.

"I'll come at once," I said.

I found Janet and Bill sitting in the drawing-room. He was reading the paper and she was playing patience. She came forward swiftly when the maid showed me in. She walked with a sort of spring, crouching a little, on silent feet, like a panther stalking his prey. I saw at once that she was in her element. She gave me her hand and turned her face away to hide her eyes brimming with tears. Her voice was low and tragic.

"I brought Margery here and put her to bed. The doctor has given her a sedative. She's all in. Isn't it awful?" She gave a sound that was something between a gasp and a sob. "I don't know why these things always happen to me."

The Bishops had never kept a servant but a charwoman went in every morning, cleaned the flat and washed up the breakfast things. She had her own key. That morning she had gone in as usual and done the sitting-room. Since his wife had left him Charlie's hours had been irregular and she was not surprised to find him asleep. But the time passed and she knew he had his work to go to. She went to the bedroom door and knocked. There was no answer. She thought she heard him groaning. She opened the door softly. He was lying in bed, on his back, and was breathing stertorously. He did not wake. She called him. Something about him frightened her. She went to the flat on the same landing. It was occupied by a journalist. He was still in bed when she rang, and opened the door to her in pyjamas.

"Beg pardon, sir," she said, "but would you just come and 'ave a look at my gentleman. I don't think he's well."

The journalist walked across the landing and into Charlie's flat. There was an empty bottle of veronal by the bed.

"I think you'd better fetch a policeman," he said.

A policeman came and rang through to the police station for an ambulance. They took Charlie to Charing Cross Hospital.

He never recovered consciousness. Margery was with him at the end.

"Of course there'll have to be an inquest," said Janet. "But it's quite obvious what happened. He'd been sleeping awfully badly for the last three or four weeks and I suppose he'd been taking veronal. He must have taken an overdose by accident."

"Is that what Margery thinks?" I asked.

"She's too upset to think anything, but I told her I was positive he hadn't committed suicide. I mean, he wasn't that sort of a man. Am I right, Bill?"

"Yes, dear," he answered.

"Did he leave any letter?"

"No, nothing. Oddly enough Margery got a letter from him this morning, well, hardly a letter, just a line. 'I'm so lonely without you, darling.' That's all. But of course that means nothing and she's promised to say nothing about it at the inquest. I mean, what is the use of putting ideas in people's heads? Everyone knows that you never can tell with veronal, I wouldn't take it myself for anything in the world, and it was quite obviously an accident. Am I right, Bill?"

"Yes, dear," he answered.

I saw that Janet was quite determined to believe that Charlie Bishop had not committed suicide, but how far in her heart she believed what she wanted to believe I was not sufficiently expert in female psychology to know. And of course it might be that she was right. It is unreasonable to suppose that a middle-aged scientist should kill himself because his middle-aged wife leaves him and it is extremely plausible that, exasperated by sleeplessness, and in all probability far from sober, he took a larger dose of the sleeping-draught than he realised. Anyhow that was the view the coroner took of the matter. It was indicated to him that of late Charles Bishop had given way to habits of intemperance which had caused his wife to leave him, and it was quite obvious that nothing was further from his thoughts than to put an end to himself. The coroner expressed his sympathy with the widow and commented very strongly on the dangers of sleeping-draughts.

I hate funerals, but Janet begged me to go to Charlie's. Several of his colleagues at the hospital had intimated their desire to come, but at Margery's wish they were dissuaded; and Janet and Bill, Margery and I were the only persons who attended it. We were to fetch the hearse from the mortuary and they offered to call for

me on their way. I was on the look-out for the car and when I
saw it drive up went downstairs, but Bill got out and met me just
inside the door.

"Half a minute," he said. "I've got something to say to you.
Janet wants you to come back afterwards and have tea. She says
it's no good Margery moping and after tea we'll play a few rubbers
of bridge. Can you come?"

"Like this?" I asked.

I had a tail coat on and a black tie and my evening dress
trousers.

"Oh, that's all right. It'll take Margery's mind off."

"Very well."

But we did not play bridge after all. Janet, with her fair hair,
was very smart in her deep mourning and she played the part of
the sympathetic friend with amazing skill. She cried a little, wiping
her eyes delicately so as not to disturb the black on her eyelashes,
and when Margery sobbed broken-heartedly put her arm tenderly
through hers. She was a very present help in trouble. We returned
to the house. There was a telegram for Margery. She took it and
went upstairs. I presumed it was a message of condolence from one
of Charlie's friends who had just heard of his death. Bill went to
change and Janet and I went up to the drawing-room and got the
bridge table out. She took off her hat and put it on the piano.

"It's no good being hypocritical," she said. "Of course Margery
has been frightfully upset, but she must pull herself together now.
A rubber of bridge will help her to get back to her normal state.
Naturally I'm dreadfully sorry about poor Charlie, but as far as
he was concerned I don't believe he'd ever have got over Margery's
leaving him and one can't deny that it has made things much easier
for her. She wired to Gerry this morning."

"What about?"

"To tell him about poor Charlie."

At that moment the maid came to the room.

"Will you go up to Mrs. Bishop, please, ma'am? She wants to
see you."

"Yes, of course."

She went out of the room quickly and I was left alone. Bill
joined me presently and we had a drink. At last Janet came back.
She handed a telegram to me. It read as follows:

For God's sake await letter. Gerry.

"What do you think it means?" she asked me.

"What it says," I replied.

"Idiot! Of course I've told Margery that it doesn't mean anything, but she's rather worried. It must have crossed her cable telling him that Charles was dead. I don't think she feels very much like bridge after all. I mean, it would be rather bad form to play on the very day her husband has been buried."

"Quite," I said.

"Of course he may wire in answer to the cable. He's sure to do that, isn't he? The only thing we can do now is to sit tight and wait for his letter."

I saw no object in continuing the conversation. I left. In a couple of days Janet rang me up to tell me that Margery had received a telegram of condolence from Morton. She repeated it to me.

Dreadfully distressed to hear sad news. Deeply sympathise with your great grief. Love. Gerry.

"What do you think of it?" she asked me.

"I think it's very proper."

"Of course he couldn't say he was as pleased as Punch, could he?"

"Not with any delicacy."

"And he did put in *love*."

I imagined how those women had examined the two telegrams from every point of view and scrutinised every word to press from it every possible shade of meaning. I almost heard their interminable conversations.

"I don't know what'll happen to Margery if he lets her down now," Janet went on. "Of course it remains to be seen if he's a gentleman."

"Rot," I said and rang off quickly.

In the course of the following days I dined with the Marshes a couple of times. Margery looked tired. I guessed that she awaited the letter that was on the way with sickening anxiety. Grief and fear had worn her to a shadow, she seemed very fragile now and she had acquired a spiritual look that I had never seen in her before. She was very gentle, very grateful for every kindness shown her, and in her smile, unsure and a little timid, was an infinite pathos. Her helplessness was very appealing. But Morton was several thousand miles away. Then one morning Janet rang me up.

"The letter has come. Margery says I can show it to you. Will you come round?"

Her tense voice told me everything. When I arrived Janet gave it to me. I read it. It was a very careful letter and I guessed that Morton had written it a good many times. It was very kind and he had evidently taken great pains to avoid saying anything that could possibly wound Margery; but what transpired was his terror. It was obvious that he was shaking in his shoes. He had felt apparently that the best way to cope with the situation was to be mildly facetious and he made very good fun of the white people in the colony. What would they say if Margery suddenly turned up? He would be given the order of the boot pretty damn quick. People thought the East was free and easy; it wasn't, it was more suburban than Clapham. He loved Margery far too much to bear the thoughts of those horrible women out there turning up their noses at her. And besides he had been sent to a station ten days from anywhere; she couldn't live in his bungalow exactly and of course there wasn't a hotel, and his work took him out into the jungle for days at a time. It was no place for a woman anyhow. He told her how much she meant to him, but she mustn't bother about him and he couldn't help thinking it would be better if she went back to her husband. He would never forgive himself if he thought he had come between her and Charlie. Yes, I am quite sure it had been a difficult letter to write.

"Of course he didn't know then that Charlie was dead. I've told Margery that changes everything."

"Does she agree with you?"

"I think she's being rather unreasonable. What do you make of the letter?"

"Well, it's quite plain that he doesn't want her."

"He wanted her badly enough two months ago."

"It's astonishing what a change of air and a change of scene will do for you. It must seem to him already like a year since he left London. He's back among his old friends and his old interests. My dear, it's no good Margery kidding herself; the life there has taken him back and there's no place for her."

"I've advised her to ignore the letter and go straight out to him."

"I hope she's too sensible to expose herself to a very terrible rebuff."

"But then what's to happen to her? Oh, it's too cruel. She's the best woman in the world. She has real goodness."

"It's funny if you come to think of it, it's her goodness that has caused all the trouble. Why on earth didn't she have an affair with Morton? Charlie would have known nothing about it and wouldn't have been a penny the worse. She and Morton could have had a grand time and when he went away they could have parted with the consciousness that a pleasant episode had come to a graceful end. It would have been a jolly recollection, and she could have gone back to Charlie satisfied and rested and continued to make him the excellent wife she had always been."

Janet pursed her lips. She gave me a look of disdain.

"There is such a thing as virtue, you know."

"Virtue be damned. A virtue that only causes havoc and unhappiness is worth nothing. You can call it virtue if you like. I call it cowardice."

"The thought of being unfaithful to Charlie while she was living with him revolted her. There are women like that, you know."

"Good gracious, she could have remained faithful to him in spirit while she was being unfaithful to him in the flesh. That is a feat of legerdemain that women find it easy to accomplish."

"What an odious cynic you are."

"If it's cynical to look truth in the face and exercise common-sense in the affairs of life, then certainly I'm a cynic and odious if you like. Let's face it, Margery's a middle-aged woman, Charlie was fifty-five and they'd been married for sixteen years. It was natural enough that she should lose her head over a young man who made a fuss of her. But don't call it love. It was physiology. She was a fool to take anything he said seriously. It wasn't himself speaking, it was his starved sex, he'd suffered from sexual starvation, at least as far as white women are concerned, for four years; it's monstrous that she should seek to ruin his life by holding him to the wild promises he made then. It was an accident that Margery took his fancy; he wanted her, and because he couldn't get her wanted her more. I dare say he thought it love; believe me, it was only letch. If they'd gone to bed together Charlie would be alive to-day. It's her damned virtue that caused the whole trouble."

"How stupid you are. Don't you see that she couldn't help herself? She just doesn't happen to be a loose woman."

"I prefer a loose woman to a selfish one and a wanton to a fool."

"Oh, shut up. I didn't ask you to come here in order to make yourself absolutely beastly."

"What did you ask me to come here for?"

"Gerry is your friend. You introduced him to Margery. If she's in the soup it's on his account. But *you* are the cause of the whole trouble. It's your duty to write to him and tell him he must do the right thing by her."

"I'm damned if I will," I said.

"Then you'd better go."

I started to do so.

"Well, at all events it's a mercy that Charlie's life was insured," said Janet.

Then I turned on her.

"And you have the nerve to call me a cynic."

I will not repeat the opprobrious word I flung at her as I slammed the door behind me. But Janet is all the same a very nice woman. I often think it would be great fun to be married to her.

❖

The Man with the Scar

IT was on account of the scar that I first noticed him, for it ran, broad and red, in a great crescent from his temple to his chin. It must have been due to a formidable wound and I wondered whether this had been caused by a sabre or by a fragment of shell. It was unexpected on that round, fat and good-humoured face. He had small and undistinguished features, and his expression was artless. His face went oddly with his corpulent body. He was a powerful man of more than common height. I never saw him in anything but a very shabby grey suit, a khaki shirt and a battered sombrero. He was far from clean. He used to come into the Palace Hotel at Guatemala City every day at cocktail time and strolling leisurely round the bar offer lottery tickets for sale. If this was the way he made his living it must have been a poor one for I never saw anyone buy, but now and then I saw him offered a drink. He never refused it. He threaded his way among the tables with a sort of rolling walk as though he were accustomed to traverse long distances on foot, paused at each table, with a little smile mentioned the numbers he had for sale and then, when no notice was taken of him, with the same smile passed on. I think he was for the most part a trifle the worse for liquor.

I was standing at the bar one evening, my foot on the rail, with an acquaintance—they make a very good dry Martini at the Palace Hotel in Guatemala City—when the man with the scar came up. I shook my head as for the twentieth time since my arrival he held out for my inspection his lottery tickets. But my companion nodded affably.

"*Qué tal, general?* How is life?"

"Not so bad. Business is none too good, but it might be worse."

"What will you have, general?"

"A brandy."

He tossed it down and put the glass back on the bar. He nodded to my acquaintance.

"*Gracias. Hasta luego.*"

Then he turned away and offered his tickets to the men who were standing next to us.

"Who is your friend?" I asked. "That's a terrific scar on his face."

"It doesn't add to his beauty, does it? He's an exile from Nicaragua. He's a ruffian of course and a bandit, but not a bad fellow. I give him a few *pesos* now and then. He was a revolutionary general, and if his ammunition hadn't given out he'd have upset the government and be Minister of War now instead of selling lottery tickets in Guatemala. They captured him, along with his staff, such as it was, and tried him by court-martial. Such things are rather summary in these countries, you know, and he was sentenced to be shot at dawn. I guess he knew what was coming to him when he was caught. He spent the night in gaol and he and the others, there were five of them altogether, passed the time playing poker. They used matches for chips. He told me he'd never had such a run of bad luck in his life; they were playing with a short pack, Jacks to open, but he never held a card; he never improved more than half a dozen times in the whole sitting and no sooner did he buy a new stack than he lost it. When day broke and the soldiers came into the cell to fetch them for execution he had lost more matches than a reasonable man could use in a lifetime.

"They were led into the patio of the gaol and placed against a wall, the five of them side by side, with the firing party facing them. There was a pause and our friend asked the officer in charge of them what the devil they were keeping him waiting for. The officer said that the general commanding the government troops wished to attend the execution and they awaited his arrival.

" 'Then I have time to smoke another cigarette,' said our friend. 'He was always unpunctual.'

"But he had barely lit it when the general—it was San Ignacio, by the way: I don't know whether you ever met him—followed by his A.D.C. came into the patio. The usual formalities were performed and San Ignacio asked the condemned men whether there was anything they wished before the execution took place. Four of the five shook their heads, but our friend spoke.

" 'Yes, I should like to say good-bye to my wife.'

" '*Bueno*,' said the general, 'I have no objection to that. Where is she?'

" 'She is waiting at the prison door.'

" 'Then it will not cause a delay of more than five minutes.'

" 'Hardly that, *Señor General*,' said our friend.

" 'Have him placed on one side.'

"Two soldiers advanced and between them the condemned rebel walked to the spot indicated. The officer in command of the firing squad on a nod from the general gave an order, there was a ragged report, and the four men fell. They fell strangely, not together, but one after the other, with movements that were almost grotesque, as though they were puppets in a toy theatre. The officer went up to them and into one who was still alive emptied two barrels of his revolver. Our friend finished his cigarette and threw away the stub.

"There was a little stir at the gateway. A woman came into the patio, with quick steps, and then, her hand on her heart, stopped suddenly. She gave a cry and with outstretched arms ran forward.

" '*Caramba*,' said the General.

"She was in black, with a veil over her hair, and her face was dead white. She was hardly more than a girl, a slim creature, with little regular features and enormous eyes. But they were distraught with anguish. Her loveliness was such that as she ran, her mouth slightly open and the agony of her face beautiful, a gasp of surprise was wrung from those indifferent soldiers who looked at her.

"The rebel advanced a step or two to meet her. She flung herself into his arms and with a hoarse cry of passion: *alma de mi corazón*, soul of my heart, he pressed his lips to hers. And at the same moment he drew a knife from his ragged shirt—I haven't a notion how he managed to retain possession of it—and stabbed her in the neck. The blood spurted from the cut vein and dyed his shirt. Then he flung his arms round her and once more pressed his lips to hers.

"It happened so quickly that many did not know what had occurred, but from the others burst a cry of horror; they sprang forward and seized him. They loosened his grasp and the girl would have fallen if the A.D.C. had not caught her. She was unconscious. They laid her on the ground and with dismay on their faces stood round watching her. The rebel knew where he was striking and it was impossible to staunch the blood. In a moment the A.D.C. who had been kneeling by her side rose.

" 'She's dead,' he whispered.

"The rebel crossed himself.

" 'Why did you do it?' asked the general.

" 'I loved her.'

"A sort of sigh passed through those men crowded together and they looked with strange faces at the murderer. The general stared at him for a while in silence.

" 'It was a noble gesture,' he said at last. 'I cannot execute this man. Take my car and have him led to the frontier. *Señor*, I offer you the homage which is due from one brave man to another.'

"A murmur of approbation broke from those who listened. The A.D.C. tapped the rebel on the shoulder, and between the two soldiers without a word he marched to the waiting car."

My friend stopped and for a little I was silent. I must explain that he was a Guatemalecan and spoke to me in Spanish. I have translated what he told me as well as I could, but I have made no attempt to tone down his rather high-flown language. To tell the truth I think it suits the story.

"But how then did he get the scar?" I asked at length.

"Oh, that was due to a bottle that burst when I was opening it. A bottle of ginger ale."

"I never liked it," said I.

❖

The Closed Shop

NOTHING would induce me to tell the name of the happy country in which the incidents occurred that I am constrained to relate; but I see no harm in admitting that it is a free and independent state on the continent of America. This is vague enough in all conscience and can give rise to no diplomatic incident. Now the president of this free and independent state had an eye to a pretty woman and there came to his capital, a wide and sunny town with a plaza, a cathedral that was not without dignity and a few old Spanish houses, a young person from Michigan of such a pleasing aspect that his heart went out to her. He lost no time in declaring his passion and was gratified to learn that it was returned, but he was mortified to discover that the young person regarded his possession of a wife and her possession of a husband as a bar to their union. She had a feminine weakness for marriage. Though it seemed unreasonable to the president, he was not the man to refuse a pretty woman the gratification of her whim and promised to make such arrangements as would enable him to offer her wedlock. He called his attorneys together and put the matter before them. He had long thought, he said, that for a progressive country their marriage laws were remarkably out of date and he proposed therefore radically to amend them. The attorneys retired and after a brief interval devised a divorce law that was satisfactory to the president. But the state of which I write was always careful to do things in a constitutional way, for it was a highly civilised, democratic and reputable country. A president who respects himself and his oath of office cannot promulgate a law, even if it is to his own interest, without adhering to certain forms, and these things take time; the president had barely signed the decree that made the new divorce law valid when a revolution broke out and he was very unfortunately hanged on a lamp-post in the plaza in front of the cathedral that was not without dignity. The young person of pleasing aspect left town in a hurry, but the law remained. Its terms were simple. On the payment of one hundred dollars gold and after a residence

of thirty days a man could divorce his wife or a wife her husband
without even apprising the other party of the intended step. Your
wife might tell you that she was going to spend a month with her
aged mother and one morning at breakfast when you looked
through your mail you might receive a letter from her informing
you that she had divorced you and was already married to another.

Now it was not long before the happy news spread here and
there that at a reasonable distance from New York was a country,
the capital of which had an equable climate and tolerable accommodation, where a woman could release herself, expeditiously and
with economy, from the irksome bonds of matrimony. The fact
that the operation could be performed without the husband's
knowledge saved her from those preliminary and acrimonious
discussions that are so wearing to the nerves. Every woman
knows that however much a man may argue about a proposition he
will generally accept a fact with resignation. Tell him you want a
Rolls-Royce and he will say he can't afford it, but buy it and he
will sign his cheque like a lamb. So in a very short time beautiful
women in considerable numbers began to come down to the
pleasant, sunny town; tired business women and women of fashion,
women of pleasure and women of leisure; they came from New
York, Chicago and San Francisco, they came from Georgia and
they came from Dakota, they came from all the states in the
Union. The passenger accommodation on the ships of the United
Fruit Line was only just adequate to the demand, and if you wanted
a stateroom to yourself you had to engage it six months in advance.
Prosperity descended upon the capital of this enterprising state
and in a very little while there was not a lawyer in it who did not
own a Ford car. Don Agosto, the proprietor of the Grand Hotel,
went to the expense of building several bathrooms, but he did not
grudge it; he was making a fortune, and he never passed the lamp-
post on which the outgoing president had been hanged without
giving it a jaunty wave of his hand.

"He was a great man," he said. "One day they will erect a
statue to him."

I have spoken as though it were only women who availed themselves of this convenient and reasonable law, and this might
indicate that in the United States it is they rather than men who
desire release from the impediment of Holy Matrimony. I have
no reason to believe that this is so. Though it was women in great
majority who travelled to this country to get a divorce, I ascribe

this to the fact that it is always easy for them to get away for six weeks (a week there, a week back and thirty days to establish a domicile) but it is difficult for men to leave their affairs so long. It is true that they could go there during their summer holidays, but then the heat is somewhat oppressive; and besides, there are no golf links: it is reasonable enough to suppose that many a man will hesitate to divorce his wife when he can only do it at the cost of a month's golf. There were of course two or three males spending their thirty days at the Grand Hotel, but they were generally, for a reason that is obscure, commercial travellers. I can but imagine that by the nature of their avocations they were able at one and the same time to pursue freedom and profit.

Be this as it may, the fact remains that the inmates of the Grand Hotel were for the most part women, and very gay it was in the patio at luncheon and at dinner when they sat at little square tables under the arches discussing their matrimonial troubles and drinking champagne. Don Agosto did a roaring trade with the generals and colonels (there were more generals than colonels in the army of this state), the lawyers, bankers, merchants and the young sparks of the town who came to look at these beautiful creatures. But the perfect is seldom realised in this world. There is always something that is not quite right and women engaged in getting rid of their husbands are very properly in an agitated condition. It makes them at times hard to please. Now it must be confessed that this delightful little city, notwithstanding its manifold advantages, somewhat lacked places of amusement. There was but one cinema and this showed films that had been wandering too long from their happy home in Hollywood. In the daytime you could have consultations with your lawyer, polish your nails and do a little shopping, but the evenings were intolerable. There were many complaints that thirty days was a long time and more than one impatient young thing asked her lawyer why they didn't put a little pep into their law and do the whole job in eight and forty hours. Don Agosto, however, was a man of resource and presently he had an inspiration: he engaged a troupe of wandering Guatemaltecans who played the marimba. There is no music in the world that sets the toes so irresistibly tingling and in a little while everyone in the patio began dancing. It is of course obvious that twenty-five beautiful women cannot dance with three commercial travellers, but there were all these generals and colonels and there were all the young sparks of the town. They danced divinely and they had great liquid black eyes. The hours flew, the days tripped one upon the heels of the other so quickly that the month passed before you realised it, and more than one of Don Agosto's guests when she bade him farewell confessed that she would willingly have stayed longer. Don Agosto was radiant. He liked to see people enjoy themselves. The marimba band was worth twice the money he paid for it, and it did his heart good to see his ladies dance with the gallant officers and the young men of the town. Since Don Agosto was thrifty he always turned off the electric light on the stairs and in the passages at ten o'clock at night and the gallant officers and the young men of the town improved their English wonderfully.

Everything went as merrily as a marriage bell, if I may use a phrase that, however hackneyed, in this connection is irresistible, till one day Madame Coralie came to the conclusion that she had had enough of it. For one man's meat is another man's poison. She dressed herself and went to call on her friend Carmencita. After she had in a few voluble words stated the purpose of her visit, Carmencita called a maid and told her to run and fetch La Gorda. They had a matter of importance which they wished to discuss with her. La Gorda, a woman of ample proportions with a heavy moustache, soon joined them and over a bottle of Malaga the three of them held a momentous conversation. The result of it was that they indited a letter to the president asking for an audience. The new president was a hefty young man in the early thirties who, a few years before, had been a stevedore in the employment of an American firm, and he had risen to his present exalted station by a natural eloquence and an effective use of his gun when he wanted to make a point or emphasise a statement. When one of his secretaries placed the letter before him he laughed.

"What do those three old faggots want with me?"

But he was a good-natured fellow and accessible. He did not forget that he had been elected by the people, as one of the people, to protect the people. He had also during his early youth been employed for some months by Madame Coralie to run errands. He told his secretary that he would see them at ten o'clock next morning. They went at the appointed hour to the palace and were led up a noble stairway to the audience chamber; the official who conducted them knocked softly on the door; a barred judas was opened and a suspicious eye appeared. The president had no intention of suffering the fate of his predecessor if he could help it and no matter who his visitors were did not receive them without precaution. The official gave the three ladies' names, the door was opened, but not too wide, and they slipped in. It was a handsome room and various secretaries at little tables, in their shirt-sleeves and with a revolver on each hip, were busy typing. One or two other young men, heavily armed, were lying on sofas reading the papers and smoking cigarettes. The president, also in his shirt-sleeves, with a revolver in his belt, was standing with his thumbs in the sleeve-holes of his waistcoat. He was tall and stout, of a handsome and even dignified presence.

"*Qué tal?*" he cried, jovially, with a flash of his white teeth. "What brings you here, *señoras?*"

"How well you're looking, Don Manuel," said La Gorda. "You are a fine figure of a man."

He shook hands with them, and his staff, ceasing their strenuous activity, leaned back and cordially waved their hands to the three ladies. They were old friends and the greetings, if a trifle sardonic, were hearty. I must disclose the fact now (which I could without doubt do in a manner so discreet that I might be misunderstood; but if you have to say something you may just as well say it plainly as not) that these three ladies were the Madams of the three principal brothels in the capital of this free and independent state. La Gorda and Carmencita were of Spanish origin and were very decently dressed in black, with black silk shawls over their heads, but Madame Coralie was French and she wore a toque. They were all of mature age and of modest demeanour.

The president made them sit down, and offered them madeira and cigarettes, but they refused.

"No, thank you, Don Manuel," said Madame Coralie. "It is on business that we have come to see you."

"Well, what can I do for you?"

La Gorda and Carmencita looked at Madame Coralie and Madame Coralie looked at La Gorda and Carmencita. They nodded and she saw that they expected her to be their spokeswoman.

"Well, Don Manuel, it is like this. We are three women who have worked hard for many years and not a breath of scandal has ever tarnished our good names. There are not in all the Americas three more distinguished houses than ours and they are a credit to this beautiful city. Why, only last year I spent five hundred dollars to supply my *sala principal* with plate-glass mirrors. We have always been respectable and we have paid our taxes with regularity. It is hard now that the fruits of our labours should be snatched away from us. I do not hesitate to say that after so many years of honest and conscientious attention to business it is unjust that we should have to submit to such treatment."

The president was astounded.

"But, Coralie, my dear, I do not know what you mean. Has anyone dared to claim money from you that the law does not sanction or that I know nothing about?"

He gave his secretaries a suspicious glance. They tried to look innocent, but though they were, only succeeded in looking uneasy.

"It is the law we complain of. Ruin stares us in the face."

"Ruin?"

"So long as this new divorce law is in existence we can do no business and we may just as well shut up our beautiful houses."

Then Madame Coralie explained in a manner so frank that I prefer to paraphrase her speech that owing to this invasion of the town by beautiful ladies from a foreign land the three elegant houses on which she and her two friends paid rates and taxes were utterly deserted. The young men of fashion preferred to spend their evenings at the Grand Hotel where they received for soft words entertainment which at the regular establishments they could only have got for hard cash.

"You cannot blame them," said the president.

"I don't," cried Madame Coralie. "I blame the women. They have no right to come and take the bread out of our mouths. Don Manuel, you are one of the people, you are not one of these aristocrats; what will the country say if you allow us to be driven out of business by blacklegs? I ask you is it just, is it honest?"

"But what can I do?" said the president. "I cannot lock them up in their rooms for thirty days. How am I to blame if these foreigners have no sense of decency?"

"It's different for a poor girl," said La Gorda. "She has her way to make. But that these women do that sort of thing when they're not obliged to, no, that I shall never understand."

"It is a bad and wicked law," said Carmencita.

The president sprang to his feet and threw his arms akimbo.

"You are not going to ask me to abrogate a law that has brought peace and plenty to this country. I am of the people and I was elected by the people, and the prosperity of my fatherland is very near my heart. Divorce is our staple industry and the law shall be repealed only over my dead body."

"Oh, *Maria Santissima*, that it should come to this," said Carmencita. "And me with two daughters in a convent in New Orleans. Ah, in this business one often has unpleasantness, but I always consoled myself by thinking that my daughters would marry well, and when the time came for me to retire they would inherit my business. Do you think I can keep them in a convent in New Orleans for nothing?"

"And who is going to keep my son at Harvard if I have to close my house, Don Manuel?" asked La Gorda.

"As for myself," said Madame Coralie, "I do not care. I shall return to France. My dear mother is eighty-seven years of age and she cannot live very much longer. It will be a comfort to her if I spend her last remaining years by her side. But it is the injustice of it that hurts. You have spent many happy evenings in my house, Don Manuel, and I am wounded that you should let us be treated like this. Did you not tell me yourself that it was the proudest day of your life when you entered as an honoured guest the house in which you had once been employed as errand boy?"

"I do not deny it. I stood champagne all round." Don Manuel walked up and down the large hall, shrugging his shoulders as he went, and now and then, deep in thought, he gesticulated. "I am of the people, elected by the people," he cried, "and the fact is, these women are blacklegs." He turned to his secretaries with a dramatic gesture. "It is a stain on my administration. It is against all my principles to allow unskilled foreign labour to take the bread out of the mouths of honest and industrious people. These ladies are quite right to come to me and appeal for my protection. I will not allow the scandal to continue."

It was of course a pointed and effective speech, but all who heard it knew that it left things exactly where they were. Madame Coralie powdered her nose and gave it, a commanding organ, a brief look in her pocket mirror.

"Of course I know what human nature is," she said, "and I can well understand that time hangs heavily on the hands of these creatures."

"We could build a golf-course," hazarded one of the secretaries. "It is true that this would only occupy them by day."

"If they want men why can't they bring them with them?" said La Gorda.

"*Caramba!*" cried the president, and with that stood on a sudden quite still. "There is the solution."

He had not reached his exalted station without being a man of insight and resource. He beamed.

"We will amend the law. Men shall come in as before without let or hindrance, but women only accompanied by their husbands or with their written consent." He saw the look of consternation which his secretaries gave him, and he waved his hand. "But the immigration authorities shall receive instructions to interpret the word husband with the widest latitude."

"*Maria Santissima!*" cried Madame Coralie. "If they come with a friend he will take care that no one else interferes with them and our customers will return to the houses where for so long they have been so hospitably entertained. Don Manuel, you are a great man and one of these days they will erect a statue to you."

It is often the simplest expedients that settle the most formidable difficulties. The law was briefly amended according to the terms of Don Manuel's suggestion and, whereas prosperity continued to pour its blessings on the wide and sunny capital of this free and independent state, Madame Coralie was enabled profitably to pursue her useful avocations, Carmencita's two daughters completed their expensive education in the convent at New Orleans, and La Gorda's son successfully graduated at Harvard.

❖

The Bum

GOD knows how often I had lamented that I had not half the time I needed to do half the things I wanted. I could not remember when last I had had a moment to myself. I had often amused my fancy with the prospect of just one week's complete idleness. Most of us when not busy working are busy playing; we ride, play tennis or golf, swim or gamble; but I saw myself doing nothing at all. I would lounge through the morning, dawdle through the afternoon and loaf through the evening. My mind would be a slate and each passing hour a sponge that wiped out the scribblings written on it by the world of sense. Time, because it is so fleeting, time, because it is beyond recall, is the most precious of human goods and to squander it is the most delicate form of dissipation in which man can indulge. Cleopatra dissolved in wine a priceless pearl, but she gave it to Antony to drink; when you waste the brief golden hours you take the beaker in which the gem is melted and dash its contents to the ground. The gesture is grand and like all grand gestures absurd. That of course is its excuse. In the week I promised myself I should naturally read, for to the habitual reader reading is a drug of which he is the slave; deprive him of printed matter and he grows nervous, moody and restless; then, like the alcoholic bereft of brandy who will drink shellac or methylated spirit, he will make do with the advertisements of a paper five years old; he will make do with a telephone directory. But the professional writer is seldom a disinterested reader. I wished my reading to be but another form of idleness. I made up my mind that if ever the happy day arrived when I could enjoy untroubled leisure I would complete an enterprise that had always tempted me, but which hitherto, like an explorer making reconnaissances into an undiscovered country, I had done little more than enter upon: I would read the entire works of Nick Carter.

But I had always fancied myself choosing my moment with surroundings to my liking, not having it forced upon me; and when I was suddenly faced with nothing to do and had to make the best of it (like a steamship acquaintance whom in the wide waste of the Pacific Ocean you have invited to stay with you in London and who turns up without warning and with all his luggage) I was not a little taken aback. I had come to Vera Cruz from Mexico City to catch one of the Ward Company's white cool ships to Yucatan; and found to my dismay that, a dock strike having been declared over-night, my ship would not put in. I was stuck in Vera Cruz. I took a room in the Hotel Diligencias overlooking the plaza, and spent the morning looking at the sights of the town. I wandered down side streets and peeped into quaint courts. I sauntered through the parish church; it is picturesque with its gargoyles and flying buttresses, and the salt wind and the blazing sun have patined its harsh and massive walls with the mellowness of age; its cupola is covered with white and blue tiles. Then I found that I had seen all that was to be seen and I sat down in the coolness of the arcade that surrounded the square and ordered a drink. The sun beat down on the plaza with a merciless splendour. The coco-palms drooped dusty and bedraggled. Great black buzzards perched on them for a moment uneasily, swooped to the ground to gather some bit of offal, and then with lumbering wings flew up to the church tower. I watched the people crossing the square; negroes, Indians, Creoles and Spanish, the motley people of the Spanish Main; and they varied in colour from ebony to ivory. As the morning wore on, the tables around me filled up, chiefly with men, who had come to have a drink before luncheon, for the most part in white ducks, but some notwithstanding the heat in the dark clothes of professional respectability. A small band, a guitarist, a blind fiddler and a harpist, played rag-time and after every other tune the guitarist came round with a plate. I had already bought the local paper and I was adamant to the newsvendors who pertinaciously sought to sell me more copies of the same sheet. I refused, oh, twenty times at least, the solicitations of grimy urchins who wanted to shine my spotless shoes; and having come to the end of my small change I could only shake my head at the beggars who importuned me. They gave one no peace. Little Indian women, in shapeless rags, each one with a baby tied in the shawl on her back, held out skinny hands and in a whimper recited a dismal screed; blind men were led up to my table by small boys; the maimed, the halt, the deformed exhibited the sores and the monstrosities with which nature or accident had afflicted them; and half naked, underfed children whined endlessly their demand for coppers. But these kept their eyes open for the fat policeman who would suddenly dart out on them with a thong and give them a sharp cut on the back or over the head. Then they would scamper, only to return again when, exhausted by the exercise of so much energy, he relapsed into lethargy.

But suddenly my attention was attracted by a beggar who, unlike the rest of them and indeed the people sitting round me, swarthy and black-haired, had hair and beard of a red so vivid that it was startling. His beard was ragged and his long mop of hair looked as though it had not been brushed for months. He wore only a pair of trousers and a cotton singlet, but they were tatters, grimy and foul, that barely held together. I have never seen anyone so thin; his legs, his naked arms were but skin and bone and through the rents of his singlet you saw every rib of his wasted body; you could count the bones of his dust-covered feet. Of that starveling band he was easily the most abject. He was not old, he could not well have been more than forty, and I could not but ask myself what had brought him to this pass. It was absurd to think that he would not have worked if work he had been able to get. He was the only one of the beggars who did not speak. The rest of them poured forth their litany of woe and if it did not bring the alms they asked continued until an impatient word from you chased them away. He said nothing. I suppose he felt that his look of destitution was all the appeal he needed. He did not even hold out his hand, he merely looked at you, but with such wretchedness in his eyes, such despair in his attitude, it was dreadful; he stood on and on, silent and immobile, gazing steadfastly, and then, if you took no notice of him, he moved slowly to the next table. If he was given nothing he showed neither disappointment nor anger. If someone offered him a coin he stepped forward a little, stretched out his claw-like hand, took it without a word of thanks and impassively went his way. I had nothing to give him and when he came to me, so that he should not wait in vain, I shook my head.

"*Dispense Usted por Dios,*" I said, using the polite Castillian formula with which the Spaniards refuse a beggar.

But he paid no attention to what I said. He stood in front of me, for as long as he stood at the other tables, looking at me with tragic eyes. I have never seen such a wreck of humanity. There was something terrifying in his appearance. He did not look quite sane. At length he passed on.

It was one o'clock and I had lunch. When I awoke from my
siesta it was still very hot, but towards evening a breath of air
coming in through the windows which I had at last ventured to
open tempted me into the plaza. I sat down under my arcade and
ordered a long drink. Presently people in greater numbers filtered
into the open space from the surrounding streets, the tables in
the restaurants round it filled up, and in the kiosk in the middle
the band began to play. The crowd grew thicker. On the free
benches people sat huddled together like dark grapes clustered on a
stalk. There was a lively hum of conversation. The big black
buzzards flew screeching overhead, swooping down when they
saw something to pick up, or scurrying away from under the feet
of the passers-by. As twilight descended they swarmed, it seemed
from all parts of the town, towards the church tower; they circled
heavily about it and hoarsely crying, squabbling and jangling,
settled themselves uneasily to roost. And again bootblacks begged
me to have my shoes cleaned, newsboys pressed dank papers upon
me, beggars whined their plaintive demand for alms. I saw once
more that strange, red-bearded fellow and watched him stand
motionless, with the crushed and piteous air, before one table
after another. He did not stop before mine. I supposed he
remembered me from the morning and having failed to get anything
from me then thought it useless to try again. You do not often
see a red-haired Mexican, and because it was only in Russia that
I had seen men of so destitute a mien I asked myself if he was by
chance a Russian. It accorded well enough with the Russian feck-
lessness that he should have allowed himself to sink to such a
depth of degradation. Yet he had not a Russian face; his emaciated
features were clear-cut, and his blue eyes were not set in the head
in a Russian manner; I wondered if he could be a sailor, English,
Scandinavian or American, who had deserted his ship and by
degrees sunk to this pitiful condition. He disappeared. Since
there was nothing else to do, I stayed on till I got hungry, and when
I had eaten came back. I sat on till the thinning crowd suggested
it was bed-time. I confess that the day had seemed long and I
wondered how many similar days I should be forced to spend
there.

But I woke after a little while and could not get to sleep again.
My room was stifling. I opened the shutters and looked out at the
church. There was no moon, but the bright stars faintly lit its
outline. The buzzards were closely packed on the cross above the

cupola and on the edges of the tower, and now and then they moved a little. The effect was uncanny. And then, I have no notion why, that red scarecrow recurred to my mind and I had suddenly a strange feeling that I had seen him before. It was so vivid that it drove away from me the possibility of sleep. I felt sure that I had come across him, but when and where I could not tell. I tried to picture the surroundings in which he might take his place, but I could see no more than a dim figure against a background of fog. As the dawn approached it grew a little cooler and I was able to sleep.

I spent my second day at Vera Cruz as I had spent the first. But I watched for the coming of the red-haired beggar, and as he stood at the tables near mine I examined him with attention. I felt certain now that I had seen him somewhere. I even felt certain that I had known him and talked to him, but I still could recall none of the circumstances. Once more he passed my table without stopping and when his eyes met mine I looked in them for some gleam of recollection. Nothing. I wondered if I had made a mistake and thought I had seen him in the same way as sometimes, by some queer motion of the brain, in the act of doing something you are convinced that you are repeating an action that you have done at some past time. I could not get out of my head the impression that at some moment he had entered into my life. I racked my brains. I was sure now that he was either English or American. But I was shy of addressing him. I went over in my mind the possible occasions when I might have met him. Not to be able to place him exasperated me as it does when you try to remember a name that is on the tip of your tongue and yet eludes you. The day wore on.

Another day came, another morning, another evening. It was Sunday and the plaza was more crowded than ever. The tables under the arcade were packed. As usual the red-haired beggar came along, a terrifying figure in his silence, his threadbare rags and his pitiful distress. He was standing in front of a table only two from mine, mutely beseeching, but without a gesture. Then I saw the policeman who at intervals tried to protect the public from the importunities of all these beggars sneak round a column and give him a resounding whack with his thong. His thin body winced, but he made no protest and showed no resentment; he seemed to accept the stinging blow as in the ordinary course of things and with his slow movements slunk away into the gathering night of the plaza. But the cruel stripe had whipped my memory and suddenly I remembered.

Not his name, that escaped me still, but everything else. He must have recognised me, for I have not changed very much in twenty years, and that was why after that first morning he had never paused in front of my table. Yes, it was twenty years since I had known him. I was spending a winter in Rome and every evening I used to dine in a restaurant in the Via Sistina where you got excellent macaroni and a good bottle of wine. It was frequented by a little band of English and American art students, and one or two writers; and we used to stay late into the night engaged in interminable arguments upon art and literature. He used to come in with a young painter who was a friend of his. He was only a boy then, he could not have been more than twenty-two; and with his blue eyes, straight nose and red hair he was pleasing to look at. I remembered that he spoke a great deal of Central America, he had had a job with the American Fruit Company, but had thrown it over because he wanted to be a writer. He was not popular among us because he was arrogant and we were none of us old enough to take the arrogance of youth with tolerance. He thought us poor fish and did not hesitate to tell us so. He would not show us his work, because our praise meant nothing to him and he despised our censure. His vanity was enormous. It irritated us; but some of us were uneasily aware that it might perhaps be justified. Was it possible that the intense consciousness of genius that he had, rested on no grounds? He had sacrificed everything to be a writer. He was so certain of himself that he infected some of his friends with his own assurance.

I recalled his high spirits, his vitality, his confidence in the future and his disinterestedness. It was impossible that it was the same man, and yet I was sure of it. I stood up, paid for my drink and went out into the plaza to find him. My thoughts were in a turmoil. I was aghast. I had thought of him now and then and idly wondered what had become of him. I could never have imagined that he was reduced to this frightful misery. There are hundreds, thousands of youths who enter upon the hard calling of the arts with extravagant hopes; but for the most part they come to terms with their mediocrity and find somewhere in life a niche where they can escape starvation. This was awful. I asked myself what had happened. What hopes deferred had broken his spirit, what disappointments shattered him and what lost illusions ground him to the dust? I asked myself if nothing could be done. I walked round the plaza. He was not in the arcades. There was no hope of finding him in the crowd that circled round the band-stand. The light was waning and I was afraid I had lost him. Then I passed the church and saw him sitting on the steps. I cannot describe what a lamentable object he looked. Life had taken him, rent him on its racks, torn him limb from limb, and then flung him, a bleeding wreck, on the stone steps of that church. I went up to him.

"Do you remember Rome?" I said.

He did not move. He did not answer. He took no more notice of me than if I were not standing before him. He did not look at me. His vacant blue eyes rested on the buzzards that were scream-ing and tearing at some object at the bottom of the steps. I did not know what to do. I took a yellow-backed note out of my pocket and pressed it in his hand. He did not give it a glance. But his hand moved a little, the thin claw-like fingers closed on the note and scrunched it up; he made it into a little ball and then edging it on to his thumb flicked it into the air so that it fell among the jangling buzzards. I turned my head instinctively and saw one of them seize it in his beak and fly off followed by two others screaming behind it. When I looked back the man was gone.

I stayed three more days in Vera Cruz. I never saw him again.

The Dream

IT chanced that in August, 1917, the work upon which I was then engaged obliged me to go from New York to Petrograd and I was instructed for safety's sake to travel by way of Vladivostok. I landed there in the morning and passed an idle day as best I could. The trans-Siberian train was due to start, so far as I remember, at about nine in the evening. I dined at the station restaurant by myself. It was crowded and I shared a small table with a man whose appearance entertained me. He was a Russian, a tall fellow, but amazingly stout, and he had so vast a paunch that he was obliged to sit well away from the table. His hands, small for his size, were buried in rolls of fat. His hair, long, dark and thin, was brushed carefully across his crown in order to conceal his baldness, and his huge sallow face, with its enormous double chin, clean-shaven, gave you an impression of indecent nakedness. His nose was small, a funny little button upon that mass of flesh, and his black shining eyes were small too. But he had a large, red and sensual mouth. He was dressed neatly enough in a black suit. It was not worn but shabby; it looked as if it had been neither pressed nor brushed since he had had it.

The service was bad and it was almost impossible to attract the attention of a waiter. We soon got into conversation. The Russian spoke good and fluent English. His accent was marked but not tiresome. He asked me many questions about myself and my plans, which—my occupation at the time making caution necessary—I answered with a show of frankness but with dissimulation. I told him I was a journalist. He asked me whether I wrote fiction and when I confessed that in my leisure moments I did, he began to talk of the later Russian novelists. He spoke intelligently. It was plain that he was a man of education.

By this time we had persuaded the waiter to bring us some cabbage soup, and my acquaintance pulled a small bottle of vodka from his pocket which he invited me to share. I do not know whether it was the vodka or the natural loquaciousness of his race that made him communicative, but presently he told me, unasked, a good deal about himself. He was of noble birth, it appeared, a lawyer by profession, and a radical. Some trouble with the authorities had made it necessary for him to be much abroad, but now he was on his way home. Business had detained him at Vladivostok, but he expected to start for Moscow in a week and if I went there he would be charmed to see me.

"Are you married?" he asked me.

I did not see what business it was of his, but I told him that I was. He sighed a little.

"I am a widower," he said. "My wife was a Swiss, a native of Geneva. She was a very cultivated woman. She spoke English, German and Italian perfectly. French, of course, was her native tongue. Her Russian was much above the average for a foreigner. She had scarcely the trace of an accent."

He called a waiter who was passing with a tray full of dishes and asked him, I suppose—for then I knew hardly any Russian—how much longer we were going to wait for the next course. The waiter, with a rapid but presumably reassuring exclamation, hurried on, and my friend sighed.

"Since the revolution the waiting in restaurants has become abominable."

He lighted his twentieth cigarette and I, looking at my watch, wondered whether I should get a square meal before it was time for me to start.

"My wife was a very remarkable woman," he continued. "She taught languages at one of the best schools for the daughters of noblemen in Petrograd. For a good many years we lived together on perfectly friendly terms. She was, however, of a jealous temperament and unfortunately she loved me to distraction."

It was difficult for me to keep a straight face. He was one of the ugliest men I had ever seen. There is sometimes a certain charm in the rubicund and jovial fat man, but this saturnine obesity was repulsive.

"I do not pretend that I was faithful to her. She was not young when I married her and we had been married for ten years. She was small and thin, and she had a bad complexion. She had a bitter tongue. She was a woman who suffered from a fury of possession, and she could not bear me to be attracted to anyone but her. She was jealous not only of the women I knew, but of my friends, my cat and my books. On one occasion in my absence she gave away a coat of mine merely because I liked none of my coats so well. But I am of an equable temperament. I will not deny that she bored me, but I accepted her acrimonious disposition as an act of God and no more thought of rebelling against it than I would against bad weather or a cold in the head. I denied her accusations as long as it was possible to deny them, and when it was impossible I shrugged my shoulders and smoked a cigarette.

"The constant scenes she made me did not very much affect me. I led my own life. Sometimes, indeed, I wondered whether it was passionate love she felt for me or passionate hate. It seemed to me that love and hate were very near allied.

"So we might have continued to the end of the chapter if one night a very curious thing had not happened. I was awakened by a piercing scream from my wife. Startled, I asked her what was the matter. She told me that she had had a fearful nightmare; she had dreamt that I was trying to kill her. We lived at the top of a large house and the well round which the stairs climbed was broad. She had dreamt that just as we had arrived at our own floor I had caught hold of her and attempted to throw her over the balusters. It was six storeys to the stone floor at the bottom and it meant certain death.

"She was much shaken. I did my best to soothe her. But next morning, and for two or three days after, she referred to the subject again and, notwithstanding my laughter, I saw that it dwelt in her mind. I could not help thinking of it either, for this dream showed me something that I had never suspected. She thought I hated her, she thought I would gladly be rid of her; she knew of course that she was insufferable, and at some time or other the idea had evidently occurred to her that I was capable of murdering her. The thoughts of men are incalculable and ideas enter our minds that we should be ashamed to confess. Sometimes I had wished that she might run away with a lover, sometimes that a painless and sudden death might give me my freedom; but never, never had the idea come to me that I might deliberately rid myself of an intolerable burden.

"The dream made an extraordinary impression upon both of us. It frightened my wife, and she became for a little less bitter and more tolerant. But when I walked up the stairs to our apartment it was impossible for me not to look over the balusters and reflect how easy it would be to do what she had dreamt. The balusters were dangerously low. A quick gesture and the thing was done. It was hard put to the thought out of my mind. Then some months later my wife awakened me one night. I was very tired and I was exasperated. She was white and trembling. She had had the dream again. She burst into tears and asked me if I hated her. I swore by all the saints of the Russian calendar that I loved her. At last she went to sleep again. It was more than I could do. I lay awake. I seemed to see her falling down the well of the stairs, and I heard her shriek and the thud as she struck the stone floor. I could not help shivering."

The Russian stopped and beads of sweat stood on his forehead. He had told the story well and fluently so that I had listened with attention. There was still some vodka in the bottle; he poured it out and swallowed it at a gulp.

"And how did your wife eventually die?" I asked after a pause.

He took out a dirty handkerchief and wiped his forehead.

"By an extraordinary coincidence she was found late one night at the bottom of the stairs with her neck broken."

"Who found her?"

"She was found by one of the lodgers who came in shortly after the catastrophe."

"And where were you?"

I cannot describe the look he gave me of malicious cunning. His little black eyes sparkled.

"I was spending the evening with a friend of mine. I did not come in till an hour later."

At that moment the waiter brought us the dish of meat that we had ordered, and the Russian fell upon it with good appetite. He shovelled the food into his mouth in enormous mouthfuls.

I was taken aback. Had he really been telling me in this hardly veiled manner that he had murdered his wife? That obese and sluggish man did not look like a murderer; I could not believe that he would have had the courage. Or was he making a sardonic joke at my expense?

In a few minutes it was time for me to go and catch my train. I left him and I have not seen him since. But I have never been able to make up my mind whether he was serious or jesting.

The Treasure

RICHARD HARENGER was a happy man. Notwithstanding what the pessimists, from Ecclesiastes onwards, have said, this is not so rare a thing to find in this unhappy world, but Richard Harenger knew it, and that is a very rare thing indeed. The golden mean which the ancients so highly prized is out of fashion, and those who follow it must put up with polite derision from those who see no merit in self-restraint and no virtue in common-sense. Richard Harenger shrugged a polite and amused shoulder. Let others live dangerously, let others burn with a hard gemlike flame, let others stake their fortunes on the turn of a card, walk the tight-rope that leads to glory or the grave, or hazard their lives for a cause, a passion or an adventure. He neither envied the fame their exploits brought them nor wasted his pity on them when their efforts ended in disaster.

But it must not be inferred from this that Richard Harenger was a selfish or a callous man. He was neither. He was considerate and of a generous disposition. He was always ready to oblige a friend and he was sufficiently well off to be able to indulge himself in the pleasure of helping others. He had some money of his own and he occupied in the Home Office a position that brought him an adequate stipend. The work suited him. It was regular, responsible and pleasant. Every day when he left the office he went to his club to play bridge for a couple of hours, and on Saturdays and Sundays he played golf. He went abroad for his holidays, staying at good hotels, and visited churches, galleries and museums. He was a regular first-nighter. He dined out a good deal. His friends liked him. He was easy to talk to. He was well-read, knowledgeable and amusing. He was besides of a personable exterior, not remarkably handsome, but tall, slim and erect of carriage, with a lean, intelligent face; his hair was growing thin, for he was now approaching the age of fifty, but his brown eyes retained their smile and his teeth were all his own. He had from nature a good constitution and he had always taken care of himself. There was no reason in the world why he should not be a happy

man, and if there had been in him a trace of self-complacency he
might have claimed that he deserved to be.

He had the good fortune even to sail safely through those
perilous, unquiet straits of marriage in which so many wise and
good men have made shipwreck. Married for love in the early
twenties, his wife and he, after some years of almost perfect
felicity, had drifted gradually apart. Neither of them wished to
marry anyone else, so there was no question of divorce (which
indeed Richard Harenger's situation in the government service
made undesirable), but for convenience sake, with the help of the
family lawyer, they arranged a separation which left them free to
lead their lives as each one wished without interference from the
other. They parted with mutual expressions of respect and good
will.

Richard Harenger sold his house in St. John's Wood and took a
flat within convenient walking distance of Whitehall. It had a
sitting-room which he lined with his books, a dining-room into
which his Chippendale furniture just fitted, a nice-sized bedroom
for himself, and beyond the kitchen a couple of maids' rooms.
He brought his cook, whom he had had for many years, from
St. John's Wood, but needing no longer so large a staff dismissed
the rest of the servants and applied at a registry office for a house-
parlourmaid. He knew exactly what he wanted and he explained
his needs to the superintendent of the agency with precision. He
wanted a maid who was not too young, first because young women
are flighty and secondly because, though he was of mature age and
a man of principle, people would talk, the porter and the tradesmen
if nobody else, and both for the sake of his own reputation and
that of the young person he considered that the applicant should
have reached years of discretion. Besides that he wanted a maid
who could clean silver well. He had always had a fancy for old
silver, and it was reasonable to demand that the forks and spoons
that had been used by a woman of quality under the reign of Queen
Anne should be treated with tenderness and respect. He was of
a hospitable nature and liked to give at least once a week little
dinners of not less than four people and not more than eight.
He could trust his cook to send in a meal that his guests would
take pleasure in eating and he desired his parlourmaid to wait
with neatness and dispatch. Then he needed a perfect valet.
He dressed well, in a manner that suited his age and condition,
and he liked his clothes to be properly looked after. The parlour-

B*

maid he was looking for must be able to press trousers and iron a tie, and he was very particular that his shoes should be well shone. He had small feet and he took a good deal of trouble to have well-cut shoes. He had a large supply and he insisted that they should be treed up the moment he took them off. Finally the flat must be kept clean and tidy. It was of course understood that any applicant for the post must be of irreproachable character, sober, honest, reliable and of a pleasing exterior. In return for this he was prepared to offer good wages, reasonable liberty and ample holidays. The superintendent listened without batting an eyelash and, telling him that she was quite sure she could suit him, sent him a string of candidates which proved that she had not paid the smallest attention to a word he said. He saw them all personally. Some were obviously inefficient, some looked fast, some were too old, others too young, some lacked the presence he thought essential; there was not one to whom he was inclined even to give a trial. He was a kindly, polite man and he declined their services with a smile and a pleasant expression of regret. He did not lose patience. He was prepared to interview house-parlourmaids till he found one who was suitable.

Now it is a funny thing about life, if you refuse to accept anything but the best you very often get it: if you utterly decline to make do with what you can get, then somehow or other you are very likely to get what you want. It is as though fate said, this man's a perfect fool, he's asking for perfection, and then just out of her feminine wilfulness flung it in his lap. One day the porter of the flats said to Richard Harenger out of a blue sky:

"I hear you're lookin' for a house-parlourmaid, sir. There's someone I know lookin' for a situation as might do."

"Can you recommend her personally?"

Richard Harenger had the sound opinion that one servant's recommendation of another was worth much more than that of an employer.

"I can vouch for her respectability. She's been in some very good situations."

"I shall be coming in to dress about seven. If that's convenient to her I could see her then."

"Very good, sir. I'll see that she's told."

He had not been in more than five minutes when the cook, having answered a ring at the front door, came in and told him that the person the porter had spoken to him about had called.

"Show her in," he said.

He turned on some more light so that he could see what the applicant looked like and, getting up, stood with his back to the fireplace. A woman came in and stood just inside the door in a respectful attitude.

"Good-evening," he said. "What is your name?"

"Pritchard, sir."

"How old are you?"

"Thirty-five, sir."

"Well, that's a reasonable age."

He gave his cigarette a puff and looked at her reflectively. She was on the tall side, nearly as tall as he, but he guessed that she wore high heels. Her black dress fitted her station. She held herself well. She had good features and a rather high colour.

"Will you take off your hat?" he asked.

She did so and he saw that she had pale brown hair. It was neatly and becomingly dressed. She looked strong and healthy. She was neither fat nor thin. In a proper uniform she would look very presentable. She was not inconveniently handsome, but she was certainly a comely, in another class of life you might almost have said a handsome, woman. He proceeded to ask her a number of questions. Her answers were satisfactory. She had left her last place for an adequate reason. She had been trained under a butler and appeared to be well acquainted with her duties. In her last place she had been head parlourmaid of three, but she did not mind undertaking the work of the flat single-handed. She had valeted a gentleman before who had sent her to a tailor's to learn how to press clothes. She was a little shy, but neither timid nor ill-at-ease. Richard asked her his questions in his amiable, leisurely way and she answered them with modest composure. He was considerably impressed. He asked her what references she could give. They seemed extremely satisfactory.

"Now look here," he said, "I'm very much inclined to engage you. But I hate changes, I've had my cook for twelve years: if you suit me and the place suits you I hope you'll stay. I mean, I don't want you to come to me in three or four months and say that you're leaving to get married."

"There's not much fear of that, sir. I'm a widow. I don't believe marriage is much catch for anyone in my position, sir. My husband never did a stroke of work from the day I married him to the day he died, and I had to keep him. What I want now is a good home."

"I'm inclined to agree with you," he smiled. "Marriage is a very good thing, but I think it's a mistake to make a habit of it."

She very properly made no reply to this, but waited for him to announce his decision. She did not seem anxious about it. He reflected that if she was as competent as she appeared she must be well aware that she would have no difficulty in finding a place. He told her what wages he was offering and these seemed to be satisfactory to her. He gave her the necessary information about the place, but she gave him to understand that she was already apprised of this, and he received the impression, which amused rather than disconcerted him, that she had made certain enquiries about him before applying for the situation. It showed prudence on her part and good sense.

"When would you be able to come in if I engaged you? I haven't got anybody at the moment. The cook's managing as best she can with a char, but I should like to get settled as soon as possible."

"Well, sir, I was going to give myself a week's holiday, but if it's a matter of obliging a gentleman I don't mind giving that up. I could come in to-morrow if it was convenient."

Richard Harenger gave her his attractive smile.

"I shouldn't like you to do without a holiday that I dare say you've been looking forward to. I can very well go on like this for another week. Go and have your holiday and come to me when it's over."

"Thank you very much, sir. Would it do if I came in to-morrow week?"

" Quite well."

When she left, Richard Harenger felt he had done a good day's work. It looked as though he had found exactly what he was after. He rang for the cook and told her he had engaged a house-parlour-maid at last.

"I think you'll like her, sir," she said. "She came in and 'ad a talk with me this afternoon. I could see at once she knew her duties. And she's not one of them flighty ones."

"We can but try, Mrs. Jeddy. I hope you gave me a good character."

"Well, I said you was particular, sir. I said you was a gentleman as liked things just so."

"I admit that."

"She said she didn't mind that. She said she liked a gentleman as knew what was what. She said there's no satisfaction in doing things proper if nobody notices. I expect you'll find she'll take a rare lot of pride in her work."

"That's what I want her to do. I think we might go farther and fare worse."

"Well, sir, there is that to it, of course. And the proof of the pudding's the eating. But if you ask my opinion I think she's going to be a real treasure."

And that is precisely what Pritchard turned out. No man was ever better served. The way she shone shoes was marvellous, and he set out of a fine morning for his walk to the office with a more jaunty step because you could almost see yourself reflected in them. She looked after his clothes with such attention that his colleagues began to chaff him about being the best-dressed man in the Civil Service. One day, coming home unexpectedly, he found a line of socks and handkerchiefs hung up to dry in the bathroom. He called Pritchard.

"D'you wash my socks and handkerchiefs yourself, Pritchard? I should have thought you had enough to do without that."

"They do ruin them so at the laundry, sir. I prefer to do them at home if you have no objection."

She knew exactly what he should wear on every occasion, and without asking him was aware whether she should put out a dinner jacket and a black tie in the evening or a dress coat and a white one. When he was going to a party where decorations were to be worn he found his neat little row of medals automatically affixed to the lapel of his coat. He soon ceased to choose every morning from his wardrobe the tie he wanted, for he found that she put out for him without fail the one he would have himself selected. Her taste was perfect. He supposed she read his letters, for she always knew what his movements were, and if he had forgotten at what hour he had an engagement he had no need to look in his book, for Pritchard could tell him. She knew exactly what tone to use with persons with whom she conversed on the telephone. Except with tradesmen, with whom she was apt to be peremptory, she was always polite, but there was a distinct difference in her manner if she was addressing one of Mr. Harenger's literary friends or the wife of a Cabinet Minister. She knew by instinct with whom he wished to speak and with whom he didn't. From his sitting-room he sometimes heard her with placid sincerity assuring a caller that he was out, and then she would come in and tell him that So-and-So had rung up, but she thought he wouldn't wish to be disturbed.

"Quite right, Pritchard," he smiled.

"I knew she only wanted to bother you about that concert," said Pritchard.

His friends made appointments with him through her, and she would tell him what she had done on his return in the evening.

"Mrs. Soames rang up, sir, and asked if you would lunch with her on Thursday, the eighth, but I said you were very sorry but you were lunching with Lady Versinder. Mr. Oakley rang up and asked if you'd go to a cocktail party at the Savoy next Tuesday at six. I said you would if you possibly could, but you might have to go to the dentist's."

"Quite right."

"I thought you could see when the time came, sir."

She kept the flat like a new pin. On one occasion soon after she entered his service, Richard coming back from a holiday took out a book from his shelves and at once noticed that it had been dusted. He rang the bell.

"I forgot to tell you when I went away under no circumstances ever to touch my books. When books are taken out to be dusted they're never put back in the right place. I don't mind my books being dirty, but I hate not being able to find them."

"I'm very sorry, sir," said Pritchard. "I know some gentlemen are very particular and I took care to put back every book exactly where I took it from."

Richard Harenger gave his books a glance. So far as he could see every one was in its accustomed place. He smiled.

"I apologise, Pritchard."

"They were in a muck, sir. I mean, you couldn't open one without getting your hands black with dust."

She certainly kept his silver as he had never had it kept before. He felt called upon to give her a special word of praise.

"Most of it's Queen Anne and George I, you know," he explained.

"Yes, I know, sir. When you've got something good like that to look after it's a pleasure to keep it like it should be."

"You certainly have a knack for it. I never knew a butler who kept his silver as well as you do."

"Men haven't the patience women have," she replied modestly.

As soon as he thought Pritchard had settled down in the place he resumed the little dinners he was fond of giving once a week. He had already discovered that she knew how to wait at table, but it was with a warm sense of complacency that he realised then how competently she could manage a party. She was quick, silent and watchful. A guest had hardly felt the need of something before Pritchard was at his elbow offering him what he wanted. She soon learned the tastes of his more intimate friends and remembered that one liked water instead of soda with his whisky and that another particularly fancied the knuckle end of a leg of lamb. She knew exactly how cold a hock should be not to ruin its taste and how long claret should have stood in the room to bring out its bouquet. It was a pleasure to see her pour out a bottle of burgundy in such a fashion as not to disturb the grounds. On one occasion she did not serve the wine Richard had ordered. He somewhat sharply pointed this out to her.

"I opened the bottle sir, and it was slightly corked. So I got the Chambertin, as I thought it was safer."

"Quite right, Pritchard."

Presently he left this matter entirely in her hands, for he discovered that she knew perfectly what wines his guests would like. Without orders from him she would provide the best in his cellar and his oldest brandy if she thought they were the sort of people who knew what they were drinking. She had no belief in the palate of women, and when they were of the party was apt to serve the champagne which had to be drunk before it went off. She had the English servant's instinctive knowledge of social differences and neither rank nor money blinded her to the fact that someone was not a gentleman, but she had favourites among his friends, and when someone she particularly liked was dining, with the air of a cat that has swallowed a canary she would pour out for him a bottle of a wine that Harenger kept for very special occasions. It amused him.

"You've got on the right side of Pritchard, old boy," he exclaimed. "There aren't many people she gives this wine to."

Pritchard became an institution. She was known very soon to be the perfect parlourmaid. People envied Harenger the possession of her as they envied nothing else that he had. She was worth her weight in gold. Her price was above rubies. Richard Harenger beamed with self-complacency when they praised her.

"Good masters make good servants," he said gaily.

One evening, when they were sitting over their port and she had left the room, they were talking about her.

"It'll be an awful blow when she leaves you."

"Why should she leave me? One or two people have tried to get her away from me, but she turned them down. She knows where she's well off."

"She'll get married one of these days."

"I don't think she's that sort."

"She's a good-looking woman."

"Yes, she has quite a decent presence."

"What are you talking about? She's a very handsome creature. In another class of life she'd be a well-known society beauty with her photograph in all the papers."

At that moment Pritchard came in with the coffee. Richard Harenger looked at her. After seeing her every day, off and on, for four years it was now—my word, how time flies—he had really forgotten what she looked like. She did not seem to have changed much since he had first seen her. She was no stouter than then, she still had the high colour, and her regular features bore the same expression which was at once intent and vacuous. The black uniform suited her. She left the room.

"She's a paragon and there's no doubt about it."

"I know she is," answered Harenger. "She's perfection. I should be lost without her. And the strange thing is that I don't very much like her."

"Why not?"

"I think she bores me a little. You see, she has no conversation. I've often tried to talk to her. She answers when I speak to her, but that's all. In four years she's never volunteered a remark of her own. I know absolutely nothing about her. I don't know if she likes me or if she's completely indifferent to me. She's an automaton. I respect her, I appreciate her, I trust her. She has every quality in the world and I've often wondered why it is that with all that I'm so completely indifferent to her. I think it must be that she is entirely devoid of charm."

They left it at that.

Two or three days after this, since it was Pritchard's night out and he had no engagement, Richard Harenger dined by himself at his club. A page-boy came to him and told him that they had just rung up from his flat to say that he had gone out without his keys and should they be brought along to him in a taxi? He put his hand to his pocket. It was a fact. By a singular chance he had forgotten to replace them when he had changed into a blue serge suit before coming out to dinner. His intention had been to play bridge, but it was an off-night at the club and there seemed little chance of a decent game; it occurred to him that it would be a good opportunity to see a picture that he had heard talked about, so he sent back the message by the page that he would call for the keys himself in half an hour.

He rang at the door of his flat and it was opened by Pritchard. She had the keys in her hand.

"What are you doing here, Pritchard?" he asked. "It's your night out, isn't it?"

"Yes, sir. But I didn't care about going, so I told Mrs. Jeddy she could go instead."

"You ought to get out when you have the chance," he said, with his usual thoughtfulness. "It's not good for you to be cooped up here all the time."

"I get out now and then on an errand, but I haven't been out in the evening for the last month."

"Why on earth not?"

"Well, it's not very cheerful going out by yourself, and somehow I don't know anyone just now that I'm particularly keen on going out with."

"You ought to have a bit of fun now and then. It's good for you."

"I've got out of the habit of it somehow."

"Look here, I'm just going to the cinema. Would you like to come along with me?"

He spoke in kindliness, on the spur of the moment, and the moment he had said the words half regretted them.

"Yes, sir, I'd like to," said Pritchard.

"Run along then and put on a hat."

"I shan't be a minute."

She disappeared and he went into the sitting-room and lit a cigarette. He was a little amused at what he was doing, and pleased too; it was nice to be able to make someone happy with so little trouble to himself. It was characteristic of Pritchard that she had shown neither surprise nor hesitation. She kept him waiting about five minutes, and when she came back he noticed that she had changed her dress. She wore a blue frock in what he supposed was artificial silk, a small black hat with a blue brooch on it, and a silver fox round her neck. He was a trifle relieved to see that she looked neither shabby nor showy. It would never occur to anyone who happened to see them that this was a distinguished official in the Home Office taking his housemaid to the pictures.

"I'm sorry to have kept you waiting, sir."

"It doesn't matter at all," he said graciously.

He opened the front door for her and she went out before him. He remembered the familiar anecdote of Louis XIV and the courtier and appreciated the fact that she had not hesitated to precede him. The cinema for which they were bound was at no great distance from Mr. Harenger's flat and they walked there. He talked about the weather and the state of the roads and Adolf Hitler. Pritchard made suitable replies. They arrived just as Mickey the Mouse was starting and this put them in a good humour. During the four years she had been in his service Richard Harenger had hardly ever seen Pritchard even smile, and now it diverted him vastly to hear her peal upon peal of joyous laughter. He enjoyed her pleasure. Then the principal attraction was thrown on the screen. It was a good picture and they both watched it with breathless excitement. Taking his cigarette-case out to help himself he automatically offered it to Pritchard.

"Thank you, sir," she said, taking one.

He lit it for her. Her eyes were on the screen and she was almost unconscious of his action. When the picture was finished they streamed out with the crowd into the street. They walked back towards the flat. It was a fine starry night.

"Did you like it?" he said.

"Like anything, sir. It was a real treat."

A thought occurred to him.

"By the way, did you have any supper to-night?"

"No, sir, I didn't have time."

"Aren't you starving?"

"I'll have a bit of bread and cheese when I get in and I'll make meself a cup of cocoa."

"That sounds rather grim." There was a feeling of gaiety in the air, and the people who poured past them, one way and another, seemed filled with a pleasant elation. In for a penny, in for a pound, he said to himself. "Look here, would you like to come and have a bit of supper with me somewhere?"

"If you'd like to, sir."

"Come on."

He hailed a cab. He was feeling very philanthropic and it was not a feeling that he disliked at all. He told the driver to go to a restaurant in Oxford Street which was gay, but at which he was confident there was no chance of meeting anyone he knew. There was an orchestra and people danced. It would amuse Pritchard to see them. When they sat down a waiter came up to them.

"They've got a set supper here," he said, thinking that was what she would like. "I suggest we have that. What would you like to drink? A little white wine?"

"What I really fancy is a glass of ginger beer," she said.

Richard Harenger ordered himself a whisky and soda. She ate the supper with hearty appetite, and though Harenger was not hungry, to put her at her ease he ate too. The picture they had just seen gave them something to talk about. It was quite true what they had said the other night, Pritchard was not a bad-looking woman, and even if someone had seen them together he would not have minded. It would make rather a good story for his friends when he told them how he had taken the incomparable Pritchard to the cinema and then afterwards to supper. Pritchard was looking at the dancers with a faint smile on her lips.

"Do you like dancing?" he said.

"I used to be a rare one for it when I was a girl. I never danced much after I was married. My husband was a bit shorter than me and somehow I never think it looks well unless the gentleman's taller, if you know what I mean. I suppose I shall be getting too old for it soon."

Richard was certainly taller than his parlourmaid. They would look all right. He was fond of dancing and he danced well. But he hesitated. He did not want to embarrass Pritchard by asking her to dance with him. It was better not to go too far perhaps. And yet what did it matter? It was a drab life she led. She was so sensible, if she thought it a mistake he was pretty sure she would find a decent excuse.

"Would you like to take a turn, Pritchard?" he said, as the band struck up again.

"I'm terribly out of practice, sir."

"What does that matter?"

"If you don't mind, sir," she answered coolly, rising from her seat. She was not in the least shy. She was only afraid that she would not be able to follow his step. They moved on to the floor. He found she danced very well.

"Why, you dance perfectly, Pritchard," he said.

"It's coming back to me."

Although she was a big woman she was light on her feet and she had a natural sense of rhythm. She was very pleasant to dance with. He gave a glance at the mirrors that lined the walls and he could not help reflecting that they looked very well together. Their eyes met in the mirror; he wondered whether she was thinking that too. They had two more dances and then Richard Harenger suggested that they should go. He paid the bill and they walked out. He noticed that she threaded her way through the crowd without a trace of self-consciousness. They got into a taxi and in ten minutes were at home.

"I'll go up the back way, sir," said Pritchard.

"There's no need to do that. Come up in the lift with me."

He took her up, giving the night-porter an icy glance, so that he should not think it strange that he came back at that somewhat late hour with his parlourmaid, and with his latch-key let her into the flat.

"Well, good-night, sir," she said. "Thank you very much. It's been a real treat for me."

"Thank *you* Pritchard. I should have had a very dull evening by myself. I hope you've enjoyed your outing."

"That I have, sir, more than I can say."

It had been a success. Richard Harenger was satisfied with himself. It was a kindly thing for him to have done. It was a very agreeable sensation to give anyone so much real pleasure. His benevolence warmed him and for a moment he felt a great love in his heart for the whole human race.

"Good-night, Pritchard," he said, and because he felt happy and good he put his arm round her waist and kissed her on the lips.

Her lips were very soft. They lingered on his and she returned his kiss. It was the warm, hearty embrace of a healthy woman in the prime of life. He found it very pleasant and he held her to him a little more closely. She put her arms round his neck.

As a general rule he did not wake till Pritchard came in with his letters, but next morning he woke at half-past seven. He had a curious sensation that he did not recognise. He was accustomed to sleep with two pillows under his head and he suddenly grew aware of the fact that he had only one. Then he remembered and with a start looked round. The other pillow was beside his own. Thank God, no sleeping head rested there, but it was plain that one had. His heart sank. He broke out into a cold sweat.

"My God, what a fool I've been!" he cried out loud.

How could he have done anything so stupid? What on earth had come over him? He was the last man to play about with servant girls. What a disgraceful thing to do! At his age and in his position. He had not heard Pritchard slip away. He must have been asleep. It wasn't even as if he'd liked her very much. She wasn't his type. And, as he had said the other night, she rather bored him. Even now he only knew her as Pritchard. He had no notion what her first name was. What madness! And what was to happen now? The position was impossible. It was obvious he couldn't keep her, and yet to send her away for what was his fault as much as hers seemed shockingly unfair. How idiotic to lose the best parlourmaid a man ever had just for an hour's folly!

"It's that damned kindness of heart of mine," he groaned.

He would never find anyone else to look after his clothes so admirably or clean the silver so well. She knew all his friends' telephone numbers and she understood wine. But of course she must go. She must see for herself that after what had happened things could never be the same. He would make her a handsome present and give her an excellent reference. At any minute she would be coming in now. Would she be arch, would she be familiar? Or would she put on airs? Perhaps even she wouldn't trouble to come in with his letters. It would be awful if he had to ring the bell and Mrs. Jeddy came in and said: Pritchard's not up yet, sir, she's having a lie in after last night.

"What a fool I've been! What a contemptible cad!"

There was a knock at the door. He was sick with anxiety.

"Come in."

Richard Harenger was a very unhappy man.

Pritchard came in as the clock struck. She wore the print dress she was in the habit of wearing during the early part of the day.

"Good-morning, sir," she said.

"Good-morning."

She drew the curtains and handed him his letters and the papers. Her face was impassive. She looked exactly as she always looked. Her movements had the same competent deliberation that they always had. She neither avoided Richard's glance nor sought it.

"Will you wear your grey, sir? It came back from the tailor's yesterday."

"Yes."

He pretended to read his letters, but he watched her from under his eyelashes. Her back was turned to him. She took his vest and drawers and folded them over a chair. She took the studs out of the shirt he had worn the day before and studded a clean one. She put out some clean socks for him and placed them on the seat of a chair with the suspenders to match by the side. Then she put out his grey suit and attached the braces to the back buttons of the trousers. She opened his wardrobe and after a moment's reflection chose a tie to go with the suit. She collected on her arm the suit of the day before and picked up the shoes.

"Will you have breakfast now, sir, or will you have your bath first?"

"I'll have breakfast now," he said.

"Very good, sir."

With her slow quiet movements, unruffled, she left the room. Her face bore that rather serious, deferential, vacuous look it always bore. What had happened might have been a dream. Nothing in Pritchard's demeanour suggested that she had the smallest recollection of the night before. He gave a sigh of relief. It was going to be all right. She need not go, she need not go. Pritchard was the perfect parlourmaid. He knew that never by word nor gesture would she ever refer to the fact that for a moment their relations had been other than those of master and servant. Richard Harenger was a very happy man.

❖

The Colonel's Lady

ALL this happened two or three years before the outbreak of the war.

The Peregrines were having breakfast. Though they were alone and the table was long they sat at opposite ends of it. From the walls George Peregrine's ancestors, painted by the fashionable painters of the day, looked down upon them. The butler brought in the morning post. There were several letters for the colonel, business letters, *The Times* and a small parcel for his wife Evie. He looked at his letters and then, opening *The Times*, began to read it. They finished breakfast and rose from the table. He noticed that his wife hadn't opened the parcel.

"What's that?" he asked.

"Only some books."

"Shall I open it for you?"

"If you like."

He hated to cut string and so with some difficulty untied the knots.

"But they're all the same," he said when he had unwrapped the parcel. "What on earth d'you want six copies of the same book for?" He opened one of them. "Poetry." Then he looked at the title page. *When Pyramids Decay*, he read, by E. K. Hamilton. Eva Katherine Hamilton: that was his wife's maiden name. He looked at her with smiling surprise. "Have you written a book, Evie? You are a slyboots."

"I didn't think it would interest you very much. Would you like a copy?"

"Well, you know poetry isn't much in my line, but—yes, I'd like a copy; I'll read it. I'll take it along to my study. I've got a lot to do this morning."

He gathered up *The Times*, his letters and the book, and went out. His study was a large and comfortable room, with a big desk, leather arm-chairs and what he called "trophies of the chase" on the walls. On the bookshelves were works of reference, books on farming, gardening, fishing and shooting, and books on the last war, in which he had won an M.C. and a D.S.O. For before his marriage he had been in the Welsh Guards. At the end of the war he retired and settled down to the life of a country gentleman in the spacious house, some twenty miles from Sheffield, which one of his forebears had built in the reign of George III. George Peregrine had an estate of some fifteen hundred acres which he managed with ability; he was a Justice of the Peace and performed his duties conscientiously. During the season he rode to hounds two days a week. He was a good shot, a golfer and though now a little over fifty could still play a hard game of tennis. He could describe himself with propriety as an all-round sportsman.

He had been putting on weight lately, but was still a fine figure of a man; tall, with grey curly hair, only just beginning to grow thin on the crown, frank blue eyes, good features and a high colour. He was a public-spirited man, chairman of any number of local organisations and, as became his class and station, a loyal member of the Conservative Party. He looked upon it as his duty to see to the welfare of the people on his estate and it was a satisfaction to him to know that Evie could be trusted to tend the sick and succour the poor. He had built a cottage hospital on the outskirts of the village and paid the wages of a nurse out of his own pocket. All he asked of the recipients of his bounty was that at elections, county or general, they should vote for his candidate. He was a friendly man, affable to his inferiors, considerate with his tenants and popular with the neighbouring gentry. He would have been pleased and at the same time slightly embarrassed if someone had told him he was a jolly good fellow. That was what he wanted to be. He desired no higher praise.

It was hard luck that he had no children. He would have been an excellent father, kindly but strict, and would have brought up his sons as gentlemen's sons should be brought up, sent them to Eton, you know, taught them to fish, shoot and ride. As it was, his heir was a nephew, son of his brother killed in a motor accident, not a bad boy, but not a chip off the old block, no, sir, far from it; and would you believe it, his fool of a mother was sending him to a co-educational school. Evie had been a sad disappointment to him. Of course she was a lady, and she had a bit of money of her own; she managed the house uncommonly well and she was a good hostess. The village people adored her. She had been a pretty little thing when he married her, with a creamy skin, light brown hair and a trim figure, healthy too and not a bad tennis player; he couldn't understand why she'd had no children; of course she was faded now, she must be getting on for five and forty; her skin was drab, her hair had lost its sheen and she was as thin as a rail. She was always neat and suitably dressed, but she didn't seem to bother how she looked, she wore no make-up and didn't even use lipstick; sometimes at night when she dolled herself up for a party you could tell that once she'd been quite attractive, but ordinarily she was—well, the sort of woman you simply didn't notice. A nice woman, of course, a good wife, and it wasn't her fault if she was barren, but it was tough on a fellow who wanted an heir of his own loins; she hadn't any vitality, that's what was the matter with her. He supposed he'd been in love with her when he asked her to marry him, at least sufficiently in love for a man who wanted to marry and settle down, but with time he discovered that they had nothing much in common. She didn't care about hunting, and fishing bored her. Naturally they'd drifted apart. He had to do her the justice to admit that she'd never bothered him. There'd been no scenes. They had no quarrels. She seemed to take it for granted that he should go his own way. When he went up to London now and then she never wanted to come with him. He had a girl there, well, she wasn't exactly a girl, she was thirty-five if she was a day, but she was blonde and luscious and he only had to wire ahead of time and they'd dine, do a show and spend the night together. Well, a man, a healthy normal man had to have some fun in his life. The thought crossed his mind that if Evie hadn't been such a good woman she'd have been a better wife; but it was not the sort of thought that he welcomed and he put it away from him.

George Peregrine finished his *Times* and being a considerate fellow rang the bell and told the butler to take it to Evie. Then he looked at his watch. It was half-past ten and at eleven he had an appointment with one of his tenants. He had half an hour to spare.

"I'd better have a look at Evie's book," he said to himself.

He took it up with a smile. Evie had a lot of highbrow books in her sitting-room, not the sort of books that interested him, but if they amused her he had no objection to her reading them. He noticed that the volume he now held in his hand contained no more than ninety pages. That was all to the good. He shared Edgar Allan Poe's opinion that poems should be short. But as he turned the pages he noticed that several of Evie's had long lines of irregular length and didn't rhyme. He didn't like that. At his first school, when he was a little boy, he remembered learning a poem that began: *The boy stood on the burning deck*, and later, at Eton, one that started: *Ruin seize thee, ruthless king*; and then there was Henry V; they'd had to take that, one half. He stared at Evie's pages with consternation.

"That's not what I call poetry," he said.

Fortunately it wasn't all like that. Interspersed with the pieces that looked so odd, lines of three or four words and then a line of ten or fifteen, there were little poems, quite short, that rhymed, thank God, with the lines all the same length. Several of the pages were just headed with the word *Sonnet*, and out of curiosity he counted the lines; there were fourteen of them. He read them. They seemed all right, but he didn't quite know what they were all about. He repeated to himself: *Ruin seize thee, ruthless king.*

"Poor Evie," he sighed.

At that moment the farmer he was expecting was ushered into the study, and putting the book down he made him welcome. They embarked on their business.

"I read your book, Evie," he said as they sat down to lunch. "Jolly good. Did it cost you a packet to have it printed?"

"No, I was lucky. I sent it to a publisher and he took it."

"Not much money in poetry, my dear," he said in his good-natured, hearty way.

"No, I don't suppose there is. What did Bannock want to see you about this morning?"

Bannock was the tenant who had interrupted his reading of Evie's poems.

"He's asked me to advance the money for a pedigree bull he wants to buy. He's a good man and I've half a mind to do it."

George Peregrine saw that Evie didn't want to talk about her book and he was not sorry to change the subject. He was glad she had used her maiden name on the title page; he didn't suppose anyone would ever hear about the book, but he was proud of his own unusual name and he wouldn't have liked it if some damned penny-a-liner had made fun of Evie's effort in one of the papers.

During the few weeks that followed he thought it tactful not to ask Evie any questions about her venture into verse, and she never referred to it. It might have been a discreditable incident that they had silently agreed not to mention. But then a strange thing happened. He had to go to London on business and he took

Daphne out to dinner. That was the name of the girl with whom he was in the habit of passing a few agreeable hours whenever he went to town.

"Oh, George," she said, "is that your wife who's written a book they're all talking about?"

"What on earth d'you mean?"

"Well, there's a fellow I know who's a critic. He took me out to dinner the other night and he had a book with him. 'Got anything for me to read?' I said. 'What's that?' 'Oh, I don't think that's your cup of tea,' he said. 'It's poetry. I've just been reviewing it.' 'No poetry for me,' I said. 'It's about the hottest stuff I ever read,' he said. 'Selling like hot cakes. And it's damned good.' "

"Who's the book by?" asked George.

"A woman called Hamilton. My friend told me that wasn't her real name. He said her real name was Peregrine. 'Funny,' I said, 'I know a fellow called Peregrine.' 'Colonel in the army,' he said. 'Lives near Sheffield.' "

"I'd just as soon you didn't talk about me to your friends," said George with a frown of vexation.

"Keep your shirt on, dearie. Who d'you take me for? I just said: 'It's not the same one.' " Daphne giggled. "My friend said: 'They say he's a regular Colonel Blimp.' "

George had a keen sense of humour.

"You could tell them better than that," he laughed. "If my wife had written a book I'd be the first to know about it, wouldn't I?"

"I suppose you would."

Anyhow the matter didn't interest her and when the colonel began to talk of other things she forgot about it. He put it out of his mind too. There was nothing to it, he decided, and that silly fool of a critic had just been pulling Daphne's leg. He was amused at the thought of her tackling that book because she had been told it was hot stuff and then finding it just a lot of bosh cut up into unequal lines.

He was a member of several clubs and next day he thought he'd lunch at one in St. James's Street. He was catching a train back to Sheffield early in the afternoon. He was sitting in a comfortable arm-chair having a glass of sherry before going into the dining-room when an old friend came up to him.

"Well, old boy, how's life?" he said. "How d'you like being the husband of a celebrity?"

George Peregrine looked at his friend. He thought he saw an amused twinkle in his eyes.

"I don't know what you're talking about," he answered.

"Come off it, George. Everyone knows E. K. Hamilton is your wife. Not often a book of verse has a success like that. Look here, Henry Dashwood is lunching with me. He'd like to meet you."

"Who the devil is Henry Dashwood and why should he want to meet me?"

"Oh, my dear fellow, what do you do with yourself all the time in the country? Henry's about the best critic we've got. He wrote a wonderful review of Evie's book. D'you mean to say she didn't show it you?"

Before George could answer his friend had called a man over. A tall, thin man, with a high forehead, a beard, a long nose and a stoop, just the sort of man whom George was prepared to dislike at first sight. Introductions were effected. Henry Dashwood sat down.

"Is Mrs. Peregrine in London by any chance? I should very much like to meet her," he said.

"No, my wife doesn't like London. She prefers the country," said George stiffly.

"She wrote me a very nice letter about my review. I was pleased. You know, we critics get more kicks than halfpence. I was simply bowled over by her book. It's so fresh and original, very modern without being obscure. She seems to be as much at her ease in free verse as in the classical metres." Then because he was a critic he thought he should criticise. "Sometimes her ear is a trifle at fault, but you can say the same of Emily Dickinson. There are several of those short lyrics of hers that might have been written by Landor."

All this was gibberish to George Peregrine. The man was nothing but a disgusting highbrow. But the colonel had good manners and he answered with proper civility: Henry Dashwood went on as though he hadn't spoken.

"But what makes the book so outstanding is the passion that throbs in every line. So many of these young poets are so anæmic, cold, bloodless, dully intellectual, but here you have real naked, earthy passion; of course deep, sincere emotion like that is tragic——ah, my dear Colonel, how right Heine was when he said that the poet makes little songs out of his great sorrows. You know, now and then, as I read and re-read those heart-rending pages I thought of Sappho."

This was too much for George Peregrine and he got up.

"Well, it's jolly nice of you to say such nice things about my wife's little book. I'm sure she'll be delighted. But I must bolt, I've got to catch a train and I want to get a bite of lunch."

"Damned fool," he said irritably to himself as he walked upstairs to the dining-room.

He got home in time for dinner and after Evie had gone to bed he went into his study and looked for her book. He thought he'd just glance through it again to see for himself what they were making such a fuss about, but he couldn't find it. Evie must have taken it away.

"Silly," he muttered.

He'd told her he thought it jolly good. What more could a fellow be expected to say? Well, it didn't matter. He lit his pipe and read the *Field* till he felt sleepy. But a week or so later it happened that he had to go into Sheffield for the day. He lunched there at his club. He had nearly finished when the Duke of Haverel came in. This was the great local magnate and of course the colonel knew him, but only to say how d'you do to; and he was surprised when the Duke stopped at his table.

"We're so sorry your wife couldn't come to us for the week-end," he said, with a sort of shy cordiality. "We're expecting rather a nice lot of people."

George was taken aback. He guessed that the Haverels had asked him and Evie over for the week-end and Evie, without saying a word to him about it, had refused. He had the presence of mind to say he was sorry too.

"Better luck next time," said the Duke pleasantly and moved on.

Colonel Peregrine was very angry and when he got home he said to his wife:

"Look here, what's this about our being asked over to Haverel? Why on earth did you say we couldn't go? We've never been asked before and it's the best shooting in the county."

"I didn't think of that. I thought it would only bore you."

"Damn it all, you might at least have asked me if I wanted to go."

"I'm sorry."

He looked at her closely. There was something in her expression that he didn't quite understand. He frowned.

"I suppose *I* was asked?" he barked.

Evie flushed a little.

"Well, in point of fact you weren't."

"I call it damned rude of them to ask you without asking me."

"I suppose they thought it wasn't your sort of party. The Duchess is rather fond of writers and people like that, you know. She's having Henry Dashwood, the critic, and for some reason he wants to meet me."

"It was damned nice of you to refuse, Evie."

"It's the least I could do," she smiled. She hesitated a moment. "George, my publishers want to give a little dinner party for me one day towards the end of the month and of course they want you to come too."

"Oh, I don't think that's quite my mark. I'll come up to London with you if you like. I'll find someone to dine with."

Daphne.

"I expect it'll be very dull, but they're making rather a point of it. And the day after, the American publisher who's taken my book is giving a cocktail party at Claridge's. I'd like to you come to that if you wouldn't mind."

"Sounds like a crashing bore, but if you really want me to come I'll come."

"It would be sweet of you."

George Peregrine was dazed by the cocktail party. There were a lot of people. Some of them didn't look so bad, a few of the women were decently turned out, but the men seemed to him pretty awful. He was introduced to everyone as Colonel Peregrine, E. K. Hamilton's husband, you know. The men didn't seem to have anything to say to him, but the women gushed.

"You *must* be proud of your wife. Isn't it *wonderful?* You know, I read it right through at a sitting, I simply couldn't put it down, and when I'd finished I started again at the beginning and read it right through a second time. I was simply *thrilled.*"

The English publisher said to him:

"We've not had a success like this with a book of verse for twenty years. I've never seen such reviews."

The American publisher said to him:

"It's swell. It'll be a smash hit in America. You wait and see."

The American publisher had sent Evie a great spray of orchids. Damned ridiculous, thought George. As they came in, people were taken up to Evie, and it was evident that they said flattering things to her, which she took with a pleasant smile and a word or two of thanks. She was a trifle flushed with the excitement, but seemed quite at her ease. Though he thought the whole thing a lot of stuff and nonsense George noted with approval that his wife was carrying it off in just the right way.

"Well, there's one thing," he said to himself, "you can see she's a lady and that's a damned sight more than you can say of anyone else here."

He drank a good many cocktails. But there was one thing that bothered him. He had a notion that some of the people he was introduced to looked at him in rather a funny sort of way, he couldn't quite make out what it meant, and once when he strolled by two women who were sitting together on a sofa he had the impression that they were talking about him and after he passed he was almost certain they tittered. He was very glad when the party came to an end.

In the taxi on their way back to their hotel Evie said to him:

"You were wonderful, dear. You made quite a hit. The girls simply raved about you: they thought you so handsome."

"Girls," he said bitterly. "Old hags."

"Were you bored, dear?"

"Stiff."

She pressed his hand in a gesture of sympathy.

"I hope you won't mind if we wait and go down by the afternoon train. I've got some things to do in the morning."

"No, that's all right. Shopping?"

"I do want to buy one or two things, but I've got to go and be photographed. I hate the idea, but they think I ought to be. For America, you know."

He said nothing. But he thought. He thought it would be a shock to the American public when they saw the portrait of the homely, desiccated little woman who was his wife. He'd always been under the impression that they liked glamour in America.

He went on thinking, and next morning when Evie had gone out he went to his club and up to the library. There he looked up recent numbers of *The Times Literary Supplement*, *The New Statesman* and *The Spectator*. Presently he found reviews of Evie's book. He didn't read them very carefully, but enough to see that they were extremely favourable. Then he went to the bookseller's in Piccadilly where he occasionally bought books. He'd made up his mind that he had to read this damned thing of Evie's properly, but he didn't want to ask her what she'd done with the copy she'd given him. He'd buy one for himself. Before going in he looked in the window and the first thing he saw was a display of *When Pyramids Decay*. Damned silly title! He went in. A young man came forward and asked if he could help him.

"No, I'm just having a look round." It embarrassed him to ask for Evie's book and he thought he'd find it for himself and then take it to the salesman. But he couldn't see it anywhere and at last, finding the young man near him, he said in a carefully casual tone: "By the way, have you got a book called *When Pyramids Decay?*"

"The new edition came in this morning. I'll get a copy."

In a moment the young man returned with it. He was a short, rather stout young man, with a shock of untidy carroty hair and spectacles. George Peregrine, tall, upstanding, very military, towered over him.

"Is this a new edition then?" he asked.

"Yes, sir. The fifth. It might be a novel the way it's selling."

George Peregrine hesitated a moment.

"Why d'you suppose it's such a success? I've always been told no one reads poetry."

"Well, it's good, you know. I've read it meself." The young man, though obviously cultured, had a slight Cockney accent, and George quite instinctively adopted a patronising attitude. "It's the story they like. Sexy, you know, but tragic."

George frowned a little. He was coming to the conclusion that the young man was rather impertinent. No one had told him anything about there being a story in the damned book and he had not gathered that from reading the reviews. The young man went on:

"Of course it's only a flash in the pan, if you know what I mean. The way I look at it, she was sort of inspired like by a personal experience, like Housman was with *The Shropshire Lad*. She'll never write anything else."

"How much is the book?" said George coldly to stop his chatter. "You needn't wrap it up, I'll just slip it into my pocket."

The November morning was raw and he was wearing a greatcoat.

At the station he bought the evening papers and magazines and he and Evie settled themselves comfortably in opposite corners of a first-class carriage and read. At five o'clock they went along to the restaurant car to have tea and chatted a little. They arrived.

They drove home in the car which was waiting for them. They bathed, dressed for dinner, and after dinner Evie, saying she was tired out, went to bed. She kissed him, as was her habit, on the forehead. Then he went into the hall, took Evie's book out of his greatcoat pocket and going into the study began to read it. He didn't read verse very easily and though he read with attention, every word of it, the impression he received was far from clear. Then he began at the beginning again and read it a second time. He read with increasing malaise, but he was not a stupid man and when he had finished he had a distinct understanding of what it was all about. Part of the book was in free verse, part in conventional metres, but the story it related was coherent and plain to the meanest intelligence. It was the story of a passionate love affair between an older woman, married, and a young man. George Peregrine made out the steps of it as easily as if he had been doing a sum in simple addition.

Written in the first person, it began with the tremulous surprise of the woman, past her youth, when it dawned upon her that the young man was in love with her. She hesitated to believe it. She thought she must be deceiving herself. And she was terrified when on a sudden she discovered that she was passionately in love with him. She told herself it was absurd; with the disparity of age between them nothing but unhappiness could come to her if she yielded to her emotion. She tried to prevent him from speaking but the day came when he told her that he loved her and forced her to tell him that she loved him too. He begged her to run away with him. She couldn't leave her husband, her home; and what life could they look forward to, she an ageing woman, he so young? How could she expect his love to last? She begged him to have mercy on her. But his love was impetuous. He wanted her, he wanted her with all his heart, and at last trembling, afraid, desirous, she yielded to him. Then there was a period of ecstatic happiness. The world, the dull, humdrum world of every day, blazed with glory. Love songs flowed from her pen. The woman worshipped the young, virile body of her lover. George flushed darkly when she praised his broad chest and slim flanks, the beauty of his legs and the flatness of his belly.

Hot stuff, Daphne's friend had said. It was that all right. Disgusting.

There were sad little pieces in which she lamented the emptiness of her life when as must happen he left her, but they ended with a cry that all she had to suffer would be worth it for the bliss that for a while had been hers. She wrote of the long, tremulous nights they passed together and the languor that lulled them to sleep in one another's arms. She wrote of the rapture of brief stolen moments when, braving all danger, their passion overwhelmed them and they surrendered to its call.

She thought it would be an affair of a few weeks, but miraculously it lasted. One of the poems referred to three years having gone by without lessening the love that filled their hearts. It looked as though he continued to press her to go away with him, far away, to a hill town in Italy, a Greek island, a walled city in Tunisia, so that they could be together always, for in another of the poems she besought him to let things be as they were. Their happiness was precarious. Perhaps it was owing to the difficulties they had to encounter and the rarity of their meetings that their love had retained for so long its first enchanting ardour. Then on a sudden the young man died. How, when or where George could not discover. There followed a long, heartbroken cry of bitter grief, grief she could not indulge in, grief that had to be hidden. She had to be cheerful, give dinner-parties and go out to dinner, behave as she had always behaved, though the light had gone out of her life and she was bowed down with anguish. The last poem of all was a set of four short stanzas in which the writer, sadly resigned to her loss, thanked the dark powers that rule man's destiny that she had been privileged at least for a while to enjoy the greatest happiness that we poor human beings can ever hope to know.

It was three o'clock in the morning when George Peregrine finally put the book down. It had seemed to him that he heard Evie's voice in every line, over and over again he came upon turns of phrase he had heard her use, there were details that were as familiar to him as to her: there was no doubt about it; it was her own story she had told, and it was as plain as anything could be that she had had a lover and her lover had died. It was not anger so much that he felt, nor horror or dismay, though he was dismayed and he was horrified, but amazement. It was as inconceivable that Evie should have had a love affair, and a wildly passionate one at that, as that the trout in a glass case over the chimney piece in his study, the finest he had ever caught, should suddenly wag its tail. He understood now the meaning of the amused look he had seen in the eyes of that man he had spoken to at the club, he understood why Daphne when she was talking about the book had seemed to be enjoying a private joke, and why those two women at the cocktail party had tittered when he strolled past them.

He broke out into a sweat. Then on a sudden he was seized with fury and he jumped up to go and awake Evie and ask her sternly for an explanation. But he stopped at the door. After all, what proof had he? A book. He remembered that he'd told Evie he thought it jolly good. True, he hadn't read it, but he'd pretended he had. He would look a perfect fool if he had to admit that.

"I must watch my step," he muttered.

He made up his mind to wait for two or three days and think it all over. Then he'd decide what to do. He went to bed, but he couldn't sleep for a long time.

"Evie," he kept on saying to himself. "Evie, of all people."

They met at breakfast next morning as usual. Evie was as she always was, quiet, demure and self-possessed, a middle-aged woman who made no effort to look younger than she was, a woman who had nothing of what he still called It. He looked at her as he hadn't looked at her for years. She had her usual placid serenity. Her pale blue eyes were untroubled. There was no sign of guilt on her candid brow. She made the same little casual remarks she always made.

"It's nice to get back to the country again after those two hectic days in London. What are you going to do this morning?"

It was incomprehensible.

Three days later he went to see his solicitor. Henry Blane was an old friend of George's as well as his lawyer. He had a place not far from Peregrine's and for years they had shot over one another's preserves. For two days a week he was a country gentleman and for the other five a busy lawyer in Sheffield. He was a tall, robust fellow, with a boisterous manner and a jovial laugh, which suggested that he liked to be looked upon essentially as a sportsman and a good fellow and only incidentally as a lawyer. But he was shrewd and worldly-wise.

"Well, George, what's brought you here today?" he boomed as the colonel was shown into his office. "Have a good time in London? I'm taking my missus up for a few days next week. How's Evie?"

"It's about Evie I've come to see you," said Peregrine, giving him a suspicious look. "Have you read her book?"

His sensitivity had been sharpened during those last days of troubled thought and he was conscious of a faint change in the lawyer's expression. It was as though he were suddenly on his guard.

"Yes, I've read it. Great success, isn't it? Fancy Evie breaking out into poetry. Wonders will never cease."

George Peregrine was inclined to lose his temper.

"It's made me look a perfect damned fool."

"Oh, what nonsense, George! There's no harm in Evie's writing a book. You ought to be jolly proud of her."

"Don't talk such rot. It's her own story. You know it and everyone else knows it. I suppose I'm the only one who doesn't know who her lover was."

"There is such a thing as imagination, old boy. There's no reason to suppose the whole thing isn't made up."

"Look here, Henry, we've known one another all our lives. We've had all sorts of good times together. Be honest with me. Can you look me in the face and tell me you believe it's a made-up story?"

Harry Blane moved uneasily in his chair. He was disturbed by the distress in old George's voice.

"You've got no right to ask me a question like that. Ask Evie."

"I daren't," George answered after an anguished pause. "I'm afraid she'd tell me the truth."

There was an uncomfortable silence.

"Who was the chap?"

Harry Blane looked at him straight in the eye.

"I don't know, and if I did I wouldn't tell you."

"You swine. Don't you see what a position I'm in? Do you think it's very pleasant to be made absolutely ridiculous?"

The lawyer lit a cigarette and for some moments silently puffed it.

"I don't see what I can do for you," he said at last.

"You've got private detectives you employ, I suppose. I want you to put them on the job and let them find everything out."

"It's not very pretty to put detectives on one's wife, old boy; and besides, taking for granted for a moment that Evie had an affair, it was a good many years ago and I don't suppose it would be possible to find out a thing. They seem to have covered their tracks pretty carefully."

"I don't care. You put the detectives on. I want to know the truth."

"I won't, George. If you're determined to do that you'd better consult someone else. And look here, even if you got evidence that

Evie had been unfaithful to you what would you do with it? You'd look rather silly divorcing your wife because she'd committed adultery ten years ago."

"At all events I could have it out with her."

"You can do that now, but you know just as well as I do that if you do she'll leave you. D'you want her to do that?"

George gave him an unhappy look.

"I don't know. I always thought she'd been a damned good wife to me. She runs the house perfectly, we never have any servant trouble; she's done wonders with the garden and she's splendid with all the village people. But damn it, I have my self-respect to think of. How can I go on living with her when I know that she was grossly unfaithful to me?"

"Have you always been faithful to her?"

"More or less, you know. After all, we've been married for nearly twenty-four years and Evie was never much for bed."

The solicitor slightly raised his eyebrows, but George was too intent on what he was saying to notice.

"I don't deny that I've had a bit of fun now and then. A man wants it. Women are different."

"We only have men's word for that," said Harry Blane, with a faint smile.

"Evie's absolutely the last woman I'd have suspected of kicking over the traces. I mean, she's a very fastidious, reticent woman. What on earth made her write the damned book?"

"I suppose it was a very poignant experience and perhaps it was a relief to her to get it off her chest like that."

"Well, if she had to write it why the devil didn't she write it under an assumed name?"

"She used her maiden name. I suppose she thought that was enough, and it would have been if the book hadn't had this amazing boom."

George Peregrine and the lawyer were sitting opposite one another with a desk between them. George, his elbow on the desk, his cheek on his hand, frowned at his thought.

"It's so rotten not to know what sort of a chap he was. One can't even tell if he was by way of being a gentleman. I mean, for all I know he may have been a farm-hand or a clerk in a lawyer's office."

Harry Blane did not permit himself to smile and when he answered there was in his eyes a kindly, tolerant look.

"Knowing Evie so well I think the probabilities are that he was all right. Anyhow I'm sure he wasn't a clerk in my office."

"It's been a shock to me," the colonel sighed. "I thought she was fond of me. She couldn't have written that book unless she hated me."

"Oh, I don't believe that. I don't think she's capable of hatred."

"You're not going to pretend that she loves me."

"No."

"Well, what does she feel for me?"

Harry Blane leaned back in his swivel chair and looked at George reflectively.

"Indifference, I should say."

The colonel gave a little shudder and reddened.

"After all, you're not in love with her, are you?"

George Peregrine did not answer directly.

"It's been a great blow to me not to have any children, but I've never let her see that I think she's let me down. I've always been kind to her. Within reasonable limits I've tried to do my duty by her."

The lawyer passed a large hand over his mouth to conceal the smile that trembled on his lips.

"It's been such an awful shock to me," Peregrine went on. "Damn it all, even ten years ago Evie was no chicken and God knows, she wasn't much to look at. It's so ugly." He sighed deeply. "What would *you* do in my place?"

"Nothing."

George Peregrine drew himself bolt upright in his chair and he looked at Harry with the stern set face that he must have worn when he inspected his regiment.

"I can't overlook a thing like this. I've been made a laughing-stock. I can never hold up my head again."

"Nonsense," said the lawyer sharply, and then in a pleasant, kindly manner. "Listen, old boy: the man's dead; it all happened a long while back. Forget it. Talk to people about Evie's book, rave about it, tell 'em how proud you are of her. Behave as though you had so much confidence in her, you *knew* she could never have been unfaithful to you. The world moves so quickly and people's memories are so short. They'll forget."

"I shan't forget."

"You're both middle-aged people. She probably does a great deal more for you than you think and you'd be awfully lonely without her. I don't think it matters if you don't forget. It'll be all to the good if you can get it into that thick head of yours that there's a lot more in Evie than you ever had the gumption to see."

"Damn it all, you talk as if *I* was to blame."

"No, I don't think you were to blame, but I'm not so sure that Evie was either. I don't suppose she wanted to fall in love with this boy. D'you remember those verses right at the end? The impression they gave me was that though she was shattered by his death, in a strange sort of way she welcomed it. All through she'd been aware of the fragility of the tie that bound them. He died in the full flush of his first love and had never known that love so seldom endures; he'd only known its bliss and beauty. In her own bitter grief she found solace in the thought that he'd been spared all sorrow."

"All that's a bit above my head, old boy. I see more or less what you mean."

George Peregrine stared unhappily at the inkstand on the desk. He was silent and the lawyer looked at him with curious, yet sympathetic, eyes.

"Do you realise what courage she must have had never by a sign to show how dreadfully unhappy she was?" he said gently.

Colonel Peregrine sighed.

"I'm broken. I suppose you're right; it's no good crying over spilt milk and it would only make things worse if I made a fuss."

"Well?"

George Peregrine gave a pitiful little smile.

"I'll take your advice. I'll do nothing. Let them think me a damned fool and to hell with them. The truth is, I don't know what I'd do without Evie. But I'll tell you what, there's one thing I shall never understand till my dying day: What in the name of heaven did the fellow ever see in her?"

❖

Miss King

IT was not till the beginning of September that Ashenden, a writer by profession, who had been abroad at the outbreak of the war, managed to get back to England. He chanced soon after his arrival to go to a party and was there introduced to a middle-aged colonel whose name he did not catch. He had some talk with him. As he was about to leave, this officer came up to him and asked:

"I say, I wonder if you'd mind coming to see me. I'd rather like to have a chat with you."

"Certainly," said Ashenden. "Whenever you like."

"What about to-morrow at eleven?"

"All right."

"I'll just write down my address. Have you a card on you?"

Ashenden gave him one and on this the colonel scribbled in pencil the name of a street and the number of a house. When Ashenden walked along next morning to keep his appointment he found himself in a street of rather vulgar red-brick houses in a part of London that had once been fashionable, but was now fallen in the esteem of the house-hunter who wanted a good address. On the house at which Ashenden had been asked to call there was a board up to announce that it was for sale, the shutters were closed and there was no sign that anyone lived in it. He rang the bell and the door was opened by a non-commissioned officer so promptly that he was startled. He was not asked his business, but led immediately into a long room at the back, once evidently a dining-room, the florid decoration of which looked oddly out of keeping with the office furniture, shabby and sparse, that was in it. It gave Ashenden the impression of a room in which the brokers had taken possession. The colonel, who was known in the Intelligence Department, as Ashenden later discovered, by the letter R., rose when he came in and shook hands with him. He was a man somewhat above the middle height, lean, with a yellow, deeply-lined face, thin grey hair and a toothbrush moustache. The thing immediately noticeable about him was the closeness with which his blue eyes were set. He only just escaped a squint. They were hard and cruel eyes, and very wary; and they gave him a cunning, shifty look. Here was a man that you could neither like nor trust at first sight. His manner was pleasant and cordial.

He asked Ashenden a good many questions and then, without further to-do, suggested that he had particular qualifications for the secret service. Ashenden was acquainted with several European languages and his profession was excellent cover; on the pretext that he was writing a book he could without attracting attention visit any neutral country. It was while they were discussing this point that R. said:

"You know, you ought to get material that would be very useful to you in your work."

"I shouldn't mind that," said Ashenden.

"I'll tell you an incident that occurred only the other day and I can vouch for its truth. I thought at the time it would make a damned good story. One of the French ministers went down to Nice to recover from a cold and he had some very important documents with him that he kept in a despatch-case. They were very important indeed. Well, a day or two after he arrived he picked up a yellow-haired lady at some restaurant or other where there was dancing, and he got very friendly with her. To cut a long story short, he took her back to his hotel—of course it was a very imprudent thing to do—and when he came to himself in the morning the lady and the despatch-case had disappeared. They had one or two drinks up in his room and his theory is that when his back was turned the woman slipped a drug into his glass."

R. finished and looked at Ashenden with a gleam in his close-set eyes.

"Dramatic, isn't it?" he asked.

"Do you mean to say that happened the other day?"

"The week before last."

"Impossible," cried Ashenden. "Why, we've been putting that incident on the stage for sixty years, we've written it in a thousand novels. Do you mean to say that life has only just caught up with us?"

R. was a trifle disconcerted.

"Well, if necessary, I could give you names and dates, and believe me, the Allies have been put to no end of trouble by the loss of the documents that the despatch-case contained."

"Well, sir, if you can't do better than that in the secret service," sighed Ashenden, "I'm afraid that as a source of inspiration to the

F*

writer of fiction it's a wash-out. We really *can't* write that story much longer."

It did not take them long to settle things and when Ashenden rose to go he had already made careful note of his instructions. He was to start for Geneva next day. The last words that R. said to him, with a casualness that made them impressive, were:

"There's just one thing I think you ought to know before you take on this job. And don't forget it. If you do well you'll get no thanks and if you get into trouble you'll get no help. Does that suit you?"

"Perfectly."

"Then I'll wish you good-afternoon."

Ashenden was on his way back to Geneva. The night was stormy and the wind blew cold from the mountains, but the stodgy little steamer plodded sturdily through the choppy waters of the lake. A scudding rain, just turning into sleet, swept the deck in angry gusts, like a nagging woman who cannot leave a subject alone. Ashenden had been to France in order to write and dispatch a report. A day or two before, about five in the afternoon, an Indian agent of his had come to see him in his rooms; it was only by a lucky chance that he was in, for he had no appointment with him, and the agent's instructions were to come to the hotel only in a case of urgent importance. He told Ashenden that a Bengali in the German service had recently come from Berlin with a black cane trunk in which were a number of documents interesting to the British Government. At that time the Central Powers were doing their best to foment such an agitation in India as would make it necessary for Great Britain to keep their troops in the country and perhaps send others from France. It had been found possible to get the Bengali arrested in Berne on a charge that would keep him out of harm's way for a while, but the black cane trunk could not be found. Ashenden's agent was a very brave and very clever fellow and he mixed freely with such of his countrymen as were disaffected to the interests of Great Britain. He had just discovered that the Bengali before going to Berne had, for greater safety, left the trunk in the cloak-room at Zürich station, and now that he was in gaol, awaiting trial, was unable to get the *bulletin* by which it might be obtained into the hands of any of his confederates. It was a matter of great urgency for the German Intelligence Department to secure the contents of the trunk without delay, and since it was impossible for them to get hold of it by the ordinary official means, they had decided to break into the station that very night and steal it. It was a bold and ingenious scheme and Ashenden felt a pleasant exhilaration (for a great deal of his work was uncommonly dull) when he heard of it. He recognised the dashing and unscrupulous touch of the head of the German secret service at Berne. But the burglary was arranged for two o'clock on the following morning and there was not a moment to lose. He could trust neither the telegraph nor the telephone to communicate with the British officer at Berne, and since the Indian agent could not go (he was taking his life in his hands by coming to see Ashenden and if he were noticed leaving his room it might easily be that he would be found one day floating in the lake with a knife-thrust in his back), there was nothing for it but to go himself.

There was a train to Berne that he could just catch and he put on his hat and coat as he ran downstairs. He jumped into a cab. Four hours later he rang the bell of the headquarters of the Intelligence Department. His name was known there but to one person, and it was for him that Ashenden asked. A tall tired-looking man, whom he had not met before, came out and without a word led him into an office. Ashenden told him his errand. The tall man looked at his watch.

"It's too late for us to do anything ourselves. We couldn't possibly get to Zürich in time."

He reflected.

"We'll put the Swiss authorities on the job. They can telephone, and when your friends attempt their little burglary, I have no doubt they'll find the station well guarded. Anyhow, you had better get back to Geneva."

He shook hands with Ashenden and showed him out. Ashenden was well aware that he would never know what happened then. Being no more than a tiny rivet in a vast and complicated machine, he never had the advantage of seeing a completed action. He was concerned with the beginning or the end of it, perhaps, or with some incident in the middle, but what his own doings led to he had seldom a chance of discovering. It was as unsatisfactory as those modern novels that give you a number of unrelated episodes and expect you by piecing them together to construct in your mind a connected narrative.

Notwithstanding his fur coat and his muffler, Ashenden was chilled to the bone. It was warm in the saloon and there were good lights to read by, but he thought it better not to sit there in case some habitual traveller, recognising him, wondered why he made these constant journeys between Geneva in Switzerland and Thonon in France; and so, making the best of what shelter could be found, he passed the tedious time in the darkness of the deck. He looked in the direction of Geneva, but could see no lights, and the sleet, turning into snow, prevented him from recognising the land-marks. Lake Leman, on fine days so trim and pretty, artificial like a piece of water in a French garden, in this tempestuous weather was as secret and as menacing as the sea. He made up his mind that, on getting back to his hotel, he would have a fire lit in his sitting-room, a hot bath, and dinner comfortably by the fireside in pyjamas and a dressing-gown. The prospect of spending an evening by himself with his pipe and a book was so agreeable that it made the misery of that journey across the lake positively worth while. Two sailors tramped past him heavily, their heads bent down to save themselves from the sleet that blew in their faces, and one of them shouted to him: *Nous arrivons*; they went to the side and withdrew a bar to allow passage for the gangway, and looking again Ashenden through the howling darkness saw mistily the lights of the quay. A welcome sight. In two or three minutes the steamer was made fast and Ashenden, muffled to the eyes, joined himself to the little knot of passengers that waited to step ashore. Though he made the journey so often—it was his duty to cross the lake into France once a week to deliver his reports and to receive instructions—he had always a faint sense of trepidation when he stood among the crowd at the gangway and waited to land. There was nothing on his passport to show that he had been in France; the steamer went round the lake touching French soil at two places, but going from Switzerland to Switzerland, so that his journey might have been to Vevey or to Lausanne; but he could never be sure that the secret police had not taken note of him, and if he had been followed and seen to land in France, the fact that there was no stamp on his passport would be difficult to explain. Of course he had his story ready, but he well knew that it was not a very convincing one, and though it might be impossible for the Swiss authorities to prove that he was anything but a casual traveller, he might nevertheless spend two or three days in gaol, which would be uncomfortable, and then be firmly conducted to the frontier, which would be mortifying. The Swiss knew well that their country was the scene of all manner of intrigues; agents of the secret service, spies, revolutionaries and agitators infested the hotels of the principal towns and, jealous of their neutrality, they were determined to prevent conduct that might embroil them with any of the belligerent powers.

There were as usual two police officers on the quay to watch the passengers disembark and Ashenden, walking past them with as unconcerned an air as he could assume, was relieved when he had got safely by. The darkness swallowed him up and he stepped out briskly for his hotel. The wild weather with a scornful gesture had swept all the neatness from the trim promenade. The shops were closed and Ashenden passed only an occasional pedestrian who sidled along, scrunched up, as though he fled from the blind wrath of the unknown. You had a feeling in that black and bitter night that civilisation, ashamed of its artificiality, cowered before the fury of elemental things. It was hail now that blew in Ashenden's face and the pavement was wet and slippery so that he had to walk with caution. The hotel faced the lake. When he reached it and a page-boy opened the door for him, he entered the hall with a flurry of wind that sent the papers on the porter's desk flying into the air. Ashenden was dazzled by the light. He stopped to ask the porter if there were letters for him. There was nothing, and he was about to get into the lift when the porter told him that two gentlemen were waiting in his room to see him. Ashenden had no friends in Geneva.

"Oh?" he answered, not a little surprised. "Who are they?"

He had taken care to get on friendly terms with the porter and his tips for trifling services had been generous. The porter gave a discreet smile.

"There is no harm in telling you. I think they are members of the police."

"What do they want?" asked Ashenden.

"They did not say. They asked me where you were, and I told them you had gone for a walk. They said they would wait till you came back."

"How long have they been there?"

"An hour."

Ashenden's heart sank, but he took care not to let his face betray his concern.

"I'll go up and see them," he said. The liftman stood aside to let him step into the lift, but Ashenden shook his head. "I'm so cold," he said, "I'll walk up."

He wished to give himself a moment to think, but as he ascended

the three flights slowly his feet were like lead. There could be small
doubt why two police officers were so bent upon seeing him. He
felt on a sudden dreadfully tired. He did not feel he could cope
with a multitude of questions. And if he were arrested as a secret
agent he must spend at least the night in a cell. He longed more than
ever for a hot bath and a pleasant dinner by his fireside. He had
half a mind to turn tail and walk out of the hotel, leaving everything
behind him; he had his passport in his pocket and he knew by
heart the hours at which trains started for the frontier: before the
Swiss authorities had made up their minds what to do he would be
in safety. But he continued to trudge upstairs. He did not like the
notion of abandoning his job so easily; he had been sent to Geneva,
knowing the risks, to do work of a certain kind, and it seemed to
him that he had better go through with it. Of course it would not
be very nice to spend two years in a Swiss prison, but the chance of
this was, like assassination to kings, one of the inconveniences of
his profession. He reached the landing of the third floor and walked
to his room. Ashenden had in him, it seems, a strain of flippancy
(on account of which, indeed, the critics had often reproached him)
and as he stood for a moment outside the door his predicament
appeared to him on a sudden rather droll. His spirits went up and
he determined to brazen the thing out. It was with a genuine smile
on his lips that he turned the handle and entering the room faced
his visitors.

"Good evening, gentlemen," said he.

The room was brightly lit, for all the lights were on, and a fire
burned in the hearth. The air was grey with smoke, since the
strangers, finding it long to wait for him, had been smoking strong
and inexpensive cigars. They sat in their greatcoats and bowler-
hats as though they had only just that moment come in; but the
ashes in the little tray on the table would alone have suggested that
they had been long enough there to make themselves familiar with
their surroundings. They were two powerful men, with black
moustaches, on the stout side, heavily built, and they reminded
Ashenden of Fafner and Fasolt, the giants in *The Rhinegold*; their
clumsy boots, the massive way they sat in their chairs and the
ponderous alertness of their expression made it obvious that they
were members of the detective force. Ashenden gave his room an
enveloping glance. He was a neat creature and saw at once that his
things, though not in disorder, were not as he had left them. He
guessed that an examination had been made of his effects. That did

not disturb him, for he kept in his room no document that would
compromise him; his code he had learned by heart and destroyed
before leaving England, and such communications as reached him
from Germany were handed to him by third parties and transmitted
without delay to the proper places. There was nothing he need fear
in a search, but the impression that it had been made confirmed his
suspicion that he had been denounced to the authorities as a
secret agent.

"What can I do for you, gentlemen?" he asked affably. "It's
warm in here, wouldn't you like to take off your coats—and hats?"

It faintly irritated him that they should sit there with their hats on.

"We're only staying a minute," said one of them. "We were
passing and as the *concierge* said you would be in at once, we thought
we would wait."

He did not remove his hat. Ashenden unwrapped his scarf and
disembarrassed himself of his heavy coat.

"Won't you have a cigar?" he asked, offering the box to the two
detectives in turn.

"I don't mind if I do," said the first, Fafner, taking one, upon
which the second, Fasolt, helped himself without a word, even of
thanks.

The name on the box appeared to have a singular effect on their
manners, for both now took off their hats.

"You must have had a very disagreeable walk in this bad
weather," said Fafner, as he bit half an inch off the end of his cigar
and spat it in the fire-place.

Now it was Ashenden's principle (a good one in life as well as in
the Intelligence Department) always to tell as much of the truth as
he conveniently could; so he answered as follows:

"What do you take me for? I wouldn't go out in such weather
if I could help it. I had to go to Vevey to-day to see an invalid
friend and I came back by boat. It was bitter on the lake."

"We come from the police," said Fafner casually.

Ashenden thought they must consider him a perfect idiot if they
imagined he had not guessed that, but it was not a piece of information to which it was discreet to reply with a pleasantry.

"Oh, really," he said.

"Have you your passport on you?"

"Yes. In these war-times I think a foreigner is wise always to
keep his passport on him."

"Very wise."

Ashenden handed the man the nice new passport, which gave no information about his movements other than that he had come from London three months before and had since then crossed no frontier. The detective looked at it carefully and passed it on to his colleague.

"It appears to be all in order," he said.

Ashenden, standing in front of the fire to warm himself, a cigarette between his lips, made no reply. He watched the detectives warily, but with an expression, he flattered himself, of amiable unconcern. Fasolt handed back the passport to Fafner, who tapped it reflectively with a thick forefinger.

"The chief of police told us to come here," he said, and Ashenden was conscious that both of them now looked at him with attention, "to make a few enquiries of you."

Ashenden knew that when you have nothing apposite to say it is better to hold your tongue; and when a man has made a remark that calls to his mind for an answer, he is apt to find silence a trifle disconcerting. Ashenden waited for the detective to proceed. He was not quite sure, but it seemed to him that he hesitated.

"It appears that there have been a good many complaints lately of the noise that people make when they come out of the Casino late at night. We wish to know if you personally have been troubled by the disturbance. It is evident that as your rooms look on the lake and the revellers pass your windows, if the noise is serious, you must have heard it."

For an instant Ashenden was dumbfounded. What balderdash was this the detective was talking to him (boom, boom, he heard the big drum as the giant lumbered on the scene), and why on earth should the chief of police send to him to find out if his beauty sleep had been disturbed by vociferous gamblers? It looked very like a trap. But nothing is so foolish as to ascribe profundity to what on the surface is merely inept; it is a pitfall into which many an ingenuous reviewer has fallen headlong. Ashenden had a confident belief in the stupidity of the human animal, which in the course of his life had stood him in good stead. It flashed across him that if the detective asked him such a question it was because he had no shadow of proof that he was engaged in any illegal practice. It was clear that he had been denounced, but no evidence had been offered, and the search of his rooms had been fruitless. But what a silly excuse was this to make for a visit and what a poverty of invention it showed! Ashenden immediately thought of three reasons the detectives might have given for seeking an interview with him and he wished that he were on terms sufficiently familiar with them to make the suggestions. This was really an insult to the intelligence. These men were even stupider than he thought; but Ashenden had always a soft corner in his heart for the stupid and now he looked upon them with a feeling of unexpected kindliness. He would have liked to pat them gently. But he answered the question with gravity.

"To tell you the truth, I am a very sound sleeper (the result doubtless of a pure heart and an easy conscience), and I have never heard a thing."

Ashenden looked at them for the faint smile that he thought his remark deserved, but their countenances remained stolid. Ashenden, as well as an agent of the British Government, was a humorist, and he stifled the beginnings of a sigh. He assumed a slightly imposing air and adopted a more serious tone.

"But even if I had been awakened by noisy people I should not dream of complaining. At a time when there is so much trouble, misery and unhappiness in the world, I cannot but think it very wrong to disturb the amusement of persons who are lucky enough to be able to amuse themselves."

"En effet," said the detective. "But the fact remains that people have been disturbed and the chief of police thought the matter should be enquired into."

His colleague, who had hitherto preserved a silence that was positively sphinx-like, now broke it.

"I notice by your passport that you are an author, monsieur," he said.

Ashenden in reaction from his previous perturbation was feeling exceedingly debonair and he answered with good-humour:

"It is true. It is a profession full of tribulation, but it has now and then its compensations."

"La gloire," said Fafner politely.

"Or shall we say notoriety?" hazarded Ashenden.

"And what are you doing in Geneva?"

The question was put so pleasantly that Ashenden felt it behoved him to be on his guard. A police officer amiable is more dangerous to the wise than a police officer aggressive.

"I am writing a play," said Ashenden.

He waved his hand to the papers on his table. Four eyes followed his gesture. A casual glance told him that the detectives had looked and taken note of his manuscripts.

"And why should you write a play here rather than in your own country?"

Ashenden smiled upon them with even more affability than before, since this was a question for which he had long been prepared, and it was a relief to give the answer. He was curious to see how it would go down.

"*Mais, monsieur*, there is the war. My country is in turmoil, it would be impossible to sit there quietly and write a play."

"Is it a comedy or a tragedy?"

"Oh, a comedy, and a light one at that," replied Ashenden. "The artist needs peace and quietness. How do you expect him to preserve that detachment of spirit that is demanded by creative work unless he can have perfect tranquillity? Switzerland has the good fortune to be neutral, and it seemed to me that in Geneva I should find the very surroundings I wanted."

Fafner nodded slight to Fasolt, but whether to indicate that he thought Ashenden an imbecile or whether in sympathy with his desire for a safe retreat from a turbulent world, Ashenden had no means of knowing. Anyhow the detective evidently came to the conclusion that he could learn nothing more from talking to Ashenden, for his remarks grew now desultory and in a few minutes he rose to go.

When Ashenden, having warmly shaken their hands, closed the door behind the pair he heaved a great sigh of relief. He turned on the water for his bath, as hot as he thought he could possibly bear it, and as he undressed reflected comfortably over his escape.

The day before, an incident had occurred that had left him on his guard. There was in his service a Swiss, known in the Intelligence Department as Bernard, who had recently come from Germany, and Ashenden, desiring to see him, had instructed him to go to a certain café at a certain time. Since he had not seen him before, so that there might be no mistake he had informed him through an intermediary what question himself would ask and what reply he was to give. He chose the luncheon hour for the meeting, since then the café was unlikely to be crowded, and it chanced that on entering he saw but one man of about the age he knew Bernard to be. He was by himself, and going up to him Ashenden casually put to him the pre-arranged question. The pre-arranged answer was given, and sitting down beside him, Ashenden ordered himself a Dubonnet. The spy was a stocky little fellow, shabbily dressed, with a bullet-shaped head, close-cropped, fair, with shifty blue eyes and a sallow skin. He did not inspire confidence, and but that Ashenden knew by experience how hard it was to find men willing to go into Germany he would have been surprised that his predecessor had engaged him. He was a German-Swiss and spoke French with a strong accent. He immediately asked for his wages and these Ashenden passed over to him in an envelope. They were in Swiss francs. He gave a general account of his stay in Germany and answered Ashenden's careful questions. He was by calling a waiter and had found a job in a restaurant near one of the Rhine bridges, which gave him good opportunity to get the information that was required of him. His reasons for coming to Switzerland for a few days were plausible and there could apparently be no difficulty in his crossing the frontier on his return. Ashenden expressed his satisfaction with his behaviour, gave him his orders and was prepared to finish the interview.

"Very good," said Bernard. "But before I go back to Germany I want two thousand francs."

"Do you?"

"Yes, and I want them now, before you leave this café. It's a sum I have to pay, and I've got to have it."

"I'm afraid I can't give it to you."

A scowl made the man's face even more unpleasant to look at than it was before.

"You've got to."

"What makes you think that?"

The spy leaned forward and, not raising his voice, but speaking so that only Ashenden could hear, burst out angrily:

"Do you think I'm going on risking my life for that beggarly sum you give me? Not ten days ago a man was caught at Mainz and shot. Was that one of your men?"

"We haven't got anyone at Mainz," said Ashenden, carelessly, and for all he knew it was true. He had been puzzled not to receive his usual communications from that place and Bernard's information might afford the explanation. "You knew exactly what you were to get when you took on the job, and if you weren't satisfied you needn't have taken it. I have no authority to give you a penny more."

"Do you see what I've got here?" said Bernard.

He took a small revolver out of his pocket and fingered it significantly.

"What are you going to do with it? Pawn it?"

With an angry shrug of the shoulders he put it back in his pocket. Ashenden reflected that had he known anything of the technique of the theatre Bernard would have been aware that it was useless to make a gesture that had no ulterior meaning.

"You refuse to give me the money?"

"Certainly."

The spy's manner, which at first had been obsequious, was now somewhat truculent, but he kept his head and never for a moment raised his voice. Ashenden could see that Bernard, however big a ruffian, was a reliable agent, and he made up his mind to suggest to R. that his salary should be raised. The scene diverted him. A little way off two fat citizens of Geneva, with black beards, were playing dominoes, and on the other side a young man with spectacles was with great rapidity writing sheet after sheet of an immensely long letter. A Swiss family (who knows, perhaps Robinson by name), consisting of a father and mother and four children, were sitting round a table making the best of two small cups of coffee. The *caissière* behind the counter, an imposing brunette with a large bust encased in black silk, was reading the local paper. The surroundings made the melodramatic scene in which Ashenden was engaged perfectly grotesque. His own play seemed to him much more real.

Bernard smiled. His smile was not engaging.

"Do you know that I have only to go to the police and tell them about you to have you arrested? Do you know what a Swiss prison is like?"

"No, I've often wondered lately. Do you?"

"Yes, and you wouldn't much like it."

One of the things that had bothered Ashenden was the possibility that he would be arrested before he finished his play. He disliked the notion of leaving it half done for an indefinite period. He did not know whether he would be treated as a political prisoner or as a common criminal and he had a mind to ask Bernard whether in the latter case (the only one Bernard was likely to know anything about) he would be allowed writing materials. He was afraid Bernard would think the inquiry an attempt to laugh at him. But he was feeling comparatively at ease and was able to answer Bernard's threat without heat.

"You could of course get me sentenced to two years' imprisonment."

"At least."

"No, that is the maximum, I understand, and I think it is quite enough. I won't conceal from you that I should find it extremely disagreeable. But not nearly so disagreeable as you would."

"What could you do?"

"Oh, we'd get you somehow. And after all, the war won't last for ever. You are a waiter, you want your freedom of action. I promise you that if I get into any trouble, you will never be admitted into any of the Allied countries for the rest of your life. I can't help thinking it would cramp your style."

Bernard did not reply, but looked down sulkily at the marble-topped table. Ashenden thought this was the moment to pay for the drinks and go.

"Think it over, Bernard," he said. "If you want to go back to your job, you have your instructions, and your usual wages shall be paid through the usual channels."

The spy shrugged his shoulders, and Ashenden, though not knowing in the least what was the result of their conversation, felt that it behoved him to walk out with dignity. He did so.

And now as he carefully put one foot into the bath, wondering if he could bear it, he asked himself what Bernard had in the end decided on. The water was just not scalding and he gradually let himself down into it. On the whole it seemed to him that the spy had thought it would be as well to go straight, and the source of his denunciation must be looked for elsewhere. Perhaps in the hotel itself. Ashenden lay back, and as his body grew used to the heat of the water gave a sigh of satisfaction.

"Really," he reflected, "there are moments in life when all this to-do that has led from the primeval slime to myself seems almost worth while."

Ashenden could not but think he was lucky to have wriggled out of the fix he had found himself in that afternoon. Had he been arrested and in due course sentenced, R., shrugging his shoulders, would merely have called him a damned fool and set about looking for someone to take his place. Already Ashenden knew his chief well enough to be aware that when he had told him that if he got into trouble he need look for no help he meant exactly what he said.

Ashenden, lying comfortably in his bath, was glad to think that in all probability he would be able to finish his play in peace. The police had drawn a blank and though they might watch him from now on with some care it was unlikely that they would take a further step until he had at least roughed out his third act. It behoved him to be prudent (only a fortnight ago his colleague at Lausanne had been sentenced to a term of imprisonment), but it would be foolish to be alarmed: his predecessor in Geneva, seeing himself, with an exaggerated sense of his own importance, shadowed from morning till night, had been so affected by the nervous strain that it had been found necessary to withdraw him. Twice a week Ashenden had to go to the market to receive instructions that were brought to him by an old peasant woman from French Savoy who sold butter and eggs. She came in with the other market-women and the search at the frontier was perfunctory. It was barely dawn when they crossed and the officials were only too glad to have done quickly with these chattering noisy women and get back to their warm fires and their cigars. Indeed this old lady looked so bland and innocent, with her corpulence, her fat red face, and her smiling good-natured mouth, it would have been a very astute detective who could imagine that if he took the trouble to put his hand deep down between those voluminous breasts of hers, he would find a little piece of paper that would land in the dock an honest old woman (who kept her son out of the trenches by taking this risk) and an English writer approaching middle age. Ashenden went to the market about nine when the housewives of Geneva for the most part had done their provisioning, stopped in front of the basket by the side of which, rain or wind, hot or cold, sat that indomitable creature and bought half a pound of butter. She slipped the note into his hand when he was given change for ten francs and he sauntered away. His only moment of risk was when he walked back to his hotel with the paper in his pocket, and after this scare he made up his mind to shorten as much as possible the period during which it could be found on him.

Ashenden sighed, for the water was no longer quite so hot; he could not reach the tap with his hand nor could he turn it with his toes (as every properly regulated tap should turn) and if he got up enough to add more hot water he might just as well get out altogether. On the other hand he could not pull out the plug with his foot in order to empty the bath and so force himself to get out, nor could he find in himself the will-power to step out of it like a man. He had often heard people tell him that he possessed character and he reflected that people judge hastily in the affairs of life because they judge on insufficient evidence: they had never seen him in a hot, but diminishingly hot, bath. His mind, however, wandered back to his play, and telling himself jokes and repartees that he knew by bitter experience would never look so neat on paper nor sound so well on the stage as they did then, he abstracted his mind from the fact that his bath was growing almost tepid, when he heard a knock at the door. Since he did not want anyone to enter, he had the presence of mind not to say come in, but the knocking was repeated.

"Who is it?" he cried irascibly.

"A letter."

"Come in then. Wait a minute."

Ashenden heard his bedroom-door open and getting out of the bath flung a towel round him and went in. A page-boy was waiting with a note. It needed only a verbal answer. It was from a lady staying in the hotel asking him to play bridge after dinner and was signed in the continental fashion Baronne de Higgins. Ashenden, longing for a cosy meal in his own room, in slippers and with a book leaned up against a reading-lamp, was about to refuse when it occurred to him that in the circumstances it might be discreet to show himself in the dining-room that night. It was absurd to suppose that in that hotel the news would not have spread that he had been visited by the police and it would be as well to prove to his fellow-guests that he was not disconcerted. It had passed through his mind that it might be someone in the hotel who had denounced him and indeed the name of the sprightly baroness had not failed to suggest itself to him. If it was she who had given him away there would be a certain humour in playing bridge with her. He gave the boy a message that he would be pleased to come and proceeded slowly to don his evening clothes.

The Baroness von Higgins was an Austrian, who on settling in Geneva during the first winter of the war had found it convenient to make her name look as French as possible. She spoke English and French perfectly. Her surname, so far from Teutonic, she owed to her grandfather, a Yorkshire stable-boy, who had been taken over to Austria by a Prince Blankenstein early in the nineteenth century. He had had a charming and romantic career; a very good-looking man, he attracted the attention of one of the arch-duchesses and then made such good use of his opportunities that he ended his life as a baron and minister plenipotentiary to an Italian court. The baroness, his only descendant, after an unhappy marriage, the particulars of which she was fond of relating to her acquaintance, had resumed her maiden name. She mentioned not infrequently the fact that her grandfather had been an ambassador, but never that he had been a stable-boy and Ashenden had learned this interesting detail from Vienna; for as he grew friendly with her he had thought it necessary to get a few particulars about her past, and he knew among other things that her private income did not permit her to live on the somewhat lavish scale on which she was living in Geneva. Since she had so many advantages for espionage, it was fairly safe to suppose that an alert secret service had enlisted her services and Ashenden took it for granted that she was engaged somehow on the same kind of work as himself. It increased if anything the cordiality of his relations with her.

When he went into the dining-room it was already full. He sat down at his table and feeling jaunty after his adventure ordered himself (at the expense of the British Government) a bottle of champagne. The baroness gave him a flashing, brilliant smile. She was a woman of more than forty, but in a hard and glittering manner extremely beautiful. She was a high-coloured blonde with golden hair of a metallic lustre, lovely no doubt but not attractive, and Ashenden had from the first reflected that it was not the sort of hair you would like to find in your soup. She had fine features, blue eyes, a straight nose, and a pink and white skin, but her skin was stretched over her bones a trifle tightly; she was generously décolletée and her white and ample bosom had the quality of marble. There was nothing in her appearance to suggest the yielding tenderness that the susceptible find so alluring. She was magnificently gowned, but scantily bejewelled, so that Ashenden, who knew something of these matters, concluded that the superior authority had given her carte blanche at a dressmaker's but had not thought it prudent or necessary to provide her with rings or pearls. She was notwithstanding so showy that but for R.'s story of the minister, Ashenden would have thought the sight of her alone must have aroused in anyone on whom she desired to exercise her wiles the sense of prudence.

While he waited for his dinner to be served, Ashenden cast his eyes over the company. Most of the persons gathered were old friends by sight. At that time Geneva was a hot-bed of intrigue and its home was the hotel at which Ashenden was staying. There were Frenchmen there, Italians and Russians, Turks, Rumanians, Greeks and Egyptians. Some had fled their country, some doubtless represented it. There was a Bulgarian, an agent of Ashenden's, whom for greater safety he had never even spoken to in Geneva; he was dining that night with two fellow-countrymen and in a day or so, if he was not killed in the interval, might have a very interesting communication to make. Then there was a little German prostitute, with china-blue eyes and a doll-like face, who made frequent journeys along the lake and up to Berne, and in the exercise of her profession got little titbits of information over which doubtless they pondered with deliberation in Berlin. She was of course of a different class from the baroness and hunted much easier game. But Ashenden was surprised to catch sight of Count von Holzminden and wondered what on earth he was doing there. This was the German agent in Vevey and he came over to Geneva only on occasion. Once Ashenden had seen him in the old quarter of the city, with its silent houses and deserted streets, talking at a corner to a man whose appearance very much suggested the spy and he would have given a great deal to hear what they said to one another. It had amused him to come across the Count, for in London before the war he had known him fairly well. He was of great family and indeed related to the Hohenzollerns. He was fond of England; he danced well, rode well and shot well; people said he was more English than the English. He was a tall, thin fellow, in well-cut clothes, with a close-cropped Prussian head, and that peculiar bend of the body as though he were just about to bow to a royalty that you feel, rather than see, in those who have spent their lives about a court. He had charming manners and was much interested in the Fine Arts. But now Ashenden and he pretended they had never seen one another before. Each of course knew on what work the other was engaged and Ashenden had had a mind to chaff him about it— it seemed absurd when he had dined with a man off and on for years and played cards with him, to act as though he did not know him from Adam—but refrained in case the German looked upon his behaviour as further proof of the British frivolity in face of war. Ashenden was perplexed: Holzminden had never set foot in that hotel before and it was unlikely that he had done so now without good reason.

Ashenden asked himself whether this event had anything to do with the unusual presence in the dining-room of Prince Ali. At that juncture it was imprudent to ascribe any occurrence, however accidental it looked, to the hazard of coincidence. Prince Ali was an Egyptian, a near relation of the Khedive, who had fled his country when the Khedive was deposed. He was a bitter enemy of the English and was known to be actively engaged in stirring up trouble in Egypt. The week before, the Khedive in great secrecy had passed three days at the hotel and the pair of them had held constant meetings in the prince's apartments. He was a little fat man with a heavy black moustache. He was living with his two daughters and a certain pasha, Mustapha by name, who was his secretary and managed his affairs. The four of them were now dining together; they drank a great deal of champagne, but sat in a stolid silence. The two princesses were emancipated young women who spent their nights dancing in restaurants with the bloods of Geneva. They were short and stout, with fine black eyes and heavy sallow faces; and they were dressed with a rich loudness that suggested the Fish-market at Cairo rather than the Rue de la Paix. His Highness usually ate upstairs but the princesses dined every evening in the public dining-room: they were chaperoned vaguely by a little old Englishwoman, a Miss King, who had been their governess; but she sat at a table by herself and they appeared to pay no attention to her. Once Ashenden, going along a corridor, had come upon the elder of the two fat princesses berating the governess in French with a violence that took his breath away. She was shouting at the top of her voice and suddenly smacked the old woman's face. When she caught sight of Ashenden she gave him a furious look and flinging into her room slammed the door. He walked on as though he had noticed nothing.

On his arrival Ashenden had tried to scrape acquaintance with Miss King, but she had received his advances not merely with frigidity but with churlishness. He had begun by taking off his hat when he met her, and she had given him a stiff bow, then he had addressed her and she had answered with such brevity that it was evident that she wished to have nothing much to do with him. But it was not his business to be discouraged, so with what assurance he could muster he took the first opportunity to enter into conversation with her. She drew herself up and said in French, but with an English accent:

" I don't wish to make acquaintance with strangers."

She turned her back on him and, next time he saw her, cut him dead.

She was a tiny woman, just a few little bones in a bag of wrinkled skin, and her face was deeply furrowed. It was obvious that she wore a wig, it was of a mousy brown, very elaborate and not always set quite straight, and she was heavily made up, with great patches of scarlet on her withered cheeks and brilliantly red lips. She dressed fantastically in gay clothes that looked as though they had been bought higgledy-piggledy from an old-clothes shop and in the day-time she wore enormous, extravagantly girlish hats. She tripped along in very small smart shoes with very high heels. Her appearance was so grotesque that it created consternation rather than amusement. People turned in the street and stared at her with open mouths.

Ashenden was told that Miss King had not been to England since she was first engaged as governess of the prince's mother and he could not but be amazed to think of all she must have seen during those long years in the harems of Cairo. It was impossible to guess how old she was. How many of those short Eastern lives must have run their course under her eyes and what dark secrets must she have known! Ashenden wondered where she came from; an exile from her own country for so long, she must possess in it neither family nor friends: he knew that her sentiments were anti-English and if she had answered him so rudely he surmised that she had been told to be on her guard against him. She never spoke anything but French. Ashenden wondered what it was she thought of as she sat there, at luncheon and dinner by herself. He wondered if ever she read. After meals she went straight upstairs and was never seen in the public sitting-rooms. He wondered what she thought of those two emancipated princesses who wore garish frocks and danced with strange men in second-rate cafés. But when Miss King passed him on her way out of the dining-room it seemed to Ashenden that her mask of a face scowled. She appeared actively to dislike him. Her gaze met his and the pair of them looked at one another for a moment; he imagined that she tried to put into her stare an unspoken insult. It would have been pleasantly absurd in that painted, withered visage if it had not been for some reason rather oddly pathetic.

But now the Baroness de Higgins, having finished her dinner, gathered up her handkerchief and her bag, and with waiters bowing on either side sailed down the spacious room. She stopped at Ashenden's table. She looked magnificent.

"I'm so glad you can play bridge to-night," she said in perfect English, with no more than a trace of German accent. "Will you come to my sitting-room when you are ready and have your coffee?"

"What a lovely dress," said Ashenden.

"It is frightful. I have nothing to wear, I don't know what I shall do now that I cannot go to Paris. Those horrible Prussians," and her r's grew guttural as she raised her voice, "why did they want to drag my poor country into this terrible war?"

She gave a sigh, and a flashing smile, and sailed on. Ashenden was among the last to finish and when he left the dining-room it was almost empty. As he walked past Count Holzminden, Ashenden feeling very gay hazarded the shadow of a wink. The German agent could not be quite sure of it and if he suspected it might rack his brains to discover what mystery it portended. Ashenden walked up to the second floor and knocked at the baroness's door.

"*Entrez, entrez,*" she said and flung it open.

She shook both his hands with cordiality and drew him into the room. He saw that the two persons who were to make the four had already arrived. They were Prince Ali and his secretary. Ashenden was astounded.

"Allow me to introduce Mr. Ashenden to Your Highness," said the baroness, speaking in her fluent French.

Ashenden bowed and took the proffered hand. The prince gave him a quick look, but did not speak. Madame de Higgins went on:

"I do not know if you have met the Pasha."

"I am delighted to make your acquaintance, Mr. Ashenden," said the prince's secretary, warmly shaking his hand. "Our beautiful baroness has talked to us of your bridge and His Highness is devoted to the game. *N'est ce pas, Altesse?*"

"*Oui, oui,*" said the prince.

Mustapha Pasha was a huge fat fellow, of forty-five perhaps, with large mobile eyes and a big black moustache. He wore a dinner jacket with a large diamond in his shirt-front and the *tarboosh* of his country. He was exceedingly voluble, and the words tumbled out of his mouth tumultuously, like marbles out of a bag. He took pains to be extremely civil to Ashenden. The prince sat in silence, looking at Ashenden quietly from under his heavy eyelids. He seemed shy.

"I have not seen you at the club, *Monsieur*," said the pasha. "Do you not like baccarat?"

"I play but seldom."

"The baroness, who has read everything, tells me that you are a remarkable writer. Unfortunately I do not read English."

The baroness paid Ashenden some very fulsome compliments

to which he listened with a proper and grateful politeness, and then, having provided her guests with coffee and liqueurs, she produced the cards. Ashenden could not but wonder why he had been asked to play. He had (he flattered himself) few illusions about himself, and so far as bridge was concerned none. He knew that he was a good player of the second class, but he had played often enough with the best players in the world to know that he was not in the same street with them. The game played now was contract, with which he was not very familiar, and the stakes were high; but the game was obviously but a pretext and Ashenden had no notion what other game was being played under the rose. It might be that knowing he was a British agent the prince and his secretary had desired to see him in order to find out what sort of person he was. Ashenden had felt for a day or two that something was in the air and this meeting confirmed his suspicions, but he had not the faintest notion of what nature this something was. His spies had told him of late nothing that signified. He was now persuaded that he owed that visit of the Swiss police to the kindly intervention of the baroness and it looked as though the bridge-party had been arranged when it was discovered that the detectives had been able to do nothing. The notion was mysterious, but diverting, and as Ashenden played one rubber after another, joining in the incessant conversation, he watched what was said by himself no less closely than what was said by the others. The war was spoken of a good deal and the baroness and the ·pasha expressed very anti-German sentiments. The baroness's heart was in England whence her family (the stable-boy from Yorkshire) had sprung and the pasha looked upon Paris as his spiritual home. When the pasha talked of Montmartre and its life by night the prince was roused from his silence.

"C'est une bien belle ville, Paris," he said.

"The Prince has a beautiful apartment there," said his secretary, "with beautiful pictures and life-sized statues."

Ashenden explained that he had the greatest sympathy for the national aspirations of Egypt and that he looked upon Vienna as the most pleasing capital in Europe. He was as friendly to them as they were to him. But if they were under the impression that they would get any information out of him that they had not already seen in the Swiss papers he had a notion that they were mistaken. At one moment he had a suspicion that he was being sounded upon the possibility of selling himself. It was done so discreetly that he could not be quite sure, but he had a feeling that a suggestion floated in the air that a clever writer could do his country a good turn and make a vast amount of money for himself if he cared to enter into an arrangement that would bring to a troubled world the peace that every humane man must so sincerely desire. It was plain that nothing very much would be said that first evening, but Ashenden as evasively as he could, more by general amiability than by words, tried to indicate that he was willing to hear more of the subject. While he talked with the pasha and the beautiful Austrian he was conscious that the watchful eyes of Prince Ali were upon him, and had an uneasy suspicion that they read too much of his thoughts. He felt rather than knew that the prince was an able and astute man. It was possible that after he left them the prince would tell the other two that they were wasting their time and there was nothing to be done with Ashenden.

Soon after midnight, a rubber having been finished, the prince rose from the table.

"It is getting late," he said, "and Mr. Ashenden has doubtless much to do to-morrow. We must not keep him up."

Ashenden looked upon this as a signal to take himself off. He left the three together to discuss the situation and retired not a little mystified. He could only trust that they were no less puzzled than he. When he got to his room he suddenly realised that he was dog-tired. He could hardly keep his eyes open while he undressed, and the moment he flung himself into bed he fell asleep.

He would have sworn that he had not been asleep five minutes when he was dragged back to wakefulness by a knocking at the door. He listened for a moment.

"Who is it?"

"It's the maid. Open. I have something to say to you."

Cursing, Ashenden turned on his light, ran a hand through his thinning and rumpled hair (for like Julius Cæsar he disliked exposing an unbecoming baldness) and unlocked and opened the door. Outside it stood a tousled Swiss maid. She wore no apron and looked as though she had thrown on her clothes in a hurry.

"The old English lady, the governess of the Egyptian princesses, is dying and she wants to see you."

"Me?" said Ashenden. "It's impossible. I don't know her. She was all right this evening."

He was confused and spoke his thoughts as they came to him.

"She asks for you. The doctor says, will you come. She cannot last much longer."

"It must be a mistake. She can't want me."

"She said your name and the number of your room. She says quick, quick."

Ashenden shrugged his shoulders. He went back into his room to put on slippers and a dressing-gown, and as an after-thought dropped a small revolver into his pocket. Ashenden believed much more in his acuteness than in a firearm, which is apt to go off at the wrong time and make a noise, but there are moments when it gives you confidence to feel your fingers round its butt, and this sudden summons seemed to him exceedingly mysterious. It was ridiculous to suppose that those two cordial stout Egyptian gentlemen were laying some sort of trap for him, but in the work upon which Ashenden was engaged the dullness of routine was apt now and again to slip quite shamelessly into the melodrama of the sixties. Just as passion will make use brazenly of the hackneyed phrase, so will chance show itself insensitive to the triteness of the literary convention.

Miss King's room was two floors higher than Ashenden's, and as he accompanied the chamber-maid along the corridor and up the stairs he asked her what was the matter with the old governess. She was flurried and stupid.

"I think she has had a stroke. I don't know. The night-porter woke me and said Monsieur Bridet wanted me to get up at once."

Monsieur Bridet was the assistant-manager.

"What is the time?" asked Ashenden.

"It must be three o'clock."

They arrived at Miss King's door and the maid knocked. It was opened by Monsieur Bridet. He had evidently been roused from his sleep; he wore slippers on his bare feet, grey trousers and a frock-coat over his pyjamas. He looked absurd. His hair as a rule plastered neatly on his head stood on end. He was extremely apologetic.

"A thousand excuses for disturbing you, Monsieur Ashenden, but she kept asking for you and the doctor said you should be sent for."

"It doesn't matter at all."

Ashenden walked in. It was a small back-room and all the lights were on. The windows were closed and the curtains drawn. It was intensely hot. The doctor, a bearded, grizzled Swiss, was standing at the bedside. Monsieur Bridet, notwithstanding his costume and his evident harassment, found in himself the presence of mind to remain the attentive manager, and with ceremony effected the proper introduction.

"This is Mr. Ashenden, for whom Miss King has been asking. Dr. Arbos of the Faculty of Medicine of Geneva."

Without a word the doctor pointed to the bed. On it lay Miss King. It gave Ashenden a shock to look at her. She wore a large white cotton nightcap (on entering Ashenden had noticed the brown wig on a stand on the dressing-table) tied under the chin and a white, voluminous nightdress that came high up in the neck. Nightcap and nightdress belonged to a past age and reminded you of Cruikshank's illustrations to the novels of Charles Dickens. Her face was greasy still with the cream she had used before going to bed to remove her make-up, but she had removed it summarily and there were streaks of black on her eyebrows and of red on her cheeks. She looked very small, lying in the bed, no larger than a child, and immensely old.

"She must be well over eighty," thought Ashenden.

She did not look human, but like a doll, the caricature of an old, old witch that an ironic toymaker had amused himself with modelling. She lay perfectly still on her back, the tiny little body hardly marked under the flatness of the blanket, her face even smaller than usual because she had removed her teeth; and you would have thought she was dead but for the black eyes, strangely large in the shrunken mask, that stared unblinkingly. Ashenden thought their expression changed when she saw him.

"Well, Miss King, I'm sorry to see you like this," he said with forced cheerfulness.

"She cannot speak," said the doctor. "She had another little stroke when the maid went to fetch you. I have just given her an injection. She may partly recover the use of her tongue in a little while. She has something to say to you."

"I will gladly wait," said Ashenden.

He fancied that in those dark eyes he saw a look of relief. For a moment or two the four of them stood round the bed and stared at the dying woman.

"Well, if there is nothing I can do, I may just as well go back to bed," said Monsieur Bridet then.

"*Allez, mon ami*," said the doctor. "You can do nothing."

Monsieur Bridet turned to Ashenden.

"May I have a word with you?" he asked.

"Certainly."

The doctor noticed a sudden fear in Miss King's eyes.

"Do not be alarmed," he said kindly. "Monsieur Ashenden is not going. He will stay as long as you wish."

The assistant-manager took Ashenden to the door and partly closed it so that those within should not hear his undertones.

"I can count on your discretion, Monsieur Ashenden, can I not? It is a very disagreeable thing to have anyone die in a hotel. The other guests do not like it and we must do all we can to prevent their knowing. I shall have the body removed the first possible moment and I shall be extremely obliged if you will not say that there has been a death."

"You can have every confidence in me," said Ashenden.

"It is very unfortunate that the manager should be away for the night. I am afraid he will be exceedingly displeased. Of course if it had been possible I would have sent for an ambulance and had her taken to the hospital, but the doctor said she might die before we got her downstairs and absolutely refused to let me. It is not my fault if she dies in the hotel."

"Death so often chooses its moments without consideration," murmured Ashenden.

"After all she is an old woman, she should have died years ago. What did this Egyptian prince want to have a governess of that age for? He ought to have sent her back to her own country. These Orientals, they are always giving trouble."

"Where is the prince now?" asked Ashenden. "She has been in his service for many years. Ought you not to wake him?"

"He is not in the hotel. He went out with his secretary. He may be playing baccarat. I do not know. Anyhow I cannot send all over Geneva to find him."

"And the princesses?"

"They have not come in. They seldom return to the hotel till dawn. They are mad about dancing. I do not know where they are; in any case they would not thank me for dragging them away from their diversions because their governess has had a stroke. I know what they are. The night-porter will tell them when they arrive and then they can please themselves. She does not want them. When the night-porter fetched me and I went into her room I asked where His Highness was and she cried with all her strength: no, no."

"She could talk then?"

"Yes, after a fashion, but the thing that surprised me was that she spoke in English. She always insisted on talking French. You know, she hated the English."

"What did she want with me?"

"That I cannot tell you. She said she had something that she must say to you at once. It is funny, she knew the number of your room. At first when she asked for you I would not let them send. I cannot have my clients disturbed in the middle of the night because a crazy old woman asks for them. You have the right to your sleep, I imagine. But when the doctor came he insisted. She gave us no peace and when I said she must wait till morning she cried."

Ashenden looked at the assistant-manager. He seemed to find nothing at all touching in the scene he related.

"The doctor asked who you were and when I told him he said that perhaps she wished to see you because you were a compatriot."

"Perhaps," said Ashenden dryly.

"Well, I shall try to get a little sleep. I shall give the night-porter orders to wake me when everything is over. Fortunately the nights are long now and if everything goes well we may be able to get the body away before it is light."

Ashenden went back into the room and immediately the dark eyes of the dying woman fixed upon him. He felt that it was incumbent upon him to say something, but as he spoke he reflected on the foolish way in which one speaks to the sick.

"I'm afraid you're feeling very ill, Miss King."

It seemed to him that a flash of anger crossed her eyes and Ashenden could not but imagine that she was exasperated by his futile words.

"You do not mind waiting?" asked the doctor.

"Of course not."

It appeared that the night-porter had been roused by the ringing of the telephone from Miss King's room, but on listening could get no one to speak. The bell continued to ring, so he went upstairs and knocked at the door. He entered with his pass-key and found Miss King lying on the floor. The telephone had fallen too. It looked as though, feeling ill, she had taken off the receiver to call for help and then collapsed. The night-porter hurried to fetch the assistant-manager and together they had lifted her back into bed. Then the maid was wakened and the doctor sent for.

It gave Ashenden a queer feeling to listen to the doctor giving him these facts in Miss King's hearing. He spoke as though she could not understand his French. He spoke as though she were already dead.

Then the doctor said: .

"Well, there is really nothing more that I can do. It is useless for me to stay. I can be rung up if there is any change."

Ashenden, knowing that Miss King might remain in that condition for hours, shrugged his shoulders.

"Very well."

The doctor patted her raddled cheek as though she were a child.

"You must try to sleep. I will come back in the morning."

He packed up the despatch-case in which he had his medical appliances, washed his hands and shuffled himself into a heavy coat. Ashenden accompanied him to the door and as he shook hands the doctor gave his prognosis in a pout of his bearded mouth. Ashenden, coming back, looked at the maid. She sat on the edge of a chair, uneasily, as though in the presence of death she feared to presume. Her broad, ugly face was bloated with fatigue.

"There's no use in your staying up," Ashenden said to her. "Why don't you go to bed?"

"*Monsieur* wouldn't like to remain here alone. Somebody must stay with him."

"But good heavens, why? You have your day's work to do to-morrow."

"In any case I have to get up at five."

"Then try to get a little sleep now. You can give me a look in when you get up. *Allez.*"

She rose heavily to her feet.

"As the gentleman wishes. But I will stay very willingly."

Ashenden smiled and shook his head.

"*Bonsoir, ma pauvre mademoiselle,*" said the maid.

She went out and Ashenden was left alone. He sat by the bedside and again his eyes met Miss King's. It was embarrassing to encounter that unshrinking stare.

"Don't worry yourself, Miss King. You've had a slight stroke. I'm sure your speech will come back to you in a minute."

He felt certain then that he saw in those dark eyes a desperate effort to speak. He could not be mistaken. The mind was shaken by desire, but the paralysed body was incapable of obedience.

For her disappointment expressed itself quite plainly, tears came to her eyes and ran down her cheeks. Ashenden took out his handkerchief and dried them.

"Don't distress yourself, Miss King. Have a little patience and I'm sure you'll be able to say anything you want."

He did not know if it was his fancy that he read in her eyes now the despairing thought that she had not the time to wait. Perhaps it was only that he ascribed to her the notions that came to himself. On the dressing-table were the governess's poor little toilet things, silver-backed embossed brushes and a silver mirror, in a corner stood a shabby black trunk and on the top of the wardrobe a large hat-box in shiny leather. It all looked poor and mean in that trim hotel room, with its suite in highly varnished rose-wood. The glare was intolerable.

"Wouldn't you be more comfortable if I turned out some of the lights?" asked Ashenden.

He put out all the lamps but the one by the bedside and then sat down again. He had a longing to smoke. Once more his eyes were held by those other eyes in which was all that remained alive of that old, old woman. He felt certain that she had something that she wanted urgently to say to him. But what was it? What was it? Perhaps she had asked him only because, feeling death near, she had had a sudden yearning, she the exile of so many years, to die with someone of her own people, so long forgotten, by her side. That was what the doctor thought. But why should she have sent for him? There were other English people in the hotel. There was an old pair, a retired Indian Civilian and his wife, to whom it seemed more natural that she should turn. No one could be more of a stranger to her than Ashenden.

"Have you got something to say to me, Miss King?"

He tried to read an answer in her eyes. They continued to stare at him meaningly, but what the meaning was he had no notion.

"Don't be afraid I shall go. I will stay as long as you want me."

Nothing, nothing. The black eyes, and as he looked at them they seemed to glow mysteriously as though there were fire behind them, the eyes continued to hold him with that insistent stare. Then Ashenden asked himself if she had sent for him because she knew that he was a British agent. Was it possible that at that last moment she had had some unexpected revulsion of feeling from everything that had signified to her for so many years? Perhaps at the moment of death a love for her country, a love

that had been dead for half a century, awakened again in her—
("I'm silly to fancy these idiotic things," thought Ashenden,
"it's cheap and tawdry fiction.")—and she had been seized with
a desire to do something for what was after all her own. No one
was quite himself just then and patriotism (in peace-time an
attitude best left to politicians, publicists and fools, but in the
dark days of war an emotion that can wring the heart-strings),
patriotism made one do odd things. It was curious that she had
been unwilling to see the prince and his daughters. Did she on a
sudden hate them? Did she feel herself a traitor on their account
and now at the last hour wish to make amends. ("It's all very
improbable, she's just a silly old maid who ought to have died
years ago.") But you couldn't ignore the improbable. Ashenden,
his common sense protesting, became strangely convinced that
she had some secret that she wished to impart to him. She had
sent for him knowing who he was because he could make use of
it. She was dying and feared nothing. But was it really important?
Ashenden leaned forward trying more eagerly to read what her
eyes had to say. Perhaps it was only some trivial thing that was
important only in her addled old brain. Ashenden was sick of
the people who saw spies in every inoffensive passer-by and plots
in the most innocent combination of circumstances. It was a
hundred to one that if Miss King recovered her speech she would
tell him something that could be of no use to anybody.

But how much must that old woman know! With her sharp eyes
and sharp ears she must have had the chance to discover matters
that were closely hidden from persons that seemed less insignificant.
Ashenden thought again how he had the impression that something of real consequence was being prepared round about him.
It was curious that Holzminden should have come to the hotel
that day; and why had Prince Ali and the pasha, those wild
gamblers, wasted an evening in playing contract-bridge with him?
It might be that some new plan was in question, it might be that
the very greatest affairs were afoot, and perhaps what the old
woman had to say might make all the difference in the world.
It might mean defeat or victory. It might mean anything. And
there she lay powerless to speak. For a long time Ashenden stared
at her in silence.

"Has it got anything to do with the war, Miss King?" he said
on a sudden, loudly.

Something passed through her eyes and a tremor shot across

her little old face. It was a distinct movement. Something strange and horrible was happening and Ashenden held his breath. The tiny frail body was suddenly convulsed and that old woman, as though by a final desperate effort of will, raised herself up in the bed. Ashenden sprang forward to support her.

"England," she said, just that one word, in a harsh cracked voice, and fell back in his arms.

When he laid her down on the pillow, he saw that she was dead.

❖

The Hairless Mexican

"Do you like macaroni?" said R.

"What do you mean by macaroni?" answered Ashenden. "It is like asking me if I like poetry. I like Keats and Wordsworth and Verlaine and Goethe. When you say macaroni, do you mean *spaghetti, tagliatelli, vermicelli, fettucini, tufali, farfalli*, or just macaroni?"

"Macaroni," replied R., a man of few words.

"I like all simple things, boiled eggs, oysters and caviare, *truite au bleu*, grilled salmon, roast lamb (the saddle by preference), cold grouse, treacle tart and rice pudding. But of all simple things the only one I can eat day in and day out, not only without disgust but with the eagerness of an appetite unimpaired by excess, is macaroni."

"I am glad of that because I want you to go down to Italy."

Ashenden had come from Geneva to meet R. at Lyons and having got there before him had spent the afternoon wandering about the dull, busy and prosaic streets of that thriving city. They were sitting now in a restaurant on the *place* to which Ashenden had taken R. on his arrival because it was reputed to give you the best food in that part of France. But since in so crowded a resort (for the Lyonese like a good dinner) you never knew what inquisitive ears were pricked up to catch any useful piece of information that might fall from your lips, they had contented themselves with talking of indifferent things. They had reached the end of an admirable repast.

"Have another glass of brandy?" said R.

"No, thank you," answered Ashenden, who was of an abstemious turn.

"One should do what one can to mitigate the rigours of war," remarked R. as he took the bottle and poured out a glass for himself and another for Ashenden.

Ashenden, thinking it would be affectation to protest, let the gesture pass, but felt bound to remonstrate with his chief on the unseemly manner in which he held the bottle.

"In my youth I was always taught that you should take a woman by the waist and a bottle by the neck," he murmured.

"I am glad you told me. I shall continue to hold a bottle by the waist and give women a wide berth."

Ashenden did not know what to reply to this and so remained silent. He sipped his brandy and R. called for his bill. It was true that he was an important person, with power to make or mar quite a large number of his fellows, and his opinions were listened to by those who held in their hands the fate of empires; but he could never face the business of tipping a waiter without an embarrassment that was obvious in his demeanour. He was tortured by the fear of making a fool of himself by giving too much or of exciting the waiter's icy scorn by giving too little. When the bill came he passed some hundred-franc notes over to Ashenden and said:

"Pay him, will you? I can never understand French figures."

The groom brought them their hats and coats.

"Would you like to go back to the hotel?" asked Ashenden.

"We might as well."

It was early in the year, but the weather had suddenly turned warm, and they walked with their coats over their arms. Ashenden knowing that R. liked a sitting-room had engaged one for him and to this, when they reached the hotel, they went. The hotel was old-fashioned and the sitting-room was vast. It was furnished with a heavy mahogany suite upholstered in green velvet and the chairs were set primly round a large table. On the walls, covered with a dingy paper, were large steel engravings of the battles of Napoleon, and from the ceiling hung an enormous chandelier once used for gas, but now fitted with electric bulbs. It flooded the cheerless room with a cold, hard light.

"This is very nice," said R., as they went in.

"Not exactly cosy," suggested Ashenden.

"No, but it looks as though it were the best room in the place. It all looks very good to me."

He drew one of the green velvet chairs away from the table and, sitting down, lit a cigar. He loosened his belt and unbuttoned his tunic.

"I always thought I liked a cheroot better than anything," he said, "but since the war I've taken quite a fancy to Havanas. Oh well, I suppose it can't last for ever." The corners of his mouth flickered with the beginning of a smile. "It's an ill wind that blows nobody any good."

Ashenden took two chairs, one to sit on and one for his feet, and when R. saw him he said: "That's not a bad idea," and swinging another chair out from the table with a sigh of relief put his boots on it.

"What room is that next door?" he asked.

"That's your bedroom."

"And on the other side?"

"A banqueting hall."

R. got up and strolled slowly about the room and when he passed the windows, as though in idle curiosity, peeped through the heavy rep curtains that covered them, and then returning to his chair once more comfortably put his feet up.

"It's just as well not to take any more risk than one need," he said.

He looked at Ashenden reflectively. There was a slight smile on his thin lips, but the pale eyes, too closely set together, remained cold and steely. R.'s stare would have been embarrassing if Ashenden had not been used to it. He knew that R. was considering how he would broach the subject that he had in mind. The silence must have lasted for two or three minutes.

"I'm expecting a fellow to come and see me to-night," he said at last. "His train gets in about ten." He gave his wrist-watch a glance. "He's known as the Hairless Mexican."

"Why?"

"Because he's hairless and because he's a Mexican."

"The explanation seems perfectly satisfactory," said Ashenden.

"He'll tell you all about himself. He talks nineteen to the dozen. He was on his uppers when I came across him. It appears that he was mixed up in some revolution in Mexico and had to get out with nothing but the clothes he stood up in. They were rather the worse for wear when I found him. If you want to please him you call him General. He claims to have been a general in Huerta's army, at least I think it was Huerta; anyhow he says that if things had gone right he would be Minister of War now and no end of a big bug. I've found him very useful. Not a bad chap. The only thing I really have against him is that he will use scent."

"And where do I come in?" asked Ashenden.

"He's going down to Italy. I've got rather a ticklish job for him to do and I want you to stand by. I'm not keen on trusting him with a lot of money. He's a gambler and he's a bit too fond of the

G*

girls. I suppose you came from Geneva on your Ashenden passport?"

"Yes."

"I've got another for you, a diplomatic one, by the way, in the name of Somerville with visas for France and Italy. I think you and he had better travel together. He's an amusing cove when he gets going, and I think you ought to know one another."

"What is the job?"

"I haven't yet quite made up my mind how much it's desirable for you to know about it."

Ashenden did not reply. They eyed one another in a detached manner, as though they were strangers who sat together in a railway carriage and each wondered who and what the other was.

"In your place I'd leave the General to do most of the talking. I wouldn't tell him more about yourself than you find absolutely necessary. He won't ask you any questions, I can promise you that, I think he's by way of being a gentleman after his own fashion."

"By the way, what is his real name?"

"I always call him Manuel, I don't know that he likes it very much, his name is Manuel Carmona."

"I gather by what you have not said that he's an unmitigated scoundrel."

R. smiled with his pale blue eyes.

"I don't know that I'd go quite so far as that. He hasn't had the advantages of a public-school education. His ideas of playing the game are not quite the same as yours or mine. I don't know that I'd leave a gold cigarette-case about when he was in the neighbourhood, but if he lost money to you at poker and had pinched your cigarette-case he would immediately pawn it to pay you. If he had half a chance he'd seduce your wife, but if you were up against it he'd share his last crust with you. The tears will run down his face when he hears Gounod's 'Ave Maria' on the gramophone, but if you insult his dignity he'll shoot you like a dog. It appears that in Mexico it's an insult to get between a man and his drink and he told me himself that once when a Dutchman who didn't know passed between him and the bar he whipped out his revolver and shot him dead."

"Did nothing happen to him?"

"No, it appears that he belongs to one of the best families. The matter was hushed up and it was announced in the papers that the Dutchman had committed suicide. He did practically. I don't believe the Hairless Mexican has a great respect for human life."

Ashenden, who had been looking intently at R., started a little and he watched more carefully than ever his chief's tired, lined and yellow face. He knew that he did not make this remark for nothing.

"Of course a lot of nonsense is talked about the value of human life. You might just as well say that the counters you use at poker have an intrinsic value, their value; is what you like to make it; for a general giving battle, men are merely counters and he's a fool if he allows himself for sentimental reasons to look upon them as human beings."

"But, you see, they're counters that feel and think and if they believe they're being squandered they are quite capable of refusing to be used any more."

"Anyhow, that's neither here nor there. We've had information that a man called Constantine Andreadi is on his way from Constantinople with certain documents that we want to get hold of. He's a Greek. He's an agent of Enver Pasha and Enver has great confidence in him. He's given him verbal messages that are too secret and too important to be put on paper. He's sailing from the Piræus, on a boat called the *Ithaca*, and will land at Brindisi on his way to Rome. He's to deliver his despatches at the German Embassy and impart what he has to say personally to the ambassador."

"I see."

At this time Italy was still neutral; the Central Powers were straining every nerve to keep her so; the Allies were doing what they could to induce her to declare war on their side.

"We don't want to get into any trouble with the Italian authorities, it might be fatal, but we've got to prevent Andreadi from getting to Rome."

"At any cost?" asked Ashenden.

"Money's no object," answered R., his lips twisting into a sardonic smile.

"What do you propose to do?"

"I don't think you need bother your head about that."

"I have a fertile imagination," said Ashenden.

"I want you to go down to Naples with the Hairless Mexican. He's very keen on getting back to Cuba. It appears that his friends are organising a show and he wants to be as near at hand as possible so that he can hop over to Mexico when things are ripe. He needs cash. I've brought money down with me, in American dollars, and I shall give it to you to-night. You'd better carry it on your person."

"Is it much?"

"It's a good deal, but I thought it would be easier for you if it wasn't bulky, so I've got it in thousand-dollar notes. You will give the Hairless Mexican the notes in return for the documents that Andreadi is bringing."

A question sprang to Ashenden's lips, but he did not ask it. He asked another instead.

"Does this fellow understand what he has to do?"

"Perfectly."

There was a knock at the door. It opened and the Hairless Mexican stood before them.

"I have arrived. Good evening, Colonel. I am enchanted to see you."

R. got up.

"Had a nice journey, Manuel? This is Mr. Somerville, who's going to Naples with you, General Carmona."

"Pleased to meet you, sir."

He shook Ashenden's hand with such force that he winced.

"Your hands are like iron, General," he murmured.

The Mexican gave them a glance.

"I had them manicured this morning. I do not think they were very well done. I like my nails much more highly polished."

They were cut to a point, stained bright red, and to Ashenden's mind shone like mirrors. Though it was not cold the General wore a fur coat with an astrakhan collar and with his every movement a wave of perfume was wafted to your nose.

"Take off your coat, General, and have a cigar," said R.

The Hairless Mexican was a tall man, and though thinnish gave you the impression of being very powerful; he was smartly dressed in a blue serge suit, with a silk handkerchief neatly tucked in the breast pocket of his coat, and he wore a gold bracelet on his wrist. His features were good, but a little larger than life-size, and his eyes were brown and lustrous. He was quite hairless. His yellow skin had the smoothness of a woman's and he had no eyebrows nor eyelashes; he wore a pale brown wig, rather long, and the locks were arranged in artistic disorder. This and the unwrinkled sallow face, combined with his dandified dress, gave him an appearance that was at first glance a trifle horrifying. He was repulsive and ridiculous, but you could not take your eyes from him. There was a sinister fascination in his strangeness.

He sat down and hitched up his trousers so that they should not bag at the knee.

"Well, Manuel, have you been breaking any hearts to-day?" said R. with his sardonic joviality.

The General turned to Ashenden.

"Our good friend, the Colonel, envies me my successes with the fair sex. I tell him he can have just as many as I if he will only listen to me. Confidence, that is all you need. If you never fear a rebuff you will never have one."

"Nonsense, Manuel, one has to have your way with the girls. There's something about you that they can't resist."

The Hairless Mexican laughed with a self-satisfaction that he did not try to disguise. He spoke English very well, with a Spanish accent, but with an American intonation.

"But since you ask me, Colonel, I don't mind telling you that I got into conversation on the train with a little woman who was coming to Lyons to see her mother-in-law. She was not very young and she was thinner than I like a woman to be, but she was possible, and she helped me to pass an agreeable hour."

"Well, let's get to business," said R.

"I am at your service, Colonel." He gave Ashenden a glance. "Is Mr. Somerville a military man?"

"No," said R., "he's an author."

"It takes all sorts to make a world, as you say. I am happy to make your acquaintance, Mr. Somerville. I can tell you many stories that will interest you; I am sure that we shall get on well together. You have a sympathetic air. I am very sensitive to that. To tell you the truth I am nothing but a bundle of nerves and if I am with a person who is antipathetic to me I go all to pieces."

"I hope we shall have a pleasant journey," said Ashenden.

"When does our friend arrive at Brindisi?" asked the Mexican, turning to R.

"He sails from the Piræus in the *Ithaca* on the fourteenth. It's probably some old tub, but you'd better get down to Brindisi in good time."

"I agree with you."

R. got up and with his hands in his pockets sat on the edge of the table. In his rather shabby uniform, his tunic unbuttoned, he looked a slovenly creature beside the neat and well-dressed Mexican.

"Mr. Somerville knows practically nothing of the errand on which you are going and I do not desire you to tell him anything. I think you had much better keep your own counsel. He is instructed to give you the funds you need for your work, but your actions are your own affair. If you need his advice of course you can ask for it."

"I seldom ask other people's advice and never take it."

"And should you make a mess of things I trust you to keep Mr. Somerville out of it. He must on no account be compromised."

"I am a man of honour, Colonel," answered the Hairless Mexican with dignity, "and I would sooner let myself be cut in a thousand pieces than betray my friends."

"That is what I have already told Mr. Somerville. On the other hand, if everything pans out O.K. Mr. Somerville is instructed to give you the sum we agreed on in return for the papers I spoke to you about. In what manner you get them is no business of his."

"That goes without saying. There is only one thing I wish to make quite plain; Mr. Somerville understands of course that I have not accepted the mission with which you have entrusted me on account of the money?"

"Quite," replied R. gravely, looking him straight in the eyes.

"I am with the Allies body and soul, I cannot forgive the Germans for outraging the neutrality of Belgium, and if I accept the money that you have offered me it is because I am first and foremost a patriot. I can trust Mr. Somerville implicitly, I suppose?"

R. nodded. The Mexican turned to Ashenden.

"An expedition is being arranged to free my unhappy country from the tyrants that exploit and ruin it and every penny that I receive will go on guns and cartridges. For myself I have no need of money; I am a soldier and I can live on a crust and a few olives. There are only three occupations that befit a gentleman, war, cards and women; it costs nothing to sling a rifle over your shoulder and take to the mountains—and that is real warfare, not this manoeuvring of battalions and firing of great guns—women love me for myself, and I generally win at cards."

Ashenden found the flamboyance of this strange creature, with his scented handkerchief and his gold bracelet, very much to his taste. This was far from being just the man in the street (whose tyranny we rail at but in the end submit to) and to the amateur of the baroque in human nature he was a rarity to be considered with delight. He was a purple patch on two legs. Notwithstanding his wig and his hairless big face, he had undoubtedly an air; he was absurd, but he did not give you the impression that he was a man to be trifled with. His self-complacency was magnificent.

"Where is your kit, Manuel?" asked R.

It was possible that a frown for an instant darkened the Mexican's brow at the abrupt question that seemed a little contemptuously to brush to one side his eloquent statement, but he gave no other sign of displeasure. Ashenden suspected that he thought the Colonel a barbarian insensitive to the finer emotions.

"I left it at the station."

"Mr. Somerville has a diplomatic passport so that he can get it through with his own things at the frontier without examination if you like."

"I have very little, a few suits and some linen, but perhaps it would be as well if Mr. Somerville would take charge of it. I bought half a dozen suits of silk pyjamas before I left Paris."

"And what about you?" asked R., turning to Ashenden.

"I've only got one bag. It's in my room."

"You'd better have it taken to the station while there's someone about. Your train goes at one ten."

"Oh?"

This was the first Ashenden had heard that they were to start that night.

"I think you'd better get down to Naples as soon as possible."

"Very well."

R. got up.

"I'm going to bed. I don't know what you fellows want to do."

"I shall take a walk about Lyons," said the Hairless Mexican. "I am interested in life. Lend me a hundred francs, Colonel, will you? I have no change on me."

R. took out his pocket-book and gave the General the note he asked for. Then to Ashenden:

"What are you going to do? Wait here?"

"No," said Ashenden, "I shall go to the station and read."

"You'd both of you better have a whisky and soda before you go, hadn't you? What about it, Manuel?"

"It is very kind of you, but I never drink anything but champagne and brandy."

"Mixed?" asked R. dryly.

"Not necessarily," returned the other with gravity.

R. ordered brandy and soda and when it came, whereas he and Ashenden helped themselves to both, the Hairless Mexican poured himself out three parts of a tumbler of neat brandy and swallowed it in two noisy gulps. He rose to his feet and put on his coat with the astrakhan collar, seized in one hand his bold black hat and, with the gesture of a romantic actor giving up the girl he loves to one more worthy of her, held out the other to R.

"Well, Colonel, I will bid you good-night and pleasant dreams. I do not expect that we shall meet again so soon."

"Don't make a hash of things, Manuel, and if you do, keep your mouth shut."

"They tell me that in one of your colleges where the sons of gentlemen are trained to become naval officers it is written in letters of gold: There is no such word as impossible in the British Navy. I do not know the meaning of the word failure."

"It has a good many synonyms," retorted R.

"I will meet you at the station, Mr. Somerville," said the Hairless Mexican, and with a flourish left them.

R. looked at Ashenden with that little smile of his that always made his face look so dangerously shrewd.

"Well, what d'you think of him?"

"You've got me beat," said Ashenden. "Is he a mountebank? He seems as vain as a peacock. And with that frightful appearance can he really be the lady's man he pretends? What makes you think you can trust him?"

R. gave a low chuckle and he washed his thin, old hands with imaginary soap.

"I thought you'd like him. He's quite a character, isn't he? I think we can trust him." R.'s eyes suddenly grew opaque. "I don't believe it would pay him to double-cross us." He paused for a moment. "Anyhow, we've got to risk it. I'll give you the tickets and the money and then you can take yourself off; I'm all in and I want to go to bed."

Ten minutes later Ashenden set out for the station with his bag on a porter's shoulder.

Having nearly two hours to wait he made himself comfortable in the waiting-room. The light was good and he read a novel.

When the time drew near for the arrival of the train from Paris that was to take them direct to Rome and the Hairless Mexican did not appear, Ashenden, beginning to grow a trifle anxious, went out on the platform to look for him. Ashenden suffered from that distressing malady known as train fever: an hour before his train was due he began to have apprehensions lest he should miss it; he was impatient with the porters who would never bring his luggage down from his room in time and he could not understand why the hotel bus cut it so fine; a block in the street would drive him to frenzy and the languid movements of the station porters infuriate him. The whole world seemed in a horrid plot to delay him; people got in his way as he passed through the barriers; others, a long string of them, were at the ticket-office getting tickets for other trains than his and they counted their change with exasperating care; his luggage took an interminable time to register; and then if he was travelling with friends they would go to buy newspapers, or would take a walk along the platform, and he was certain they would be left behind, they would stop to talk to a casual stranger or suddenly be seized with a desire to telephone and disappear at a run. In fact the universe conspired to make him miss every train he wanted to take and he was not happy unless he was settled in his corner, his things on the rack above him, with a good half-hour to spare. Sometimes by arriving at the station too soon he had caught an earlier train than the one he had meant to, but that was nerve-racking and caused him all the anguish of very nearly missing it.

The Rome express was signalled and there was no sign of the Hairless Mexican; it came in and he was not to be seen. Ashenden became more and more harassed. He walked quickly up and down the platform, looked in all the waiting-rooms, went to the *consigne* where the luggage was left; he could not find him. There were no sleeping-cars, but a number of people got out and he took two seats in a first-class carriage. He stood by the door, looking up and down the platform and up at the clock; it was useless to go if his travelling companion did not turn up, and Ashenden made up his mind to take his things out of the carriage as the porter cried *en voiture*; but, by George! he would give the brute hell when he found him. There were three minutes more, then two minutes, then one; at that late hour there were few persons about and all who were travelling had taken their seats. Then he saw the Hairless Mexican, followed by two porters with his luggage and accompanied by a man in a bowler-hat, walk leisurely on to the platform. He caught sight of Ashenden and waved to him.

"Ah, my dear fellow, there you are, I wondered what had become of you."

"Good God, man, hurry up or we shall miss the train."

"I never miss a train. Have you got good seats? The *chef de gare* has gone for the night; this is his assistant."

The man in the bowler-hat took it off when Ashenden nodded to him.

"But this is an ordinary carriage. I am afraid I could not travel in that." He turned to the stationmaster's assistant with an affable smile. "You must do better for me than that, *mon cher*."

"*Certainement, mon général*, I will put you into a *salon-lit*. Of course."

The assistant stationmaster led them along the train and opened the door of an empty compartment where there were two beds. The Mexican eyed it with satisfaction and watched the porters arrange the luggage.

"That will do very well. I am much obliged to you." He held out his hand to the man in the bowler-hat. "I shall not forget you and next time I see the Minister I will tell him with what civility you have treated me."

"You are too good, General. I shall be very grateful."

A whistle was blown and the train started.

"This is better than an ordinary first-class carriage, I think, Mr. Somerville," said the Mexican. "A good traveller should learn how to make the best of things."

But Ashenden was still extremely cross.

"I don't know why the devil you wanted to cut it so fine. We should have looked a pair of damned fools if we'd missed the train."

"My dear fellow, there was never the smallest chance of that. When I arrived I told the stationmaster that I was General Carmona, Commander-in-Chief of the Mexican Army, and that I had to stop off in Lyons for a few hours to hold a conference with the British Field-Marshal. I asked him to hold the train for me if I was delayed and suggested that my government might see its way to conferring an order on him. I have been to Lyons before, I like the girls here; they have not the *chic* of the Parisians, but they have something, there is no denying that they have

something. Will you have a mouthful of brandy before you go
to sleep?"

"No, thank you," said Ashenden morosely.

"I always drink a glass before going to bed, it settles the nerves."

He looked in his suit-case and without difficulty found a bottle.
He put it to his lips and had a long drink, wiped his mouth with
the back of his hand and lit a cigarette. Then he took off his boots
and lay down. Ashenden dimmed the light.

"I have never yet made up my mind," said the Hairless Mexican
reflectively, "whether it is pleasanter to go to sleep with the kisses
of a beautiful woman on your mouth or with a cigarette between
your lips. Have you ever been to Mexico? I will tell you about
Mexico to-morrow. Good-night."

Soon Ashenden heard from his steady breathing that he was
asleep and in a little while himself dozed off. Presently he woke.
The Mexican, deep in slumber, lay motionless; he had taken off
his fur coat and was using it as a blanket; he still wore his wig.
Suddenly there was a jolt and the train with a noisy grinding
of brakes stopped; in the twinkling of an eye, before Ashenden
could realize that anything had happened, the Mexican was on
his feet with his hand to his hip.

"What is it?" he cried.

"Nothing. Probably only a signal against us."

The Mexican sat down heavily on his bed. Ashenden turned on
the light.

"You wake quickly for such a sound sleeper," he said.

"You have to in my profession."

Ashenden would have liked to ask him whether this was murder,
conspiracy or commanding armies, but was not sure that it would
be discreet. The General opened his bag and took out the bottle.

"Will you have a nip?" he asked. "There is nothing like it
when you wake suddenly in the night."

When Ashenden refused he put the bottle once more to his
lips and poured a considerable quantity of liquor down his throat.
He sighed and lit a cigarette. Although Ashenden had seen him
now drink nearly a bottle of brandy, and it was probable that he
had had a good deal more when he was going about the town, he
was certainly quite sober. Neither in his manner nor in his speech
was there any indication that he had drunk during the evening
anything but lemonade.

The train started and Ashenden again fell asleep. When he

awoke it was morning and turning round lazily he saw that the Mexican was awake too. He was smoking a cigarette. The floor by his side was strewn with burnt-out butts and the air was thick and grey. He had begged Ashenden not to insist on opening a window, for he said the night air was dangerous.

"I did not get up, because I was afraid of waking you. Will you do your toilet first or shall I?"

"I'm in no hurry," said Ashenden.

"I am an old campaigner, it will not take me long. Do you wash your teeth every day?"

"Yes," said Ashenden.

"So do I. It is a habit I learned in New York. I always think that a fine set of teeth are an adornment to a man."

There was a wash-basin in the compartment and the General scrubbed his teeth, with gurglings and garglings, energetically. Then he got a bottle of eau-de-Cologne from his bag, poured some of it on a towel and rubbed it over his face and hands. He took a comb and carefully arranged his wig; either it had not moved in the night or else he had set it straight before Ashenden awoke. He got another bottle out of his bag, with a spray attached to it, and squeezing a bulb covered his shirt and coat with a fine cloud of scent, did the same to his handkerchief, and then with a beaming face, like a man who has done his duty by the world and is well pleased, turned to Ashenden and said:

"Now I am ready to brave the day. I will leave my things for you, you need not be afraid of the eau-de-Cologne, it is the best you can get in Paris."

"Thank you very much," said Ashenden. "All I want is soap and water."

"Water? I never use water except when I have a bath. Nothing can be worse for the skin."

When they approached the frontier, Ashenden, remembering the General's instructive gesture when he was suddenly awakened in the night, said to him:

"If you've got a revolver on you I think you'd better give it to me. With my diplomatic passport they're not likely to search me, but they might take it into their heads to go through you and we don't want to have any bothers."

"It is hardly a weapon, it is only a toy," returned the Mexican, taking out of his hip-pocket a fully loaded revolver of formidable dimensions. "I do not like parting with it even for an hour, it gives me the feeling that I am not fully dressed. But you are quite right, we do not want to take any risks; I will give you my knife as well. I would always rather use a knife than a revolver; I think it is a more elegant weapon."

"I dare say it is only a matter of habit," answered Ashenden. "Perhaps you are more at home with a knife."

"Anyone can pull a trigger, but it needs a man to use a knife."

To Ashenden it looked as though it were in a single movement that he tore open his waistcoat and from his belt snatched and opened a long knife of murderous aspect. He handed it to Ashenden with a pleased smile on his large, ugly and naked face.

"There's a pretty piece of work for you, Mr. Somerville. I've never seen a better bit of steel in my life, it takes an edge like a razor and it's strong; you can cut a cigarette-paper with it and you can hew down an oak. There is nothing to get out of order and when it is closed it might be the knife a schoolboy uses to cut notches in his desk."

He shut it with a click and Ashenden put it along with the revolver in his pocket.

"Have you anything else?"

"My hands," replied the Mexican with arrogance, "but those I dare say the Custom officials will not make trouble about."

Ashenden remembered the iron grip he had given him when they shook hands and slightly shuddered. They were large and long and smooth; there was not a hair on them or on the wrists, and with the pointed, rosy, manicured nails there was really something sinister about them.

Ashenden and General Carmona went through the formalities at the frontier independently and when they returned to their carriage Ashenden handed back to his companion the revolver and the knife. He sighed.

"Now I feel more comfortable. What do you say to a game of cards?"

"I should like it," said Ashenden.

The Hairless Mexican opened his bag again and from a corner extracted a greasy pack of French cards. He asked Ashenden whether he played écarté and when Ashenden told him that he did not suggested piquet. This was a game that Ashenden was not unfamiliar with, so they settled the stakes and began. Since both were in favour of quick action, they played the game of four hands, doubling the first and last. Ashenden had good enough cards, but the General seemed notwithstanding always to have better. Ashenden kept his eyes open and he was not careless of the possibility that his antagonist might correct the inequalities of chance, but he saw nothing to suggest that everything was not above board. He lost game after game. He was capoted and rubiconed. The score against him mounted up and up till he had lost something like a thousand francs, which at that time was a tidy sum. The General smoked innumerable cigarettes. He made them himself with a twist of the finger, a lick of his tongue and incredible celerity. At last he flung himself against the back of his seat.

"By the way, my friend, does the British Government pay your card losses when you are on a mission?" he asked.

"It certainly doesn't."

"Well, I think you have lost enough. If it went down on your expense account I would have proposed playing till we reached Rome, but you are sympathetic to me. If it is your own money I do not want to win any more of it."

He picked up the cards and put them aside. Ashenden somewhat ruefully took out a number of notes and handed them to the Mexican. He counted them and with his usual neatness put them carefully folded into his pocket-book. Then, leaning forward, he patted Ashenden almost affectionately on the knee.

"I like you, you are modest and unassuming, you have not the arrogance of your countrymen, and I am sure that you will take my advice in the spirit in which it is meant. Do not play piquet with people you don't know."

Ashenden was somewhat mortified and perhaps his face showed it, for the Mexican seized his hand.

"My dear fellow, I have not hurt your feelings? I would not do that for the world. You do not play piquet worse than most piquet players. It is not that. If we were going to be together longer I would teach you how to win at cards. One plays cards to win money and there is no sense in losing."

"I thought it was only in love and war that all things were fair," said Ashenden, with a chuckle.

"Ah, I am glad to see you smile. That is the way to take a loss. I see that you have good humour and good sense. You will go far in life. When I get back to Mexico and am in possession of my estates again you must come and stay with me. I will treat you like a king. You shall ride my best horses, we will go to bullfights together, and if there are girls you fancy you have only to say the word and you shall have them."

He began telling Ashenden of the vast territories, the *haciendas* and the mines in Mexico, of which he had been dispossessed. He told him of the feudal state in which he lived. It did not matter whether what he said was true or not, for those sonorous phrases of his were fruity with the rich-distilled perfumes of romance. He described a spacious life that seemed to belong to another age and his eloquent gestures brought before the mind's eye tawny distances and vast green plantations, great herds of cattle and in the moonlit night the song of the blind singers that melted in the air and the twanging of guitars.

"Everything I lost, everything. In Paris I was driven to earn a pittance by giving Spanish lessons or showing Americans— *Americanos del Norte*, I mean—the night life of the city. I who have flung away a thousand *duros* on a dinner have been forced to beg my bread like a blind Indian. I who have taken pleasure in clasping a diamond bracelet round the wrist of a beautiful woman have been forced to accept a suit of clothes from a hag old enough to be my mother. Patience. Man is born to trouble as the sparks fly upward, but misfortune cannot last for ever. The time is ripe and soon we shall strike our blow."

He took up the greasy pack of cards and set them out in a number of little piles.

"Let us see what the cards say. They never lie. Ah, if I had only had greater faith in them I should have avoided the only action of my life that has weighed heavily on me. My conscience is at ease. I did what any man would do under the circumstances, but I regret that necessity forced upon me an action that I would willingly have avoided."

He looked through the cards, set some of them on one side on a system Ashenden did not understand, shuffled the remainder and once more put them in little piles.

"The cards warned me, I will never deny that, their warning was clear and definite. Love and a dark woman, danger, betrayal and death. It was as plain as the nose on your face. Any fool would have known what it meant and I have been using the cards all my life. There is hardly an action that I make without consulting them. There are no excuses. I was besotted. Ah, you of the Northern races do not know what love means, you do not know how it can prevent you from sleeping, how it can take your appetite for food away so that you dwindle as if from a fever, you do not understand what a frenzy it is so that you are like a madman and you will stick at nothing to satisfy your desire. A man like me is capable of every folly and every crime when he is in love, si, Señor, and of heroism. He can scale mountains higher than Everest and swim seas broader than the Atlantic. He is god, he is devil. Women have been my ruin."

Once more the Hairless Mexican glanced at the cards, took some out of the little piles and left others in. He shuffled them again.

"I have been loved by multitudes of women. I do not say it in vanity. I offer no explanation. It is mere matter of fact. Go to Mexico City and ask them what they know of Manuel Carmona and of his triumphs. Ask them how many women have resisted Manuel Carmona."

Ashenden, frowning a little, watched him reflectively. He wondered whether R., that shrewd fellow who chose his instruments with such a sure instinct, had not this time made a mistake, and he was uneasy. Did the Hairless Mexican really believe that he was irresistible or was he merely a blatant liar? In the course of his manipulations he had thrown out all the cards in the pack but four, and these now lay in front of him face downwards and side by side. He touched them one by one but did not turn them up.

"There is fate," he said, "and no power on earth can change it. I hesitate. This is a moment that ever fills me with apprehension and I have to steel myself to turn over the cards that may tell me that disaster awaits me. I am a brave man, but sometimes I have reached this stage and not had the courage to look at the four vital cards."

Indeed now he eyed the backs of them with an anxiety he did not try to hide.

"What was I saying to you?"

"You were telling me that women found your fascinations irresistible," replied Ashenden dryly.

"Once all the same I found a woman who resisted me. I saw her first in a house, a casa de mujeres in Mexico City, she was going down the stairs as I went up; she was not very beautiful, I had had a hundred more beautiful, but she had something that took my fancy and I told the old woman who kept the house to send her to me. You will know her when you go to Mexico City; they call her La Marqueza. She said that the girl was not an inmate, but came there only from time to time and had left. I told her to have her there next evening and not to let her go till I came. But I was delayed and when I arrived La Marqueza told me that the girl had said she was not used to being kept waiting and had gone. I am a good-natured fellow and I do not mind if women are capricious and teasing, that is part of their charm, so with a laugh I sent her a note of a hundred *duros* and promised that on the following day I would be punctual. But when I went, on the minute, La Marqueza handed me back my hundred *duros* and told me the girl did not fancy me. I laughed at her impertinence. I took off the diamond ring I was wearing and told the old woman to give her that and see whether it would induce her to change her mind. In the morning La Marqueza brought me in return for my ring—a red carnation. I did not know whether to be amused or angry. I am not used to being thwarted in my passions, I never hesitate to spend money (what is it for but to squander on pretty women?), and I told La Marqueza to go to the girl and say that I would give her a thousand *duros* to dine with me that night. Presently she came back with the answer that the girl would come on the condition that I allowed her to go home immediately after dinner. I accepted with a shrug of the shoulders. I did not think she was serious. I thought that she was saying that only to make herself more desired. She came to dinner at my house. Did I say she was not beautiful? She was the most beautiful, the most exquisite creature I had ever met. I was intoxicated. She had charm and she had wit. She had all the *gracia* of the Andalusian. In one word she was adorable. I asked her why she had treated me so casually and she laughed in my face. I laid myself out to be agreeable. I exercised all my skill. I surpassed myself. But when we finished dinner she rose from her seat and bade me good-night. I asked her where she was going. She said I had promised to let her go and she trusted me as a man of honour to keep my word. I expostulated, I reasoned, I raved, I stormed. She held me to my word. All I could induce her to do was to consent to dine with me the following night on the same terms.

"You will think I was a fool, I was the happiest man alive; for seven days I paid her a thousand silver *duros* to dine with me. Every evening I waited for her with my heart in my mouth, as nervous as a *novillero* at his first bull-fight, and every evening she played with me, laughed at me, coquetted with me and drove me frantic. I was madly in love with her. I have never loved anyone so much before or since. I could think of nothing else. I was distracted. I neglected everything. I am a patriot and I love my country. A small band of us had got together and made up our minds that we could no longer put up with the misrule from which we were suffering. All the lucrative posts were given to other people, we were being made to pay taxes as though we were tradesmen, and we were exposed to abominable affronts. We had money and men. Our plans were made and we were ready to strike. I had an infinity of things to do, meetings to go to, ammunition to get, orders to give, I was so besotted over this woman that I could attend to nothing.

"You would have thought that I should be angry with her for making such a fool of me, me who had never known what it was not to gratify my smallest whim; I did not believe that she refused me to inflame my desires, I believed that she told the plain truth when she said that she would not give herself to me until she loved me. She said it was for me to make her love me. I thought her an angel. I was ready to wait. My passion was so consuming that sooner or later, I felt, it must communicate itself to her; it was like a fire on the prairie that devours everything around it; and at last—at last she said she loved me. My emotion was so terrific that I thought I should fall down and die. Oh, what rapture! Oh, what madness! I would have given her everything I possessed in the world, I would have torn down the stars from heaven to deck her hair; I wanted to do something to prove to her the extravagance of my love, I wanted to do the impossible, the incredible, I wanted to give her myself, my soul, my honour, all, all I had and all I was; and that night when she lay in my arms I told her of our plot and who we were that were concerned in it. I felt her body stiffen with attention, I was conscious of a flicker of her eyelids, there was something, I hardly knew what, the hand that stroked my face was dry and cold; a sudden suspicion seized me and all at once I remembered what the cards had told me: love and a dark woman, danger, betrayal and death. Three times they'd said it and I wouldn't heed. I made no sign that I had noticed anything. She nestled up against my heart and told me that she was frightened to hear such things and asked me if So-and-so was concerned. I answered her. I wanted to make sure. One after the other, with infinite cunning, between her kisses she cajoled me into giving every detail of the plot, and now I was certain, as certain as I am that you sit before me, that she was a spy. She was a spy of the President's and she had been set to allure me with her devilish charm and now she had wormed out of me all our secrets. The lives of all of us were in her hands and I knew that if she left that room in twenty-four hours we should be dead men. And I loved her, I loved her; oh, words cannot tell you the agony of desire that burned my heart; love like that is no pleasure; it is pain, pain, but the exquisite pain that transcends all pleasure. It is that heavenly anguish that the saints speak of when they are seized with a divine ecstasy. I knew that she must not leave the room alive and I feared that if I delayed my courage would fail me.

" 'I think I shall sleep,' she said.

" 'Sleep, my dove,' I answered.

" '*Alma de mi corazon*,' she called me. 'Soul of my heart.' They were the last words she spoke. Those heavy lids of hers, dark like a grape and faintly humid, those heavy lids of hers closed over her eyes and in a little while I knew by the regular movement of her breast against mine that she slept. You see, I loved her, I could not bear that she should suffer; she was a spy, yes, but my heart bade me spare her the terror of knowing what must happen. It is strange, I felt no anger because she had betrayed me, I should have hated her because of her vileness; I could not, I only felt that my soul was enveloped in night. Poor thing, poor thing. I could have cried in pity for her. I drew my arm very gently from around her, my left arm that was, my right was free, and raised myself on my hand. But she was so beautiful, I turned my face away when I drew the knife with all my strength across her lovely throat. Without awaking she passed from sleep to death."

He stopped and stared frowning at the four cards that still lay, their backs upward, waiting to be turned up.

"It was in the cards. Why did I not take their warning? I will not look at them. Damn them. Take them away."

With a violent gesture he swept the whole pack on to the floor.

"Though I am a free-thinker I had masses said for her soul." He leaned back and rolled himself a cigarette. He inhaled a long breathful of smoke. He shrugged his shoulders. "The Colonel said you were a writer. What do you write?"

"Stories," replied Ashenden.

"Detective stories?"

"No."

"Why not? They are the only ones I read. If I were a writer I should write detective stories."

"They are very difficult. You need an incredible amount of

invention. I devised a murder story once, but the murder was so ingenious that I could never find a way of bringing it home to the murderer, and, after all, one of the conventions of the detective story is that the mystery should in the end be solved and the criminal brought to justice."

"If your murder is as ingenious as you think the only means you have of proving the murderer's guilt is by the discovery of his motives. When once you have found a motive the chances are that you will hit upon evidence that till then had escaped you. If there is no motive the most damning evidence will be inconclusive. Imagine for instance that you went up to a man in a lonely street on a moonless night and stabbed him to the heart. Who would ever think of you? But if he was your wife's lover, or your brother, or had cheated or insulted you, then a scrap of paper, a bit of string or a chance remark would be enough to hang you. What were your movements at the time he was killed? Are there not a dozen people who saw you before and after? But if he was a total stranger you would never for a moment be suspected. It was inevitable that Jack the Ripper should escape unless he was caught in the act."

Ashenden had more than one reason to change the conversation. They were parting at Rome and he thought it necessary to come to an understanding with his companion about their respective movements. The Mexican was going to Brindisi and Ashenden to Naples. He meant to lodge at the Hotel de Belfast, which was a large second-rate hotel near the harbour frequented by commercial travellers and the thriftier kind of tripper. It would be as well to let the General have the number of his room so that he could come up if necessary without enquiring of the porter, and at the next stopping-place Ashenden got an envelope from the station-buffet and made him address it in his own writing to himself at the post-office in Brindisi. All Ashenden had to do then was to scribble a number on a sheet of paper and post it.

The Hairless Mexican shrugged his shoulders.

"To my mind all these precautions are rather childish. There is absolutely no risk. But whatever happens you may be quite sure that I will not compromise you."

"This is not the sort of job which I'm very familiar with," said Ashenden. "I'm content to follow the Colonel's instructions and know no more about it than it's essential I should."

"Quite so. Should the exigencies of the situation force me to take a drastic step and I get into trouble I shall of course be treated as a political prisoner. Sooner or later Italy is bound to come into the war on the side of the Allies and I shall be released. I have considered everything. But I beg you very seriously to have no more anxiety about the outcome of our mission than if you were going for a picnic on the Thames."

But when at last they separated and Ashenden found himself alone in a carriage on the way to Naples he heaved a great sigh of relief. He was glad to be rid of that chattering, hideous and fantastic creature. He was gone to meet Constantine Andreadi at Brindisi and if half of what he had told Ashenden was true, Ashenden could not but congratulate himself that he did not stand in the Greek spy's shoes. He wondered what sort of a man he was. There was a grimness in the notion of his coming across the blue Ionian, with his confidential papers and his dangerous secrets, all unconscious of the noose into which he was putting his head. Well, that was war, and only fools thought it could be waged with kid gloves on.

Ashenden arrived in Naples and, having taken a room at the hotel, wrote its number on a sheet of paper in block letters and posted it to the Hairless Mexican. He went to the British Consulate, where R. had arranged to send any instructions he might have for him, and found that they knew about him and everything was in order. Then he put aside these matters and made up his mind to amuse himself. Here in the South the spring was well advanced and in the busy streets the sun was hot. Ashenden knew Naples pretty well. The Piazza di San Ferdinando, with its bustle, the Piazza del Plebiscito, with its handsome church, stirred in his heart pleasant recollections. The Strada di Chiara was as noisy as ever. He stood at corners and looked up the narrow alleys that climbed the hill precipitously, those alleys of high houses with the washing set out to dry on lines across the street like pennants flying to mark a feast-day: and he sauntered along the shore, looking at the burnished sea with Capri faintly outlined against the bay, till he came to Posilippo, where there was an old, rambling and bedraggled *palazzo* in which in his youth he had spent many a romantic hour. He observed the curious little pain with which the memories of the past wrung his heart-strings. Then he took a fly drawn by a small and scraggy pony and rattled back over the stones to the *Galleria*, where he sat in the cool and drank an *americano* and looked at the people who loitered there, talking, for ever talking with vivacious gestures, and, exercising his fancy, sought from their appearance to divine their reality.

For three days Ashenden led the idle life that fitted so well the fantastical, untidy and genial city. He did nothing from morning till night but wander at random, looking, not with the eye of the tourist who seeks for what ought to be seen, nor with the eye of the writer who looks for his own (seeing in a sunset a melodious phrase or in a face the inkling of a character), but with that of the tramp to whom whatever happens is absolute. He went to the museum to look at the statue of Agrippina the Younger, which he had particular reasons for remembering with affection, and took the opportunity to see once more the Titian and the Brueghel in the picture gallery. But he always came back to the church of Santa Chiara. Its grace, its gaiety, the airy persiflage with which it seemed to treat religion and at the back of this its sensual emotion; its extravagance, its elegance of line; to Ashenden it seemed to express, as it were in one absurd and grandiloquent metaphor, the sunny, dusty, lovely city and its bustling inhabitants. It said that life was charming and sad; it's a pity one hadn't any money, but money wasn't everything, and anyway why bother when we are here to-day and gone to-morrow, and it was all very exciting and amusing, and after all we must make the best of things: *facciamo una piccola combinazione.*

But on the fourth morning, when Ashenden, having just stepped out of his bath, was trying to dry himself on a towel that absorbed no moisture, his door was quickly opened and a man slipped into his room.

"What d'you want?" cried Ashenden.

"It's all right. Don't you know me?"

"Good Lord, it's the Mexican. What have you done to yourself?"

He had changed his wig and wore now a black one, close-cropped, that fitted on his head like a cap. It entirely altered the look of him and though this was still odd enough, it was quite different from that which he had borne before. He wore a shabby grey suit.

"I can only stop a minute. He's getting shaved."

Ashenden felt his cheeks suddenly redden.

"You found him then?"

"That wasn't difficult. He was the only Greek passenger on the ship. I went on board when she got in and asked for a friend who had sailed from the Piræus. I said I had come to meet a Mr. George Diogenidis. I pretended to be much puzzled at his not coming, and I got into conversation with Andreadi. He's travelling under a false name. He calls himself Lombardos. I followed him when he landed and do you know the first thing he did? He went into a barber's and had his beard shaved. What do you think of that?"

"Nothing. Anyone might have his beard shaved."

"That is not what I think. He wanted to change his appearance. Oh, he's cunning. I admire the Germans, they leave nothing to chance, he's got his whole story pat, but I'll tell you that in a minute."

"By the way, you've changed your appearance too."

"Ah, yes, this is a wig I'm wearing; it makes a difference, doesn't it?"

"I should never have known you."

"One has to take precautions. We are bosom friends. We had to spend the day in Brindisi and he cannot speak Italian. He was glad to have me help him and we travelled up together. I have brought him to this hotel. He says he is going to Rome to-morrow, but I shall not let him out of my sight; I do not want him to give me the slip. He says that he wants to see Naples and I have offered to show him everything there is to see."

"Why isn't he going to Rome to-day?"

"That is part of the story. He pretends he is a Greek business man who has made money during the war. He says he was the owner of two coasting steamers and has just sold them. Now he means to go to Paris and have his fling. He says he has wanted to go to Paris all his life and at last has the chance. He is close. I tried to get him to talk. I told him I was a Spaniard and had been to Brindisi to arrange communications with Turkey about war material. He listened to me and I saw he was interested, but he told me nothing and of course I did not think it wise to press him. He has the papers on his person."

"How do you know?"

"He is not anxious about his grip, but he feels every now and then round his middle, they're either in a belt or in the lining of his vest."

"Why the devil did you bring him to this hotel?"

"I thought it would be more convenient. We may want to search his luggage."

"Are you staying here too?"

"No, I am not such a fool as that. I told him I was going to Rome by the night train and would not take a room. But I must go, I promised to meet him outside the barber's in fifteen minutes."

"All right."

"Where shall I find you to-night if I want you?"

Ashenden for an instant eyed the Hairless Mexican, then with a slight frown looked away.

"I shall spend the evening in my room."

"Very well. Will you just see that there's nobody in the passage?"

Ashenden opened the door and looked out. He saw no one. The hotel in point of fact at that season was nearly empty. There were few foreigners in Naples and trade was bad.

"It's all right," said Ashenden.

The Hairless Mexican walked boldly out. Ashenden closed the door behind him. He shaved and slowly dressed. The sun was shining as brightly as usual on the square and the people who passed, the shabby little carriages with their scrawny horses, had the same air as before, but they did not any longer fill Ashenden with gaiety. He was not comfortable. He went out and called as was his habit at the Consulate to ask if there was a telegram for him. Nothing. Then he went to Cook's and looked out the trains to Rome: there was one soon after midnight and another at five in the morning. He wished he could catch the first. He did not know what were the Mexican's plans; if he really wanted to get to Cuba he would do well to make his way to Spain, and, glancing at the notices in the office, Ashenden saw that next day there was a ship sailing from Naples to Barcelona.

Ashenden was bored with Naples. The glare in the streets tired his eyes, the dust was intolerable, the noise was deafening. He went to the *Galleria* and had a drink. In the afternoon he went to a cinema. Then, going back to his hotel, he told the clerk that since he was starting so early in the morning he preferred to pay his bill at once, and he took his luggage to the station, leaving in his room only a despatch-case in which were the printed part of his code and a book or two. He dined. Then returning to the hotel he sat down to wait for the Hairless Mexican. He could not conceal from himself the fact that he was exceedingly nervous. He began to read, but the book was tiresome, and he tried another; his attention wandered and he glanced at his watch. It was desperately early; he took up his book again, making up his mind that he would not look at his watch till he had read thirty pages, but though he ran his eyes conscientiously down one page after another he could not tell more than vaguely what it was he read. He looked at the time again. Good God, it was only half-past ten. He wondered where the Hairless Mexican was, and what he was doing; he was afraid he would make a mess of things. It was a horrible business. Then it struck him that he had better shut the window and draw the curtains. He smoked innumerable cigarettes. He looked at his watch and it was a quarter past eleven. A thought struck him and his heart began to beat against his chest; out of curiosity he counted his pulse and was surprised to find that it was normal. Though it was a warm night and the room was stuffy his hands and feet were icy. What a nuisance it was, he reflected irritably, to have an imagination that conjured up pictures of things that you didn't in the least want to see! From his standpoint as a writer he had often considered murder and his mind went to that fearful description of one in *Crime and Punishment*. He did not want to think of this topic, but it forced itself upon him; his book dropped to his knees and staring at the wall in front of him (it had a brown wall-paper with a pattern of dingy roses) he asked himself how, if one had to, one would commit a murder in Naples. Of course there was the Villa, the great leafy garden facing the bay in which stood the aquarium; that was deserted at night and very dark; things happened there that did not bear the light of day and prudent persons after dusk avoided its sinister paths. Beyond Posilippo the road was very solitary and there were byways that led up the hill in which by night you would never meet a soul, but how would you induce a man who had any nerves to go there? You might suggest a row in the bay, but the boatman who hired the boat would see you; it was doubtful indeed if he would let you go on the water alone; there were disreputable hotels down by the harbour where no questions were asked of persons who arrived late at night without luggage; but here again the waiter who showed you your room had the chance of a good look at you and you had on entering to sign an elaborate questionnaire.

Ashenden looked once more at the time. He was very tired. He sat now not even trying to read, his mind a blank.

Then the door opened softly and he sprang to his feet. His flesh crept. The Hairless Mexican stood before him.

"Did I startle you?" he asked smiling. "I thought you would prefer me not to knock."

"Did anyone see you come in?"

H

"I was let in by the night-watchman; he was asleep when I rang and didn't even look at me. I'm sorry I'm so late, but I had to change."

The Hairless Mexican wore now the clothes he had travelled down in and his fair wig. It was extraordinary how different he looked. He was bigger and more flamboyant; the very shape of his face was altered. His eyes were shining and he seemed in excellent spirits. He gave Ashenden a glance.

"How white you are, my friend! Surely you're not nervous?"

"Have you got the documents?"

"No. He hadn't got them on him. This is all he had."

He put down on the table a bulky pocket-book and a passport.

"I don't want them," said Ashenden quickly. "Take them."

With a shrug of the shoulders the Hairless Mexican put the things back in his pocket.

"What was in his belt? You said he kept feeling round his middle."

"Only money. I've looked through the pocket-book. It contains nothing but private letters and photographs of women. He must have locked the documents in his grip before coming out with me this evening."

"Damn," said Ashenden.

"I've got the key of his room. We'd better go and look through his luggage."

Ashenden felt a sensation of sickness in the pit of his stomach. He hesitated. The Mexican smiled not unkindly.

"There's no risk, amigo," he said, as though he were reassuring a small boy, "but if you don't feel happy, I'll go alone."

"No, I'll come with you," said Ashenden.

"There's no one awake in the hotel and Mr. Andreadi won't disturb us. Take off your shoes if you like."

Ashenden did not answer. He frowned because he noticed that his hands were slightly trembling. He unlaced his shoes and slipped them off. The Mexican did the same.

"You'd better go first," he said. "Turn to the left and go straight along the corridor. It's number thirty-eight."

Ashenden opened the door and stepped out. The passage was dimly lit. It exasperated him to feel so nervous when he could not but be aware that his companion was perfectly at ease. When they reached the door the Hairless Mexican inserted the key, turned the lock and went in. He switched on the light. Ashenden followed him and closed the door. He noticed that the shutters were shut.

"Now we're all right. We can take our time."

He took a bunch of keys out of his pocket, tried one or two and at last hit upon the right one. The suitcase was filled with clothes.

"Cheap clothes," said the Mexican contemptuously as he took them out. "My own principle is that it's always cheaper in the end to buy the best. After all one is a gentleman or one isn't a gentleman."

"Are you obliged to talk?" asked Ashenden.

"A spice of danger affects people in different ways. It only excites me, but it puts you in a bad temper, *amigo*."

"You see, I'm scared and you're not," replied Ashenden with candour.

"It's merely a matter of nerves."

Meanwhile he felt the clothes, rapidly but with care, as he took them out. There were no papers of any sort in the suitcase. Then he took out his knife and slit the lining. It was a cheap piece and the lining was gummed to the material of which the suitcase was made. There was no possibility of anything being concealed in it.

"They're not here. They must be hidden in the room."

"Are you sure he didn't deposit them in some office? At one of the consulates, for example?"

"He was never out of my sight for a moment except when he was getting shaved."

The Hairless Mexican opened the drawers and the cupboard. There was no carpet on the floor. He looked under the bed, in it, and under the mattress. His dark eyes shot up and down the room, looking for a hiding-place, and Ashenden felt that nothing escaped him.

"Perhaps he left them in charge of the clerk downstairs?"

"I should have known it. And he wouldn't dare. They're not here. I can't understand it."

He looked about the room irresolutely. He frowned in the attempt to guess at a solution of the mystery.

"Let's get out of here," said Ashenden.

"In a minute."

The Mexican went down on his knees, quickly and neatly folded the clothes, and packed them up again. He locked the bag and stood up. Then, putting out the light, he slowly opened the door and looked out. He beckoned to Ashenden and slipped into the passage. When Ashenden had followed him he stopped and locked the door, put the key in his pocket and walked with Ashenden to his room. When they were inside it and the bolt drawn Ashenden wiped his clammy hands and his forehead. .

"Thank God, we're out of that!"

"There wasn't really the smallest danger. But what are we to do now? The Colonel will be angry that the papers haven't been found."

"I'm taking the five o'clock train to Rome. I shall wire for instructions there."

"Very well, I will come with you."

"I should have thought it would suit you better to get out of the country more quickly. There's a boat to-morrow that goes to Barcelona. Why don't you take that and if necessary I can come to see you there?"

The Hairless Mexican gave a little smile.

"I see that you are anxious to be rid of me. Well, I won't thwart a wish that your inexperience in these matters excuses. I will go to Barcelona. I have a visa for Spain."

Ashenden looked at his watch. It was a little after two. He had nearly three hours to wait. His companion comfortably rolled himself a cigarette.

"What do you say to a little supper?" he asked. "I'm as hungry as a wolf."

The thought of food sickened Ashenden, but he was terribly thirsty. He did not want to go out with the Hairless Mexican, but neither did he want to stay in that hotel by himself.

"Where could one go at this hour?"

"Come along with me. I'll find you a place."

Ashenden put on his hat and took his despatch-case in his hand. They went downstairs. In the hall the porter was sleeping soundly on a mattress on the floor. As they passed the desk, walking softly in order not to wake him, Ashenden noticed in the pigeon-hole belonging to his room a letter. He took it out and saw that it was addressed to him. They tiptoed out of the hotel and shut the door behind them. Then they walked quickly away. Stopping after a hundred yards or so under a lamp-post Ashenden took the letter out of his pocket and read it; it came from the Consulate and said: *The enclosed telegram arrived to-night and in case it is urgent I am sending it round to your hotel by messenger.* It had apparently been left some time before midnight while Ashenden was sitting in his room. He opened the telegram and saw that it was in code.

"Well, it'll have to wait," he said, putting it back in his pocket.

The Hairless Mexican walked as though he knew his way through the deserted streets and Ashenden walked by his side. At last they came to a tavern in a blind alley, noisome and evil, and this the Mexican entered.

"It's not the Ritz," he said, "but at this hour of the night it's only in a place like this that we stand a chance of getting something to eat."

Ashenden found himself in a long sordid room at one end of which a wizened young man sat at a piano; there were tables standing out from the wall on each side and against them benches. A number of persons, men and women, were sitting about. They were drinking beer and wine. The women were old, painted, and hideous; and their harsh gaiety was at once noisy and lifeless. When Ashenden and the Hairless Mexican came in they all stared and when they sat down at one of the tables Ashenden looked away in order not to meet the leering eyes, just ready to break into a smile, that sought his insinuatingly. The wizened pianist strummed a tune and several couples got up and began to dance. Since there were not enough men to go round some of the women danced together. The General ordered two plates of spaghetti and a bottle of Capri wine. When the wine was brought he drank a glassful greedily and then waiting for the *pasta* eyed the women who were sitting at the other tables.

"Do you dance?" he asked Ashenden. "I'm going to ask one of these girls to have a turn with me."

He got up and Ashenden watched him go up to one who had at least flashing eyes and white teeth to recommend her; she rose and he put his arm round her. He danced well. Ashenden saw him begin talking; the woman laughed and presently the look of indifference with which she had accepted his offer changed to one of interest. Soon they were chatting gaily. The dance came to an end and putting her back at her table he returned to Ashenden and drank another glass of wine.

"What do you think of my girl?" he asked. "Not bad, is she? It does one good to dance. Why don't you ask one of them? This is a nice place, is it not? You can always trust me to find anything like this. I have an instinct."

The pianist started again. The woman looked at the Hairless Mexican and when with his thumb he pointed to the floor she jumped up with alacrity. He buttoned up his coat, arched his back

and standing up by the side of the table waited for her to come to
him. He swung her off, talking, smiling, and already he was on
familiar terms with everyone in the room. In fluent Italian, with
his Spanish accent, he exchanged badinage with one and the other.
They laughed at his sallies. Then the waiter brought two heaped
platefuls of macaroni and when the Mexican saw them he stopped
dancing without ceremony and, allowing his partner to get back to
her table as she chose, hurried to his meal.

"I'm ravenous," he said. "And yet I ate a good dinner. Where
did you dine? You're going to eat some macaroni, aren't you?"

"I have no appetite," said Ashenden.

But he began to eat and to his surprise found that he was hungry.
The Hairless Mexican ate with huge mouthfuls, enjoying himself
vastly; his eyes shone and he was loquacious. The woman he had
danced with had in that short time told him all about herself and he
repeated now to Ashenden what she had said. He stuffed huge
pieces of bread into his mouth. He ordered another bottle of wine.

"Wine?" he cried scornfully. "Wine is not a drink, only
champagne; it does not even quench your thirst. Well, *amigo*, are
you feeling better?"

"I'm bound to say I am," smiled Ashenden.

"Practice, that is all you want, practice."

He stretched out his hand to pat Ashenden on the arm.

"What's that?" cried Ashenden with a start. "What's that stain
on your cuff?"

The Hairless Mexican gave his sleeve a glance.

"That? Nothing. It's only blood. I had a little accident and cut
myself."

Ashenden was silent. His eyes sought the clock that hung over
the door.

"Are you anxious about your train? Let me have one more
dance and then I'll accompany you to the station."

The Mexican got up and with his sublime self-assurance seized in
his arms the woman who sat nearest to him and danced away with
her. Ashenden watched him moodily. He was a monstrous, terrible
figure with that blond wig and his hairless face, but he moved with
a matchless grace; his feet were small and seemed to hold the
ground like the pads of a cat or a tiger; his rhythm was wonderful
and you could not but see that the bedizened creature he danced
with was intoxicated by his gestures. There was music in his toes
and in the long arms that held her so firmly, and there was music

in those long legs that seemed to move strangely from the hips. Sinister and grotesque though he was, there was in him now a feline elegance, even something of beauty, and you felt a secret, shameful fascination. To Ashenden he suggested one of those sculptures of the pre-Aztec hewers of stone, in which there is barbarism and vitality, something terrible and cruel, and yet withal a brooding and significant loveliness. All the same he would gladly have left him to finish the night by himself in that sordid dance-hall, but he knew that he must have a business conversation with him. He did not look forward to it without misgiving. He had been instructed to give Manuel Carmona certain sums in return for certain documents. Well, the documents were not forthcoming, and as for the rest—Ashenden knew nothing about that; it was no business of his. The Hairless Mexican waved gaily as he passed him.

"I will come the moment the music stops. Pay the bill and then I shall be ready."

Ashenden wished he could have seen into his mind. He could not even make a guess at its workings. Then the Mexican, with his scented handkerchief wiping the sweat from his brow, came back.

"Have you had a good time, General?" Ashenden asked him.

"I always have a good time. Poor white trash, but what do I care? I like to feel the body of a woman in my arms and see her eyes grow languid and her lips part as her desire for me melts the marrow in her bones like butter in the sun. Poor white trash, but women."

They sallied forth. The Mexican proposed that they should walk and in that quarter, at that hour, there would have been little chance of finding a cab; but the sky was starry. It was a summer night and the air was still. The silence walked beside them like the ghost of a dead man. When they neared the station the houses seemed on a sudden to take on a greyer, more rigid line, and you felt that the dawn was at hand. A little shiver trembled through the night. It was a moment of apprehension and the soul for an instant was anxious; it was as though, inherited down the years in their countless millions, it felt a witless fear that perhaps another day would not break. But they entered the station and the night once more enwrapped them. One or two porters lolled about like stage-hands after the curtain has rung down and the scene is struck. Two soldiers in dim uniforms stood motionless.

The waiting-room was empty, but Ashenden and the Hairless Mexican went to sit in the most retired part of it.

"I still have an hour before my train goes. I'll just see what this cable's about."

He took it out of his pocket and from the despatch-case got his code. He was not then using a very elaborate one. It was in two parts, one contained in a slim book and the other, given him on a sheet of paper and destroyed by him before he left allied territory, committed to memory. Ashenden put on his spectacles and set to work. The Hairless Mexican sat in a corner of the seat, rolling himself cigarettes and smoking; he sat there placidly, taking no notice of what Ashenden did, and enjoyed his well-earned repose. Ashenden deciphered the groups of numbers one by one and as he got it out jotted down each word on a piece of paper. His method was to abstract his mind from the sense till he had finished, since he had discovered that if you took notice of the words as they came along you often jumped to a conclusion and sometimes were led into error. So he translated quite mechanically, without paying attention to the words as he wrote them one after the other. When at last he had done he read the complete message. It ran as follows:

Constantine Andreadi has been detained by illness at Piræus. He will be unable to sail. Return Geneva and await instructions.

At first Ashenden could not understand. He read it again. He shook from head to foot. Then, for once robbed of his self-possession, he blurted out, in a hoarse, agitated and furious whisper: "You bloody fool, you've killed the wrong man."

❖

Giulia Lazzari

ASHENDEN was in the habit of asserting that he was never bored. It was one of his notions that only such persons were as had no resources in themselves and it was but the stupid that depended on the outside world for their amusement. Ashenden had no illusions about himself and such success in current letters as had come to him had left his head unturned. He distinguished acutely between fame and the notoriety that rewards the author of a successful novel or a popular play; and he was indifferent to this except in so far as it was attended with tangible benefits. He was perfectly ready to take advantage of his familiar name to get a better state-room in a ship than he had paid for, and if a Customs-house officer passed his luggage unopened because he had read his short stories Ashenden was pleased to admit that the pursuit of literature had its compensations. He sighed when eager young students of the drama sought to discuss its technique with him, and when gushing ladies tremulously whispered in his ear their admiration of his books he often wished he was dead. But he thought himself intelligent and so it was absurd that he should be bored. It was a fact that he could talk with interest to persons commonly thought so excruciatingly dull that their fellows fled from them as though they owed them money. It may be that here he was but indulging the professional instinct that was seldom dormant in him; they, his raw material, did not bore him any more than fossils bore the geologist. And now he had everything that a reasonable man could want for his entertainment. He had pleasant rooms in a good hotel and Geneva is one of the most agreeable cities in Europe to live in. He hired a boat and rowed on the lake or hired a horse and trotted sedately, for in that neat and orderly canton it is difficult to find a stretch of turf where you can have a good gallop, along the macadamised roads in the environs of the town. He wandered on foot about its old streets, trying among those grey stone houses, so quiet and dignified, to recapture the spirit of a past age. He read again with delight Rousseau's *Confessions*, and for the second or third time tried in vain to get on with *La Nouvelle Héloïse*. He wrote. He knew few people, for it was his business to keep in the background, but he had picked up a chatting acquaintance with several persons living in his hotel and he was not lonely. His life was sufficiently filled, it was varied, and when he had nothing else to do he could enjoy his own reflections; it was absurd to think that under these circumstances he could possibly be bored, and yet, like a little lonely cloud in the sky, he did see in the offing the possibility of boredom. There is a story that Louis XIV, having summoned a courtier to attend him on a ceremonial occasion, found himself ready to go as the courtier appeared; he turned to him and with icy majesty said, *J'ai failli attendre*, of which the only translation I can give, but a poor one, is, I have but just escaped waiting: so Ashenden might have admitted that he now but just escaped being bored.

It might be, he mused, as he rode along the lake on a dappled horse with a great rump and a short neck, like one of those prancing steeds that you see in old pictures, but this horse never pranced and he needed a firm jab with the spur to break even into a smart trot—it might be, he mused, that the great chiefs of the secret service in their London offices, their hands on the throttle of this great machine, led a life full of excitement; they moved their pieces here and there, they saw the pattern woven by the multitudinous threads (Ashenden was lavish with his metaphors), they made a picture out of the various pieces of the jigsaw puzzle; but it must be confessed that for the small fry like himself to be a member of the secret service was not as adventurous an affair as the public thought. Ashenden's official existence was as orderly and monotonous as a city clerk's. He saw his spies at stated intervals and paid them their wages; when he could get hold of a new one he engaged him, gave him his instructions and sent him off to Germany; he waited for the information that came through and despatched it; he went into France once a week to confer with his colleague over the frontier and to receive his orders from London; he visited the market-place on market-day to get any message the old butter-woman had brought him from the other side of the lake; he kept his eyes and ears open; and he wrote long reports which he was convinced no one read, till having inadvertently slipped a jest into one of them he received a sharp reproof for his levity. The work he was doing was evidently necessary, but it could not be called anything but monotonous. At one moment for something better to do he had considered the possibility of a flirtation with the Baroness von Higgins. He was confident now that she was an agent in the service of the Austrian Government and he looked forward to a certain entertainment in the duel he foresaw. It would be amusing to set his wits against hers. He was quite aware that she would lay snares for him and to avoid them would give him something to keep his mind from rusting. He found her not unwilling to play the game. She wrote him gushing little notes when he sent her flowers. She went for a row with him on the lake and letting her long white hand drag through the water talked of Love and hinted at a Broken Heart. They dined together and went to see a performance, in French and in prose, of *Romeo and Juliet*. Ashenden had not made up his mind how far he was prepared to go when he received a sharp note from R. to ask him what he was playing at: information "had come to hand" that he (Ashenden) was much in the society of a woman calling herself the Baroness de Higgins, who was known to be an agent of the Central Powers and it was most undesirable that he should be on any terms with her but those of frigid courtesy. Ashenden shrugged his shoulders. R. did not think him as clever as he thought himself. But he was interested to discover, what he had not known before, that there was someone in Geneva part of whose duties at all events was to keep an eye on him. There was evidently someone who had orders to see that he did not neglect his work or get into mischief. Ashenden was not a little amused. What a shrewd, unscrupulous old thing was R.! He took no risks; he trusted nobody; he made use of his instruments, but, high or low, had no opinion of them. Ashenden looked about to see whether he could spot the person who had told R. what he was doing. He wondered if it was one of the waiters in the hotel. He knew that R. had a great belief in waiters; they had the chance of seeing so much and could so easily get into places where information was lying about to be picked up. He even wondered whether R. had got his news from the Baroness herself; it would not be so strange if after all she was employed by the secret service of one of the Allied nations. Ashenden continued to be polite to the Baroness, but ceased to be attentive.

He turned his horse and trotted gently back to Geneva. An ostler from the riding-stables was waiting at the hotel door and slipping out of the saddle Ashenden went into the hotel. At the desk the porter handed him a telegram. It was to the following effect:

Aunt Maggie not at all well. Staying at Hôtel Lotti, Paris. If possible please go and see her. Raymond.

Raymond was one of R.'s facetious *noms de guerre*, and since Ashenden was not so fortunate as to possess an Aunt Maggie he concluded that this was an order to go to Paris. It had always seemed to Ashenden that R. had spent much of his spare time in reading detective fiction and especially when he was in a good humour he found a fantastic pleasure in aping the style of the shilling shocker. If R. was in a good humour it meant that he was about to bring off a coup, for when he had brought one off he was filled with depression and then vented his spleen on his subordinates.

Ashenden, leaving his telegram with deliberate carelessness on the desk, asked at what time the express left for Paris. He glanced at the clock to see whether he had time to get to the Consulate before it closed and secure his visa. When he went upstairs to fetch his passport the porter, just as the lift doors were closed, called him.

"*Monsieur* has forgotten his telegram," he said.

"How stupid of me," said Ashenden.

Now Ashenden knew that if an Austrian baroness by any chance wondered why he had so suddenly gone to Paris she would discover that it was owing to the indisposition of a female relative. In those troublous times of war it was just as well that everything should be clear and above board. He was known at the French Consulate and so lost little time there. He had told the porter to get him a ticket and on his return to the hotel bathed and changed. He was not a little excited at the prospect of this unexpected jaunt. He liked the journey. He slept well in a sleeping-car and was not disturbed if a sudden jolt waked him; it was pleasant to lie a while smoking a cigarette and to feel oneself in one's little cabin so enchantingly alone; the rhythmical sound as the wheels rattled over the points was an agreeable background to the pattern of one's reflections, and to speed through the open country and the night made one feel like a star speeding through space. And at the end of the journey was the unknown.

When Ashenden arrived in Paris it was chilly and a light rain was falling; he felt unshaved and he wanted a bath and clean linen; but he was in excellent spirits. He telephoned from the station to R. and asked how Aunt Maggie was.

"I'm glad to see that your affection for her was great enough to allow you to waste no time in getting here," answered R., with the ghost of a chuckle in his voice. "She's very low, but I'm sure it'll do her good to see you."

Ashenden reflected that this was the mistake the amateur humorist, as opposed to the professional, so often made; when he made a joke he harped on it. The relations of the joker to his joke should be as quick and desultory as those of a bee to its flower. He should make his joke and pass on. There is of course no harm if, like the bee approaching the flower, he buzzes a little; for it is just as well to announce to a thick-headed world that a joke is intended. But Ashenden, unlike most professional humorists, had a kindly tolerance for other people's humour and now he answered R. on his own lines.

"When would she like to see me, do you think?" he asked. "Give her my love, won't you?"

Now R. quite distinctly chuckled. Ashenden sighed.

"She'll want to titivate a little before you come, I expect. You know what she is, she likes to make the best of herself. Shall we say half-past ten, and then when you've had a talk to her we might go out and lunch together somewhere."

"All right," said Ashenden. "I'll come to the Lotti at ten-thirty."

When Ashenden, clean and refreshed, reached the hotel an orderly whom he recognised met him in the hall and took him up to R.'s apartment. He opened the door and showed Ashenden in. R. was standing with his back to a bright log fire dictating to his secretary.

"Sit down," said R. and went on with his dictation.

It was a nicely furnished sitting-room and a bunch of roses in a bowl gave the impression of a woman's hand. On a large table was a litter of papers. R. looked older than when last Ashenden had seen him. His thin yellow face was more lined and his hair was greyer. The work was telling on him. He did not spare himself. He was up at seven every morning and he worked late into the night. His uniform was spick and span, but he wore it shabbily.

"That'll do," he said. "Take all this stuff away and get on with the typing. I'll sign before I go out to lunch." Then he turned to the orderly. "I don't want to be disturbed."

The secretary, a second-lieutenant in the thirties, obviously a civilian with a temporary commission, gathered up a mass of papers and left the room. As the orderly was following, R. said:

"Wait outside. If I want you I'll call."

"Very good, sir."

When they were alone R. turned to Ashenden with what for him was cordiality.

"Have a nice journey up?"

"Yes, sir."

"What do you think of this?" he asked, looking round the room. "Not bad, is it? I never see why one shouldn't do what one can to mitigate the hardships of war."

While he was idly chatting R. gazed at Ashenden with a singular fixity. The stare of those pale eyes of his, too closely set together, gave you the impression that he looked at your naked brain and had a very poor opinion of what he saw there. R. in rare moments of expansion made no secret of the fact that he looked upon his fellow-men as fools or knaves. That was one of the obstacles he had to contend with in his calling. On the whole he preferred them knaves; you knew then what you were up against and could take steps accordingly. He was a professional soldier and had spent his career in India and the Colonies. At the outbreak of the war he was stationed in Jamaica and someone in the War Office who had had dealings with him, remembering him, brought him over and put him in the Intelligence Department. His astuteness was so great that he very soon occupied an important post. He had an immense energy and a gift for organisation, no scruples, but resource, courage and determination. He had perhaps but one weakness. Throughout his life he had never come in contact with persons, especially women, of any social consequence; the only women he had ever known were the wives of his brother officers, the wives of government officials and of business men; and when, coming to London at the beginning of the war, his work brought him into contact with brilliant, beautiful and distinguished women he was unduly dazzled. They made him feel shy, but he cultivated their society; he became quite a lady's man, and to Ashenden, who knew more about him than R. suspected, that bowl of roses told a story.

Ashenden knew that R. had not sent for him to talk about the weather and the crops, and wondered when he was coming to the point. He did not wonder long.

"You've been doing pretty well in Geneva," he said.

"I'm glad you think that, sir," replied Ashenden.

Suddenly R. looked very cold and stern. He had done with idle talk.

"I've got a job for you," he said.

Ashenden made no reply, but he felt a happy little flutter somewhere about the pit of his stomach.

"Have you ever heard of Chandra Lal?"

"No, sir."

A frown of impatience for an instant darkened the Colonel's brow. He expected his subordinates to know everything he wished them to know.

"Where have you been living all these years?"

"At 36, Chesterfield Street, Mayfair," returned Ashenden.

The shadow of a smile crossed R.'s yellow face. The somewhat impertinent reply was after his own sardonic heart. He went over to the big table and opened a despatch-case that lay upon it. He took out a photograph and handed it to Ashenden.

"That's him."

To Ashenden, unused to Oriental faces, it looked like any of a hundred Indians that he had seen. It might have been the photograph of one or other of the rajahs who come periodically to England and are portrayed in the illustrated papers. It showed a fat-faced, swarthy man, with full lips and a fleshy nose; his hair was black, thick and straight, and his very large eyes even in the photograph were liquid and cow-like. He looked ill-at-ease in European clothes.

"Here he is in native dress," said R., giving Ashenden another photograph.

This was full-length, whereas the first had shown only the head and shoulders, and it had evidently been taken some years earlier. He was thinner and his great, serious eyes seemed to devour his face. It was done by a native photographer in Calcutta and the surroundings were naïvely grotesque. Chandra Lal stood against a background on which had been painted a pensive palm tree and a view of the sea. One hand rested on a heavily carved table on which was a rubber-plant in a flower-pot. But in his turban and long, pale tunic he was not without dignity.

"What d'you think of him?" asked R.

"I should have said he was a man not without personality. There is a certain force there."

"Here's his dossier. Read it, will you?"

R. gave Ashenden a couple of typewritten pages and Ashenden sat down. R. put on his spectacles and began to read the letters that awaited his signature. Ashenden skimmed the report and then read it a second time more attentively. It appeared that Chandra Lal was a dangerous agitator. He was a lawyer by profession, but had taken up politics and was bitterly hostile to the British rule in India. He was a partisan of armed force and had been on more than one occasion responsible for riots in which life had been lost. He was once arrested, tried and sentenced to two years' imprisonment; but he was at liberty at the beginning of the war and seizing his opportunity began to foment active rebellion. He was at the heart of plots to embarrass the British in India and so prevent them from transferring troops to the seat of war and with the help of immense sums given to him by German agents he was able to cause a great deal of trouble. He was concerned in two or three bomb outrages which, though beyond killing a few innocent bystanders they did little harm, yet shook the nerves of the public and so damaged its morale. He evaded all attempts to arrest him, his activity was formidable, he was here and there; but the police could never lay hands on him, and they only learned that he had been in some city when, having done his work, he had left it. At last a high reward was offered for his arrest on a charge of murder, but he escaped the country, got to America, from there went to Sweden and eventually reached Berlin. Here he busied himself with schemes to create disaffection among the native troops that had been brought to Europe. All this was narrated dryly, without comment or explanation, but from the very frigidity of the narrative you got a sense of mystery and adventure, of hairbreadth escapes and dangers dangerously encountered. The report ended as follows:

"C. has a wife in India and two children. He is not known to have anything to do with women. He neither drinks nor smokes. He is said to be honest. Considerable sums of money have passed through his hands and there has never been any question as to his not having made a proper (!) use of them. He has undoubted courage and is a hard worker. He is said to pride himself on keeping his word."

Ashenden returned the document to R.

"Well?"

"A fanatic." Ashenden thought there was about the man something rather romantic and attractive, but he knew that R. did not want any nonsense of that sort from him. "He looks like a very dangerous fellow."

"He is the most dangerous conspirator in or out of India. He's done more harm than all the rest of them put together. You know that there's a gang of these Indians in Berlin; well, he's the brains of it. If he could be got out of the way I could afford to ignore the others; he's the only one who has any guts. I've been trying to catch him for a year, I thought there wasn't a hope; but now at last I've got a chance and, by God, I'm going to take it."

"And what'll you do then?"

R. chuckled grimly.

"Shoot him and shoot him damn quick."

Ashenden did not answer. R. walked once or twice across the small room and then, again with his back to the fire, faced Ashenden. His thin mouth was twisted by a sarcastic smile.

"Did you notice at the end of that report I gave you it said he wasn't known to have anything to do with women? Well, that *was* true, but it isn't any longer. The damned fool has fallen in love."

R. stepped over to his despatch-case and took out a bundle tied up with pale blue ribbon.

"Look, here are his love-letters. You're a novelist, it might amuse you to read them. In fact you should read them, it will help you to deal with the situation. Take them away with you."

R. flung the neat little bundle back into the despatch-case.

"One wonders how an able man like that can allow himself to get besotted over a woman. It was the last thing I ever expected of him."

Ashenden's eyes travelled to the bowl of beautiful roses that stood on the table, but he said nothing. R., who missed little, saw the glance and his look suddenly darkened. Ashenden knew that he felt like asking him what the devil he was staring at. At that moment R. had no friendly feelings towards his subordinate, but he made no remark. He went back to the subject in hand.

"Anyhow that's neither here nor there. Chandra has fallen madly in love with a woman called Giulia Lazzari. He's crazy about her."

"Do you know how he picked her up?"

"Of course I do. She's a dancer, and she does Spanish dances, but she happens to be an Italian. For stage purposes she calls herself La Malagueña. You know the kind of thing. Popular Spanish music and a mantilla, a fan and a high comb. She's been dancing all over Europe for the last ten years."

"Is she any good?"

"No, rotten. She's been in the provinces in England and she's had a few engagements in London. She never got more than ten pounds a week. Chandra met her in Berlin in a Tingel-tangel, you know what that is, a cheap sort of music-hall. I take it that on the Continent she looked upon her dancing chiefly as a means to enhance her value as a prostitute."

"How did she get to Berlin during the war?"

"She's been married to a Spaniard at one time; I think she still is though they don't live together, and she travelled on a Spanish passport. It appears Chandra made a dead set for her." R. took up the Indian's photograph again and looked at it thoughtfully. "You wouldn't have thought there was anything very attractive in that greasy little nigger. God, how they run to fat! The fact remains that she fell very nearly as much in love with him as he did with her. I've got her letters too, only copies, of course, he's got the originals and I dare say he keeps them tied up in pink ribbon. She's mad about him. I'm not a literary man, but I think I know when a thing rings true; anyhow you'll be reading them, and you can tell me what you think. And then people say there's no such thing as love at first sight."

R. smiled with faint irony. He was certainly in a good humour this morning.

"But how did you get hold of all these letters?"

"How did I get hold of them? How do you imagine? Owing to her Italian nationality Giulia Lazzari was eventually expelled from Germany. She was put over the Dutch frontier. Having an engagement to dance in England she was granted a visa and"—R. looked up a date among the papers—"and on the twenty-fourth of October last sailed from Rotterdam to Harwich. Since then she has danced in London, Birmingham, Portsmouth and other places. She was arrested a fortnight ago at Hull."

"What for?"

"Espionage. She was transferred to London and I went to see her myself at Holloway."

Ashenden and R. looked at one another for a moment without speaking and it may be that each was trying his hardest to read the other's thoughts. Ashenden was wondering where the truth in all this lay and R. wondered how much of it he could advantageously tell him.

"How did you get on to her?"

"I thought it odd that the Germans should allow her to dance quite quietly in Berlin for weeks and then for no particular reason decide to put her out of the country. It would be a good introduction for espionage. And a dancer who was not too careful of her virtue might make opportunities of learning things that it would be worth somebody's while in Berlin to pay a good price for. I thought it might be as well to let her come to England and see what she was up to. I kept track of her. I discovered that she was sending letters to an address in Holland two or three times a week and two or three times a week was receiving answers from Holland. Hers were written in a queer mixture of French, German and English; she speaks English a little and French quite well, but the answers were written entirely in English; it was good English, but not an Englishman's English, flowery and rather grandiloquent; I wondered who was writing them. They seemed to be just ordinary love-letters, but they were by way of being rather hot stuff. It was plain enough that they were coming from Germany and the writer was neither English, French nor German. Why did he write in English? The only foreigners who know English better than any continental language are Orientals, and not Turks or Egyptians either; they know French. A Jap would write English and so would an Indian. I came to the conclusion that Giulia's lover was one of that gang of Indians that were making trouble for us in Berlin. I had no idea it was Chandra Lal till I found the photograph."

"How did you get that?"

"She carried it about with her. It was a pretty good bit of work, that. She kept it locked up in her trunk, with a lot of theatrical photographs, of comic singers and clowns and acrobats; it might easily have passed for the picture of some music-hall artiste in his stage dress. In fact, later, when she was arrested and asked who the photograph represented she said she didn't know, it was an Indian conjuror who had given it her and she had no idea what his name was. Anyhow I put a very smart lad on the job and he thought it queer that it should be the only photograph in the lot that came from Calcutta. He noticed that there was a number on the back, and he took it, the number, I mean; of course the photograph was replaced in the box."

"By the way, just as a matter of interest how did your very smart lad get at the photograph at all?"

R.'s eyes twinkled.

"That's none of your business. But I don't mind telling you that he was a good-looking boy. Anyhow it's of no consequence. When we got the number of the photograph we cabled to Calcutta and in a little while I received the grateful news that the object of Giulia's affections was no less a person than the incorruptible

Chandra Lal. Then I thought it my duty to have Giulia watched a little more carefully. She seemed to have a sneaking fondness for naval officers. I couldn't exactly blame her for that; they are attractive, but it is unwise for ladies of easy virtue and doubtful nationality to cultivate their society in war-time. Presently I got a very pretty little body of evidence against her."

"How was she getting her stuff through?"

"She wasn't getting it through. She wasn't trying to. The Germans had turned her out quite genuinely; she wasn't working for them, she was working for Chandra. After her engagement was through in England she was planning to go to Holland again and meet him. She wasn't very clever at the work; she was nervous, but it looked easy; no one seemed to bother about her, it grew rather exciting; she was getting all sorts of interesting information without any risk. In one of her letters she said: 'I have so much to tell you, *mon petit chou* darling, and what you will be *extrêmement intéressé* to know,' and she underlined the French words."

R. paused and rubbed his hands together. His tired face bore a look of devilish enjoyment of his own cunning.

"It was espionage made easy. Of course I didn't care a damn about her, it was him I was after. Well, as soon as I'd got the goods on her I arrested her. I had enough evidence to convict a regiment of spies."

R. put his hands in his pockets and his pale lips twisted to a smile that was almost a grimace.

"Holloway's not a very cheerful place, you know."

"I imagine no prison is," remarked Ashenden.

"I left her to stew in her own juice for a week before I went to see her. She was in a very pretty state of nerves by then. The wardress told me she'd been in violent hysterics most of the time. I must say she looked like the devil."

"Is she handsome?"

"You'll see for yourself. She's not my type. I dare say she's better when she's made up and that kind of thing. I talked to her like a Dutch uncle. I put the fear of God into her. I told her she'd get ten years. I think I scared her, I know I tried to. Of course she denied everything, but the proofs were there, I assured her she hadn't got a chance. I spent three hours with her. She went all to pieces and at last she confessed everything. Then I told her that I'd let her go scot-free if she'd get Chandra to come to France. She absolutely refused, she said she'd rather die; she was very hysterical and tiresome, but I let her rave. I told her to think it over and said I'd see her in a day or two and we'd have another talk about it. In point of fact I left her for a week. She'd evidently had time to reflect, because when I came again she asked me quite calmly what it was exactly that I proposed. She'd been in a gaol a fortnight then and I expect she'd had about enough of it. I put it to her as plainly as I could and she accepted."

"I don't think I quite understand," said Ashenden.

"Don't you? I should have thought it was clear to the meanest intelligence. If she can get Chandra to cross the Swiss frontier and come into France she's to go free, either to Spain or to South America, with her passage paid."

"And how the devil is she to get Chandra to do that?"

"He's madly in love with her. He's longing to see her. His letters are almost crazy. She's written to him to say that she can't get a visa to Holland (I told you she was to join him there when her tour was over), but she can get one for Switzerland. That's a neutral country and he's safe there. He jumped at the chance. They've arranged to meet at Lausanne."

"Yes."

"When he reaches Lausanne he'll get a letter from her to say that the French authorities won't let her cross the frontier and that she's going to Thonon, which is just on the other side of the lake from Lausanne, in France, and she's going to ask him to come there."

"What makes you think he will?"

R. paused for an instant. He looked at Ashenden with a pleasant expression.

"She must make him if she doesn't want to go to penal servitude for ten years."

"I see."

"She's arriving from England this evening in custody and I should like you to take her down to Thonon by the night train."

"Me?" said Ashenden.

"Yes, I thought it the sort of job you could manage very well. Presumably you know more about human nature than most people. It'll be a pleasant change for you to spend a week or two at Thonon. I believe it's a pretty little place, fashionable too—in peace-time. You might take the baths there."

"And what do you expect me to do when I get the lady down to Thonon?"

"I leave you a free hand. I've made a few notes that may be useful to you. I'll read them to you, shall I?"

Ashenden listened attentively. R.'s plan was simple and explicit. Ashenden could not but feel unwilling admiration for the brain that had so neatly devised it.

Presently R. suggested that they should have luncheon and he asked Ashenden to take him to some place where they could see smart people. It amused Ashenden to see R., so sharp, sure of himself and alert in his office, seized as he walked into the restaurant with shyness. He talked a little too loud in order to show that he was at his ease and made himself somewhat unnecessarily at home. You saw in his manner the shabby and commonplace life he had led till the hazards of war raised him to a position of consequence. He was glad to be in that fashionable restaurant cheek by jowl with persons who bore great or distinguished names, but he felt like a schoolboy in his first top-hat, and he quailed before the steely eye of the *maître d'hôtel*. His quick glance darted here and there and his sallow face beamed with a self-satisfaction of which he was slightly ashamed. Ashenden drew his attention to an ugly woman in black, with a lovely figure, wearing a long row of pearls.

"That is Madame de Brides. She is the mistress of the Grand Duke Theodore. She's probably one of the most influential women in Europe, she's certainly one of the cleverest."

R.'s clever eyes rested on her and he flushed a little.

"By George, this is life," he said.

Ashenden watched him curiously. Luxury is dangerous to people who have never known it and to whom its temptations are held out too suddenly. R., that shrewd, cynical man, was captivated by the vulgar glamour and the shoddy brilliance of the scene before him. Just as the advantage of culture is that it enables you to talk nonsense with distinction, so the habit of luxury allows you to regard its frills and furbelows with a proper contumely.

But when they had eaten their luncheon and were drinking their coffee Ashenden, seeing that R. was mellowed by the good meal and his surroundings, went back to the subject that was in his thoughts.

"That Indian fellow must be a rather remarkable chap," he said.

"He's got brains, of course."

"One can't help being impressed by a man who had the courage to take on almost single-handed the whole British power in India."

"I wouldn't get sentimental about him if I were you. He's nothing but a dangerous criminal."

"I don't suppose he'd use bombs if he could command a few batteries and half a dozen battalions. He uses what weapons he can. You can hardly blame him for that. After all, he's aiming at nothing for himself, is he? He's aiming at freedom for his country. On the face of it it looks as though he were justified in his actions."

But R. had no notion of what Ashenden was talking.

"That's very far-fetched and morbid," he said. "We can't go into all that. Our job is to get him and when we've got him to shoot him."

"Of course. He's declared war and he must take his chance. I shall carry out your instructions, that's what I'm here for, but I see no harm in realising that there's something to be admired and respected in him."

R. was once more the cool and astute judge of his fellows.

"I've not yet made up my mind whether the best men for this kind of job are those who do it with passion or those who keep their heads. Some of them are filled with hatred for the people we're up against and when we down them it gives them a sort of satisfaction like satisfying a personal grudge. Of course they're very keen on their work. You're different, aren't you? You look at it like a game of chess and you don't seem to have any feeling one way or the other. I can't quite make it out. Of course for some sort of jobs it's just what one wants."

Ashenden did not answer. He called for the bill and walked back with R. to the hotel.

The train started at eight. When he had disposed of his bag Ashenden walked along the platform. He found the carriage in which Giulia Lazzari was, but she sat in a corner, looking away from the light, so that he could not see her face. She was in charge of two detectives who had taken her over from English police at Boulogne. One of them worked with Ashenden on the French side of the Lake Geneva and as Ashenden came up he nodded to him.

"I've asked the lady if she will dine in the restaurant-car, but she prefers to have dinner in the carriage, so I've ordered a basket. Is that quite correct?"

"Quite," said Ashenden.

"My companion and I will go into the diner in turn so that she will not remain alone."

' "That is very considerate of you. I will come along when we've started and have a chat with her."

"She's not disposed to be very talkative," said the detective.

"One could hardly expect it," replied Ashenden.

He walked on to get his ticket for the second service and then returned to his own carriage. Giulia Lazzari was just finishing her meal when he went back to her. From a glance at the basket he judged that she had not eaten with too poor an appetite. The detective who was guarding her opened the door when Ashenden appeared and at Ashenden's suggestion left them alone.

Giulia Lazzari gave him a sullen look.

"I hope you've had what you wanted for dinner," he said as he sat down in front of her.

She bowed slightly, but did not speak. He took out his case.

"Will you have a cigarette?"

She gave him a glance, seemed to hesitate, and then, still without a word, took one. He struck a match and, lighting it, looked at her. He was surprised. For some reason he had expected her to be fair, perhaps from some notion that an Oriental would be more likely to fall for a blonde; but she was almost swarthy. Her hair was hidden by a close-fitting hat, but her eyes were coal-black. She was far from young, she might have been thirty-five, and her skin was lined and sallow. She had at the moment no make-up on and she looked haggard. There was nothing beautiful about her but her magnificent eyes. She was big, and Ashenden thought she must be too big to dance gracefully; it might be that in Spanish costume she was a bold and flaunting figure, but there in the train, shabbily dressed, there was nothing to explain the Indian's infatuation. She gave Ashenden a long, appraising stare. She wondered evidently what sort of man he was. She blew a cloud of smoke through her nostrils and gave it a glance, then looked back at Ashenden. He could see that her sullenness was only a mask, she was nervous and frightened. She spoke in French with an Italian accent.

"Who are you?"

"My name would mean nothing to you, *madame*. I am going to Thonon. I have taken a room for you at the Hotel de la Place. It is the only one open now. I think you will find it quite comfortable."

"Ah, it is you the Colonel spoke to me of. You are my gaoler."

"Only as a matter of form. I shall not intrude upon you."

"All the same you are my gaoler."

"I hope not for very long. I have in my pocket your passport with all the formalities completed to permit you to go to Spain."

She threw herself back into the corner of the carriage. White with those great black eyes, in the poor light, her face was suddenly a mask of despair.

"It's infamous. Oh, I think I could die happy if I could only kill that old Colonel. He has no heart. I'm so unhappy."

"I am afraid you have got yourself into a very unfortunate situation. Did you not know that espionage was a dangerous game?"

"I never sold any of the secrets. I did no harm."

"Surely only because you had no opportunity. I understand that you signed a full confession."

Ashenden spoke to her as amiably as he could, a little as though he were talking to a sick person, and there was no harshness in his voice.

"Oh, yes, I made a fool of myself. I wrote the letter the Colonel said I was to write. Why isn't that enough? What is to happen to me if he does not answer? I cannot force him to come if he does not want to."

"He has answered," said Ashenden. "I have the answer with me."

She gave a gasp and her voice broke.

"Oh, show it to me, I beseech you to let me see it."

"I have no objection to doing that. But you must return it to me."

He took Chandra's letter from his pocket and gave it to her. She snatched it from his hand. She devoured it with her eyes, there were eight pages of it, and as she read the tears streamed down her cheeks. Between her sobs she gave little exclamations of love, calling the writer by pet names French and Italian. This was the letter that Chandra had written in reply to hers telling him, on R.'s instructions, that she would meet him in Switzerland. He was mad with joy at the prospect. He told her in passionate phrases how long the time had seemed to him since they were parted, and how he had yearned for her, and now that he was to see her again so soon he did not know how he was going to bear his impatience. She finished it and let it drop to the floor.

"You can see he loves me, can't you? There's no doubt about that. I know something about it, believe me."

"Do you really love him?" asked Ashenden.

"He's the only man who's ever been kind to me. It's not very gay, the life one leads in these music-halls, all over Europe, never resting, and men—they are not much, the men who haunt those places. At first I thought he was just like the rest of them."

Ashenden picked up the letter and replaced it in his pocket-book.

"A telegram was sent in your name to the address in Holland to say that you would be at the Hotel Gibbons at Lausanne on the 14th."

"That is to-morrow."

"Yes."

She threw up her head and her eyes flashed.

"Oh, it is an infamous thing that you are forcing me to do. It is shameful."

"You are not obliged to do it," said Ashenden.

"And if I don't?"

"I'm afraid you must take the consequences."

"I can't go to prison," she cried out suddenly, "I can't, I can't; I have such a short time before me; he said ten years. Is it possible I could be sentenced to ten years?"

"If the Colonel told you so it is very possible."

"Oh, I know him. That cruel face. He would have no mercy. And what should I be in ten years? Oh, no no."

At that moment the train stopped at a station and the detective waiting in the corridor tapped on the window. Ashenden opened the door and the man gave him a picture-postcard. It was a dull little view of Pontarlier, the frontier station between France and Switzerland, and showed a dusty *place* with a statue in the middle and a few plane-trees. Ashenden handed her a pencil.

"Will you write this postcard to your lover. It will be posted at Pontarlier. Address it to the hotel at Lausanne."

She gave him a glance, but without answering took it and wrote as he directed.

"Now on the other side write: 'Delayed at frontier but everything all right. Wait at Lausanne.' Then add whatever you like, *tendresses*, if you lie."

He took the postcard from her, read it to see that she had done as he directed and then reached for his hat.

"Well, I shall leave you now, I hope you will have a sleep. I will fetch you in the morning when we arrive at Thonon."

The second detective had now returned from his dinner and

as Ashenden came out of the carriage the two men went in. Giulia Lazzari huddled back into her corner. Ashenden gave the post-card to an agent who was waiting to take it to Pontarlier and then made his way along the crowded train to his sleeping-car.

It was bright and sunny, though cold, next morning when they reached their destination. Ashenden, having given his bags to a porter, walked along the platform to where Giulia Lazzari and the two detectives were standing. Ashenden nodded to them.

"Well, good-morning. You need not trouble to wait."

They touched their hats, gave a word of farewell to the woman, and walked away.

"Where are they going?" she asked.

"Off. You will not be bothered with them any more."

"Am I in your custody then?"

"You're in nobody's custody. I'm going to permit myself to take you to your hotel and then I shall leave you. You must try to get a good rest."

Ashenden's porter took her hand-luggage and she gave him the ticket for her trunk. They walked out of the station. A cab was waiting for them and Ashenden begged her to get in. It was a longish drive to the hotel and now and then Ashenden felt that she gave him a sidelong glance. She was perplexed. He sat without a word. When they reached the hotel the proprietor—it was a small hotel, prettily situated at the corner of a little promenade and it had a charming view—showed them the room that had been prepared for Madame Lazzari. Ashenden turned to him.

"That'll do very nicely, I think. I shall come down in a minute."

The proprietor bowed and withdrew.

"I shall do my best to see that you are comfortable, *madame*," said Ashenden. "You are here absolutely your own mistress and you may order pretty well anything you like. To the proprietor you are just a guest of the hotel like any other. You are absolutely free."

"Free to go out?" she asked quickly.

"Of course."

"With a policeman on either side of me, I suppose."

"Not at all. You are as free in the hotel as though you were in your own house and you are free to go out and come in when you choose. I should like an assurance from you that you will not write letters without my knowledge or attempt to leave Thonon without my permission."

She gave Ashenden a long stare. She could not make it out at all. She looked as though she thought it a dream.

"I am in a position that forces me to give you any assurance you ask. I give you my word of honour that I will not write a letter without showing it to you or attempt to leave this place."

"Thank you. Now I will leave you. I will do myself the pleasure of coming to see you to-morrow morning."

Ashenden nodded and went out. He stopped for five minutes at the police-station to see that everything was in order and then took the cab up the hill to a little secluded house on the outskirts of the town at which on his periodical visits to this place he stayed. It was pleasant to have a bath and a shave and get into slippers. He felt lazy and spent the rest of the morning reading a novel.

Soon after dark, for even at Thonon, though it was in France, it was thought desirable to attract attention to Ashenden as little as possible, an agent from the police-station came to see him. His name was Felix. He was a little dark Frenchman with sharp eyes and an unshaven chin, dressed in a shabby grey suit and rather down at heel, so that he looked like a lawyer's clerk out of work. Ashenden offered him a glass of wine and they sat down by the fire.

"Well, your lady lost no time," he said. "Within a quarter of an hour of her arrival she was out of the hotel with a bundle of clothes and trinkets that she sold in a shop near the market. When the afternoon boat came in she went down to the quay and bought a ticket to Evian."

Evian, it should be explained, was the next place along the lake in France and from there, crossing over, the boat went to Switzerland.

"Of course she hadn't a passport, so permission to embark was denied her."

"How did she explain that she had no passport?"

"She said she'd forgotten it. She said she had an appointment to see friends in Evian and tried to persuade the official in charge to let her go. She attempted to slip a hundred francs into his hand."

"She must be a stupider woman than I thought," said Ashenden.

But when next day he went about eleven in the morning to see her he made no reference to her attempt to escape. She had had time to arrange herself, and now, her hair elaborately done, her lips and cheeks painted, she looked less haggard than when he had first seen her.

"I've brought you some books," said Ashenden. "I'm afraid the time hangs heavy on your hands."

"What does that matter to you?"

"I have no wish that you should suffer anything that can be avoided. Anyhow, I will leave them and you can read them or not as you choose."

"If you only knew how I hated you."

"It would doubtless make me very uncomfortable. But I really don't know why you should. I am only doing what I have been ordered to do."

"What do you want of me now? I do not suppose you have come only to ask after my health."

Ashenden smiled.

"I want you to write a letter to your lover telling him that owing to some irregularity in your passport the Swiss authorities would not let you cross the frontier, so you have come here where it is very nice and quiet, so quiet that one can hardly realise there is a war, and you propose that Chandra should join you."

"Do you think he is a fool? He will refuse."

"Then you must do your best to persuade him."

She looked at Ashenden a long time before she answered. He suspected that she was debating within herself whether by writing the letter and so seeming docile she could not gain time.

"Well, dictate and I will write what you say."

"I should prefer you to put it in your own words."

"Give me half an hour and the letter shall be ready."

"I will wait here," said Ashenden.

"Why?"

"Because I prefer to."

Her eyes flashed angrily, but controlling herself she said nothing. On the chest of drawers were writing materials. She sat down at the dressing-table and began to write. When she handed Ashenden the letter he saw that even through her rouge she was very pale. It was the letter of a person not much used to expressing herself by means of pen and ink, but it was well enough, and when towards the end, starting to say how much she loved the man, she had been carried away and wrote with all her heart, it had really a certain passion.

"Now add: The man who is bringing this is Swiss, you can trust him absolutely. I didn't want the censor to see it."

She hesitated an instant, but then wrote as he directed.

"How do you spell, absolutely?"

"As you like. Now address an envelope and I will relieve you of my unwelcome presence."

He gave the letter to the agent who was waiting to take it across the lake. Ashenden brought her the reply the same evening. She snatched it from his hands and for a moment pressed it to her heart. When she read it she uttered a little cry of relief.

"He won't come."

The letter, in the Indian's flowery, stilted English, expressed his bitter disappointment. He told her how intensely he had looked forward to seeing her and implored her to do everything in the world to smooth the difficulties that prevented her from crossing the frontier. He said that it was impossible for him to come, impossible, there was a price on his head, and it would be madness for him to think of risking it. He attempted to be jocular, she did not want her little fat lover to be shot, did she?

"He won't come," she repeated, "he won't come."

"You must write and tell him that there is no risk. You must say that if there were you would not dream of asking him. You must say that if he loves you he will not hesitate."

"I won't. I won't."

"Don't be a fool. You can't help yourself."

She burst into a sudden flood of tears. She flung herself on the floor and seizing Ashenden's knees implored him to have mercy on her.

"I will do anything in the world for you if you will let me go."

"Don't be absurd," said Ashenden. "Do you think I want to become your lover? Come, come, you must be serious. You know the alternative."

She raised herself to her feet and changing on a sudden to fury flung at Ashenden one foul name after another.

"I like you much better like that," he said. "Now will you write or shall I send for the police?"

"He will not come. It is useless."

"It is very much to your interest to make him come."

"What do you mean by that? Do you mean that if I do everything in my power and fail, that . . ."

She looked at Ashenden with wild eyes.

"Yes, it means either you or him."

She staggered. She put her hand to her heart. Then without a word she reached for pen and paper. But the letter was not to Ashenden's liking and he made her write it again. When she had finished she flung herself on the bed and burst once more into passionate weeping. Her grief was real, but there was something theatrical in the expression of it that prevented it from being peculiarly moving to Ashenden. He felt his relation to her as impersonal as a doctor's in the presence of a pain that he cannot alleviate. He saw now why R. had given him this peculiar task; it needed a cool head and an emotion well under control.

He did not see her next day. The answer to the letter was not delivered to him till after dinner, when it was brought to Ashenden's little house by Felix.

"Well, what news have you?"

"Our friend is getting desperate," smiled the Frenchman. "This afternoon she walked up to the station just as a train was about to start for Lyons. She was looking up and down uncertainly so I went to her and asked if there was anything I could do. I introduced myself as an agent of the Sureté. If looks could kill I should not be standing here now."

"Sit down, *mon ami*," said Ashenden.

"*Merci*. She walked away, she evidently thought it was no use to try to get on the train, but I have something more interesting to tell you. She has offered a boatman on the lake a thousand francs to take her across to Lausanne."

"What did he say to her?"

"He said he couldn't risk it."

"Yes?"

The little agent gave his shoulders a slight shrug and smiled.

"She's asked him to meet her on the road that leads to Evian at ten o'clock to-night so that they can talk of it again, and she's given him to understand that she will not repulse too fiercely the advances of a lover. I have told him to do what he likes so long as he comes and tells me everything that is of importance."

"Are you sure you can trust him?" asked Ashenden.

"Oh, quite. He knows nothing, of course, but that she is under surveillance. You need have no fear about him. He is a good boy. I have known him all his life."

Ashenden read Chandra's letter. It was eager and passionate. It throbbed strangely with the painful yearning of his heart.

Love? Yes, if Ashenden knew anything of it there was the real thing. He told her how he spent the long hours walking by the lakeside and looking towards the coast of France. How near they were and yet so desperately parted! He repeated again and again that he could not come, and begged her not to ask him, he would do everything in the world for her, but that he dared not do, and yet if she insisted how could he resist her? He besought her to have mercy on him. And then he broke into a long wail at the thought that he must go away without seeing her, he asked her if there were not some means by which she could slip over, he swore that if he could ever hold her in his arms again he would never let her go. Even the forced and elaborate language in which it was written could not dim the hot fire that burned the pages; it was the letter of a madman.

"When will you hear the result of her interview with the boatman?" asked Ashenden.

"I have arranged to meet him at the landing-stage between eleven and twelve."

Ashenden looked at his watch.

"I will come with you."

They walked down the hill and reaching the quay for shelter from the cold wind stood in the lea of the custom-house. At last they saw a man approaching and Felix stepped out of the shadow that hid them.

"Antoine."

"*Monsieur Félix?* I have a letter for you; I promised to take it to Lausanne by the first boat to-morrow."

Ashenden gave the man a brief glance, but did not ask what had passed between him and Giulia Lazzari. He took the letter and by the light of Felix's electric torch read it. It was in faulty German.

"*On no account come. Pay no attention to my letters. Danger. I love you. Sweetheart. Don't come.*"

He put it in his pocket, gave the boatman fifty francs, and went home to bed. But the next day when he went to see Giulia Lazzari he found her door locked. He knocked for some time, there was no answer. He called her.

"Madame Lazzari, you must open the door. I want to speak to you."

"I am in bed. I am ill and can see no one."

"I am sorry, but you must open the door. If you are ill I will send for a doctor."

"No, go away. I will see no one."

"If you do not open the door I shall send for a locksmith and have it broken open."

There was a silence and then he heard the key turned in the lock. He went in. She was in a dressing-gown and her hair was dishevelled. She had evidently just got out of bed.

"I am at the end of my strength. I can do nothing more. You have only to look at me to see that I am ill. I have been sick all night."

"I shall not keep you long. Would you like to see a doctor?"

"What good can a doctor do me?"

He took out of his pocket the letter she had given the boatman and handed it to her.

"What is the meaning of this?" he asked.

She gave a gasp at the sight of it and her sallow face went green.

"You gave me your word that you would neither attempt to escape nor write a letter without my knowledge."

"Did you think I would keep my word?" she cried, her voice ringing with scorn.

"No. To tell you the truth it was not entirely for your convenience that you were placed in a comfortable hotel rather than in the local gaol, but I think I should tell you that though you have your freedom to go in and out as you like you have no more chance of getting away from Thonon than if you were chained by the leg in a prison cell. It is silly to waste your time writing letters that will never be delivered.

"*Cochon.*"

She flung the opprobrious word at him with all the violence that was in her.

"But you must sit down and write a letter that *will* be delivered."

"Never. I will do nothing more. I will not write another word."

"You came here on the understanding that you would do certain things."

"I will not do them. It is finished."

"You had better reflect a little."

"Reflect! I have reflected. You can do what you like; I don't care."

"Very well, I will give you five minutes to change your mind."

Ashenden took out his watch and looked at it. He sat down on the edge of the unmade bed.

"Oh, it has got on my nerves, this hotel. Why did you not put me in the prison? Why, why? Everywhere I went I felt that spies were on my heels. It is infamous what you are making me do. Infamous! What is my crime? I ask you, what have I done? Am I not a woman? It is infamous what you are asking me to do. Infamous."

She spoke in a high shrill voice. She went on and on. At last the five minutes were up. Ashenden had not said a word. He rose.

"Yes, go, go," she shrieked at him.

She flung foul names at him.

"I shall come back," said Ashenden.

He took the key out of the door as he went out of the room and locked it behind him. Going downstairs he hurriedly scribbled a note, called the boots and dispatched him with it to the police-station. Then he went up again. Giulia Lazzari had thrown herself on her bed and turned her face to the wall. Her body was shaken with hysterical sobs. She gave no sign that she heard him come in. Ashenden sat down on the chair in front of the dressing-table and looked idly at the odds and ends that littered it. The toilet things were cheap and tawdry and none too clean. There were little shabby pots of rouge and cold-cream and little bottles of black for the eyebrows and eyelashes. The hairpins were horrid and greasy. The room was untidy and the air was heavy with the smell of cheap scent. Ashenden thought of the hundreds of rooms she must have occupied in third-rate hotels in the course of her wandering life from provincial town to provincial town in one country after another. He wondered what had been her origins. She was a coarse and vulgar woman, but what had she been when young? She was not the type he would have expected to adopt that career, for she seemed to have no advantages that could help her, and he asked himself whether she came of a family of entertainers (there are all over the world families in which for generations the members have become dancers or acrobats or comic singers) or whether she had fallen into the life accidentally through some lover in the business who had for a time made her his partner. And what men must she have known in all these years, the comrades of the shows she was in, the agents and managers who looked upon it as a perquisite of their position that they should enjoy her favours, the merchants or well-to-do tradesmen, the young sparks of the various towns she played in, who were attracted for the moment by the glamour of the dancer or the blatent sensuality of the woman! To her they were the paying customers and she accepted them indifferently as the recognised and admitted supplement to her miserable salary, but to them perhaps she was romance. In her bought arms they caught sight for a moment of the brilliant world of the capitals, and ever so distantly and however shoddily of the adventure and the glamour of a more spacious life.

There was a sudden knock at the door and Ashenden immediately cried out:

"*Entrez.*"

Giulia Lazzari sprang up in bed to a sitting posture.

"Who is it?" she called.

She gave a gasp as she saw the two detectives who had brought her from Boulogne and handed her over to Ashenden at Thonon.

"You! What do you want?" she shrieked.

"*Allons, levez vous,*" said one of them, and his voice had a sharp abruptness that suggested that he would put up with no nonsense.

"I'm afraid you must get up, Madame Lazzari," said Ashenden. "I am delivering you once more to the care of these gentlemen."

"How can I get up! I'm ill, I tell you. I cannot stand. Do you want to kill me?"

"If you won't dress yourself, we shall have to dress you, and I'm afraid we shouldn't do it very cleverly. Come, come, it's no good making a scene."

"Where are you going to take me?"

"They're going to take you back to England."

One of the detectives took hold of her arm.

"Don't touch me, don't come near me," she screamed furiously.

"Let her be," said Ashenden. "I'm sure she'll see the necessity of making as little trouble as possible."

"I'll dress myself."

Ashenden watched her as she took off her dressing-gown and slipped a dress over her head. She forced her feet into shoes obviously too small for her. She arranged her hair. Every now and then she gave the detectives a hurried, sullen glance. Ashenden wondered if she would have the nerve to go through with it. R. would call him a damned fool, but he almost wished she would. She went up to the dressing-table and Ashenden stood up in order to let her sit down. She greased her face quickly and then rubbed off the grease with a dirty towel, she powdered herself and made up her eyes. But her hand shook. The three men watched her in silence. She rubbed the rouge on her cheeks and painted her mouth. Then she crammed a hat down on her head. Ashenden made a gesture to the first detective and he took a pair of handcuffs out of his pocket and advanced towards her.

At the sight of them she started back violently and flung her arms wide.

"*Non, non, non, Je ne veux pas.* No, not them. No. No."

"Come, *ma fille*, don't be silly," said the detective roughly.

As though for protection (very much to his surprise) she flung her arms round Ashenden.

"Don't let them take me, have mercy on me, I can't, I can't."

Ashenden extricated himself as best he could.

"I can do nothing more for you."

The detective seized her wrists and was about to affix the handcuffs when with a great cry she threw herself down on the floor.

"I will do what you wish. I will do everything."

On a sign from Ashenden the detectives left the room. He waited for a little till she had regained a certain calm. She was lying on the floor, sobbing passionately. He raised her to her feet and made her sit down.

"What do you want me to do?" she gasped.

"I want you to write another letter to Chandra."

"My head is in a whirl. I could not put two phrases together. You must give me time."

But Ashenden felt that it was better to get her to write a letter while she was under the effect of her terror. He did not want to give her time to collect herself.

"I will dictate the letter to you. All you have to do is to write exactly what I tell you."

She gave a deep sigh, but took the pen and the paper and sat down before them at the dressing-table.

"If I do this and . . . and you succeed, how do I know that I shall be allowed to go free?"

"The Colonel promised that you should. You must take my word for it that I shall carry out his instructions."

"I *should* look a fool if I betrayed my friend and then went to prison for ten years."

"I'll tell you your best guarantee of our good faith. Except by reason of Chandra you are not of the smallest importance to us.

Why should we put ourselves to the bother and expense of keeping you in prison when you can do us no harm?"

She reflected for an instant. She was composed now. It was as though, having exhausted her emotion, she had become on a sudden a sensible and practical woman.

"Tell me what you want me to write."

Ashenden hesitated. He thought he could put the letter more or less in the way she would naturally have put it, but he had to give it consideration. It must be neither fluent nor literary. He knew that in moments of emotion people are inclined to be melodramatic and stilted. In a book or on the stage this always rings false and the author has to make his people speak more simply and with less emphasis than in fact they do. It was a serious moment, but Ashenden felt that there were in it elements of the comic.

"I didn't know I loved a coward," he started. "If you loved me you couldn't hesitate when I ask you to come. . . . Underline *couldn't* twice." He went on. "When I promise you there is no danger. If you don't love me, you are right not to come. Don't come. Go back to Berlin where you are in safety. I am sick of it. I am alone here. I have made myself ill by waiting for you and every day I have said he is coming. If you loved me you would not hesitate so much. It is quite clear to me that you do not love me. I am sick and tired of you. I have no money. This hotel is impossible. There is nothing for me to stay for. I can get an engagement in Paris. I have a friend there who has made me serious propositions. I have wasted long enough over you and look what I have got from it. It is finished. Good-bye. You will never find a woman who will love you as I have loved you. I cannot afford to refuse the proposition of my friend, so I have telegraphed to him and as soon as I shall receive his answer I go to Paris. I do not blame you because you do not love me, that is not your fault, but you must see that I should be a stupid to go on wasting my life. One is not young for ever. Good-bye. Giulia."

When Ashenden read over the letter he was not altogether satisfied. But it was the best he could do. It had an air of verisimilitude which the words lacked because, knowing little English, she had written phonetically, the spelling was atrocious and the handwriting like a child's; she had crossed out words and written them over again. Some of the phrases he had put in French.

Once or twice tears had fallen on the pages and blurred the ink.

"I leave you now," said Ashenden. "It may be that when next you see me I shall be able to tell you that you are free to go where you choose. Where do you want to go?"

"Spain."

"Very well, I will have everything prepared."

She shrugged her shoulders. He left her.

There was nothing now for Ashenden to do but wait. He sent a messenger to Lausanne in the afternoon, and next morning went down to the quay to meet the boat. There was a waiting-room next to the ticket-office and here he told the detectives to hold themselves in readiness. When a boat arrived the passengers advanced along the pier in line and their passports were examined before they were allowed to go ashore. If Chandra came and showed his passport, and it was very likely that he was travelling with a false one, issued probably by a neutral nation, he was to be asked to wait and Ashenden was to identify him. Then he would be arrested. It was with some excitement that Ashenden watched the boat come in and the little group of people gathered at the gangway. He scanned them closely but saw no one who looked in the least like an Indian. Chandra had not come. Ashenden did not know what to do. He had played his last card. There were not more than half a dozen passengers for Thonon, and when they had been examined and gone their way he strolled along the pier.

"Well, it's no go," he said to Felix, who had been examining the passports. "The gentleman I expected hasn't turned up."

"I have a letter for you."

He handed Ashenden an envelope addressed to Madame Lazzari on which he immediately recognized the spidery handwriting of Chandra Lal. At that moment the steamer from Geneva which was going to Lausanne and the end of the lake hove in sight. It arrived at Thonon every morning twenty minutes after the steamer going in the opposite direction had left. Ashenden had an inspiration.

"Where is the man who brought it?"

"He's in the ticket-office."

"Give him the letter and tell him to return to the person who gave it to him. He is to say that he took it to the lady and she sent it back. If the person asks him to take another letter he is to say that it is not much good as she is packing her trunk and leaving Thonon."

He saw the letter handed over and the instructions given and then walked back to his little house in the country.

The next boat on which Chandra could possibly come arrived about five and having at that hour an important engagement with an agent working in Germany he warned Felix that he might be a few minutes late. But if Chandra came he could easily be detained; there was no great hurry since the train in which he was to be taken to Paris did not start till shortly after eight. When Ashenden had finished his business he strolled leisurely down to the lake. It was light still and from the top of the hill he saw the steamer pulling out. It was an anxious moment and instinctively he quickened his steps. Suddenly he saw someone running towards him and recognised the man who had taken the letter.

"Quick, quick," he cried. "He's there."

Ashenden's heart gave a great thud against his chest.

"At last."

He began to run too and as they ran the man, panting, told him how he had taken back the unopened letter. When he put it in the Indian's hand he turned frightfully pale ("I should never have thought an Indian could turn that colour," he said), and turned it over and over in his hand as though he could not understand what his own letter was doing there. Tears sprang to his eyes and rolled down his cheeks. ("It was grotesque, he's fat, you know.") He said something in a language the man did not understand and then in French asked him when the boat went to Thonon. When he got on board he looked about, but did not see him, then he caught sight of him, huddled up in an ulster with his hat drawn down over his eyes, standing alone in the bows. During the crossing he kept his eyes fixed on Thonon.

"Where is he now?" asked Ashenden.

"I got off first and Monsieur Felix told me to come for you."

"I suppose they're holding him in the waiting-room."

Ashenden was out of breath when they reached the pier. He burst into the waiting-room. A group of men, talking at the top of their voices and gesticulating wildly, were clustered round a man lying on the ground.

"What's happened?" he cried.

"Look," said Monsieux Felix.

Chandra Lal lay there, his eyes wide open and a thin line of foam on his lips, dead. His body was horribly contorted.

"He's killed himself. We've sent for the doctor. He was too quick for us."

A sudden thrill of horror passed through Ashenden.

When the Indian landed Felix recognised from the description that he was the man they wanted. There were only four passengers. He was the last. Felix took an exaggerated time to examine the passports of the first three, and then took the Indian's. It was a Spanish one and it was all in order. Felix asked the regulation questions and noted them on the official sheet. Then he looked at him pleasantly and said:

"Just come into the waiting-room for a moment. There are one or two formalities to fulfil."

"Is my passport not in order?" the Indian asked.

"Perfectly."

Chandra hesitated, but then followed the official to the door of the waiting-room. Felix opened it and stood aside.

"*Entrez.*"

Chandra went in and the two detectives stood up. He must have suspected at once that they were police-officers and realised that he had fallen into a trap.

"Sit down," said Felix. "I have one or two questions to put to you."

"It is hot in here," he said, and in point of fact they had a little stove there that kept the place like an oven. "I will take off my coat if you permit."

"Certainly," said Felix graciously.

He took off his coat, apparently with some effort, and he turned to put it on a chair, and then before they realised what had happened they were startled to see him stagger and fall heavily to the ground. While taking off his coat Chandra had managed to swallow the contents of a bottle that was still clasped in his hand. Ashenden put his nose to it. There was a very distinct odour of almonds.

For a little while they looked at the man who lay on the floor. Felix was apologetic.

"Will they be very angry?" he asked nervously.

"I don't see that it was your fault," said Ashenden. "Anyhow, he can do no more harm. For my part I am just as glad he killed himself. The notion of his being executed did not make me very comfortable."

In a few minutes the doctor arrived and pronounced life extinct.

"Prussic acid," he said to Ashenden.

Ashenden nodded.

"I will go and see Madame Lazzari," he said. "If she wants to stay a day or two longer I shall let her. But if she wants to go to-night of course she can. Will you give the agents at the station instructions to let her pass?"

"I shall be at the station myself," said Felix.

Ashenden once more climbed the hill. It was night now, a cold, bright night with an unclouded sky and the sight of the new moon, a white shining thread, made him turn three times the money in his pocket. When he entered the hotel he was seized on a sudden with distaste for its cold banality. It smelt of cabbage and boiled mutton. On the walls of the hall were coloured posters of railway companies advertising Grenoble, Carcassonne and the bathing places of Normandy. He went upstairs and after a brief knock opened the door of Giulia Lazzari's room. She was sitting in front of her dressing-table, looking at herself in the glass, just idly, despairingly, apparently doing nothing, and it was in this that she saw Ashenden as he came in. Her face changed suddenly as she caught sight of his and she sprang up so vehemently that the chair fell over.

"What is it? Why are you so white?" she cried.

She turned round and stared at him and her features were gradually twisted to a look of horror.

"*Il est pris*," she gasped.

"*Il est mort*," said Ashenden.

"Dead! He took the poison. He had the time for that. He's escaped you after all."

"What do you mean? How did you know about the poison?"

"He always carried it with him. He said that the English should never take him alive."

Ashenden reflected for an instant. She had kept that secret well. He supposed the possibility of such a thing should have occurred to him. How was he to anticipate these melodramatic devices?

"Well, now you are free. You can go wherever you like and no obstacle shall be put in your way. Here are your ticket and your passport and here is the money that was in your possession when you were arrested. Do you wish to see Chandra?"

She started.

"No, no."

"There is no need. I thought you might care to."

She did not weep. Ashenden supposed that she had exhausted all her emotion. She seemed apathetic.

"A telegram will be sent to-night to the Spanish frontier to instruct the authorities to put no difficulties in your way. If you will take my advice you will get out of France as soon as you can."

She said nothing, and since Ashenden had no more to say he made ready to go.

"I am sorry that I have had to show myself so hard to you. I am glad to think that now the worst of your troubles are over and I hope that time will assuage the grief that I know you must feel for the death of your friend."

Ashenden gave her a little bow and turned to the door. But she stopped him.

"One little moment," she said. "There is one thing I should like to ask. I think you have some heart."

"Whatever I can do for you, you may be sure I will."

"What are they going to do with his things?"

"I don't know. Why?"

Then she said something that confounded Ashenden. It was the last thing he expected.

"He had a wrist-watch that I gave him last Christmas. It cost twelve pounds. Can I have it back?"

❖

The Traitor

WHEN Ashenden, given charge of a number of spies working from Switzerland, was first sent there, R., wishing him to see the sort of reports that he would be required to obtain, handed him the communications, a sheaf of typewritten documents, of a man known in the secret service as Gustav.

"He's the best fellow we've got," said R. "His information is always very full and circumstantial. I want you to give his reports your very best attention. Of course Gustav is a clever little chap, but there's no reason why we shouldn't get just as good reports from the other agents. It's merely a question of explaining exactly what we want."

Gustav, who lived at Basle, represented a Swiss firm with branches at Frankfort, Mannheim and Cologne, and by virtue of his business was able to go in and out of Germany without risk. He travelled up and down the Rhine, and gathered material about the movement of troops, the manufacture of munitions, the state of mind of the country (a point on which R. laid stress) and other matters upon which the Allies desired information. His frequent letters to his wife hid an ingenious code and the moment she received them in Basle she sent them to Ashenden in Geneva, who extracted from them the important facts and communicated these in the proper quarter. Every two months Gustav came home and prepared one of the reports that served as models to the other spies in this particular section of the secret service.

His employers were pleased with Gustav and Gustav had reason to be pleased with his employers. His services were so useful that he was not only paid more highly than the others, but for particular scoops had received from time to time a handsome bonus.

This went on for more than a year. Then something aroused R.'s quick suspicions; he was a man of an amazing alertness, not so much of mind, as of instinct, and he had suddenly a feeling that some hanky-panky was going on. He said nothing definite to Ashenden (whatever R. surmised he was disposed to keep to himself), but told him to go to Basle, Gustav being then in Germany, and have a talk with Gustav's wife. He left it to Ashenden to decide the tenor of the conversation.

Having arrived at Basle, and leaving his bag at the station, for he did not yet know whether he would have to stay or not, he took a tram to the corner of the street in which Gustav lived and, with a quick look to see that he was not followed, walked along to the house he sought. It was a block of flats that gave you the impression of decent poverty and Ashenden conjectured that they were inhabited by clerks and small tradespeople. Just inside the door was a cobbler's shop and Ashenden stopped.

"Does Herr Grabow live here?" he asked in his none too fluent German.

"Yes, I saw him go up a few minutes ago. You'll find him in."

Ashenden was startled, for he had but the day before received through Gustav's wife a letter addressed from Mannheim in which Gustav by means of his code gave the numbers of certain regiments that had just crossed the Rhine. Ashenden thought it unwise to ask the cobbler the question that rose to his lips, so thanked him and went up to the third floor, on which he knew already that Gustav lived. He rang the bell and heard it tinkle within. In a moment the door was opened by a dapper little man with a close-shaven round head and spectacles. He wore carpet slippers.

"Herr Grabow?" asked Ashenden.

"At your service," said Gustav.

"May I come in?"

Gustav was standing with his back to the light and Ashenden could not see the look on his face. He felt a momentary hesitation and gave the name under which he received Gustav's letters from Germany.

"Come in, come in. I am very glad to see you."

Gustav led the way into a stuffy little room, heavy with carved oak furniture, and on the large table covered with a table-cloth of green velveteen was a typewriter. Gustav was apparently engaged in composing one of his invaluable reports. A woman was sitting at the open window darning socks, but at a word from Gustav rose, gathered up her things and left. Ashenden had disturbed a pretty picture of connubial bliss.

"Sit down, please. How very fortunate that I was in Basle! I have long wanted to make your acquaintance. I have only just this minute returned from Germany." He pointed to the sheets of paper by the typewriter. "I think you will be pleased with the news

I bring. I have some very valuable information." He chuckled. "One is never sorry to earn a bonus."

He was very cordial, but to Ashenden his cordiality rang false. Gustav kept his eyes, smiling behind the glasses, fixed watchfully on Ashenden, and it was possible that they held a trace of nervousness.

"You must have travelled quickly to get here only a few hours after your letter, sent here and then sent on by your wife, reached me in Geneva."

"That is very probable. One of the things I had to tell you is that the Germans suspect that information is getting through by means of commercial letters and so they have decided to hold up all mail at the frontier for eight-and-forty hours."

"I see," said Ashenden amiably. "And was it on that account that you took the precaution of dating your letter forty-eight hours after you sent it?"

"Did I do that? That was very stupid of me. I must have mistaken the day of the month."

Ashenden looked at Gustav with a smile. That was very thin; Gustav, a business man, knew too well how important in his particular job was the exactness of a date. The circuitous routes by which it was necessary to get information from Germany made it difficult to transmit news quickly and it was essential to know precisely on what days certain events had taken place.

"Let me look at your passport a minute," said Ashenden.

"What do you want with my passport?"

"I want to see when you went into Germany and when you came out."

"But you do not imagine that my comings and goings are marked on my passport? I have methods of crossing the frontier."

Ashenden knew a good deal of this matter. He knew that both the Germans and the Swiss guarded the frontier with severity.

"Oh? Why should you not cross in the ordinary way? You were engaged because your connection with a Swiss firm supplying necessary goods to Germany made it easy for you to travel backwards and forwards without suspicion. I can understand that you might get past the German sentries with the connivance of the Germans, but what about the Swiss?"

Gustav assumed a look of indignation.

"I do not understand you. Do you mean to suggest that I am in the service of the Germans? I give you my word of honour . . . I will not allow my integrity to be impugned."

"You would not be the only one to take money from both sides and provide information of value to neither."

"Do you pretend that my information is of no value? Why then have you given me more bonuses than any other agent has received? The Colonel has repeatedly expressed the highest satisfaction with my services."

It was Ashenden's turn now to be cordial.

"Come, come, my dear fellow, do not try to ride the high horse. You do not wish to show me your passport and I will not insist. You are not under the impression that we leave the statements of our agents without corroboration or that we are so foolish as not to keep track of their movements? Even the best of jokes cannot bear an indefinite repetition. I am in peace-time a humorist by profession and I tell you that from bitter experience." Now Ashenden thought the moment had arrived to attempt his bluff; he knew something of the excellent but difficult game of poker. "We have information that you have not been to Germany now, nor since you were engaged by us, but have sat here quietly in Basle, and all your reports are merely due to your fertile imagination."

Gustav looked at Ashenden and saw a face expressive of nothing but tolerance and good-humour. A smile slowly broke on his lips and he gave his shoulders a little shrug.

"Did you think I was such a fool as to risk my life for fifty pounds a month? I love my wife."

Ashenden laughed outright.

"I congratulate you. It is not everyone who can flatter himself that he has made a fool of our secret service for a year."

"I had the chance of earning money without any difficulty. My firm stopped sending me into Germany at the beginning of the war, but I learned what I could from the other travellers. I kept my ears open in restaurants and beer-cellars, and I read the German papers. I got a lot of amusement out of sending you reports and letters."

"I don't wonder," said Ashenden.

"What are you going to do?"

"Nothing. What can we do? You are not under the impression that we shall continue to pay you a salary?"

"No, I cannot expect that."

"By the way, if it is not indiscreet, may I ask if you have been playing the same game with the Germans?"

"Oh, no," Gustav cried vehemently. "How can you think it?

My sympathies are absolutely pro-Ally. My heart is entirely with you."

"Well, why not?" asked Ashenden. "The Germans have all the money in the world and there is no reason why you should not get some of it. We could give you information from time to time that the Germans would be prepared to pay for."

Gustav drummed his fingers on the table. He took up a sheet of the now useless report.

"The Germans are dangerous people to meddle with."

"You are a very intelligent man. And after all, even if your salary is stopped, you can always earn a bonus by bringing us news that can be useful to us. But it will have to be substantiated; in future we pay only by results."

"I will think of it."

For a moment or two Ashenden left Gustav to his reflections. He lit a cigarette and watched the smoke he had inhaled fade into the air. He thought too.

"Is there anything particular you want to know?" asked Gustav suddenly.

Ashenden smiled.

"It would be worth a couple of thousand Swiss francs to you if you could tell me what the Germans are doing with a spy of theirs in Lucerne. He is an Englishman and his name is Grantley Caypor."

"I have heard the name," said Gustav. He paused a moment. "How long are you staying here?"

"As long as necessary. I will take a room at the hotel and let you know the number. If you have anything to say to me you can be sure of finding me in my room at nine every morning and at seven every night."

"I should not risk coming to the hotel. But I can write."

"Very well."

Ashenden rose to go and Gustav accompanied him to the door. "We part without ill-feeling then?" he asked.

"Of course. Your reports will remain in our archives as models of what a report should be."

Ashenden spent two or three days visiting Basle. It did not much amuse him. He passed a good deal of time in the book-shops turning over the pages of books that would have been worth reading if life were a thousand years long. Once he saw Gustav in the street. On the fourth morning a letter was brought up with his coffee. The envelope was that of a commercial firm unknown to him and inside it was a typewritten sheet. There was no address and no signature. Ashenden wondered if Gustav was aware that a typewriter could betray its owner as certainly as a handwriting. Having twice carefully read the letter, he held the paper up to the light to see the watermark (he had no reason for doing this except that the sleuths of detective novels always did it), then struck a match and watched it burn. He scrunched up the charred fragments in his hand.

He got up, for he had taken advantage of his situation to break-fast in bed, packed his bag and took the next train to Berne. From there he was able to send a code telegram to R. His instructions were given to him verbally two days later, in the bedroom of his hotel at an hour when no one was likely to be seen walking along a corridor, and within twenty-four hours, though by a circuitous route, he arrived at Lucerne.

Having taken a room at the hotel at which he had been instructed to stay, Ashenden went out; it was a lovely day, early in August, and the sun shone in an unclouded sky. He had not been to Lucerne since he was a boy and but vaguely remembered a covered bridge, a great stone lion and a church in which he had sat, bored yet impressed, while they played an organ; and, now wandering along a shady quay (and the lake looked just as tawdry and unreal as it looked on the picture-postcards) he tried not so much to find his way about a half-forgotten scene as to reform in his mind some recollection of the shy and eager lad, so impatient for life (which he saw not in the present of his adolescence but only in the future of his manhood) who so long ago had wandered there. But it seemed to him that the most vivid of his memories was not of himself, but of the crowd; he seemed to remember sun and heat and people; the train was crowded and so was the hotel, the lake steamers were packed and on the quays and in the streets you threaded your way among the throng of holiday-makers. They were fat and old and ugly and odd, and they stank. Now, in war-time, Lucerne was as deserted as it must have been before the world at large discovered that Switzerland was the playground of Europe. Most of the hotels were closed, the streets were empty, the rowing boats for hire rocked idly at the water's edge and there was none to take them, and in the avenues by the lake the only persons to be seen were serious Swiss taking their neutrality, like a dachshund, for a walk with them. Ashenden felt exhilarated by the solitude and, sitting down on a bench that faced the water, surrendered himself deliberately to the sensation. It was true that the lake was absurd, the water was too blue, the mountains too snowy, and its beauty, hitting you in the face, exasperated rather than thrilled; but all the same there was something pleasing in the prospect, an artless candour, like one of Mendelssohn's *Songs Without Words*, that made Ashenden smile with complacency. Lucerne reminded him of wax flowers under glass cases and cuckoo clocks and fancy-work in Berlin wool. So long at all events as the fine weather lasted he was prepared to enjoy himself. He did not see why he should not at least try to combine pleasure to himself with profit to his country. He was travelling with a brand-new passport in his pocket, under a borrowed name, and this gave him an agreeable sense of owning a new personality. He was often slightly tired of himself and it diverted him for a while to be merely a creature of R.'s facile invention. The experience he had just enjoyed appealed to his acute sense of the absurd. R., it is true, had not seen the fun of it: what humour R. possessed was of a sardonic turn and he had no facility for taking in good part a joke at his own expense. To do that you must be able to look at yourself from the outside and be at the same time spectator and actor in the pleasant comedy of life. R. was a soldier and regarded introspection as unhealthy, un-English and unpatriotic.

Ashenden got up and strolled slowly to his hotel. It was a small German hotel, of the second class, spotlessly clean, and his bedroom had a nice view; it was furnished with brightly varnished pitch-pine, and though on a cold wet day it would have been wretched, in that warm and sunny weather it was gay and pleasing. There were tables in the hall and he sat down at one of these and ordered a bottle of beer. The landlady was curious to know why in that dead season he had come to stay and he was glad to satisfy her curiosity. He told her that he had recently recovered from an attack of typhoid and had come to Lucerne to get back his strength. He was employed in the Censorship Department and was taking the opportunity to brush up his rusty German. He asked her if she could recommend to him a German teacher. The landlady was a blond and blowsy Swiss, good-humoured and talkative, so that Ashenden felt pretty sure that she would repeat in the proper quarter the information he gave her. It was his turn now to ask a few questions. She was voluble on the subject of the war on account of which the hotel, in that month so full that rooms had

to be found for visitors in neighbouring houses, was nearly empty.
A few people came in from outside to eat their meals *en pension*
but she had only two lots of resident guests. One was an old
Irish couple who lived in Vevey and passed their summers in
Lucerne and the other was an Englishman and his wife. She was
a German and they were obliged on that account to live in a
neutral country. Ashenden took care to show little curiosity
about them—he recognised in the description Grantley Caypor—
but of her own accord she told him that they spent most of the
day walking about the mountains. Herr Caypor was a botanist
and much interested in the flora of the country. His lady was a
very nice woman and she felt her position keenly. Ah, well, the
war could not last for ever. The landlady bustled away and
Ashenden went upstairs.

Dinner was at seven, and, wishing to be in the dining-room
before anyone else so that he could take stock of his fellow-
guests as they entered, he went down as soon as he heard the bell.
It was a very plain, stiff, white-washed room, with chairs of the
same shiny pitch-pine as in his bedroom, and on the walls were
oleographs of Swiss lakes. On each little table was a bunch of
flowers. It was all neat and clean and presaged a bad dinner.
Ashenden would have liked to make up for it by ordering a bottle
of the best Rhine wine to be found in the hotel, but did not
venture to draw attention to himself by extravagance (he saw
on two or three tables half-empty bottles of table hock, which
made him surmise that his fellow-guests drank thriftily), and so
contented himself with ordering a pint of lager. Presently one
or two persons came in, single men with some occupation in
Lucerne and obviously Swiss, and sat down each at his own little
table and untied the napkins that at the end of luncheon they
had neatly tied up. They propped newspapers against their water-
jugs and read while they somewhat noisily ate their soup. Then
entered a very old tall bent man, with white hair and a drooping
white moustache, accompanied by a little old white-haired lady
in black. These were certainly the Irish colonel and his wife of
whom the landlady had spoken. They took their seats and the
colonel poured out a thimbleful of wine for his wife and a thimbleful for himself. They waited in silence for their dinner to be
served to them by the buxom, hearty maid.

At last the persons arrived for whom Ashenden had been
waiting. He was doing his best to read a German book and it

was only by an exercise of self-control that he allowed himself only for one instant to raise his eyes as they came in. His glance showed him a man of about forty-five with short dark hair, somewhat grizzled, of middle height, but corpulent, with a broad red clean-shaven face. He wore a shirt open at the neck, with a wide collar, and a grey suit. He walked ahead of his wife, and of her Ashenden only caught the impression of a German woman self-effaced and dusty. Grantley Caypor sat down and began in a loud voice explaining to the waitress that they had taken an immense walk. They had been up some mountain the name of which meant nothing to Ashenden, but which excited in the maid expressions of astonishment and enthusiasm. Then Caypor, still in fluent German but with a marked English accent, said that they were so late they had not even gone up to wash, but had just rinsed their hands outside. He had a resonant voice and a jovial manner.

"Serve me quick, we're starving with hunger, and bring beer, bring three bottles. *Lieber Gott*, what a thirst I have!"

He seemed to be a man of exuberant vitality. He brought into that dull, overclean dining-room the breath of life and everyone in it appeared on a sudden more alert. He began to talk to his wife, in English, and everything he said could be heard by all; but presently she interrupted him with a remark made in an undertone. Caypor stopped and Ashenden felt that his eyes were turned in his direction. Mrs. Caypor had noticed the arrival of a stranger and had drawn her husband's attention to it. Ashenden turned the page of the book he was pretending to read, but he felt that Caypor's gaze was fixed intently upon him. When he addressed his wife again it was in so low a tone that Ashenden could not even tell what language he used, but when the maid brought them their soup Caypor, his voice still low, asked her a question. It was plain that he was enquiring who Ashenden was. Ashenden could catch of the maid's reply but the one word *länder*.

One or two people finished their dinner and went out picking their teeth. The old Irish colonel and his old wife rose from their table and he stood aside to let her pass. They had eaten their meal without exchanging a word. She walked slowly to the door; but the colonel stopped to say a word to a Swiss who might have been a local attorney, and when she reached it she stood there, bowed and with a sheep-like look, patiently waiting for her husband to come and open it for her. Ashenden realised that she had never opened a door for herself. She did not know how to. In a minute the colonel with his old, old gait came to the door and opened it; she passed out and he followed. The little incident offered a key to their whole lives, and from it Ashenden began to reconstruct their histories, circumstances and characters; but he pulled himself up; he could not allow himself the luxury of creation. He finished his dinner.

When he went into the hall he saw tied to the leg of a table a bull-terrier and in passing mechanically put down his hand to fondle the dog's drooping, soft ears. The landlady was standing at the foot of the stairs.

"Whose is this lovely beast?" asked Ashenden.

"He belongs to Herr Caypor. Fritzi, he is called. Herr Caypor says he has a longer pedigree than the King of England."

Fritzi rubbed himself against Ashenden's leg and with his nose sought the palm of his hand. Ashenden went upstairs to fetch his hat, and when he came down saw Caypor standing at the entrance of the hotel talking with the landlady. From the sudden silence and their constrained manner he guessed that Caypor had been making enquiries about him. When he passed between them, into the street, out of the corner of his eye he saw Caypor give a suspicious stare. That frank, jovial red face bore then a look of shifty cunning.

Ashenden strolled along till he found a tavern where he could have his coffee in the open and to compensate himself for the bottle of beer that his sense of duty had urged him to drink at dinner ordered the best brandy the house provided. He was pleased at last to have come face to face with the man of whom he had heard so much and in a day or two hoped to become acquainted with him. It is never very difficult to get to know anyone who has a dog. But he was in no hurry; he would let things take their course: with the object he had in view he could not afford to be hasty.

Ashenden reviewed the circumstances. Grantley Caypor was an Englishman, born according to his passport in Birmingham, and he was forty-two years of age. His wife, to whom he had been married for eleven years, was of German birth and parentage. That was public knowledge. Information about his antecedents was contained in a private document. He had started life, according to this, in a lawyer's office in Birmingham and then had drifted into journalism. He had been connected with an English paper in

Cairo and with another in Shanghai. There he got into trouble for attempting to get money on false pretences and was sentenced to a short term of imprisonment. All trace of him was lost for two years after his release, when he reappeared in a shipping-office in Marseilles. From there, still in the shipping business, he went to Hamburg, where he married, and to London. In London he set up for himself in the export business, but after some time failed and was made a bankrupt. He returned to journalism. At the outbreak of war he was once more in the shipping business, and in August, 1914, was living quietly with his German wife at Southampton. In the beginning of the following year he told his employers that owing to the nationality of his wife his position was intolerable; they had no fault to find with him and, recognising that he was in an awkward fix, granted his request that he should be transferred to Genoa. Here he remained till Italy entered the war, but then gave notice and with his papers in perfect order crossed the border and took up his residence in Switzerland.

All this indicated a man of doubtful honesty and unsettled disposition, with no background and of no financial standing; but the facts were of no importance to anyone till it was discovered that Caypor, certainly from the beginning of the war and perhaps sooner, was in the service of the German Intelligence Department. He had a salary of forty pounds a month. But though dangerous and wily no steps would have been taken to deal with him if he had contented himself with transmitting such news as he was able to get in Switzerland. He could do no great harm there and it might even be possible to make use of him to convey information that it was desirable to let the enemy have. He had no notion that anything was known of him. His letters, and he received a good many, were closely censored; there were few codes that the people who dealt with such matters could not in the end decipher and it might be that sooner or later through him it would be possible to lay hands on the organisation that still flourished in England. But then he did something that drew R.'s attention to him. Had he known it none could have blamed him for shaking in his shoes: R. was not a very nice man to get on the wrong side of. Caypor scraped acquaintance in Zurich with a young Spaniard, Gomez by name, who had lately entered the British secret service, by his nationality inspired him with confidence, and managed to worm out of him the fact that he was engaged in espionage. Probably the Spaniard, with a very human desire to seem important, had done no more than talk mysteriously; but on Caypor's information he was watched when he went to Germany and one day caught just as he was posting a letter in a code that was eventually deciphered. He was tried, convicted and shot. It was bad enough to lose a useful and disinterested agent, but it entailed besides the changing of a safe and simple code. R. was not pleased. But R. was not the man to let any desire of revenge stand in the way of his main object, and it occurred to him that if Caypor was merely betraying his country for money it might be possible to get him to take more money to betray his employers. The fact that he had succeeded in delivering into their hands an agent of the Allies must seem to them an earnest of his good faith. He might be very useful. But R. had no notion what kind of man Caypor was, he had lived his shabby, furtive life obscurely, and the only photograph that existed of him was one taken for a passport. Ashenden's instructions were to get acquainted with Caypor and see whether there was any chance that he would work honestly for the British: if he thought there was, he was entitled to sound him and if his suggestions were met with favour to make certain propositions. It was a task that needed tact and a knowledge of men. If on the other hand Ashenden came to the conclusion that Caypor could not be bought, he was to watch and report his movements. The information he had obtained from Gustav was vague, but important; there was only one point in it that was interesting, and this was that the head of the German Intelligence Department in Berne was growing restive at Caypor's lack of activity. Caypor was asking for a higher salary and Major von P. had told him that he must earn it. It might be that he was urging him to go to England. If he could be induced to cross the frontier Ashenden's work was done.

"How the devil do you expect *me* to persuade him to put his head in a noose?" asked Ashenden.

"It won't be a noose, it'll be a firing squad," said R.

"Caypor's clever."

"Well, be cleverer, damn your eyes."

Ashenden made up his mind that he would take no steps to make Caypor's acquaintance, but allow the first advances to be made by him. If he was being pressed for results it must surely occur to him that it would be worth while to get into conversation with an Englishman who was employed in the Censorship Department. Ashenden was prepared with a supply of information that it could not in the least benefit the Central Powers to possess. With a false name and a false passport he had little to fear that Caypor would guess that he was a British agent.

Ashenden did not have to wait long. Next day he was sitting in the doorway of the hotel, drinking a cup of coffee and already half asleep after a substantial *mittagessen*, when the Caypors came out of the dining-room. Mrs. Caypor went upstairs and Caypor released his dog. The dog bounded along and in a friendly fashion leaped up against Ashenden.

"Come here, Fritzi," cried Caypor, and then to Ashenden: "I'm so sorry. But he's quite gentle."

"Oh, that's all right. He won't hurt me."

Caypor stopped at the doorway.

"He's a bull-terrier. You don't often see them on the Continent." He seemed while he spoke to be taking Ashenden's measure; he called to the maid: "A coffee, please, *fräulein*. You've just arrived, haven't you?"

"Yes, I came yesterday."

"Really? I didn't see you in the dining-room last night. Are you making a stay?"

"I don't know. I've been ill and I've come here to recuperate."

The maid came with the coffee and seeing Caypor talking to Ashenden put the tray on the table at which he was sitting. Caypor gave a laugh of faint embarrassment.

"I don't want to force myself upon you. I don't know why the maid put my coffee on your table."

"Please sit down," said Ashenden.

"It's very good of you. I've lived so long on the Continent that I'm always forgetting that my countrymen are apt to look upon it as confounded cheek if you talk to them. Are you English, by the way, or American?"

"English," said Ashenden.

Ashenden was by nature a very shy person, and he had in vain tried to cure himself of a failing that at his age was unseemly, but on occasion he knew how to make effective use of it. He explained now in a hesitating and awkward manner the facts that he had the day before told the landlady and that he was convinced she had already passed on to Caypor.

"You couldn't have come to a better place than Lucerne. It's an oasis of peace in this war-weary world. When you're here you might almost forget that there is such a thing as a war going on. That is why I've come here. I'm a journalist by profession."

"I couldn't help wondering if you wrote," said Ashenden, with an eagerly timid smile.

It was clear that he had not learnt that 'oasis of peace in a war-weary world' at the shipping-office.

"You see, I married a German lady," said Caypor gravely.

"Oh, really?"

"I don't think anyone could be more patriotic than I am. I'm English through and through and I don't mind telling you that in my opinion the British Empire is the greatest instrument for good that the world has ever seen, but having a German wife I naturally see a good deal of the reverse of the medal. You don't have to tell me that the Germans have faults, but frankly I'm not prepared to admit that they're devils incarnate. At the beginning of the war my poor wife had a very rough time in England and I for one couldn't have blamed her if she'd felt rather bitter about it. Everyone thought she was a spy. It'll make you laugh when you know her. She's the typical German *hausfrau* who cares for nothing but her house and her husband and our only child Fritzi." Caypor fondled his dog and gave a little laugh. "Yes, Fritzi, you are our child, aren't you? Naturally it made my position very awkward. I was connected with some very important papers, and my editors weren't quite comfortable about it. Well, to cut a long story short I thought the most dignified course was to resign and come to a neutral country till the storm blew over. My wife and I never discuss the war, though I'm bound to tell you that it's more on my account than hers, she's much more tolerant than I am and she's more willing to look upon this terrible business from my point of view than I am from hers."

"That is strange," said Ashenden. "As a rule women are so much more rabid than men."

"My wife is a very remarkable person. I should like to introduce you to her. By the way, I don't know if you know my name. Grantley Caypor."

"My name is Somerville," said Ashenden.

He told him then of the work he had been doing in the Censorship Department, and he fancied that into Caypor's eyes came a certain intentness. Presently he told him that he was looking for someone to give him conversation-lessons in German so that he might rub up his rusty knowledge of the language; and as he spoke a notion flashed across his mind: he gave Caypor a look and saw that the same notion had come to him. It had occurred to them at the same instant that it would be a very good plan for Ashenden's teacher to be Mrs. Caypor.

"I asked our landlady if she could find me someone and she said she thought she could. I must ask her again. It ought not to be very hard to find a man who is prepared to come and talk German to me for an hour a day."

"I wouldn't take anyone on the landlady's recommendation," said Caypor. "After all you want someone with a good North-German accent and she only talks Swiss. I'll ask my wife if she knows anyone. My wife's a very highly educated woman and you could trust her recommendation."

"That's very kind of you."

Ashenden observed Grantley Caypor at his ease. He noticed how the small, grey-green eyes, which last night he had not been able to see, contradicted the red good-humoured frankness of the face. They were quick and shifty, but when the mind behind them was seized by an unexpected notion they were suddenly still. It gave one a peculiar feeling of the working of the brain. They were not eyes that inspired confidence; Caypor did that with his jolly, good-natured smile, the openness of his broad, weather-beaten face, his comfortable obesity and the cheeriness of his loud, deep voice. He was doing his best now to be agreeable. While Ashenden talked to him, a little shyly still but gaining confidence from that breezy, cordial manner, capable of putting anyone at his ease, it intrigued him to remember that the man was a common spy. It gave a tang to his conversation to reflect that he had been ready to sell his country for no more than forty pounds a month. Ashenden had known Gomez, the young Spaniard whom Caypor had betrayed. He was a high-spirited youth, with a love of adventure, and he had undertaken his dangerous mission not for the money he earned by it, but from a passion for romance. It amused him to outwit the clumsy German and it appealed to his sense of the absurd to play a part in a shilling shocker. It was not very nice to think of him now six feet underground in a prison yard. He was young and he had a certain grace of gesture. Ashenden wondered whether Caypor had felt a qualm when he delivered him up to destruction.

"I suppose you know a little German?" asked Caypor, interested in the stranger.

"Oh, yes, I was a student in Germany, and I used to talk it

fluently, but that is long ago and I have forgotten. I can still read it very comfortably."

"Oh, yes, I noticed you were reading a German book last night."

Fool! It was only a little while since he had told Ashenden that he had not seen him at dinner. He wondered whether Caypor had observed the slip. How difficult it was never to make one! Ashenden must be on his guard; the thing that made him most nervous was the thought that he might not answer readily enough to his assumed name of Somerville. Of course there was always the chance that Caypor had made the slip on purpose to see by Ashenden's face whether he noticed anything. Caypor got up.

"There is my wife. We go for a walk up one of the mountains every afternoon. I can tell you some charming walks. The flowers even now are lovely."

"I'm afraid I must wait till I'm a bit stronger," said Ashenden, with a little sigh.

He had naturally a pale face and never looked as robust as he was. Mrs. Caypor came downstairs and her husband joined her. They walked down the road, Fritzi bounding round them, and Ashenden saw that Caypor immediately began to speak with volubility. He was evidently telling his wife the results of his interview with Ashenden. Ashenden looked at the sun shining so gaily on the lake; the shadow of a breeze fluttered the green leaves of the trees; everything invited to a stroll: he got up, went to his room and throwing himself on his bed had a very pleasant sleep.

He went into dinner that evening as the Caypors were finishing, for he had wandered melancholy about Lucerne in the hope of finding a cocktail that would enable him to face the potato salad that he foresaw, and on their way out of the dining-room Caypor stopped and asked him if he would drink coffee with them. When Ashenden joined them in the hall Caypor got up and introduced him to his wife. She bowed stiffly and no answering smile came to her face to respond to Ashenden's civil greeting. It was not hard to see that her attitude was definitely hostile. It put Ashenden at his ease. She was a plainish woman, nearing forty, with a muddy skin and vague features; her drab hair was arranged in a plait round her head like that of Napoleon's Queen of Prussia; and she was squarely built, plump rather than fat, and solid.

But she did not look stupid; she looked, on the contrary, a woman of character and Ashenden, who had lived enough in Germany to recognise the type, was ready to believe that though capable of doing the housework, cooking the dinner and climbing a mountain, she might be also prodigiously well-informed. She wore a white blouse that showed a sunburned neck, a black skirt and heavy walking boots. Caypor addressing her in English told her in his jovial way, as though she did not know it already, what Ashenden had told him about himself. She listened grimly.

"I think you told me you understood German," said Caypor, his big red face wreathed in polite smiles but his little eyes darting about restlessly.

"Yes, I was for some time a student in Heidelberg."

"Really?" said Mrs. Caypor in English, an expression of faint interest for a moment chasing away the sullenness from her face. "I know Heidelberg very well. I was at school there for one year."

Her English was correct, but throaty, and the mouthing emphasis she gave her words was disagreeable. Ashenden was diffuse in praise of the old university town and the beauty of the neighbourhood. She heard him, from the standpoint of her Teutonic superiority, with toleration rather than with enthusiasm.

"It is well known that the valley of the Neckar is one of the beauty places of the whole world," she said.

"I have not told you, my dear," said Caypor then, "that Mr. Somerville is looking for someone to give him conversation lessons while he is here. I told him that perhaps you could suggest a teacher."

"No, I know no one whom I could conscientiously recommend," she answered. "The Swiss accent is hateful beyond words. It could do Mr. Somerville only harm to converse with a Swiss."

"If I were in your place, Mr. Somerville, I would try and persuade my wife to give you lessons. She is, if I may say so, a very cultivated and highly educated woman."

"Ach, Grantley, I have not the time. I have my own work to do."

Ashenden saw that he was being given his opportunity. The trap was prepared and all he had to do was to fall in. He turned to Mrs. Caypor with a manner that he tried to make shy, deprecating and modest.

"Of course it would be too wonderful if you would give me lessons. I should look upon it as a real privilege. Naturally I wouldn't want to interfere with your work. I am just here to get well, with nothing in the world to do, and I would suit my time entirely to your convenience."

He felt a flash of satisfaction pass from one to the other and in Mrs. Caypor's blue eyes he fancied that he saw a dark glow.

"Of course it would be a purely business arrangement," said Caypor. "There's no reason that my good wife shouldn't earn a little pin-money. Would you think ten francs an hour too much?"

"No," said Ashenden, "I should think myself lucky to get a first-rate teacher for that."

"What do you say, my dear? Surely you can spare an hour, and you would be doing this gentleman a kindness. He would learn that all Germans are not the devilish fiends that they think them in England."

On Mrs. Caypor's brow was an uneasy frown and Ashenden could not but think with apprehension of that hour's conversation a day that he was going to exchange with her. Heaven only knew how he would have to rack his brain for subjects of discourse with that heavy and morose woman. Now she made a visible effort.

"I shall be very pleased to give Mr. Somerville conversation lessons."

"I congratulate you, Mr. Somerville," said Caypor noisily. "You're in for a treat. When will you start, to-morrow at eleven?"

"That would suit me very well if it suits Mrs. Caypor."

"Yes, that is as good an hour as another," she answered.

Ashenden left them to discuss the happy outcome of their diplomacy. But when, punctually at eleven next morning, he heard a knock at his door (for it had been arranged that Mrs. Caypor should give him his lesson in his room) it was not without trepidation that he opened it. It behoved him to be frank, a trifle indiscreet, but obviously wary of a German woman, sufficiently intelligent, and impulsive. Mrs. Caypor's face was dark and sulky. She plainly hated having anything to do with him. But they sat down and she began, somewhat peremptorily, to ask him questions about his knowledge of German literature. She corrected his mistakes with exactness and when he put before her some difficulty in German construction explained it with clearness and precision. It was obvious that though she hated giving him a lesson she meant to give it conscientiously. She seemed to have not only an aptitude for teaching, but a love of it, and as the hour went on she began to speak with greater earnestness. It was already only by an effort that she remembered that he was a brutal Englishman. Ashenden, noticing the unconscious struggle within her, found himself not a little entertained; and it was with truth that, when later in the day Caypor asked him how the lesson had gone, he answered that it was highly satisfactory; Mrs. Caypor was an excellent teacher and a most interesting person.

"I told you so. She's the most remarkable woman I know."

And Ashenden had a feeling that when in his hearty, laughing way Caypor said this he was for the first time entirely sincere.

In a day or two Ashenden guessed that Mrs. Caypor was giving him lessons only in order to enable Caypor to arrive at a closer intimacy with him, for she confined herself strictly to matters of literature, music and painting; and when Ashenden, by way of experiment, brought the conversation round to the war, she cut him short.

"I think that is a topic that we had better avoid, Herr Somerville," she said.

She continued to give her lessons with the greatest thoroughness, and he had his money's worth, but every day she came with the same sullen face and it was only in the interest of teaching that she lost for a moment her instinctive dislike of him. Ashenden exercised in turn, but in vain, all his wiles. He was ingratiating, ingenuous humble, grateful, flattering, simple and timid. She remained coldly hostile. She was a fanatic. Her patriotism was aggressive, but disinterested, and obsessed with the notion of the superiority of all things German she loathed England with a virulent hatred because in that country she saw the chief obstacle to their diffusion. Her ideal was a German world in which the rest of the nations under a hegemony greater than that of Rome should enjoy the benefits of German science and German art and German culture. There was in the conception a magnificent impudence that appealed to Ashenden's sense of humour. She was no fool. She had read much, in several languages, and she could talk of the books she had read with good sense. She had a knowledge of modern painting and modern music that not a little impressed Ashenden. It was amusing once to hear her before luncheon play one of those silvery little pieces of Debussy; she played it disdainfully because it was French and so light, but with an angry appreciation of its grace and gaiety. When Ashenden congratulated her she shrugged her shoulders.

"The decadent music of a decadent nation." she said. Then with powerful hands she struck the first resounding chords of a sonata by Beethoven; but she stopped. "I cannot play, I am out of practice, and you English, what do you know of music? You have not produced a composer since Purcell!"

"What do you think of that statement?" Ashenden, smiling, asked Caypor, who was standing near.

"I confess its truth. The little I know of music my wife taught me. I wish you could hear her play when she is in practice." He put his fat hand, with its square, stumpy fingers, on her shoulder. "She can wring your heartstrings with pure beauty."

"*Dummer Kerl,*" she said, in a soft voice, "Stupid fellow," and Ashenden saw her mouth for a moment quiver, but she quickly recovered. "You English, you cannot paint, you cannot model, you cannot write music."

"Some of us can at times write pleasing verses," said Ashenden, with good-humour, for it was not his business to be put out, and, he did not know why, two lines occurring to him he said them:

"*Whither, O splendid ship, thy white sails crowding,*
  Leaning across the bosom of the urgent West."

"Yes," said Mrs. Caypor, with a strange gesture, "you can write poetry. I wonder why."

And to Ashenden's surprise she went on, in her guttural English, to recite the next two lines of the poem he had quoted.

"Come, Grantley, *mittagessen* is ready, let us go into the dining-room."

They left Ashenden reflective.

Ashenden admired goodness, but was not outraged by wickedness. People sometimes thought him heartless because he was more often interested in others than attached to them, and even in the few to whom he was attached his eyes saw with equal clearness the merits and the defects. When he liked people it was not because he was blind to their faults, he did not mind their faults but accepted them with a tolerant shrug of the shoulders, or because he ascribed to them excellencies that they did not possess; and since he judged his friends with candour they never disappointed him and so he seldom lost one. He asked from none more than he could give. He was able to pursue his study of the Caypors without prejudice and without passion. Mrs. Caypor seemed to him more of a piece and therefore the easier of the two to understand; she obviously detested him; though it was necessary for her to be civil to him her antipathy was strong enough to wring from her now and then an expression of rudeness; and had she been safely able to do so she would have killed him without a qualm. But in the pressure of Caypor's chubby hand on his wife's shoulder and in the fugitive trembling of her lips Ashenden had divined that this unprepossessing woman and that mean fat man were joined together by a deep and sincere love. It was touching. Ashenden assembled the observations that he had been making for the past few days and little things that he had noticed but to which he had attached no significance returned to him. It seemed to him that Mrs. Caypor loved her husband because she was of a stronger character than he and because she felt his dependence on her; she loved him for his admiration of her, and you might guess that till she met him this dumpy, plain woman with her dullness, good sense and want of humour could not have much enjoyed the admiration of men; she enjoyed his heartiness and his noisy jokes, and his high spirits stirred her sluggish blood; he was a great big bouncing boy and he would never be anything else and she felt like a mother towards him; she had made him what he was, and he was her man and she was his woman, and she loved him, notwithstanding his weakness (for with her clear head she must always have been conscious of that), she loved him, *ach*, *was*, as Isolde loved Tristan. But then there was the espionage. Even Ashenden with all his tolerance for human frailty could not but feel that to betray your country for money is not a very pretty proceeding. Of course she knew of it, indeed it was probably through her that Caypor had first been approached; he would never have undertaken such work if she had not urged him to it. She loved him and she was an honest and an upright woman. By what devious means had she persuaded herself to force her husband to adopt so base and dishonourable a calling? Ashenden lost himself in a labyrinth of conjecture as he tried to piece together the actions of her mind.

Grantley Caypor was another story. There was little to admire in him, but at that moment Ashenden was not looking for an object of admiration; but there was much that was singular and much that was unexpected in that gross and vulgar fellow. Ashenden watched with entertainment the suave manner in which the spy tried to inveigle him in his toils. It was a couple of days after his first lesson that Caypor after dinner, his wife having gone upstairs, threw himself heavily into a chair by Ashenden's side. His faithful Fritzi came up to him and put his long muzzle with its black nose on his knee.

"He has no brain," said Caypor, "but a heart of gold. Look at those little pink eyes. Did you ever see anything so stupid? And what an ugly face, but what incredible charm!"

"Have you had him long?" asked Ashenden.

"I got him in 1914 just before the outbreak of war. By the way, what do you think of the news to-day? Of course my wife and I never discuss the war. You can't think what a relief to me it is to find a fellow-countryman to whom I can open my heart."

He handed Ashenden a cheap Swiss cigar and Ashenden, making a rueful sacrifice to duty, accepted it.

"Of course, they haven't got a chance, the Germans," said Caypor, "not a dog's chance. I knew they were beaten the moment we came in."

His manner was earnest, sincere and confidential. Ashenden made a commonplace rejoinder.

"It's the greatest grief of my life that owing to my wife's nationality I was unable to do any war work. I tried to enlist the day war broke out, but they wouldn't have me on account of my age, but I don't mind telling you, if the war goes on much longer, wife or no wife, I'm going to do something. With my knowledge of languages I ought to be of some service in the Censorship Department. That's where you were, wasn't it?"

That was the mark at which he had been aiming and in answer now to his well-directed questions Ashenden gave him the information that he had already prepared. Caypor drew his chair a little nearer and dropped his voice.

"I'm sure you wouldn't tell me anything that anyone shouldn't know, but after all these Swiss are absolutely pro-German and we don't want to give anyone the chance of overhearing."

Then he went on another tack. He told Ashenden a number of things that were of a certain secrecy.

"I wouldn't tell this to anybody else, you know, but I have one or two friends who are in pretty influential positions, and they know they can trust me."

Thus encouraged, Ashenden was a little more deliberately indiscreet and when they parted both had reason to be satisfied. Ashenden guessed that Caypor's typewriter would be kept busy next morning and that extremely energetic Major in Berne would shortly receive a most interesting report.

One evening, going upstairs after dinner, Ashenden passed an open bathroom. He caught sight of the Caypors.

"Come in," cried Caypor in his cordial way. "We're washing our Fritzi."

The bull-terrier was constantly getting himself very dirty, and it was Caypor's pride to see him clean and white. Ashenden went in. Mrs. Caypor with her sleeves turned up and a large white apron was standing at one end of the bath, while Caypor, in a pair of trousers and a singlet, his fat, freckled arms bare, was soaping the wretched hound.

"We have to do it at night," he said, "because the Fitzgeralds use this bath and they'd have a fit if they knew we washed the dog in it. We wait till they go to bed. Come along, Fritzi, show the gentleman how beautifully you behave when you have your face scrubbed."

The poor brute, woebegone but faintly wagging his tail to show that however foul was this operation performed on him he bore no malice to the god who did it, was standing in the middle of the bath in six inches of water. He was soaped all over and Caypor, talking the while, shampooed him with his great fat hands.

"Oh, what a beautiful dog he's going to be when he's as white as the driven snow. His master will be as proud as Punch to walk out with him and all the little lady-dogs will say: Good gracious, who's that beautiful aristocratic-looking bull-terrier walking as though he owned the whole of Switzerland? Now stand still while you have your ears washed. You couldn't bear to go out into the street with dirty ears, could you? like a nasty little Swiss schoolboy. *Noblesse oblige*. Now the black nose. Oh, and all the soap is going into his little pink eyes and they'll smart."

Mrs. Caypor listened to this nonsense with a good-humoured sluggish smile on her broad, plain face, and presently gravely took a towel.

"Now he's going to have a ducking. Upsie-daisy."

Caypor seized the dog by the fore-legs and ducked him once and ducked him twice. There was a struggle, a flurry and a splashing. Caypor lifted him out of the bath.

"Now go to mother and she'll dry you."

Mrs. Caypor sat down and taking the dog between her strong legs rubbed him till the sweat poured off her forehead. And Fritzi, a little shaken and breathless, but happy it was all over, stood, with his sweet stupid face, white and shining.

"Blood will tell," cried Caypor exultantly. "He knows the names of no less than sixty-four of his ancestors, and they were all nobly born."

Ashenden was faintly troubled. He shivered a little as he walked upstairs.

Then, one Sunday, Caypor told him that he and his wife were going on an excursion and would eat their luncheon at some little mountain restaurant; and he suggested that Ashenden, each paying his share, should come with them. After three weeks at Lucerne Ashenden thought that his strength would permit him to venture the exertion. They started early, Mrs. Caypor business-like in her walking boots and Tyrolese hat and alpenstock, and Caypor in stockings and plus-fours looking very British. The situation amused Ashenden and he was prepared to enjoy his day; but he meant to keep his eyes open; it was not inconceivable that the Caypors had discovered what he was and it would not do to go too near a precipice; Mrs. Caypor would not hesitate to give him a push and Caypor for all his jolliness was an ugly customer. But on the face of it there was nothing to mar Ashenden's pleasure in the golden morning. The air was fragrant. Caypor was full of conversation. He told funny stories. He was gay and jovial. The sweat rolled off his great red face and he laughed at himself because he was so fat. To Ashenden's astonishment he showed a peculiar knowledge of the mountain flowers. Once he went out of the way to pick one he saw a little distance from the path and brought it back to his wife. He looked at it tenderly.

"Isn't it lovely?" he cried, and his shifty grey-green eyes for a moment were as candid as a child's. "It's like a poem by Walter Savage Landor."

"Botany is my husband's favourite science," said Mrs. Caypor. "I laugh at him sometimes. He is devoted to flowers. Often when we have hardly had enough money to pay the butcher he has spent everything in his pocket to bring me a bunch of roses."

"*Qui fleurit sa maison fleurit son coeur,*" said Grantley Caypor.

Ashenden had once or twice seen Caypor, coming in from a walk, offer Mrs. Fitzgerald a nosegay of mountain flowers with an elephantine courtesy that was not entirely displeasing; and what he had just learned added a certain significance to the pretty little action. His passion for flowers was genuine and when he gave them to the old Irish lady he gave her something he valued. It showed a real kindness of heart. Ashenden had always thought botany a tedious science, but Caypor, talking exuberantly as they walked along, was able to impart to it life and interest. He must have given it a good deal of study.

"I've never written a book," he said. "There are too many books already and any desire to write I have is satisfied by the more immediately profitable and quite ephemeral composition of an article for a daily paper. But if I stay here much longer I have half a mind to write a book about the wild flowers of Switzerland. Oh, I wish you'd been here a little earlier. They were marvellous. But one wants to be a poet for that, and I'm only a poor newspaper-man."

It was curious to observe how he was able to combine real emotion with false fact.

When they reached the inn, with its view of the mountains and the lake, it was good to see the sensual pleasure with which he poured down his throat a bottle of ice-cold beer. You could not but feel sympathy for a man who took so much delight in simple things. They lunched deliciously off scrambled eggs and mountain trout. Even Mrs. Caypor was moved to an unwonted gentleness by her surroundings; the inn was in an agreeably rural spot, it looked like a picture of a Swiss chalet in a book of early nineteenth-century travels; and she treated Ashenden with something less than her usual hostility. When they arrived she had burst into loud German exclamations on the beauty of the scene, and now, softened perhaps too by food and drink, her eyes, dwelling on the grandeur before her, filled with tears. She stretched out her hand.

"It is dreadful and I am ashamed, notwithstanding this horrible and unjust war I can feel in my heart at the moment nothing but happiness and gratitude."

Caypor took her hand and pressed it and, an unusual thing with him, addressing her in German, called her little pet-names. It was absurd, but touching. Ashenden, leaving them to their emotions, strolled through the garden and sat down on a bench that had been prepared for the comfort of the tourist. The view was of course spectacular, but it captured you; it was like a piece of music that was obvious and meretricious, but for the moment shattered your self-control.

And as Ashenden lingered idly in that spot he pondered over the mystery of Grantley Caypor's treachery. If he liked strange people he had found in him one who was strange beyond belief. It would be foolish to deny that he had amiable traits. His joviality was not assumed, he was without pretence a hearty fellow, and he had real good nature. He was always ready to do a kindness. Ashenden had often watched him with the old Irish colonel and his wife who were the only other residents of the hotel; he would listen good-humouredly to the old man's tedious stories of the Egyptian war, and he was charming with her. Now that Ashenden had arrived at terms of some familiarity with Caypor he found that he regarded him less with repulsion than with curiosity. He did not think that he had become a spy merely for the money; he was a man of modest tastes and what he had earned in a shipping-office must have sufficed to so good a manager as Mrs. Caypor; and after war was declared there was no lack of remunerative work for men over the military age. It might be that he was one of those men who prefer devious ways to straight for some intricate pleasure they get in fooling their fellows; and that he had turned spy, not from hatred of the country that had imprisoned him, not even from love of his wife, but from a desire to score off the big-wigs who never even knew of his existence. It might be that it was vanity that impelled him, a feeling that his talents had not received the recognition they merited, or just a puckish, impish desire to do mischief. He was a crook. It is true that only two cases of dishonesty had been brought home to him, but if he had been caught twice it might be surmised that he had often been dishonest without being caught. What did Mrs. Caypor think of this? They were so united that she must be aware of it. Did it make her ashamed, for her own uprightness surely none could doubt, or did she accept it as an inevitable kink in the man she loved? Did she do all she could to prevent it or did she close her eyes to something she could not help?

How much easier life would be if people were all black or all white and how much simpler it would be to act in regard to them! Was Caypor a good man who loved evil or a bad man who loved good? And how could such unreconcilable elements exist side by side and in harmony within the same heart? For one thing was clear, Caypor was disturbed by no gnawing of conscience;

he did his mean and despicable work with gusto. He was a traitor who enjoyed his treachery. Though Ashenden had been studying human nature more or less consciously all his life, it seemed to him that he knew as little about it now in middle age as he had done when he was a child. Of course R. would have said to him: Why the devil do you waste your time with such nonsense? The man's a dangerous spy and your business is to lay him by the heels.

That was true enough. Ashenden had decided that it would be useless to attempt to make any arrangement with Caypor. Though doubtless he would have no feeling about betraying his employers he could certainly not be trusted. His wife's influence was too strong. Besides, notwithstanding what he had from time to time told Ashenden, he was in his heart convinced that the Central Powers must win the war, and he meant to be on the winning side. Well, then Caypor must be laid by the heels, but how he was to effect that Ashenden had no notion. Suddenly he heard a voice.

"There you are. We've been wondering where you had hidden yourself."

He looked round and saw the Caypors strolling towards him. They were walking hand in hand.

"So this is what has kept you so quiet," said Caypor as his eyes fell on the view. "What a spot!"

Mrs. Caypor clasped her hands.

"*Ach Gott, wie schön!*" she cried. "*Wie schön.* When I look at that blue lake and those snowy mountains I feel inclined, like Goethe's Faust, to cry to the passing moment: Tarry."

"This is better than being in England with the excursions and alarums of war, isn't it?" said Caypor.

"Much," said Ashenden.

"By the way, did you have any difficulty in getting out?"

"No, not the smallest."

"I'm told they make rather a nuisance of themselves at the frontier nowadays."

"I came through without the smallest difficulty. I don't fancy they bother much about the English. I thought the examination of passports was quite perfunctory."

A fleeting glance passed between Caypor and his wife. Ashenden wondered what it meant. It would be strange if Caypor's thoughts were occupied with the chances of a journey to England at the very moment when he was himself reflecting on its possibility. In a little while Mrs. Caypor suggested that they had better be starting back and they wandered together in the shade of trees down the mountain paths.

Ashenden was watchful. He could do nothing (and his inactivity irked him) but wait with his eyes open to seize the opportunity that might present itself. A couple of days later an incident occurred that made him certain something was in the wind. In the course of his morning lesson Mrs. Caypor remarked:

"My husband has gone to Geneva to-day. He had some business to do there."

"Oh," said Ashenden, "will he be gone long?"

"No, only two days."

It is not everyone who can tell a lie and Ashenden had the feeling, he hardly knew why, that Mrs. Caypor was telling one then. Her manner perhaps was not quite as indifferent as you would have expected when she was mentioning a fact that could be of no interest to Ashenden. It flashed across his mind that Caypor had been summoned to Berne to see the redoubtable head of the German secret service. When he had the chance he said casually to the waitress:

"A little less work for you to do, *fräulein*. I hear that Herr Caypor has gone to Berne."

"Yes. But he'll be back to-morrow."

That proved nothing, but it was something to go upon. Ashenden knew in Lucerne a Swiss who was willing on emergency to do odd jobs and, looking him up, asked him to take a letter to Berne. It might be possible to pick up Caypor and trace his movements. Next day Caypor appeared once more with his wife at the dinner-table, but merely nodded to Ashenden and afterwards both went straight upstairs. They looked troubled. Caypor, as a rule so animated, walked with bowed shoulders and looked neither to the right nor to the left. Next morning Ashenden received a reply to his letter: Caypor had seen Major von P. It was possible to guess what the Major had said to him. Ashenden well knew how rough he could be; he was a hard man and a brutal, clever and unscrupulous, and he was not accustomed to mince his words. They were tired of paying Caypor a salary to sit still in Lucerne and do nothing; the time was come for him to go to England. Guess-work? Of course it was guess-work, but in that trade it mostly was; you had to deduce the animal from its jawbone. Ashenden knew from Gustav that the Germans wanted to send someone to England. He drew a long breath; if Caypor went he would have to get busy.

When Mrs. Caypor came in to give him his lesson she was dull and listless. She looked tired and her mouth was set obstinately. It occurred to Ashenden that the Caypors had spent most of the night talking. He wished he knew what they had said. Did she urge him to go or did she try to dissuade him? Ashenden watched them again at luncheon. Something was the matter, for they hardly spoke to one another and as a rule they found plenty to talk about. They left the room early, but when Ashenden went out he saw Caypor sitting in the hall by himself.

"Hulloa," he cried jovially, but surely the effort was patent, "how are you getting on? I've been to Geneva."

"So I heard," said Ashenden.

"Come and have your coffee with me. My poor wife's got a headache. I told her she'd better go and lie down." In his shifty green eyes was an expression that Ashenden could not read. "The fact is, she's rather worried, poor dear; I'm thinking of going to England."

Ashenden's heart gave a sudden leap against his ribs, but his face remained impassive:

"Oh, are you going for long? We shall miss you."

"To tell you the truth, I'm fed up with doing nothing. The war looks as though it were going on for years and I can't sit here indefinitely. Besides, I can't afford it, I've got to earn my living. I may have a German wife, but I am an Englishman, hang it all, and I want to do my bit. I could never face my friends again if I just stayed here in ease and comfort till the end of the war and never attempted to do a thing to help the country. My wife takes her German point of view and I don't mind telling you that she's a bit upset. You know what women are."

Now Ashenden knew what it was that he saw in Caypor's eyes. Fear. It gave him a nasty turn. Caypor didn't want to go to England, he wanted to stay safely in Switzerland; Ashenden knew now what the major had said to him when he went to see him in Berne. He had got to go or lose his salary. What was it that his wife had said when he told her what had happened? He had wanted her to press him to stay, but, it was plain, she hadn't done that; perhaps he had not dared tell her how frightened he was; to her he had always been gay, bold, adventurous and devil-may-care; and now, the prisoner of his own lies, he had not found it in him to confess himself the mean and sneaking coward he was.

"Are you going to take your wife with you?" asked Ashenden.

"No, she'll stay here."

It had been arranged very neatly. Mrs. Caypor would receive his letters and forward the information they contained to Berne.

"I've been out of England so long that I don't quite know how to set about getting war-work. What would you do in my place?"

"I don't know; what sort of work are you thinking of?"

"Well, you know, I imagine I could do the same thing as you did. I wonder if there's anyone in the Censorship Department that you could give me a letter of introduction to."

It was only by a miracle that Ashenden saved himself from showing by a smothered cry or by a broken gesture how startled he was; but not by Caypor's request, by what had just dawned upon him. What an idiot he had been! He had been disturbed by the thought that he was wasting his time at Lucerne, he was doing nothing, and though in fact, as it turned out, Caypor was going to England it was due to no cleverness of his. He could take to himself no credit for the result. And now he saw that he had been put in Lucerne, told how to describe himself and given the proper information, so that what actually had occurred should occur. It would be a wonderful thing for the German secret service to get an agent into the Censorship Department; and by a happy accident there was Grantley Caypor, the very man for the job, on friendly terms with someone who had worked there. What a bit of luck! Major von P. was a man of culture and, rubbing his hands, he must surely have murmured: *stultum facit fortuna quem vult perdere*. It was a trap of that devilish R. and the grim major at Berne had fallen into it. Ashenden had done his work just by sitting still and doing nothing. He almost laughed as he thought what a fool R. had made of him.

"I was on very good terms with the chief of my department, I could give you a note to him if you liked."

"That would be just the thing."

"But of course I must give the facts. I must say I've met you here and only known you a fortnight."

"Of course. But you'll say what else you can for me, won't you?"

"Oh, certainly."

"I don't know yet if I can get a visa. I'm told they're rather fussy."

"I don't see why. I shall be very sick if they refuse me one when I want to go back."

"I'll go and see how my wife is getting on," said Caypor suddenly, getting up. "When will you let me have that letter?"

"Whenever you like. Are you going at once?"

"As soon as possible."

Caypor left him. Ashenden waited in the hall for a quarter of an hour so that there should appear in him no sign of hurry. Then he went upstairs and prepared various communications. In one he informed R. that Caypor was going to England; in another he made arrangements through Berne that wherever Caypor applied for a visa it should be granted to him without question; and these he despatched forthwith. When he went down to dinner he handed Caypor a cordial letter of introduction.

Next day but one Caypor left Lucerne.

Ashenden waited. He continued to have his hour's lesson with Mrs. Caypor and under her conscientious tuition began now to speak German with ease. They talked of Goethe and Winckelmann, of art and life and travel. Fritzi sat quietly by her chair.

"He misses his master," she said, pulling his ears. "He only really cares for him, he suffers me only as belonging to him."

After his lesson Ashenden went every morning to Cook's to ask for his letters. It was here that all communications were addressed to him. He could not move till he received instructions, but R. could be trusted not to leave him idle long; and meanwhile there was nothing for him to do but have patience. Presently he received a letter from the consul in Geneva to say that Caypor had there applied for his visa and had set out for France. Having read this Ashenden went on for a little stroll by the lake and on his way back happened to see Mrs. Caypor coming out of Cook's office. He guessed that she was having her letters addressed there too. He went up to her.

"Have you had news of Herr Caypor?" he asked her.

"No," she said. "I suppose I could hardly expect to yet."

He walked along by her side. She was disappointed, but not yet anxious; she knew how irregular at that time was the post. But next day during the lesson he could not but see that she was impatient to have done with it. The post was delivered at noon and at five minutes to she looked at her watch and him. Though Ashenden knew very well that no letter would ever come for her he had not the heart to keep her on tenter-hooks.

"Don't you think that's enough for the day? I'm sure you want to go down to Cook's," he said.

"Thank you. That is very amiable of you."

When a little later he went there himself he found her standing in the middle of the office. Her face was distraught. She addressed him wildly.

"My husband promised to write from Paris. I am sure there is a letter for me, but these stupid people say there's nothing. They're so careless, it's a scandal."

Ashenden did not know what to say. While the clerk was looking through the bundle to see if there was anything for him she came up to the desk again.

"When does the next post come in from France?" she asked.

"Sometimes there are letters about five."

"I'll come then."

She turned and walked rapidly away. Fritzi followed her with his tail between his legs. There was no doubt of it, already the fear had seized her that something was wrong. Next morning she looked dreadful; she could not have closed her eyes all night; and in the middle of the lesson she started up from her chair.

"You must excuse me, Herr Somerville, I cannot give you a lesson to-day. I am not feeling well."

Before Ashenden could say anything she had flung nervously from the room, and in the evening he got a note from her to say that she regretted that she must discontinue giving him con-versation lessons. She gave no reason. Then Ashenden saw no more of her; she ceased coming in to meals; except to go morning and afternoon to Cook's she spent apparently the whole day in her room. Ashenden thought of her sitting there hour after hour with that hideous fear gnawing at her heart. Who could help feeling sorry for her? The time hung heavy on his hands too. He read a good deal and wrote a little, he hired a canoe and went for long leisurely paddles on the lake; and at last one morning the clerk at Cook's handed him a letter. It was from R. It had all the appearance of a business communication, but between the lines he read a good deal.

Dear Sir, it began, *The goods, with accompanying letter, despatched by you from Lucerne have been duly delivered. We are obliged to you for executing our instructions with such promptness.*

It went on in this strain. R. was exultant. Ashenden guessed that Caypor had been arrested and by now had paid the penalty of his crime. He shuddered. He remembered a dreadful scene. Dawn. A cold, grey dawn, with a drizzling rain falling. A man, blindfolded, standing against a wall, an officer very pale giving an order, a volley, and then a young soldier, one of the firing-party, turning round and holding on to his gun for support, vomiting. The officer turning paler still, and he, Ashenden, feeling dreadfully faint. How terrified Caypor must have been! It was awful when the tears ran down their faces. Ashenden shook himself. He went to the ticket-office and obedient to his orders bought himself a ticket for Geneva.

As he was waiting for his change Mrs. Caypor came in. He was shocked at the sight of her. She was blowsy and dishevelled and there were heavy rings round her eyes. She was deathly pale. She staggered up to the desk and asked for a letter. The clerk shook his head.

"I'm sorry, madam, there's nothing yet."

"But look, look. Are you sure? Please look again."

The misery in her voice was heartrending. The clerk with a shrug of the shoulders took out the letters from a pigeon-hole and sorted them once more.

"No, there's nothing, madam."

She gave a hoarse cry of despair and her face was distorted with anguish.

"Oh, God, oh, God," she moaned.

She turned away, the tears streaming from her weary eyes, and for a moment she stood there like a blind man groping and not knowing which way to go. Then a fearful thing happened, Fritzi, the bull-terrier, sat down on his haunches and threw back his head and gave a long, long melancholy howl. Mrs. Caypor looked at him with terror; her eyes seemed really to start from her head. The doubt, the gnawing doubt that had tortured her during those dreadful days of suspense, was a doubt no longer. She knew. She staggered blindly into the street.

❖

His Excellency

WHEN Ashenden was sent to X and looked about him he could not but see that his situation was equivocal. X was the capital of an important belligerent state; but a state divided against itself; there was a large party antagonistic to the war and revolution was possible if not imminent. Ashenden was instructed to see what under the circumstances could best be done; he was to suggest a policy and, if it was approved by the exalted personages who had sent him, to carry it out. A vast amount of money was put at his disposal. The Ambassadors of Great Britain and the United States had been directed to afford him such facilities as were at their command, but Ashenden had been told privately to keep himself to himself; he was not to make difficulties for the official representatives of the two powers by divulging to them facts that it might be inconvenient for them to know; and since it might be necessary for him to give support under cover to a party that was at daggers drawn with that in office and with which the relations of the United States and Great Britain were extremely cordial it was just as well that Ashenden should keep his own counsel. The exalted personages did not wish the ambassadors to suffer the affront of discovering that an obscure agent had been sent to work at cross-purposes with them. On the other hand it was thought just as well to have a representative in the opposite camp, who in the event of a sudden upheaval would be at hand with adequate funds and in the confidence of the new leaders of the country.

But ambassadors are sticklers for their dignity and they have a keen nose to scent any encroachment on their authority. When Ashenden on his arrival at X paid an official call on Sir Herbert Witherspoon, the British Ambassador, he was received with a politeness to which no exception could be taken, but with a frigidity that would have sent a little shiver down the spine of a polar bear. Sir Herbert was a diplomat *de carrière* and he cultivated the manner of his profession to a degree that filled the observer with admiration. He did not ask Ashenden anything about his mission because he knew that Ashenden would reply evasively, but he allowed him to see that it was a perfectly foolish one. He talked with acidulous tolerance of the exalted personages who had sent Ashenden to X. He told Ashenden that he had instructions to meet any demands for help that he made and stated that if Ashenden at any time desired to see him he had only to say so.

"I have received the somewhat singular request to dispatch telegrams for you in a private code which I understand has been given to you and to hand over to you telegrams in code as they arrive."

"I hope they will be few and far between, sir," answered Ashenden. "I know nothing so tedious as coding and decoding."

Sir Herbert paused for an instant. Perhaps that was not quite the answer he expected. He rose.

"If you will come into the Chancellery I will introduce you to the Counsellor and to the Secretary to whom you can take your telegrams."

Ashenden followed him out of the room, and after handing him over to the Counsellor the ambassador gave him a limp hand to shake.

"I hope I shall have the pleasure of seeing you again one of these days," he said, and with a curt nod left him.

Ashenden bore his reception with composure. It was his business to remain in obscurity and he did not wish any official attentions to attract notice to him. But when on the afternoon of the same day he made his call at the American Embassy he discovered why Sir Herbert Witherspoon had shown him so much coldness. The American ambassador was Mr. Wilbur Schäfer; he came from Kansas City and had been given his post when few suspected that a war was on the point of breaking out, as a reward for political services. He was a big stout man, no longer young, for his hair was white, but well-preserved and exceedingly robust. He had a square, red face, clean-shaven, with a little snub nose and a determined chin. His face was very mobile and he twisted it continually into odd and amusing grimaces. It looked as though it were made out of the red india-rubber from which they make hot-water bottles. He greeted Ashenden with cordiality. He was a hearty fellow.

"I suppose you've seen Sir Herbert. I reckon you've got his dander up. What do they mean in Washington and London by telling us to dispatch your code telegrams without knowing what they're all about? You know, they've got no right to do that."

"Oh, Your Excellency, I think it was only done to save time and trouble," said Ashenden.

"Well, what is this mission anyway?"

This of course was a question that Ashenden was not prepared to answer, but not thinking it politic to say so, he determined to give a reply from which the ambassador could learn little. He had already made up his mind from the look of him that Mr. Schäfer, though doubtless possessed of the gifts that enable a man to swing a presidential election this way or that, had not, at least nakedly for all men to see, the acuteness that his position perhaps demanded. He gave you the impression of a bluff, good-humoured creature who liked good cheer. Ashenden would have been wary when playing poker with him, but where the matter in hand was concerned felt himself fairly safe. He began to talk in a loose, vague way of the world at large and before he had gone far managed to ask the ambassador his opinion of the general situation. It was as the sound of the trumpet to the war-horse: Mr. Schäfer made him a speech that lasted without a break for twenty-five minutes, and when at last he stopped in exhaustion, Ashenden with warm thanks for his friendly reception was able to take his leave.

Making up his mind to give both the ambassadors a wide berth, he set about his work and presently devised a plan of campaign. But by chance he was able to do Sir Herbert Witherspoon a good turn and so was thrown again into contact with him. It has been suggested that Mr. Schäfer was more of a politician than a diplomat, and it was his position rather than his personality that gave weight to his opinions. He looked upon the eminence to which he had risen as an opportunity to enjoy the good things of life and his enthusiasm led him to lengths that his constitution could ill support. His ignorance of foreign affairs would in any case have made his judgment of doubtful value, but his state at meetings of the Allied ambassadors so often approached the comatose that he seemed hardly capable of forming a judgment at all. He was known to have succumbed to the fascination of a Swedish lady of undoubted beauty, but of antecedents that from the point of view of a secret service agent were suspect. Her relations with Germany were such as to make her sympathy with the Allies dubious. Mr. Schäfer saw her every day and was certainly much under her influence. Now it was noticed that there was from time to time a leakage of very secret information and the question arose whether Mr. Schäfer did not in these daily interviews inadvertently say things that were promptly passed on to the headquarters of the enemy. No one could have doubted Mr. Schäfer's honesty and patriotism, but it was permissible to be uncertain of his discretion. It was an awkward matter to deal with, but the concern was as great in Washington as in London and Paris, and Ashenden was instructed to deal with it. He had of course not been sent to X without help to do the work he was expected to do, and among his assistants was an astute, powerful and determined man, a Galician Pole, named Herbartus. After consultation with him it happened by one of those fortunate coincidences that occasionally come about in the secret service that a maid in the service of the Swedish lady fell ill and in her place the countess (for such she was) was very luckily able to engage an extremely respectable person from the neighbourhood of Cracow. The fact that before the war she had been secretary to an eminent scientist made her doubtless no less competent a housemaid.

The result of this was that Ashenden received every two or three days a neat report upon the goings-on at this charming lady's apartment, and though he learned nothing that could confirm the vague suspicions that had arisen he learned something else of no little importance. From conversations held at the cosy little tête-à-tête dinners that the countess gave the ambassador it appeared that His Excellency was harbouring a bitter grievance against his English colleague. He complained that the relations between himself and Sir Herbert were deliberately maintained on a purely official level. In his blunt way he said he was sick of the frills that damned Britisher put on. He was a he-man and a hundred-per-cent American and he had no more use for protocol and etiquette than for a snowball in hell. Why didn't they get together, like a couple of regular fellows, and have a good old crack? Blood was thicker than water, he'd say, and they'd do more towards winning the war by sitting down in their shirt-sleeves and talking things out over a bottle of rye than by all their diplomacy and white spats. Now it was obviously very undesirable that there should not exist between the two ambassadors a perfect cordiality, so Ashenden thought it well to ask Sir Herbert whether he might see him.

He was ushered into Sir Herbert's library.

"Well, Mr. Ashenden, what can I do for you? I hope you're quite satisfied with everything. I understand that you've been keeping the telegraph lines busy."

Ashenden, as he sat down, gave the ambassador a glance. He was beautifully dressed in a perfectly cut tail-coat that fitted his slim figure like a glove, in his black silk tie was a handsome pearl, there was a perfect line in his grey trousers, with their quiet and distinguished stripe, and his neat, pointed shoes looked as though he had never worn them before. You could hardly imagine him sitting in his shirt-sleeves over a whisky high-ball. He was a tall, thin man, with exactly the figure to show off modern clothes, and he sat in his chair, rather upright, as though he were sitting for an official portrait. In his cold and uninteresting way he was really a very handsome fellow. His neat grey hair was parted on one side, his pale face was clean-shaven, he had a delicate, straight nose and grey eyes under grey eyebrows, his mouth in youth might have been sensual and well-shaped, but now it was set to an expression of sarcastic determination and the lips were pallid. It was the kind of face that suggested centuries of good breeding, but you could not believe it capable of expressing emotion. You would never expect to see it break into the hearty distortion of laughter, but at the most be for a moment frigidly kindled by an ironic smile.

Ashenden was uncommonly nervous.

"I'm afraid you'll think I'm meddling in what doesn't concern me, sir. I'm quite prepared to be told to mind my own business."

"We'll see. Pray go on."

Ashenden told his story and the ambassador listened attentively. He did not turn his cold, grey eyes from Ashenden's face, and Ashenden knew that his embarrassment was obvious.

"How did you find out all this?"

"I have means of getting hold of little bits of information that are sometimes useful," said Ashenden.

"I see."

Sir Herbert maintained his steady gaze, but Ashenden was surprised to see on a sudden in the steely eyes a little smile. The bleak, supercilious face became for an instant quite attractive.

"There is another little bit of information that perhaps you'd be good enough to give me. What does one do to be a regular fellow?"

"I am afraid one can do nothing, Your Excellency," replied Ashenden gravely. "I think it is a gift of God."

The light vanished from Sir Herbert's eyes, but his manner was slightly more urbane than when Ashenden was brought into the room. He rose and held out his hand.

"You did quite right to come and tell me this, Mr. Ashenden. I have been very remiss. It is inexcusable on my part to offend that inoffensive old gentleman. But I will do my best to repair my error. I will call at the American Embassy this afternoon."

"But not in too great state, sir, if I may venture a suggestion."

The ambassador's eyes twinkled. Ashenden began to think him almost human.

"I can do nothing but in state, Mr. Ashenden. That is one of the misfortunes of my temperament." Then as Ashenden was leaving he added: "Oh, by the way, I wonder if you'd care to come to dinner with me tomorrow night. Black tie. At eight-fifteen."

He did not wait for Ashenden's assent, but took it for granted, and with a nod of dismissal sat down once more at his great writing-table.

Ashenden looked forward with misgiving to the dinner to which Sir Herbert Witherspoon had invited him. The black tie suggested a small party, perhaps only Lady Anne, the ambassador's wife, whom Ashenden did not know, or one or two young secretaries. It did not presage a hilarious evening. It was possible that they might play bridge after dinner, but Ashenden knew that professional diplomats do not play bridge with skill: it may be supposed that they find it difficult to bend their great minds to the triviality of a parlour game. On the other hand he was interested to see a little more of the ambassador in circumstances of less formality. For it was evident that Sir Herbert Witherspoon was not an ordinary person. He was in appearance and manner a perfect specimen of his class and it is always entertaining to come upon good examples of a well-known type. He was exactly what you expected an ambassador to be. If any of his characteristics had been ever so slightly exaggerated he would have been a caricature. He escaped being ridiculous only by a hair's breadth and you watched him with a kind of breathlessness as you might watch a tight-rope dancer doing perilous feats at a dizzy height. He was certainly a man of character. His rise in the diplomatic service had been rapid and though doubtless it helped him to be connected by marriage with powerful families his rise had been due chiefly to his merit. He knew how to be determined when determination was necessary and conciliatory when conciliation was opportune. His manners were perfect; he could speak half a dozen languages with ease and accuracy; he had a clear and logical brain. He was never afraid to think out his thoughts to the end, but was wise enough to suit his actions

to the exigencies of the situation. He had reached his post at
X at the early age of fifty-three and had borne himself in the
exceedingly difficult conditions created by the war and contending
parties within the state with tact, confidence and once at least
with courage. For on one occasion, a riot having arisen, a band
of revolutionaries forced their way into the British Embassy and
Sir Herbert from the head of his stairs had harangued them and
notwithstanding revolvers flourished at him had persuaded them
to go to their homes. He would end his career in Paris. That was
evident. He was a man whom you could not but admire but whom
it was not easy to like. He was a diplomat of the school of those
Victorian ambassadors to whom could confidently be entrusted
great affairs and whose self-reliance, sometimes it must be admitted
tinctured with arrogance, was justified by its results.

When Ashenden drove up to the doors of the Embassy they
were flung open and he was received by a stout and dignified
English butler and three footmen. He was ushered up that magnificent flight of stairs on which had taken place the dramatic incident
just related and shown into an immense room, dimly lit with
shaded lamps, in which at the first glance he caught sight of large
pieces of stately furniture and over the chimney-piece an immense
portrait in coronation robes of King George IV. But there was
a bright fire blazing on the hearth and from a deep sofa by the side
of it his host, as his name was announced, slowly rose. Sir Herbert
looked very elegant as he came towards him. He wore his dinner
jacket, the most difficult costume for a man to look well in, with
notable distinction.

"My wife has gone to a concert, but she'll come in later. She
wants to make your acquaintance. I haven't asked anybody else.
I thought I would give myself the pleasure of enjoying your company en tête-à-tête."

Ashenden murmured a civil rejoinder, but his heart sank. He
wondered how he was going to pass at least a couple of hours
alone with this man who made him, he was bound to confess,
feel extremely shy.

The door was opened again and the butler and a footman
entered bearing very heavy silver salvers.

"I always have a glass of sherry before my dinner," said the
ambassador, "but in case you have acquired the barbarous custom
of drinking cocktails I can offer you what I believe is called a
dry Martini."

Shy though he might be, Ashenden was not going to give in to this sort of thing with complete tameness.

"I move with the times," he replied. "To drink a glass of sherry when you can get a dry Martini is like taking a stage-coach when you can travel by the Orient Express."

A little desultory conversation after this fashion was interrupted by the throwing open of two great doors and the announcement that His Excellency's dinner was served. They went into the dining-room. This was a vast apartment in which sixty people might have comfortably dined, but there was now only a small round table in it so that Sir Herbert and Ashenden sat intimately. There was an immense mahogany sideboard on which were massive pieces of gold plate, and above it, facing Ashenden, was a fine picture by Canaletto. Over the chimney-piece was a three-quarter-length portrait of Queen Victoria as a girl with a little gold crown on her small, prim head. Dinner was served by the corpulent butler and the three very tall English footmen. Ashenden had the impression that the ambassador enjoyed in his well-bred way the sensation of ignoring the pomp in which he lived. They might have been dining in one of the great country houses of England; it was a ceremony they performed, sumptuous without ostentation, and it was saved from a trifling absurdity only because it was in a tradition; but the experience gained for Ashenden a kind of savour from the thought that dwelt with him that on the other side of the wall was a restless, turbulent population that might at any moment break into bloody revolution, while not two hundred miles away men in the trenches were sheltering in their dug-outs from the bitter cold and the pitiless bombardment.

Ashenden need not have feared that the conversation would proceed with difficulty and the notion he had had that Sir Herbert had asked him in order to question him about his secret mission was quickly dispelled. The ambassador behaved to him as though he were a travelling Englishman who had presented a letter of introduction and to whom he desired to show civility. You would hardly have thought that a war was raging, for he made to it only such references as showed that he was not deliberately avoiding a distressing subject. He spoke of art and literature, proving himself to be a diligent reader of catholic taste, and when Ashenden talked to him, from personal acquaintance, of the writers whom Sir Herbert knew only through their works, he listened with the friendly condescension which the great ones of the earth affect towards the artist. (Sometimes, however, they paint a picture or write a book, and then the artist gets a little of his own back.) He mentioned in passing a character in one of Ashenden's novels, but did not make any other reference to the fact that his guest was a writer. Ashenden admired his urbanity. He disliked people to talk to him of his books, in which indeed, once written, he took small interest, and it made him self-conscious to be praised or blamed to his face. Sir Herbert Witherspoon flattered his self-esteem by showing that he had read him, but spared his delicacy by withholding his opinion of what he had read. He spoke too of the various countries in which during his career he had been stationed and of various persons, in London and elsewhere, that he and Ashenden knew in common. He talked well, not without a pleasant irony that might very well have passed for humour, and intelligently. Ashenden did not find his dinner dull, but neither did he find it exhilarating. He would have been more interested if the ambassador had not so invariably said the right, wise and sensible thing upon every topic that was introduced. Ashenden was finding it something of an effort to keep up with this distinction of mind and he would have liked the conversation to get into its shirt-sleeves, so to speak, and put its feet on the table. But of this there was no chance and Ashenden once or twice caught himself wondering how soon after dinner he could decently take his leave. At eleven he had an appointment with Herbartus at the Hotel de Paris.

The dinner came to an end and coffee was brought in. Sir Herbert knew good food and good wine and Ashenden was obliged to admit that he had fared excellently. Liqueurs were served with the coffee, and Ashenden took a glass of brandy.

"I have some very old Benedictine," said the ambassador. "Won't you try it?"

"To tell you the honest truth I think brandy is the only liqueur worth drinking."

"I'm not sure that I don't agree with you. But in that case I must give you something better than that."

He gave an order to the butler, who presently brought in a cobwebbed bottle and two enormous glasses.

"I don't really want to boast," said the ambassador as he watched the butler pour the golden liquid into Ashenden's glass, "but I venture to think that if you like brandy you'll like this. I got it when I was counsellor for a short time in Paris."

"I've had a good deal to do lately with one of your successors then."

"Byring?"

"Yes."

"What do you think of the brandy?"

"I think it's marvellous."

"And of Byring?"

The question came so oddly on the top of the other that it sounded faintly comic.

"Oh, I think he's a damned fool."

Sir Herbert leaned back in his chair, holding the huge glass with both hands in order to bring out the aroma, and looked slowly round the stately and spacious room. The table had been cleared of superfluous things. There was a bowl of roses between Ashenden and his host. The servants switched off the electric light as they finally left the room and it was lit now only by the candles that were on the table and by the fire. Notwithstanding its size it had an air of sober comfort. The ambassador's eyes rested on the really distinguished portrait of Queen Victoria that hung over the chimney-piece.

"I wonder," he said at last.

"He'll have to leave the diplomatic service."

"I'm afraid so."

Ashenden gave him a quick glance of enquiry. He was the last man from whom he would have expected sympathy for Byring.

"Yes, in the circumstances," he proceeded, "I suppose it's inevitable that he should leave the service. I'm sorry. He's an able fellow and he'll be missed. I think he had a career before him."

"Yes, that is what I've heard. I'm told that at the F.O. they thought very highly of him."

"He has many of the gifts that are useful in this rather dreary trade," said the ambassador, with a slight smile, in his cold and judicial manner. "He's handsome, he's a gentleman, he has nice manners, he speaks excellent French and he has a good head on his shoulders. He'd have done well."

"It seems a pity that he should waste such golden opportunities."

"I understand he's going into the wine business at the end of the war. Oddly enough he's going to represent the very firm from whom I got this brandy."

Sir Herbert raised the glass to his nose and inhaled the fragrance. Then he looked at Ashenden. He had a way of looking at people, when he was thinking of something else perhaps, that suggested that he thought them somewhat peculiar but rather disgusting insects.

"Have you ever seen the woman?" he asked.

"I dined with her and Byring at Larue's."

"How very interesting. What is she like?"

"Charming."

Ashenden tried to describe her to his host, but meanwhile with another part of his mind he recollected the impression she had made on him at the restaurant when Byring had introduced him to her. He had been not a little interested to meet a woman of whom for some years he had heard so much. She called herself Rose Auburn, but what her real name was few knew. She had gone to Paris originally as one of a troupe of dancers, called the Glad Girls, who performed at the Moulin Rouge, but her astonishing beauty had soon caused her to be noticed and a wealthy French manufacturer fell in love with her. He gave her a house and loaded her with jewels, but could not long meet the demands she made upon him, and she passed in rapid succession from lover to lover. She became in a short time the best known courtesan in France. Her expenditure was prodigal and she ruined her admirers with cynical unconcern. The richest men found themselves unable to cope with her extravagance. Ashenden, before the war, had seen her once at Monte Carlo lose a hundred and eighty thousand francs at a sitting and that then was an important sum. She sat at the big table, surrounded by curious onlookers, throwing down packets of thousand-franc notes with a self-possession that would have been admirable if it had been her own money that she was losing.

When Ashenden met her she had been leading this riotous life, dancing and gambling all night, racing most afternoons a week, for twelve or thirteen years and she was no longer very young; but there was hardly a line on that lovely brow, scarcely a crowsfoot round those liquid eyes, to betray the fact. The most astonishing thing about her was that notwithstanding this feverish and unending round of senseless debauchery she had preserved an air of virginity. Of course she cultivated the type. She had an exquisitely graceful and slender figure, and her innumerable frocks were always made with a perfect simplicity. Her brown hair was very plainly done. With her oval face, charming little nose and large blue eyes she had all the air of one or other of Anthony Trollope's charming heroines. It was the keepsake style raised to such rareness that it made you catch your breath. She had a lovely skin, very white and red, and if she painted it was not from necessity but from wantonness. She irradiated a sort of dewy innocence that was as attractive as it was unexpected.

Ashenden had heard of course that Byring for a year or more had been her lover. Her notoriety was such that a hard light of publicity was shed on everyone with whom she had any affair, but in this instance the gossips had more to say than usual because Byring had no money to speak of and Rose Auburn had never been known to grant her favours for anything that did not in some way represent hard cash. Was it possible that she loved him? It seemed incredible and yet what other explanation was there? Byring was a young man with whom any woman might have fallen in love. He was somewhere in the thirties, very tall and good-looking with a singular charm of manner and of an appearance so debonair that people turned round in the street to look at him; but unlike most handsome men he seemed entirely unaware of the impression he created. When it became known that Byring was the *amant de coeur* (a prettier phrase than our English fancy man) of this famous harlot be became an object of admiration to many women and of envy to many men; but when a rumour spread abroad that he was going to marry her consternation seized his friends and ribald laughter everyone else. It became known that Byring's chief had asked him if it was true and he had admitted it. Pressure was put upon him to relinquish a plan that could only end in disaster. It was pointed out to him that the wife of a diplomat has social obligations that Rose Auburn could not fulfil. Byring replied that he was prepared to resign his post whenever by so doing he would not cause inconvenience. He brushed aside every expostulation and every argument; he was determined to marry.

When first Ashenden met Byring he did not very much take to him. He found him slightly aloof. But as the hazards of his work brought him from time to time into contact with him he discerned that the distant manner was due merely to shyness and as he came to know him better he was charmed by the uncommon sweetness of his disposition. Their relations, however, remained purely official so that it was a trifle unexpected when Byring one day asked him to dinner to meet Miss Auburn, and he could not but wonder whether it was because already people were beginning to turn the cold shoulder on him. When he went he discovered that the invitation was due to the lady's curiosity. But the surprise he got on learning that she had found time to read (with admiration, it appeared) two or three of his novels was not the only surprise he got that evening. Leading on the whole a quiet and studious life he had never had occasion to penetrate into the world of the higher prostitution and the great courtesans of the period were known to him only by name. It was somewhat astonishing to Ashenden to discover that Rose Auburn differed so little in air and manner from the smart women of Mayfair with whom through his books he had become more or less intimately acquainted. She was perhaps a little more anxious to please (indeed one of her agreeable traits was the interest she took in whomever she was talking to), but she was certainly no more made-up and her conversation was as intelligent. It lacked only the coarseness that society has lately affected. Perhaps she felt instinctively that those lovely lips should never disfigure themselves with foul words; perhaps only she was at heart still a trifle suburban. It was evident that she and Byring were madly in love with one another. It was really moving to see their mutual passion. When Ashenden took his leave of them, as he shook hands with her (and she held his hand a moment and with her blue, starry eyes looked into his) she said to him:

"You will come and see us when we're settled in London, won't you? You know we're going to be married."

"I heartily congratulate you," said Ashenden.

"And him?" she smiled, and her smile was like an angel's; it had the freshness of dawn and the tender rapture of a southern spring.

"Have you never looked at yourself in the glass?"

Sir Herbert Witherspoon watched him intently while Ashenden (he thought not without a trace of humour) was describing the dinner-party. No flicker of a smile brightened his cold eyes.

"Do you think it'll be a success?" he asked now.

"No."

"Why not?"

The question took Ashenden aback.

"A man not only marries his wife, he marries her friends. Do you realise the sort of people Byring will have to mix with, painted women of tarnished reputation and men who've gone down in the social scale, parasites and adventurers? Of course they'll have money, her pearls must be worth a hundred thousand pounds, and they'll be able to cut a dash in the smart Bohemia of London. Do you know the gold fringe of society? When a woman of bad character marries she earns the admiration of her set, she has worked the trick, she's caught a man and become respectable, but he, the man, only earns its ridicule. Even her own friends, the old hags with their gigolos and the abject men who earn a shabby living by introducing the unwary to tradesmen on a ten per cent commission, even they despise him. He is the mug. Believe me, to conduct yourself gracefully in such a position you need either great dignity of character or an unparalleled effrontery. Besides, do you think there's a chance of its lasting? Can a woman who's led that wild career settle down to domestic life? In a little while she'll grow bored and restless. And how long does love last? Don't you think Byring's reflections will be bitter when, caring for her no longer, he compares what he is with what he might have been?"

Witherspoon helped himself to another drop of his old brandy. Then he looked up at Ashenden with a curious expression.

"I'm not sure if a man isn't wiser to do what he wants very much to do and let the consequences take care of themselves."

"It must be very pleasant to be an ambassador," said Ashenden.

Sir Herbert smiled thinly.

"Byring rather reminds me of a fellow I knew when I was a very junior clerk at the F.O. I won't tell you his name because he's by way of being very well-known now and highly respected. He's made a great success of his career. There is always something a little absurd in success."

Ashenden slightly raised his eyebrows at this statement, somewhat unexpected in the mouth of Sir Herbert Witherspoon, but did not say anything.

"He was one of my fellow-clerks. He was a brilliant creature, I don't think anyone ever denied that, and everyone prophesied from the beginning that he would go far. I venture to say that he had pretty well all the qualifications necessary for a diplomatic career. He was of a family of soldiers and sailors, nothing very grand, but eminently respectable, and he knew how to behave in the great world without bumptiousness or timidity. He was well-read. He took an interest in painting. I dare say he made himself a trifle ridiculous; he wanted to be in the movement, he was very anxious to be modern, and at a time when little was known of Gauguin and Cézanne he raved over their pictures. There was perhaps a certain snobbishness in his attitude, a desire to shock and astonish the conventional, but at heart his admiration of the arts was genuine and sincere. He adored Paris and whenever he had the chance ran over and put up at a little hotel in the Latin Quarter, where he could rub shoulders with painters and writers. As is the habit with gentry of that sort they patronised him a little because he was nothing but a diplomat and laughed at him a little because he was evidently a gentleman. But they liked him because he was always ready to listen to their speeches, and when he praised their works they were even willing to admit that, though a philistine, he had a certain instinct for the Right Stuff."

Ashenden noted the sarcasm and smiled at the fling at his own profession. He wondered what this long description was leading to. The ambassador seemed to linger over it partly because he liked it, but also because for some reason he hesitated to come to the point.

"But my friend was modest. He enjoyed himself enormously and he listened open-mouthed when these young painters and unknown scribblers tore to pieces established reputations and talked with enthusiasm of persons of whom the sober but cultured secretaries in Downing Street had never even heard. At the back of his mind he knew that they were rather a common, second-rate lot, and when he went back to his work in London it was with no regret, but with the feeling that he had been witnessing an odd and diverting play; now the curtain had fallen he was quite ready to go home. I haven't told you that he was ambitious. He knew that his friends expected him to do considerable things and he had no notion of disappointing them. He was perfectly conscious of his abilities. He meant to succeed. Unfortunately he was not rich, he had only a few hundreds a year, but his father and mother were dead and he had neither brother nor sister. He was aware that this freedom from close ties was an asset. His opportunity to make connections that would be of use to him was unrestricted. Do you think he sounds a very disagreeable young man?"

"No," said Ashenden in answer to the sudden question. "Most clever young men are aware of their cleverness, and there is generally a certain cynicism in their calculations with regard to the future. Surely young men should be ambitious."

"Well, on one of these little trips to Paris my friend became acquainted with a talented young Irish painter called O'Malley. He's an R.A. now and paints highly paid portraits of Lord Chancellors and Cabinet Ministers. I wonder if you remember one he did of my wife, which was exhibited a couple of years ago."

"No, I don't. But I know his name."

"My wife was delighted with it. His art always seems to me very refined and agreeable. He's able to put on canvas the distinction of his sitters in a very remarkable way. When he paints a woman of breeding, you know that it is a woman of breeding and not a trollop."

"It is a charming gift," said Ashenden. "Can he also paint a slut and make her look like one?"

"He could. Now doubtless he would scarcely wish to. He was living then in a small and dirty studio in the rue du Cherche Midi with a little Frenchwoman of the character you describe and he painted several portraits of her which were extremely like."

It seemed to Ashenden that Sir Herbert was going into somewhat excessive detail, and he asked himself whether the friend of whom he was telling a story that till now seemed to lead nowhither was in point of fact himself. He began to give it more of his attention.

"My friend liked O'Malley. He was good company, the type of the agreeable rattle, and he had a truly Irish gift of the gab. He talked incessantly and in my friend's opinion brilliantly. He found it very amusing to go and sit in the studio while O'Malley was painting and listen to him chattering away about the technique of his art. O'Malley was always saying that he would paint a portrait of him and his vanity was tickled. O'Malley thought him far from plain and said it would do him good to exhibit the portrait of someone who at least looked like a gentleman."

"By the way, when was all this?" asked Ashenden.

"Oh, thirty years ago. . . . They used to talk of their future and when O'Malley said the portrait he was going to paint of my friend would look very well in the National Portrait Gallery, my friend had small doubt in the back of his mind, whatever he modestly said, that it would eventually find its way there. One evening when my friend—shall we call him Brown?—was sitting in the studio and O'Malley, desperately taking advantage of the

last light of day, was trying to get finished for the Salon that
portrait of his mistress which is now in the Tate Gallery, O'Malley
asked him if he would like to come and dine with them. He was
expecting a friend of hers, she was called Yvonne by the way,
and he would be glad if Brown would make a fourth. This friend
of Yvonne's was an acrobat and O'Malley was anxious to get
her to pose for him in the nude. Yvonne said she had a marvellous figure. She had seen O'Malley's work and was willing
enough to sit and dinner was to be devoted to settling the matter.
She was not performing then, but was about to open at the Gáités
Montparnasses and with her days free was not disinclined to
oblige a friend and earn a little money. The notion amused Brown,
who had never met an acrobat, and he accepted. Yvonne suggested
that he might find her to his taste and if he did she could promise
him that he would not find her very difficult to persuade. With
his grand air and English clothes she would take him for a *milord
anglais*. My friend laughed. He did not take the suggestion very
seriously. 'On ne sait jamais,' he said. Yvonne looked at him
with mischievous eyes. He sat on. It was Easter time and cold,
but the studio was comfortably warm, and though it was small
and everything was higgledy-piggledy and the dust lay heavy on
the rim of the window, it was most friendly and cosy. Brown
had a tiny flat in Waverton Street, in London, with very good
mezzotints on the walls and several pieces of early Chinese pottery
here and there, and he wondered to himself why his tasteful
sitting-room had none of the comforts of home nor the romance
that he found in that disorderly studio.

"Presently there was a ring at the door and Yvonne ushered
in her friend. Her name, it appeared, was Alix, and she shook
hands with Brown, uttering a stereotyped phrase, with the mincing
politeness of a fat woman in a *bureau de tabac*. She wore a long
cloak in imitation mink and an enormous scarlet hat. She looked
incredibly vulgar. She was not even pretty. She had a broad flat
face, a wide mouth and an upturned nose. She had a great deal
of hair, golden, but obviously dyed, and large china-blue eyes.
She was heavily made-up."

Ashenden began to have no doubt that Witherspoon was
narrating an experience of his own, for otherwise he could never
have remembered after thirty years what hat the young woman
wore and what coat, and he was amused at the ambassador's
simplicity in thinking that so thin a subterfuge could disguise

the truth. Ashenden could not but guess how the story would end and it tickled him to think that this cold, distinguished and exquisite person should ever have had anything like an adventure.

"She began to talk away to Yvonne and my friend noticed that she had one feature that oddly enough he found very attractive: she had a deep and husky voice as though she were just recovering from a bad cold and, he didn't know why, it seemed to him exceedingly pleasant to listen to. He asked O'Malley if that was her natural voice and O'Malley said she had had it as long as ever he had known her. He called it a whisky voice. He told her what Brown said about it and she gave him a smile of her wide mouth and said it wasn't due to drink, it was due to standing so much on her head. That was one of the inconveniences of her profession. Then the four of them went to a beastly little restaurant off the boulevard St. Michel where for two francs fifty including wine my friend ate a dinner that seemed to him more delicious than any he had ever eaten at the Savoy or Claridge's. Alix was a very chatty young person and Brown listened with amusement, with amazement even, while in her rich, throaty voice she talked of the varied incidents of the day. She had a great command of slang and though he could not understand half of it, he was immensely tickled with its picturesque vulgarity. It was pungent of the heated asphalt, the zinc bars of cheap taverns and racy of the crowded squares in the poorer districts of Paris. There was an energy in those apt and vivid metaphors that went like champagne to his anæmic head. She was a guttersnipe, yes, that's what she was, but she had a vitality that warmed you like a blazing fire. He was conscious that Yvonne had told her that he was an unattached Englishman, with plenty of money; he saw the appraising glance she gave him and then, pretending that he had noticed nothing, he caught the phrase, *il n'est pas mal.* It faintly amused him: he had a notion himself that he was not so bad. There were places, indeed, where they went further than that. She did not pay much attention to him, in point of fact they were talking of things of which he was ignorant and he could do little more than show an intelligent interest, but now and again she gave him a long look, passing her tongue quickly round her lips, that suggested to him that he only had to ask for her to give. He shrugged a mental shoulder. She looked healthy and young, she had an agreeable vivacity, but beyond her husky voice there was nothing particularly attractive in her. But the notion of having

a little affair in Paris did not displease him, it was life, and the
thought that she was a music-hall artiste was mildly diverting:
in middle age it would doubtless amuse him to remember that
he had enjoyed the favours of an acrobat. Was it la Rochefoucauld
or Oscar Wilde who said that you should commit errors in youth
in order to have something to regret in old age? At the end of
dinner (and they sat over their coffee and brandy till late), they
went out into the street and Yvonne proposed that he should
take Alix home. He said he would be delighted. Alix said it
was not far and they walked. She told him that she had a little
apartment, of course mostly she was on tour, but she liked to
have a place of her own, a woman, you know, had to be in her
furniture, without that she received no consideration; and presently they reached a shabby house in a bedraggled street. She
rang the bell for the *concierge* to open the door. She did not
press him to enter. He did not know if she looked upon it as
a matter of course. He was seized with timidity. He racked his
brains, but could not think of a single thing to say. Silence fell
upon them. It was absurd. With a little click the door opened;
she looked at him expectantly; she was puzzled; a wave of shyness
swept over him. Then she held out her hand, thanked him for
bringing her to the door, and bade him good-night. His heart
beat nervously. If she had asked him to come in he would have
gone. He wanted some sign that she would like him to. He
shook her hand, said good night, raised his hat and walked away.
He felt a perfect fool. He could not sleep; he tossed from side to
side of his bed, thinking for what a noodle she must take him,
and he could hardly wait for the day that would permit him to
take steps to efface the contemptible impression he must have
made on her. His pride was lacerated. Wanting to lose no time
he went round to her house at eleven to ask her to lunch with
him, but she was out; he sent round some flowers and later in
the day called again. She had been in, but was gone out once
more. He went to see O'Malley on the chance of finding her,
but she was not there, and O'Malley facetiously asked him how
he had fared. To save his face he told him that he had come to
the conclusion that she did not mean very much to him and so
like a perfect gentleman he had left her. But he had an uneasy
feeling that O'Malley saw through his story. He sent her a *pneumatique* asking her to dine with him next day. She did not answer.
He could not understand it, he asked the porter of his hotel a

dozen times if there was nothing for him, and at last, almost in desperation, just before dinner went to her house. The *concierge* told him she was in and he went up. He was very nervous, inclined to be angry because she had treated his invitation so cavalierly, but at the same time anxious to appear at his ease. He climbed the four flights of stairs, dark and smelly, and rang at the door to which he had been directed. There was a pause, he heard sounds within and rang again. Presently she opened. He had an absolute certitude that she did not in the least know who he was. He was taken aback, it was a blow to his vanity; but he assumed a cheerful smile.

" 'I came to find out if you were going to dine with me to-night. I sent you a *pneumatique*.'

"Then she recognised him. But she stood at the door and did not ask him in.

" 'Oh, no, I can't dine with you to-night. I have terrible megrim and I am going to bed. I couldn't answer your *pneumatique*, I mislaid it, and I'd forgotten your name. Thank you for the flowers. It was nice of you to send them.'

" 'Then won't you come and dine with me to-morrow night?'

" '*Justement*, I have an engagement to-morrow night. I'm sorry.'

"There was nothing more to say. He had not the nerve to ask her anything else and so bade her good-night and went. He had the impression that she was not vexed with him, but that she had entirely forgotten him. It was humiliating. When he went back to London without having seen her again, it was with a curious sense of dissatisfaction. He was not in the least in love with her, he was annoyed with her, but he could not get her quite out of his mind. He was honest enough to realise that he was suffering from nothing more than wounded vanity.

"During that dinner at the little restaurant off the Boul' Mich' she had mentioned that her troupe was going to London in the spring and in one of his letters to O'Malley he slipped in casually a phrase to the effect that if his young friend Alix happened to be coming to town he (O'Malley) might let him know and he would look her up. He would like to hear from her own ingenuous lips what she thought of the nude O'Malley had painted of her. When the painter some time afterwards wrote and told him that she was appearing a week later at the Metropolitan in the Edgware Road, he felt a sudden rush of blood to his head. He went to see her play. If he had not taken the precaution to go earlier in the day and look at the programme he would have missed her, for her turn was the first on the list. There were two men, a stout one and a thin one, with large black moustaches, and Alix. They were dressed in ill-fitting pink tights with green satin trunks. The men did various exercises on twin trapezes while Alix tripped about the stage, giving them handkerchiefs to wipe their hands on, and occasionally turned a somersault. When the fat man raised the thin one on his shoulders she climbed up and stood on the shoulders of the second, kissing her hand to the audience. They did tricks with safety bicycles. There is often grace, and even beauty, in the performance of clever acrobats, but this one was so crude, so vulgar that my friend felt positively embarrassed. There is something shameful in seeing grown men publicly make fools of themselves. Poor Alix, with a fixed and artificial smile on her lips, in her pink tights and green satin trunks, was so grotesque that he wondered how he could have let himself feel a moment's annoyance because when he went to her apartment she had not recognised him. It was with a shrug of the shoulders, condescendingly, that he went round to the stage door afterwards and gave the doorkeeper a shilling to take her his card. In a few minutes she came out. She seemed delighted to see him.

" 'Oh, how good it is to see the face of someone you know in this sad city,' she said. 'Ah, now you can give me that dinner you asked me to in Paris. I'm dying of hunger. I never eat before the show. Imagine that they should have given us such a bad place on the programme. It's an insult. But we shall see the agent to-morrow. If they think they can put upon us like that they are mistaken. Ah, *non, non et non!* And what an audience! No enthusiasm, no applause, nothing.'

"My friend was staggered. Was it possible that she took her performance seriously? He almost burst out laughing. But she still spoke with that throaty voice that had such a queer effect on his nerves. She was dressed all in red and wore the same red hat in which he had first seen her. She looked so flashy that he did not fancy the notion of asking her to a place where he might be seen and so suggested Soho. There were hansoms still in those days, and the hansom was more conducive to love-making, I imagine, than is the taxi of the present time. My friend put his arm round Alix's waist and kissed her. It left her calm, but on the other hand did not wildly excite him. While they ate a late dinner he made himself very gallant and she played up to him agreeably;

but when they got up to go and he proposed that she should come round to his rooms in Waverton Street she told him that a friend had come over from Paris with her and that she had to meet him at eleven: she had only been able to dine with Brown because her companion had a business engagement. Brown was exasperated, but did not want to show it, and when, as they walked down Wardour Street (for she said she wanted to go to the Café Monico), pausing in front of a pawnbroker's to look at the jewellery in the window, she went into ecstasies over a bracelet of sapphires and diamonds that Brown thought incredibly vulgar, he asked her if she would like it.

" 'But it's marked fifteen pounds,' she said.

"He went in and bought it for her. She was delighted. She made him leave her just before they came to Piccadilly Circus.

" 'Now listen, *mon petit*,' she said, 'I cannot see you in London because of my friend, he is jealous as a wolf, that is why I think it is more prudent for you to go now, but I am playing at Boulogne next week, why do you not come over? I shall be alone there. My friend has to go back to Holland, where he lives.'

" 'All right,' said Brown, 'I'll come.'

"When he went to Boulogne—he had two days' leave—it was with the one idea of salving the wound to his pride. It was odd that he should care. I daresay to you it seems inexplicable. He could not bear the notion that Alix looked upon him as a fool and he felt that when once he had removed that impression from her he would never bother about her again. He thought of O'Malley too, and of Yvonne. She must have told them and it galled him to think that people whom in his heart he despised should laugh at him behind his back. Do you think he was very contemptible?"

"Good gracious, no," said Ashenden. "All sensible people know that vanity is the most devastating, the most universal and the most ineradicable of the passions that afflict the soul of man, and it is only vanity that makes him deny its power. It is more consuming than love. With advancing years, mercifully, you can snap your fingers at the terror and the servitude of love, but age cannot free you from the thraldom of vanity. Time can assuage the pangs of love, but only death can still the anguish of wounded vanity. Love is simple and seeks no subterfuge, but vanity cozens you with a hundred disguises. It is part and parcel of every virtue: it is the mainspring of courage and the strength of ambition; it gives constancy to the lover and endurance to the stoic; it adds

20   L

fuel to the fire of the artist's desire for fame and is at once the support and the compensation of the honest man's integrity; it leers even cynically in the humility of the saint. You cannot escape it, and should you take pains to guard against it, it will make use of those very pains to trip you up. You are defenceless against its onslaught because you know not on what unprotected side it will attack you. Sincerity cannot protect you from its snare nor humour from its mockery."

Ashenden stopped, not because he had said all he had to say, but because he was out of breath. He noticed also that the ambassador, desiring to talk rather than to listen, heard him with a politeness that was strained. But he had made this speech not so much for his host's edification as for his own entertainment.

"It is vanity finally that makes man support his abominable lot."

For a minute Sir Herbert was silent. He looked straight in front of him as though his thoughts lingered distressfully on some far horizon of memory.

"When my friend came back from Boulogne he knew that he was madly in love with Alix and he had arranged to meet her again in a fortnight's time when she would be performing at Dunkirk. He thought of nothing else in the interval and the night before he was to start, he only had thirty-six hours this time, he could not sleep, so devouring was the passion that consumed him. Then he went over for a night to Paris to see her and once when she was disengaged for a week he persuaded her to come to London. He knew that she did not love him. He was just a man among a hundred others and she made no secret of the fact that he was not her only lover. He suffered agonies of jealousy but knew that it would only excite her ridicule or her anger if he showed it. She had not even a fancy for him. She liked him because he was a gentleman and well dressed. She was quite willing to be his mistress so long as the claims he made on her were not irksome. But that was all. His means were not large enough to enable him to make her any serious offers, but even if they had been, liking her freedom, she would have refused."

"But what about the Dutchman?" asked Ashenden.

"The Dutchman? He was a pure invention. She made him up on the spur of the moment because for one reason or another she did not just then want to be bothered with Brown. What should one lie more or less matter to her? Don't think he didn't struggle against his passion. He knew it was madness; he knew that a permanent connection between them could only lead to disaster for him. He had no illusions about her: she was common, coarse and vulgar. She could talk of none of the things that interested him, nor did she try, she took it for granted that he was concerned with her affairs and told him interminable stories of her quarrels with fellow-performers, her disputes with managers and her wrangles with hotel-keepers. What she said bored him to death, but the sound of her throaty voice made his heart beat so that sometimes he thought he would suffocate."

Ashenden sat uneasily in his chair. It was a Sheraton chair very good to look at, but hard and straight; and he wished that Sir Herbert had had the notion of going back to the other room where there was a comfortable sofa. It was quite plain now that the story he was telling was about himself and Ashenden felt a certain indelicacy in the man's stripping his soul before him so nakedly. He did not desire this confidence to be forced upon him. Sir Herbert Witherspoon meant nothing to him. By the light of the shaded candles Ashenden saw that he was deathly pale and there was a wildness in his eyes that in that cold and composed man was strangely disconcerting. He poured himself out a glass of water; his throat was dry so that he could hardly speak. But he went on pitilessly.

"At last my friend managed to pull himself together. He was disgusted by the sordidness of his intrigue; there was no beauty in it, nothing but shame; and it was leading to nothing. His passion was as vulgar as the woman for whom he felt it. Now it happened that Alix was going to spend six months in the North of Africa with her troupe and for that time at least it would be impossible for him to see her. He made up his mind that he must seize the opportunity and make a definite break. He knew bitterly that it would mean nothing to her. In three weeks she would have forgotten him.

"And then there was something else. He had come to know very well some people, a man and his wife, whose social and political connections were extremely important. They had an only daughter and, I don't know why, she fell in love with him. She was everything that Alix was not, pretty in the real English way, with blue eyes and pink and white cheeks, tall and fair; she might have stepped out of one of du Maurier's pictures in *Punch*. She was clever and well-read, and since she had lived all her life in political circles she could talk intelligently of the sort of things that interested him. He had reason to believe that if he asked her to marry him she would accept. I have told you that he was ambitious. He knew that he had great abilities and he wanted the chance to use them. She was related to some of the greatest families in England and he would have been a fool not to realise that a marriage of this kind must make his path infinitely easier. The opportunity was golden. And what a relief to think that he could put behind him definitely that ugly little episode, and what a happiness, instead of that wall of cheerful indifference and matter-of-fact good nature against which in his passion for Alix he had vainly battered his head, what a happiness to feel that to someone else he really meant something! How could he help being flattered and touched when he saw her face light up as he came into the room? He wasn't in love with her, but he thought her charming, and he wanted to forget Alix and the vulgar life into which she had led him. At last he made up his mind. He asked her to marry him and was accepted. Her family was delighted. The marriage was to take place in the autumn, since her father had to go on some political errand to South America and was taking his wife and daughter with him. They were to be gone the whole summer. My friend Brown was transferring from the F.O. to the diplomatic service and had been promised a post at Lisbon. He was to go there immediately.

"He saw his fiancée off. Then it happened that owing to some hitch the man whom Brown was going to replace was kept at Lisbon three months longer and so for that period my friend found himself at a loose end. And just when he was making up his mind what to do with himself he received a letter from Alix. She was coming back to France and had a tour booked; she gave him a long list of the places she was going to, and in her casual, friendly way said that they would have fun if he could manage to run over for a day or two. An insane, a criminal notion seized him. If she had shown any eagerness for him to come he might have resisted, it was her airy, matter-of-fact indifference that took him. On a sudden he longed for her. He did not care if she was gross and vulgar, he had got her in his bones, and it was his last chance. In a little while he was going to be married. It was now or never. He went down to Marseilles and met her as she stepped off the boat that had brought her from Tunis. His heart leaped at the pleasure she showed on seeing him. He knew he loved her madly. He told her that he was going to be married in three months and

asked her to spend the last of his freedom with him. She refused
to abandon her tour. How could she leave her companions in the
lurch? He offered to compensate them, but she would not hear of
it; they could not find someone to take her place at a moment's
notice, nor could they afford to throw over a good engagement that
might lead to others in the future; they were honest people, and
they kept their word, they had their duty to their managers and
their duty to their public. He was exasperated; it seemed absurd
that his whole happiness should be sacrificed to that wretched tour.
And at the end of the three months? What was to happen to her
then? Oh, no, he was asking something that wasn't reasonable.
He told her that he adored her. He did not know till then how
insanely he loved her. Well, then, she said, why did he not come
with her and make the tour with them? She would be glad of his
company; they could have a good time together and at the end of
three months he could go and marry his heiress and neither of
them would be any the worse. For a moment he hesitated, but
now that he saw her again he could not bear the thought of being
parted from her so soon. He accepted. And then she said:

" 'But listen, my little one, you mustn't be silly, you know. The
managers won't be too pleased with me if I make a lot of *chichi*,
I have to think of my future, and they won't be so anxious to have
me back if I refuse to please old customers of the house. It won't
be very often, but it must be understood that you are not to make
me scenes if now and then I give myself to someone whose fancy
I take. It will mean nothing, that is business, you will be my
amant de cœur.'

"He felt a strange, excruciating pain in his heart, and I think he
went so pale that she thought he was going to faint. She looked at
him curiously.

" 'Those are the terms,' she said. 'You can either take them or
leave them.'

"He accepted."

Sir Herbert Witherspoon leaned forward in his chair and he was
so white that Ashenden thought too that he was going to faint.
His skin was drawn over his skull so that his face looked like a
death's head, but the veins on his forehead stood out like knotted
cords. He had lost all reticence. And Ashenden once more wished
that he would stop, it made him shy and nervous to see the man's
naked soul: no one has the right to show himself to another in
that destitute state. He was inclined to cry:

"Stop, stop. You mustn't tell me any more. You'll be so ashamed."

But the man had lost all shame.

"For three months they travelled together from one dull provincial town to another, sharing a filthy little bedroom in frowsy hotels; Alix would not let him take her to good hotels, she said she had not the clothes for them and she was more comfortable in the sort of hotel she was used to; she did not want her companions in the business to say that she was putting on side. He sat interminable hours in shabby cafés. He was treated as a brother by members of the troupe, they called him by his Christian name and chaffed him coarsely and slapped him on the back. He ran errands for them when they were busy with their work. He saw the good-humoured contempt in the eyes of managers and was obliged to put up with the familiarity of stage-hands. They travelled third-class from place to place and he helped to carry the luggage. He with whom reading was a passion never opened a book because Alix was bored by reading and thought that anyone who did was just giving himself airs. Every night he went to the music-hall and watched her go through that grotesque and ignoble performance. He had to fall in with her pathetic fancy that it was artistic. He had to congratulate her when it had gone well and condole with her when some feat of agility had gone amiss. When she had finished he went to a café and waited for her while she changed, and sometimes she would come in rather hurriedly and say:

" 'Don't wait for me to-night, *mon chou*, I'm busy.'

"And then he would undergo agonies of jealousy. He would suffer as he never knew a man could suffer. She would come back to the hotel at three or four in the morning. She wondered why he was not asleep. Sleep! How could he sleep with that misery gnawing at his heart? He had promised he would not interfere with her. He did not keep his promise. He made her terrific scenes. Sometimes he beat her. Then she would lose her patience and tell him she was sick of him, she would pack her things to go, and then he would go grovelling to her, promising anything, any submission, vowing to swallow any humiliation, if she would not leave him. It was horrible and degrading. He was miserable. Miserable? No, he was happier than he'd ever been in his life. It was the gutter that he wallowed in, but he wallowed in it with delight. Oh, he was so bored with the life he'd led hitherto, and this one seemed to him amazing and romantic. This was reality. And that frowsy, ugly woman with the whisky voice, she had such a splendid vitality, such a zest for life that she seemed to raise his own to some more vivid level. It really did seem to him to burn with a pure, gem-like flame. Do people still read Pater?"

"I don't know," said Ashenden. "I don't."

"There was only three months of it. Oh, how short the time seemed and how quickly the weeks sped by! Sometimes he had wild dreams of abandoning everything and throwing in his lot with the acrobats. They had come to have quite a liking for him and they said he could easily train himself to take a part in the turn. He knew they said it more in jest than in earnest, but the notion vaguely tickled him. But these were only dreams and he knew that nothing would come of them. He never really chaffered with the thought that when the three months came to an end he would not return to his own life with its obligations. With his mind, that cold, logical mind of his, he knew it would be absurd to sacrifice everything for a woman like Alix; he was ambitious, he wanted power; and besides, he could not break the heart of that poor child who loved and trusted him. She wrote to him once a week. She was longing to get back, the time seemed endless to her and he, he had a secret wish that something would happen to delay her arrival. If he could only have a little more time! Perhaps if he had six months he would have got over his infatuation. Already sometimes he hated Alix.

"The last day came. They seemed to have little to say to one another. They were both sad; but he knew that Alix only regretted the breaking of an agreeable habit, in twenty-four hours she would be as gay and full of spirits with her stray companion as though he had never crossed her path; he could only think that next day he was going to Paris to meet his fiancée and her family. They spent their last night in one another's arms weeping. If she'd asked him then not to leave her it may be that he would have stayed; but she didn't, it never occurred to her, she accepted his going as a settled thing, and she wept not because she loved him, she wept because he was unhappy.

"In the morning she was sleeping so soundly that he had not the heart to wake her to say good-bye. He slipped out very quietly, with his bag in his hand, and took the train to Paris."

Ashenden turned away his head, for he saw two tears form themselves in Witherspoon's eyes and roll down his cheeks. He did not even try to hide them. Ashenden lit another cigar.

"In Paris they cried out when they saw him. They said he looked like a ghost. He told them he'd been ill and hadn't said anything about it in order not to worry them. They were very kind. A month later he was married. He did very well for himself. He was given opportunities to distinguish himself and he distinguished himself. His rise was spectacular. He had the well-ordered and distinguished establishment that he had wanted. He had the power for which he had craved. He was loaded with honours. Oh, he made a success of life and there were hundreds who envied him. It was all ashes. He was bored, bored to distraction, bored by that distinguished, beautiful lady he had married, bored by the people his life forced him to live with; it was a comedy he was playing and sometimes it seemed intolerable to live for ever and ever behind a mask, sometimes he felt he couldn't bear it. But he bore it. Sometimes he longed for Alix so fiercely that he felt it would be better to shoot himself than to suffer such anguish. He never saw her again. Never. He heard from O'Malley that she had married and left her troupe. She must be a fat old woman now and it doesn't matter any more. But he had wasted his life. And he never even made that poor creature whom he married happy. How could he go on hiding from her year after year that he had nothing to give her but pity? Once in his agony he told her about Alix and she tortured him ever after with her jealousy. He knew that he should never have married her; in six months she would have got over her grief if he had told her he could not bear to, and in the end would have happily married somebody else. So far as she was concerned his sacrifice was vain. He was terribly conscious that he had only one life and it seemed so sad to think that he had wasted it. He could never surmount his immeasurable regret. He laughed when people spoke of him as a strong man: he was as weak and unstable as water. And that's why I tell you that Byring is right. Even though it only lasts five years, even though he ruins his career, even though this marriage of his ends in disaster, it will have been worth while. He will have been satisfied. He will have fulfilled himself."

At that moment the door opened and a lady came in. The ambassador glanced at her and for an instant a look of cold hatred crossed his face, but it was only for an instant; then, rising from the table, he composed his ravaged features to an expression of courteous suavity. He gave the incomer a haggard smile.

"Here is my wife. This is Mr. Ashenden."

"I couldn't imagine where you were. Why didn't you go and sit in your study? I'm sure Mr. Ashenden's been dreadfully uncomfortable."

She was a tall, thin woman of fifty, rather drawn and faded, but she looked as though she had once been pretty. It was obvious that she was very well-bred. She vaguely reminded you of an exotic plant, reared in a hot-house, that had begun to lose its bloom. She was dressed in black.

"What was the concert like?" asked Sir Herbert.

"Oh, not bad at all. They gave a Brahms Concerto and the Fire-music from the *Walküre*, and some Hungarian dances of Dvořák. I thought them rather showy." She turned to Ashenden. "I hope you haven't been bored all alone with my husband. What have you been talking about? Art and Literature?"

"No, its raw material," said Ashenden.

He took his leave.

❖

Mr. Harrington's Washing

WHEN Ashenden went on deck and saw before him a low-lying coast and a white town he felt a pleasant flutter of excitement. It was early and the sun had not long risen, but the sea was glassy and the sky was blue; it was warm already and one knew that the day would be sweltering. Vladivostok. It really gave one the sensation of being at the end of the world. It was a long journey that Ashenden had made from New York to San Francisco, across the Pacific in a Japanese boat to Yokohama, then from Tsuruki in a Russian boat, he the only Englishman on board, up the Sea of Japan. From Vladivostok he was to take the Trans-Siberian to Petrograd. It was the most important mission that he had ever had and he was pleased with the sense of responsibility that it gave him. He had no one to give him orders, unlimited funds (he carried in a belt next to his skin bills of exchange for a sum so enormous that he was staggered when he thought of them), and though he had been set to do something that was beyond human possibility he did not know this and was prepared to set about his task with confidence. He believed in his own astuteness. Though he had both esteem and admiration for the sensibility of the human race, he had little respect for their intelligence: man has always found it easier to sacrifice his life than to learn the multiplication table.

Ashenden did not much look forward to ten days on a Russian train, and in Yokohama he had heard rumours that in one or two places bridges had been blown up and the line cut. He was told that the soldiers, completely out of hand, would rob him of every-thing he possessed and turn him out on the steppe to shift for himself. It was a cheerful prospect. But the train was certainly starting and whatever happened later (and Ashenden had always a feeling that things never turned out as badly as you expected) he was determined to get a place on it. His intention on landing was to go at once to the British Consulate and find out what arrange-ments had been made for him; but as they neared the shore and he was able to discern the untidy and bedraggled town he felt not a little forlorn. He knew but a few words of Russian. The only man on the ship who spoke English was the purser and though he promised Ashenden to do anything he could to help him, Ashenden had the impression that he must not too greatly count upon him. It was a relief then, when they docked, to have a young man, small and with a mop of untidy hair, obviously a Jew, come up to him and ask if his name was Ashenden.

"Mine is Benedict. I'm the interpreter at the British Consulate. I've been told to look after you. We've got you a place on the train to-night."

Ashenden's spirits went up. They landed. The little Jew looked after his luggage and had his passport examined and then, getting into a car that waited for them, they drove off to the Consulate.

"I've had instructions to offer you every facility," said the Consul, "and you've only got to tell me what you want. I've fixed you up all right on the train, but God knows if you'll ever get to Petrograd. Oh, by the way, I've got a travelling companion for you. He's a man called Harrington, an American, and he's going to Petrograd for a firm in Philadelphia. He's trying to fix up some deal with the Provisional Government."

"What's he like?" asked Ashenden.

"Oh, he's all right. I wanted him to come with the American Consul to luncheon, but they've gone for an excursion in the country. You must get to the station a couple of hours before the train starts. There's always an awful scrimmage and if you're not there in good time someone will pinch your seat."

The train started at midnight and Ashenden dined with Benedict at the station restaurant, which was, it appeared, the only place in that slatternly town where you could get a decent meal. It was crowded. The service was intolerably slow. Then they went on to the platform, where, though they had still two hours to spare, there was already a seething mob. Whole families, sitting on piles of luggage, seemed to be camped there. People rushed to and fro, or stood in little groups violently arguing. Women screamed. Others were silently weeping. Here two men were engaged in a fierce quarrel. It was a scene of indescribable confusion. The light in the station was wan and cold and the white faces of all those people were like the white faces of the dead waiting, patient or anxious, distraught or penitent, for the judgment of the last day. The train was made up and most of the carriages were already filled to overflowing. When at last Benedict found that in which Ashenden had his place a man sprang out of it excitedly.

"Come in and sit down," he said. "I've had the greatest difficulty in keeping your seat. A fellow wanted to come in here with a wife and two children. My Consul has just gone off with him to see the stationmaster."

"This is Mr. Harrington," said Benedict.

Ashenden stepped into the carriage. It had two berths in it. The porter stowed his luggage away. He shook hands with his travelling companion.

Mr. John Quincy Harrington was a very thin man of somewhat less than middle height, he had a yellow, bony face, with large, pale-blue eyes and when he took off his hat to wipe his brow wet from the perturbation he had endured he showed a large, bald skull; it was very bony and the ridges and protuberances stood out disconcertingly. He wore a bowler-hat, a black coat and waistcoat, and a pair of striped trousers; a very high white collar and a neat, unobtrusive tie. Ashenden did not know precisely how you should dress in order to take a ten days' journey across Siberia, but he could not but think that Mr. Harrington's costume was eccentric. He spoke with precision in a high-pitched voice and in an accent that Ashenden recognised as that of New England.

In a minute the stationmaster came accompanied by a bearded Russian, suffering evidently from profound emotion, and followed by a lady holding two children by the hand. The Russian, tears running down his face, was talking with quivering lips to the stationmaster, and his wife between her sobs was apparently telling him the story of her life. When they arrived at the carriage the altercation became more violent and Benedict joined in with his fluent Russian. Mr. Harrington did not know a word of the language, but being obviously of an excitable turn broke in and explained in voluble English that these seats had been booked by the Consuls of Great Britain and the United States respectively, and though he didn't know about the King of England, he could tell them straight and they could take it from him that the President of the United States would never permit an American citizen to be done out of a seat on the train that he had duly paid for. He would yield to force, but to nothing else, and if they touched him he would register a complaint with the Consul at once. He said all this and a great deal more to the stationmaster, who of course had no notion what he was talking about, but with much emphasis and a good deal of gesticulation made him in reply a passionate speech. This roused Mr. Harrington to the utmost pitch of indignation, for shaking his fist in the stationmaster's face, his own pale with fury, he cried out:

"Tell him I don't understand a word he says and I don't want to understand. If the Russians want us to look upon them as a civilised people, why don't they talk a civilised language? Tell him that I am Mr. John Quincy Harrington and I'm travelling on behalf of Messrs. Crewe and Adams of Philadelphia with a special letter of introduction to Mr. Kerensky and if I'm not left in peaceful possession of this carriage Mr. Crewe will take the matter up with the Administration in Washington."

Mr. Harrington's manner was so truculent and his gestures so menacing that the stationmaster, throwing up the sponge, turned on his heel without another word and walked moodily away. He was followed by the bearded Russian and his wife arguing heatedly with him and the two apathetic children. Mr. Harrington jumped back into the carriage.

"I'm terribly sorry to have to refuse to give up my seat to a lady with two children," he said. "No one knows better than I the respect due to a woman and a mother, but I've got to get to Petrograd by this train if I don't want to lose a very important order and I'm not going to spend ten days in a corridor for all the mothers in Russia."

"I don't blame you," said Ashenden.

"I am a married man and I have two children myself. I know that travelling with your family is a difficult matter, but there's nothing that I know to prevent you from staying at home."

When you are shut up with a man for ten days in a railway carriage you can hardly fail to learn most of what there is to know about him, and for ten days (for eleven to be exact) Ashenden spent twenty-four hours a day with Mr. Harrington. It is true that they went into the dining-room three times a day for their meals, but they sat opposite to one another; it is true that the train stopped for an hour morning and afternoon so that they were able to have a tramp up and down the platform, but they walked side by side. Ashenden made acquaintance with some of his fellow-travellers and sometimes they came into the compartment to have a chat, but if they only spoke French or German Mr. Harrington would watch them with acidulous disapproval and if they spoke English he would never let them get a word in. For Mr. Harrington was a

talker. He talked as though it were a natural function of the
human being, automatically, as men breathe or digest their food;
he talked not because he had something to say, but because he
could not help himself, in a high-pitched, nasal voice, without
inflection, at one dead level of tone. He talked with precision,
using a copious vocabulary and forming his sentences with deliberation; he never used a short word when a longer one would do; he
never paused. He went on and on. It was not a torrent, for there
was nothing impetuous about it, it was like a stream of lava pouring
irresistibly down the side of a volcano. It flowed with a quiet
and steady force that overwhelmed everything that was in its path.

Ashenden thought he had never known as much about anyone
as he knew about Mr. Harrington, and not only about him, with
all his opinions, habits and circumstances, but about his wife and
his wife's family, his children and their schoolfellows, his employers
and the alliances they had made for three or four generations with
the best families of Philadelphia. His own family had come from
Devonshire early in the eighteenth century and Mr. Harrington
had been to the village where the graves of his forebears were still
to be seen in the churchyard. He was proud of his English ancestry,
but proud too of his American birth, though to him America was
a little strip of land along the Atlantic coast and Americans were a
small number of persons of English or Dutch origin whose blood
had never been sullied by foreign admixture. He looked upon the
Germans, Swedes, Irish and the inhabitants of Central and Eastern
Europe who for the last hundred years have descended upon the
United States as interlopers. He turned his attention away from
them as a maiden lady who lived in a secluded manor might avert
her eyes from the factory chimneys that had trespassed upon her
retirement.

When Ashenden mentioned a man of vast wealth who owned
some of the finest pictures in America Mr. Harrington said:

"I've never met him. My great-aunt Maria Penn Warmington
always said his grandmother was a very good cook. My great-aunt
Maria was terribly sorry when she left her to get married. She
said she never knew anyone who could make an apple pancake as
she could."

Mr. Harrington was devoted to his wife and he told Ashenden
at unbelievable length how cultivated and what a perfect mother
she was. She had delicate health and had undergone a great
number of operations all of which he described in detail. He had

had two operations himself, one on his tonsils and one to remove his appendix and he took Ashenden day by day through his experiences. All his friends had had operations and his knowledge of surgery was encyclopædic. He had two sons, both at school, and he was seriously considering whether he would not be well-advised to have them operated on. It was curious that one of them should have enlarged tonsils, and he was not at all happy about the appendix of the other. They were more devoted to one another than he had ever seen two brothers be and a very good friend of his, the brightest surgeon in Philadelphia, had offered to operate on them both together so that they should not be separated. He showed Ashenden photographs of the boys and their mother. This journey of his to Russia was the first time in their lives that he had been separated from them and every morning he wrote a long letter to his wife telling her everything that had happened and a good deal of what he had said during the day. Ashenden watched him cover sheet after sheet of paper with his neat, legible and precise handwriting.

Mr. Harrington had read all the books on conversation and knew its technique to the last detail. He had a little book in which he noted down the stories he heard and he told Ashenden that when he was going out to dinner he always looked up half a dozen so that he should not be at a loss. They were marked with a G if they could be told in general society and with an M (for men) if they were more fit for rough masculine ears. He was a specialist in that peculiar form of anecdote that consists in narrating a long serious incident, piling detail upon detail, till a comic end is reached. He spared you nothing and Ashenden foreseeing the point long before it arrived would clench his hands and knit his brows in the strenuous effort not to betray his impatience and at last force from his unwilling mouth a grim and hollow laugh. If someone came into the compartment in the middle Mr. Harrington would greet him with cordiality.

"Come right in and sit down. I was just telling my friend a story. You must listen to it, it's one of the funniest things you ever heard."

Then he would begin again from the very beginning and repeat it word for word, without altering a single apt epithet, till he reached the humorous end. Ashenden suggested once that they should see whether they could find two people on the train who played cards so that they might while away the time with a game of bridge, but Mr. Harrington said he never touched cards and when Ashenden in desperation began to play patience he pulled a wry face.

"It beats me how an intelligent man can waste his time card-playing, and of all the unintellectual pursuits I have ever seen it seems to me that solitaire is the worst. It kills conversation. Man is a social animal and he exercises the highest part of his nature when he takes part in social intercourse."

"There is a certain elegance in wasting time," said Ashenden. "Any fool can waste money, but when you waste time you waste what is priceless. Besides," he added with bitterness, "you can still talk."

"How can I talk when your attention is taken up by whether you are going to get a black seven to put on a red eight? Conversation calls forth the highest powers of the intellect and if you have made a study of it you have the right to expect that the person you're talking to will give you the fullest attention he is capable of."

He did not say this acrimoniously, but with the good-humoured patience of a man who has been much tried. He was just stating a plain fact and Ashenden could take it or leave it. It was the claim of the artist to have his work taken seriously.

Mr. Harrington was a diligent reader. He read pencil in hand, underlining passages that attracted his attention and on the margin making in his neat writing comments on what he read. This he was fond of discussing and when Ashenden himself was reading and felt on a sudden that Mr. Harrington, book in one hand and pencil in the other, was looking at him with his large pale eyes he began to have violent palpitations of the heart. He dared not look up, he dared not even turn the page, for he knew that Mr. Harrington would regard this as ample excuse to break into a discourse, but remained with his eyes fixed desperately on a single word, like a chicken with its beak to a chalk line, and only ventured to breathe when he realised that Mr. Harrington, having given up the attempt, had resumed his reading. He was then engaged on a History of the American Constitution in two volumes and for recreation was perusing a stout volume that purported to contain all the great speeches of the world. For Mr. Harrington was an after-dinner speaker and had read all the best books on speaking in public. He knew exactly how to get on good terms with his audience, just where to put in the serious words that touched their hearts, how to catch their attention by a few apt stories and finally with what degree of eloquence, suiting the occasion, to deliver his peroration.

Mr. Harrington was very fond of reading aloud. Ashenden had had frequent occasion to observe the distressing propensity ot Americans for this pastime. In hotel drawing-rooms at night after dinner he had often seen the father of a family seated in a retired corner and surrounded by his wife, his two sons and his daughter, reading to them. On ships crossing the Atlantic he had sometimes watched with awe the tall, spare gentleman of commanding aspect who sat in the centre of fifteen ladies no longer in their first youth and in a resonant voice read to them the history of Art. Walking up and down the promenade deck he had passed honeymooning couples lying on deck-chairs and caught the unhurried tones of the bride as she read to her young husband the pages of a popular novel. It had always seemed to him a curious way of showing affection. He had had friends who had offered to read to him and he had known women who had said they loved being read to, but he had always politely refused the invitation and firmly ignored the hint. He liked neither reading aloud nor being read aloud to. In his heart he thought the national predilection for this form of entertainment the only flaw in the perfection of the American character. But the immortal gods love a good laugh at the expense of human beings and now delivered him, bound and helpless, to the knife of the high priest. Mr. Harrington flattered himself that he was a very good reader and he explained to Ashenden the theory and practice of the art. Ashenden learned that there were two schools, the dramatic and the natural: in the first you imitated the voices of those who spoke (if you were reading a novel), and when the heroine wailed you wailed and when emotion choked her you choked too; but in the other you read as impassively as though you were reading the price-list of a mail-order house in Chicago. This was the school Mr. Harrington belonged to. In the seventeen years of his married life he had read aloud to his wife, and to his sons as soon as they were old enough to appreciate them, the novels of Sir Walter Scott, Jane Austen, Dickens, the Brontë Sisters, Thackeray, George Eliot, Nathaniel Hawthorne and W. D. Howells. Ashenden came to the conclusion that it was second nature with Mr. Harrington to read aloud and to prevent him from doing so made him as uneasy as cutting off his tobacco made the confirmed smoker. He would take you unawares.

"Listen to this," he would say, "you must listen to this," as though he were suddenly struck by the excellence of a maxim or the neatness of a phrase. "Now just tell me if you don't think this is remarkably well put. It's only three lines."

He read them and Ashenden was willing to give him a moment's attention, but having finished them, without pausing for a moment to take breath, he went on. He went right on. On and on. In his measured high-pitched voice, without emphasis or expression, he read page after page. Ashenden fidgeted, crossed and uncrossed his legs, lit cigarettes and smoked them, sat first in one position, then in another. Mr. Harrington went on and on. The train went leisurely through the interminable steppes of Siberia. They passed villages and crossed rivers. Mr. Harrington went on and on. When he finished a great speech by Edmund Burke he put down the book in triumph.

"Now that in my opinion is one of the finest orations in the English language. It is certainly a part of our common heritage that we can look upon with genuine pride."

"Doesn't it seem to you a little ominous that the people to whom Edmund Burke made that speech are all dead?" asked Ashenden gloomily.

Mr. Harrington was about to reply that this was hardly to be wondered at since the speech was made in the eighteenth century, when it dawned upon him that Ashenden (bearing up wonderfully under affliction as any unprejudiced person could not fail to admit) was making a joke. He slapped his knee and laughed heartily.

"Gee, that's a good one," he said. "I'll write that down in my little book. I see exactly how I can bring it in one time when I have to speak at our luncheon club."

Mr. Harrington was a highbrow; but that appellation, invented by the vulgar as a term of abuse, he had accepted like the instrument of a saint's martyrdom, the gridiron of Saint Laurence for instance or the wheel of Saint Catherine, as an honorific title. He gloried in it.

"Emerson was a highbrow," he said. "Longfellow was a high-brow. Oliver Wendell Holmes was a highbrow. James Russell Lowell was a highbrow."

Mr. Harrington's study of American literature had taken him no further down the years than the period during which those eminent, but not precisely thrilling, authors flourished.

Mr. Harrington was a bore. He exasperated Ashenden, and enraged him; he got on his nerves, and drove him to frenzy. But Ashenden did not dislike him. His self-satisfaction was enormous but so ingenuous that you could not resent it; his conceit was so childlike that you could only smile at it. He was so well-meaning, so thoughtful, so deferential, so polite that though Ashenden would willingly have killed him he could not but own that in that short while he had conceived for Mr. Harrington something very like affection. His manners were perfect, formal, a trifle elaborate perhaps (there is no harm in that, for good manners are the product of an artificial state of society and so can bear a touch of the powdered wig and the lace ruffle), but though natural to his good breeding they gained a pleasant significance from his good heart. He was ready to do anyone a kindness and seemed to find nothing too much trouble if he could thereby oblige his fellow-man. He was eminently *serviable*. And it may be that this is a word for which there is no exact translation because the charming quality it denotes is not very common among our practical people. When Ashenden was ill for a couple of days Mr. Harrington nursed him with devotion. Ashenden was embarrassed by the care he took of him and though racked with pain could not help laughing at the fussy attention with which Mr. Harrington took his temperature, from his neatly packed valise extracted a whole regiment of tabloids and firmly doctored him; and he was touched by the trouble he gave himself to get from the dining-car the things that he thought Ashenden could eat. He did everything in the world for him but stop talking.

It was only when he was dressing that Mr. Harrington was silent, for then his maidenly mind was singly occupied with the problem of changing his clothes before Ashenden without indelicacy. He was extremely modest. He changed his linen every day, neatly taking it out of his suitcase and neatly putting back what was soiled; but he performed miracles of dexterity in order during the process not to show an inch of bare skin. After a day or two Ashenden gave up the struggle to keep neat and clean in that dirty train, with one lavatory for the whole carriage, and soon was as grubby as the rest of the passengers; but Mr. Harrington refused to yield to the difficulties. He performed his toilet with deliberation notwithstanding the impatient persons who rattled the door-handle, and returned from the lavatory every morning washed, shining and smelling of soap. Once dressed, in his black coat, striped trousers and well-polished shoes, he looked as spruce as though he had just stepped out of his tidy little red-brick house in Philadelphia and was about to board the street-car that would take

him downtown to his office. At one point of the journey it was
announced that an attempt had been made to blow up a bridge
and that there were disturbances at the next station over the river;
it might be that the train would be stopped and the passengers
turned adrift or taken prisoner. Ashenden, thinking he might
be separated from his luggage, took the precaution to change into
his thickest clothes so that if he had to pass the winter in Siberia
he need suffer as little as necessary from the cold; but Mr. Harrington would not listen to reason; he made no preparations for the
possible experience and Ashenden had the conviction that if he
spent three months in a Russian prison he would still preserve
that smart and natty appearance. A troop of Cossacks boarded
the train and stood on the platform of each carriage with their guns
loaded, and the train rattled gingerly over the damaged bridge;
then they came to the station at which they had been warned of
danger, put on steam and dashed straight through it. Mr. Harrington was mildly satirical when Ashenden changed back into a light
summer suit.

Mr. Harrington was a keen business man. It was obvious that
it would need someone very astute to overreach him and Ashenden
was sure that his employers had been well-advised to send him on
this errand. He would safeguard their interests with all his might
and if he succeeded in driving a bargain with the Russians it would
be a hard one. His loyalty to his firm demanded that. He spoke of
the partners with affectionate reverence. He loved them and was
proud of them; but he did not envy them because their wealth was
great. He was quite content to work on a salary and thought
himself adequately paid; so long as he could educate his boys and
leave his widow enough to live on, what was money to him?
He thought it a trifle vulgar to be rich. He looked upon culture
as more important than money. He was careful of it and after
every meal put down in his note-book exactly what it had cost him.
His firm might be certain that he would not charge a penny more
for his expenses than he had spent. But having discovered that
poor people came to the station at the stopping places of the train
to beg and seeing that the war had really brought them to destitution
he took care before each halt to supply himself with ample small
change and in a shame-faced way, mocking himself for being taken
in by such impostors, distributed everything in his pocket.

"Of course I know they don't deserve it," he said, "and I don't
do it for them. I do it entirely for my own peace of mind. I should

feel so terribly badly if I thought some man really was hungry and I'd refused to give him the price of a meal."

Mr. Harrington was absurd, but lovable. It was inconceivable that anyone should be rude to him, it would have seemed as dreadful as hitting a child; and Ashenden, chafing inwardly but with a pretence of amiability, suffered meekly and with a truly Christian spirit the affliction of the gentle, ruthless creature's society. It took eleven days at that time to get from Vladivostok to Petrograd and Ashenden felt that he could not have borne another day. If it had been twelve he would have killed Mr. Harrington.

When at last (Ashenden tired and dirty, Mr. Harrington neat, sprightly and sententious) they reached the outskirts of Petrograd and stood at the window looking at the crowded houses of the city, Mr. Harrington turned to Ashenden and said:

"Well, I never would have thought that eleven days in the train would pass so quickly. We've had a wonderful time. I've enjoyed your company and I know you've enjoyed mine. I'm not going to pretend I don't know that I'm a pretty good conversationalist. But now we've come together like this we must take care to stay together. We must see as much of one another as we can while I'm in Petrograd."

"I shall have a great deal to do," said Ashenden. "I'm afraid my time won't be altogether my own."

"I know," answered Mr. Harrington cordially. "I expect to be pretty busy myself, but we can have breakfast together anyway and we'll meet in the evening and compare notes. It would be too bad if we drifted apart now."

"Too bad," sighed Ashenden.

When Ashenden found himself alone in his bedroom for the first time, he sat down and looked about him. It had seemed an age. He had not the energy to start immediately to unpack. How many of these hotel bedrooms had he known since the beginning of the war, grand or shabby, in one place and one land after another! It seemed to him that he had been living in his luggage for as long as he could remember. He was weary. He asked himself how he was going to set about the work that he had been sent to do. He felt lost in the immensity of Russia and very solitary. He had protested when he was chosen for this mission, it looked too large an order, but his protests were ignored. He was chosen not because those in authority thought him particularly suited for the job, but because there was no one to be found who was more suited. There was a knock at the door and Ashenden, pleased to make use of the few words of the language he knew, called out in Russian. The door was opened. He sprang to his feet.

"Come in, come in," he cried. "I'm awfully glad to see you."

Three men entered. He knew them by sight, since they had travelled in the same ship with him from San Francisco to Yokohama, but following their instructions no communications had passed between them and Ashenden. They were Czechs, exiled from their country for their revolutionary activity and long settled in America, who had been sent over to Russia to help Ashenden in his mission and put him in touch with Professor Z., whose authority over the Czechs in Russia was absolute. Their chief was a certain Dr. Egon Orth, a tall thin man, with a little grey head; he was minister to some church in the Middle West and a doctor of divinity; but had abandoned his cure to work for the liberation of his country, and Ashenden had the impression that he was an intelligent fellow who would not put too fine a point on matters of conscience. A parson with a fixed idea has this advantage over common men, that he can persuade himself of the Almighty's approval for almost any goings-on. Dr. Orth had a merry twinkle in his eye and a dry humour.

Ashenden had had two secret interviews with him in Yokohama and had learnt that Professor Z., though eager to free his country from the Austrian rule and, since he knew that this could only come about by the downfall of the Central Powers, with the Allies body and soul, yet had scruples; he would not do things that outraged his conscience, all must be straightforward and above board, and so some things that it was necessary to do had to be done without his knowledge. His influence was so great that his wishes could not be disregarded, but on occasion it was felt better not to let him know too much of what was going on.

Dr. Orth had arrived in Petrograd a week before Ashenden and now put before him what he had learned of the situation. It seemed to Ashenden that it was critical and if anything was to be done it must be done quickly. The army was dissatisfied and mutinous, the Government under the weak Kerensky was tottering and held power only because no one else had the courage to seize it, famine was staring the country in the face and already the possibility had to be considered that the Germans would march on Petrograd. The Ambassadors of Great Britain and the United States had been apprised of Ashenden's coming, but his mission was secret even from them, and there were particular reasons why he could demand no assistance from them. He arranged with Dr. Orth to make an appointment with Professor Z. so that he could learn his views and explain to him that he had the financial means to support any scheme that seemed likely to prevent the catastrophe that the Allied governments foresaw of Russia's making a separate peace. But he had to get in touch with influential persons in all classes. Mr. Harrington with his business proposition and his letters to Ministers of State would be thrown in contact with members of the Government and Mr. Harrington wanted an interpreter. Dr. Orth spoke Russian almost as well as his own language and it struck Ashenden that he would be admirably suited to the post. He explained the circumstances to him and it was arranged that while Ashenden and Mr. Harrington were at luncheon Dr. Orth should come in, greeting Ashenden as though he had not seen him before, and be introduced to Mr. Harrington; then Ashenden, guiding the conversation, would suggest to Mr. Harrington that the heavens had sent in Dr. Orth the ideal man for his purpose.

But there was another person on whom Ashenden had fixed as possibly useful to him and now he said:

"Have you ever heard of a woman called Anastasia Alexandrovna Leonidov? She's the daughter of Alexander Denisiev."

"I know all about him of course."

"I have reason to believe she's in Petrograd. Will you find out where she lives and what she's doing?"

"Certainly."

Dr. Orth spoke in Czech to one of the two men who accompanied him. They were sharp-looking fellows, both of them, one was tall and fair and the other was short and dark, but they were younger than Dr. Orth and Ashenden understood that they were there to do as he bade them. The man nodded, got up, shook hands with Ashenden and went out.

"You shall have all the information possible this afternoon."

"Well, I think there's nothing more we can do for the present," said Ashenden. "To tell you the truth I haven't had a bath for eleven days and I badly want one."

Ashenden had never quite made up his mind whether the pleasure of reflection was better pursued in a railway carriage or in a bath. So far as the act of invention was concerned he was inclined to prefer a train that went smoothly and not too fast, and many of his best ideas had come to him when he was thus traversing the plains of France; but for the delight of reminiscence or the entertainment of embroidery upon a theme already in his head he had no doubt that nothing could compare with a hot bath. He considered now, wallowing in soapy water like a water-buffalo in a muddy pond, the grim pleasantry of his relations with Anastasia Alexandrovna Leonidov.

In these stories no more than the barest suggestion has been made that Ashenden was capable on occasions of the passion ironically called tender. The specialists in this matter, those charming creatures who make a business of what philosophers know is but a diversion, assert that writers, painters and musicians, all in short who are connected with the arts, in the relation of love cut no very conspicuous figure. There is much cry but little wool. They rave or sigh, make phrases and strike many a romantic attitude, but in the end, loving art or themselves (which with them is one and the same thing) better than the object of their emotion, offer a shadow when the said object, with the practical common sense of the sex, demands a substance. It may be so and this may be the reason (never before suggested) why women in their souls look upon art with such a virulent hatred. Be this as it may Ashenden in the last twenty years had felt his heart go pit-a-pat because of one charming person after another. He had had a good deal of fun and had paid for it with a great deal of misery, but even when suffering most acutely from the pangs of unrequited love he had been able to say to himself, albeit with a wry face, after all, it's grist to the mill.

Anastasia Alexandrovna Leonidov was the daughter of a revolutionary who had escaped from Siberia after being sentenced to penal servitude for life and had settled in England. He was an able man and had supported himself for thirty years by the activity of a restless pen and had even made himself a distinguished position in English letters. When Anastasia Alexandrovna reached a suitable age she married Vladimir Semenovich Leonidov, also an exile from his native country, and it was after she had been married to him for some years that Ashenden made her acquaintance. It was at the time when Europe discovered Russia. Everyone was reading the Russian novelists, the Russian dancers captivated the civilised world, and the Russian composers set shivering the sensibility of persons who were beginning to want a change from Wagner. Russian art seized upon Europe with the virulence of an epidemic of influenza. New phrases became the fashion, new colours, new emotions, and the highbrows described themselves without a moment's hesitation as members of the intelligentsia. It was a difficult word to spell but an easy one to say. Ashenden fell like the rest, changed the cushions of his sitting-room, hung an eikon on the wall, read Chekoff and went to the ballet.

Anastasia Alexandrovna was by birth, circumstances and education very much a member of the intelligentsia. She lived with her husband in a tiny house near Regent's Park and here all the literary folk in London might gaze with humble reverence at pale-faced bearded giants who leaned against the wall like caryatids taking a day off; they were revolutionaries to a man and it was a miracle that they were not in the mines of Siberia. Women of letters tremulously put their lips to a glass of vodka. If you were lucky and greatly favoured you might shake hands there with Diaghileff, and now and again, like a peach-blossom wafted by the breeze, Pavlova herself hovered in and out. At this time Ashenden's success had not been so great as to affront the highbrows, he had very distinctly been one of them in his youth, and though some already looked askance, others (optimistic creatures with a faith in human nature) still had hopes of him. Anastasia Alexandrovna told him to his face that he was a member of the intelligentsia. Ashenden was quite ready to believe it. He was in a state when he was ready to believe anything. He was thrilled and excited. It seemed to him that at last he was about to capture that illusive spirit of romance that he had so long been chasing. Anastasia Alexandrovna had fine eyes and a good, though for these days too voluptuous, figure, high cheek-bones and a snub nose (this was very Tartar), a wide mouth full of large square teeth and a pale skin. She dressed somewhat flamboyantly. In her dark melancholy eyes Ashenden saw the boundless steppes of Russia, and the Kremlin with its pealing bells, and the solemn ceremonies of Easter at St. Isaac's, and forests of silver beeches and the Nevsky Prospekt; it was astonishing how much he saw in her eyes. They were round and shining and slightly protuberant like those of a Pekinese. They talked together of Alyosha in the *Brothers Karamazov*, of Natasha in *War and Peace*, of Anna Karenina and of *Fathers and Sons*.

Ashenden soon discovered that her husband was quite unworthy of her and presently learned that she shared his opinion. Vladimir Semenovich was a little man with a large, long head that looked as though it had been pulled like a piece of liquorice, and he had a great shock of unruly Russian hair. He was a gentle, unobtrusive creature and it was hard to believe that the Czarist government had really feared his revolutionary activities. He taught Russian and wrote for papers in Moscow. He was amiable and obliging. He needed these qualities, for Anastasia Alexandrovna was a woman of character: when she had a toothache Vladimir Semenovich suffered the agonies of the damned and when her heart was wrung by the suffering of her unhappy country Vladimir Semenovich might well have wished he had never been born. Ashenden could not help admitting that he was a poor thing, but he was so harmless that he conceived quite a liking for him, and when in due course he had disclosed his passion to Anastasia Alexandrovna and to his joy found it was returned he was puzzled to know what to do about Vladimir Semenovich. Neither Anastasia Alexandrovna nor he felt that they could live another minute out of one another's pockets, and Ashenden feared that, with her revolutionary views and all that, she would never consent to marry him; but somewhat to his surprise, and very much to his relief, she accepted the suggestion with alacrity.

"Would Vladimir Semenovich let himself be divorced, do you think?" he asked, as he sat on the sofa, leaning against cushions the colour of which reminded him of raw meat just gone bad, and held her hand.

"Vladimir adores me," she answered. "It'll break his heart."

"He's a nice fellow, I shouldn't like him to be very unhappy. I hope he'll get over it."

"He'll never get over it. That is the Russian spirit. I know that when I leave him he'll feel that he has lost everything that made life worth living for him. I've never known anyone so wrapped up in a woman as he is in me. But of course he wouldn't want to stand in the way of my happiness. He's far too great for that. He'll see that when it's a question of my own self-development I haven't the right to hesitate. Vladimir will give me my freedom without question."

At that time the divorce law in England was even more complicated and absurd than it is now and in case she was not acquainted with its peculiarities Ashenden explained to Anastasia Alexandrovna the difficulties of the case. She put her hand gently on his.

"Vladimir would never expose me to the vulgar notoriety of the divorce court. When I tell him that I have decided to marry you he will commit suicide."

"That would be terrible," said Ashenden.

He was startled, but thrilled. It was really very much like a Russian novel and he saw the moving and terrible pages, pages and pages, in which Dostoievsky would have described the situation. He knew the lacerations his characters would have suffered, the broken bottles of champagne, the visits to the gipsies, the vodka, the swoonings, the catalepsy and the long, long speeches everyone would have made. It was all very dreadful and wonderful and shattering.

"It would make us horribly unhappy," said Anastasia Alexandrovna, "but I don't know what else he could do. I couldn't ask him to live without me. He would be like a ship without a rudder or a car without a carburettor. I know Vladimir so well. He will commit suicide."

"How?" asked Ashenden, who had the realist's passion for the exact detail.

"He will blow his brains out."

Ashenden remembered *Rosmersholm*. In his day he had been an ardent Ibsenite and had even flirted with the notion of learning Norwegian so that he might, by reading the master in the original, get at the secret essence of his thought. He had once seen Ibsen in the flesh drink a glass of Munich beer.

"But do you think we could ever pass another easy hour if we had the death of that man on our conscience?" he asked. "I have a feeling that he would always be between us."

"I know we shall suffer, we shall suffer dreadfully," said Anastasia Alexandrovna, "but how can we help it? Life is like that. We must think of Vladimir. There is his happiness to be considered too. He will prefer to commit suicide."

She turned her face away and Ashenden saw that the heavy tears were coursing down her cheeks. He was much moved. For he had a soft heart and it was dreadful to think of poor Vladimir lying there with a bullet in his brain.

These Russians, what fun they have!

But when Anastasia Alexandrovna had mastered her emotion she turned to him gravely. She looked at him with her humid, round and slightly protuberant eyes.

"We must be quite sure that we're doing the right thing," she said. "I should never forgive myself if I'd allowed Vladimir to commit suicide and then found I'd made a mistake. I think we ought to make sure that we really love one another."

"But don't you know?" exclaimed Ashenden in a low, tense voice. "I know."

"Let's go over to Paris for a week and see how we get on. Then we shall know."

Ashenden was a trifle conventional and the suggestion took him by surprise. But only for a moment. Anastasia was wonderful. She was very quick and she saw the hesitation that for an instant troubled him.

"Surely you have no bourgeois prejudices?" she said.

"Of course not," he assured her hurriedly, for he would much sooner have been thought knavish than bourgeois, "I think it's a splendid idea."

"Why should a woman hazard her whole life on a throw? It's impossible to know what a man is really like till you've lived with him. It's only fair to give her the opportunity to change her mind before it's too late."

"Quite so," said Ashenden.

Anastasia Alexandrovna was not a woman to let the grass grow under her feet and so having made their arrangements forthwith on the following Saturday they started for Paris.

"I shall not tell Vladimir that I am going with you," she said. "It would only distress him."

"It would be a pity to do that," said Ashenden.

"And if at the end of the week I come to the conclusion that we've made a mistake he need never know anything about it."

"Quite so," said Ashenden.

They met at Victoria Station.

"What class have you got?" she asked him.

"First."

"I'm glad of that. Father and Vladimir travel third on account of their principles, but I always feel sick on a train and I like to be able to lean my head on somebody's shoulder. It's easier in a first-class carriage."

When the train started Anastasia Alexandrovna said she felt dizzy, so she took off her hat and leaned her head on Ashenden's shoulder. He put his arm round her waist.

"Keep quite still, won't you?" she said.

When they got on to the boat she went down to the ladies' cabin and at Calais was able to eat a very hearty meal, but when they got into the train she took off her hat again and rested her head on

Ashenden's shoulder. He thought he would like to read and took up a book.

"Do you mind not reading?" she said. "I have to be held and when you turn the pages it makes me feel all funny."

Finally they reached Paris and went to a little hotel on the Left Bank that Anastasia Alexandrovna knew of. She said it had atmosphere. She could not bear those great big grand hotels on the other side; they were hopelessly vulgar and bourgeois.

"I'll go anywhere you like," said Ashenden, "as long as there's a bathroom."

She smiled and pinched his cheek.

"How adorably English you are. Can't you do without a bathroom for a week? My dear, my dear, you have so much to learn."

They talked far into the night about Maxim Gorki and Karl Marx, human destiny, love and the brotherhood of man; and drank innumerable cups of Russian tea, so that in the morning Ashenden would willingly have breakfasted in bed and got up for luncheon; but Anastasia Alexandrovna was an early riser. When life was so short and there was so much to do it was a sinful thing to have breakfast a minute after half-past eight. They sat down in a dingy little dining-room the windows of which showed no signs of having been opened for a month. It was full of atmosphere. Ashenden asked Anastasia Alexandrovna what she would have for breakfast.

"Scrambled eggs," she said.

She ate heartily. Ashenden had already noticed that she had a healthy appetite. He supposed it was a Russian trait: you could not picture Anna Karenina making her midday meal off a bath-bun and a cup of coffee, could you?

After breakfast they went to the Louvre and in the afternoon they went to the Luxembourg. They dined early in order to go to the Comédie Française; then they went to a Russian cabaret where they danced. When next morning at eight-thirty they took their places in the dining-room and Ashenden asked Anastasia Alexandrovna what she fancied, her reply was:

"Scrambled eggs."

"But we had scrambled eggs yesterday," he expostulated.

"Let's have them again to-day," she smiled.

"All right."

They spent the day in the same manner except that they went to the Carnavalet instead of the Louvre and the Musée Guimet instead of the Luxembourg. But when the morning after in answer to

Ashenden's enquiry Anastasia Alexandrovna again asked for scrambled eggs, his heart sank.

"But we had scrambled eggs yesterday and the day before," he said.

"Don't you think that's a very good reason to have them again to-day?"

"No, I don't."

"Is it possible that your sense of humour is a little deficient this morning?" she asked. "I eat scrambled eggs every day. It's the only way I like them."

"Oh, very well. In that case of course we'll have scrambled eggs."

But the following morning he could not face them.

"Will you have scrambled eggs as usual?" he asked her.

"Of course," she smiled affectionately, showing him two rows of large square teeth.

"All right, I'll order them for you; I shall have mine fried."

The smile vanished from her lips.

"Oh?" She paused a moment. "Don't you think that's rather inconsiderate? Do you think it's fair to give the cook unnecessary work? You English, you're all the same, you look upon servants as machines. Does it occur to you that they have hearts like yours, the same feelings and the same emotions? How can you be surprised that the proletariat are seething with discontent when the bourgeoisie like you are so monstrously selfish?"

"Do you really think that there'll be a revolution in England if I have my eggs in Paris fried rather than scrambled?"

She tossed her pretty head in indignation.

"You don't understand. It's the principle of the thing. You think it's a jest, of course I know you're being funny, I can laugh at a joke as well as anyone, Chekoff was well-known in Russia as a humorist; but don't you see what is involved? Your whole attitude is wrong. It's a lack of feeling. You wouldn't talk like that if you had been through the events of 1905 in Petersburg. When I think of the crowds in front of the Winter Palace kneeling in the snow while the Cossacks charged them, women and children! No, no, no."

Her eyes filled with tears and her face was all twisted with pain. She took Ashenden's hand.

"I know you have a good heart. It was just thoughtless on your part and we won't say anything more about it. You have imagination. You're very sensitive. I know. You'll have your eggs done in the same way as mine, won't you?"

"Of course," said Ashenden.

He ate scrambled eggs for breakfast every morning after that. The waiter said: *"Monsieur aime les œufs brouillés."* At the end of the week they returned to London. He held Anastasia Alexandrovna in his arms, her head resting on his shoulder, from Paris to Calais and again from Dover to London. He reflected that the journey from New York to San Francisco took five days. When they arrived at Victoria and stood on the platform waiting for a cab she looked at him with her round, shining and slightly protuberant eyes.

"We've had a wonderful time, haven't we?" she said.

"Wonderful."

"I've quite made up my mind. The experiment has justified itself. I'm willing to marry you whenever you like."

But Ashenden saw himself eating scrambled eggs every morning for the rest of his life. When he had put her in a cab, he called another for himself, went to the Cunard office and took a berth on the first ship that was going to America. No immigrant, eager for freedom and a new life, ever looked upon the statue of Liberty with more heartfelt thankfulness than did Ashenden, when on that bright and sunny morning his ship steamed into the harbour of New York.

Some years had passed since then and Ashenden had not seen Anastasia Alexandrovna again. He knew that on the outbreak of the revolution in March she and Vladimir Semenovich had gone to Russia. It might be that they would be able to help him, in a way Vladimir Semenovich owed him his life, and he made up his mind to write to Anastasia Alexandrovna to ask if he might come to see her.

When Ashenden went down to lunch he felt somewhat rested. Mr. Harrington was waiting for him and they sat down. They ate what was put before them.

"Ask the waiter to bring us some bread," said Mr. Harrington.

"Bread?" replied Ashenden. "There's no bread."

"I can't eat without bread," said Mr. Harrington.

"I'm afraid you'll have to. There's no bread, no butter, no sugar, no eggs, no potatoes. There's fish and meat and green vegetables, and that's all."

Mr. Harrington's jaw dropped.

"But this is war," he said.

"It looks very much like it."

Mr. Harrington was for a moment speechless; then he said: "I'll tell you what I'm going to do, I'm going to get through with my business as quick as I can and then I'm going to get out of this country. I'm sure Mrs. Harrington wouldn't like me to go without sugar or butter. I've got a very delicate stomach. The firm would never have sent me here if they'd thought I wasn't going to have the best of everything."

In a little while Dr. Egan Orth came in and gave Ashenden an envelope. On it was written Anastasia Alexandrovna's address. He introduced him to Mr. Harrington. It was soon clear that he was pleased with Dr. Egan Orth and so without further to-do he suggested that here was the perfect interpreter for him.

"He talks Russian like a Russian. But he's an American citizen so that he won't do you down. I've known him a considerable time and I can assure you that he's absolutely trustworthy."

Mr. Harrington was pleased with the notion and after luncheon Ashenden left them to settle the matter by themselves. He wrote a note to Anastasia Alexandrovna and presently received an answer to say that she was going to a meeting, but would look in at his hotel about seven. He awaited her with apprehension. Of course he knew now that he had not loved her, but Tolstoi and Dostoievsky, Rimsky-Korsakoff, Stravinsky and Bakst; but he was not quite sure if the point had occurred to her. When between eight and half-past she arrived he suggested that she should join Mr. Harrington and him at dinner. The presence of a third party, he thought, would prevent any awkwardness their meeting might have; but he need not have had any anxiety, for five minutes after they had sat down to a plate of soup it was borne in upon him that the feelings of Anastasia Alexandrovna towards him were as cool as were his towards her. It gave him a momentary shock. It is very hard for a man, however modest, to grasp the possibility that a woman who has once loved him may love him no longer, and though of course he did not imagine that Anastasia Alexandrovna had languished for five years with a hopeless passion for him, he did think that by a heightening of colour, a flutter of the eyelashes, or a quiver of the lips she would betray the fact that she had still a soft place in her heart for him. Not at all. She talked to him as though he were a friend she was very glad to see again after an absence of a few days, but whose intimacy with her was purely social. He asked after Vladimir Semenovich.

"He has been a disappointment to me," she said. "I never thought he was a clever man, but I thought he was an honest one. He's going to have a baby."

Mr. Harrington who was about to put a piece of fish into his mouth, stopped, his fork in the air, and stared at Anastasia Alexandrovna with astonishment. In extenuation it must be explained that he had never read a Russian novel in his life. Ashenden, slightly perplexed too, gave her a questioning look.

"I'm not the mother," she said with a laugh. "I am not interested in that sort of thing. The mother is a friend of mine and a well-known writer on Political Economy. I do not think her views are sound, but I should be the last to deny that they deserve considera-tion. She has a good brain, quite a good brain." She turned to Mr. Harrington. "Are you interested in Political Economy?"

For once in his life Mr. Harrington was speechless. Anastasia Alexandrovna gave them her views on the subject and they began to speak on the situation in Russia. She seemed to be on intimate terms with the leaders of the various political parties and Ashenden made up his mind to sound her on the possibility of her working with him. His infatuation had not blinded him to the fact that she was an extremely intelligent woman. After dinner he told Mr. Harrington that he wished to talk business with Anastasia Alexan-drovna and took her to a retired corner of the lounge. He told her all he thought necessary and found her interested and anxious to help. She had a passion for intrigue and a desire for power. When he hinted that he had command of large sums of money she saw at once that through him she might acquire an influence in the affairs of Russia. It tickled her vanity. She was immensely patriotic, but like many patriots she had an impression that her own aggrandisement tended to the good of her country. When they parted they had come to a working agreement.

"That was a very remarkable woman," said Mr. Harrington next morning when they met at breakfast.

"Don't fall in love with her," smiled Ashenden.

This, however, was not a matter on which Mr. Harrington was prepared to jest.

"I have never looked at a woman since I married Mrs. Harring-ton," he said. "That husband of hers must be a bad man."

"I could do with a plate of scrambled eggs," said Ashenden,

20   M

irrelevantly, for their breakfast consisted of a cup of tea without milk and a little jam instead of sugar.

With Anastasia Alexandrovna to help him and Dr. Orth in the background, Ashenden set to work. Things in Russia were going from bad to worse. Kerensky, the head of the Provisional Government, was devoured by vanity and dismissed any minister who gave evidence of a capacity that might endanger his own position. He made speeches. He made endless speeches. At one moment there was a possibility that the Germans would make a dash for Petrograd. Kerensky made speeches. The food shortage grew more serious, the winter was approaching and there was no fuel. Kerensky made speeches. In the background the Bolsheviks were active, Lenin was hiding in Petrograd, it was said that Kerensky knew where he was, but dared not arrest him. He made speeches.

It amused Ashenden to see the unconcern with which Mr. Harrington wandered through this turmoil. History was in the making and Mr. Harrington minded his own business. It was uphill work. He was made to pay bribes to secretaries and underlings under the pretence that the ear of great men would be granted to him. He was kept waiting for hours in antechambers and then sent away without ceremony. When at last he saw the great men he found they had nothing to give him but idle words. They made him promises and in a day or two he discovered that the promises meant nothing. Ashenden advised him to throw in his hand and return to America; but Mr. Harrington would not hear of it; his firm had sent him to do a particular job, and by gum, he was going to do it or perish in the attempt. Then Anastasia Alexandrovna took him in hand. A singular friendship had arisen between the pair. Mr. Harrington thought her a very remarkable and deeply wronged woman; he told her all about his wife and his two sons, he told her all about the Constitution of the United States; she on her side told him all about Vladimir Semenovich, and she told him about Tolstoi, Turgenev and Dostoievsky. They had great times together. He said he couldn't manage to call her Anastasia Alexandrovna, it was too much of a mouthful; so he called her Delilah. And now she placed her inexhaustible energy at his service and they went together to the persons who might be useful to him. But things were coming to a head. Riots broke out and the streets were growing dangerous. Now and then armoured cars filled with discontented reservists careered wildly along the Nevsky Prospekt and in order to show that they were not happy took pot-shots at the passers-by. On one occasion when Mr. Harrington and Anastasia Alexandrovna were in a tram together shots peppered the windows and they had to lie down on the floor for safety. Mr. Harrington was highly indignant.

"An old fat woman was lying right on top of me and when I wriggled to get out Delilah caught me a clip on the side of the head and said: Stop still, you fool. I don't like your Russian ways, Delilah."

"Anyhow you stopped still," she giggled.

"What you want in this country is a little less art and a little more civilisation."

"You are bourgeoisie, Mr. Harrington, you are not a member of the intelligentsia."

"You are the first person who's ever said that, Delilah. If I'm not a member of the intelligentsia I don't know who is," retorted Mr. Harrington with dignity.

Then one day when Ashenden was working in his room there was a knock at the door and Anastasia Alexandrovna stalked in followed somewhat sheepishly, by Mr. Harrington. Ashenden saw that she was excited.

"What's the matter?" he asked.

"Unless this man goes back to America he'll get killed. You really must talk to him. If I hadn't been there something very unpleasant might have happened to him."

"Not at all, Delilah," said Mr. Harrington, with asperity. "I'm perfectly capable of taking care of myself and I wasn't in the smallest danger."

"What is it all about?" asked Ashenden.

"I'd taken Mr. Harrington to the Lavra of Alexander Nevsky to see Dostoievsky's grave," said Anastasia Alexandrovna, "and on our way back we saw a soldier being rather rough with an old woman."

"Rather rough!" cried Mr. Harrington. "There was an old woman walking along the pavement with a basket of provisions on her arm. Two soldiers came up behind her and one of them snatched the basket from her and walked off with it. She burst out screaming and crying, I don't know what she was saying, but I can guess, and the other soldier took his gun and with the butt-end of it hit her over the head. Isn't that right, Delilah?"

"Yes," she answered, unable to help smiling. "And before I could prevent it Mr. Harrington jumped out of the cab and ran up to the soldier who had the basket, wrenched it from him and began to abuse the pair of them like pickpockets. At first they were so taken aback they didn't know what to do and then they got in a rage. I ran after Mr. Harrington and explained to them that he was a foreigner and drunk."

"Drunk?" cried Mr. Harrington.

"Yes, drunk. Of course a crowd collected. It looked as though it wasn't going to be very nice."

Mr. Harrington smiled with those large, pale-blue eyes of his.

"It sounded to me as though you were giving them a piece of your mind, Delilah. It was as good as a play to watch you."

"Don't be stupid, Mr. Harrington," cried Anastasia, in a sudden fury, stamping her foot. "Don't you know that those soldiers might very easily have killed you and me too, and not one of the bystanders would have raised a finger to help us?"

"Me? I'm an American citizen, Delilah. They wouldn't dare touch a hair of my head."

"They'd have difficulty in finding one," said Anastasia Alexandrovna, who when she was in a temper had no manners. "But if you think Russian soldiers are going to hesitate to kill you because you're an American citizen you'll get a big surprise one of these days."

"Well, what happened to the old woman?" asked Ashenden.

"The soldiers went off after a little and we went back to her."

"Still with the basket?"

"Yes. Mr. Harrington clung on to that like grim death. She was lying on the ground with the blood pouring from her head. We got her into the cab and when she could speak enough to tell us where she lived we drove her home. She was bleeding dreadfully and we had some difficulty in staunching the blood."

Anastasia Alexandrovna gave Mr. Harrington an odd look and to his surprise Ashenden saw him turn scarlet.

"What's the matter now?"

"You see, we had nothing to bind her up with. Mr. Harrington's handkerchief was soaked. There was only one thing about me that I could get off quickly and so I took off my . . ."

But before she could finish Mr. Harrington interrupted her.

"You need not tell Mr. Ashenden what you took off. I'm a married man and I know ladies wear them, but I see no need to refer to them in general society."

Anastasia Alexandrovna giggled.

"Then you must kiss me, Mr. Harrington. If you don't I shall say."

Mr. Harrington hesitated a moment, considering evidently the pros and cons of the matter, but he saw that Anastasia Alexandrovna was determined.

"Go on then, you may kiss me, Delilah, though I'm bound to say I don't see what pleasure it can be to you."

She put her arms round his neck and kissed him on both cheeks, then without a word of warning burst into a flood of tears.

"You're a brave little man, Mr. Harrington. You're absurd but magnificent," she sobbed.

Mr. Harrington was less surprised than Ashenden would have expected him to be. He looked at Anastasia with a thin, quizzical smile and gently patted her.

"Come, come, Delilah, pull yourself together. It gave you a nasty turn, didn't it? You're quite upset. I shall have terrible rheumatism in my shoulder if you go on weeping all over it."

The scene was ridiculous and touching. Ashenden laughed, but he had the beginnings of a lump in his throat.

When Anastasia Alexandrovna had left them Mr. Harrington sat in a brown study.

"They're very queer, these Russians. Do you know what Delilah did?" he said, suddenly. "She stood up in the cab, in the middle of the street, with people passing on both sides, and took her pants off. She tore them in two and gave me one to hold while she made a bandage of the other. I was never so embarrassed in my life."

"Tell me what gave you the idea of calling her Delilah?" smiled Ashenden.

Mr. Harrington reddened a little.

"She's a very fascinating woman, Mr. Ashenden. She's been deeply wronged by her husband and I naturally felt a great deal of sympathy for her. These Russians are very emotional people and I did not want her to mistake my sympathy for anything else. I told her I was very much attached to Mrs. Harrington."

"You're not under the impression that Delilah was Potiphar's wife?" asked Ashenden.

"I don't know what you mean by that, Mr. Ashenden," replied Mr. Harrington. "Mrs. Harrington has always given me to understand that I'm very fascinating to women, and I thought if I called our little friend Delilah it would make my position quite clear."

"I don't think Russia's any place for you, Mr. Harrington," said Ashenden smiling. "If I were you I'd get out of it as quick as I could."

"I can't go now. I've got them to agree to my terms at last and we're going to sign next week. Then I shall pack my grip and go."

"I wonder if your signatures will be worth the paper they're written on," said Ashenden.

He had at length devised a plan of campaign. It took him twenty-four hours' hard work to code a telegram in which he put his scheme before the persons who had sent him to Petrograd. It was accepted and he was promised all the money he needed. Ashenden knew he could do nothing unless the Provisional Government remained in power for another three months; but winter was at hand and food was getting scarcer every day. The army was mutinous. The people clamoured for peace. Every evening at the Europe Ashenden drank a cup of chocolate with Professor Z. and discussed with him how best to make use of his devoted Czechs. Anastasia Alexandrovna had a flat in a retired spot and here he had meetings with all manner of persons. Plans were drawn up. Measures were taken. Ashenden argued, persuaded, promised. He had to overcome the vacillation of one and wrestle with the fatalism of another. He had to judge who was resolute and who was self-sufficient, who was honest and who was infirm of purpose. He had to curb his impatience with the Russian verbosity; he had to be good-tempered with people who were willing to talk of everything but the matter in hand; he had to listen sympathetically to ranting and rhodomontade. He had to beware of treachery. He had to humour the vanity of fools and elude the greed of the ambitious. Time was pressing. The rumours grew hot and many of the activities of the Bolsheviks. Kerensky ran hither and thither like a frightened hen.

Then the blow fell. On the night of November 7th, 1917, the Bolsheviks rose, Kerensky's ministers were arrested and the Winter Palace was sacked by the mob; the reins of power were seized by Lenin and Trotsky.

Anastasia Alexandrovna came to Ashenden's room at the hotel early in the morning. Ashenden was coding a telegram. He had been up all night, first at the Smolny, and then at the Winter Palace. He was tired out. Her face was white and her shining brown eyes were tragic.

"Have you heard?" she asked Ashenden.

He nodded.

"It's all over then. They say Kerensky has fled. They never even showed fight." Rage seized her. "The buffoon!" she screamed.

At that moment there was a knock at the door and Anastasia Alexandrovna looked at it with sudden apprehension.

"You know the Bolsheviks have got a list of people they've decided to execute. My name is on it, and it may be that yours is too."

"If it's they and they want to come in they only have to turn the handle," said Ashenden, smiling, but with ever so slightly odd a feeling at the pit of his stomach. "Come in."

The door was opened and Mr. Harrington stepped into the room. He was as dapper as ever, in his short black coat and striped trousers, his shoes neatly polished and a derby on his bald head. He took it off when he saw Anastasia Alexandrovna.

"Oh, fancy finding you here so early. I looked in on my way out, I wanted to tell you my news. I tried to find you yesterday evening, but couldn't. You didn't come in to dinner."

"No, I was at a meeting," said Ashenden.

"You must both congratulate me, I got my signatures yesterday, and my business is done."

Mr. Harrington beamed on them, the picture of self-satisfaction, and he arched himself like a bantam-cock who has chased away all rivals. Anastasia Alexandrovna burst into a sudden shriek of hysterical laughter. He stared at her in perplexity.

"Why, Delilah, what is the matter?" he said.

Anastasia laughed till the tears ran from her eyes and then began to sob in earnest. Ashenden explained.

"The Bolsheviks have overthrown the Government. Kerensky's ministers are in prison. The Bolsheviks are out to kill. Delilah says her name is on the list. Your minister signed your documents yesterday because he knew it did not matter what he did then. Your contracts are worth nothing. The Bolsheviks are going to make peace with Germany as soon as they can."

Anastasia Alexandrovna had recovered her self-control as quickly as she had lost it.

"You had better get out of Russia as soon as you can, Mr. Harrington. It's no place for a foreigner now and it may be that in a few days you won't be able to."

Mr. Harrington looked from one to the other.

"O my," he said. "O my!" It seemed inadequate. "Are you going to tell me that that Russian minister was just making a fool of me?"

Ashenden shrugged his shoulders.

"How can one tell what he was thinking of? He may have a keen sense of humour and perhaps he thought it funny to sign a fifty-million-dollar contract yesterday when there was every chance of his being stood against the wall and shot to-day. Anastasia Alexandrovna's right, Mr. Harrington, you'd better take the first train that'll get you to Sweden."

"And what about you?"

"There's nothing for me to do here any more. I'm cabling for instructions and I shall go as soon as I get leave. The Bolsheviks have got ahead of us and the people I was working with will have their work cut out to save their lives."

"Boris Petrovich was shot this morning," said Anastasia Alexandrovna with a frown.

They both looked at Mr. Harrington and he stared at the floor. His pride in this achievement of his was shattered and he sagged like a pricked balloon. But in a minute he looked up. He gave Anastasia Alexandrovna a little smile and for the first time Ashenden noticed how attractive and kindly his smile was. There was something peculiarly disarming about it.

"If the Bolsheviks are after you, Delilah, don't you think you'd better come with me? I'll take care of you and if you like to come to America I'm sure Mrs. Harrington would be glad to do anything she could for you."

"I can see Mrs. Harrington's face if you arrived in Philadelphia with a Russian refugee," laughed Anastasia Alexandrovna. "I'm afraid it would need more explaining than you could ever manage. No, I shall stay here."

"But if you're in danger?"

"I'm a Russian. My place is here. I will not leave my country when most my country needs me."

"That is bunk, Delilah," said Mr. Harrington very quietly.

Anastasia Alexandrovna had spoken with deep emotion, but now with a little start she shot a sudden quizzical look at him.

"I know it is, Samson," she answered. "To tell you the truth I think we're all going to have a hell of a time, God knows what's going to happen, but I want to see; I wouldn't miss a minute of it for the world."

Mr. Harrington shook his head.

"Curiosity is the bane of your sex, Delilah," he said.

"Go along and do your packing, Mr. Harrington," said Ashenden, smiling, "and then we'll take you to the station. The train will be besieged."

"Very well, I'll go. And I shan't be sorry either. I haven't had a decent meal since I came here and I've done a thing I never thought I should have to do in my life, I've drunk my coffee without sugar and when I've been lucky enough to get a little piece of black bread I've had to eat it without butter. Mrs. Harrington will never believe me when I tell her what I've gone through. What this country wants is organisation."

When he left them Ashenden and Anastasia Alexandrovna talked over the situation. Ashenden was depressed because all his careful schemes had come to nothing, but Anastasia Alexandrovna was excited and she hazarded every sort of guess about the outcome of this new revolution. She pretended to be very serious, but in her heart she looked upon it all very much as a thrilling play. She wanted more and more things to happen. Then there was another knock at the door and before Ashenden could answer Mr. Harrington burst in.

"Really the service at this hotel is a scandal," he cried heatedly, "I've been ringing my bell for fifteen minutes and I can't get anyone to pay the smallest attention to me."

"Service?" exclaimed Anastasia Alexandrovna. "There is not a servant left in the hotel."

"But I want my laundry. They promised to let me have it back last night."

"I'm afraid you haven't got much chance of getting it now," said Ashenden.

"I'm not going to leave without my laundry. Four shirts, two union suits, a pair of pyjamas, and four collars. I wash my handkerchiefs and socks in my room. I want my laundry and I'm not going to leave this hotel without it."

"Don't be a fool," cried Ashenden. "What you've got to do is to get out of here while the going's good. If there are no servants to get it you'll just have to leave your washing behind you."

"Pardon me, sir, I shall do nothing of the kind. I'll go and fetch it myself. I've suffered enough at the hands of this country and

I'm not going to leave four perfectly good shirts to be worn by a lot of dirty Bolsheviks. No, sir. I do not leave Russia till I have my laundry."

Anastasia Alexandrovna stared at the floor for a moment; then with a little smile looked up. It seemed to Ashenden that there was something in her that responded to Mr. Harrington's futile obstinacy. In her Russian way she understood that Mr. Harrington could not leave Petrograd without his washing. His insistence had given it the value of a symbol.

"I'll go downstairs and see if I can find anybody about who knows where the laundry is, and if I can I'll go with you and you can bring your washing away with you."

Mr. Harrington unbent. He answered with that sweet and disarming smile of his.

"That's terribly kind of you, Delilah. I don't mind if it's ready or not, I'll take it just as it is."

Anastasia Alexandrovna left them.

"Well, what do you think of Russia and the Russians now?" Mr. Harrington asked Ashenden.

"I'm fed up with them. I'm fed up with Tolstoi, I'm fed up with Turgenev and Dostoievski, I'm fed up with Chekoff. I'm fed up with the Intelligentsia. I hanker after people who know their mind from one minute to another, who mean what they say an hour after they've said it, whose word you can rely on; I'm sick of fine phrases, and oratory and attitudinising."

Ashenden, bitten by the prevailing ill, was about to make a speech when he was interrupted by a rattle as of peas on a drum. In the city, so strangely silent, it sounded abrupt and odd.

"What's that?" asked Mr. Harrington.

"Rifle-firing. On the other side of the river, I should think."

Mr. Harrington gave a funny little look. He laughed, but his face was a trifle pale; he did not like it, and Ashenden did not blame him.

"I think it's high time I got out. I shouldn't so much mind for myself, but I've got a wife and children to think of. I haven't had a letter from Mrs. Harrington for so long I'm a bit worried." He paused an instant. "I'd like you to know Mrs. Harrington, she's a very wonderful woman. She's the best wife a man ever had. Until I came here I'd not been separated from her for more than three days since we were married."

Anastasia Alexandrovna came back and told them that she had found the address.

"It's about forty minutes' walk from here and if you'll come now I'll go with you," she said.

"I'm ready."

"You'd better look out," said Ashenden. "I don't believe the streets are very healthy to-day."

Anastasia Alexandrovna looked at Mr. Harrington.

"I must have my laundry, Delilah," he said. "I should never rest in peace if I left it behind me and Mrs. Harrington would never let me hear the last of it."

"Come on then."

They set out and Ashenden went on with the dreary business of translating into a very complicated code the shattering news he had to give. It was a long message, and then he had to ask for instructions upon his own movements. It was a mechanical job and yet it was one in which you could not allow your attention to wander. The mistake of a single figure might make a whole sentence incomprehensible.

Suddenly his door was burst open and Anastasia Alexandrovna flung into the room. She had lost her hat and was dishevelled. She was panting. Her eyes were starting out of her head and she was obviously in a state of great excitement.

"Where's Mr. Harrington?" she cried. "Isn't he here?"

"No."

"Is he in his bedroom?"

"I don't know. Why, what's the matter? We'll go and look if you like. Why didn't you bring him along with you?"

They walked down the passage and knocked at Mr. Harrington's door; there was no answer; they tried the handle; the door was locked.

"He's not there."

They went back to Ashenden's room. Anastasia Alexandrovna sank into a chair.

"Give me a glass of water, will you? I'm out of breath. I've been running."

She drank the water Ashenden poured out for her. She gave a sudden sob.

"I hope he's all right. I should never forgive myself if he was hurt. I was hoping he would have got here before me. He got his washing all right. We found the place. There was only an old woman there and they didn't want to let us take it, but we insisted. Mr. Harrington was furious because it hadn't been touched. It was exactly as he had sent it. They'd promised it last night and it was still in the bundle that Mr. Harrington had made himself. I said that was Russia and Mr. Harrington said he preferred coloured people. I'd led him by side streets because I thought it was better, and we started to come back again. We passed at the top of a street and at the bottom of it I saw a little crowd. There was a man addressing them.

" 'Let's go and hear what's he's saying,' I said.

"I could see they were arguing. It looked exciting. I wanted to know what was happening.

" 'Come along, Delilah,' he said. 'Let us mind our own business.'

" 'You go back to the hotel and do your packing. I'm going to see the fun,' I said.

"I ran down the street and he followed me. There were about two or three hundred people there and a student was addressing them. There were some working-men and they were shouting at him. I love a row and I edged my way into the crowd. Suddenly we heard the sound of shots and before you could realise what was happening two armoured cars came dashing down the street. There were soldiers in them and they were firing as they went. I don't know why. For fun, I suppose, or because they were drunk. We all scattered like a lot of rabbits. We just ran for our lives. I lost Mr. Harrington. I can't make out why he isn't here. Do you think something has happened to him?"

Ashenden was silent for a while.

"We'd better go out and look for him," he said. "I don't know why the devil he couldn't leave his washing."

"I understand, I understand so well."

"That's a comfort," said Ashenden irritably. "Let's go."

He put on his hat and coat, and they walked downstairs. The hotel seemed strangely empty. They went out into the street. There was hardly anyone to be seen. They walked along. The trams were not running and the silence in the great city was uncanny. The shops were closed. It was quite startling when a motor-car dashed by at breakneck speed. The people they passed looked frightened and downcast. When they had to go through a main thoroughfare they hastened their steps. A lot of people were there and they stood about irresolutely as though they did not know what to do next. Reservists in their shabby grey were walking down the middle of the roadway in little bunches. They did not speak.

They looked like sheep looking for their shepherd. Then they came to the street down which Anastasia Alexandrovna had run, but they entered it from the opposite end. A number of windows had been broken by the wild shooting. It was quite empty. You could see where the people had scattered, for strewn about were articles they had dropped in their haste, books, a man's hat, a lady's bag and a basket. Anastasia Alexandrovna touched Ashenden's arm to draw his attention: sitting on the pavement, her head bent right down to her lap, was a woman and she was dead. A little way on two men had fallen together. They were dead too. The wounded, one supposed, had managed to drag themselves away or their friends had carried them. Then they found Mr. Harrington. His derby had rolled in the gutter. He lay on his face, in a pool of blood, his bald head, with its prominent bones, very white; his neat black coat smeared and muddy. But his hand was clenched tight on the parcel that contained four shirts, two union suits, a pair of pyjamas and four collars. Mr. Harrington had not let his washing go.

❖

Lord Mountdrago

DR. AUDLIN looked at the clock on his desk. It was twenty minutes to six. He was surprised that his patient was late, for Lord Mountdrago prided himself on his punctuality; he had a sentencious way of expressing himself which gave the air of an epigram to a commonplace remark, and he was in the habit of saying that punctuality is a compliment you pay to the intelligent and a rebuke you administer to the stupid. Lord Mountdrago's appointment was for five-thirty.

There was in Dr. Audlin's appearance nothing to attract attention. He was tall and spare, with narrow shoulders and something of a stoop; his hair was grey and thin; his long, sallow face deeply lined. He was not more than fifty, but he looked older. His eyes, pale-blue and rather large, were weary. When you had been with him for a while you noticed that they moved very little; they remained fixed on your face, but so empty of expression were they that it was no discomfort. They seldom lit up. They gave no clue to his thoughts nor changed with the words he spoke. If you were of an observant turn it might have struck you that he blinked much less often than most of us. His hands were on the large side, with long, tapering fingers; they were soft, but firm, cool but not clammy. You could never have said what Dr. Audlin wore unless you had made a point of looking. His clothes were dark. His tie was black. His dress made his sallow lined face paler, and his pale eyes more wan. He gave you the impression of a very sick man.

Dr. Audlin was a psycho-analyst. He had adopted the profession by accident and practised it with misgiving. When the war broke out he had not been long qualified and was getting experience at various hospitals; he offered his services to the authorities, and after a time was sent out to France. It was then that he discovered his singular gift. He could allay certain pains by the touch of his cool, firm hands, and by talking to them often induce sleep in men who were suffering from sleeplessness. He spoke slowly. His voice had no particular colour, and its tone did not alter with the words he uttered, but it was musical, soft and lulling. He told the men that they must rest, that they mustn't worry, that they must sleep; and rest stole into their jaded bones, tranquillity pushed their anxieties away, like a man finding a place for himself on a crowded bench, and slumber fell on their tired eyelids like the light rain of spring upon the fresh-turned earth. Dr. Audlin found that by speaking to men with that low, monotonous voice of his, by looking at them with his pale, quiet eyes, by stroking their weary foreheads with his long firm hands, he could soothe their perturbations, resolve the conflicts that distracted them and banish the phobias that made their lives a torment. Sometimes he effected cures that seemed miraculous. He restored speech to a man who, after being buried under the earth by a bursting shell, had been struck dumb, and he gave back the use of his limbs to another who had been paralysed after a crash in a plane. He could not understand his powers; he was of a sceptical turn, and though they say that in circumstances of this kind the first thing is to believe in yourself, he never quite succeeded in doing that; and it was only the outcome of his activities, patent to the most incredulous observer, that obliged him to admit that he had some faculty, coming from he knew not where, obscure and uncertain, that enabled him to do things for which he could offer no explanation. When the war was over he went to Vienna and studied there, and afterwards to Zurich; and then settled down in London to practise the art he had so strangely acquired. He had been practising now for fifteen years, and had attained, in the speciality he followed, a distinguished reputation. People told one another of the amazing things he had done, and though his fees were high, he had as many patients as he had time to see. Dr. Audlin knew that he had achieved some very extraordinary results; he had saved men from suicide, others from the lunatic asylum, he had assuaged griefs that embittered useful lives, he had turned unhappy marriages into happy ones, he had eradicated abnormal instincts and thus delivered not a few from a hateful bondage, he had given health to the sick in spirit; he had done all this, and yet at the back of his mind remained the suspicion that he was little more than a quack.

It went against his grain to exercise a power that he could not understand, and it offended his honesty to trade on the faith of the people he treated when he had no faith in himself. He was rich enough now to live without working, and the work exhausted him; a dozen times he had been on the point of giving up practice. He knew all that Freud and Jung and the rest of them had written. He was not satisfied; he had an intimate conviction that all their theory was hocus-pocus, and yet there the results were, incomprehensible, but manifest. And what had he not seen of human nature during the fifteen years that patients had been coming to his dingy back room in Wimpole Street? The revelations that had been poured into his ears, sometimes only too willingly, sometimes with shame, with reservations, with anger, had long ceased to surprise him. Nothing could shock him any longer. He knew by now that men were liars, he knew how extravagant was their vanity; he knew far worse than that about them; but he knew that it was not for him to judge or to condemn. But year by year as these terrible confidences were imparted to him his face grew a little greyer, its lines a little more marked and his pale eyes more weary. He seldom laughed, but now and again when for relaxation he read a novel he smiled. Did their authors really think the men and women they wrote of were like that? If they only knew how much more complicated they were, how much more unexpected, what irreconcilable elements co-existed within their souls and what dark and sinister contentions afflicted them!

It was a quarter to six. Of all the strange cases he had been called upon to deal with Dr. Audlin could remember none stranger than that of Lord Mountdrago. For one thing the personality of his patient made it singular. Lord Mountdrago was an able and a distinguished man. Appointed Secretary for Foreign Affairs when still under forty, now after three years in office he had seen his policy prevail. It was generally acknowledged that he was the ablest politician in the Conservative Party and only the fact that his father was a peer, on whose death he would no longer be able to sit in the House of Commons, made it impossible for him to aim at the premiership. But if in these democratic times it is out of the question for a Prime Minister of England to be in the House of Lords, there was nothing to prevent Lord Mountdrago from continuing to be Secretary for Foreign Affairs in successive Conservative administrations and so for long directing the foreign policy of his country.

Lord Mountdrago had many good qualities. He had intelligence and industry. He was widely travelled, and spoke several languages fluently. From early youth he had specialised in foreign affairs, and had conscientiously made himself acquainted with the political and economic circumstances of other countries. He had courage, insight and determination. He was a good speaker, both on the platform and in the House, clear, precise and often witty. He was a brilliant debater and his gift of repartee was celebrated. He had a fine presence: he was a tall, handsome man, rather bald and somewhat too stout, but this gave him solidity and an air of maturity that were of service to him. As a young man he had been something of an athlete and had rowed in the Oxford boat, and he was known to be one of the best shots in England. At twenty-four he had married a girl of eighteen whose father was a duke and her mother a great American heiress, so that she had both position and wealth, and by her he had had two sons. For several years they had lived privately apart, but in public united, so that appearances were saved, and no other attachment on either side had given the gossips occasion to whisper. Lord Mountdrago indeed was too ambitious, too hard-working, and it must be added too patriotic, to be tempted by any pleasures that might interfere with his career. He had, in short, a great deal to make him a popular and successful figure. He had unfortunately great defects.

He was a fearful snob. You would not have been surprised at this if his father had been the first holder of the title. That the son of an ennobled lawyer, a manufacturer or a distiller should attach an inordinate importance to his rank is understandable. The earldom held by Lord Mountdrago's father was created by Charles II, and the barony held by the first Earl dated from the Wars of the Roses. For three hundred years the successive holders of the title had allied themselves with the noblest families of England. But Lord Mountdrago was as conscious of his birth as a *nouveau riche* is conscious of his money. He never missed an opportunity of impressing it upon others. He had beautiful manners when he chose to display them, but this he did only with people whom he regarded as his equals. He was coldly insolent to those whom he looked upon as his social inferiors. He was rude to his servants and insulting to his secretaries. The subordinate officials in the government offices to which he had been successively attached feared and hated him. His arrogance was horrible. He knew that he was a great deal cleverer than most of the persons he had to do with, and never hesitated to apprise them of the fact. He had no patience with the infirmities of human nature. He felt himself born to command and was irritated with people who expected him to listen to their arguments or wished to hear the reasons for his decisions. He was immeasurably selfish. He looked upon any service that was rendered him as a right due to his rank and intelligence and therefore deserving of no gratitude. It never entered his head that he was called upon to do anything for others. He had many enemies: he despised them. He knew no one who merited his assistance, his sympathy or his compassion. He had no friends. He was distrusted by his chiefs, because they doubted his loyalty; he was unpopular with his party, because he was over-bearing and discourteous; and yet his merit was so great, his patriotism so evident, his intelligence so solid and his management of affairs so brilliant that they had to put up with him. And what made it possible to do this was that on occasion he could be enchanting: when he was with persons whom he considered his equals, or whom he wished to captivate, in the company of foreign dignitaries or women of distinction, he could be gay, witty and debonair; his manners then reminded you that in his veins ran the same blood as had run in the veins of Lord Chesterfield; he could tell a story with point, he could be natural, sensible and even profound. You were surprised at the extent of his knowledge and the sensitiveness of his taste. You thought him the best company in the world; you forgot that he had insulted you the day before and was quite capable of cutting you dead the next.

Lord Mountdrago almost failed to become Dr. Audlin's patient. A secretary rang up the doctor and told him that his lordship, wishing to consult him, would be glad if he would come to his house at ten o'clock on the following morning. Dr. Audlin answered that he was unable to go to Lord Mountdrago's house, but would be pleased to give him an appointment at his consulting-room at five o'clock on the next day but one. The secretary took the message and presently rang back to say that Lord Mountdrago insisted on seeing Dr. Audlin in his own house and the doctor could fix his own fee. Dr. Audlin replied that he only saw patients in his consulting-room and expressed his regret that unless Lord Mountdrago was prepared to come to him he could not give him his attention. In a quarter of an hour a brief message was delivered to him that his lordship would come not next day but one, but next day, at five.

When Lord Mountdrago was then shown in he did not come forward, but stood at the door and insolently looked the doctor up and down. Dr. Audlin perceived that he was in a rage; he gazed at him, silently, with still eyes. He saw a big heavy man, with greying hair, receding on the forehead so that it gave nobility to his brow, a puffy face with bold regular features and an expression of haughtiness. He had somewhat the look of one of the Bourbon sovereigns of the eighteenth century.

"It seems that it is as difficult to see you as a Prime Minister, Dr. Audlin. I'm an extremely busy man."

"Won't you sit down?" said the doctor.

His face showed no sign that Lord Mountdrago's speech in any way affected him. Dr. Audlin sat in his chair at the desk. Lord Mountdrago still stood and his frown darkened.

"I think I should tell you that I am His Majesty's Secretary for Foreign Affairs," he said acidly.

"Won't you sit down?" the doctor repeated.

Lord Mountdrago made a gesture, which might have suggested that he was about to turn on his heel and stalk out of the room; but if that was his intention he apparently thought better of it. He seated himself. Dr. Audlin opened a large book and took up his pen. He wrote without looking at his patient.

"How old are you?"

"Forty-two."

"Are you married?"

"Yes."

"How long have you been married?"

"Eighteen years."

"Have you any children?"

"I have two sons."

Dr. Audlin noted down the facts as Lord Mountdrago abruptly answered his questions. Then he leaned back in his chair and looked at him. He did not speak; he just looked, gravely, with pale eyes that did not move.

"Why have you come to see me?" he asked at length.

"I've heard about you. Lady Canute is a patient of yours, I understand. She tells me you've done her a certain amount of good."

Dr. Audlin did not reply. His eyes remained fixed on the other's face, but they were so empty of expression that you might have thought he did not even see him.

"I can't do miracles," he said at length. Not a smile, but the shadow of a smile flickered in his eyes. "The Royal College of Physicians would not approve of it if I did."

Lord Mountdrago gave a brief chuckle. It seemed to lessen his hostility. He spoke more amiably.

"You have a very remarkable reputation. People seem to believe in you."

"Why have you come to me?" repeated Dr. Audlin.

Now it was Lord Mountdrago's turn to be silent. It looked as though he found it hard to answer. Dr. Audlin waited. At last Lord Mountdrago seemed to make an effort. He spoke.

"I'm in perfect health. Just as a matter of routine I had myself examined by my own doctor the other day, Sir Augustus Fitzherbert, I daresay you've heard of him, and he tells me I have the physique of a man of thirty. I work hard, but I'm never tired, and I enjoy my work. I smoke very little and I'm an extremely moderate drinker. I take a sufficiency of exercise and I lead a regular life. I am a perfectly sound, normal, healthy man. I quite expect you to think it very silly and childish of me to consult you."

Dr. Audlin saw that he must help him.

"I don't know if I can do anything to help you. I'll try. You're distressed?"

Lord Mountdrago frowned.

"The work that I'm engaged in is important. The decisions I am called upon to make can easily affect the welfare of the country and even the peace of the world. It is essential that my judgment should be balanced and my brain clear. I look upon it as my duty to eliminate any cause of worry that may interfere with my usefulness."

Dr. Audlin had never taken his eyes off him. He saw a great deal. He saw behind his patient's pompous manner and arrogant pride an anxiety that he could not dispel.

"I asked you to be good enough to come here because I know by experience that it's easier for someone to speak openly in the dingy surroundings of a doctor's consulting-room than in his accustomed environment."

"They're certainly dingy," said Lord Mountdrago acidly. He paused. It was evident that this man who had so much self-assurance, so quick and decided a mind that he was never at a loss, at this moment was embarrassed. He smiled in order to show the doctor that he was at his ease, but his eyes betrayed his disquiet. When he spoke again it was with unnatural heartiness.

"The whole thing's so trivial that I can hardly bring myself to bother you with it. I'm afraid you'll just tell me not to be a fool and waste your valuable time."

"Even things that seem very trivial may have their importance. They can be a symptom of a deep-seated derangement. And my time is entirely at your disposal."

Dr. Audlin's voice was low and grave. The monotone in which he spoke was strangely soothing. Lord Mountdrago at length made up his mind to be frank.

"The fact is I've been having some very tiresome dreams lately. I know it's silly to pay any attention to them, but—well, the honest truth is that I'm afraid they've got on my nerves."

"Can you describe any of them to me?"

Lord Mountdrago smiled, but the smile that tried to be careless was only rueful.

"They're so idiotic, I can hardly bring myself to narrate them."

"Never mind."

"Well, the first I had was about a month ago. I dreamt that I was at a party at Connemara House. It was an official party. The King and Queen were to be there and of course decorations were worn. I was wearing my ribbon and my star. I went into a sort of cloakroom they have to take off my coat. There was a little man there called Owen Griffiths, who's a Welsh Member of Parliament, and to tell you the truth, I was surprised to see him. He's very common, and I said to myself: 'Really, Lydia Connemara is going too far, whom will she ask next?' I thought he looked at me rather curiously, but I didn't take any notice of him; in fact I cut the little bounder and walked upstairs. I suppose you've never been there?"

"Never."

"No, it's not the sort of house you'd ever be likely to go to. It's a rather vulgar house, but it's got a very fine marble staircase, and the Connemaras were at the top receiving their guests. Lady Connemara gave me a look of surprise when I shook hands with her, and began to giggle; I didn't pay much attention, she's a very silly, ill-bred woman and her manners are no better than those of her ancestors whom King Charles II made a duchess. I must say the reception rooms at Connemara House are stately. I walked through, nodding to a number of people and shaking hands; then I saw the German Ambassador talking with one of the Austrian Archdukes. I particularly wanted to have a word with him, so I went up and held out my hand. The moment the Archduke saw me he burst into a roar of laughter. I was deeply affronted. I looked him up and down sternly, but he only laughed the more. I was about to speak to him rather sharply, when there was a sudden hush and I realised that the King and Queen had come. Turning my back on the Archduke, I stepped forward, and then, quite suddenly, I noticed that I hadn't got any trousers on. I was in short silk drawers, and I wore scarlet sock-suspenders. No wonder Lady Connemara had giggled; no wonder the Archduke had laughed! I can't tell you what that moment was. An agony of shame. I awoke in a cold sweat. Oh, you don't know the relief I felt to find it was only a dream."

"It's the kind of dream that's not so very uncommon," said Dr. Audlin.

"I dare say not. But an odd thing happened next day. I was in the lobby of the House of Commons, when that fellow Griffiths walked slowly past me. He deliberately looked down at my legs and then he looked me full in the face and I was almost certain he winked. A ridiculous thought came to me. He'd been there the night before and seen me make that ghastly exhibition of myself and was enjoying the joke. But of course I knew that was impossible because it was only a dream. I gave him an icy glare and he walked on. But he was grinning his head off."

Lord Mountdrago took his handkerchief out of his pocket and wiped the palms of his hands. He was making no attempt now to conceal his perturbation. Dr. Audlin never took his eyes off him.

"Tell me another dream."

"It was the night after, and it was even more absurd than the first one. I dreamt that I was in the House. There was a debate on foreign affairs which not only the country, but the world, had been looking forward to with the gravest concern. The government had decided on a change in their policy which vitally affected the future of the Empire. The occasion was historic. Of course the House was crowded. All the ambassadors were there. The galleries were packed. It fell to me to make the important speech of the evening. I had prepared it carefully. A man like me has enemies, there are a lot of people who resent my having achieved the position I have at an age when even the cleverest men are content with situations of relative obscurity, and I was determined that my speech should not only be worthy of the occasion, but should silence my detractors. It excited me to think that the whole world was hanging on my lips. I rose to my feet. If you've ever been in the House you'll know how members chat to one another during a debate, rustle papers and turn over reports. The silence was the silence of the grave when I began to speak. Suddenly I caught sight of that odious little bounder on one of the benches opposite, Griffiths the Welsh member; he put out his tongue at me. I don't know if you've ever heard a vulgar music-hall song called *A Bicycle Made for Two*. It was very popular a great many years ago. To show Griffiths how completely I despised him I began to sing it. I sang the first verse right through. There was a moment's surprise, and when I finished they cried 'Hear, hear,' on the opposite benches. I put up my hand to silence them and sang the second verse. The House listened to me in stony silence and I felt the song wasn't going down very well. I was vexed, for I have a good baritone voice, and I was determined that they should do me justice. When I started the third verse the members began to laugh; in an instant the laughter spread; the ambassadors, the strangers in the Distinguished Strangers' Gallery, the ladies in the Ladies' Gallery, the reporters, they shook, they bellowed, they held their sides, they rolled in their seats; everyone was overcome with laughter except the ministers on the Front Bench immediately behind me. In that incredible, in that unprecedented uproar, they sat petrified. I gave them a glance, and suddenly the enormity of what I had done fell upon me. I had made myself the laughing-stock of the whole world. With misery I realised that I should have to resign. I woke and knew it was only a dream."

Lord Mountdrago's grand manner had deserted him as he narrated this, and now having finished he was pale and trembling. But with an effort he pulled himself together. He forced a laugh to his shaking lips.

"The whole thing was so fantastic that I couldn't help being amused. I didn't give it another thought, and when I went into the House on the following afternoon I was feeling in very good form. The debate was dull, but I had to be there, and I read some documents that required my attention. For some reason I chanced to look up and I saw that Griffiths was speaking. He has an unpleasant Welsh accent and an unprepossessing appearance. I couldn't imagine that he had anything to say that it was worth my while to listen to, and I was about to return to my papers when he quoted two lines from *A Bicycle Made for Two*. I couldn't help glancing at him and I saw that his eyes were fixed on me with a grin of bitter mockery. I faintly shrugged my shoulders. It was comic that a scrubby little Welsh member should look at me like that. It was an odd coincidence that he should quote two lines from that disastrous song that I'd sung all through in my dream. I began to read my papers again, but I don't mind telling you that I found it difficult to concentrate on them. I was a little puzzled. Owen Griffiths had been in my first dream, the one at Connemara House, and I'd received a very definite impression afterwards that he knew the sorry figure I'd cut. Was it a mere coincidence that he had just quoted those two lines? I asked myself if it was possible that he was dreaming the same dreams as I was. But of course the idea was preposterous and I determined not to give it a second thought."

There was a silence. Dr. Audlin looked at Lord Mountdrago and Lord Mountdrago looked at Dr. Audlin.

"Other people's dreams are very boring. My wife used to dream occasionally and insist on telling me her dreams next day with circumstantial detail. I found it maddening."

Dr. Audlin faintly smiled.

"You're not boring me."

"I'll tell you one more dream I had a few days later. I dreamt that I went into a public-house at Limehouse. I've never been to Limehouse in my life and I don't think I've ever been in a public-house since I was at Oxford, and yet I saw the street and the place I went into as exactly as if I were at home there. I went into a room, I don't know whether they call it the saloon bar or the private bar; there was a fireplace and a large leather arm-chair on one side of it, and on the other a small sofa; a bar ran the whole length of the room and over it you could see into the public bar. Near the door was a round marble-topped table and two arm-chairs beside it. It was a Saturday night and the place was packed. It was brightly lit, but the smoke was so thick that it made my eyes smart. I was dressed like a rough, with a cap on my head and a handkerchief round my neck. It seemed to me that most of the people there were drunk. I thought it rather amusing. There was a gramophone going, or the radio, I don't know which, and in front of the fireplace two women were doing a grotesque dance. There was a little crowd round them, laughing, cheering and singing. I went up to have a look and some man said to me: ' 'Ave a drink, Bill?' There were glasses on the table full of a dark liquid which I understand is called brown ale. He gave me a glass and not wishing to be conspicuous I drank it. One of the women who were dancing broke away from the other and took hold of the glass. ' 'Ere, what's the idea?' she said. 'That's my beer you're putting away.' 'Oh, I'm so sorry,' I said, 'this gentleman offered it me and I very naturally thought it was his to offer.' 'All right, mate,' she said, 'I don't mind. You come an' 'ave a dance with me.' Before I could protest she'd caught hold of me and we were dancing together. And then I found myself sitting in the arm-chair with the woman on my lap and we were sharing a glass of beer. I should tell you that sex has never played any great part in my life. I married young because in my position it was desirable that I should marry, but also in order to settle once for all the question of sex. I had the two sons I had made up my mind to have, and then I put the whole matter on one side. I've always been too busy to give much thought to that kind of thing, and living so much in the public eye as I do it would have been madness to do anything that might give rise to scandal. The greatest asset a politician can have is a blameless record as far as women are concerned. I have no patience with the men who smash up their careers for women. I only despise them. The woman I had on my knees was drunk; she wasn't pretty and she wasn't young: in fact, she was just a blowsy old prostitute. She filled me with disgust, and yet when she put her mouth to mine and kissed me, though her breath stank of beer and her teeth were decayed, though I loathed myself, I wanted her—I wanted her with all my soul. Suddenly I heard a voice. 'That's right, old boy, have a good time.' I looked up and there was Owen Griffiths. I tried to spring out of the chair, but that horrible woman wouldn't let me. 'Don't you pay no attention to 'im,' she said, ' 'e's only one of them nosy-parkers.' 'You go to it,' he said. 'I know Moll. She'll give you your money's worth all right.' You know, I wasn't so much annoyed at his seeing me in that absurd situation as angry that he should address me as 'old boy'. I pushed the woman aside and stood up and faced him. 'I don't know you and I don't want to know you,' I said. 'I know you all right,' he said. 'And my advice to you, Molly, is, see that you get your money, he'll bilk you if he can.' There was a bottle of beer standing on the table close by. Without a word I seized it by the neck and hit him over the head with it as hard as I could. I made such a violent gesture that it woke me up."

"A dream of that sort is not incomprehensible," said Dr. Audlin.

"It is the revenge nature takes on persons of unimpeachable character."

"The story's idiotic. I haven't told it you for its own sake. I've told it you for what happened next day. I wanted to look up something in a hurry and I went into the library of the House. I got the book and began reading. I hadn't noticed when I sat down that Griffiths was sitting in a chair close by me. Another of the Labour Members came in and went up to him. 'Hullo, Owen,' he said to him, 'you're looking pretty dicky to-day.' 'I've got an awful headache,' he answered. 'I feel as if I'd been cracked over the head with a bottle.' "

Now Lord Mountdrago's face was grey with anguish.

"I knew then that the idea I'd had and dismissed as preposterous was true. I knew that Griffiths was dreaming my dreams and that he remembered them as well as I did."

"It may also have been a coincidence."

"When he spoke he didn't speak to his friend, he deliberately spoke to me. He looked at me with sullen resentment."

"Can you offer any suggestion why this same man should come into your dreams?"

"None."

Dr. Audlin's eyes had not left his patient's face and he saw that he lied. He had a pencil in his hand and he drew a straggling line or two on his blotting-paper. It often took a long time to get people to tell the truth, and yet they knew that unless they told it he could do nothing for them.

"The dream you've just described to me took place just over three weeks ago. Have you had any since?"

"Every night."

"And does this man Griffiths come into them all?"

"Yes."

The doctor drew more lines on his blotting-paper. He wanted the silence, the drabness, the dull light of that little room to have its effect on Lord Mountdrago's sensibility. Lord Mountdrago threw himself back in his chair and turned his head away so that he should not see the other's grave eyes.

"Dr. Audlin, you must do something for me. I'm at the end of my tether. I shall go mad if this goes on. I'm afraid to go to sleep. Two or three nights I haven't. I've sat up reading and when I felt drowsy put on my coat and walked till I was exhausted. But I must have sleep. With all the work I have to do I must be at concert pitch; I must be in complete control of all my faculties. I need rest; sleep brings me none. I no sooner fall asleep than my dreams begin, and he's always there, that vulgar little cad, grinning at me, mocking me, despising me. It's a monstrous persecution. I tell you, doctor, I'm not the man of my dreams; it's not fair to judge me by them. Ask anyone you like. I'm an honest, upright, decent man. No one can say anything against my moral character either private or public. My whole ambition is to serve my country and maintain its greatness. I have money, I have rank, I'm not exposed to many of the temptations of lesser men, so that it's no credit to me to be incorruptible; but this I can claim, that no honour, no personal advantage, no thought of self would induce me to swerve by a hair's breadth from my duty. I've sacrificed everything to become the man I am. Greatness is my aim. Greatness is within my reach and I'm losing my nerve. I'm not that mean, despicable, cowardly, lewd creature that horrible little man sees. I've told you three of my dreams; they're nothing; that man has seen me do things that are so beastly, so horrible, so shameful, that even if my life depended on it I wouldn't tell them. And he remembers them. I can hardly meet the derision and disgust I see in his eyes and I even hesitate to speak because I know my words can seem to him nothing but utter humbug. He's seen me do things that no man with any self-respect would do, things for which men are driven out of the society of their fellows and sentenced to long terms of imprisonment; he's heard the foulness of my speech; he's seen me not only ridiculous, but revolting. He despises me and he no longer pretends to conceal it. I tell you that if you can't do something to help me I shall either kill myself or kill him."

"I wouldn't kill him if I were you," said Dr. Audlin, coolly, in that soothing voice of his. "In this country the consequences of killing a fellow-creature are awkward."

"I shouldn't be hanged for it, if that's what you mean. Who would know that I'd killed him? That dream of mine has shown me how. I told you, the day after I'd hit him over the head with a beer-bottle he had such a headache that he couldn't see straight. He said so himself. That shows that he can feel with his waking body what happens to his body asleep. It's not with a bottle I shall hit him next time. One night, when I'm dreaming, I shall find myself with a knife in my hand or a revolver in my pocket, I must because I want to so intensely, and then I shall seize my opportunity. I'll stick him like a pig; I'll shoot him like a dog. In the heart. And then I shall be free of this fiendish persecution."

Some people might have thought that Lord Mountdrago was mad; after all the years during which Dr. Audlin had been treating the diseased souls of men he knew how thin a line divides those whom we call sane from those whom we call insane. He knew how often in men who to all appearance were healthy and normal, who were seemingly devoid of imagination, and who fulfilled the duties of common life with credit to themselves and with benefit to their fellows, when you gained their confidence, when you tore away the mask they wore to the world, you found not only hideous abnormality, but kinks so strange, mental extravagances so fantastic, that in that respect you could only call them lunatic. If you put them in an asylum not all the asylums in the world would be large enough. Anyhow, a man was not certifiable because he had strange dreams and they had shattered his nerve. The case was singular, but it was only an exaggeration of others that had come under Dr. Audlin's observation; he was doubtful, however, whether the methods of treatment that he had so often found efficacious would here avail.

"Have you consulted any other member of my profession?" he asked.

"Only Sir Augustus. I merely told him that I suffered from nightmares. He said I was overworked and recommended me to go for a cruise. That's absurd. I can't leave the Foreign Office just now when the international situation needs constant attention. I'm indispensable, and I know it. On my conduct at the present juncture my whole future depends. He gave me sedatives. They had no effect. He gave me tonics. They were worse than useless. He's an old fool."

"Can you give any reason why it should be this particular man who persists in coming into your dreams?"

"You asked me that question before. I answered it."

That was true. But Dr. Audlin had not been satisfied with the answer.

"Just now you talked of persecution. Why should Owen Griffiths want to persecute you?"

"I don't know."

Lord Mountdrago's eyes shifted a little. Dr. Audlin was sure that he was not speaking the truth.

"Have you ever done him an injury?"

"Never."

Lord Mountdrago made no movement, but Dr. Audlin had a queer feeling that he shrank into his skin. He saw before him a large, proud man who gave the impression that the questions put to him were an insolence, and yet for all that, behind that façade, was something shifting and startled that made you think of a frightened animal in a trap. Dr. Audlin leaned forward and by the power of his eyes forced Lord Mountdrago to meet them.

"Are you quite sure?"

"Quite sure. You don't seem to understand that our ways lead along different paths. I don't wish to harp on it, but I must remind you that I am a Minister of the Crown and Griffiths is an obscure member of the Labour Party. Naturally there's no social connection between us; he's a man of very humble origin, he's not the sort of person I should be likely to meet at any of the houses I go to; and politically our respective stations are so far separated that we could not possibly have anything in common."

"I can do nothing for you unless you tell me the complete truth."

Lord Mountdrago raised his eyebrows. His voice was rasping.

"I'm not accustomed to having my word doubted, Dr. Audlin. If you're going to do that I think to take up any more of your time can only be a waste of mine. If you will kindly let my secretary know what your fee is he will see that a cheque is sent to you."

For all the expression that was to be seen on Dr. Audlin's face you might have thought that he simply had not heard what Lord Mountdrago said. He continued to look steadily into his eyes and his voice was grave and low.

"Have you done anything to this man that *he* might look upon as an injury?"

Lord Mountdrago hesitated. He looked away, and then, as though there were in Dr. Audlin's eyes a compelling force that he could not resist, looked back. He answered sulkily:

"Only if he was a dirty, second-rate little cad."

"But that is exactly what you've described him to be."

Lord Mountdrago sighed. He was beaten. Dr. Audlin knew that the sigh meant he was going at last to say what he had till then held back. Now he had no longer to insist. He dropped his eyes and began again drawing vague geometrical figures on his blotting-paper. The silence lasted two or three minutes.

"I'm anxious to tell you everything that can be of any use to you. If I didn't mention this before, it's only because it was so unimportant that I didn't see how it could possibly have anything to do with the case. Griffiths won a seat at the last election and he began to make a nuisance of himself almost at once. His father's a miner, and he worked in a mine himself when he was a boy; he's been a schoolmaster in the board schools and a journalist. He's that half-baked, conceited intellectual, with inadequate knowledge, ill-considered ideas and impracticable plans, that compulsory education has brought forth from the working-classes. He's a scrawny, grey-faced man, who looks half-starved, and he's always very slovenly in appearance; heaven knows members nowadays don't bother much about their dress, but his clothes are an outrage to the dignity of the House. They're ostentatiously shabby, his collar's never clean and his tie's never tied properly; he looks as if he hadn't had a bath for a month and his hands are filthy. The Labour Party have two or three fellows on the Front Bench who've got a certain ability, but the rest of them don't amount to much. In the kingdom of the blind the one-eyed man is king: because Griffiths is glib and has a lot of superficial information on a number of subjects, the Whips on his side began to put him up to speak whenever there was a chance. It appeared that he fancied himself on foreign affairs, and he was continually asking me silly, tiresome questions. I don't mind telling you that I made a point of snubbing him as soundly as I thought he deserved. From the beginning I hated the way he talked, his whining voice and his vulgar accent; he had nervous mannerisms that intensely irritated me. He talked rather shyly, hesitatingly, as though it were torture to him to speak and yet he was forced to by some inner passion, and often he used to say some very disconcerting things. I'll admit that now and again he had a sort of tub-thumping eloquence. It had a certain influence over the ill-regulated minds of the members of his party. They were impressed by his earnestness and they weren't, as I was, nauseated by his sentimentality. A certain sentimentality is the common coin of political debate. Nations are governed by self-interest, but they prefer to believe that their aims are altruistic, and the politician is justified if with fair words and fine phrases he can persuade the electorate that the hard bargain he is driving for his country's advantage tends to the good of humanity. The mistake people like Griffiths make is to take these fair words and fine phrases at their face value. He's a crank, and a noxious crank. He calls himself an idealist. He has at his tongue's end all the tedious blather that the intelligentsia have been boring us with for years. Non-resistance. The brotherhood of man. You know the hopeless rubbish. The worst of it was that it impressed not only his own party, it even shook some of the sillier, more sloppy-minded members of ours. I heard rumours that Griffiths was likely to get office when a Labour Government came in; I even heard it suggested that he might get the Foreign Office. The notion was grotesque but not impossible. One day I had occasion to wind up a debate on foreign affairs which Griffiths had opened. He'd spoken for an hour. I thought it a very good opportunity to cook his goose, and by God, sir, I cooked it. I tore his speech to pieces. I pointed out the faultiness of his reasoning and emphasised the deficiency of his knowledge. In the House of Commons the most devastating weapon is ridicule: I mocked him; I bantered him; I was in good form that day and the House rocked with laughter. Their laughter excited me and I excelled myself. The Opposition sat glum and silent, but even some of them couldn't help laughing once or twice; it's not intolerable, you know, to see a colleague, perhaps a rival, made a fool of. And if ever a man was made a fool of I made a fool of Griffiths. He shrank down in a seat, I saw his face go white, and presently he buried it in his hands. When I sat down I'd killed him. I'd destroyed his prestige for ever; he had no more chance of getting office when a Labour Government came in than the policeman at the door. I heard afterwards that his father, the old miner, and his mother had come up from Wales, with various supporters of his in the constituency, to watch the triumph they expected him to have. They had seen only his utter humiliation. He'd won the constituency by the narrowest margin. An incident like that might very easily lose him his seat. But that was no business of mine."

"Should I be putting it too strongly if I said you had ruined his career?" asked Dr. Audlin.

"I don't suppose you would."

"That is a very serious injury you've done him."

"He brought it on himself."

"Have you never felt any qualms about it?"

"I think perhaps if I'd known that his father and mother were there I might have let him down a little more gently."

There was nothing further for Dr. Audlin to say, and he set about treating his patient in such a manner as he thought might avail. He sought by suggestion to make him forget his dreams when he awoke; he sought to make him sleep so deeply that he would not dream. He found Lord Mountdrago's resistance impossible to break down. At the end of an hour he dismissed him. Since then he had seen Lord Mountdrago half a dozen times. He had done him no good. The frightful dreams continued every night to harass the unfortunate man, and it was clear that his general condition was growing rapidly worse. He was worn out. His irritability was uncontrollable. Lord Mountdrago was angry because he received no benefit from his treatment, and yet continued it, not only because it seemed his only hope, but because it was a relief to him to have someone with whom he could talk openly. Dr. Audlin came to the conclusion at last that there was only one way in which Lord Mountdrago could achieve deliverance, but he knew him well enough to be assured that of his own free will he would never, never take it. If Lord Mountdrago was to be saved from the breakdown that was threatening he must be induced to take a step that must be abhorrent to his pride of birth and his self-complacency. Dr. Audlin was convinced that to delay was impossible. He was treating his patient by suggestion, and after several visits found him more susceptible to it. At length he managed to get him into a condition of somnolence. With his low, soft, monotonous voice he soothed his tortured nerves. He repeated the same words over and over again. Lord Mountdrago lay quite still, his eyes closed; his breathing was regular, and his limbs were relaxed. Then Dr. Audlin in the same quiet tone spoke the words he had prepared.

"You will go to Owen Griffiths and say that you are sorry that you caused him that great injury. You will say that you will do whatever lies in your power to undo the harm that you have done him."

The words acted on Lord Mountdrago like the blow of a whip across his face. He shook himself out of his hypnotic state and sprang to his feet. His eyes blazed with passion and he poured forth upon Dr. Audlin a stream of angry vituperation such as even he had never heard. He swore at him. He cursed him. He used language of such obscenity that Dr. Audlin, who had heard every sort of foul word, sometimes from the lips of chaste and distinguished women, was surprised that he knew it.

"Apologise to that filthy little Welshman? I'd rather kill myself."

"I believe it to be the only way in which you can regain your balance."

Dr. Audlin had not often seen a man presumably sane in such a condition of uncontrollable fury. He grew red in the face and his eyes bulged out of his head. He did really foam at the mouth. Dr. Audlin watched him coolly, waiting for the storm to wear itself out, and presently he saw that Lord Mountdrago, weakened by the strain to which he had been subjected for so many weeks, was exhausted.

"Sit down," he said then, sharply.

Lord Mountdrago crumpled up into a chair.

"Christ, I feel all in. I must rest a minute and then I'll go."

For five minutes perhaps they sat in complete silence. Lord Mountdrago was a gross, blustering bully, but he was also a gentleman. When he broke the silence he had recovered his self-control.

"I'm afraid I've been very rude to you. I'm ashamed of the things I've said to you and I can only say you'd be justified if you refused to have anything more to do with me. I hope you won't do that. I feel that my visits to you do help me. I think you're my only chance."

"You mustn't give another thought to what you said. It was of no consequence."

"But there's one thing you mustn't ask me to do, and that is to make excuses to Griffiths."

"I've thought a great deal about your case. I don't pretend to understand it, but I believe that your only chance of release is to do what I proposed. I have a notion that we're none of us one self, but many, and one of the selves in you has risen up against the injury you did Griffiths and has taken on the form of Griffiths in your mind and is punishing you for what you cruelly did. If I were a priest I should tell you that it is your conscience that has adopted the shape and lineaments of this man to scourge you to repentance and persuade you to reparation."

"My conscience is clear. It's not my fault if I smashed the man's career. I crushed him like a slug in my garden. I regret nothing."

It was on these words that Lord Mountdrago had left him. Reading through his notes, while he waited, Dr. Audlin considered how best he could bring his patient to the state of mind that, now that his usual methods of treatment had failed, he thought alone could help him. He glanced at his clock. It was six. It was strange that Lord Mountdrago did not come. He knew he had intended to because a secretary had rung up that morning to say that he would be with him at the usual hour. He must have been detained by pressing work. This notion gave Dr. Audlin something else to think of: Lord Mountdrago was quite unfit to work and in no condition to deal with important matters of state. Dr. Audlin wondered whether it behoved him to get in touch with someone in authority, the Prime Minister or the Permanent Under-Secretary for Foreign Affairs, and impart to him his conviction that Lord Mountdrago's mind was so unbalanced that it was dangerous to leave affairs of moment in his hands. It was a ticklish thing to do. He might cause needless trouble and get roundly snubbed for his pains. He shrugged his shoulders.

"After all," he reflected, "the politicians have made such a mess of the world during the last five-and-twenty years, I don't suppose it makes much odds if they're mad or sane."

He rang the bell.

"If Lord Mountdrago comes now will you tell him that I have another appointment at six-fifteen and so I'm afraid I can't see him."

"Very good, sir."

"Has the evening paper come yet?"

"I'll go and see."

In a moment the servant brought it in. A huge headline ran across the front page: Tragic Death of Foreign Minister.

"My God!" cried Dr. Audlin.

For once he was wrenched out of his wonted calm. He was shocked, horribly shocked, and yet he was not altogether surprised. The possibility that Lord Mountdrago might commit suicide had occurred to him several times, for that it was suicide he could not doubt. The paper said that Lord Mountdrago had been waiting in a Tube station, standing on the edge of the platform, and as the train came in was seen to fall on the rail. It was supposed that he had had a sudden attack of faintness. The paper went on to say that Lord Mountdrago had been suffering for some weeks from the effects of overwork, but had felt it impossible to absent himself while the foreign situation demanded his unremitting attention. Lord Mountdrago was another victim of the strain that modern politics placed upon those who played the more important parts in it. There was a neat little piece about the talents and industry, the patriotism and vision, of the deceased statesman, followed by various surmises upon the Prime Minister's choice of his successor. Dr. Audlin read all this. He had not liked Lord Mountdrago. The chief emotion that his death caused in him was dissatisfaction with himself because he had been able to do nothing for him.

Perhaps he had done wrong in not getting into touch with Lord Mountdrago's doctor. He was discouraged, as always when failure frustrated his conscientious efforts, and repulsion seized him for the theory and practice of this empiric doctrine by which he earned his living. He was dealing with dark and mysterious forces that it was perhaps beyond the powers of the human mind to understand. He was like a man blindfold trying to feel his way to he knew not whither. Listlessly he turned the pages of the paper. Suddenly he gave a great start, and an exclamation once more was forced from his lips. His eyes had fallen on a small paragraph near the bottom of a column. Sudden Death of an M.P., he read. Mr. Owen Griffiths, member for so-and-so, had been taken ill in Fleet Street that afternoon and when he was brought to Charing Cross Hospital life was found to be extinct. It was supposed that death was due to natural causes, but an inquest would be held. Dr. Audlin could hardly believe his eyes. Was it possible that the night before Lord Mountdrago had at last in his dream found himself possessed of the weapon, knife or gun, that he had wanted, and had killed his tormentor, and had that ghostly murder, in the same way as the blow with the bottle had given him a racking headache on the following day, taken effect a certain number of hours later on the waking man? Or was it, more mysterious and more frightful, that when Lord Mountdrago sought relief in death, the enemy he had so cruelly wronged, unappeased, escaping from his own mortality, had pursued him to some other sphere there to torment him still? It was strange. The sensible thing was to look upon it merely as an odd coincidence. Dr. Audlin rang the bell.

"Tell Mrs. Milton that I'm sorry I can't see her this evening. I'm not well."

It was true; he shivered as though of an ague. With some kind of spiritual sense he seemed to envisage a bleak, a horrible void. The dark night of the soul engulfed him, and he felt a strange, primeval terror of he knew not what.

Sanatorium

FOR the first six weeks that Ashenden was at the sanatorium he stayed in bed. He saw nobody but the doctor who visited him morning and evening, the nurses who looked after him and the maid who brought him his meals. He had contracted tuberculosis of the lungs and since at the time there were reasons that made it difficult for him to go to Switzerland the specialist he saw in London had sent him up to a sanatorium in the north of Scotland. At last the day came that he had been patiently looking forward to when the doctor told him he could get up; and in the afternoon his nurse, having helped him to dress, took him down to the verandah, placed cushions behind him, wrapped him up in rugs and left him to enjoy the sun that was streaming down from a cloudless sky. It was mid-winter. The sanatorium stood on the top of a hill and from it you had a spacious view of the snow-clad country. There were people lying all along the verandah in deck-chairs, some chatting with their neighbours and some reading. Every now and then one would have a fit of coughing and you noticed that at the end of it he looked anxiously at his handkerchief. Before the nurse left Ashenden she turned with a kind of professional briskness to the man who was lying in the next chair.

"I want to introduce Mr. Ashenden to you," she said. And then to Ashenden: "This is Mr. McLeod. He and Mr. Campbell have been here longer than anyone else."

On the other side of Ashenden was lying a pretty girl, with red hair and bright blue eyes; she had on no make-up, but her lips were very red and the colour on her cheeks was high. It emphasised the astonishing whiteness of her skin. It was lovely even when you realised that its delicate texture was due to illness. She wore a fur coat and was wrapped up in rugs, so that you could see nothing of her body, but her face was extremely thin, so thin that it made her nose, which wasn't really large, look a trifle prominent. She gave Ashenden a friendly look, but did not speak, and Ashenden, feeling rather shy among all those strange people, waited to be spoken to.

"First time they've let you get up, is it?" said McLeod.

"Yes."

"Where's your room?"

Ashenden told him.

"Small. I know every room in the place. I've been here for seventeen years. I've got the best room here and so I damned well ought to have. Campbell's been trying to get me out of it, he wants it himself, but I'm not going to budge; I've got a right to it, I came here six months before he did."

McLeod, lying there, gave you the impression that he was immensely tall; his skin was stretched tight over his bones, his cheeks and temples hollow, so that you could see the formation of his skull under it; and in that emaciated face, with its great bony nose, the eyes were preternaturally large.

"Seventeen years is a long time," said Ashenden, because he could think of nothing else to say.

"Time passes very quickly. I like it here. At first, after a year or two, I went away in the summer, but I don't any more. It's my home now. I've got a brother and two sisters; but they're married and now they've got families; they don't want me. When you've been here a few years and you go back to ordinary life, you feel a bit out of it, you know. Your pals have gone their own ways and you've got nothing in common with them any more. It all seems an awful rush. Much ado about nothing, that's what it is. It's noisy and stuffy. No, one's better off here. I shan't stir again till they carry me out feet first in my coffin."

The specialist had told Ashenden that if he took care of himself for a reasonable time he would get well, and he looked at McLeod with curiosity.

"What do you do with yourself all day long?" he asked.

"Do? Having T.B. is a whole time job, my boy. There's my temperature to take and then I weigh myself. I don't hurry over my dressing. I have breakfast, I read the papers and go for a walk. Then I have my rest. I lunch and play bridge. I have another rest and then I dine. I play a bit more bridge and I go to bed. They've got quite a decent library here, we get all the new books, but I don't really have much time for reading. I talk to people. You meet all sorts here, you know. They come and they go. Sometimes they go because they think they're cured, but a lot of them come back, and sometimes they go because they die. I've seen a lot of people out and before I go I expect to see a lot more."

The girl sitting on Ashenden's other side suddenly spoke.

"I should tell you that few persons can get a heartier laugh out of a hearse than Mr. McLeod," she said.

McLeod chuckled.

"I don't know about that, but it wouldn't be human nature if I didn't say to myself: Well, I'm just as glad it's him and not me they're taking for a ride."

It occurred to him that Ashenden didn't know the pretty girl, so he introduced him.

"By the way, I don't think you've met Mr. Ashenden—Miss Bishop. She's English, but not a bad girl."

"How long have you been here?" asked Ashenden.

"Only two years. This is my last winter. Dr. Lennox says I shall be all right in a few months and there's no reason why I shouldn't go home."

"Silly, I call it," said McLeod. "Stay where you're well off, that's what I say."

At that moment a man, leaning on a stick, came walking slowly along the verandah.

"Oh, look, there's Major Templeton," said Miss Bishop, a smile lighting up her blue eyes; and then, as he came up: "I'm glad to see you up again."

"Oh, it was nothing. Only a bit of a cold. I'm quite all right now."

The words were hardly out of his mouth when he began to cough. He leaned heavily on his stick. But when the attack was over he smiled gaily.

"Can't get rid of this damned cough," he said. "Smoking too much. Dr. Lennox says I ought to give it up, but it's no good— I can't."

He was a tall fellow, good-looking in a slightly theatrical way, with a dusky, sallow face, fine very dark eyes and a neat black moustache. He was wearing a fur coat with an Astrakhan collar. His appearance was smart and perhaps a trifle showy. Miss Bishop made Ashenden known to him. Major Templeton said a few civil words in an easy, cordial way, and then asked the girl to go for a stroll with him; he had been ordered to walk to a certain place in the wood behind the sanatorium and back again. McLeod watched them as they sauntered off.

"I wonder if there's anything between those two," he said. "They do say Templeton was a devil with the girls before he got ill."

"He doesn't look up to much in that line just now," said Ashenden.

"You never can tell. I've seen a lot of rum things here in my day. I could tell you no end of stories if I wanted to."

"You evidently do, so why don't you?"

McLeod grinned.

"Well, I'll tell you one. Three or four years ago there was a woman here who was pretty hot stuff. Her husband used to come and see her every other week-end, he was crazy about her, used to fly up from London; but Dr. Lennox was pretty sure she was carrying on with somebody here, but he couldn't find out who. So one night when we'd all gone to bed he had a thin coat of paint put down just outside her room and next day he had everyone's slippers examined. Neat, wasn't it? The fellow whose slippers had paint on them got the push. Dr. Lennox has to be particular, you know. He doesn't want the place to get a bad name."

"How long has Templeton been here?"

"Three or four months. He's been in bed most of the time. He's for it all right. Ivy Bishop'll be a damned fool if she gets stuck on him. She's got a good chance of getting well. I've seen so many of them, you know, I can tell. When I look at a fellow I make up my mind at once whether he'll get well or whether he won't, and if he won't I can make a pretty shrewd guess how long he'll last. I'm very seldom mistaken. I give Templeton about two years myself."

McLeod gave Ashenden a speculative look and Ashenden, knowing what he was thinking, though he tried to be amused, could not help feeling somewhat concerned. There was a twinkle in McLeod's eyes. He plainly knew what was passing through Ashenden's mind.

"You'll get all right. I wouldn't have mentioned if if I hadn't been pretty sure of that. I don't want Dr. Lennox to hoof me out for putting the fear of God into his bloody patients."

Then Ashenden's nurse came to take him back to bed. Even though he had only sat out for an hour, he was tired, and was glad to find himself once more between the sheets. Dr. Lennox came in to see him in the course of the evening. He looked at his temperature chart.

"That's not so bad," he said.

Dr. Lennox was small, brisk and genial. He was a good enough doctor, an excellent business man, and an enthusiastic fisherman. When the fishing season began he was inclined to leave the care of his patients to his assistants; the patients grumbled a little, but were glad enough to eat the young salmon he brought back to vary their meals. He was fond of talking, and now, standing at the end of Ashenden's bed, he asked him, in his broad Scots, whether he had got into conversation with any of the patients that afternoon. Ashenden told him the nurse had introduced him to McLeod. Dr. Lennox laughed.

"The oldest living inhabitant. He knows more about the sanatorium and its inmates than I do. How he gets his information I haven't an idea, but there's not a thing about the private lives of anyone under this roof that he doesn't know. There's not an old maid in the place with a keener nose for a bit of scandal. Did he tell you about Campbell?"

"He mentioned him."

"He hates Campbell, and Campbell hates him. Funny, when you come to think of it, those two men, they've been here for seventeen years and they've got about one sound lung between them. They loathe the sight of one another. I've had to refuse to listen to the complaints about one another that they come to me with. Campbell's room is just below McLeod's and Campbell plays the fiddle. It drives McLeod wild. He says he's been listening to the same tunes for fifteen years, but Campbell says McLeod doesn't know one tune from another. McLeod wants me to stop Campbell playing, but I can't do that, he's got a perfect right to play so long as he doesn't play in the silence hours. I've offered to change McLeod's room, but he won't do that. He says Campbell only plays to drive him out of the room because it's the best in the house, and he's damned if he's going to have it. It's queer, isn't it, that two middle-aged men should think it worth while to make life hell for one another. Neither can leave the other alone. They have their meals at the same table, they play bridge together; and not a day passes without a row. Sometimes I've threatened to turn them both out if they don't behave like sensible fellows. That keeps them quiet for a bit. They don't want to go. They've been here so long, they've got no one any more who gives a damn for them, and they can't cope with the world outside. Campbell went away for a couple of months' holiday some years ago. He came back after a week; he said he couldn't stand the racket, and the sight of so many people in the streets scared him."

It was a strange world into which Ashenden found himself thrown when, his health gradually improving, he was able to mix with his fellow patients. One morning Dr. Lennox told him he could thenceforward lunch in the dining-room. This was a large, low room, with great window space; the windows were always wide open and on fine days the sun streamed in. There seemed to be a great many people and it took him some time to sort them out. They were of all kinds, young, middle-aged and old. There were some, like McLeod and Campbell, who had been at the sanatorium for years and expected to die there. Others had only been there for a few months. There was one middle-aged spinster called Miss Atkin who had been coming every winter for a long time and in the summer went to stay with friends and relations. She had nothing much the matter with her any more, and might just as well have stayed away altogether, but she liked the life. Her long residence had given her a sort of position, she was honorary librarian and hand in glove with the matron. She was always ready to gossip with you, but you were soon warned that everything you said was passed on. It was useful to Dr. Lennox to know that his patients were getting on well together and were happy, that they did nothing imprudent and followed his instructions. Little escaped Miss Atkin's sharp eyes, and from her it went to the matron and so to Dr. Lennox. Because she had been coming for so many years, she sat at the same table as McLeod and Campbell, together with an old general who had been put there on account of his rank. The table was in no way different from any other, and it was not more advantageously placed, but because the oldest residents sat there it was looked upon as the most desirable place to sit, and several elderly women were bitterly resentful because Miss Atkin, who went away for four or five months every summer, should be given a place there while they who spent the whole year in the sanatorium sat at other tables. There was an old Indian Civilian who had been at the sanatorium longer than anyone but McLeod and Campbell; he was a man who in his day had ruled a province, and he was waiting irascibly for either McLeod or Campbell to die so that he might take his place at the first table. Ashenden made the acquaintance of Campbell. He was a long, big-boned fellow with a bald head, so thin that you wondered how his limbs held together; and when he sat crumpled in an arm-chair he gave you the uncanny impression of a mannikin in a puppet-show. He was brusque, touchy and bad-tempered. The first thing he asked Ashenden was:

"Are you fond of music?"

"Yes."

"No one here cares a damn for it. I play the violin. But if you like it, come to my room one day and I'll play to you."

"Don't you go," said McLeod, who heard him. "It's torture."

"How can you be so rude?" cried Miss Atkin. "Mr. Campbell plays very nicely."

"There's no one in this beastly place that knows one note from another," said Campbell.

With a derisive chuckle McLeod walked off. Miss Atkin tried to smooth things down.

"You mustn't mind what McLeod said."

"Oh, I don't. I'll get back on him all right."

He played the same tune over and over again all that afternoon. McLeod banged on the floor, but Campbell went on. He sent a message by a maid to say that he had a headache and would Mr. Campbell mind not playing; Campbell replied that he had a perfect right to play and if Mr. McLeod didn't like it he could lump it. When next they met high words passed.

Ashenden was put at a table with the pretty Miss Bishop, with Templeton, and with a London man, an accountant, called Henry Chester. He was a stocky, broad-shouldered, wiry little fellow, and the last person you would ever have thought would be attacked by T.B. It had come upon him as a sudden and unexpected blow. He was a perfectly ordinary man, somewhere between thirty, and forty, married, with two children. He lived in a decent suburb. He went up to the City every morning and read the morning paper; he came down from the City every evening and read the evening paper. He had no interests except his business and his family. He liked his work; he made enough money to live in comfort, he put by a reasonable sum every year, he played golf on Saturday afternoon and on Sunday, he went every August for a three weeks' holiday to the same place on the east coast; his children would grow up and marry, then he would turn his business over to his son and retire with his wife to a little house in the country where he could potter about till death claimed him at a ripe old age. He asked nothing more from life than that, and it was a life that thousands upon thousands of his fellow-men lived with satisfaction. He was the average citizen. Then this thing happened. He had caught cold playing golf, it had gone to his chest, and he had had a cough that he couldn't shake off. He had always been strong and healthy, and had no opinion of doctors; but at last at his wife's persuasion he had consented to see one. It was a shock to him, a fearful shock, to learn that there was tubercle in both his lungs and that his only chance of life was to go immediately to a sanatorium. The specialist he saw then told him that he might be able to go back to work in a couple of years, but two years had passed and Dr. Lennox advised him not to think of it for at least a year more. He showed him the bacilli in his sputum, and in an X-ray photograph the actively-diseased patches in his lungs. He lost heart. It seemed to him a cruel and unjust trick that fate had played upon him. He could have understood it if he had led a wild life, if he had drunk too much, played around with women or kept late hours. He would have deserved it then. But he had done none of these things. It was monstrously unfair. Having no resources in himself, no interest in books, he had nothing to do but think of his health. It became an obsession. He watched his symptoms anxiously. They had to deprive him of a thermometer because he took his temperature a dozen times a day. He got it into his head that the doctors were taking his case too indifferently, and in order to force their attention used every method he could devise to make the thermometer register a temperature that would alarm; and when his tricks were foiled he grew sulky and querulous. But he was by nature a jovial, friendly creature, and when he forgot himself he talked and laughed gaily; then on a sudden he remembered that he was a sick man and you would see in his eyes the fear of death.

At the end of every month his wife came up to spend a day or two in a lodging-house near-by. Dr. Lennox did not much like the visits that relatives paid the patients, it excited and unsettled them. It was moving to see the eagerness with which Henry Chester looked forward to his wife's arrival; but it was strange to notice that once she had come he seemed less pleased than one would have expected. Mrs. Chester was a pleasant, cheerful little woman, not pretty, but neat, as commonplace as her husband, and you only had to look at her to know that she was a good wife and mother, a careful housekeeper, a nice, quiet body who did her duty and interfered with nobody. She had been quite happy in the dull, domestic life they had led for so many years, her only dissipation a visit to the pictures, her great thrill the sales in the big London shops; and it had never occurred to her that it was monotonous. It completely satisfied her. Ashenden liked her. He listened with interest while she prattled about her children and her house in the suburbs, her neighbours and her trivial occupations. On one occasion he met her in the road. Chester for some reason connected with his treatment had stayed in and she was alone. Ashenden suggested that they should walk together. They talked for a little of indifferent things. Then she suddenly asked him how he thought her husband was.

"I think he seems to be getting on all right."

"I'm so terribly worried."

"You must remember it's a slow, long business. One has to have patience."

They walked on a little and then he saw she was crying.

"You mustn't be unhappy about him," said Ashenden gently.

"Oh, you don't know what I have to put up with when I come here. I know I ought not to speak about it, but I must. I can trust you, can't I?"

"Of course."

"I love him. I'm devoted to him. I'd do anything in the world I could for him. We've never quarrelled, we've never even differed about a single thing. He's beginning to hate me and it breaks my heart."

"Oh, I can't believe that. Why, when you're not here he talks of you all the time. He couldn't talk more nicely. He's devoted to you."

"Yes, that's when I'm not here. It's when I'm here, when he sees me well and strong, that it comes over him. You see, he resents it so terribly that he's ill and I'm well. He's afraid he's going to die and he hates me because I'm going to live. I have to be on my guard all the time; almost everything I say, if I speak of the children, if I speak of the future, exasperates him, and he says bitter, wounding things. When I speak of something I've had to do to the house or a servant I've had to change it irritates him beyond endurance. He complains that I treat him as if he didn't count any more. We used to be so united, and now I feel there's a great wall of antagonism between us. I know I shouldn't blame him, I know it's only his illness, he's a dear good man really, and kindness itself, normally he's the easiest man in the world to get on with; and now I simply dread coming here and I go with relief. He'd be terribly sorry if I had T.B. but I know that in his heart of hearts it would be a relief. He could forgive me, he could forgive fate, if he thought I was going to die too. Sometimes he tortures me by talking about what I shall do when he's dead, and when I get hysterical and cry out to him to stop, he says I needn't grudge him a little pleasure when he'll be dead so soon and I can go on living for years and years and have a good time. Oh, it's so frightful to think that this love we've had for one another all these years should die in this sordid, miserable way."

Mrs. Chester sat down on a stone by the roadside and gave way to passionate weeping. Ashenden looked at her with pity, but could find nothing to say that might comfort her. What she had told him did not come quite as a surprise.

"Give me a cigarette," she said at last. "I mustn't let my eyes get all red and swollen, or Henry'll know I've been crying and he'll think I've had bad news about him. Is death so horrible? Do we all fear death like that?"

"I don't know," said Ashenden.

"When my mother was dying she didn't seem to mind a bit. She knew it was coming and she even made little jokes about it. But she was an old woman."

Mrs. Chester pulled herself together and they set off again. They walked for a while in silence.

"You won't think any the worse of Henry for what I've told you?" she said at last.

"Of course not."

"He's been a good husband and a good father. I've never known a better man in my life. Until this illness I don't think an unkind or ungenerous thought ever passed through his head."

The conversation left Ashenden pensive. People often said he had a low opinion of human nature. It was because he did not always judge his fellows by the usual standards. He accepted, with a smile, a tear or a shrug of the shoulders, much that filled others with dismay. It was true that you would never have expected that good-natured, commonplace little chap to harbour such bitter and unworthy thoughts; but who has ever been able to tell to what depths man may fall or to what heights rise? The fault lay in the poverty of his ideals. Henry Chester was born and bred to lead an average life, exposed to the normal vicissitudes of existence, and when an unforeseeable accident befell him he had no means of coping with it. He was like a brick made to take its place with a million others in a huge factory, but by chance with a flaw in it so that it is inadequate to its purpose. And the brick too, if it had a mind, might cry: What have I done that I cannot fulfil my modest end, but must be taken away from all these other bricks that support me and thrown on the dust-heap? It was no fault of Henry Chester's that he was incapable of the conceptions that might have enabled him to bear his calamity with resignation. It is not everyone who can find solace in art or thought. It is the tragedy of our day that these humble souls have lost their faith in God, in whom lay hope, and their belief in a resurrection that might bring them the happiness that has been denied them on earth; and have found nothing to put in their place.

There are people who say that suffering ennobles. It is not true. As a general rule it makes man petty, querulous and selfish; but here in this sanatorium there was not much suffering. In certain stages of tuberculosis the slight fever that accompanies it excites rather than depresses, so that the patient feels alert and, upborne by hope, faces the future blithely; but for all that the idea of death haunts the subconscious. It is a sardonic theme song that runs through a sprightly operetta. Now and again the gay, melodious arias, the dance measures, deviate strangely into tragic strains that throb menacingly down the nerves; the petty interests of every day, the small jealousies and trivial concerns are as nothing; pity and terror make the heart on a sudden stand still and the awfulness of death broods as the silence that precedes a tropical storm broods over the tropical jungle. After Ashenden had been for some time at the sanatorium there came a boy of twenty. He was in the navy, a sub-lieutenant in a submarine, and he had what they used to call in novels galloping consumption. He was a tall, good-looking youth, with curly brown hair, blue eyes and a very sweet smile. Ashenden saw him two or three times lying on the terrace in the sun and passed the time of day with him. He was a cheerful lad. He talked of musical shows and film stars; and he read the paper for the football results and the boxing news. Then he was put to bed and Ashenden saw him no more. His relations were sent for and in two months he was dead. He died uncomplaining. He understood what was happening to him as little as an animal. For a day or two there was the same malaise in the sanatorium as there is in a prison when a man has been hanged; and then, as though by universal consent, in obedience to an instinct of self-preservation, the boy was put out of mind: life, with its three meals a day, its golf on the miniature course, its regulated exercise, its prescribed rests, its quarrels and jealousies, its scandal-mongering and petty vexations, went on as before. Campbell, to the exasperation of McLeod, continued to play the prize-song and "Annie Laurie" on his fiddle. McLeod continued to boast of his bridge and gossip about other people's health and morals. Miss Atkin continued to backbite. Henry Chester continued to complain that the doctors gave him insufficient attention and railed against fate because, after the model life he had led, it had played him such a dirty trick. Ashenden continued to read, and with amused tolerance to watch the vagaries of his fellow-creatures.

He became intimate with Major Templeton. Templeton was perhaps a little more than forty years of age. He had been in the Grenadier Guards, but had resigned his commission after the war. A man of ample means, he had since then devoted himself entirely to pleasure. He raced in the racing season, shot in the shooting season and hunted in the hunting season. When this was over he went to Monte Carlo. He told Ashenden of the large sums he had made and lost at baccarat. He was very fond of women and if his stories could be believed they were very fond of him. He loved good food and good drink. He knew by their first names the head waiters of every restaurant in London where you ate well. He belonged to half a dozen clubs. He had led for years a useless, selfish, worthless life, the sort of life which maybe it will be impossible for anyone to live in the future, but he had lived it without misgiving and had enjoyed it. Ashenden asked him once what he would do if he had his time over again and he answered that he would do exactly what he had done. He was an amusing talker, gay and pleasantly ironic, and he dealt with the surface of things, which was all he knew, with a light, easy and assured touch. He always had a pleasant word for the dowdy spinsters in the sanatorium and a joking one for the peppery old gentlemen, for he combined good manners with a natural kindliness. He knew his way about the superficial world of the people who have more money than they know what to do with as well as he knew his way about Mayfair. He was the kind of man who would always have been willing to take a bet, to help a friend and to give a tenner to a rogue. If he had never done much good in the world he had never done much harm. He amounted to nothing. But he was a more agreeable companion than many of more sterling character and of more admirable qualities. He was very ill now. He was dying and he knew it. He took it with the same easy, laughing nonchalance as he had taken all the rest. He'd had a thundering good time, he regretted nothing, it was rotten tough luck getting T.B. but to hell with it, no one can live for ever, and when you came to think of it, he might have been killed in the war or broken his bloody neck in a point-to-point. His principle all through life had been, when you've made a bad bet, pay up and forget about it. He'd had a good run for his money and he was ready to call it a day. It had been a damned good party while it lasted, but every party's got to come to an end, and next day it doesn't matter much if you went home with the milk or if you left while the fun was in full swing.

Of all those people in the sanatorium he was probably from the moral standpoint the least worthy, but he was the only one who genuinely accepted the inevitable with unconcern. He snapped his fingers in the face of death, and you could choose whether to call his levity unbecoming or his insouciance gallant.

The last thing that ever occurred to him when he came to the sanatorium was that he might fall more deeply in love there than he had ever done before. His amours had been numerous, but they had been light; he had been content with the politely mercenary love of chorus girls and with ephemeral unions with women of easy virtue whom he met at house parties. He had always taken care to avoid any attachment that might endanger his freedom. His only aim in life had been to get as much fun out of it as possible, and where sex was concerned he found every advantage and no inconvenience in ceaseless variety. But he liked women. Even when they were quite old he could not talk to them without a caress in his eyes and a tenderness in his voice. He was prepared to do anything to please them. They were conscious of his interest in them and were agreeably flattered, and they felt, quite mistakenly, that they could trust him never to let them down. He once said a thing that Ashenden thought showed insight:

"You know, any man can get any woman he wants if he tries hard enough, there's nothing in that, but once he's got her, only a man who thinks the world of women can get rid of her without humiliating her."

It was simply from habit that he began to make love to Ivy Bishop. She was the prettiest and the youngest girl in the sanatorium. She was in point of fact not so young as Ashenden had first thought her, she was twenty-nine, but for the last eight years she had been wandering from one sanatorium to another, in Switzerland, England and Scotland, and the sheltered invalid life had preserved her youthful appearance so that you might easily have taken her for twenty. All she knew of the world she had learnt in these establishments, so that she combined rather curiously extreme innocence with extreme sophistication. She had seen a number of love affairs run their course. A good many men, of various nationalities, had made love to her; she accepted their attentions with self-possession and humour, but she had at her disposal plenty of firmness when they showed an inclination to go too far. She had a force of character unexpected in anyone who looked so flower-like and when it came to a show-down knew how to express her meaning in plain, cool and decisive words. She was quite ready to have a flirtation with George Templeton. It was a game she understood, and though always charming to him, it was with a bantering lightness that showed quite clearly that she had summed him up and had no mind to take the affair more seriously than he did. Like Ashenden, Templeton went to bed every evening at six and dined in his room, so that he saw Ivy only by day. They went for little walks together, but otherwise were seldom alone. At lunch the conversation between the four of them, Ivy, Templeton, Henry Chester and Ashenden, was general, but it was obvious that it was for neither of the two men that Templeton took so much trouble to be entertaining. It seemed to Ashenden that he was ceasing to flirt with Ivy to pass the time, and that his feeling for her was growing deeper and more sincere; but he could not tell whether she was conscious of it nor whether it meant anything to her. Whenever Templeton hazarded a remark that was more intimate than the occasion warranted she countered it with an ironic one that made them all laugh. But Templeton's laugh was rueful. He was no longer content to have her take him as a play-boy. The more Ashenden knew Ivy Bishop the more he liked her. There was something pathetic in her sick beauty, with that lovely transparent skin, the thin face in which the eyes were so large and so wonderfully blue; and there was something pathetic in her plight, for like so many others in the sanatorium she seemed to be alone in the world. Her mother led a busy social life, her sisters were married; they took but a perfunctory interest in the young woman from whom they had been separated now for eight years. They corresponded, they came to see her occasionally, but there was no longer very much between them. She accepted the situation without bitterness. She was friendly with everyone and prepared always to listen with sympathy to the complaints and the distress of all and sundry. She went out of her way to be nice to Henry Chester and did what she could to cheer him.

"Well, Mr. Chester," she said to him one day at lunch, "it's the end of the month, your wife will be coming to-morrow. That's something to look forward to."

"No, she's not coming this month," he said quietly, looking down at his plate.

"Oh, I am sorry. Why not? The children are all right, aren't they?"

"Dr. Lennox thinks it's better for me that she shouldn't come." There was a silence. Ivy looked at him with troubled eyes.

"That's tough luck, old man," said Templeton in his hearty way. "Why didn't you tell Lennox to go to hell?"

"He must know best," said Chester.

Ivy gave him another look and began to talk of something else. Looking back, Ashenden realised that she had at once suspected the truth. For next day he happened to walk with Chester.

"I'm awfully sorry your wife isn't coming," he said. "You'll miss her visit dreadfully."

"Dreadfully."

He gave Ashenden a sidelong glance. Ashenden felt that he had something he wanted to say, but could not bring himself to say it. He gave his shoulders an angry shrug.

"It's my fault if she's not coming. I asked Lennox to write and tell her not to. I couldn't stick it any more. I spend the whole month looking forward to her coming and then when she's here I hate her. You see, I resent so awfully having this filthy disease. She's strong and well and full of beans. It maddens me when I see the pain in her eyes. What does it matter to her really? Who cares if you're ill? They pretend to care, but they're jolly glad it's you and not them. I'm a swine, aren't I?"

Ashenden remembered how Mrs. Chester had sat on a stone by the side of the road and wept.

"Aren't you afraid you'll make her very unhappy, not letting her come?"

"She must put up with that. I've got enough with my own unhappiness without bothering with hers."

Ashenden did not know what to say and they walked on in silence. Suddenly Chester broke out irritably.

"It's all very well for you to be disinterested and unselfish, you're going to live. I'm going to die, and God damn it, I don't want to die. Why should I? It's not fair."

Time passed. In a place like the sanatorium where there was little to occupy the mind it was inevitable that soon everyone should know that George Templeton was in love with Ivy Bishop. But it was not so easy to tell what her feelings were. It was plain that she liked his company, but she did not seek it, and indeed it looked as though she took pains not to be alone with him. One or two of the middle-aged ladies tried to trap her into some compromising admission, but ingenuous as she was, she was easily a match for them. She ignored their hints and met their straight questions with incredulous laughter. She succeeded in exasperating them.

"She can't be so stupid as not to see that he's mad about her."

"She has no right to play with him like that."

"I believe she's just as much in love with him as he is with her."

"Dr. Lennox ought to tell her mother."

No one was more incensed than McLeod.

"Too ridiculous. After all, nothing can come of it. He's riddled with T.B. and she's not much better."

Campbell on the other hand was sardonic and gross.

"I'm all for their having a good time while they can. I bet there's a bit of hanky-panky going on if one only knew, and I don't blame 'em."

"You cad," said McLeod.

"Oh, come off it. Templeton isn't the sort of chap to play bumble-puppy bridge with a girl like that unless he's getting something out of it, and she knows a thing or two, I bet."

Ashenden, who saw most of them, knew them better than any of the others. Templeton at last had taken him into his confidence. He was rather amused at himself.

"Rum thing at my time of life, falling in love with a decent girl. Last thing I'd ever expected of myself. And it's no good denying it, I'm in it up to the neck; if I were a well man I'd ask her to marry me to-morrow. I never knew a girl could be as nice as that. I've always thought girls, decent girls, I mean, damned bores. But she isn't a bore, she's as clever as she can stick. And pretty too. My God, what a skin! And that hair: but it isn't any of that that's bowled me over like a row of ninepins. D'you know what's got me? Damned ridiculous when you come to think of it. An old rip like me. Virtue. Makes me laugh like a hyena. Last thing

I've ever wanted in a woman, but there it is, no getting away from it, she's good, and it makes me feel like a worm. Surprises you, I suppose?"

"Not a bit," said Ashenden. "You're not the first rake who's fallen to innocence. It's merely the sentimentality of middle age."

"Dirty dog," laughed Templeton.

"What does she say to it?"

"Good God, you don't supoose I've told her. I've never said a word to her that I wouldn't have said before anyone else. I may be dead in six months, and besides, what have I got to offer a girl like that?"

Ashenden by now was pretty sure that she was just as much in love with Templeton as he was with her. He had seen the flush that coloured her cheeks when Templeton came into the dining-room and he had noticed the soft glance she gave him now and then when he was not looking at her. There was a peculiar sweetness in her smile when she listened to him telling some of his old experiences. Ashenden had the impression that she basked comfortably in his love as the patients on the terrace, facing the snow, basked in the hot sunshine; but it might very well be that she was content to leave it at that, and it was certainly no business of his to tell Templeton what perhaps she had no wish that he should know.

Then an incident occurred to disturb the monotony of life. Though McLeod and Campbell were always at odds they played bridge together because, till Templeton came, they were the best players in the sanatorium. They bickered incessantly, their post-mortems were endless, but after so many years each knew the other's game perfectly and they took a keen delight in scoring off one another. As a rule Templeton refused to play with them; though a fine player he preferred to play with Ivy Bishop, and McLeod and Campbell were agreed on this, that she ruined the game. She was the kind of player who, having made a mistake that lost the rubber, would laugh and say: Well, it only made the difference of a trick. But one afternoon, since Ivy was staying in her room with a headache, Templeton consented to play with Campbell and McLeod. Ashenden was the fourth. Though it was the end of March there had been heavy snow for several days, and they played, in a verandah open on three sides to the wintry air, in fur coats and caps, with mittens on their hands. The stakes were too small for a gambler like Templeton to take the game seriously and his bidding was overbold, but he played so much better than the other three that he generally managed to make his contract or at least to come near it. But there was much doubling and redoubling. The cards ran high, so that an inordinate number of small slams were bid; it was a tempestuous game, and McLeod and Campbell lashed one another with their tongues. Half-past five arrived and the last rubber was started, for at six the bell rang to send everyone to rest. It was a hard-fought rubber, with sets on both sides, for McLeod and Campbell were opponents and each was determined that the other should not win. At ten minutes to six it was game all and the last hand was dealt. Templeton was McLeod's partner and Ashenden Campbell's. The bidding started with two clubs from McLeod; Ashenden said nothing; Templeton showed that he had substantial help, and finally McLeod called a grand slam. Campbell doubled and McLeod redoubled. Hearing this, the players at other tables who had broken off gathered round and the hands were played in deadly silence to a little crowd of onlookers. McLeod's face was white with excitement and there were beads of sweat on his brow. His hands trembled. Campbell was very grim. McLeod had to take two finesses and they both came off. He finished with a squeeze and got the last of the thirteen tricks. There was a burst of applause from the onlookers. McLeod, arrogant in victory, sprang to his feet. He shook his clenched fist at Campbell.

"Play that off on your blasted fiddle," he shouted. "Grand slam doubled and redoubled. I've wanted to get it all my life and now I've got it. By God. By God."

He gasped. He staggered forward and fell across the table. A stream of blood poured from his mouth. The doctor was sent for. Attendants came. He was dead.

He was buried two days later, early in the morning so that the patients should not be disturbed by the sight of a funeral. A relation in black came from Glasgow to attend it. No one had liked him. No one regretted him. At the end of a week so far as one could tell, he was forgotten. The Indian Civilian took his place at the principal table and Campbell moved into the room he had so long wanted.

"Now we shall have peace," said Dr. Lennox to Ashenden. "When you think that I've had to put up with the quarrels and complaints of those two men for years and years . . . Believe me, one has to have patience to run a sanatorium. And to think that after all the trouble he's given me he had to end up like that and scare all those people out of their wits."

"It was a bit of a shock, you know," said Ashenden.

"He was a worthless fellow and yet some of the women have been quite upset about it. Poor little Miss Bishop cried her eyes out."

"I suspect that she was the only one who cried for him and not for herself."

But presently it appeared that there was one person who had not forgotten him. Campbell went about like a lost dog. He wouldn't play bridge. He wouldn't talk. There was no doubt about it, he was moping for McLeod. For several days he remained in his room, having his meals brought to him, and then went to Dr. Lennox and said he didn't like it as well as his old one and wanted to be moved back. Dr. Lennox lost his temper, which he rarely did, and told him he had been pestering him to give him that room for years and now he could stay there or get out of the sanatorium. He returned to it and sat gloomily brooding.

"Why don't you play your violin?" the matron asked him at length. "I haven't heard you play for a fortnight."

"I haven't."

"Why not?"

"It's no fun any more. I used to get a kick out of playing because I knew it maddened McLeod. But now nobody cares if I play or not. I shall never play again."

Nor did he for all the rest of the time that Ashenden was at the sanatorium. It was strange, now that McLeod was dead life had lost its savour for him. With no one to quarrel with, no one to infuriate, he had lost his incentive and it was plain that it would not be long before he followed his enemy to the grave.

But on Templeton McLeod's death had another effect, and one which was soon to have unexpected consequences. He talked to Ashenden about it in his cool, detached way.

"Grand, passing out like that in his moment of triumph. I can't make out why everyone got in such a state about it. He'd been here for years, hadn't he?"

"Eighteen, I believe."

"I wonder if it's worth it. I wonder if it's not better to have one's fling and take the consequences."

"I suppose it depends on how much you value life."

"But is this life?"

Ashenden had no answer. In a few months he could count on being well, but you only had to look at Templeton to know that he was not going to recover. The death-look was on his face.

"D'you know what I've done?" asked Templeton. "I've asked Ivy to marry me."

Ashenden was startled.

"What did she say?"

"Bless her little heart, she said it was the most ridiculous idea she'd ever heard in her life and I was crazy to think of such a thing."

"You must admit she was right."

"Quite. But she's going to marry me."

"It's madness."

"I dare say it is; but anyhow, we're going to see Lennox and ask him what he thinks about it."

The winter had broken at last; there was still snow on the hills, but in the valleys it was melted and on the lower slopes the birch-trees were in bud all ready to burst into delicate leaf. The enchant-ment of spring was in the air. The sun was hot. Everyone felt alert and some felt happy. The old stagers who came only for the winter were making their plans to go south. Templeton and Ivy went to see Dr. Lennox together. They told him what they had in mind. He examined them; they were X-rayed and various tests were taken. Dr. Lennox fixed a day when he would tell them the results and in the light of this discuss their proposal. Ashenden saw them just before they went to keep the appointment. They were anxious, but did their best to make a joke of it. Dr. Lennox showed them the results of his examinations and explained to them in plain language what their condition was.

"All that's very fine and large," said Templeton then, "but what we want to know is whether we can get married."

"It would be highly imprudent."

"We know that, but does it matter?"

"And criminal if you had a child."

"We weren't thinking of having one," said Ivy.

"Well, then I'll tell you in very few words how the matter stands. Then you must decide for yourselves."

Templeton gave Ivy a little smile and took her hand. The doctor went on.

"I don't think Miss Bishop will ever be strong enough to lead a normal life, but if she continues to live as she has been doing for the last eight years . . ."

"In sanatoriums?"

"Yes. There's no reason why she shouldn't live very comfortably, if not to a ripe old age, as long as any sensible person wants to live. The disease is quiescent. If she marries, if she attempts to live an ordinary life, the foci of infection may very well light up again, and what the results of that may be no one can foretell. So far as you are concerned, Templeton, I can put it even more shortly. You've seen the X-ray photos yourself. Your lungs are riddled with tubercle. If you marry you'll be dead in six months."

"And if I don't how long can I live?"

The doctor hesitated.

"Don't be afraid. You can tell me the truth."

"Two or three years."

"Thank you, that's all we wanted to know."

They went as they had come, hand in hand; Ivy was crying softly. No one knew what they said to one another; but when they came into luncheon they were radiant. They told Ashenden and Chester that they were going to be married as soon as they could get a licence. Then Ivy turned to Chester.

"I should so much like your wife to come up for my wedding. D'you think she would?"

"You're not going to be married here?"

"Yes. Our respective relations will only disapprove, so we're not going to tell them until it's all over. We shall ask Dr. Lennox to give me away."

She looked mildly at Chester, waiting for him to speak, for he had not answered her. The other two men watched him. His voice shook a little when he spoke.

"It's very kind of you to want her. I'll write and ask her."

When the news spread among the patients, though everyone congratulated them, most of them privately told one another that it was very injudicious; but when they learnt, as sooner or later everything that happened in the sanatorium was learnt, that Dr. Lennox had told Templeton that if he married he would be dead in six months, they were awed to silence. Even the dullest were moved at the thought of these two persons who loved one another so much that they were prepared to sacrifice their lives. A spirit of kindliness and good will descended on the sanatorium: people who hadn't been speaking spoke to one another again; others forgot for a brief space their own anxieties. Everyone seemed to share in the happiness of the happy pair. And it was not only the spring that filled those sick hearts with new hope, the great love that had taken possession of the man and the girl seemed to spread its effulgence on all that came near them. Ivy was quietly blissful; the excitement became her and she looked younger and prettier. Templeton seemed to walk on air. He laughed and joked as if he hadn't a care in the world. You would have said that he looked forward to long years of uninterrupted felicity. But one day he confided in Ashenden.

"This isn't a bad place, you know," he said. "Ivy's promised me that when I hand in my checks she'll come back here. She knows the people and she won't be so lonely."

"Doctors are often mistaken," said Ashenden. "If you live reasonably I don't see why you shouldn't go on for a long time yet."

"I'm only asking for three months. If I can only have that it'll be worth it."

Mrs. Chester came up two days before the wedding. She had not seen her husband for several months and they were shy with one another. It was easy to guess that when they were alone they felt awkward and constrained. Yet Chester did his best to shake off the depression that was now habitual and at all events at meal-times showed himself the jolly, hearty little fellow that he must have been before he fell ill. On the eve of the wedding day they all dined together, Templeton and Ashenden both sitting up for dinner; they drank champagne and stayed up till ten joking, laughing and enjoying themselves. The wedding took place next morning in the kirk. Ashenden was best man. Everyone in the sanatorium who could stand on his feet attended it. The newly married couple were setting out by car immediately after lunch. Patients, doctors and nurses assembled to see them off. Someone had tied an old shoe on the back of the car, and as Templeton and his wife came out of the door of the sanatorium rice was flung over them. A cheer was raised as they drove away, as they drove away to love and death. The crowd separated slowly. Chester and his wife went silently side by side. After they had gone a little way he shyly took her hand. Her heart seemed to miss a beat. With a sidelong glance she saw that his eyes were wet with tears.

"Forgive me, dear," he said. "I've been very unkind to you."

"I knew you didn't mean it," she faltered.

"Yes, I did. I wanted you to suffer because I was suffering. But not any more. All this about Templeton and Ivy Bishop— I don't know how to put it, it's made me see everything differently. I don't mind dying any more. I don't think death's very important, not so important as love. And I want you to live and be happy. I don't grudge you anything any more and I don't resent anything. I'm glad now it's me that must die and not you. I wish for you everything that's good in the world. I love you."

❖

The Social Sense

I DO not like long-standing engagements. How can you tell whether on a certain day three or four weeks ahead you will wish to dine with a certain person? The chances are that in the interval something will turn up that you would much sooner do and so long a notice presages a large and formal party. But what help is there? The date has been fixed thus far away so that the guests bidden may be certainly disengaged and it needs a very adequate excuse to prevent your refusal from seeming churlish. You accept, and for a month the engagement hangs over you with gloomy menace. It interferes with your cherished plans. It disorganises your life. There is really only one way to cope with the situation and that is to put yourself off at the last moment. But it is one that I have never had the courage or the want of scruple to adopt.

It was with a faint sense of resentment then that one June evening towards half-past eight I left my lodging in Half Moon Street to walk round the corner to dine with the Macdonalds. I liked them. Many years ago I made up my mind not to eat the food of persons I disliked or despised, and though I have on this account enjoyed the hospitality of far fewer people than I otherwise should have done I still think the rule a good one. The Macdonalds were nice, but their parties were a toss-up. They suffered from the delusion that if they asked six persons to dine with them who had nothing in the world to say to one another the party would be a failure, but if they multiplied it by three and asked eighteen it must be a success. I arrived a little late, which is almost inevitable when you live so near the house you are going to that it is not worth while to take a taxi, and the room into which I was shown was filled with people. I knew few of them and my heart sank as I saw myself laboriously making conversation through a long dinner with two total strangers. It was a relief to me when I saw Thomas and Mary Warton come in and an unexpected pleasure when I found on going in to dinner that I had been placed next to Mary.

Thomas Warton was a portrait-painter who at one time had had considerable success, but he had never fulfilled the promise of his youth and had long ceased to be taken seriously by the critics. He made an adequate income, but at the Private View of the Royal Academy no one gave more than a passing glance at the dull but conscientious portraits of fox-hunting squires and prosperous merchants which with unfailing regularity he sent to the annual exhibition. One would have liked to admire his work because he was an amiable and kindly man. If you happened to be a writer he was so genuinely enthusiastic over anything you had done, so charmed with any success you might have had, that you wished your conscience would allow you to speak with decent warmth of his own productions. It was impossible and you were driven to the last refuge of the portrait painter's friend.

"It looks as if it were a marvellous likeness," you said.

Mary Warton had been in her day a well-known concert singer and she had still the remains of a lovely voice. She must in her youth have been very handsome. Now, at fifty-three, she had a haggard look. Her features were rather mannish and her skin was weather-beaten; but her short grey hair was thick and curly and her fine eyes were bright with intelligence. She dressed picturesquely rather than fashionably and she had a weakness for strings of beads and fantastic ear-rings. She had a blunt manner, a quick sense of human folly and a sharp tongue, so that many people did not like her. But no one could deny that she was clever. She was not only an accomplished musician, but she was a great reader and she was passionately interested in painting. She had a very rare feeling for art. She liked the modern, not from pose but from natural inclination, and she had bought for next to nothing the pictures of unknown painters who later became famous. You heard at her house the most recent and difficult music and no poet or novelist in Europe could offer the world something new and strange without her being ready to fight on his behalf the good fight against the philistines. You might say she was a highbrow; she was; but her taste was almost faultless, her judgment sound and her enthusiasm honest.

No one admired her more than Thomas Warton. He had fallen in love with her when she was still a singer and had pestered her to marry him. She had refused him half a dozen times and I had a notion that she had married him in the end with hesitation. She thought that he would become a great painter and when he turned out to be no more than a decent craftsman, without originality or imagination, she felt that she had been cheated. She was mortified by the contempt with which the connoisseurs regarded him. Thomas Warton loved his wife. He had the greatest respect for her judgment and would sooner have had a word of praise from her than columns of eulogy in all the papers in London. She was too honest to say what she did not think. It wounded him bitterly that she held his work in such poor esteem, and though he pretended to make a joke of it you could see that at heart he resented her outspoken comments. Sometimes his long, horse-like face grew red with the anger he tried to control and his eyes dark with hatred. It was notorious among their friends that the couple did not get on. They had the distressing habit of fripping in public. Warton never spoke to others of Mary but with admiration, but she was less discreet and her confidants knew how exasperating she found him. She admitted his goodness, his generosity, his unselfishness; she admitted them ungrudgingly; but his defects were of the sort that make a man hard to live with, for he was narrow, argumentative and conceited. He was not an artist and Mary Warton cared more for art than for anything in the world. It was a matter on which she could not compromise. It blinded her to the fact that the faults in Warton that maddened her were due in large part to his hurt feelings. She wounded him continually and he was dogmatic and intolerant in self-protection. There cannot be anything much worse than to be despised by the one person whose approval is all in all to you; and though Thomas Warton was intolerable it was impossible not to feel sorry for him. But if I have given the impression that Mary was a discontented, rather tiresome, pretentious woman I have been unjust to her. She was a loyal friend and a delightful companion. You could talk to her of any subject under the sun. Her conversation was humorous and witty. Her vitality was immense.

She was sitting now on the left hand of her host and the talk around her was general. I was occupied with my next-door neighbour, but I guessed by the laughter with which Mary's sallies were greeted that she was at her brilliant best. When she was in the vein no one could approach her.

"You're in great form to-night," I remarked, when at last she turned to me.

"Does it surprise you?"

"No, it's what I expect of you. No wonder people tumble over one another to get you to their houses. You have the inestimable gift of making a party go."

"I do my little best to earn my dinner."

"By the way, how's Manson? Someone told me the other day that he was going into a nursing-home for an operation. I hope it's nothing serious."

Mary paused for a moment before answering, but she still smiled brightly.

"Haven't you seen the paper to-night?"

"No, I've been playing golf. I only got home in time to jump into a bath and change."

"He died at two o'clock this afternoon." I was about to make an exclamation of horrified surprise, but she stopped me. "Take care. Tom is watching me like a lynx. They're all watching me. They all know I adored him, but they none of them know for certain if he was my lover, even Tom doesn't know; they want to see how I'm taking it. Try to look as if you were talking of the Russian Ballet."

At that moment someone addressed her from the other side of the table, and throwing back her head a little with a gesture that was habitual with her, a smile on her large mouth, she flung at the speaker so quick and apt an answer that everyone round her burst out laughing. The talk once more became general and I was left to my consternation.

I knew, everyone knew, that for five and twenty years there had existed between Gerrard Manson and Mary Warton a passionate attachment. It had lasted so long that even the more strait-laced of their friends, if ever they had been shocked by it, had long since learnt to accept it with tolerance. They were middle-aged people, Manson was sixty and Mary not much younger, and it was absurd that at their age they should not do what they liked. You met them sometimes sitting in a retired corner of an obscure restaurant or walking together in the Zoo and you wondered why they still took care to conceal an affair that was nobody's business but their own. But of course there was Thomas. He was insanely jealous of Mary. He made many violent scenes and indeed, at the end of one tempestuous period, not so very long ago, he forced her to promise never to see Manson again. Of course she broke the promise, and though she knew that Thomas suspected this, she took precautions to prevent him from discovering it for a fact.

It was hard on Thomas. I think he and Mary would have jogged on well enough together and she would have resigned herself to the fact that he was a second-rate painter if her intercourse with Manson had not embittered her judgment. The contrast between her husband's mediocrity and her lover's brilliance was too galling.

"With Tom I feel as if I were stifling in a closed room full of dusty knick-knacks," she told me. "With Gerrard I breathe the pure air of the mountain tops."

"Is it possible for a woman to fall in love with a man's mind?" I asked in a pure spirit of enquiry.

"What else is there in Gerrard?"

That, I admit, was a poser. For my part I thought, nothing; but the sex is extraordinary and I was quite ready to believe that Mary saw in Gerrard Manson a charm and a physical attractiveness to which most people were blind. He was a shrivelled little man, with a pale intellectual face, faded blue eyes behind his spectacles, and a high dome of shiny bald head. He had none of the appearance of a romantic lover. On the other hand he was certainly a very subtle critic and a felicitous essayist. I resented somewhat his contemptuous attitude towards English writers unless they were safely dead and buried; but this was only to his credit with the intelligentsia, who are ever ready to believe that there can be no good in what is produced in their own country, and with them his influence was great. On one occasion I told him that one had only to put a commonplace in French for him to mistake it for an epigram and he had thought well enough of the joke to use it as his own in one of his essays. He reserved such praise as he was willing to accord his contemporaries to those who wrote in a foreign tongue. The exasperating thing was that no one could deny that he was himself a brilliant writer. His style was exquisite. His knowledge was vast. He could be profound without pomposity, amusing without frivolity, and polished without affectation. His slightest article was readable. His essays were little masterpieces. For my part I did not find him a very agreeable companion. Perhaps I did not get the best out of him. Though I knew him a great many years I never heard him say an amusing thing. He was not talkative and when he made a remark it was oracular. The prospect of spending an evening alone with him would have filled me with dismay. It never ceased to puzzle me that this dull and mannered little man should be able to write with so much grace, wit and gaiety.

It puzzled me even more that a gallant and vivacious creature like Mary Warton should have cherished for him so consuming a passion. These things are inexplicable and there was evidently something in that odd, crabbed, irascible creature that appealed to women. His wife adored him. She was a fat, frowsy boring person. She had led Gerrard a dog's life, but had always refused to give him his freedom. She swore to kill herself if he left her and since she was unbalanced and hysterical he was never quite certain that she would not carry out her threat. One day, when I was having tea with Mary, I saw that she was distraught and nervous and when I asked her what was the matter she burst into tears. She had been lunching with Manson and had found him shattered after a terrific scene with his wife.

"We can't go on like this," Mary cried. "It's ruining his life. It's ruining all our lives."

"Why don't you take the plunge?"

"What do you mean?"

"You've been lovers so long, you know the best and the worst of one another by now; you're getting old and you can't count on many more years of life; it seems a pity to waste a love that has endured so long. What good are you doing to Mrs. Manson or to Tom? Are they happy because you two are making yourselves miserable?"

"No."

"Then why don't you chuck everything and just go off together and let come what may?"

Mary shook her head.

"We've talked that over endlessly. We've talked it over for a quarter of a century. It's impossible. For years Gerrard couldn't on account of his daughters. Mrs. Manson may have been a very fond mother, but she was a very bad one, and there was no one to see the girls were properly brought up but Gerrard. And now that they're married off he's set in his habits. What should we do? Go to France or Italy? I couldn't tear Gerrard away from his surroundings. He'd be wretched. He's too old to make a fresh start. And besides, though Thomas nags me and makes scenes and we frip and get on one another's nerves, he loves me. When it came to the point I simply shouldn't have the heart to leave him. He'd be lost without me."

"It's a situation without an issue. I'm dreadfully sorry for you."

On a sudden Mary's haggard, weather-beaten face was lit by a smile that broke on her large red mouth; and upon my word at that moment she was beautiful.

"You need not be. I was rather low a little while ago, but now I've had a good cry I feel better. Notwithstanding all the pain, all the unhappiness this affair has caused me, I wouldn't have missed it for all the world. For those few moments of ecstasy my love has brought me I would be willing to live all my life over again. And I think he'd tell you the same thing. Oh, it's been so infinitely worth while."

I could not help but be moved.

"There's no doubt about it," I said. "That's love all right."

"Yes, it's love, and we've just got to go through with it. There's no way out."

And now with this tragic suddenness the way out had come. I turned a little to look at Mary and she, feeling my eyes upon her, turned too. There was a smile on her lips.

"Why did you come here to-night? It must be awful for you."

She shrugged her shoulders.

"What could I do? I read the news in the evening paper while I was dressing. He'd asked me not to ring up the nursing-home on account of his wife. It's death to me. Death. I had to come. We'd been engaged for a month. What excuse could I give Tom? I'm not supposed to have seen Gerrard for two years. Do you know that for twenty years we've written to one another every day?" Her lower lip trembled a little, but she bit it and for a moment her face was twisted to a strange grimace; then with a smile she pulled herself together. "He was everything I had in the world, but I couldn't let the party down, could I? He always said I had a social sense."

"Happily we shall break up early and you can go home."

"I don't want to go home. I don't want to be alone. I daren't cry because my eyes will get red and swollen, and we've got a lot of people lunching with us to-morrow. Will you come, by the way? I want an extra man. I must be in good form; Tom expects to get a commission for a portrait out of it."

"By George, you've got courage."

"D'you think so? I'm heartbroken, you know. I suppose that's what makes it easier for me. Gerrard would have liked me to put a good face on it. He would have appreciated the irony of the situation. It's the sort of thing he always thought the French novelists described so well."

The Verger

THERE had been a christening that afternoon at St. Peter's, Neville Square, and Albert Edward Foreman still wore his verger's gown. He kept his new one, its folds as full and stiff as though it were made not of alpaca but of perennial bronze, for funerals and weddings (St. Peter's, Neville Square, was a church much favoured by the fashionable for these ceremonies) and now he wore only his second-best. He wore it with complacence, for it was the dignified symbol of his office, and without it (when he took it off to go home) he had the disconcerting sensation of being somewhat insufficiently clad. He took pains with it; he pressed it and ironed it himself. During the sixteen years he had been verger of this church he had had a succession of such gowns, but he had never been able to throw them away when they were worn out and the complete series, neatly wrapped up in brown paper, lay in the bottom drawers of the wardrobe in his bedroom.

The verger busied himself quietly, replacing the painted wooden cover on the marble font, taking away a chair that had been brought for an infirm old lady, and waited for the vicar to have finished in the vestry so that he could tidy up in there and go home. Presently he saw him walk across the chancel, genuflect in front of the high altar and come down the aisle; but he still wore his cassock.

"What's he 'anging about for?" the verger said to himself. "Don't 'e know I want my tea?"

The vicar had been but recently appointed, a red-faced energetic man in the early forties, and Albert Edward still regretted his predecessor, a clergyman of the old school who preached leisurely sermons in a silvery voice and dined out a great deal with his more aristocratic parishioners. He liked things in church to be just so, but he never fussed; he was not like this new man who wanted to have his finger in every pie. But Albert Edward was tolerant. St. Peter's was in a very good neighbourhood and the parishioners were a very nice class of people. The new vicar had come from the East End and he couldn't be expected to fall in all at once with the discreet ways of his fashionable congregation.

"All this 'ustle," said Albert Edward. "But give 'im time, he'll learn."

When the vicar had walked down the aisle so far that he could address the verger without raising his voice more than was becoming in a place of worship he stopped.

"Foreman, will you come into the vestry for a minute. I have something to say to you."

"Very good, sir."

The vicar waited for him to come up and they walked up the church together.

"A very nice christening, I thought, sir. Funny 'ow the baby stopped cryin' the moment you took him."

"I've noticed they very often do," said the vicar, with a little smile. "After all I've had a good deal of practice with them."

It was a source of subdued pride to him that he could nearly always quiet a whimpering infant by the manner in which he held it and he was not unconscious of the amused admiration with which mothers and nurses watched him settle the baby in the crook of his surpliced arm. The verger knew that it pleased him to be complimented on his talent.

The vicar preceded Albert Edward into the vestry. Albert Edward was a trifle surprised to find the two churchwardens there. He had not seen them come in. They gave him pleasant nods.

"Good-afternoon, my lord. Good-afternoon, sir," he said to one after the other.

They were elderly men, both of them, and they had been church-wardens almost as long as Albert Edward had been verger. They were sitting now at a handsome refectory table that the old vicar had brought many years before from Italy and the vicar sat down in the vacant chair between them. Albert Edward faced them, the table between him and them, and wondered with slight uneasiness what was the matter. He remembered still the occasion on which the organist had got into trouble and the bother they had all had to hush things up. In a church like St. Peter's, Neville Square, they couldn't afford a scandal. On the vicar's red face was a look of resolute benignity, but the others bore an expression that was slightly troubled.

"He's been naggin' them, he 'as," said the verger to himself. "He's jockeyed them into doin' something, but they don't 'alf like it. That's what it is, you mark my words."

But his thoughts did not appear on Albert Edward's clean-cut and distinguished features. He stood in a respectful but not obsequious attitude. He had been in service before he was appointed to his ecclesiastical office, but only in very good houses, and his deportment was irreproachable. Starting as a page-boy in the household of a merchant-prince, he had risen by due degrees from the position of fourth to first footman, for a year he had been single-handed butler to a widowed peeress and, till the vacancy occurred at St. Peter's, butler with two men under him in the house of a retired ambassador. He was tall, spare, grave and dignified. He looked, if not like a duke, at least like an actor of the old school who specialised in dukes' parts. He had tact, firmness and self-assurance. His character was unimpeachable.

The vicar began briskly.

"Foreman, we've got something rather unpleasant to say to you. You've been here a great many years and I think his lordship and the general agree with me that you've fulfilled the duties of your office to the satisfaction of everybody concerned."

The two churchwardens nodded.

"But a most extraordinary circumstance came to my knowledge the other day and I felt it my duty to impart it to the churchwardens. I discovered to my astonishment that you could neither read nor write."

The verger's face betrayed no sign of embarrassment.

"The last vicar knew that, sir," he replied. "He said it didn't make no difference. He always said there was a great deal too much education in the world for 'is taste."

"It's the most amazing thing I ever heard," cried the general. "Do you mean to say that you've been verger of this church for sixteen years and never learned to read or write?"

"I went into service when I was twelve, sir. The cook in the first place tried to teach me once, but I didn't seem to 'ave the knack for it, and then what with one thing and another I never seemed to 'ave the time. I've never really found the want of it. I think a lot of these young fellows waste a rare lot of time readin' when they might be doin' something useful."

"But don't you want to know the news?" said the other churchwarden. "Don't you ever want to write a letter?"

"No, me lord, I seem to manage very well without. And of late years now they've all these pictures in the papers I get to know what's goin' on pretty well. Me wife's quite a scholar and if I want to write a letter she writes it for me. It's not as if I was a bettin' man."

The two churchwardens gave the vicar a troubled glance and then looked down at the table.

"Well, Foreman, I've talked the matter over with these gentlemen and they quite agree with me that the situation is impossible. At a church like St. Peter's, Neville Square, we cannot have a verger who can neither read nor write."

Albert Edward's thin, sallow face reddened and he moved uneasily on his feet, but he made no reply.

"Understand me, Foreman, I have no complaint to make against you. You do your work quite satisfactorily; I have the highest opinion both of your character and of your capacity; but we haven't the right to take the risk of some accident that might happen owing to your lamentable ignorance. It's a matter of prudence as well as of principle."

"But couldn't you learn, Foreman?" asked the general.

"No, sir, I'm afraid I couldn't, not now. You see, I'm not as young as I was and if I couldn't seem able to get the letters in me 'ead when I was a nipper I don't think there's much chance of it now."

"We don't want to be harsh with you, Foreman," said the vicar. "But the churchwardens and I have quite made up our minds. We'll give you three months and if at the end of that time you cannot read and write I'm afraid you'll have to go."

Albert Edward had never liked the new vicar. He'd said from the beginning that they'd made a mistake when they gave him St. Peter's. He wasn't the type of man they wanted with a classy congregation like that. And now he straightened himself a little. He knew his value and he wasn't going to allow himself to be put upon.

"I'm very sorry, sir, I'm afraid it's no good. I'm too old a dog to learn new tricks. I've lived a good many years without knowin' 'ow to read and write, and without wishin' to praise myself, self-praise is no recommendation, I don't mind sayin' I've done my duty in that state of life in which it 'as pleased a merciful providence to place me, and if I *could* learn now I don't know as I'd want to."

"In that case, Foreman, I'm afraid you must go."

"Yes, sir, I quite understand. I shall be 'appy to 'and in my resignation as soon as you've found somebody to take my place."

But when Albert Edward with his usual politeness had closed

the church door behind the vicar and the two churchwardens he could not sustain the air of unruffled dignity with which he had borne the blow inflicted upon him and his lips quivered. He walked slowly back to the vestry and hung up on its proper peg his verger's gown. He sighed as he thought of all the grand funerals and smart weddings it had seen. He tidied everything up, put on his coat, and hat in hand walked down the aisle. He locked the church door behind him. He strolled across the square, but deep in his sad thoughts he did not take the street that led him home, where a nice strong cup of tea awaited him; he took the wrong turning. He walked slowly along. His heart was heavy. He did not know what he should do with himself. He did not fancy the notion of going back to domestic service; after being his own master for so many years, for the vicar and churchwardens could say what they liked, it was he that had run St. Peter's, Neville Square, he could scarcely demean himself by accepting a situation. He had saved a tidy sum, but not enough to live on without doing something, and life seemed to cost more every year. He had never thought to be troubled with such questions. The vergers of St. Peter's, like the popes of Rome, were there for life. He had often thought of the pleasant reference the vicar would make in his sermon at evensong the first Sunday after his death to the long and faithful service, and the exemplary character of their late verger, Albert Edward Foreman. He sighed deeply. Albert Edward was a non-smoker and a total abstainer, but with a certain latitude; that is to say he liked a glass of beer with his dinner and when he was tired he enjoyed a cigarette. It occurred to him now that one would comfort him and since he did not carry them he looked about him for a shop where he could buy a packet of Gold Flakes. He did not at once see one and walked on a little. It was a long street, with all sorts of shops in it, but there was not a single one where you could buy cigarettes.

"That's strange," said Albert Edward.

To make sure he walked right up the street again. No, there was no doubt about it. He stopped and looked reflectively up and down.

"I can't be the only man as walks along this street and wants a fag," he said. "I shouldn't wonder but what a fellow might do very well with a little shop here. Tobacco and sweets, you know."

He gave a sudden start.

"That's an idea," he said. "Strange 'ow things come to you when you least expect it."

He turned, walked home, and had his tea.

"You're very silent this afternoon, Albert," his wife remarked.

"I'm thinkin'," he said.

He considered the matter from every point of view and next day he went along the street and by good luck found a little shop to let that looked as though it would exactly suit him. Twenty-four hours later he had taken it and when a month after that he left St. Peter's, Neville Square, for ever, Albert Edward Foreman set up in business as a tobacconist and newsagent. His wife said it was a dreadful come-down after being verger of St. Peter's, but he answered that you had to move with the times, the church wasn't what it was, and 'enceforward he was going to render unto Cæsar what was Cæsar's. Albert Edward did very well. He did so well that in a year or so it struck him that he might take a second shop and put a manager in. He looked for another long street that hadn't got a tobacconist in it and when he found it, and a shop to let, took it and stocked it. This was a success too. Then it occurred to him that if he could run two he could run half a dozen, so he began walking about London, and whenever he found a long street that had no tobacconist and a shop to let he took it. In the course of ten years he had acquired no less than ten shops and he was making money hand over fist. He went round to all of them himself every Monday, collected the week's takings and took them to the bank.

One morning when he was there paying in a bundle of notes and a heavy bag of silver the cashier told him that the manager would like to see him. He was shown into an office and the manager shook hands with him.

"Mr. Foreman, I wanted to have a talk to you about the money you've got on deposit with us. D'you know exactly how much it is?"

"Not within a pound or two, sir; but I've got a pretty rough idea."

"Apart from what you paid in this morning it's a little over thirty thousand pounds. That's a very large sum to have on deposit and I should have thought you'd do better to invest it."

"I wouldn't want to take no risk, sir. I know it's safe in the bank."

"You needn't have the least anxiety. We'll make you out a list of absolutely gilt-edged securities. They'll bring you in a better rate of interest than we can possibly afford to give you."

A troubled look settled on Mr. Foreman's distinguished face. "I've never 'ad anything to do with stocks and shares and I'd 'ave to leave it all in your 'ands," he said.

The manager smiled. "We'll do everything. All you'll have to do next time you come in is just to sign the transfers."

"I could do that all right," said Albert uncertainly. "But 'ow should I know what I was signin'?"

"I suppose you can read," said the manager a trifle sharply.

Mr. Foreman gave him a disarming smile.

"Well, sir, that's just it. I can't. I know it sounds funny-like, but there it is, I can't read or write, only me name, an' I only learnt to do that when I went into business."

The manager was so surprised that he jumped up from his chair. "That's the most extraordinary thing I ever heard."

"You see, it's like this, sir, I never 'ad the opportunity until it was too late and then some'ow I wouldn't. I got obstinate-like."

The manager stared at him as though he were a prehistoric monster.

"And do you mean to say that you've built up this important business and amassed a fortune of thirty thousand pounds without being able to read or write? Good God, man, what would you be now if you had been able to?"

"I can tell you that, sir," said Mr. Foreman, a little smile on his still aristocratic features. "I'd be verger of St. Peter's, Nevill Square."

❖

In a Strange Land

I AM of a roving disposition; but I travel not to see imposing monuments, which indeed somewhat bore me, nor beautiful scenery, of which I soon tire; I travel to see men. I avoid the great. I would not cross the road to meet a president or a king; I am content to know the writer in the pages of his book and the painter in his picture; but I have journeyed a hundred leagues to see a missionary of whom I had heard a strange story and I have spent a fortnight in a vile hotel in order to improve my acquaintance with a billiard-marker. I should be inclined to say that I am not surprised to meet any sort of person were it not that there is one sort that I am constantly running against and that never fails to give me a little shock of amused astonishment. This is the elderly Englishwoman, generally of adequate means, who is to be found living alone, up and down the world, in unexpected places. You do not wonder when you hear of her living in a villa on a hill outside a small Italian town, the only Englishwoman in the neighbourhood, and you are almost prepared for it when a lonely hacienda is pointed out to you in Andalusia and you are told that there has dwelt for many years an English lady. But it is more surprising when you hear that the only white person in a Chinese city is an Englishwoman, not a missionary, who lives there none knows why; and there is another who inhabits an island in the South Seas and a third who has a bungalow on the outskirts of a large village in the centre of Java. They live solitary lives, these women, without friends, and they do not welcome the stranger. Though they may not have seen one of their own race for months they will pass you on the road as though they did not see you, and if, presuming on your nationality, you should call, as likely as not they will decline to see you; but if they do, they will give you a cup of tea from a silver teapot and on a plate of Old Worcester you will find Scotch scones. They will talk to you politely, as though they were entertaining you in a Kentish vicarage, but when you take your leave will show no particular desire to continue the acquaintance. One wonders in vain what strange instinct it is that has driven them to separate themselves from their kith and kin and thus to live apart from all their natural interests in an alien land. Is it romance they have sought or freedom?

But of all these Englishwomen whom I have met or perhaps only heard of (for as I have said they are difficult of access) the one who remains most vividly in my memory is an elderly person who lived in Asia Minor. I had arrived after a tedious journey at a little town from which I proposed to make the ascent of a celebrated mountain and I was taken to a rambling hotel that stood at its foot. I arrived late at night and signed my name in the book. I went up to my room. It was cold and I shivered as I undressed, but in a moment there was a knock at the door and the dragoman came in.

"Signora Niccolini's compliments," he said.

To my astonishment he handed me a hot-water bottle. I took it with grateful hands.

"Who is Signora Niccolini?" I asked.

"She is the proprietor of this hotel," he answered.

I sent her my thanks and he withdrew. The last thing I expected in a scrubby hotel in Asia Minor kept by an old Italian woman was a beautiful hot-water bottle. There is nothing I like more (if we were not all sick to death of the war I would tell you the story of how six men risked their lives to fetch a hot-water bottle from a château in Flanders that was being bombarded); and next morning, so that I might thank her in person, I asked if I might see the Signora Niccolini. While I waited for her I racked my brains to think what hot-water bottle could possibly be in Italian. In a moment she came in. She was a little stout woman, not without dignity, and she wore a black apron trimmed with lace and a small black lace cap. She stood with her hands crossed. I was astonished at her appearance for she looked exactly like a house-keeper in a great English house.

"Did you wish to speak to me, sir?"

She was an Englishwoman and in those few words I surely recognised the trace of a cockney accent.

"I wanted to thank you for the hot-water bottle," I replied in some confusion.

"I saw by the visitors' book that you were English, sir, and I always send up a 'ot-water bottle to English gentlemen."

"Believe me, it was very welcome."

"I was for many years in the service of the late Lord Ormskirk, sir. He always used to travel with a 'ot-water bottle. Is there anything else, sir?"

"Not at the moment, thank you."

She gave me a polite little nod and withdrew. I wondered how on earth it came about that a funny old Englishwoman like that should be the landlady of a hotel in Asia Minor. It was not easy to make her acquaintance, for she knew her place, as she would herself have put it, and she kept me at a distance. It was not for nothing that she had been in service in a noble English family. But I was persistent and I induced her at last to ask me to have a cup of tea in her own little parlour. I learnt that she had been lady's-maid to a certain Lady Ormskirk, and Signor Niccolini (for she never alluded to her deceased husband in any other way) had been his lordship's chef. Signor Niccolini was a very handsome man and for some years there had been an "understanding" between them. When they had both saved a certain amount of money they were married, retired from service, and looked about for a hotel. They had bought this one on an advertisement because Signor Niccolini thought he would like to see something of the world. That was nearly thirty years ago and Signor Niccolini had been dead for fifteen. His widow had not once been back to England. I asked her if she was never homesick.

"I don't say as I wouldn't like to go back on a visit, though I expect I'd find many changes. But my family didn't like the idea of me marrying a foreigner and I 'aven't spoken to them since. Of course there are many things here that are not the same as what they 'ave at 'ome, but it's surprising what you get used to. I see a lot of life. I don't know as I should care to live the 'umdrum life they do in a place like London."

I smiled. For what she said was strangely incongruous with her manner. She was a pattern of decorum. It was extraordinary that she could have lived for thirty years in this wild and almost barbaric country without its having touched her. Though I knew no Turkish and she spoke it with ease I was convinced that she spoke it most incorrectly and with a cockney accent. I suppose she had remained the precise, prim English lady's-maid, knowing her place, through all these vicissitudes because she had no faculty of surprise. She took everything that came as a matter of course. She looked upon everyone who wasn't English as a foreigner and therefore as someone, almost imbecile, for whom allowances must be made. She ruled her staff despotically—for did she not know how an upper servant in a great house should exercise his authority over the under servants?—and everything about the hotel was clean and neat.

"I do my best," she said, when I congratulated her on this, standing, as always when she spoke to me, with her hands respectfully crossed. "Of course one can't expect foreigners to 'ave the same ideas what we 'ave, but as his lordship used to say to me, what we've got to do, Parker, he said to me, what we've got to do in this life is to make the best of our raw material."

But she kept her greatest surprise for the eve of my departure.

"I'm glad you're not going before you've seen my two sons, sir."

"I didn't know you had any."

"They've been away on business, but they've just come back. You'll be surprised when you've seen them. I've trained them with me own 'ands so to speak, and when I'm gone they'll carry on the 'otel between them."

In a moment two tall, swarthy, strapping young fellows entered the hall. Her eyes lit up with pleasure. They went up to her and took her in their arms and gave her resounding kisses.

"They don't speak English, sir, but they understand a little, and of course they speak Turkish like natives, and Greek and Italian."

I shook hands with the pair and then Signora Niccolini said something to them and they went away.

"They're handsome fellows, Signora," I said. "You must be very proud of them."

"I am, sir, and they're good boys, both of them. They've never give me a moment's trouble from the day they was born and they're the very image of Signor Niccolini."

"I must say no one would think they had an English mother."

"I'm not exactly their mother, sir. I've just sent them along to say 'ow do you do to 'er."

I dare say I looked a little confused.

"They're the sons that Signor Niccolini 'ad by a Greek girl that used to work in the 'otel, and 'aving no children of me own I adopted them."

I sought for some remark to make.

"I 'ope you don't think that there's any blame attaches to Signor Niccolini," she said, drawing herself up a little. "I shouldn't like you to think that, sir." She folded her hands again and with a mixture of pride, primness and satisfaction added the final word: "Signor Niccolini was a very full-blooded man."

❖

The Taipan

No one knew better than he that he was an important person. He was number one in not the least important branch of the most important English firm in China. He had worked his way up through solid ability and he looked back with a faint smile at the callow clerk who had come out to China thirty years before. When he remembered the modest home he had come from, a little red house in a long row of little red houses, in Barnes, a suburb which, aiming desperately at the genteel, achieves only a sordid melancholy, and compared it with the magnificent stone mansion, with its wide verandahs and spacious rooms, which was at once the office of the company and his own residence, he chuckled with satisfaction. He had come a long way since then. He thought of the high tea to which he sat down when he came home from school (he was at St. Paul's), with his father and mother and his two sisters, a slice of cold meat, a great deal of bread and butter and plenty of milk in his tea, everybody helping himself, and then he thought of the state in which now he ate his evening meal. He always dressed and whether he was alone or not he expected the three boys to wait at table. His number one boy knew exactly what he liked and he never had to bother himself with the details of housekeeping; but he always had a set dinner with soup and fish, entrée, roast, sweet and savoury, so that if he wanted to ask anyone in at the last moment he could. He liked his food and he did not see why when he was alone he should have less good a dinner than when he had a guest.

He had indeed gone far. That was why he did not care to go home now, he had not been to England for ten years, and he took his leave in Japan or Vancouver, where he was sure of meeting old friends from the China coast. He knew no one at home. His sisters had married in their own station, their husbands were clerks and their sons were clerks; there was nothing between him and them; they bored him. He satisfied the claims of relationship by sending them every Christmas a piece of fine silk, some elaborate embroidery, or a case of tea. He was not a mean man and as long as his mother lived he had made her an allowance. But when the time came for him to retire he had no intention of going back to England, he had seen too many men do that and he knew how often it was a failure; he meant to take a house near the race-course in Shanghai: what with bridge and his ponies and golf he expected to get through the rest of his life very comfortably. But he had a good many years before he need think of retiring. In another five or six Higgins would be going home and then he would take charge of the head office in Shanghai. Meanwhile he was very happy where he was, he could save money, which you couldn't do in Shanghai, and have a good time into the bargain. This place had another advantage over Shanghai: he was the most prominent man in the community and what he said went. Even the consul took care to keep on the right side of him. Once a consul and he had been at loggerheads and it was not he who had gone to the wall. The taipan thrust out his jaw pugnaciously as he thought of the incident.

But he smiled, for he felt in an excellent humour. He was walking back to his office from a capital luncheon at the Hong-Kong and Shanghai Bank. They did you very well there. The food was first-rate and there was plenty of liquor. He had started with a couple of cocktails, then he had some excellent sauterne and he had finished up with two glasses of port and some fine old brandy. He felt good. And when he left he did a thing that was rare with him; he walked. His bearers with his chair kept a few paces behind him in case he felt inclined to slip into it, but he enjoyed stretching his legs. He did not get enough exercise these days. Now that he was too heavy to ride it was difficult to get exercise. But if he was too heavy to ride he could still keep ponies, and as he strolled along in the balmy air he thought of the spring meeting. He had a couple of griffins that he had hopes of and one of the lads in his office had turned out a fine jockey (he must see they didn't sneak him away, old Higgins in Shanghai would give a pot of money to get him over there) and he ought to pull off two or three races. He flattered himself that he had the finest stable in the city. He pouted his broad chest like a pigeon. It was a beautiful day, and it was good to be alive.

He paused as he came to the cemetery. It stood there, neat and orderly, as an evident sign of the community's opulence. He never passed the cemetery without a little glow of pride. He was pleased to be an Englishman. For the cemetery stood in a place, valueless when it was chosen, which with the increase of the city's affluence was now worth a great deal of money. It had been suggested that the graves should be moved to another spot and the land sold for building, but the feeling of the community was against it. It gave the taipan a sense of satisfaction to think that their dead rested on the most valuable site on the island. It showed that there were things they cared for more than money. Money be blowed! When it came to "the things that mattered" (this was a favourite phrase with the taipan), well, one remembered that money wasn't everything.

And now he thought he would take a stroll through. He looked at the graves. They were neatly kept and the pathways were free from weeds. There was a look of prosperity. And as he sauntered along he read the names on the tombstones. Here were three side by side; the captain, the first mate, and the second mate of the barque *Mary Baxter*, who had all perished together in the typhoon of 1908. He remembered it well. There was a little group of two missionaries, their wives and children, who had been massacred during the Boxer troubles. Shocking thing that had been! Not that he took much stock in missionaries; but, hang it all, one couldn't have these damned Chinese massacring them. Then he came to a cross with a name on it he knew. Good chap, Edward Mulock, but he couldn't stand his liquor, drank himself to death, poor devil, at twenty-five; the taipan had known a lot of them do that; there were several more neat crosses with a man's name on them and the age, twenty-five, twenty-six, or twenty-seven; it was always the same story: they had come out to China; they had never seen so much money before, they were good fellows and they wanted to drink with the rest: they couldn't stand it, and there they were in the cemetery. You had to have a strong head and a fine constitution to drink drink for drink on the China coast. Of course it was very sad, but the taipan could hardly help a smile when he thought how many of those young fellows he had drunk underground. And there was a death that had been useful, a fellow in his own firm, senior to him and a clever chap too: if that fellow had lived he might not have been taipan now. Truly the ways of fate were inscrutable. Ah, and here was little Mrs. Turner, Violet Turner, she had been a pretty little thing, he had had quite an affair with her; he had been devilish cut up when she died. He looked at her age on the tombstone. She'd be no chicken if she were alive now. And as he thought of all those dead people a sense of satisfaction spread through him. He had beaten them all. They were dead and he was alive, and by George he'd scored them off. His eyes collected in one picture all those crowded graves and he smiled scornfully. He very nearly rubbed his hands.

"No one ever thought I was a fool," he muttered.

He had a feeling of good-natured contempt for the gibbering dead. Then, as he strolled along, he came suddenly upon two coolies digging a grave. He was astonished, for he had not heard that anyone in the community was dead.

"Who the devil's that for?" he said aloud.

The coolies did not even look at him, they went on with their work, standing in the grave, deep down, and they shovelled up heavy clods of earth. Though he had been so long in China he knew no Chinese, in his day it was not thought necessary to learn the damned language, and he asked the coolies in English whose grave they were digging. They did not understand. They answered him in Chinese and he cursed them for ignorant fools. He knew that Mrs. Broome's child was ailing and it might have died, but he would certainly have heard of it, and besides, that wasn't a child's grave, it was a man's and a big man's too. It was uncanny. He wished he hadn't gone into that cemetery; he hurried out and stepped into his chair. His good-humour had all gone and there was an uneasy frown on his face. The moment he got back to his office he called to his number two:

"I say, Peters, who's dead, d'you know?"

But Peters knew nothing. The taipan was puzzled. He called one of the native clerks and sent him to the cemetery to ask the coolies. He began to sign his letters. The clerk came back and said the coolies had gone and there was no one to ask. The taipan began to feel vaguely annoyed: he did not like things to happen of which he knew nothing. His own boy would know, his boy always knew everything, and he sent for him; but the boy had heard of no death in the community.

"I knew no one was dead," said the taipan irritably. "But what's the grave for?"

He told the boy to go to the overseer of the cemetery and find out what the devil he had dug a grave for when no one was dead.

"Let me have a whisky and soda before you go," he added, as the boy was leaving the room.

He did not know why the sight of the grave had made him uncomfortable. But he tried to put it out of his mind. He felt better when he had drunk the whisky, and he finished his work. He went upstairs and turned over the pages of *Punch*. In a few minutes he would go to the club and play a rubber or two of bridge before dinner. But it would ease his mind to hear what his boy had to say and he waited for his return. In a little while the boy came back and he brought the overseer with him.

"What are you having a grave dug for?" he asked the overseer point-blank. "Nobody's dead."

"I no dig glave," said the man.

"What the devil do you mean by that? There were two coolies digging a grave this afternoon."

The two Chinese looked at one another. Then the boy said they had been to the cemetery together. There was no new grave there.

The taipan only just stopped himself from speaking.

"But damn it all, I saw it myself," were the words on the tip of his tongue.

But he did not say them. He grew very red as he choked them down. The two Chinese looked at him with their steady eyes. For a moment his breath failed him.

"All right. Get out," he gasped.

But as soon as they were gone he shouted for the boy again, and when he came, maddeningly impassive, he told him to bring some whisky. He rubbed his sweating face with a handkerchief. His hand trembled when he lifted the glass to his lips. They could say what they liked, but he had seen the grave. Why, he could hear still the dull thud as the coolies threw the spadefuls of earth on the ground above them. What did it mean? He could feel his heart beating. He felt strangely ill at ease. But he pulled himself together. It was all nonsense. If there was no grave there it must have been an hallucination. The best thing he could do was to go to the club, and if he ran across the doctor he would ask him to give him a look over.

Everyone in the club looked just the same as ever. He did not know why he should have expected them to look different. It was a comfort. These men, living for many years with one another lives that were methodically regulated, had acquired a number of little idiosyncrasies—one of them hummed incessantly while he played bridge, another insisted on drinking beer through a straw —and these tricks which had so often irritated the taipan now gave him a sense of security. He needed it, for he could not get out of his head that strange sight he had seen; he played bridge very badly; his partner was censorious, and the taipan lost his temper. He thought the men were looking at him oddly. He wondered what they saw in him that was unaccustomed.

Suddenly he felt he could not bear to stay in the club any longer. As he went out he saw the doctor reading *The Times* in the reading-room, but he could not bring himself to speak to him. He wanted to see for himself whether that grave was really there and stepping into his chair he told his bearers to take him to the cemetery. You couldn't have an hallucination twice, could you? And besides, he would take the overseer in with him and if the grave was not there he wouldn't see it, and if it was he'd give the overseer the soundest thrashing he'd ever had. But the overseer was nowhere to be found. He had gone out and taken the keys with him. When the taipan found he could not get into the cemetery he felt suddenly exhausted. He got back into his chair and told his bearers to take him home. He would lie down for half an hour before dinner. He was tired out. That was it. He had heard that people had hallucinations when they were tired. When his boy came in to put out his clothes for dinner it was only by an effort of will that he got up. He had a strong inclination not to dress that evening, but he resisted it: he made it a rule to dress, he had dressed every evening for twenty years and it would never do to break his rule. But he ordered a bottle of champagne with his dinner and that made him feel more comfortable. Afterwards he told the boy to bring him the best brandy. When he had drunk a couple of glasses of this he felt himself again. Hallucinations be damned! He went to the billiard-room and practised a few difficult shots. There could not be much the matter with him when his eye was so sure. When he went to bed he sank immediately into a sound sleep.

But suddenly he awoke. He had dreamed of that open grave and the coolies digging leisurely. He was sure he had seen them. It was absurd to say it was an hallucination when he had seen them with his own eyes. Then he heard the rattle of the night-watchman going his rounds. It broke upon the stillness of the night so harshly that it made him jump out of his skin. And then terror seized him. He felt a horror of the winding multitudinous streets of the Chinese city, and there was something ghastly and terrible in the convoluted roofs of the temples with their devils grimacing and tortured. He loathed the smells that assaulted his nostrils. And the people. Those myriads of blue-clad coolies, and the beggars in their filthy rags, and the merchants and the magistrates, sleek, smiling, and inscrutable, in their long black gowns. They seemed to press upon him with menace. He hated the country. China. Why had he ever come? He was panic-stricken now. He must get out. He would not stay another year, another month. What did he care about Shanghai?

"Oh, my God," he cried, "if I were only safely back in England."

He wanted to go home. If he had to die he wanted to die in England. He could not bear to be buried among all these yellow men, with their slanting eyes and their grinning faces. He wanted to be buried at home, not in that grave he had seen that day. He could never rest there. Never. What did it matter what people thought? Let them think what they liked. The only thing that mattered was to get away while he had the chance.

He got out of bed and wrote to the head of the firm and said he had discovered he was dangerously ill. He must be replaced. He could not stay longer than was absolutely necessary. He must go home at once.

They found the letter in the morning clenched in the taipan's hand. He had slipped down between the desk and the chair. He was stone dead.

❖

The Consul

MR. PETE was in a state of the liveliest exasperation. He had been in the consular service for more than twenty years and he had had to deal with all manner of vexatious people, officials who would not listen to reason, merchants who took the British Government for a debt-collecting agency, missionaries who resented as gross injustice any attempt at fair play; but he never recollected a case which had left him more completely at a loss. He was a mild-mannered man, but for no reason he flew into a passion with his writer and he very nearly sacked the Eurasian clerk because he had wrongly spelt two words in a letter placed before him for his official signature. He was a conscientious man and he could not persuade himself to leave his office before the clock struck four, but the moment it did he jumped up and called for his hat and stick. Because his boy did not bring them at once he abused him roundly. They say that the consuls all grow a little odd; and the merchants who can live for thirty-five years in China without learning enough of the language to ask their way in the street say that it is because they have to study Chinese; and there was no doubt that Mr. Pete was decidedly odd. He was a bachelor and on that account had been sent to a series of posts which by reason of their isolation were thought unsuited to married men. He had lived so much alone that his natural tendency to eccentricity had developed to an extravagant degree, and he had habits which surprised the stranger. He was very absent-minded. He paid no attention to his house, which was always in great disorder, nor to his food; his boys gave him to eat what they liked and for everything he had made him pay through the nose. He was untiring in his efforts to suppress the opium traffic, but he was the only person in the city who did not know that his servants kept opium in the consulate itself, and a busy traffic in the drug was openly conducted at the back door of the compound. He was an ardent collector and the house provided for him by the government was filled with the various things which he had collected one after the other, pewter, brass, carved wood; these were his more legitimate enterprises; but he also collected stamps, birds' eggs, hotel labels, and postmarks: he boasted that he had a collection of postmarks which was unequalled in the Empire. During his long sojourning in lonely places he had read a great deal, and though he was no sinologue he had a greater knowledge of China, its history, literature, and people, than most of his colleagues; but from his wide reading he had acquired not toleration but vanity. He was a man of a singular appearance. His body was small and frail and when he walked he gave you the idea of a dead leaf dancing before the wind; and then there was something extraordinarily odd in the small Tyrolese hat, with a cock's feather in it, very old and shabby, which he wore perched rakishly on the side of his large head. He was exceedingly bald. You saw that his eyes, blue and pale, were weak behind the spectacles, and a drooping, ragged, dingy moustache did not hide the peevishness of his mouth. And now, turning out of the street in which was the consulate, he made his way on to the city wall, for there only in the multitudinous city was it possible to walk with comfort.

He was a man who took his work hardly, worrying himself to death over every trifle, but as a rule a walk on the wall soothed and rested him. The city stood in the midst of a great plain and often at sundown from the wall you could see in the distance the snow-capped mountains, the mountains of Tibet; but now he walked quickly, looking neither to the right nor to the left, and his fat spaniel frisked about him unobserved. He talked to himself rapidly in a low monotone. The cause of his irritation was a visit that he had that day received from a lady who called herself Mrs. Yü and whom he with a consular passion for precision insisted on calling Miss Lambert. This in itself sufficed to deprive their intercourse of amenity. She was an Englishwoman married to a Chinese. She had arrived two years before with her husband from England, where he had been studying at the University of London; he had made her believe that he was a great personage in his own country and she had imagined herself to be coming to a gorgeous palace and a position of consequence. It was a bitter surprise when she found herself brought to a shabby Chinese house crowded with people: there was not even a foreign bed in it, nor a knife and fork: everything seemed to her very dirty and smelly. It was a shock to find that she had to live with her husband's father and mother and he told her that she must do exactly what his mother bade her; but in her complete ignorance of Chinese it was not till she had been two or three days in the house that she realised that she was not her husband's only wife. He had been married as a boy before he left his native city to acquire the knowledge of the barbarians. When she bitterly upbraided him for deceiving her he shrugged his shoulders. There was nothing to prevent a Chinese from having two wives if he wanted them and, he added with some disregard to truth, no Chinese woman looked upon it as a hardship. It was upon making this discovery that she paid her first visit to the consul. He had already heard of her arrival—in China everyone knows everything about everyone— and he received her without surprise. Nor had he much sympathy to show her. That a foreign woman should marry a Chinese at all filled him with indignation, but that she should do so without making proper inquiries vexed him like a personal affront. She was not at all the sort of woman whose appearance led you to imagine that she would be guilty of such a folly. She was a solid, thick-set, young person, short, plain, and matter-of-fact. She was cheaply dressed in a tailor-made suit and she wore a tam-o'-shanter. She had bad teeth and a muddy skin. Her hands were large and red and ill-cared for. You could tell that she was not unused to hard work. She spoke English with a cockney whine.

"How did you meet Mr. Yü?" asked the consul frigidly.

"Well, you see, it's like this," she answered. "Dad was in a very good position, and when he died mother said: 'Well, it seems a sinful waste to keep all these rooms empty, I'll put a card in the window.'"

The consul interrupted her.

"He had lodgings with you?"

"Well, they weren't exactly lodgings," she said.

"Shall we say apartments then?" replied the consul, with his thin, slightly vain smile.

That was generally the explanation of these marriages. Then because he thought her a very foolish vulgar woman he explained bluntly that according to English law she was not married to Yü and that the best thing she could do was to go back to England at once. She began to cry and his heart softened a little to her. He promised to put her in charge of some missionary ladies who would look after her on the long journey, and indeed, if she liked, he would see if meanwhile she could not live in one of the missions. But while he talked Miss Lambert dried her tears.

"What's the good of going back to England?" she said at last. "I 'aven't got nowhere to go to."

"You can go to your mother."

"She was all against my marrying Mr. Yü. I should never hear the last of it if I was to go back now."

The consul began to argue with her, but the more he argued the more determined she became, and at last he lost his temper.

"If you like to stay here with a man who isn't your husband it's your own look-out, but I wash my hands of all responsibility."

Her retort had often rankled.

"Then you've got no cause to worry," she said, and the look on her face returned to him whenever he thought of her.

That was two years ago and he had seen her once or twice since then. It appeared that she got on very badly both with her mother-in-law and with her husband's other wife, and she had come to the consul with preposterous questions about her rights according to Chinese law. He repeated his offer to get her away, but she remained steadfast in her refusal to go, and their interview always ended in the consul's flying into a passion. He was almost inclined to pity the rascally Yü who had to keep the peace between three warring women. According to his English wife's account he was not unkind to her. He tried to act fairly by both his wives. Miss Lambert did not improve. The consul knew that ordinarily she wore Chinese clothes, but when she came to see him she put on European dress. She was become extremely blowsy. Her health suffered from the Chinese food she ate and she was beginning to look wretchedly ill. But really he was shocked when she had been shown into his office that day. She wore no hat and her hair was dishevelled. She was in a highly hysterical state.

"They're trying to poison me," she screamed and she put before him a bowl of some foul-smelling food. "It's poisoned," she said. "I've been ill for the last ten days, it's only by a miracle I've escaped."

She gave him a long story, circumstantial and probable enough to convince him: after all, nothing was more likely than that the Chinese women should use familiar methods to get rid of an intruder who was hateful to them.

"Do they know you've come here?"

"Of course they do; I told them I was going to show them up."

Now at last was the moment for decisive action. The consul looked at her in his most official manner.

"Well, you must never go back there. I refuse to put up with your nonsense any longer. I insist on your leaving this man who isn't your husband."

But he found himself helpless against the woman's insane obstinacy. He repeated all the arguments he had used so often, but she would not listen, and as usual he lost his temper. It was then, in answer to his final, desperate question, that she had made the remark which had entirely robbed him of his calm.

"But what on earth makes you stay with the man?" he cried.

She hesitated for a moment and a curious look came into her eyes.

"There's something in the way his hair grows on his forehead that I can't help liking," she answered.

The consul had never heard anything so outrageous. It really was the last straw. And now while he strode along, trying to walk off his anger, though he was not a man who often used bad language he really could not restrain himself, and he said fiercely:

"Women are simply bloody."

❖

A Friend in Need

FOR thirty years now I have been studying my fellow-men. I do not know very much about them. I should certainly hesitate to engage a servant on his face, and yet I suppose it is on the face that for the most part we judge the persons we meet. We draw our conclusions from the shape of the jaw, the look in the eyes, the contour of the mouth. I wonder if we are more often right than wrong. Why novels and plays are so often untrue to life is because their authors, perhaps of necessity, make their characters all of a piece. They cannot afford to make them self-contradictory, for then they become incomprehensible, and yet self-contradictory is what most of us are. We are a haphazard bundle of inconsistent qualities. In books on logic they will tell you that it is absurd to say that yellow is tubular or gratitude heavier than air; but in that mixture of incongruities that makes up the self yellow may very well be a horse and cart and gratitude the middle of next week. I shrug my shoulders when people tell me that their first impressions of a person are always right. I think they must have small insight or great vanity. For my own part I find that the longer I know people the more they puzzle me: my oldest friends are just those of whom I can say that I don't know the first thing about them.

These reflections have occurred to me because I read in this morning's paper that Edward Hyde Burton had died at Kobe. He was a merchant and he had been in business in Japan for many years. I knew him very little, but he interested me because once he gave me a great surprise. Unless I had heard the story from his own lips I should never have believed that he was capable of such an action. It was more startling because both in appearance and manner he suggested a very definite type. Here if ever was a man all of a piece. He was a tiny little fellow, not much more than five feet four in height, and very slender, with white hair, a red face much wrinkled, and blue eyes. I suppose he was about sixty when I knew him. He was always neatly and quietly dressed in accordance with his age and station.

Though his offices were in Kobe Burton often came down to Yokohama. I happened on one occasion to be spending a few days there, waiting for a ship, and I was introduced to him at the British Club. We played bridge together. He played a good game and a generous one. He did not talk very much, either then or later when we were having drinks, but what he said was sensible. He had a quiet, dry humour. He seemed to be popular at the club and afterwards, when he had gone, they described him as one of the best. It happened that we were both staying at the Grand Hotel and next day he asked me to dine with him. I met his wife, fat, elderly and smiling, and his two daughters. It was evidently a united and affectionate family. I think the chief thing that struck me about Burton was his kindliness. There was something very pleasing in his mild blue eyes. His voice was gentle; you could not imagine that he could possibly raise it in anger; his smile was benign. Here was a man who attracted you because you felt in him a real love for his fellows. He had charm. But there was nothing mawkish in him: he liked his game of cards and his cocktail, he could tell with point a good and spicy story, and in his youth he had been something of an athlete. He was a rich man and he had made every penny himself. I suppose one thing that made you like him was that he was so small and frail; he aroused your instincts of protection. You felt that he could not bear to hurt a fly.

One afternoon I was sitting in the lounge of the Grand Hotel. This was before the earthquake and they had leather arm-chairs there. From the windows you had a spacious view of the harbour with its crowded traffic. There were great liners on their way to Vancouver and San Francisco or to Europe by way of Shanghai, Hong-Kong and Singapore; there were tramps of all nations, battered and sea-worn, junks with their high sterns and great coloured sails, and innumerable sampans. It was a busy, exhilarating scene, and yet, I know not why, restful to the spirit. Here was romance and it seemed that you had but to stretch out your hand to touch it.

Burton came into the lounge presently and caught sight of me. He seated himself in the chair next to mine.

"What do you say to a little drink?"

He clapped his hands for a boy and ordered two gin fizzes. As the boy brought them a man passed along the street outside and seeing me waved his hand.

"Do you know Turner?" said Burton as I nodded a greeting.

"I've met him at the club. I'm told he's a remittance man."

"Yes, I believe he is. We have a good many here."

"He plays bridge well."

"They generally do. There was a fellow here last year, oddly enough a namesake of mine, who was the best bridge player I ever met. I suppose you never came across him in London. Lenny Burton he called himself. I believe he'd belonged to some very good clubs."

"No, I don't believe I remember the name."

"He was quite a remarkable player. He seemed to have an instinct about the cards. It was uncanny. I used to play with him a lot. He was in Kobe for some time."

Burton sipped his gin fizz.

"It's rather a funny story," he said. "He wasn't a bad chap. I liked him. He was always well-dressed and smart-looking. He was handsome in a way with curly hair and pink-and-white cheeks. Women thought a lot of him. There was no harm in him, you know, he was only wild. Of course he drank too much. Those sort of fellows always do. A bit of money used to come in for him once a quarter and he made a bit more by card-playing. He won a good deal of mine, I know that."

Burton gave a kindly chuckle. I knew from my own experience that he could lose money at bridge with a good grace. He stroked his shaven chin with his thin hand; the veins stood out on it and it was almost transparent.

"I suppose that is why he came to me when he went broke, that and the fact that he was a namesake of mine. He came to see me in my office one day and asked me for a job. I was rather surprised. He told me that there was no more money coming from home and he wanted to work. I asked him how old he was.

" 'Thirty-five,' he said.

" 'And what have you been doing hitherto?' I asked him.

" 'Well, nothing very much,' he said.

"I couldn't help laughing.

" 'I'm afraid I can't do anything for you just yet,' I said. 'Come back and see me in another thirty-five years, and I'll see what I can do.'

"He didn't move. He went rather pale. He hesitated for a moment and then he told me that he had had bad luck at cards for some time. He hadn't been willing to stick to bridge, he'd been playing poker, and he'd got trimmed. He hadn't a penny. He'd pawned everything he had. He couldn't pay his hotel bill and they wouldn't give him any more credit. He was down and out. If he couldn't get something to do he'd have to commit suicide.

"I looked at him for a bit. I could see now that he was all to pieces. He'd been drinking more than usual and he looked fifty. The girls wouldn't have thought so much of him if they'd seen him then.

" 'Well, isn't there anything you can do except play cards?' I asked him.

" 'I can swim,' he said.

" 'Swim!'

"I could hardly believe my ears; it seemed such an insane answer to give.

" 'I swam for my university.'

"I got some glimmering of what he was driving at. I've known too many men who were little tin gods at their university to be impressed by it.

" 'I was a pretty good swimmer myself when I was a young man,' I said.

"Suddenly I had an idea."

Pausing in his story, Burton turned to me.

"Do you know Kobe?" he asked.

"No," I said, "I passed through it once, but I only spent a night there."

"Then you don't know the Shioya Club. When I was a young man I swam from there round the beacon and landed at the creek of Tarumi. It's over three miles and it's rather difficult on account of the currents round the beacon. Well, I told my young namesake about it and I said to him that if he'd do it I'd give him a job.

"I could see he was rather taken aback.

" 'You say you're a swimmer,' I said.

" 'I'm not in very good condition,' he answered.

"I didn't say anything. I shrugged my shoulders. He looked at me for a moment and then he nodded.

" 'All right,' he said. 'When do you want me to do it?'

"I looked at my watch. It was just after ten.

" 'The swim shouldn't take you much over an hour and a quarter. I'll drive round to the creek at half-past twelve and meet you. I'll take you back to the club to dress and then we'll have lunch together.'

" 'Done,' he said.

"We shook hands. I wished him good luck and he left me. I had a lot of work to do that morning and I only just managed to get to the creek at Tarumi at half-past twelve. But I needn't have hurried; he never turned up."

"Did he funk it at the last moment?" I asked.

"No, he didn't funk it. He started all right. But of course he'd ruined his constitution by drink and dissipation. The currents round the beacon were more than he could manage. We didn't get the body for about three days."

I didn't say anything for a moment or two. I was a trifle shocked. Then I asked Burton a question.

"When you made him that offer of a job, did you know he'd be drowned?"

He gave a little mild chuckle and he looked at me with those kind and candid blue eyes of his. He rubbed his chin with his hand.

"Well, I hadn't got a vacancy in my office at the moment."

The Round Dozen

I LIKE Elsom. It is a seaside resort in the South of England, not very far from Brighton, and it has something of the late Georgian charm of that agreeable town. But it is neither bustling nor garish. Ten years ago, when I used to go there not infrequently, you might still see here and there an old house, solid and pretentious in no unpleasing fashion (like a decayed gentlewoman of good family whose discreet pride in her ancestry amuses rather than offends you), which was built in the reign of the First Gentleman in Europe and where a courtier of fallen fortunes may well have passed his declining years. The main street had a lackadaisical air and the doctor's motor seemed a trifle out of place. The house-wives did their housekeeping in a leisurely manner. They gossiped with the butcher as they watched him cut from his great joint of South Down a piece of the best end of the neck, and they asked amiably after the grocer's wife as he put half a pound of tea and a packet of salt into their string bag. I do not know whether Elsom was ever fashionable: it certainly was not so then; but it was respectable and cheap. Elderly ladies, maiden and widowed, lived there, Indian Civilians and retired soldiers: they looked forward with little shudders of dismay to August and September which would bring holiday-makers; but did not disdain to let them their houses and on the proceeds spend a few worldly weeks in a Swiss pension. I never knew Elsom at that hectic time when the lodging-houses were full and young men in blazers sauntered along the front, when Pierrots performed on the beach and in the billiard-room at the Dolphin you heard the click of balls till eleven at night. I only knew it in winter. Then in every house on the sea-front, stucco houses with bow-windows built a hundred years ago, there was a sign to inform you that apartments were to let; and the guests of the Dolphin were waited on by a single waiter and the boots. At ten o'clock the porter came into the smoking-room and looked at you in so marked a manner that you got up and went to bed. Then Elsom was a restful place and the Dolphin a very comfortable inn. It was pleasing to think that the Prince Regent drove over with Mrs. Fitzherbert more than once to drink a dish of tea in its coffee-room. In the hall was a framed letter from Mr. Thackeray ordering a sitting-room and two bedrooms overlooking the sea and giving instructions that a fly should be sent to the station to meet him.

One November, two or three years after the war, having had a bad attack of influenza, I went down to Elsom to regain my strength. I arrived in the afternoon and when I had unpacked my things went for a stroll on the front. The sky was overcast and the calm sea grey and cold. A few seagulls flew close to the shore. Sailing-boats, their masts taken down for the winter, were drawn up high on the shingly beach and the bathing-huts stood side by side in a long, grey and tattered row. No one was sitting on the benches that the town council had put here and there, but a few people were trudging up and down for exercise. I passed an old colonel with a red nose who stamped along in plus-fours followed by a terrier, two elderly women in short skirts and stout shoes and a plain girl in a tam-o'-shanter. I had never seen the front so deserted. The lodging-houses looked like bedraggled old maids waiting for lovers who would never return, and even the friendly Dolphin seemed wan and desolate. My heart sank. Life on a sudden seemed very drab. I returned to the hotel, drew the curtains of my sitting-room, poked the fire and with a book sought to dispel my melancholy. But I was glad enough when it was time to dress for dinner. I went into the coffee-room and found the guests of the hotel already seated. I gave them a casual glance. There was one lady of middle age by herself and there were two elderly gentlemen, golfers probably, with red faces and baldish heads, who ate their food in moody silence. The only other persons in the room were a group of three who sat in the bow-window, and they immediately attracted my surprised attention. The party consisted of an old gentleman and two ladies, one of whom was old and probably his wife, while the other was younger and possibly his daughter. It was the old lady who first excited my interest. She wore a voluminous dress of black silk and a black lace cap; on her wrists were heavy gold bangles and round her neck a substantial gold chain from which hung a large gold locket; at her neck was a large gold brooch. I did not know that anyone still wore jewellery of that sort. Often, passing second-hand jewellers and pawnbrokers, I had lingered for a moment to look at these strangely old-fashioned articles, so solid, costly and hideous, and thought, with a smile in which there was a tinge of sadness, of the women long since dead who had worn them. They suggested the period when the bustle and the flounce were taking the place of the crinoline and the pork-pie hat was ousting the poke-bonnet. The British people liked things solid and good in those days. They went to church on Sunday morning and after church walked in the Park. They gave dinner-parties of twelve courses where the master of the house carved the beef and the chickens, and after dinner the ladies who could play favoured the company with Mendelssohn's *Songs without Words* and the gentleman with the fine baritone voice sang an old English ballad.

The younger woman had her back turned to me and at first I could see only that she had a slim and youthful figure. She had a great deal of brown hair which seemed to be elaborately arranged. She wore a grey dress. The three of them were chatting in low tones and presently she turned her head so that I saw her profile. It was astonishingly beautiful. The nose was straight and delicate, the line of the cheek exquisitely modelled; I saw then that she wore her hair after the manner of Queen Alexandra. The dinner proceeded to its close and the party got up. The old lady sailed out of the room, looking neither to the right nor to the left, and the young one followed her. Then I saw with a shock that she was old. Her frock was simple enough, the skirt was longer than was at that time worn, and there was something slightly old-fashioned in the cut, I dare say the waist was more clearly indicated than was then usual, but it was a girl's frock. She was tall, like a heroine of Tennyson's, slight, with long legs and a graceful carriage. I had seen the nose before, it was the nose of a Greek goddess, her mouth was beautiful, and her eyes were large and blue. Her skin was of course a little tight on the bones and there were wrinkles on her forehead and about her eyes, but in youth it must have been lovely. She reminded you of those Roman ladies with features of an exquisite regularity whom Alma-Tadema used to paint, but who, notwithstanding their antique dress, were so stubbornly English. It was a type of cold perfection that one had not seen for five-and-twenty years. Now it is as dead as the epigram. I was like an archæologist who finds some long-buried statue and I was thrilled in so unexpected a manner to hit upon this survival of a past era. For no day is so dead as the day before yesterday.

The gentleman rose to his feet when the two ladies left, and then resumed his chair. A waiter brought him a glass of heavy port. He smelt it, sipped it, and rolled it round his tongue. I observed him. He was a little man, much shorter than his imposing wife, well-covered without being stout, with a fine head of curling grey hair. His face was much wrinkled and it bore a faintly humorous expression. His lips were tight and his chin was square. He was, according to our present notions, somewhat extravagantly dressed. He wore a black velvet jacket, a frilled shirt with a low collar and a large black tie, and very wide evening trousers. It gave you vaguely the effect of costume. Having drunk his port with deliberation, he got up and sauntered out of the room.

When I passed through the hall, curious to know who these singular people were, I glanced at the visitors' book. I saw written in an angular feminine hand, the writing that was taught to young ladies in modish schools forty years or so ago, the names: Mr. and Mrs. Edwin St. Clair and Miss Porchester. Their address was given as 68, Leinster Square, Bayswater, London. These must be the names and this the address of the persons who had so much interested me. I asked the manageress who Mr. St. Clair was and she told me that she believed he was something in the City. I went into the billiard-room and knocked the balls about for a little while and then on my way upstairs passed through the lounge. The two red-faced gentlemen were reading the evening paper and the elderly lady was dozing over a novel. The party of three sat in a corner. Mrs. St. Clair was knitting, Miss Porchester was busy with embroidery, and Mr. St. Clair was reading aloud in a discreet but resonant tone. As I passed I discovered that he was reading *Bleak House*.

I read and wrote most of the next day, but in the afternoon I went for a walk and on my way home I sat down for a little on one of those convenient benches on the sea-front. It was not quite so cold as the day before and the air was pleasant. For want of anything better to do I watched a figure advancing towards me from a distance. It was a man and as he came nearer I saw that it was rather a shabby little man. He wore a thin black greatcoat and a somewhat battered bowler. He walked with his hands in his pockets and looked cold. He gave me a glance as he passed by, went on a few steps, hesitated, stopped and turned back. When he came up once more to the bench on which I sat he took a hand out of his pocket and touched his hat. I noticed that he wore shabby black gloves, and surmised that he was a widower in straitened circumstances. Or he might have been a mute recovering, like myself, from influenza.

"Excuse me, sir," he said, "but could you oblige me with a match?"

"Certainly."

He sat down beside me and while I put my hand in my pocket for matches he hunted in his for cigarettes. He took out a small packet of Gold Flake and his face fell.

"Dear, dear, how very annoying! I haven't got a cigarette left."

"Let me offer you one," I replied, smiling.

I took out my case and he helped himself.

"Gold?" he asked, giving the case a tap as I closed it. "Gold? That's a thing I never could keep. I've had three. All stolen."

His eyes rested in a melancholy way on his boots, which were sadly in need of repair. He was a wizened little man with a long thin nose and pale-blue eyes. His skin was sallow and he was much lined. I could not tell what his age was; he might have been five-and-thirty or he might have been sixty. There was nothing remarkable about him except his insignificance. But though evidently poor he was neat and clean. He was respectable and he clung to respectability. No, I did not think he was a mute, I thought he was a solicitor's clerk who had lately buried his wife and been sent to Elsom by an indulgent employer to get over the first shock of his grief.

"Are you making a long stay, sir?" he asked me.

"Ten days or a fortnight."

"Is this your first visit to Elsom, sir?"

"I have been here before."

"I know it well, sir. I flatter myself there are very few seaside resorts that I have not been to at one time or another. Elsom is hard to beat, sir. You get a very nice class of people here. There's nothing noisy or vulgar about Elsom, if you understand what I mean. Elsom has very pleasant recollections for me, sir. I knew Elsom well in bygone days. I was married in St. Martin's Church, sir."

"Really," I said feebly.

"It was a very happy marriage, sir."

"I'm very glad to hear it," I returned.

"Nine months, that one lasted," he said reflectively.

Surely the remark was a trifle singular. I had not looked forward with any enthusiasm to the probability which I so clearly foresaw that he would favour me with an account of his matrimonial experiences, but now I waited if not with eagerness at least with curiosity for a further observation. He made none. He sighed a little. At last I broke the silence.

"There don't seem to be very many people about," I remarked.

"I like it so. I'm not one for crowds. As I was saying just now, I reckon I've spent a good many years at one seaside resort after the other, but I never came in the season. It's the winter I like."

"Don't you find it a little melancholy?"

He turned towards me and placed his black-gloved hand for an instant on my arm.

"It is melancholy. And because it's melancholy a little ray of sunshine is very welcome."

The remark seemed to me perfectly idiotic and I did not answer. He withdrew his hand from my arm and got up.

"Well, I mustn't keep you, sir. Pleased to have made your acquaintance."

He took off his dingy hat very politely and strolled away. It was beginning now to grow chilly and I thought I would return to the Dolphin. As I reached its broad steps a landau drove up, drawn by two scraggy horses, and from it stepped Mr. St. Clair. He wore a hat that looked like the unhappy result of a union between a bowler and a top-hat. He gave his hand to his wife and then to his niece. The porter carried in after them rugs and cushions. As Mr. St. Clair paid the driver I heard him tell him to come at the usual time next day and I understood that the St. Clairs took a drive every afternoon in a landau. It would not have surprised me to learn that none of them had ever been in a motor-car.

The manageress told me that they kept very much to themselves and sought no acquaintance among the other persons staying at the hotel. I rode my imagination on a loose rein. I watched them eat three meals a day. I watched Mr. and Mrs. St. Clair sit at the top of the hotel steps in the morning. He read *The Times* and she knitted. I suppose Mrs. St. Clair had never read a paper in her life, for they never took anything but *The Times* and Mr. St. Clair of course took it with him every day to the City. At about twelve Miss Porchester joined them.

"Have you enjoyed your walk, Eleanor?" asked Mrs. St. Clair.

"It was very nice, Aunt Gertrude," answered Miss Porchester.

And I understood that just as Mrs. St. Clair took "her drive" every afternoon Miss Porchester took "her walk" every morning.

"When you have come to the end of your row, my dear," said Mr. St. Clair, with a glance at his wife's knitting, "we might go for a constitutional before luncheon."

"That will be very nice," answered Mrs. St. Clair. She folded up her work and gave it to Miss Porchester. "If you're going upstairs, Eleanor, will you take my work?"

"Certainly, Aunt Gertrude."

"I dare say you're a little tired after your walk, my dear."

"I shall have a little rest before luncheon."

Miss Porchester went into the hotel and Mr. and Mrs. St. Clair walked slowly along the sea-front, side by side, to a certain point, and then walked slowly back.

When I met one of them on the stairs I bowed and received an unsmiling, polite bow in return, and in the morning I ventured upon a good-day, but there the matter ended. It looked as though I should never have a chance to speak to any of them. But presently I thought that Mr. St. Clair gave me now and then a glance, and thinking he had heard my name I imagined, perhaps vainly, that he looked at me with curiosity. And a day or two after that I was sitting in my room when the porter came in with a message.

"Mr. St. Clair presents his compliments and could you oblige him with the loan of *Whitaker's Almanack*."

I was astonished.

"Why on earth should he think that I have a *Whitaker's Almanack?*"

"Well, sir, the manageress told him you wrote."

I could not see the connection.

"Tell Mr. St. Clair that I'm very sorry that I haven't got a *Whitaker's Almanack*, but if I had I would very gladly lend it to him."

Here was my opportunity. I was by now filled with eagerness to know these fantastic persons more closely. Now and then in the heart of Asia I have come upon a lonely tribe living in a little village among an alien population. No one knows how they came there or why they settled in that spot. They live their own lives, speak their own language, and have no communication with their neighbours. No one knows whether they are the descendants of a band that was left behind when their nation swept in a vast horde across the continent or whether they are the dying remnant of some great people that in that country once held empire. They are a mystery. They have no future and no history. This odd little family seemed to me to have something of the same character. They were of an era that is dead and gone. They reminded me of persons in one of those leisurely, old-fashioned novels that one's father read. They belonged to the 'eighties and they had not moved since then. How extraordinary it was that they could have lived through the last forty years as though the world stood still! They took me back to my childhood and I recollected people who are long since dead. I wonder if it is only distance that gives me the impression that they were more peculiar than anyone is now. When a person was described then as "quite a character", by heaven, it meant something.

So that evening after dinner I went into the lounge and boldly addressed Mr. St. Clair.

"I'm so sorry I haven't got a *Whitaker's Almanack*," I said, "but if I have any other book that can be of service to you I shall be delighted to lend it to you."

Mr. St. Clair was obviously startled. The two ladies kept their eyes on their work. There was an embarrassed hush.

"It does not matter at all, but I was given to understand by the manageress that you were a novelist."

I racked my brain. There was evidently some connection between my profession and *Whitaker's Almanack* that escaped me.

"In days gone by Mr. Trollope used often to dine with us in Leinster Square and I remember him saying that the two most useful books to a novelist were the Bible and *Whitaker's Almanack*."

"I see that Thackeray once stayed in this hotel," I remarked, anxious not to let the conversation drop.

"I never very much cared for Mr. Thackeray, though he dined more than once with my wife's father, the late Mr. Sargeant Saunders. He was too cynical for me. My niece has not read *Vanity Fair* to this day."

Miss Porchester blushed slightly at this reference to herself. A waiter brought in the coffee and Mrs. St. Clair turned to her husband.

"Perhaps, my dear, this gentleman would do us the pleasure to have his coffee with us."

Although not directly addressed I answered promptly:

"Thank you very much."

I sat down.

"Mr. Trollope was always my favourite novelist," said Mr. St. Clair. "He was so essentially a gentleman. I admire Charles Dickens. But Charles Dickens could never draw a gentleman. I am given to understand that young people nowadays find Mr. Trollope a little slow. My niece, Miss Porchester, prefers the novels of Mr. William Black."

"I'm afraid I've never read any," I said.

"Ah, I see that you are like me; you are not up to date. My niece once persuaded me to read a novel by a Miss Rhoda Broughton, but I could not manage more than a hundred pages of it."

"I did not say I liked it, Uncle Edwin," said Miss Porchester, defending herself, with another blush, "I told you it was rather fast, but everybody was talking about it."

"I'm quite sure it is not the sort of book your Aunt Gertrude would have wished you to read, Eleanor."

"I remember Miss Broughton telling me once that when she was young people said her books were fast and when she was old they said they were slow, and it was very hard since she had written exactly the same sort of book for forty years."

"Oh, did you know Miss Broughton?" asked Miss Porchester, addressing me for the first time. "How very interesting! And did you know Ouida?"

"My dear Eleanor, what will you say next! I'm quite sure you've never read anything by Ouida."

"Indeed, I have, Uncle Edwin. I've read *Under Two Flags* and I liked it very much."

"You amaze and shock me. I don't know what girls are coming to nowadays."

"You always said that when I was thirty you gave me complete liberty to read anything I liked."

"There is a difference, my dear Eleanor, between liberty and licence," said Mr. St. Clair, smiling a little in order not to make his reproof offensive, but with a certain gravity.

I do not know if in recounting this conversation I have managed to convey the impression it gave me of a charming and old-fashioned air. I could have listened all night to them discussing the depravity of an age that was young in the eighteen-eighties. I would have given a good deal for a glimpse of their large and roomy house in Leinster Square. I should have recognised the suite covered in red brocade that stood stiffly about the drawing-room, each piece in its appointed place; and the cabinets filled with Dresden china would have brought me back my childhood. In the dining-room, where they habitually sat, for the drawing-room was used only for parties, was a Turkey carpet and a vast mahogany sideboard "groaning" with silver. On the walls were the pictures that had excited the admiration of Mrs. Humphrey Ward and her uncle Matthew in the Academy of eighteen-eighty.

Next morning, strolling through a pretty lane at the back of Elsom, I met Miss Porchester, who was taking "her walk". I should have liked to go a little way with her, but felt certain that it would embarrass this maiden of fifty to saunter alone with a man even of my respectable years. She bowed as I passed her and blushed. Oddly enough, a few yards behind her I came upon the funny shabby little man in black gloves with whom I had spoken for a few minutes on the front. He touched his old bowler hat.

"Excuse me, sir, but could you oblige me with a match?" he said.

"Certainly," I retorted, "but I'm afraid I have no cigarettes on me."

"Allow me to offer you one of mine," he said, taking out the paper case. It was empty. "Dear, dear, I haven't got one either. What a curious coincidence!"

He went on and I had a notion that he a little hastened his steps. I was beginning to have my doubts about him. I hoped he was not going to bother Miss Porchester. For a moment I thought of walking back, but I did not. He was a civil little man and I did not believe he would make a nuisance of himself to a single lady.

I saw him again that very afternoon. I was sitting on the front. He walked towards me with little, halting steps. There was something of a wind and he looked like a dried leaf being driven before it. This time he did not hesitate, but sat down beside me.

"We meet again, sir. The world is a small place. If it will not inconvenience you perhaps you will allow me to rest a few minutes. I am a wee bit tired."

"This is a public bench, and you have just as much right to sit on it as I."

I did not wait for him to ask me for a match, but at once offered him a cigarette.

"How very kind of you, sir! I have to limit myself to so many cigarettes a day, but I enjoy those I smoke. As one grows older the pleasures of life diminish, but my experience is that one enjoys more those that remain."

"That is a very consoling thought."

"Excuse me, sir, but am I right in thinking that you are the well-known author?"

"I am an author," I replied. "But what made you think it?"

"I have seen your portrait in the illustrated papers. I suppose you don't recognise me?"

I looked at him again, a weedy little man in neat but shabby black clothes, with a long nose and watery blue eyes.

"I'm afraid I don't."

"I dare say I've changed," he sighed. "There was a time when my photograph was in every paper in the United Kingdom. Of course, those press photographs never do you justice. I give you my word, sir, that if I hadn't seen my name underneath I should never have guessed that some of them were meant for me."

He was silent for a while. The tide was out and beyond the shingle of the beach was a strip of yellow mud. The breakwaters were half buried in it like the backbones of prehistoric beasts.

"It must be a wonderfully interesting thing to be an author, sir. I've often thought I had quite a turn for writing myself. At one time and another I've done a rare lot of reading. I haven't kept up with it much lately. For one thing my eyes are not so good as they used to be. I believe I could write a book if I tried."

"They say anybody can write one," I answered.

"Not a novel, you know. I'm not much of a one for novels; I prefer histories and that-like. But memoirs. If anybody was to make it worth my while I wouldn't mind writing my memoirs."

"It's very fashionable just now."

"There are not many people who've had the experiences I've had in one way and another. I did write to one of the Sunday papers about it some little while back, but they never answered my letter."

He gave me a long, appraising look. He had too respectable an air to be about to ask me for half a crown.

"Of course you don't know who I am, sir, do you?"

"I honestly don't."

He seemed to ponder for a moment, then he smoothed down his black gloves on his fingers, looked for a moment at a hole in one of them, and then turned to me not without self-consciousness.

"I am the celebrated Mortimer Ellis," he said.

"Oh?"

I did not know what other ejaculation to make, for to the best of my belief I had never heard the name before. I saw a look of disappointment come over his face, and I was a trifle embarrassed.

"Mortimer Ellis," he repeated. "You're not going to tell me you don't know."

"I'm afraid I must. I'm very often out of England."

I wondered to what he owed his celebrity. I passed over in my mind various possibilities. He could never have been an athlete, which alone in England gives a man real fame, but he might have been a faith-healer or a champion billiard-player. There is of course no one so obscure as a Cabinet Minister out of office and he might have been the President of the Board of Trade in a defunct administration. But he had none of the look of a politician.

"That's fame for you," he said bitterly. "Why, for weeks I was the most talked-about man in England. Look at me. You must have seen my photograph in the papers. Mortimer Ellis."

"I'm sorry," I said, shaking my head.

He paused a moment to give his disclosure effectiveness.

"I am the well-known bigamist."

Now what are you to reply when a person who is practically a stranger to you informs you that he is a well-known bigamist? I will confess that I have sometimes had the vanity to think that I am not as a rule at a loss for a retort, but here I found myself speechless.

"I've had eleven wives, sir," he went on.

"Most people find one about as much as they can manage."

"Ah, that's want of practice. When you've had eleven there's very little you don't know about women."

"But why did you stop at eleven?"

"There now, I knew you'd say that. The moment I set eyes on you I said to myself, he's got a clever face. You know, sir, that's the thing that always grizzles me. Eleven does seem a funny number, doesn't it? There's something unfinished about it. Now three anyone might have, and seven's all right, they say nine's lucky, and there's nothing wrong with ten. But eleven! That's the one thing I regret. I shouldn't have minded anything if I could have brought it up to the Round Dozen."

He unbuttoned his coat and from an inside pocket produced a bulging and very greasy pocket-book. From this he took a large bundle of newspaper cuttings; they were worn and creased and dirty. But he spread out two or three.

"Now just you look at those photographs. I ask you, are they like me? It's an outrage. Why, you'd think I was a criminal to look at them."

The cuttings were of imposing length. In the opinion of sub-editors Mortimer Ellis had obviously been a news item of value. One was headed, A Much Married Man; another, Heartless Ruffian Brought to Book; a third, Contemptible Scoundrel Meets his Waterloo.

"Not what you would call a good press," I murmured.

"I never pay any attention to what the newspapers say," he answered, with a shrug of his thin shoulders. "I've known too many journalists myself for that. No, it's the judge I blame. He treated me shocking and it did him no good, mind you; he died within the year."

I ran my eyes down the report I held.

"I see he gave you five years."

"Disgraceful, I call it, and see what it says." He pointed to a place with his forefinger. " 'Three of his victims pleaded for mercy to be shown to him.' That shows what they thought of me. And after that he gave me five years. And just look what he called me, a heartless scoundrel—me, the best-hearted man that ever lived—a pest of society and a danger to the public. Said he wished he had the power to give me the cat. I don't so much mind his giving me five years, though you'll never get me to say it wasn't excessive, but I ask you, had he the right to talk to me like that? No, he hadn't, and I'll never forgive him, not if I live to be a hundred."

The bigamist's cheeks flushed and his watery eyes were filled for a moment with fire. It was a sore subject with him.

"May I read them?" I asked him.

"That's what I gave them you for. I want you to read them, sir. And if you can read them without saying that I'm a much wronged man, well, you're not the man I took you for."

As I glanced through one cutting after another I saw why Mortimer Ellis had so wide an acquaintance with the seaside resorts of England. They were his hunting-ground. His method was to go to some place when the season was over and take apartments in one of the empty lodging-houses. Apparently it did not take him long to make acquaintance with some woman or other, widow or spinster, and I noticed that their ages at the time were between thirty-five and fifty. They stated in the witness-box that they had met him first on the sea-front. He generally proposed marriage to them within a fortnight of this and they were married shortly after. He induced them in one way or another to entrust him with their savings and in a few months, on the pretext that he had to go to London on business, he left them never to return. Only one had ever seen him again till, obliged to give evidence, they saw him in the dock. They were women of a certain respectability; one was the daughter of a doctor and another of a clergyman; there was a lodging-house keeper, there was the widow of a commercial traveller, and there was a retired dressmaker. For the most part, their fortunes ranged from five hundred to a thousand pounds, but whatever the sum the misguided women were stripped of every penny. Some of them told really pitiful stories of the destitution to which they had been reduced. But they all acknowledged that he had been a good husband to them. Not only had three actually pleaded for mercy to be shown him, but one said in the witness-box that, if he was willing to come, she was ready to take him back. He noticed that I was reading this.

"And she'd have worked for me," he said, "there's no doubt about that. But I said, better let bygones be bygones. No one likes a cut off the best end of the neck better than I do, but I'm not much of a one for cold roast mutton, I will confess."

It was only by an accident that Mortimer Ellis did not marry his twelfth wife and so achieve the Round Dozen which I understand appealed to his love of symmetry. For he was engaged to be married to a Miss Hubbard—"two thousand pounds she had, if she had a penny, in war-loan," he confided to me—and the banns had been read, when one of his former wives saw him, made enquiries, and communicated with the police. He was arrested on the very day before his twelfth wedding.

"She was a bad one, she was," he told me. "She deceived me something cruel."

"How did she do that?"

"Well, I met her at Eastbourne, one December it was, on the pier, and she told me in course of conversation that she'd been in the millinery business and had retired. She said she'd made a tidy bit of money. She wouldn't say exactly how much it was, but she gave me to understand it was something like fifteen hundred pounds. And when I married her, would you believe it, she hadn't got three hundred. And that's the one who gave me away. And mind you, I'd never blamed her. Many a man would have cut up rough when he found out he'd been made a fool of. I never showed her that I was disappointed even, I just went away without a word."

"But not without the three hundred pounds, I take it."

"Oh come, sir, you must be reasonable," he returned in an injured tone. "You can't expect three hundred pounds to last for ever and I'd been married to her four months before she confessed the truth."

"Forgive my asking," I said, "and pray don't think my question suggests a disparaging view of your personal attractions, but— why did they marry you?"

"Because I asked them," he answered, evidently very much surprised at my enquiry.

"But did you never have any refusals?"

"Very seldom. Not more than four or five in the whole course of my career. Of course I didn't propose till I was pretty sure of my ground and I don't say I didn't draw a blank sometimes. You can't expect to click every time, if you know what I mean, and I've often wasted several weeks making up to a woman before I saw there was nothing doing."

I surrendered myself for a time to my reflections. But I noticed presently that a broad smile spread over the mobile features of my friend.

"I understand what you mean," he said. "It's my appearance that puzzles you. You don't know what it is they see in me. That's what comes of reading novels and going to the pictures. You think what women want is the cowboy type, or the romance of old Spain touch, flashing eyes, an olive skin, and a beautiful dancer. You make me laugh."

"I'm glad," I said.

"Are you a married man, sir?"

"I am. But I only have one wife."

"You can't judge by that. You can't generalise from a single instance, if you know what I mean. Now, I ask you, what would you know about dogs if you'd never had anything but one bull-terrier?"

The question was rhetorical and I felt sure did not require an answer. He paused for an effective moment and went on.

"You're wrong, sir. You're quite wrong. They may take a

fancy to a good-looking young fellow, but they don't want to marry him. They don't really care about looks."

"Douglas Jerrold, who was as ugly as he was witty, used to say that if he was given ten minutes' start with a woman he could cut out the handsomest man in the room."

"They don't want wit. They don't want a man to be funny; they think he's not serious. They don't want a man who's too handsome; they think he's not serious either. That's what they want, they want a man who's serious. Safety first. And then— attention. I may not be handsome and I may not be amusing, but believe me, I've got what every woman wants. Poise. And the proof is, I've made every one of my wives happy."

"It certainly is much to your credit that three of them pleaded for mercy to be shown to you and that one was willing to take you back."

"You don't know what an anxiety that was to me all the time I was in prison. I thought she'd be waiting for me at the gate when I was released and I said to the Governor: For God's sake, sir, smuggle me out so as no one can see me."

He smoothed his gloves again over his hands and his eye once more fell upon the hole in the first finger.

"That's what comes of living in lodgings, sir. How's a man to keep himself neat and tidy without a woman to look after him? I've been married too often to be able to get along without a wife. There are men who don't like being married. I can't understand them. The fact is, you can't do a thing really well unless you've got your heart in it, and I like being a married man. It's no difficulty to me to do the little things that women like and that some men can't be bothered with. As I was saying just now, it's attention a woman wants. I never went out of the house without giving my wife a kiss and I never came in without giving her another. And it was very seldom I came in without bringing her some chocolates or a few flowers. I never grudged the expense."

"After all, it was her money you were spending," I interposed.

"And what if it was? It's not the money that you've paid for a present that signifies, it's the spirit you give it in. That's what counts with women. No, I'm not one to boast, but I will say this of myself, I am a good husband."

I looked desultorily at the reports of the trial which I still held.

"I'll tell you what surprises me," I said. "All these women

were very respectable, of a certain age, quiet, decent persons. And yet they married you without any enquiry after the shortest possible acquaintance."

He put his hand impressively on my arm.

"Ah, that's what you don't understand, sir. Women have got a craving to be married. It doesn't matter how young they are or how old they are, if they're short or tall, dark or fair, they've all got one thing in common: they want to be married. And mind you, I married them in church. No woman feels really safe unless she's married in church. You say I'm no beauty, well, I never thought I was, but if I had one leg and a hump on my back I could find any number of women who'd jump at the chance of marrying me. It's a mania with them. It's a disease. Why, there's hardly one of them who wouldn't have accepted me the second time I saw her only I like to make sure of my ground before I commit myself. When it all came out there was a rare to-do because I'd married eleven times. Eleven times? Why, it's nothing, it's not even a Round Dozen. I could have married thirty times if I'd wanted to. I give you my word, sir, when I consider my opportunities, I'm astounded at my moderation."

"You told me you were very fond of reading history."

"Yes, Warren Hastings said that, didn't he? It struck me at the time I read it. It seemed to fit me like a glove."

"And you never found these constant courtships a trifle monotonous?"

"Well, sir, I think I've got a logical mind, and it always gave me a rare lot of pleasure to see how the same effects followed on the same causes, if you know what I mean. Now, for instance, with a woman who'd never been married before I always passed myself off as a widower. It worked like a charm. You see, a spinster likes a man who knows a thing or two. But with a widow I always said I was a bachelor: a widow's afraid a man who's been married before knows too much."

I gave him back his cuttings; he folded them up neatly and replaced them in his greasy pocket-book.

"You know, sir, I always think I've been misjudged. Just see what they say about me: a pest of society, unscrupulous villain, contemptible scoundrel. Now just look at me. I ask you, do I look that sort of man? You know me, you're a judge of character, I've told you all about myself; do you think me a bad man?"

"My acquaintance with you is very slight," I answered with what I thought considerable tact.

"I wonder if the judge, I wonder if the jury, I wonder if the public ever thought about my side of the question. The public booed me when I was taken into the court and the police had to protect me from their violence. Did any of them think what what I'd done for these women?"

"You took their money."

"Of course I took their money. I had to live the same as anybody has to live. But what did I give them in exchange for their money?"

This was another rhetorical question and though he looked at me as though he expected an answer I held my tongue. Indeed I did not know the answer. His voice was raised and he spoke with emphasis. I could see that he was serious.

"I'll tell you what I gave them in exchange for their money. Romance. Look at this place." He made a wide, circular gesture that embraced the sea and the horizon. "There are a hundred places in England like this. Look at that sea and that sky; look at these lodging-houses; look at that pier and the front. Doesn't it make your heart sink? It's dead as mutton. It's all very well for you who come down here for a week or two because you're run down. But think of all those women who live here from one year's end to another. They haven't a chance. They hardly know anyone. They've just got enough money to live on and that's all. I wonder if you know how terrible their lives are. Their lives are just like the front, a long, straight, cemented walk that goes on and on from one seaside resort to another. Even in the season there's nothing for them. They're out of it. They might as well be dead. And then I come along. Mind you, I never made advances to a woman who wouldn't have gladly acknowledged to thirty-five. And I give them love. Why, many of them had never known what it was to have a man do them up behind. Many of them had never known what it was to sit on a bench in the dark with a man's arm round their waist. I bring them change and excitement. I give them a new pride in themselves. They were on the shelf and I come along quite quietly and I deliberately take them down. A little ray of sunshine in those drab lives, that's what I was. No wonder they jumped at me, no wonder they wanted me to go back to them. The only one who gave me away was the milliner; she said she was a widow, my private opinion is that she'd never been married at all. You say I did the dirty on them; why, I brought happiness and glamour into eleven lives that never thought they had even a dog's chance of it again. You say I'm a villain and a scoundrel, you're wrong. I'm a philanthropist. Five years, they gave me; they should have given me the medal of the Royal Humane Society."

He took out his empty packet of Gold Flake and looked at it with a melancholy shake of the head. When I handed him my cigarette case he helped himself without a word. I watched the spectacle of a good man struggling with his emotion.

"And what did I get out of it, I ask you?" he continued presently. "Board and lodging and enough to buy cigarettes. But I never was able to save, and the proof is that now, when I'm not so young as I was, I haven't got half a crown in my pocket." He gave me a sidelong glance. "It's a great come-down for me to find myself in this position. I've always paid my way and I've never asked a friend for a loan in all my life. I was wondering, sir, if you could oblige me with a trifle. It's humiliating to me to have to suggest it, but the fact is, if you could oblige me with a pound it would mean a great deal to me."

Well, I had certainly had a pound's worth of entertainment out of the bigamist and I dived for my pocket-book.

"I shall be very glad," I said.

He looked at the notes I took out.

"I suppose you couldn't make it two, sir?"

"I think I could."

I handed him a couple of pound notes and he gave a little sigh as he took them.

"You don't know what it means to a man who's used to the comforts of home life not to know where to turn for a night's lodging."

"But there is one thing I should like you to tell me," I said. "I shouldn't like you to think me cynical, but I had a notion that women on the whole take the maxim, 'It is more blessed to give than to receive,' as applicable exclusively to our sex. How did you persuade these respectable, and no doubt thrifty, women to entrust you so confidently with all their savings?"

An amused smile spread over his undistinguished features.

"Well, sir, you know what Shakespeare said about ambition o'erleaping itself. That's the explanation. Tell a woman you'll double her capital in six months if she'll give it you to handle and she won't be able to give you the money quick enough. Greed, that's what it is. Just greed."

It was a sharp sensation, stimulating to the appetite (like hot sauce with ice cream), to go from this diverting ruffian to the respectability, all lavender bags and crinolines, of the St. Clairs and Miss Porchester. I spent every evening with them now. No sooner had the ladies left him than Mr. St. Clair sent his compliments to my table and asked me to drink a glass of port with him. When we had finished it we went into the lounge and drank coffee. Mr. St. Clair enjoyed his glass of old brandy. The hour I thus spent with them was so exquisitely boring that it had for me a singular fascination. They were told by the manageress that I had written plays.

"We used often to go to the theatre when Sir Henry Irving was at the Lyceum," said Mr. St. Clair. "I once had the pleasure of meeting him. I was taken to supper at the Garrick Club by Sir Everard Millais and I was introduced to Mr. Irving, as he then was."

"Tell him what he said to you, Edwin," said Mrs. St. Clair.

Mr. St. Clair struck a dramatic attitude and gave not at all a bad imitation of Henry Irving.

" 'You have the actor's face, Mr. St. Clair,' he said to me. 'If you ever think of going on the stage, come to me and I will give you a part.' " Mr. St. Clair resumed his natural manner. "It was enough to turn a young man's head."

"But it didn't turn yours," I said.

"I will not deny that if I had been otherwise situated I might have allowed myself to be tempted. But I had my family to think of. It would have broken my father's heart if I had not gone into the business."

"What is that?" I asked.

"I am a tea merchant, sir. My firm is the oldest in the City of London. I have spent forty years of my life in combating to the best of my ability the desire of my fellow-countrymen to drink Ceylon tea instead of the China tea which was universally drunk in my youth."

I thought it charmingly characteristic of him to spend a lifetime in persuading the public to buy something they didn't want rather than something they did.

"But in his younger days my husband did a lot of amateur acting and he was thought very clever," said Mrs. St. Clair.

"Shakespeare, you know, and sometimes *The School for Scandal*. I would never consent to act trash. But that is a thing of the past. I had a gift, perhaps it was a pity to waste it, but it's too late now. When we have a dinner-party I sometimes let the ladies persuade me to recite the great soliloquies of Hamlet. But that is all I do."

Oh! Oh! Oh! I thought with shuddering fascination of those dinner-parties and wondered whether I should ever be asked to one of them. Mrs. St. Clair gave me a little smile, half shocked, half prim.

"My husband was very Bohemian as a young man," she said.

"I sowed my wild oats. I knew quite a lot of painters and writers, Wilkie Collins, for instance, and even men who wrote for the papers. Watts painted a portrait of my wife, and I bought a picture of Millais. I knew a number of the pre-Raphaelites."

"Have you a Rossetti?" I asked.

"No. I admired Rossetti's talent, but I could not approve of his private life. I would never buy a picture by an artist whom I should not care to ask to dinner at my house."

My brain was reeling when Miss Porchester, looking at her watch, said: "Are you not going to read to us to-night, Uncle Edwin?"

I withdrew.

It was while I was drinking a glass of port with Mr. St. Clair one evening that he told me the sad story of Miss Porchester. She was engaged to be married to a nephew of Mrs. St. Clair, a barrister, when it was discovered that he had had an intrigue with the daughter of his laundress.

"It was a terrible thing," said Mr. St. Clair. "A terrible thing. But of course my niece took the only possible course. She returned him his ring, his letters and his photograph, and said that she could never marry him. She implored him to marry the young person he had wronged and said she would be a sister to her. It broke her heart. She has never cared for anyone since."

"And did he marry the young person?"

Mr. St. Clair shook his head and sighed.

"No, we were greatly mistaken in him. It has been a sore grief to my dear wife to think that a nephew of hers should behave in such a dishonourable manner. Some time later we heard that he was engaged to a young lady in a very good position with ten thousand pounds of her own. I considered it my duty to write to her father and put the facts before him. He answered my letter in a most insolent fashion. He said he would much rather his son-in-law had a mistress before marriage than after."

"What happened then?"

"They were married and now my wife's nephew is one of His Majesty's Judges of the High Court, and his wife is My Lady. But we've never consented to receive them. When my wife's nephew was knighted Eleanor suggested that we should ask them to dinner, but my wife said that he should never darken our doors and I upheld her."

"And the laundress's daughter?"

"She married in her own class of life and has a public-house at Canterbury. My niece, who has a little money of her own, did everything for her and is godmother to her eldest child."

Poor Miss Porchester. She had sacrificed herself on the altar of Victorian morality and I am afraid the consciousness that she had behaved beautifully was the only benefit she had got from it.

"Miss Porchester is a woman of striking appearance," I said. "When she was younger she must have been perfectly lovely. I wonder she never married somebody else."

"Miss Porchester was considered a great beauty. Alma-Tadema admired her so much that he asked her to sit as a model for one of his pictures, but of course we couldn't very well allow that." Mr. St. Clair's tone conveyed that the suggestion had deeply outraged his sense of decency. "No, Miss Porchester never cared for anyone but her cousin. She never speaks of him and it is now thirty years since they parted, but I am convinced that she loves him still. She is a true woman, my dear sir, one life, one love, and though perhaps I regret that she has been deprived of the joys of marriage and motherhood I am bound to admire her fidelity."

But the heart of woman is incalculable and rash is the man who thinks she will remain in one stay. Rash, Uncle Edwin. You have known Eleanor for many years, for when, her mother having fallen into a decline and died, you brought the orphan to your comfortable and even luxurious house in Leinster Square, she was but a child; but what, when it comes down to brass tacks, Uncle Edwin, do you really know of Eleanor?

It was but two days after Mr. St. Clair had confided to me the touching story which explained why Miss Porchester had remained a spinster that, coming back to the hotel in the afternoon after a round of golf, the manageress came up to me in an agitated manner.

"Mr. St. Clair's compliments and will you go up to number twenty-seven the moment you come in."

"Certainly. But why?"

"Oh, there's a rare upset. They'll tell you."

I knocked at the door. I heard a "Come in, come in," which reminded me that Mr. St. Clair had played Shakespearean parts in probably the most refined amateur dramatic company in London. I entered and found Mrs. St. Clair lying on the sofa with a handkerchief soaked in eau-de-Cologne on her brow and a bottle of smelling-salts in her hand. Mr. St. Clair was standing in front of the fire in such a manner as to prevent anyone else in the room from obtaining any benefit from it.

"I must apologise for asking you to come up in this unceremonious fashion, but we are in great distress, and we thought you might be able to throw some light on what has happened."

His perturbation was obvious.

"What *has* happened?"

"Our niece, Miss Porchester, has eloped. This morning she sent in a message to my wife that she had one of her sick headaches. When she has one of her sick headaches she likes to be left absolutely alone and it wasn't till this afternoon that my wife went to see if there was anything she could do for her. The room was empty. Her trunk was packed. Her dressing-case with silver fittings was gone. And on the pillow was a letter telling us of her rash act."

"I'm very sorry," I said. "I don't know exactly what I can do."

"We were under the impression that you were the only gentleman at Elsom with whom she had any acquaintance."

His meaning flashed across me.

"I haven't eloped with her," I said. "I happen to be a married man."

"I see you haven't eloped with her. At the first moment we thought perhaps . . . but if it isn't you, who is it?"

"I'm sure I don't know."

"Show him the letter, Edwin," said Mrs. St. Clair from the sofa.

"Don't move, Gertrude. It will bring on your lumbago."

Miss Porchester had "her" sick headaches and Mrs. St. Clair

had "her" lumbago. What had Mr. St. Clair? I was willing to bet a fiver that Mr. St. Clair had "his" gout. He gave me the letter and I read it with an air of decent commiseration.

Dearest Uncle Edwin and Aunt Gertrude,

When you receive this I shall be far away. I am going to be married this morning to a gentleman who is very dear to me. I know I am doing wrong in running away like this, but I was afraid you would endeavour to set obstacles in the way of my marriage and since nothing would induce me to change my mind I thought it would save us all much unhappiness if I did it without telling you anything about it. My fiancé is a very retiring man, owing to his long residence in tropical countries not in the best of health, and he thought it much better that we should be married quite privately. When you know how radiantly happy I am I hope you will forgive me. Please send my box to the luggage office at Victoria Station.

Your loving niece,
Eleanor.

"I will never forgive her," said Mr. St. Clair as I returned him the letter. "She shall never darken my doors again. Gertrude, I forbid you ever to mention Eleanor's name in my hearing."

Mrs. St. Clair began to sob quietly.

"Aren't you rather hard?" I said. "Is there any reason why Miss Porchester shouldn't marry?"

"At her age," he answered angrily. "It's ridiculous. We shall be the laughing-stock of everyone in Leinster Square. Do you know how old she is? She's fifty-one."

"Fifty-four," said Mrs. St. Clair through her sobs.

"She's been the apple of my eye. She's been like a daughter to us. She's been an old maid for years. I think it's positively improper for her to think of marriage."

"She was always a girl to us, Edwin," pleaded Mrs. St. Clair.

"And who is this man she's married? It's the deception that rankles. She must have been carrying on with him under our very noses. She does not even tell us his name. I fear the very worst."

Suddenly I had an inspiration. That morning after breakfast I had gone out to buy myself some cigarettes and at the tobacconist's I ran across Mortimer Ellis. I had not seen him for some days.

"You're looking very spruce," I said.

His boots had been repaired and were neatly blacked, his

hat was brushed, he was wearing a clean collar and new gloves. I thought he had laid out my two pounds to advantage.

"I have to go to London this morning on business," he said.

I nodded and left the shop.

I remembered that a fortnight before, walking in the country, I had met Miss Porchester and, a few yards behind, Mortimer Ellis. Was it possible that they had been walking together and he had fallen back as they caught sight of me? By heaven, I saw it all.

"I think you said that Miss Porchester had money of her own," I said.

"A trifle. She has three thousand pounds."

Now I was certain. I looked at them blankly. Suddenly Mrs. St. Clair, with a cry, sprang to her feet.

"Edwin, Edwin, supposing he doesn't marry her?"

Mr. St. Clair at this put his hand to his head and in a state of collapse sank into a chair.

"The disgrace would kill me," he groaned.

"Don't be alarmed," I said. "He'll marry her all right. He always does. He'll marry her in church."

They paid no attention to what I said. I suppose they thought I'd suddenly taken leave of my senses. I was quite sure now. Mortimer Ellis had achieved his ambition after all. Miss Porchester completed the Round Dozen.

❖

The Human Element

I SEEM never to find myself in Rome but at the dead season. I pass through in August or September on my way somewhere or other and spend a couple of days revisiting places or pictures that are endeared to me by old associations. It is very hot then and the inhabitants of the city spend their day interminably strolling up and down the Corso. The Caffé Nazionale is crowded with people sitting at little tables for long hours with an empty cup of coffee in front of them and a glass of water. In the Sistine Chapel you see blond and sunburned Germans, in knickerbockers and shirts open at the neck, who have walked down the dusty roads of Italy with knapsacks on their shoulders; and in St. Peter's little groups of the pious, tired but eager, who have come on pilgrimage (at an inclusive rate) from some distant country. They are under the charge of a priest and they speak strange tongues. The Hotel Plaza then is cool and restful. The public rooms are dark, silent and spacious. In the lounge at tea-time the only persons are a young, smart officer and a woman with fine eyes, drinking iced lemonade, and they talk intimately, in low tones, with the unwearying fluency of their race. You go up to your room and read and write letters and come down again two hours later and they are still talking. Before dinner a few people saunter into the bar, but for the rest of the day it is empty and the barman has time to tell you of his mother in Switzerland and his experiences in New York. You discuss life and love and the high cost of liquor.

And on this occasion too I found that I had the hotel almost to myself. When the reception clerk took me to my room he told me that they were pretty full, but when, having bathed and changed, I came down again to the hall, the liftman, an old acquaintance, informed me that there were not more than a dozen people staying there. I was tired after a long and hot journey down Italy and had made up my mind to dine quietly in the hotel and go to bed early. It was late when I went into the dining-room, vast and brightly lit, but not more than three or four tables were occupied. I looked round me with satisfaction. It is very agreeable to find yourself alone in a great city which is yet not quite strange to you and in a large empty hotel. It gives you a delectable sense of freedom. I felt the wings of my spirit give a little flutter of delight. I had paused for ten minutes in the bar and had a dry Martini. I ordered myself a bottle of good red wine. My limbs were weary, but my soul responded wonderfully to food and drink and I began to feel a singular lightness of heart. I ate my soup and my fish and pleasant thoughts filled my mind. Scraps of dialogue occurred to me and my fancy played happily with the persons of a novel I was then at work on. I rolled a phrase on my tongue and it tasted better than the wine. I began to think of the difficulty of describing the looks of people in such a way as to make the reader see them as you see them. To me it has always been one of the most difficult things in fiction. What does the reader really get when you describe a face feature by feature? I should think nothing. And yet the plan some writers adopt of taking a salient characteristic, a crooked smile or shifty eyes, and emphasising that, though effective, avoids rather than solves the problem. I looked about me and wondered how I would describe the people at the tables round me. There was one man by himself just opposite and for practice I asked myself in what way I should treat him. He was a tall, spare fellow, and what I believe is generally called loose-limbed. He wore a dinner jacket and a boiled shirt. He had a rather long face and pale eyes; his hair was fairish and wavy, but it was growing thin, and the baldness of his temples gave him a certain nobility of brow. His features were undistinguished. His mouth and nose were like everybody else's; he was clean-shaven; his skin was naturally pale, but at the moment sunburned. His appearance suggested an intellectual but slightly commonplace distinction. He looked as though he might have been a lawyer or a don who played a pretty game of golf. I felt that he had good taste and was well-read and would be a very agreeable guest at a luncheon-party in Chelsea. But how the devil one was to describe him so as in a few lines to give a vivid, interesting and accurate picture I could not imagine. Perhaps it would be better to let all the rest go and dwell only on that rather fatigued distinction which on the whole was the most definite impression he gave. I looked at him reflectively. Suddenly he leaned forwards and gave me a stiff but courtly little bow. I have a ridiculous habit of flushing when I am taken aback and now I felt my cheeks redden. I was startled. I had been staring at him for several minutes as though he were a dummy. He must have thought me extremely rude. I nodded with a good deal of embarrassment and looked away. Fortunately at that moment the waiter was handing me a dish. To the best of my belief I had never seen the fellow before. I asked myself whether his bow was due to my insistent stare, which made him think that he had met me somewhere, or whether I had really run across him and completely forgotten. I have a bad memory for faces and I had in this case the excuse that he looked exactly like a great many other people. You saw a dozen of him at every golf course round London on a fine Sunday.

He finished his dinner before me. He got up, but on his way out stopped at my table. He stretched out his hand.

"How d'you do?" he said. "I didn't recognise you when you first came in. I wasn't meaning to cut you."

He spoke in a pleasant voice with the tones cultivated at Oxford and copied by many who have never been there. It was evident that he knew me and evident too that he had no notion that I did not also know him. I had risen and since he was a good deal taller than I he looked down on me. He held himself with a sort of languor. He stooped a little, which added to the impression he gave me of having about him an air that was vaguely apologetic. His manner was a trifle condescending and at the same time a trifle shy,

"Won't you come and have your coffee with me?" he said. "I'm quite alone."

"Yes, I shall be glad to."

He left me and I still had no notion who he was or where I had met him. I had noticed one curious thing about him. Not once during the few sentences we exchanged, when we shook hands, or when with a nod he left me, did even the suspicion of a smile cross his face. Seeing him more closely I observed that he was in his way good-looking; his features were regular, his grey eyes were handsome, he had a slim figure; but it was a way that I found uninteresting. A silly woman would say he looked romantic. He reminded you of one of the knights of Burne-Jones though he was on a larger scale and there was no suggestion that he suffered from the chronic colitis that afflicted those unfortunate creatures. He was the sort of man whom you expected to look wonderful in fancy dress till you saw him in it and then you found that he looked absurd.

Presently I finished my dinner and went into the lounge. He

was sitting in a large arm-chair and when he saw me he called a waiter. I sat down. The waiter came up and he ordered coffee and liqueurs. He spoke Italian very well. I was wondering by what means I could find out who he was without offending him. People are always a little disconcerted when you do not recognise them, they are so important to themselves, it is a shock to discover of what small importance they are to others. The excellence of his Italian recalled him to me. I remembered who he was and remembered at the same time that I did not like him. His name was Humphrey Carruthers. He was in the Foreign Office and he had a position of some importance. He was in charge of I know not what department. He had been attached to various embassies and I supposed that a sojourn in Rome accounted for his idiomatic Italian. It was stupid of me not to have seen at once that he was connected with the diplomatic service. He had all the marks of the profession. He had the supercilious courtesy that is so well calculated to put up the backs of the general public and the aloofness due to the consciousness the diplomat has that he is not as other men are, joined with the shyness occasioned by his uneasy feeling that other men do not quite realise it. I had known Carruthers for a good many years, but had met him infrequently, at luncheon-parties where I said no more than how do you do to him and at the opera where he gave me a cool nod. He was generally thought intelligent; he was certainly cultured. He could talk of all the right things. It was inexcusable of me not to have remembered him, for he had lately acquired a very considerable reputation as a writer of short stories. They had appeared first in one or other of those magazines that are founded now and then by well-disposed persons to give the intelligent reader something worthy of his attention and that die when their proprietors have lost as much money as they want to; and in their discreet and handsomely printed pages had excited as much attention as an exiguous circulation permitted. Then they were published in book form. They created a sensation. I have seldom read such unanimous praise in the weekly papers. Most of them gave the book a column and the Literary Supplement of *The Times* reviewed it not among the common ruck of novels but in a place by itself cheek by jowl with the memoirs of a distinguished statesman. The critics welcomed Humphrey Carruthers as a new star in the firmament. They praised his distinction, his subtlety, his delicate irony and his insight. They praised his style, his sense of beauty and his atmosphere. Here at last was a writer who had raised the short story from the depths into which in English-speaking countries it had fallen and here was work to which an Englishman could point with pride; it bore comparison with the best compositions in this manner of Finland, Russia and Czecho-Slovakia.

Three years later Humphrey Carruthers brought out his second book and the critics commented on the interval with satisfaction. Here was no hack prostituting his talent for money! The praise it received was perhaps a little cooler than that which welcomed his first volume, the critics had had time to collect themselves, but it was enthusiastic enough to have delighted any common writer who earns his living by his pen and there was no doubt that his position in the world of letters was secure and honourable. The story that attracted most commendation was called *The Shaving Mop* and all the best critics pointed out with what beauty the author in three or four pages had laid bare the tragic soul of a barber's assistant.

But his best known story, which was also his longest, was called *Week End*. It gave its title to his first book. It narrated the adventures of a number of people who left Paddington Station on Saturday afternoon to stay with friends at Taplow and on Monday morning returned to London. It was so delicate that it was a little difficult to know exactly what happened. A young man, parliamentary secretary to a Cabinet Minister, very nearly proposed to a baronet's daughter, but didn't. Two or three others went on the river in a punt. They all talked a great deal in an allusive way, but none of them ever finished a sentence and what they meant was very subtly indicated by dots and dashes. There were a good many descriptions of flowers in the garden and a sensitive picture of the Thames under the rain. It was all seen through the eyes of the German governess and everyone agreed that Carruthers had conveyed her outlook on the situation with quite delicious humour.

I read both Humphrey Carruthers' books. I think it part of the writer's business to make himself aware of what is being written by his contemporaries. I am very willing to learn and I thought I might discover in them something that would be useful to me. I was disappointed. I like a story to have a beginning, a middle, and an end. I have a weakness for a point. I think atmosphere is all very well, but atmosphere without anything else is like a frame without a picture; it has not much significance. But it may be that I could not see the merit of Humphrey Carruthers on account of defects in myself, and if I have described his two most successful stories without enthusiasm the cause perhaps lies in my own wounded vanity. For I was perfectly conscious that Humphrey Carruthers looked upon me as a writer of no account. I am convinced that he had never read a word I had written. The popularity I enjoyed was sufficient to persuade him that there was no occasion for him to give me any of his attention. For a moment, such was the stir he created, it looked as though he might himself be faced with that ignominy, but it soon appeared that his exquisite work was above the heads of the public. One can never tell how large the intelligentsia is, but one can tell fairly well how many of its members are prepared to pay money to patronise the arts they cherish. The plays that are of too fine a quality to attract the patrons of the commercial theatre can count on an audience of ten thousand, and the books that demand from their readers more comprehension than can be expected from the common herd sell twelve hundred copies. For the intelligentsia, notwithstanding their sensitiveness to beauty, prefer to go to the theatre on the nod and to get a book from the library.

I am sure this did not distress Carruthers. He was an artist. He was also a clerk in the Foreign Office. His reputation as a writer was distinguished; he was not interested in the vulgar, and to sell well would possibly have damaged his career. I could not surmise what had induced him to invite me to have coffee with him. It is true he was alone, but I should have supposed he found his thoughts excellent company, and I could not believe he imagined that I had anything to say that would interest him. Nevertheless I could not but see that he was doing his dreary best to be affable. He reminded me of where we had last met and we talked for a moment of common friends in London. He asked me how I came to be in Rome at this season and I told him. He volunteered the information that he had arrived that morning from Brindisi. Our conversation did not go easily and I made up my mind that as soon as I civilly could I would get up and leave him. But presently I had an odd sensation, I hardly know what caused it, that he was conscious of this and was desperately anxious not to give me the opportunity. I was surprised. I gathered my wits about me. I noticed that whenever I paused he broke in with a new topic. He was trying to find something to interest me so that I should stay. He was straining every nerve to be agreeable.

Surely he could not be lonely; with his diplomatic connections he must know plenty of people with whom he could have spent the evening. I wondered indeed that he was not dining at the Embassy; even though it was summer there must be someone there he knew. I noticed also that he never smiled. He talked with a sort of harsh eagerness as though he were afraid of a moment's silence and the sound of his voice shut out of his mind something that tortured him. It was very strange. Though I did not like him, though he meant nothing to me and to be with him irked me somewhat, I was against my will a trifle interested. I gave him a searching glance. I wondered if it was my fancy that I saw in those pale eyes of his the cowed look of a hunted dog and notwithstanding his neat features and his expression so civilly controlled, in his aspect something that suggested the grimace of a soul in pain. I could not understand. A dozen absurd notions flashed through my mind. I was not particularly sympathetic: like an old war horse scenting the fray I roused myself. I had been feeling very tired, but now I grew alert. My sensibilities put out tentacles. I was suddenly alive to every expression of his face and every gesture. I put aside the thought that had come to me that he had written a play and wanted my advice. These exquisite persons succumb strangely to the glamour of the footlights and they are not averse from getting a few tips from the craftsman whose competence they superciliously despise. No, it was not that. A single man in Rome, of æsthetic leanings, is liable to get into trouble, and I asked myself whether Carruthers had got into some difficulty to extricate himself from which the Embassy was the last place he could go to. The idealist, I have noticed, is apt at times to be imprudent in the affairs of the flesh. He sometimes finds love in places which the police inconveniently visit. I tittered in my heart. Even the gods laugh when a prig is caught in an equivocal situation.

Suddenly Carruthers said something that staggered me.

"I'm so desperately unhappy," he muttered.

He said it without warning. He obviously meant it. There was in his tone a sort of gasp. It might very well have been a sob. I cannot describe what a shock it was to me to hear him say those words. I felt as you do when you turn a corner of the street and on a sudden a great blast of wind meets you, takes your breath away, and nearly blows you off your feet. It was so unexpected. After all I hardly knew the fellow. We were not friends. I did not like him; he did not like me. I had never looked on him as quite human. It was amazing that a man so self-controlled, so urbane, accustomed to the usages of polite society, should break in upon a stranger with such a confession. I am naturally reticent. I should be ashamed, whatever I was suffering, to disclose my pain to another. I shivered. His weakness outraged me. For a moment I was filled with a passion of anger. How dared he thrust the anguish of his soul on me? I very nearly cried:

"What the hell do I care?"

But I didn't. He was sitting huddled up in the big arm-chair. The solemn nobility of his features, which reminded one of the marble statue of a Victorian statesman, had strangely crumpled and his face sagged. He looked almost as though he were going to cry. I hesitated. I faltered. I had flushed when he spoke and now I felt my face go white. He was a pitiable object.

"I'm awfully sorry," I said.

"Do you mind if I tell you about it?"

"No."

It was not the moment for many words. I suppose Carruthers was in the early forties. He was a well-made man, athletic in his way, and with a confident bearing. Now he looked twenty years older and strangely shrivelled. He reminded me of the dead soldiers I had seen during the war and how oddly small death had made them. I was embarrassed and looked away, but I felt his eyes claiming mine and I looked back.

"Do you know Betty Welldon-Burns?" he asked me.

"I used to meet her sometimes in London years ago. I've not seen her lately."

"She lives in Rhodes now, you know. I've just come from there. I've been staying with her."

"Oh?"

He hesitated.

"I'm afraid you'll think it awfully strange of me to talk to you like this. I'm at the end of my tether. If I don't talk to somebody I shall go off my head."

He had ordered double brandies with the coffee and now calling the waiter he ordered himself another. We were alone in the lounge. There was a little shaded lamp on the table between us. Because it was a public room he spoke in a low voice. The place gave one oddly enough a sense of intimacy. I cannot repeat all that Carruthers said to me in the words he said it; it would be impossible for me to remember them; it is more convenient for me to put it in my own fashion. Sometimes he could not bring himself to say a thing right out and I had to guess at what he meant. Sometimes he had not understood, and it seemed to me that in certain ways I saw the truth more clearly than he. Betty Welldon-Burns had a very keen sense of humour and he had none. I perceived a good deal that had escaped him.

I had met her a good many times, but I knew her chiefly from hearsay. In her day she had made a great stir in the little world of London and I had heard of her often before I met her. This was at a dance in Portland Place soon after the war. She was then already at the height of her celebrity. You could not open an illustrated paper without seeing in it a portrait of her, and her mad pranks were a staple of conversation. She was twenty-four. Her mother was dead, her father, the Duke of St. Erth, old and none too rich, spent most of the year in his Cornish castle and she lived in London with a widowed aunt. At the outbreak of the war she went to France. She was just eighteen. She was a nurse in a hospital at the Base and then drove a car. She acted in a theatrical tour designed to amuse the troops; she posed in tableaux at home for charitable purposes, held auctions for this object and that and sold flags in Piccadilly. Every one of her activities was widely advertised and in every new rôle she was profusely photographed. I suppose that she managed to have a very good time. But now that the war was over she was having her fling with a vengeance. Just then everybody a little lost his head. The young, relieved of the burden that for five years had oppressed them, indulged in one wild escapade after another. Betty took part in them all. Sometimes, for one reason or another, an account of them found its way into the newspapers and her name was always in the headline. At that time night clubs were in the first flush of their success and she was to be seen at them every night. She lived a life of hectic gaiety. It can only be described in a hackneyed phrase, because it was a hackneyed thing. The British public in its odd way took her to its heart and Lady Betty was a sufficient description of her throughout the British islands. Women mobbed her when she went to a wedding and the gallery applauded her at first nights as though she were a popular actress. Girls copied the way she did her hair and manufacturers of soap and face cream paid her money to use her photograph to advertise their wares.

Of course dull, stodgy people, the people who remembered and regretted the old order, disapproved of her. They sneered at her constant appearance in the limelight. They said she had an insane passion for self-advertisement. They said she was fast. They said she drank too much. They said she smoked too much. I will admit that nothing I had heard of her had predisposed me to think very well of her. I held cheap the women who seemed to look upon the war as an occasion to enjoy themselves and be talked about. I am bored by the papers in which you see photographs of persons in society walking in Cannes or playing golf at St. Andrew's. I have always found the Bright Young People extremely tedious. The gay life seems dull and stupid to the onlooker, but the moralist is unwise to judge it harshly. It is as absurd to be angry with the young things who lead it as with a litter of puppies scampering aimlessly around, rolling one another over and chasing their tails. It is well to bear it with fortitude if they cause havoc in the flower beds or break a piece of china. Some of them will be drowned because their points are not up to the mark and the rest will grow up into well-behaved dogs. Their unruliness is due only to the vitality of youth.

And it was vitality that was Betty's most shining characteristic. The urge of life flowed through her with a radiance that dazzled you. I do not think I shall ever forget the impression she made on me at the party at which I first saw her. She was like a mænad. She danced with an abandon that made you laugh, so obvious was her intense enjoyment of the music and the movement of her young limbs. Her hair was brown, slightly disordered by the vigour of her gestures, but her eyes were deep blue, and her skin was milk and roses. She was a great beauty, but she had none of the coldness of great beauty. She laughed constantly and when she was not laughing she smiled and her eyes danced with the joy of living. She was like a milkmaid on the farmstead of the gods. She had the strength and health of the people; and yet the independence of her bearing, a sort of noble frankness of carriage, suggested the great lady. I do not quite know how to put the feeling she gave me, that though so simple and unaffected she was not unconscious of her station. I fancied that if occasion arose she could get on her dignity and be very grand indeed. She was charming to everybody because, probably without being quite aware of it, in the depths of her heart she felt that the rest of the world was perfectly insignificant. I understood why the factory girls in the East End adored her and why half a million people who had never seen her except in a photograph looked upon her with the intimacy of personal friendship. I was introduced to her and she spent a few minutes talking to me. It was extraordinarily flattering to see the interest she showed in you; you knew she could not really be so pleased to meet you as she seemed or so delighted with what you said, but it was very attractive. She had the gift of being able to jump over the first difficult phases of acquaintance and you had not known her for five minutes before you felt you had known her all her life. She was snatched away from me by someone who wanted to dance with her and she surrendered herself to her partner's arms with just the same eager happiness as she had shown when she sank into a chair by my side. I was surprised when I met her at luncheon a fortnight later to find that she remembered exactly what we had talked about during those noisy ten minutes at the dance. A young woman with all the social graces.

I mentioned the incident to Carruthers.

"She was no fool," he said. "Very few people knew how intelligent she was. She wrote some very good poetry. Because she was so gay, because she was so reckless and never cared a damn for anybody, people thought she was scatter-brained. Far from it. She was as clever as a monkey. You would never have thought she'd had the time to read all the things she had. I don't suppose anyone knew that side of her as well as I did. We used to take walks together, in the country at week-ends, and in London we'd drive out to Richmond Park and walk there, and talk. She loved flowers and trees and grass. She was interested in everything. She had a lot of information and a lot of sense. There was nothing she couldn't talk about. Sometimes when we'd been for a walk in the afternoon and we met at a night club and she'd had a couple of glasses of champagne, that was enough to make her completely buffy, you know, and she was the life and soul of the party, I couldn't help thinking how amazed the rest of them would be if they knew how seriously we'd been talking only a few hours before. It was an extraordinary contrast. There seemed to be two entirely different women in her."

Carruthers said all this without a smile. He spoke with the melancholy he might have used if he had been speaking of some person snatched from the pleasant company of the living by untimely death. He gave a deep sigh.

"I was madly in love with her. I proposed to her half a dozen times. Of course I knew I hadn't a chance, I was only a very junior clerk at the F.O., but I couldn't help myself. She refused me, but she was always frightfully nice about it. It never made any difference to our friendship. You see, she really liked me. I gave her something that other people didn't. I always thought that she was really fonder of me than of anybody. I was crazy about her."

"I don't suppose you were the only one," I said, having to say something.

"Far from it. She used to get dozens of love letters from men she'd never seen or heard of, farmers in Africa, miners, and policemen in Canada. All sorts of people proposed to her. She could have married anyone she liked."

"Even royalty, one heard."

"Yes, she said she couldn't stand the life. And then she married Jimmie Welldon-Burns."

"People were rather surprised, weren't they?"

"Did you ever know him?"

"No, I don't think so. I may have met him, but he left no impression on me."

"He wouldn't. He was the most insignificant fellow that ever breathed. His father was a big manufacturer up in the North. He'd made a lot of money during the war and bought a baronetcy. I believe he hadn't an aitch to his name. Jimmy was at Eton with me, they'd tried hard to make a gentleman of him, and in London after the war he was about a good deal. He was always willing to throw a party. No one ever paid any attention to him. He just paid the bill. He was the most crashing bore. You know, rather prim, terribly polite; he made you rather uncomfortable because he was so anxious not to do the wrong thing. He always wore his clothes as though he'd just put them on for the first time and they were a little too tight for him."

When Carruthers innocently opened his *Times* one morning and casting his eyes down the fashionable intelligence of the day saw that a marriage had been arranged between Elizabeth, only daughter of the Duke of St. Erth, and James, eldest son of Sir John Welldon-Burns, Bart., he was dumbfounded. He rang Betty up and asked if it was true.

"Of course," she said.

He was so shocked that for the moment he found nothing to say. She went on speaking.

"He's bringing his family to luncheon to-day to meet father. I dare say it'll be a bit grim. You might stand me a cocktail at Claridge's to fortify me, will you?"

"At what time?" he asked.

"One."

"All right. I'll meet you there."

He was waiting for her when she came in. She walked with a sort of spring as though her eager feet itched to break into a dance. She was smiling. Her eyes shone with the joy that suffused her because she was alive and the world was such a pleasant place to live in. People recognising her whispered to one another as she came in. Carruthers really felt that she brought sunshine and the scent of flowers into the sober but rather overwhelming splendour of Claridge's lounge. He did not wait to say how do you do to her.

"Betty, you can't do it," he said. "It's simply out of the question."

"Why?"

"He's awful."

"I don't think he is. I think he's rather nice."

A waiter came up and took their order. Betty looked at Carruthers with those beautiful blue eyes of hers that managed to be at the same time so gay and so tender.

"He's such a frightful bounder, Betty."

"Oh, don't be so silly, Humphrey. He's just as good as anybody else. I think you're rather a snob."

"He's so dull."

"No, he's rather quiet. I don't know that I want a husband who's too brilliant. I think he'll make a very good background. He's quite good-looking and he has nice manners."

"My God, Betty."

"Oh, don't be idiotic, Humphrey."

"Are you going to pretend you're in love with him?"

"I think it would be tactful, don't you?"

"Why are you going to marry him?"

She looked at him coolly.

"He's got pots of money. I'm nearly twenty-six."

There was nothing much more to be said. He drove her back to her aunt's house. She had a very grand marriage, with dense crowds lining the approach to St. Margaret's, Westminster, presents from practically all the royal family, and the honeymoon was passed on the yacht her father-in-law had lent them. Carruthers applied for a post abroad and was sent to Rome (I was right in guessing that he had thus acquired his admirable Italian) and later to Stockholm. Here he was counsellor and here he wrote the first of his stories.

Perhaps Betty's marriage had disappointed the British public who expected much greater things of her, perhaps only that as a young married woman she no longer appealed to the popular sense of romance; the fact was plain that she soon lost her place in the public eye. You ceased to hear very much about her. Not long after the marriage it was rumoured that she was going to have a baby and a little later that she had had a miscarriage. She did not drop out of society, I suppose she continued to see her friends, but her activities were no longer spectacular. She was certainly but seldom seen any more in those raffish assemblies where the members of a tarnished aristocracy hob-nob with the hangers-on of the arts and flatter themselves that they are being at once smart and cultured. People said she was settling down. They wondered how she was getting on with her husband and no sooner did they do this than they concluded that she was not getting on very well. Presently gossip said that Jimmie was drinking too much and then, a year or two later, one heard that he had contracted tuberculosis. The Welldon-Burns' spent a couple of winters in Switzerland. Then the news spread that they had separated and Betty had gone to live in Rhodes. An odd place to choose.

"It must be deadly," her friends said.

A few of them went to stay with her now and then and came back with reports of the beauty of the island and the leisurely charm of the life. But of course it was very lonely. It seemed strange that Betty, with her brilliance and her energy, should be content to settle there. She had bought a house. She knew no one but a few Italian officials, there was indeed no one to know; but she seemed perfectly happy. Her visitors could not make it out. But the life of London is busy and memories are short. People ceased to concern themselves with her. She was forgotten. Then, a few weeks before I met Humphrey Carruthers in Rome, *The Times* announced the death of Sir James Welldon-Burns, second baronet. His younger brother succeeded him in the title. Betty had never had a child.

Carruthers continued to see her after the marriage. Whenever he came to London they lunched together. She had the ability to take up a friendship after a long separation as though no passage of time had intervened, so that there was never any strangeness in their meetings. Sometimes she asked him when he was going to marry.

"You're getting on, you know, Humphrey. If you don't marry soon you'll get rather old-maidish."

"D'you recommend marriage?"

It was not a very kindly thing to say, because like everyone else he had heard that she was not getting on too well with her husband, but her remark piqued him.

"On the whole. I think probably an unsatisfactory marriage is better than no marriage at all."

"You know quite well that nothing would induce me to marry and you know why."

"Oh, my dear, you're not going to pretend that you're still in love with me?"

"I am."

"You are a damned fool."

"I don't care."

She smiled at him. Her eyes always had that look, partly bantering, partly tender, that gave him such a happy pain in his heart. Funny, he could almost localise it.

"You're rather sweet, Humphrey. You know I'm devoted to you, but I wouldn't marry you even if I were free."

When she left her husband and went to live in Rhodes Carruthers ceased to see her. She never came to England. They maintained an active correspondence.

"Her letters were wonderful," he said. "You seemed to hear her talking. They were just like her. Clever and witty, inconsequent and yet so shrewd."

He suggested coming to Rhodes for a few days, but she thought he had better not. He understood why. Everyone knew he had been madly in love with her. Everyone knew he was still. He did not know in what circumstances exactly the Welldon-Burns' had separated. It might be that there had been a good deal of bad feeling. Betty might think that his presence on the island would compromise her.

"She wrote a charming letter to me when my first book came out. You know I dedicated it to her. She was surprised that I had done anything so good. Everyone was very nice about it, and she was delighted with that. I think her pleasure was the chief thing that pleased me. After all I'm not a professional writer, you know: I don't attach much importance to literary success."

Fool, I thought, and liar. Did he think I had not noticed the self-satisfaction that consumed him on account of the favourable reception of his books? I did not blame him for feeling that, nothing could be more pardonable, but why be at such pains to deny it. But it was doubtless true that it was mostly for Betty's sake that he relished the notoriety they had brought him. He had a positive achievement to offer her. He could lay at her feet now not only his love, but a distinguished reputation. Betty was not very young any more, she was thirty-six; her marriage, her sojourn abroad, had changed things; she was no longer surrounded by suitors; she had lost the halo with which the public admiration had surrounded her. The distance between them was no longer insuperable. He alone had remained faithful through the years. It was absurd that she should continue to bury her beauty, her wit, her social grace in an island in a corner of the Mediterranean. He knew she was fond of him. She could hardly fail to be touched by his long devotion. And the life he had to offer her now was one that he knew would appeal to her. He made up his mind to ask her once more to marry him. He was able to get away towards the end of July. He wrote and said that he was going to spend his leave in the Greek islands and if she would be glad to see him he would stop off at Rhodes for a day or two, where he had heard the Italians had opened a very good hotel. He put his suggestion in this casual way out of delicacy. His training at the Foreign Office had taught him to eschew abruptness. He never willingly put himself in a position from which he could not if necessary withdraw with tact. Betty sent him a telegram in reply. She said it was too marvellous that he was coming to Rhodes and of course he must come and stay with her, for at least a fortnight, and he was to wire what boat he was coming by.

He was in a state of wild excitement when at last the ship he had taken at Brindisi steamed, soon after sunrise, into the neat and pretty harbour of Rhodes. He had hardly slept a wink all night and getting up early had watched the island loom grandly out of the dawn and the sun rise over the summer sea. Boats came out as the ship dropped her anchor. The gangway was lowered. Humphrey, leaning over the rail, watched the doctor and the port officials and the hotel couriers swarm up it. He was the only

Englishman on board. His nationality was obvious. A man came on deck and immediately walked up to him.

"Are you Mr. Carruthers?"

"Yes."

He was about to smile and put out his hand, but he perceived in the twinkling of an eye that the person who addressed him, an Englishman like himself, was not a gentleman. Instinctively his manner, remaining exceedingly polite, became a trifle stiff. Of course Carruthers did not tell me this, but I see the scene so clearly that I have no hesitation in describing it.

"Her ladyship hopes you don't mind her not coming to meet you, but the boat got in so early and it's more than an hour's drive to where we live."

"Oh, of course. Her ladyship well?"

"Yes, thank you. Got your luggage ready?"

"Yes."

"If you'll show me where it is I'll tell one of these fellows to put it in a boat. You won't have any difficulty at the Customs. I've fixed that up all right, and then we'll get off. Have you had breakfast?"

"Yes, thank you."

The man was not quite sure of his aitches. Carruthers wondered who he was. You could not say he was uncivil, but he was certainly a little offhand. Carruthers knew that Betty had rather a large estate; perhaps he was her agent. He seemed very competent. He gave the porters instructions in fluent Greek and when they got in the boat and the boatmen asked for more money than he gave them, he said something that made them laugh and they shrugged their shoulders satisfied. The luggage was passed through the Customs without examination, Humphrey's guide shaking hands with the officials, and they went into a sunny place where a large yellow car was standing.

"Are you going to drive me?" asked Carruthers.

"I'm her ladyship's chauffeur."

"Oh, I see. I didn't know."

He was not dressed like a chauffeur. He wore white duck trousers and espadrilles on his bare feet, a white tennis shirt, with no tie and open at the neck, and a straw hat. Carruthers frowned. Betty oughtn't to let her chauffeur drive the car like that. It was true that he had had to get up before daybreak and it looked like being a hot drive up to the villa. Perhaps under ordinary conditions he wore uniform. Though not so tall as Carruthers, who was six feet one in his socks, he was not short; but he was broad-shouldered and squarely built, so that he looked stocky. He was not fat, but plump rather; he looked as though he had a hearty appetite and ate well. Young still, thirty perhaps or thirty-one, he had already a massive look and one day would be very beefy. Now he was a hefty fellow. He had a broad face deeply sunburned, a short thickish nose and a somewhat sullen look. He wore a short fair moustache. Oddly enough Carruthers had a vague feeling that he had seen him before.

"Have you been with her ladyship long?" he asked.

"Well, I have, in a manner of speaking."

Carruthers became a trifle stiffer. He did not quite like the manner in which the chauffeur spoke. He wondered why he did not say "sir" to him. He was afraid Betty had let him get a little above himself. It was like her to be a bit careless about such things. But it was a mistake. He'd give her a hint when he got a chance. Their eyes met for an instant and he could have sworn that there was a twinkle of amusement in the chauffeur's. Carruthers could not imagine why. He was not aware that there was anything amusing in him.

"That, I suppose, is the old city of the Knights," he said distantly, pointing to the battlemented walls.

"Yes. Her ladyship'll take you over. We get a rare lot of tourists here in the season."

Carruthers wished to be affable. He thought it would be nicer of him to offer to sit by the chauffeur rather than behind by himself and was just going to suggest it when the matter was taken out of his hands. The chauffeur told the porters to put Carruther's bags at the back, and settling himself at the wheel said:

"Now if you'll hop in we'll get along."

Carruthers sat down beside him and they set off along a white road that ran by the sea. In a few minutes they were in the open country. They drove in silence. Carruthers was a little on his dignity. He felt that the chauffeur was inclined to be familiar and he did not wish to give him occasion to be so. He flattered himself that he had a manner with him that puts his inferiors in their place. He thought with sardonic grimness that it would not be long before the chauffeur would be calling him "sir". But the morning was lovely; the white road ran between olive groves and the farmhouses they passed now and then, with their white walls and flat roofs, had an Oriental look that took the fancy. And Betty was waiting for him. The love in his heart disposed him to kindliness towards all men and lighting himself a cigarette he thought it would be a generous act to offer the chauffeur one too. After all, Rhodes was very far away from England and the age was democratic. The chauffeur accepted the gift and stopped the car to light up.

"Have you got the baccy?" he asked suddenly.

"Have I got what?"

The chauffeur's face fell.

"Her ladyship wired to you to bring two pounds of Player's Navy Cut. That's why I fixed it up with the Customs people not to open your luggage."

"I never got the wire."

"Damn!"

"What on earth does her ladyship want with two pounds of Player's Navy Cut?"

He spoke with hauteur. He did not like the chauffeur's exclamation. The fellow gave him a sidelong glance in which Carruthers read a certain insolence.

"We can't get it here," he said briefly.

He threw away with what looked very like exasperation the Egyptian cigarette Carruthers had given him and started off again. He looked sulky. He said nothing more. Carruthers felt that his efforts at sociability had been a mistake. For the rest of the journey he ignored the chauffeur. He adopted the frigid manner that he had used so successfully as secretary at the Embassy when a member of the British public came to him for assistance. For some time they had been running up hill and now they came to a long low wall and then to an open gate. The chauffeur turned in.

"Have we arrived?" cried Carruthers.

"Sixty-five kilometres in fifty-seven minutes," said the chauffeur, a smile suddenly showing his fine white teeth. "Not so bad considering the road."

He sounded his klaxon shrilly. Carruthers was breathless with excitement. They drove up a narrow road through an olive grove, and came to a low, white, rambling house. Betty was standing at the door. He jumped out of the car and kissed her on both cheeks. For a moment he could not speak. But subconsciously he noticed that at the door stood an elderly butler in white ducks and a couple of footmen in the fustanellas of their country. They were smart and picturesque. Whatever Betty permitted her chauffeur it was evident that the house was run in the civilised style suited to her station. She led him through the hall, a large apartment with whitewashed walls in which he was vaguely conscious of handsome furniture, into the drawing-room. This also was large and low, with the same whitewashed walls, and he had immediately an impression of comfort and luxury.

"The first thing you must do is to come and look at my view," she said.

"The first thing I must do is to look at you."

She was dressed in white. Her arms, her face, her neck, were deeply burned by the sun; her eyes were bluer than he had ever seen them and the whiteness of her teeth was startling. She looked extremely well. She was very trim and neat. Her hair was waved, her nails were manicured; he had had a moment's anxiety that in the easy life she led on this romantic isle she had let herself go.

"Upon my word you look eighteen, Betty. How do you manage it?"

"Happiness," she smiled.

It gave him a momentary pang to hear her say this. He did not want her to be too happy. He wanted to give her happiness. But now she insisted on taking him out on the terrace. The drawing-room had five long windows that led out to it and from the terrace the olive-clad hill tumbled steeply to the sea. There was a tiny bay below in which a white boat, mirrored on the calm water, lay at anchor. On a further hill, round the corner, you saw the white houses of a Greek village and beyond it a huge grey crag surmounted by the battlements of a medieval castle.

"It was one of the strongholds of the Knights," she said. "I'll take you up there this evening."

The scene was quite lovely. It took your breath away. It was peaceful and yet it had a strange air of life. It moved you not to contemplation, but stirred you to activity.

"You've got the tobacco all right, I suppose."

He started.

"I'm afraid I haven't. I never got your wire."

"But I wired to the Embassy and I wired to the Excelsior."

"I stayed at the Plaza."

"What a bore! Albert'll be furious."

"Who is Albert?"

"He drove you out. Player's is the only tobacco he likes and he can't get it here."

"Oh, the chauffeur." He pointed to the boat that lay gleaming beneath them. "Is that the yacht I've heard about?"

"Yes."

It was a large caïque that Betty had bought, fitted with a motor auxiliary and smartened up. In it she wandered about the Greek islands. She had been as far north as Athens and as far south as Alexandria.

"We'll take you for a trip if you can spare the time," she said. "You ought to see Cos while you're here."

"Who runs it for you?"

"Of course I have a crew, but Albert chiefly. He's very clever with motors and all that."

He did not know why it gave him a vague discomfort to hear her speak of the chauffeur again. Carruthers wondered if she did not leave too much in his hands. It was a mistake to give a servant too much leeway.

"You know, I couldn't help thinking I'd seen Albert before somewhere. But I can't place him."

She smiled brightly, her eyes shining, with that sudden gaiety of hers that gave her face its delightful frankness.

"You ought to remember him. He was the second footman at Aunt Louise's. He must have opened the door to you hundreds of times."

Aunt Louise was the aunt with whom Betty had lived before her marriage.

"Oh, is that who he is? I suppose I must have seen him there without noticing him. How does he happen to be here?"

"He comes from our place at home. When I married he wanted to come with me, so I took him. He was Jimmie's valet for some time and then I sent him to some motor works, he was mad about cars, and eventually I took him on as my chauffeur. I don't know what I should do without him now."

"Don't you think it's rather a mistake to get too dependent on a servant?"

"I don't know. It never occurred to me."

Betty showed him the rooms that had been got ready for him, and when he had changed they strolled down to the beach. A dinghy was waiting for them and they rowed out to the caïque and bathed from there. The water was warm and they sunned themselves on the deck. The caïque was roomy, comfortable and luxurious. Betty showed him over and they came upon Albert tinkering with the engines. He was in filthy overalls, his hands were black and his face was smeared with grease.

"What's the matter, Albert?" said Betty.

He raised himself and faced her respectfully.

"Nothing, m'lady. I was just 'aving a look round."

"There are only two things Albert loves in the world. One is the car and the other's the yacht. Isn't that true, Albert?"

She gave him a gay smile and Albert's rather stolid face lit up. He showed his beautiful white teeth.

"That's true, m'lady."

"He sleeps on board, you know. We rigged up a very nice cabin for him aft."

Carruthers fell into the life very easily. Betty had bought the estate from a Turkish pasha exiled to Rhodes by Abdul Hamid and she had added a wing to the picturesque house. She had made a wild garden of the olive grove that surrounded it. It was planted with rosemary and lavender and asphodel, broom that she had had sent from England and the roses for which the island was famous. In the spring, she told him, the ground was carpeted with anemones. But when she showed him her property, telling him her plans and what alterations she had in mind, Carruthers could not help feeling a little uneasy.

"You talk as though you were going to live here all your life," he said.

"Perhaps I am," she smiled.

"What nonsense! At your age."

"I'm getting on for forty, old boy," she answered lightly.

He discovered with satisfaction that Betty had an excellent cook and it gratified his sense of propriety to dine with her in the splendid dining-room, with its Italian furniture, and be waited on by the dignified Greek butler and the two handsome footmen in their flamboyant uniforms. The house was furnished with taste; the rooms contained nothing that was not essential, but every piece was good. Betty lived in considerable state. When, the day after his arrival, the Governor with several members of his staff came over to dinner she displayed all the resources of the household. The Governor entering the house passed between a double row of flunkeys magnificent in their starched petticoats, embroidered jackets and velvet caps. It was almost a bodyguard. Carruthers liked the grand style. The dinner-party was very gay. Betty's Italian was fluent and Carruthers spoke it perfectly. The young officers in the Governor's suite were uncommonly smart in their uniforms. They were very attentive to Betty and she treated them with easy cordiality. She chaffed them. After dinner the gramophone was turned on and they danced with her one after the other.

When they were gone Carruthers asked her:

"Aren't they all madly in love with you?"

"I don't know about that. They hint occasionally at alliances permanent or otherwise, but they take it very good-naturedly when I decline with thanks."

They were not serious. The young ones were callow and the not so young were fat and bald. Whatever they might feel about her Carruthers could not for a moment believe that Betty would make a fool of herself with a middle-class Italian. But a day or two later a curious thing happened. He was in his rooms dressing for dinner; he heard a man's voice outside in the passage, he could not hear what was said or what language was spoken, and then ringing out suddenly Betty's laughter. It was a charming laugh, rippling and gay, like a young girl's, and it had a joyous abandon that was infectious. But whom could she be laughing with? It was not the way you would laugh with a servant. It had a curious intimacy. It may seem strange that Carruthers read all this into a peal of laughter, but it must be remembered that Carruthers was very subtle. His stories were remarkable for such touches.

When they met presently on the terrace and he was shaking a cocktail he sought to gratify his curiosity.

"What were you laughing your head off over just now? Has anyone been here?"

"No."

She looked at him with genuine surprise.

"I thought one of your Italian officers had come to pass the time of day."

"No."

Of course the passage of years had had its effect on Betty. She was beautiful, but her beauty was mature. She had always had assurance, but now she had repose; her serenity was a feature, like her blue eyes and her candid brow, that was part of her beauty. She seemed to be at peace with all the world; it rested you to be with her as it rested you to lie among the olives within sight of the wine-coloured sea. Though she was as gay and witty as ever, the seriousness which once he had been alone to know was now patent. No one could accuse her any longer of being scatter-brained; it was impossible not to perceive the fineness of her character. It had even nobility. That was not a trait it was usual to find in the modern woman and Carruthers said to himself that she was a throw-back; she reminded him of the great ladies of the eighteenth century. She had always had a feeling for literature, the poems she wrote as a girl were graceful and melodious, and he was more interested than surprised when she told him that she had undertaken a solid historical work. She was getting materials together for an account of the Knights of St. John in Rhodes. It was a story of romantic incidents. She took Carruthers to the city and showed him the noble battlements and together they wandered through austere and stately buildings. They strolled up the silent Street of the Knights with the lovely stone façades and the great coats of arms that recalled a dead chivalry. She had a surprise for him here. She had bought one of the old houses and with affectionate care had restored it to its old state. When you entered the little courtyard, with its carved stone stairway, you were taken back into the middle ages. It had a tiny walled garden in which a fig-tree grew and roses. It was small and secret and silent. The old knights had been in contact with the East long enough to have acquired Oriental ideas of privacy.

"When I'm tired of the villa I come here for two or three days and picnic. It's a relief sometimes not to be surrounded by people."

"But you're not alone here?"

"Practically."

There was a little parlour austerely furnished.

"What is this?" said Carruthers pointing with a smile to a copy of *The Sporting Times* that lay on a table.

"Oh, that's Albert's. I suppose he left it here when he came to meet you. He has *The Sporting Times* and the *News of the World* sent him every week. That is how he keeps abreast of the great world."

She smiled tolerantly. Next to the parlour was a bedroom with nothing much in it but a large bed.

"The house belonged to an Englishman. That's partly why I bought it. He was a Sir Giles Quern, and one of my ancestors married a Mary Quern who was a cousin of his. They were Cornish people."

Finding that she could not get on with her history without such a knowledge of Latin as would enable her to read the medieval documents with ease, Betty had set about learning the classical language. She troubled to acquire only the elements of grammar and then started, with a translation by her side, to read the authors that interested her. It is a very good method of learning a language and I have often wondered that it is not used in schools. It saves all the endless turning over of dictionaries and the fumbling search for meaning. After nine months Betty could read Latin as fluently as most of us can read French. It seemed a trifle ridiculous to Carruthers that this lovely, brilliant creature should take her work so seriously and yet he was moved; he would have liked to snatch her in his arms and kiss her, not at that moment as a woman, but as a precocious child whose cleverness suddenly enchants you. But later he reflected upon what she had told him. He was of course a very clever man, otherwise he could not have attained the position he held in the Foreign Office, and it would be silly to claim that those two books of his could have made so much stir without some merit; if I have made him look a bit of a fool it is only because I did not happen to like him, and if I have derided his stories it is merely because stories of that sort seem to me rather silly. He had tact and insight. He had a conviction that there was but one way to win her. She was in a groove and happy in it, her plans were definite; but her life at Rhodes was so well-ordered, so complete and satisfying, that for that very reason its hold over her could be combated. His chance was to arouse in her the restlessness that lies deep in the heart of the English. So he talked to Betty of England and London, their common friends and the painters, writers and musicians with whom his literary success had brought him acquaintance. He talked of the Bohemian parties in Chelsea, and of the opera, of trips to Paris *en bande* for a fancy-dress ball or to Berlin to see the new plays. He recalled to her imagination a life rich and easy, varied, cultured, intelligent and highly civilised. He tried to make her feel that she was stagnating in a backwater. The world was hurrying on, from one new and interesting phase to another, and she was standing still. They were living in a thrilling age and she was missing it. Of course he did not tell her this; he left her to infer it. He was amusing and spirited, he had an excellent memory for a good

story, he was whimsical and gay. I know I have not made Humphrey
Carruthers witty any more than I have shown Lady Betty brilliant.
The reader must take my word for it that they were. Carruthers
was generally reckoned an entertaining companion, and that is
half the battle; people were willing to find him amusing and they
vowed the things he said were marvellous. Of course his wit
was social. It needed a particular company, who understood his
allusions and shared his exclusive sense of humour. There are a
score of journalists in Fleet Street who could knock spots off the
most famous of the society wits; it is their business to be witty
and brilliance is in their day's work. There are few of the society
beauties whose photographs appear in the papers who could get a
job at three pounds a week in the chorus of a song-and-dance show.
Amateurs must be judged with tolerance. Carruthers knew that
Betty enjoyed his society. They laughed a great deal together.
The days passed in a flash.

"I shall miss you terribly when you go," she said in her frank
way. "It's been a treat having you here. You are a sweet,
Humphrey."

"Have you only just discovered it?"

He patted himself on the back. His tactics had been right.
It was interesting to see how well his simple plan had worked.
Like a charm. The vulgar might laugh at the Foreign Office, but
there was no doubt it taught you how to deal with difficult people.
Now he had but to choose his opportunity. He felt that Betty had
never been more attached to him. He would wait till the end of
his visit. Betty was emotional. She would be sorry that he was
going. Rhodes would seem very dull without him. Whom would
she have to talk to when he was gone? After dinner they usually
sat on the terrace looking at the starry sea; the air was warm and
balmy and vaguely scented: it was then he would ask her to marry
him, on the eve of his departure. He felt it in his bones that she
would accept him.

One morning when he had been in Rhodes a little over a week,
he happened to be coming upstairs as Betty was walking along the
passage.

"You've never shown me your room, Betty," he said.

"Haven't I? Come in and have a look now. It's rather nice."

She turned back and he followed her in. It was over the drawing-
room and nearly as large. It was furnished in the Italian style,
and as is the present way more like a sitting-room than a bedroom.

There were fine Paninis on the walls and one or two handsome cabinets. The bed was Venetian and beautifully painted.

"That's a couch of rather imposing dimensions for a widow lady," he said facetiously.

"It is enormous, isn't it? But it was so lovely, I had to buy it. It cost a fortune."

His eye took in the bed-table by the side. There were two or three books on it, a box of cigarettes, and on an ash-tray a briar pipe. Funny! What on earth had Betty got a pipe by her bed for?

"Do look at this *cassone*. Isn't the painting marvellous? I almost cried when I found it."

"I suppose that cost a fortune too."

"I daren't tell you what I paid."

When they were leaving the room he cast another glance at the bed-table. The pipe had vanished.

It was odd that Betty should have a pipe in her bedroom, she certainly didn't smoke one herself, and if she had would have made no secret of it, but of course there were a dozen reasonable explanations. It might be a present she was making to somebody, one of the Italians or even Albert, he had not been able to see if it was new or old, or it might be a pattern that she was going to ask him to take home to have others of the same sort sent out to her. After the moment's perplexity, not altogether unmingled with amusement, he put the matter out of his mind. They were going for a picnic that day, taking their luncheon with them, and Betty was driving him herself. They had arranged to go for a cruise of a couple of days before he left so that he should see Patmos and Cos, and Albert was busy with the engines of the caïque. They had a wonderful day. They visited a ruined castle and climbed a mountain on which grew asphodel, hyacinth and narcissus, and returned dead beat. They separated not long after dinner and Carruthers went to bed. He read for a little and then turned out his light. But he could not sleep. It was hot under his mosquito-net. He turned and tossed. Presently he thought he would go down to the little beach at the foot of the hill and bathe. It was not more than three minutes' walk. He put on his espadrilles and took a towel. The moon was full and he saw it shining on the sea through the olive-trees. But he was not alone to have thought that this radiant night would be lovely to bathe in, for just before he came out on to the beach sounds reached his ears. He muttered a little damn of vexation, some of Betty's servants were bathing, and he could not very well disturb them. The olive-trees came almost to the water's edge and undecided he stood in their shelter. He heard a voice that gave him a sudden start.

"Where's my towel?"

English. A woman waded out of the water and stood for a moment at its edge. From the darkness a man came forward with nothing but a towel round his loins. The woman was Betty. She was stark naked. The man wrapped a bath-robe round her and began drying her vigorously. She leaned on him while she put on first one shoe and then the other and to support her he placed his arm round her shoulders. The man was Albert.

Carruthers turned and fled up the hill. He stumbled blindly. Once he nearly fell. He was gasping like a wounded beast. When he got into his room he flung himself on the bed and clenched his fists and the dry, painful sobs that tore his chest broke into tears. He evidently had a violent attack of hysterics. It was all clear to him, clear with the ghastly vividness with which on a stormy night a flash of lightning can disclose a ravaged landscape, clear, horribly clear. The way the man had dried her and the way she leaned against him pointed not to passion, but to a long-continued intimacy, and the pipe by the bedside, the pipe had a hideously conjugal air. It suggested the pipe a man might smoke while he was reading in bed before going to sleep. *The Sporting Times!* That was why she had that little house in the Street of the Knights, so that they could spend two or three days together in domestic familiarity. They were like an old married couple. Humphrey asked himself how long the hateful thing had lasted and suddenly he knew the answer; for years. Ten, twelve, fourteen; it had started when the young footman first came to London, he was a boy then and it was obvious enough that it was not he who had made the advances; all through those years when she was the idol of the British public, when everyone adored her and she could have married anyone she liked, she was living with the second footman at her aunt's house. She took him with her when she married. Why had she made that surprising marriage? And the still-born child that came before its time. Of course that was why she had married Jimmie Welldon-Burns, because she was going to have a child by Albert. Oh, shameless, shameless! And then, when Jimmie's health broke down she had made him take Albert as his valet. And what had Jimmie known and what had he suspected? He drank, that was what had started his tuberculosis;

but why had he started drinking? Perhaps it was to still a suspicion that was so ugly that he could not face it. And it was to live with Albert that she had left Jimmie and it was to live with Albert that she had settled in Rhodes. Albert, his hands with their broken nails stained by his work on the motors, coarse of aspect and stocky, rather like a butcher with his high colour and clumsy strength, Albert not even very young any more and running to fat, uneducated and vulgar, with his common way of speaking. Albert, Albert, how could she?

Carruthers got up and drank some water. He threw himself into a chair. He could not bear his bed. He smoked cigarette after cigarette. He was a wreck in the morning. He had not slept at all. They brought him in his breakfast; he drank the coffee but could eat nothing. Presently there was a brisk knock on his door.

"Coming down to bathe, Humphrey?"

That cheerful voice sent the blood singing through his head. He braced himself and opened the door.

"I don't think I will to-day. I don't feel very well."

She gave him a look.

"Oh, my dear, you look all in. What's the matter with you?"

"I don't know. I think I must have got a touch of the sun."

His voice was dead and his eyes were tragic. She looked at him more closely. She did not say anything for a moment. He thought she went pale. *He knew.* Then a faintly mocking smile crossed her eyes; she thought the situation comic.

"Poor old boy, go and lie down, I'll send you in some aspirin. Perhaps you'll feel better at luncheon."

He lay in his darkened room. He would have given anything to get away then so that he need not set eyes on her again, but there was no means of that, the ship that was to take him back to Brindisi did not touch at Rhodes till the end of the week. He was a prisoner. And the next day they were to go to the islands. There was no escape from her there; in the caïque they would be in one another's pockets all day long. He couldn't face that. He was so ashamed. But she wasn't ashamed. At that moment when it had been plain to her that nothing was hidden from him any longer she had smiled. She was capable of telling him all about it. He could not bear that. That was too much. After all she couldn't be certain that he knew, at best she could only suspect; if he behaved as if nothing had happened, if at luncheon and during the days that remained he was as gay and jolly as usual she would think she had been mistaken. It was enough to know what he knew, he would not suffer the crowning humiliation of hearing from her own lips the disgraceful story. But at luncheon the first thing she said was:

"Isn't it a bore. Albert says something's gone wrong with the motor, we shan't be able to go on our trip after all. I daren't trust to sail at this time of the year. We might be becalmed for a week."

She spoke lightly and he answered in the same casual fashion.

"Oh, I'm sorry, but still I don't really care. It's so lovely here, I really didn't much want to go."

He told her that the aspirin had done him good and he felt much better; to the Greek butler and the two footmen in fustanellas it must have seemed that they talked as vivaciously as usual. That night the British consul came to dinner and the night after some Italian officers. Carruthers counted the days, he counted the hours. Oh, if the moment would only come when he could step on the ship and be free from the horror that every moment of the day obsessed him! He was growing so tired. But Betty's manner was so self-possessed that sometimes he asked himself if she really knew that he was aware of her secret. Was it the truth that she had told about the caïque and not, as had at once struck him, an excuse; and was it an accident that a succession of visitors prevented them from ever being alone together? The worst of having so much tact was that you never quite knew whether other people were acting naturally or being tactful too. When he looked at her, so easy and calm, so obviously happy, he could not believe the odious truth. And yet he had seen with his own eyes. And the future. What would her future be? It was horrible to think of. Sooner or later the truth must become notorious. And to think of Betty a mock and an outcast, in the power of a coarse and common man, growing older, losing her beauty; and the man was five years younger than she. One day he would take a mistress, one of her own maids, perhaps, with whom he would feel at home as he had never felt with the great lady, and what could she do then? What humiliation then must she be prepared to put up with! He might be cruel to her. He might beat her. Betty. Betty.

Carruthers wrung his hands. And on a sudden an idea came to him that filled him with a painful exaltation; he put it away from him, but it returned; it would not let him be. He must save her, he had loved her too much and too long to let her sink, sink as she was sinking; a passion of self-sacrifice welled up in him. Notwithstanding everything, though his love now was dead and he felt for her an almost physical repulsion, he would marry her. He laughed mirthlessly. What would his life be? He couldn't help that. He didn't matter. It was the only thing to do. He felt wonderfully uplifted, and yet very humble, for he was awed at the thought of the heights which the divine spirit of man could reach.

His ship was to sail on Saturday and on Thursday when the guests who had been dining left them, he said:

"I hope we're going to be alone to-morrow."

"As a matter of fact I've asked some Egyptians who spend the summer here. She's a sister of the ex-Khedive and very intelligent. I'm sure you'll like her."

"Well, it's my last evening. Couldn't we spend it alone?"

She gave him a glance. There was a faint amusement in her eyes, but his were grave.

"If you like. I can put them off."

"Then do."

He was to start early in the morning and his luggage was packed. Betty had told him not to dress, but he had answered that he preferred to. For the last time they sat down to dinner facing one another. The dining-room, with its shaded lights, was bare and formal, but the summer night flooding in through the great open windows gave it a sober richness. It had the effect of the private refectory in a convent to which a royal lady had retired in order to devote the remainder of her life to a piety not too austere. They had their coffee on the terrace. Carruthers drank a couple of liqueurs. He was feeling very nervous.

"Betty, my dear, I've got something I want to say to you," he began.

"Have you? I wouldn't say it if I were you."

She answered gently. She remained perfectly calm, watching him shrewdly, but with the glimmer of a smile in her blue eyes.

"I must."

She shrugged her shoulders and was silent. He was conscious that his voice trembled a little and he was angry with himself.

"You know I've been madly in love with you for many years. I don't know how many times I've asked you to marry me. But, after all, things change and people change too, don't they? We're neither of us so young as we were. Won't you marry me now, Betty?"

She gave him the smile that had always been such an attractive thing in her; it was so kindly, so frank, and still, still so wonderfully innocent.

"You're very sweet, Humphrey. It's awfully nice of you to ask me again. I can't tell you how touched I am. But you know, I'm a creature of habit, I've got in the habit of saying no to you now, and I can't change it."

"Why not?"

There was something aggressive in his tone, something almost ominous, that made her give him a quick look. Her face blanched with sudden anger, but she immediately controlled herself.

"Because I don't want to," she smiled.

"Are you going to marry anyone else?"

"I? No. Of course not."

For a moment she seemed to draw herself up as though a wave of ancestral pride swept through her and then she began to laugh. But whether she laughed at the thought that had passed through her mind or because something in Humphrey's proposal had amused her none but she could have told.

"Betty. I implore you to marry me."

"Never."

"You can't go on living this life."

He put into his voice all the anguish of his heart and his face was drawn and tortured. She smiled affectionately.

"Why not? Don't be such a donkey. You know I adore you, Humphrey, but you are rather an old woman."

"Betty. Betty."

Did she not see that it was for her sake that he wanted it? It was not love that made him speak, but human pity and shame. She got up.

"Don't be tiresome, Humphrey. You'd better go to bed, you know you have to be up with the lark. I shan't see you in the morning. Good-bye and God bless you. It's been wonderful having you here."

She kissed him on both cheeks.

Next morning, early, for he had to be on board at eight, when Carruthers stepped out of the front door he found Albert waiting for him in the car. He wore a singlet, duck trousers and a beret basque. Carruthers' luggage was in the back. He turned to the butler.

"Put my bags beside the chauffeur," he said. "I'll sit behind."

Albert made no remark. Carruthers got in and they drove off. When they arrived at the harbour, porters ran up. Albert got out of the car. Carruthers looked down at him from his greater height.

"You need not see me on board. I can manage perfectly well by myself. Here's a tip for you."

He gave him a five-pound note. Albert flushed. He was taken aback, he would have liked to refuse it, but did not know how to, and the servility of years asserted itself. Perhaps he did not know what he said.

"Thank you, sir."

Carruthers gave him a curt nod and walked away. He had forced Betty's lover to call him "sir". It was as though he had struck her a blow across that smiling mouth of hers and flung in her face an opprobrious word. It filled him with a bitter satisfaction.

He shrugged his shoulders and I could see that even this small triumph now seemed vain. For a little while we were silent. There was nothing for me to say. Then he began again.

"I dare say you think it's very strange that I should tell you all this. I don't care. You know, I feel as if nothing mattered any more. I feel as if decency no longer existed in the world. Heaven knows, I'm not jealous. You can't be jealous unless you love and my love is dead. It was killed in a flash. After all those years. I can't think of her now without horror. What destroys me, what makes me so frightfully unhappy is to think of her unspeakable degradation."

So it has been said that it was not jealousy that caused Othello to kill Desdemona, but an agony that the creature that he believed angelic should be proved impure and worthless. What broke his noble heart was that virtue should so fall.

"I thought there was no one like her. I admired her so much. I admired her courage and her frankness, her intelligence and her love of beauty. She's just a sham and she's never been anything else."

"I wonder if that's true. Do you think any of us are all of a piece? Do you know what strikes me? I should have said that Albert was only the instrument, her toll to the solid earth, so to speak, that left her soul at liberty to range the empyrean. Perhaps the mere fact that he was so far below her gave her a sense of freedom in her relations with him that she would have lacked with a man of her own class. The spirit is very strange, it never soars so high as when the body has wallowed for a period in the gutter."

"Oh, don't talk such rot," he answered angrily.

"I don't think it is rot. I don't put it very well, but the idea's sound."

"Much good it does me. I'm broken and done for. I'm finished."

"Oh, nonsense. Why don't you write a story about it?"

"I?"

"You know, that's the great pull a writer has over other people. When something has made him terribly unhappy, and he's tortured and miserable, he can put it all into a story and it's astonishing what a comfort and relief it is."

"It would be monstrous. Betty was everything in the world to me. I couldn't do anything so caddish."

He paused for a little and I saw him reflect. I saw that notwithstanding the horror that my suggestion caused him he did for one minute look at the situation from the standpoint of the writer. He shook his head.

"Not for her sake, for mine. After all I have some self-respect. Besides, there's no story there."

Jane

I REMEMBER very well the occasion on which I first saw Jane Fowler. It is indeed only because the details of the glimpse I had of her then are so clear that I trust my recollection at all, for, looking back, I must confess that I find it hard to believe that it has not played me a fantastic trick. I had lately returned to London from China and was drinking a dish of tea with Mrs. Tower. Mrs. Tower had been seized with the prevailing passion for decoration; and with the ruthlessness of her sex had sacrificed chairs in which she had comfortably sat for years, tables, cabinets, ornaments on which her eyes had dwelt in peace since she was married, pictures that had been familiar to her for a generation; and delivered herself into the hands of an expert. Nothing remained in her drawing-room with which she had any association, or to which any sentiment was attached; and she had invited me that day to see the fashionable glory in which she now lived. Everything that could be pickled was pickled and what couldn't be pickled was painted. Nothing matched, but everything harmonised.

"Do you remember that ridiculous drawing-room suite that I used to have?" asked Mrs. Tower.

The curtains were sumptuous yet severe; the sofa was covered with Italian brocade; the chair on which I sat was in *petit point*. The room was beautiful, opulent without garishness and original without affectation; yet to me it lacked something; and while I praised with my lips I asked myself why I so much preferred the rather shabby chintz of the despised suite, the Victorian water-colours that I had known so long, and the ridiculous Dresden china that had adorned the chimney-piece. I wondered what it was that I missed in all these rooms that the decorators were turning out with a profitable industry. Was it heart? But Mrs. Tower looked about her happily.

"Don't you like my alabaster lamps?" she said. "They give such a soft light."

"Personally I have a weakness for a light that you can see by," I smiled.

"It's so difficult to combine that with a light that you can't be too much seen by," laughed Mrs. Tower.

I had no notion what her age was. When I was quite a young man she was a married woman a good deal older than I, but now she treated me as her contemporary. She constantly said that she made no secret of her age, which was forty, and then added with a smile that all women took five years off. She never sought to conceal the fact that she dyed her hair (it was a very pretty brown with reddish tints), and she said she did this because hair was hideous while it was going grey; as soon as hers was white she would cease to dye it.

"Then they'll say what a young face I have."

Meanwhile it was painted, though with discretion, and her eyes owed not a little of their vivacity to art. She was a handsome woman, exquisitely gowned, and in the sombre glow of the alabaster lamps did not look a day more than the forty she gave herself.

"It is only at my dressing-table that I can suffer the naked brightness of a thirty-two-candle electric bulb," she added with smiling cynicism. "There I need it to tell me first the hideous truth and then to enable me to take the necessary steps to correct it."

We gossiped pleasantly about our common friends and Mrs. Tower brought me up to date in the scandal of the day. After roughing it here and there it was very agreeable to sit in a comfortable chair, the fire burning brightly on the hearth, charming tea-things set out on a charming table, and talk with this amusing, attractive woman. She treated me as a prodigal returned from his husks and was disposed to make much of me. She prided herself on her dinner-parties; she took no less trouble to have her guests suitably assorted than to give them excellent food; and there were few persons who did not look upon it as a treat to be bidden to one of them. Now she fixed a date and asked me whom I would like to meet.

"There's only one thing I must tell you. If Jane Fowler is still here I shall have to put it off."

"Who is Jane Fowler?" I asked.

Mrs. Tower gave a rueful smile.

"Jane Fowler is my cross."

"Oh!"

"Do you remember a photograph that I used to have on the piano before I had my room done, of a woman in a tight dress with tight sleeves and a gold locket, with her hair drawn back from a broad forehead and her ears showing and spectacles on a rather blunt nose? Well, that was Jane Fowler."

"You had so many photographs about the room in your unregenerate days," I said, vaguely.

"It makes me shudder to think of them. I've made them into a huge brown-paper parcel and hidden them in an attic."

"Well, who is Jane Fowler?" I asked again, smiling.

"She's my sister-in-law. She was my husband's sister and she married a manufacturer in the North. She's been a widow for many years, and she's very well-to-do."

"And why is she your cross?"

"She's worthy, she's dowdy, she's provincial. She looks twenty years older than I do and she's quite capable of telling anyone she meets that we were at school together. She has an overwhelming sense of family affection and because I am her only living connection she's devoted to me. When she comes to London it never occurs to her that she should stay anywhere but here—she thinks it would hurt my feelings—and she'll pay me visits of three or four weeks. We sit here and she knits and reads. And sometimes she insists on taking me to dine at Claridge's and she looks like a funny old charwoman and everyone I particularly don't want to be seen by is sitting at the next table. When we are driving home she says she loves giving me a little treat. With her own hands she makes me tea-cosies that I am forced to use when she is here and doilies and centrepieces for the dining-room table."

Mrs. Tower paused to take breath.

"I should have thought a woman of your tact would find a way to deal with a situation like that."

"Ah, but don't you see, I haven't a chance. She's so immeasurably kind. She has a heart of gold. She bores me to death, but I wouldn't for anything let her suspect it."

"And when does she arrive?"

"To-morrow."

But the answer was hardly out of Mrs. Tower's mouth when the bell rang. There were sounds in the hall of a slight commotion and in a minute or two the butler ushered in an elderly lady.

"Mrs. Fowler," he announced.

"Jane," cried Mrs. Tower, springing to her feet. "I wasn't expecting you to-day."

"So your butler has just told me. I certainly said to-day in my letter."

Mrs. Tower recovered her wits.

"Well, it doesn't matter. I'm very glad to see you whenever you come. Fortunately I'm doing nothing this evening."

"You mustn't let me give you any trouble. If I can have a boiled egg for my dinner that's all I shall want."

A faint grimace for a moment distorted Mrs. Tower's handsome features. A boiled egg!

"Oh, I think we can do a little better than that."

I chuckled inwardly when I recollected that the two ladies were contemporaries. Mrs. Fowler looked a good fifty-five. She was a rather big woman; she wore a black straw hat with a wide brim and from it a black lace veil hung over her shoulders, a cloak that oddly combined severity with fussiness, a long black dress, voluminous as though she wore several petticoats under it, and stout boots. She was evidently short-sighted, for she looked at you through large gold-rimmed spectacles.

"Won't you have a cup of tea?" asked Mrs. Tower.

"If it wouldn't be too much trouble. I'll take off my mantle."

She began by stripping her hands of the black gloves she wore, and then took off her cloak. Round her neck was a solid gold chain from which hung a large gold locket in which I felt certain was a photograph of her deceased husband. Then she took off her hat and placed it neatly with her gloves and cloak on the sofa corner. Mrs. Tower pursed her lips. Certainly those garments did not go very well with the austere but sumptuous beauty of Mrs. Tower's redecorated drawing-room. I wondered where on earth Mrs. Fowler had found the extraordinary clothes she wore. They were not old and the materials were expensive. It was astounding to think that dressmakers still made things that had not been worn for a quarter of a century. Mrs. Fowler's grey hair was very plainly done, showing all her forehead and her ears, with a parting in the middle. It had evidently never known the tongs of Monsieur Marcel. Now her eyes fell on the tea-table with its teapot of Georgian silver and its cups in old Worcester.

"What have you done with the tea-cosy I gave you last time I came up, Marion?" she asked. "Don't you use it?"

"Yes, I used it every day, Jane," answered Mrs. Tower glibly. "Unfortunately we had an accident with it a little while ago. It got burnt."

"But the last one I gave you got burnt."

"I'm afraid you'll think us very careless."

"It doesn't really matter," smiled Mrs. Fowler. "I shall enjoy making you another. I'll go to Liberty's to-morrow and buy some silks."

Mrs. Tower kept her face bravely.

"I don't deserve it, you know. Doesn't your vicar's wife need one?"

"Oh, I've just made her one," said Mrs. Fowler brightly.

I noticed that when she smiled she showed white, small and regular teeth. They were a real beauty. Her smile was certainly very sweet.

But I felt it high time for me to leave the two ladies to themselves, so I took my leave.

Early next morning Mrs. Tower rang me up and I heard at once from her voice that she was in high spirits.

"I've got the most wonderful news for you," she said. "Jane is going to be married."

"Nonsense."

"Her fiancé is coming to dine here to-night to be introduced to me and I want you to come too."

"Oh, but I shall be in the way."

"No, you won't. Jane suggested herself that I should ask you. Do come."

She was bubbling over with laughter.

"Who is he?"

"I don't know. She tells me he's an architect. Can you imagine the sort of man Jane would marry?"

I had nothing to do and I could trust Mrs. Tower to give me a good dinner.

When I arrived Mrs. Tower, very splendid in a tea-gown a little too young for her, was alone.

"Jane is putting the finishing touches to her appearance. I'm longing for you to see her. She's all in a flutter. She says he adores her. His name is Gilbert and when she speaks of him her voice gets all funny and tremulous. It makes me want to laugh."

"I wonder what he's like."

"Oh, I'm sure I know. Very big and massive, with a bald head and an immense gold chain across an immense tummy. A large, fat, clean-shaven, red face and a booming voice."

Mrs. Fowler came in. She wore a very stiff black silk dress with a wide skirt and a train. At the neck it was cut into a timid V and the sleeves came down to the elbows. She wore a necklace of diamonds set in silver. She carried in her hands a long pair of black gloves and a fan of black ostrich feathers. She managed (as so few people do) to look exactly what she was. You could never have thought her anything in the world but the respectable relict of a North-country manufacturer of ample means.

"You've really got quite a pretty neck, Jane," said Mrs. Tower with a kindly smile.

It was indeed astonishingly young when you compared it with her weather-beaten face. It was smooth and unlined and the skin was white. And I noticed then that her head was very well placed on her shoulders.

"Has Marion told you my news?" she said, turning to me with that really charming smile of hers as if we were already old friends.

"I must congratulate you," I said.

"Wait to do that till you've seen my young man."

"I think it's too sweet to hear you talk of your young man," smiled Mrs. Tower.

Mrs. Fowler's eyes certainly twinkled behind her preposterous spectacles.

"Don't expect anyone too old. You wouldn't like me to marry a decrepit old gentleman with one foot in the grave, would you?"

This was the only warning she gave us. Indeed there was no time for any further discussion, for the butler flung open the door and in a loud voice announced:

"Mr. Gilbert Napier."

There entered a youth in a very well-cut dinner jacket. He was slight, not very tall, with fair hair in which there was a hint of a natural wave, clean-shaven and blue-eyed. He was not particularly good-looking, but he had a pleasant, amiable face. In ten years he would probably be wizened and sallow; but now, in extreme youth, he was fresh and clean and blooming. For he was certainly not more than twenty-four. My first thought was that this was the son of Jane Fowler's fiancé (I had not known he was a widower) come to say that his father was prevented from dining by a sudden attack of gout. But his eyes fell immediately on Mrs. Fowler, his face lit up, and he went towards her with both hands outstretched. Mrs. Fowler gave him hers, a demure smile on her lips, and turned to her sister-in-law.

"This is my young man, Marion," she said.

He held out his hand.

"I hope you'll like me, Mrs. Tower," he said. "Jane tells me you're the only relation she has in the world."

Mrs. Tower's face was wonderful to behold. I saw then to admiration how bravely good breeding and social usage could combat the instincts of the natural woman. For the astonishment and then the dismay that for an instant she could not conceal were quickly driven away, and her face assumed an expression of affable welcome. But she was evidently at a loss for words. It was not unnatural if Gilbert felt a certain embarrassment and I was too busy preventing myself from laughing to think of anything to say. Mrs. Fowler alone kept perfectly calm.

"I know you'll like him, Marion. There's no one enjoys good food more than he does." She turned to the young man. "Marion's dinners are famous."

"I know," he beamed.

Mrs. Tower made some quick rejoinder and we went downstairs. I shall not soon forget the exquisite comedy of that meal. Mrs. Tower could not make up her mind whether the pair of them were playing a practical joke on her or whether Jane by wilfully concealing her fiancé's age had hoped to make her look foolish. But then Jane never jested and she was incapable of doing a malicious thing. Mrs. Tower was amazed, exasperated and perplexed. But she had recovered her self-control, and for nothing would she have forgotten that she was a perfect hostess whose duty it was to make her party go. She talked vivaciously; but I wondered if Gilbert Napier saw how hard and vindictive was the expression of her eyes behind the mask of friendliness that she turned to him. She was measuring him. She was seeking to delve into the secret of his soul. I could see that she was in a passion, for under her rouge her cheeks glowed with an angry red.

"You've got a very high colour, Marion," said Jane, looking at her amiably through her great round spectacles.

"I dressed in a hurry. I dare say I put on too much rouge."

"Oh, is it rouge? I thought it was natural. Otherwise I shouldn't have mentioned it." She gave Gilbert a shy little smile. "You know, Marion and I were at school together. You would never think it to look at us now, would you? But of course I've lived a very quiet life."

I do not know what she meant by these remarks; it was almost incredible that she made them in complete simplicity; but anyhow they goaded Mrs. Tower to such a fury that she flung her own vanity to the winds. She smiled brightly.

"We shall neither of us see fifty again, Jane," she said.

If the observation was meant to discomfit the widow it failed.

"Gilbert says I mustn't acknowledge to more than forty-nine for his sake," she answered blandly.

Mrs. Tower's hands trembled slightly, but she found a retort.

"There is of course a certain disparity of age between you," she smiled.

"Twenty-seven years," said Jane. "Do you think it's too much? Gilbert says I'm very young for my age. I told you I shouldn't like to marry a man with one foot in the grave."

I was really obliged to laugh and Gilbert laughed too. His laughter was frank and boyish. It looked as though he were amused at everything Jane said. But Mrs. Tower was almost at the end of her tether and I was afraid that unless relief came she would for once forget that she was a woman of the world. I came to the rescue as best I could.

"I suppose you're very busy buying your trousseau," I said.

"No. I wanted to get my things from the dressmaker in Liverpool I've been to ever since I was first married. But Gilbert won't let me. He's very masterful, and of course he has wonderful taste."

She looked at him with a little affectionate smile, demurely, as though she were a girl of seventeen.

Mrs. Tower went quite pale under her make-up.

"We're going to Italy for our honeymoon. Gilbert has never had a chance of studying Renaissance architecture and of course it's important for an architect to see things for himself. And we shall stop in Paris on the way and get my clothes there."

"Do you expect to be away long?"

"Gilbert has arranged with his office to stay away for six months. It will be such a treat for him, won't it? You see, he's never had more than a fortnight's holiday before."

"Why not?" asked Mrs. Tower in a tone that no effort of will could prevent from being icy.

"He's never been able to afford it, poor dear."

"Ah!" said Mrs. Tower, and into the exclamation put volumes.

Coffee was served and the ladies went upstairs. Gilbert and I began to talk in the desultory way in which men talk who have nothing whatever to say to one another; but in two minutes a note was brought in to me by the butler. It was from Mrs. Tower and ran as follows:

"Come upstairs quickly and then go as soon as you can. Take him with you. Unless I have it out with Jane at once I shall have a fit."

I told a facile lie.

"Mrs. Tower has a headache and wants to go to bed. I think if you don't mind we'd better clear out."

"Certainly," he answered.

We went upstairs and five minutes later were on the doorstep. I called a taxi and offered the young man a lift.

"No, thanks," he answered. "I'll just walk to the corner and jump on a bus."

Mrs. Tower sprang to the fray as soon as she heard the front-door close behind us.

"Are you crazy, Jane?" she cried.

"Not more than most people who don't habitually live in a lunatic asylum, I trust," Jane answered blandly.

"May I ask why you're going to marry this young man?" asked Mrs. Tower with formidable politeness.

"Partly because he won't take no for an answer. He's asked me five times. I grew positively tired of refusing him."

"And why do you think he's so anxious to marry you?"

"I amuse him."

Mrs. Tower gave an exclamation of annoyance.

"He's an unscrupulous rascal. I very nearly told him so to his face."

"You would have been wrong, and it wouldn't have been very polite."

"He's penniless and you're rich. You can't be such a besotted fool as not to see that he's marrying you for your money."

Jane remained perfectly composed. She observed her sister-in-law's agitation with detachment.

"I don't think he is, you know," she replied. "I think he's very fond of me."

"You're an old woman, Jane."

"I'm the same age as you are, Marion," she smiled.

"I've never let myself go. I'm very young for my age. No one would think I was more than forty. But even I wouldn't

R

dream of marrying a boy twenty years younger than myself."

"Twenty-seven," corrected Jane.

"Do you mean to tell me that you can bring yourself to believe that it's possible for a young man to care for a woman old enough to be his mother?"

"I've lived very much in the country for many years. I dare say there's a great deal about human nature that I don't know. They tell me there's a man called Freud, an Austrian, I believe . . ."

But Mrs. Tower interrupted her without any politeness at all.

"Don't be ridiculous, Jane. It's so undignified. It's so ungraceful. I always thought you were a sensible woman. Really you're the last person I should ever have thought likely to fall in love with a boy."

"But I'm not in love with him. I've told him that. Of course I like him very much or I wouldn't think of marrying him. I thought it only fair to tell him quite plainly what my feelings were towards him."

Mrs. Tower gasped. The blood rushed to her head and her breathing oppressed her. She had no fan, but she seized the evening paper and vigorously fanned herself with it.

"If you're not in love with him why do you want to marry him?"

"I've been a widow a very long time and I've led a very quiet life. I thought I'd like a change."

"If you want to marry just to be married why don't you marry a man of your own age?"

"No man of my own age has asked me five times. In fact no man of my own age has asked me at all."

Jane chuckled as she answered. It drove Mrs. Tower to the final pitch of frenzy.

"Don't laugh, Jane. I won't have it. I don't think you can be right in your mind. It's dreadful."

It was altogether too much for her and she burst into tears. She knew that at her age it was fatal to cry, her eyes would be swollen for twenty-four hours and she would look a sight. But there was no help for it. She wept. Jane remained perfectly calm. She looked at Marion through her large spectacles and reflectively smoothed the lap of her black silk dress.

"You're going to be so dreadfully unhappy," Mrs. Tower sobbed, dabbing her eyes cautiously in the hope that the black on her lashes would not smudge.

"I don't think so, you know," Jane answered in those equable,

mild tones of hers, as if there were a little smile behind the words.
"We've talked it over very thoroughly. I always think I'm a very
easy person to live with. I think I shall make Gilbert very happy
and comfortable. He's never had anyone to look after him properly.
We're only marrying after mature consideration. And we've
decided that if either of us wants his liberty the other will place
no obstacles in the way of his getting it."

Mrs. Tower had by now recovered herself sufficiently to make a
cutting remark.

"How much has he persuaded you to settle on him?"

"I wanted to settle a thousand a year on him, but he wouldn't
hear of it. He was quite upset when I made the suggestion. He
says he can earn quite enough for his own needs."

"He's more cunning than I thought," said Mrs. Tower acidly.

Jane paused a little and looked at her sister-in-law with kindly
but resolute eyes.

"You see, my dear, it's different for you," she said. "You've
never been so very much a widow, have you?"

Mrs. Tower looked at her. She blushed a little. She even felt
slightly uncomfortable. But of course Jane was much too simple
to intend an innuendo. Mrs. Tower gathered herself together with
dignity.

"I'm so upset that I really must go to bed," she said. "We'll
resume the conversation to-morrow morning."

"I'm afraid that won't be very convenient, dear. Gilbert and
I are going to get the licence to-morrow morning."

Mrs. Tower threw up her hands in a gesture of dismay, but she
found nothing more to say.

The marriage took place at a registrar's office. Mrs. Tower and
I were the witnesses. Gilbert in a smart blue suit looked absurdly
young and he was obviously nervous. It is a trying moment for
any man. But Jane kept her admirable composure. She might
have been in the habit of marrying as frequently as a woman of
fashion. Only a slight colour on her cheeks suggested that beneath
her calm was some faint excitement. It is a thrilling moment for
any woman. She wore a very full dress of silvery grey velvet in the
cut of which I recognised the hand of the dressmaker in Liverpool
(evidently a widow of unimpeachable character) who had made
her gowns for so many years; but she had so far succumbed to the
frivolity of the occasion as to wear a large picture hat covered with

blue ostrich feathers. Her gold-rimmed spectacles made it extraordinarily grotesque. When the ceremony was over the registrar (somewhat taken aback, I thought, by the difference of age between the pair he was marrying) shook hands with her, tendering his strictly official congratulations; and the bridegroom, blushing slightly, kissed her. Mrs. Tower, resigned but implacable, kissed her; and then the bride looked at me expectantly. It was evidently fitting that I should kiss her too. I did. I confess that I felt a little shy as we walked out of the registrar's office past loungers who waited cynically to see the bridal pairs, and it was with relief that I stepped into Mrs. Tower's car. We drove to Victoria Station, for the happy couple were to go over to Paris by the two o'clock train, and Jane had insisted that the wedding-breakfast should be eaten at the station restaurant. She said it always made her nervous not to be on the platform in good time. Mrs. Tower, present only from a strong sense of family duty, was able to do little to make the party go off well; she ate nothing (for which I could not blame her, since the food was execrable, and anyway I hate champagne at luncheon) and talked in a strained voice. But Jane went through the menu conscientiously.

"I always think one should make a hearty meal before starting out on a journey," she said.

We saw them off, and I drove Mrs. Tower back to her house.

"How long do you give it?" she said. "Six months?"

"Let's hope for the best," I smiled.

"Don't be so absurd. There can be no 'best'. You don't think he's marrying her for anything but her money, do you? Of course it can't last. My only hope is that she won't have to go through as much suffering as she deserves."

I laughed. The charitable words were spoken in such a tone as to leave me in small doubt of Mrs. Tower's meaning.

"Well, if it doesn't last you'll have the consolation of saying: 'I told you so'," I said.

"I promise you I'll never do that."

"Then you'll have the satisfaction of congratulating yourself on your self-control in not saying: 'I told you so'."

"She's old and dowdy and dull."

"Are you sure she's dull?" I said. "It's true she doesn't say very much, but when she says anything it's very much to the point."

"I've never heard her make a joke in my life."

I was once more in the Far East when Gilbert and Jane returned from their honeymoon and this time I remained away for nearly two years. Mrs. Tower was a bad correspondent and though I sent her an occasional picture-postcard I received no news from her. But I met her within a week of my return to London; I was dining out and found that I was seated next to her. It was an immense party, I think we were four-and-twenty, like the blackbirds in the pie, and, arriving somewhat late, I was too confused by the crowd in which I found myself to notice who was there. But when we sat down, looking round the long table I saw that a good many of my fellow-guests were well known to the public from their photographs in the illustrated papers. Our hostess had a weakness for the persons technically known as celebrities and this was an unusually brilliant gathering. When Mrs. Tower and I had exchanged the conventional remarks that two people make when they have not seen one another for a couple of years I asked about Jane.

"She's very well," said Mrs. Tower with a certain dryness.

"How has the marriage turned out?"

Mrs. Tower paused a little and took a salted almond from the dish in front of her.

"It appears to be quite a success."

"You were wrong then?"

"I said it wouldn't last and I still say it won't last. It's contrary to human nature."

"Is she happy?"

"They're both happy."

"I suppose you don't see very much of them."

"At first I saw quite a lot of them. But now . . ." Mrs. Tower pursed her lips a little. "Jane is becoming very grand."

"What *do* you mean?" I laughed.

"I think I should tell you that she's here to-night."

"Here?"

I was startled. I looked round the table again. Our hostess was a delightful and an entertaining woman, but I could not imagine that she would be likely to invite to a dinner such as this the elderly and dowdy wife of an obscure architect. Mrs. Tower saw my perplexity and was shrewd enough to see what was in my mind. She smiled thinly.

"Look on the left of our host."

I looked. Oddly enough the woman who sat there had by her

fantastic appearance attracted my attention the moment I was ushered into the crowded drawing-room. I thought I noticed a gleam of recognition in her eye, but to the best of my belief I had never seen her before. She was not a young woman, for her hair was iron-grey; it was cut very short and clustered thickly round her well-shaped head in tight curls. She made no attempt at youth, for she was conspicuous in that gathering by using neither lipstick, rouge nor powder. Her face, not a particularly handsome one, was red and weather-beaten; but because it owed nothing to artifice had a naturalness that was very pleasing. It contrasted oddly with the whiteness of her shoulders. They were really magnificent. A woman of thirty might have been proud of them. But her dress was extraordinary. I had not often seen anything more audacious. It was cut very low, with short skirts, which were then the fashion, in black and yellow; it had almost the effect of fancy-dress and yet so became her that though on anyone else it would have been outrageous, on her it had the inevitable simplicity of nature. And to complete the impression of an eccentricity in which there was no pose and of an extravagance in which there was no ostentation she wore, attached by a broad black ribbon, a single eyeglass.

"You're not going to tell me *that* is your sister-in-law," I gasped.

"That is Jane Napier," said Mrs. Tower icily.

At that moment she was speaking. Her host was turned towards her with an anticipatory smile. A baldish white-haired man, with a sharp, intelligent face, who sat on her left, was leaning forward eagerly, and the couple who sat opposite, ceasing to talk with one another, listened intently. She said her say and they all, with a sudden movement, threw themselves back in their chairs and burst into vociferous laughter. From the other side of the table a man addressed Mrs. Tower: I recognised a famous statesman.

"Your sister-in-law has made another joke, Mrs. Tower," he said.

Mrs. Tower smiled.

"She's priceless, isn't she?"

"Let me have a long drink of champagne and then for heaven's sake tell me all about it," I said.

Well, this is how I gathered it had all happened. At the beginning of their honeymoon Gilbert took Jane to various dressmakers in Paris and he made no objection to her choosing a number of "gowns" after her own heart; but he persuaded her to have a "frock" or two made according to his own design. It appeared that he had a knack for that kind of work. He engaged a smart French maid. Jane had never had such a thing before. She did her own mending and when she wanted "doing up" was in the habit of ringing for the housemaid. The dresses Gilbert had devised were very different from anything she had worn before; but he had been careful not to go too far too quickly, and because it pleased him she persuaded herself, though not without misgivings, to wear them in preference to those she had chosen herself. Of course she could not wear them with the voluminous petticoats she had been in the habit of using, and these, though it cost her an anxious moment, she discarded.

"Now if you please," said Mrs. Tower, with something very like a sniff of disapproval, "she wears nothing but thin silk tights. It's a wonder to me she doesn't catch her death of cold at her age."

Gilbert and the French maid taught her how to wear her clothes, and, unexpectedly enough, she was very quick at learning. The French maid was in raptures over Madame's arms and shoulders. It was a scandal not to show anything so fine.

"Wait a little, Alphonsine," said Gilbert. "The next lot of clothes I design for Madame we'll make the most of her."

The spectacles of course were dreadful. No one could look really well in gold-rimmed spectacles. Gilbert tried some with tortoiseshell rims. He shook his head.

"They'd look all right on a girl," he said. "You're too old to wear spectacles, Jane." Suddenly he had an inspiration. "By George, I've got it. You must wear an eyeglass."

"Oh, Gilbert, I couldn't."

She looked at him and his excitement, the excitement of the artist, made her smile. He was so sweet to her she wanted to do what she could to please him.

"I'll try," she said.

When they went to an optician and, suited with the right size, she placed an eyeglass jauntily in her eye Gilbert clapped his hands. There and then, before the astonished shopman, he kissed her on both cheeks.

"You look wonderful," he cried.

So they went down to Italy and spent happy months studying Renaissance and Baroque architecture. Jane not only grew accustomed to her changed appearance, but found she liked it.

At first she was a little shy when she went into the dining-room of an hotel and people turned round to stare at her, no one had ever raised an eyelid to look at her before, but presently she found that the sensation was not disagreeable. Ladies came up to her and asked her where she got her dress.

"Do you like it?" she answered demurely. "My husband designed it for me."

"I should like to copy it if you don't mind."

Jane had certainly for many years lived a very quiet life, but she was by no means lacking in the normal instincts of her sex. She had her answer ready.

"I'm so sorry, but my husband's very particular and he won't hear of anyone copying my frocks. He wants me to be unique."

She had an idea that people would laugh when she said this, but they didn't; they merely answered:

"Oh, of course I quite understand. You *are* unique."

But she saw them making mental notes of what she wore, and for some reason this quite "put her about". For once in her life that she wasn't wearing what everybody else did, she reflected, she didn't see why everybody else should want to wear what she did.

"Gilbert," she said, quite sharply for her, "next time you're designing dresses for me I wish you'd design things that people *can't* copy."

"The only way to do that is to design things that only you can wear."

"Can't you do that?"

"Yes, if you'll do something for me."

"What is it?"

"Cut off your hair."

I think this was the first time that Jane jibbed. Her hair was long and thick and as a girl she had been quite vain of it; to cut it off was a very drastic proceeding. This really was burning her boats behind her. In her case it was not the first step that cost so much, it was the last; but she took it ("I know Marion will think me a perfect fool, and I shall *never* be able to go to Liverpool again," she said), and when they passed through Paris on their way home Gilbert led her (she felt quite sick, her heart was beating so fast) to the best hairdresser in the world. She came out of his shop with a jaunty, saucy, impudent head of crisp grey curls. Pygmalion had finished his fantastic masterpiece: Galatea was come to life.

"Yes," I said, "but that isn't enough to explain why Jane is here to-night amid this crowd of duchesses, Cabinet Ministers and such-like; nor why she is sitting on one side of her host with an Admiral of the Fleet on the other."

"Jane is a humorist," said Mrs. Tower. "Didn't you see them all laughing at what she said?"

There was no doubt now of the bitterness in Mrs. Tower's heart.

"When Jane wrote and told me they were back from their honeymoon I thought I must ask them both to dinner. I didn't much like the idea, but I felt it had to be done. I knew the party would be deadly and I wasn't going to sacrifice any of the people who really mattered. On the other hand I didn't want Jane to think I hadn't any nice friends. You know I never have more than eight, but on this occasion I thought it would make things go better if I had twelve. I'd been too busy to see Jane until the evening of the party. She kept us all waiting a little—that was Gilbert's cleverness—and at last she sailed in. You could have knocked me down with a feather. She made the rest of the women look dowdy and provincial. She made me feel like a painted old trollop."

Mrs. Tower drank a little champagne.

"I wish I could describe the frock to you. It would have been quite impossible on anyone else; on her it was perfect. And the eyeglass! I'd known her for thirty-five years and I'd never seen her without spectacles."

"But you knew she had a good figure."

"How should I? I'd never seen her except in the clothes you first saw her in. Did you think she had a good figure? She seemed not to be unconscious of the sensation she made but to take it as a matter of course. I thought of my dinner and I heaved a sigh of relief. Even if she was a little heavy in hand, with that appearance it didn't so very much matter. She was sitting at the other end of the table and I heard a good deal of laughter, I was glad to think that the other people were playing up well; but after dinner I was a good deal taken aback when no less than three men came up to me and told me that my sister-in-law was priceless, and did I think she would allow them to call on her? I didn't quite know whether I was standing on my head or my heels. Twenty-four hours later our hostess of to-night rang me up and said she had heard my sister-in-law was in London and she was priceless and would I ask her to luncheon to meet her? She has an infallible instinct, that woman: in a month everyone was talking about Jane. I am here to-night, not because I've known our hostess for twenty years and have asked her to dinner a hundred times, but because I'm Jane's sister-in-law."

Poor Mrs. Tower. The position was galling, and though I could not help being amused, for the tables were turned on her with a vengeance, I felt that she deserved my sympathy.

"People never can resist those who make them laugh," I said, trying to console her.

"She never makes *me* laugh."

Once more from the top of the table I heard a guffaw and guessed that Jane had said another amusing thing.

"Do you mean to say that you are the only person who doesn't think her funny?" I asked, smiling.

"Had it struck *you* that she was a humorist?"

"I'm bound to say it hadn't."

"She says just the same things as she's said for the last thirty-five years. I laugh when I see everyone else does because I don't want to seem a perfect fool, but I am not amused."

"Like Queen Victoria," I said.

It was a foolish jest and Mrs. Tower was quite right sharply to tell me so. I tried another tack.

"Is Gilbert here?" I asked, looking down the table.

"Gilbert was asked because she won't go out without him, but to-night he's at a dinner of the Architects' Institute or whatever it's called."

"I'm dying to renew my acquaintance with her."

"Go and talk to her after dinner. She'll ask you to her Tuesdays."

"Her Tuesdays?"

"She's at home every Tuesday evening. You'll meet there everyone you ever heard of. They're the best parties in London. She's done in one year what I've failed to do in twenty."

"But what you tell me is really miraculous. How has it been done?"

Mrs. Tower shrugged her handsome but adipose shoulders.

"I shall be glad if you'll tell me," she replied.

After dinner I tried to make my way to the sofa on which Jane was sitting, but I was intercepted and it was not till a little later that my hostess came up to me and said:

"I must introduce you to the star of my party. Do you know

Jane Napier? She's priceless. She's much more amusing than your comedies."

I was taken up to the sofa. The admiral who had been sitting beside her at dinner was with her still. He showed no sign of moving and Jane, shaking hands with me, introduced me to him.

"Do you know Sir Reginald Frobisher?"

We began to chat. It was the same Jane as I had known before, perfectly simple, homely and unaffected, but her fantastic appearance certainly gave a peculiar savour to what she said. Suddenly I found myself shaking with laughter. She had made a remark, sensible and to the point, but not in the least witty, which her manner of saying and the bland look she gave me through her eyeglass made perfectly irresistible. I felt light-hearted and buoyant. When I left her she said to me:

"If you've got nothing better to do, come and see us on Tuesday evening. Gilbert will be so glad to see you."

"When he's been a month in London he'll know that he *can* have nothing better to do," said the admiral.

So, on Tuesday but rather late, I went to Jane's. I confess I was a little surprised at the company. It was quite a remarkable collection of writers, painters and politicians, actors, great ladies and great beauties: Mrs. Tower was right, it was a grand party; I had seen nothing like it in London since Stafford House was sold. No particular entertainment was provided. The refreshments were adequate without being luxurious. Jane in her quiet way seemed to be enjoying herself; I could not see that she took a great deal of trouble with her guests, but they seemed to like being there and the gay, pleasant party did not break up till two in the morning. After that I saw much of her. I not only went often to her house, but seldom went out to luncheon or to dinner without meeting her. I am an amateur of humour and I sought to discover in what lay her peculiar gift. It was impossible to repeat anything she said, for the fun, like certain wines, would not travel. She had no gift for epigram. She never made a brilliant repartee. There was no malice in her remarks nor sting in her rejoinders. There are those who think that impropriety, rather than brevity, is the soul of wit; but she never said a thing that could have brought a blush to a Victorian cheek. I think her humour was unconscious and I am sure it was unpremeditated. It flew like a butterfly from flower to flower, obedient only to its own caprice and pursuivant of neither method nor intention. It depended on the way she spoke and on the way she looked. Its subtlety gained by the flaunting and extravagant appearance that Gilbert had achieved for her; but her appearance was only an element in it. Now of course she was the fashion and people laughed if she but opened her mouth. They no longer wondered that Gilbert had married a wife so much older than himself. They saw that Jane was a woman with whom age did not count. They thought him a devilish lucky young fellow. The admiral quoted Shakespeare to me: "Age cannot wither her, nor custom stale her infinite variety." Gilbert was delighted with her success. As I came to know him better I grew to like him. It was quite evident that he was neither a rascal nor a fortune-hunter. He was not only immensely proud of Jane but genuinely devoted to her. His kindness to her was touching. He was a very unselfish and sweet-tempered young man.

"Well, what do you think of Jane now?" he said to me once, with boyish triumph.

"I don't know which of you is more wonderful," I said. "You or she."

"Oh, I'm nothing."

"Nonsense. You don't think I'm such a fool as not to see that it's you, and you only, who've made Jane what she is."

"My only merit is that I saw what was there when it wasn't obvious to the naked eye," he answered.

"I can understand your seeing that she had in her the possibility of that remarkable appearance, but how in the world have you made her into a humorist?"

"But I always thought the things she said a perfect scream. She was always a humorist."

"You're the only person who ever thought so."

Mrs. Tower, not without magnanimity, acknowledged that she had been mistaken in Gilbert. She grew quite attached to him. But notwithstanding appearances she never faltered in her opinion that the marriage could not last. I was obliged to laugh at her.

"Why, I've never seen such a devoted couple," I said.

"Gilbert is twenty-seven now. It's just the time for a pretty girl to come along. Did you notice the other evening at Jane's that pretty little niece of Sir Reginald's? I thought Jane was looking at them both with a good deal of attention, and I wondered to myself."

"I don't believe Jane fears the rivalry of any girl under the sun."

"Wait and see," said Mrs. Tower.

"You gave it six months."

"Well, now I give it three years."

When anyone is very positive in an opinion it is only human nature to wish him proved wrong. Mrs. Tower was really too cocksure. But such a satisfaction was not mine, for the end that she had always and confidently predicted to the ill-assorted match did in point of fact come. Still, the fates seldom give us what we want in the way we want it, and though Mrs. Tower could flatter herself that she had been right, I think after all she would sooner have been wrong. For things did not happen at all in the way she expected.

One day I received an urgent message from her and fortunately went to see her at once. When I was shown into the room Mrs. Tower rose from her chair and came towards me with the stealthy swiftness of a leopard stalking his prey. I saw that she was excited.

"Jane and Gilbert have separated," she said.

"Not really? Well, you were right after all."

Mrs. Tower looked at me with an expression I could not under-stand.

"Poor Jane," I muttered.

"Poor Jane!" she repeated, but in tones of such derision that I was dumbfounded.

She found some difficulty in telling me exactly what had occurred.

Gilbert had left her a moment before she leaped to the telephone to summon me. When he entered the room, pale and distraught, she saw at once that something terrible had happened. She knew what he was going to say before he said it.

"Marion, Jane has left me."

She gave him a little smile and took his hand.

"I knew you'd behave like a gentleman. It would have been dreadful for her for people to think that you had left her."

"I've come to you because I knew I could count on your sympathy."

"Oh, I don't blame you, Gilbert," said Mrs. Tower, very kindly. "It was bound to happen."

He sighed.

"I suppose so. I couldn't hope to keep her always. She was too wonderful and I'm a perfectly commonplace fellow."

Mrs. Tower patted his hand. He was really behaving beautifully.

"And what is going to happen now?"

"Well, she's going to divorce me."

"Jane always said she'd put no obstacle in your way if ever you wanted to marry a girl."

"You don't think it's likely I should ever be willing to marry anyone else after being Jane's husband," he answered.

Mrs. Tower was puzzled.

"Of course you mean that *you've* left Jane."

"I? That's the last thing I should ever do."

"Then why is she divorcing you?"

"She's going to marry Sir Reginald Frobisher as soon as the decree is made absolute."

Mrs. Tower positively screamed. Then she felt so faint that she had to get her smelling salts.

"After all you've done for her?"

"I've done nothing for her."

"Do you mean to say you're going to allow yourself to be made use of like that?"

"We arranged before we married that if either of us wanted his liberty the other should put no hindrance in the way."

"But that was done on your account. Because you were twenty-seven years younger than she was."

"Well, it's come in very useful for her," he answered bitterly.

Mrs. Tower expostulated, argued and reasoned; but Gilbert insisted that no rules applied to Jane, and he must do exactly what she wanted. He left Mrs. Tower prostrate. It relieved her a good deal to give me a full account of this interview. It pleased her to see that I was as surprised as herself and if I was not so indignant with Jane as she was she ascribed that to the criminal lack of morality incident to my sex. She was still in a state of extreme agitation when the door was opened and the butler showed in —Jane herself. She was dressed in black and white as no doubt befitted her slightly ambiguous position, but in a dress so original and fantastic, in a hat so striking, that I positively gasped at the sight of her. But she was as ever bland and collected. She came forward to kiss Mrs. Tower, but Mrs. Tower withdrew herself with icy dignity.

"Gilbert has been here," she said.

"Yes, I know," smiled Jane. "I told him to come and see you. I'm going to Paris to-night and I want you to be very kind to him while I am away. I'm afraid just at first he'll be rather lonely and

I shall feel more comfortable if I can count on your keeping an eye on him."

Mrs. Tower clasped her hands.

"Gilbert has just told me something that I can hardly bring myself to believe. He tells me that you're going to divorce him to marry Reginald Frobisher."

"Don't you remember, before I married Gilbert you advised me to marry a man of my own age? The admiral is fifty-three."

"But, Jane, you owe everything to Gilbert," said Mrs. Tower indignantly. "You wouldn't exist without him. Without him to design your clothes, you'll be nothing."

"Oh, he's promised to go on designing my clothes," Jane answered blandly.

"No woman could want a better husband. He's always been kindness itself to you."

"Oh, I know he's been sweet."

"How can you be so heartless?"

"But I was never in love with Gilbert," said Jane. "I always told him that. I'm beginning to feel the need of the companionship of a man of my own age. I think I've probably been married to Gilbert long enough. The young have no conversation." She paused a little and gave us both a charming smile. "Of course I shan't lose sight of Gilbert. I've arranged that with Reginald. The admiral has a niece that would just suit him. As soon as we're married we'll ask them to stay with us at Malta—you know that the admiral is to have the Mediterranean Command—and I shouldn't be at all surprised if they fell in love with one another."

Mrs. Tower gave a little sniff.

"And have you arranged with the admiral that if you want your liberty neither should put any hindrance in the way of the other?"

"I suggested it," Jane answered with composure. "But the admiral says he knows a good thing when he sees it and he won't want to marry anyone else, and if anyone wants to marry me—he has eight twelve-inch guns on his flagship and he'll discuss the matter at short range." She gave us a look through her eyeglass which even the fear of Mrs. Tower's wrath could not prevent me from laughing at. "I think the admiral's a very passionate man."

Mrs. Tower indeed gave me an angry frown.

"I never thought you funny, Jane," she said. "I never understood why people laughed at the things you said."

'I never thought I was funny myself, Marion," smiled Jane, showing her bright, regular teeth. "I am glad to leave London before too many people come round to our opinion."

"I wish you'd tell me the secret of your astonishing success," I said.

She turned to me with that bland, homely look I knew so well.

"You know, when I married Gilbert and settled in London and people began to laugh at what I said no one was more surprised than I was. I'd said the same things for thirty years and no one ever saw anything to laugh at. I thought it must be my clothes or my bobbed hair or my eyeglass. Then I discovered it was because I spoke the truth. It was so unusual that people thought it humorous. One of these days someone else will discover the secret and when people habitually tell the truth of course there'll be nothing funny in it."

"And why am I the only person not to think it funny?" asked Mrs. Tower.

Jane hesitated a little as though she were honestly searching for a satisfactory explanation.

"Perhaps you don't know the truth when you see it, Marion dear," she answered in her mild good-natured way.

It certainly gave her the last word. I felt that Jane would always have the last word. She *was* priceless.